THE SPELL OF MARY STEWART

Three Complete Books

THE SPELL OF
MARY
STEWART

NELSON DOUBLEDAY, INC.   *Garden City, New York*

THIS
ROUGH
MAGIC

THIS ROUGH MAGIC

CHAPTER
ONE

ॐ

. . . a relation for a breakfast . . .
The Tempest, Act v, Scene 1

"And if it's a boy," said Phyllida cheerfully, "we'll call him Prospero."
I laughed. "Poor little chap, why on earth? Oh, of course . . . Has someone been telling you that Corfu was Shakespeare's magic island for *The Tempest?*"

"As a matter of fact, yes, the other day, but for goodness' sake don't ask me about it now. Whatever you may be used to, I draw the line at Shakespeare for breakfast." My sister yawned, stretched out a foot into the sunshine at the edge of the terrace, and admired the expensive beach sandal on it. "I didn't mean that, anyway, I only meant that we've already got a Miranda here, and a Spiro, which may not be short for Prospero, but sounds very like it."

"Oh? It sounds highly romantic. Who are they?"

"A local boy and girl: they're twins."

"Good heavens. Papa must be a literary gent?"

Phyllida smiled. "You could say so."

Something in her expression roused my curiosity, just as something else told me she had meant to; so I—who can be every bit as provoking as Phyllida when I try—said merely, "Well, in that case hadn't you better have a change? How about Caliban for your unborn young? It fits like a glove."

"Why?" she demanded indignantly.

"'This blue-eyed hag was hither brought with child,'" I quoted. "Is there some more coffee?"

"Of course. Here. Oh, my goodness, it's nice to have you here, Lucy! I suppose I oughtn't to call it luck that you were free to come just now, but I'm awfully glad you could. This is heaven after Rome."

"And paradise after London. I feel different already. When I think where I was this time yesterday . . . and when I *think* about the rain . . ."

I shuddered, and drank my coffee, leaning back in my chair to gaze out across pine tops furry with gold towards the sparkling sea, and surrendering myself to the dreamlike feeling that marks the start of a holiday in a place like this when one is tired and has been transported overnight from the April chill of England to the sunlight of a magic island in the Ionian Sea.

Perhaps I should explain (for those who are not so lucky as I) that Corfu is an island off the west coast of Greece. It is long and sickle-shaped, and lies along the curve of the coast; at its nearest, in the north, it is barely two miles off the Albanian mainland, but from the town of Corfu, which is about halfway down the curve of the sickle, the coast of Greece is about seven or eight miles distant. At its northern end the island is broad and mountainous, tailing off through rich valleys and ever decreasing hills into the long, flat scorpion's tail of the south from which some think that Corfu, or Kerkyra, gets its name.

My sister's house lies some twelve miles north of Corfu town, where the coast begins its curve towards the mainland, and where the foothills of Mount Pantokrator provide shelter for the rich little pocket of land which has been part of her husband's family property for a good many years.

My sister Phyllida is three years older than I, and when she was twenty she married a Roman banker, Leonardo Forli. His family had settled in Corfu during the Venetian occupation of that island, and had managed somehow to survive the various subsequent "occupations" with their small estate more or less intact, and had even, like the Vicar of Bray, contrived to prosper. It was under the British Protectorate that Leo's great-grandfather had built the pretentious and romantic Castello dei Fiori in the woods above the little bay where the estate runs down to the sea. He had planted vineyards, and orange orchards, including a small plantation (if that is the word) of the Japanese miniature oranges called *koùm koyàt* for which the Forli estate later became famous. He even cleared space in the woods for a garden, and built—beyond the southern arm of the bay and just out of sight of the Castello—a jetty and a vast boathouse, which (according to Phyllida) would almost have housed the Sixth Fleet, and had indeed housed the complicated flock of vessels in which his guests used to visit him. In his day, I gathered, the Castello had been the scene of one large and continuous house party: in summer they sailed and fished, and in the fall there were hunting parties, when thirty or so guests would invade the Greek and Albanian mainlands to harry the birds and ibexes.

But those days had vanished with the first war, and the family moved to Rome, though without selling the Castello, which remained, through the twenties and thirties, their summer home. The shifting fortunes of the Second World War almost destroyed the estate, but the Forlis emerged in postwar Rome with the family fortunes mysteriously repaired, and the then Forli Senior—Leo's father—turned his attention once more to the Corfu property. He had done something to restore the place, but after his death three years ago his son had decided that the Castello's rubbed and faded splendours were no longer for him, and had built a pair of smallish modern villas—in reality twin bungalows—on the two headlands enclosing the bay of which the Castello overlooked the centre. He and Phyllida themselves used the Villa Forli, as they called the house on the northern headland; its twin, the Villa Rotha, stood to the south of the bay, above the creek where the boathouse was. The Villa Rotha had been rented by an Englishman, a Mr. Manning, who had been there since the previous autumn working on a book ("you know the kind," said my sister, "all photographs, with a thin trickle of text in large type, but they're *good*"). The three houses were connected with the road by the main drive to the Castello, and with one another by various paths through the woods and down into the bay.

This year the hot spring in Rome, with worse promised, had driven the Forlis early to Corfu. Phyllida, who was pregnant, had been feeling the heat badly, so had been persuaded to leave the two older children (whose school term was still running) with their grandmother, and Leo had brought her over a few days before I arrived, but had had to go back to his business in Rome, with the promise to fly over when he could at weekends, and to bring the children for Easter. So Phyllida, hearing that I was currently at a loose end, had written begging me to join her in Corfu and keep her company.

The invitation couldn't have been better timed. The play I was in had just folded after the merest face-saver of a run, and I was out of a job. That the job had been my first in London—my "big chance"—accounted partly for my present depression. There was nothing more on the cards: the agencies were polite, but evasive; and besides, we had had a dreadful winter and I was tired, dispirited, and seriously wondering, at twenty-five, if I had made a fool of myself in insisting against all advice on the stage as a career. But—as everyone knows who has anything to do with it—the stage is not a profession, but a virus, and I had it. So I had worked and scraped my way through the usual beginnings until last year, when I finally decided, after three years of juvenile leads in provincial rep., that it was time to try my luck in London. And luck had seemed at last to be with me. After ten months or so of television walk-ons and the odd commercial, I had landed a promising part, only to have the play fold under me like a dying camel, after a two-month run.

But at least I could count myself luckier than the other few thousand still fighting their way towards the bottom rung of the ladder: while they were sitting in the agents' stuffy offices, here was I on the terrace of the Villa Forli, with as many weeks in front of me as I cared to take in the dazzling sunshine of Corfu.

The terrace was a wide tiled platform perched at the end of the promontory where wooded cliffs fell steeply to the sea. Below the balustrade hung cloud on cloud of pines, already smelling warm and spicy in the morning sun. Behind the house and to either side sloped the cool woods where small birds flashed and twittered. The bay itself was hidden by trees, but the view ahead was glorious—a stretch of the calm, shimmering gulf that lies in the curved arm of Corfu. Away northward, across the dark blue strait, loomed, insubstantial as mist, the ghostly snows of Albania.

It was a scene of the most profound and enchanted peace. No sound but the birds; nothing in sight but trees and sky and sun-reflecting sea.

I sighed. "Well, if it isn't Prospero's magic island it ought to be. . . . Who are these romantic twins of yours, anyway?"

"Spiro and Miranda? Oh, they belong to the woman who works for us here, Maria. She has that cottage at the main Castello gate—you'd see it last night on your way in from the airport."

"I remember a light there . . . A tiny place, wasn't it? So they're Corfu people—what's the word? Corfusians?"

She laughed. "Idiot. Corfiotes. Yes, they're Corfiote peasants. The brother works for Godfrey Manning over at the Villa Rotha. Miranda helps her mother here."

"Peasants?" Mildly intrigued, I gave her the lead I thought she wanted. "It does seem a bit odd to find those names here. Who was this well-read father of theirs, then? Leo?"

"Leo," said his loving wife, "has to my certain knowledge read nothing but the Roman *Financial Times* for the last eight years. He'd think 'Prospero and Miranda' was the name of an investment trust. No, it's even odder than you think, my love . . ." She gave her small cat-and-canary smile, the one I recognized as preceding the more farfetched flights of gossip that she calls "interesting facts that I feel you ought to know." . . . "Actually, Spiro's officially called after the island Saint—every second boy's called Spiridion in Corfu—but since our distinguished tenant at the Castello was responsible for the christening—and for the twins as well, one gathers—I'll bet he's down as Prospero in the parish register, or whatever they have here."

"Your 'distinguished tenant'?" This was obviously the *bonne bouche* she had been saving for me, but I looked at her in some surprise, remembering the vivid description she had once given me of the Castello dei Fiori: "tatty beyond words, sort of Wagnerian Gothic, like a set for a musical version of *Dracula*." I wondered who could have been persuaded to pay for these operatic splendours. "Someone's rented Valhalla, then? Aren't you lucky. Who?"

"Julian Gale."

"*Julian Gale?*" I sat up abruptly, staring at her. "You can't mean—do you mean Julian Gale? The actor?"

"As ever was." My sister looked pleased with the effect she had produced. I was wide awake now, as I had certainly not been during the long recital of our family affairs earlier. Sir Julian Gale was not only "an actor," he had been one of the more brilliant lights of the English theatre for more years than I could well remember . . . And, more recently, one of its mysteries.

"Well!" I said. "So this is where he went."

"I thought you'd be interested," said Phyl, rather smugly.

"I'll say I am! Everyone's still wondering, on and off, why he packed it in like that two years ago. Of course I knew he'd been ill after that ghastly accident, but to give it up and then just quietly vanish . . . You should have heard the rumours."

"I can imagine. We've our own brand here. But don't go all shiny-eyed and imagine you'll get anywhere near him, my child. He's here for privacy, and I mean for privacy. He doesn't go out at all—socially, that is—except to the houses of a couple of friends, and they've got TRESPASSERS WILL BE SHOT plastered at intervals of one yard all over the grounds, and the gardener throws all callers over the cliff into the sea."

"I shan't worry him. I think too darned much of him for that. I suppose you must have met him. How is he?"

"Oh, I—he seems all right. Just doesn't get around, that's all. I've only met him a couple of times. Actually, it was he who told me that Corfu was supposed to be the setting of *The Tempest*." She glanced at me sideways. "I, er, I suppose you'd allow him to be 'a literary gent'?"

But this time I ignored the lead. "*The Tempest* was his swan song,"

I said. "I saw it at Stratford, the last performance, and cried my eyes out over the 'this rough magic I here abjure' bit. Is that what made him choose Corfu to retire to?"

She laughed. "I doubt it. Didn't you know he was practically a native? He was here during the war, and apparently stayed on for a bit after it was over, and then, I'm told, he used to bring his family back almost every year for holidays, when the children were young. They had a house near Ipsos, and kept it on till quite recently, but it was sold after his wife and daughter were killed. However, I suppose he still had . . . connections . . . here, so when he thought of retiring he remembered the Castello. We hadn't meant to let the place, it wasn't really fit, but he was so anxious to find somewhere quite isolated and quiet, and it really did seem a godsend that the Castello was empty, with Maria and her family just next door; so Leo let it go. Maria and the twins turned to and fixed up a few of the rooms, and there's a couple who live at the far side of the orange orchards; they look after the place, and their grandson does the Castello garden and helps around, so for anyone who really only wants peace and privacy I suppose it's a pretty fair bargain . . . Well, that's our little colony. I won't say it's just another Saint-Trop. in the height of the season, but there's plenty of what you want, if it's only peace and sunshine and bathing."

"Suits me," I said dreamily. "Oh, how it suits me."

"D'you want to go down this morning?"

"I'd love to. Where?"

"Well, the bay, of course. It's down that way." She pointed vaguely through the trees.

"I thought you said there were notices warning trespassers off."

"Oh, goodness, not literally, and not from the beach, anyway, only the grounds. We'd never let anyone else have the bay, that's what we come here for! Actually, it's quite nice straight down from here on the north side of the headland where our own little jetty is, but there's sand in the bay, and it's heaven for lying about, and quite private . . . Well, you do as you like. I might go down later, but if you want to swim this morning, I'll get Miranda to show you the way."

"She's here now?"

"Darling," said my sister, "you're in the lap of vulgar luxury now, remember? Did you think I made the coffee myself?"

"Get you, Contessa," I said crudely. "I can remember the day—"

I broke off as a girl came out on to the terrace with a tray, to clear away the breakfast things. She eyed me curiously, with that unabashed stare of the Greeks which one learns to get used to, as it is virtually impossible to stare it down in return, and smiled at me, the smile broadening into a grin as I tried a "Good morning" in Greek—a phrase which was, as yet, my whole vocabulary. She was short and stockily built, with a thick neck and round face, and heavy brows almost meeting over her nose. Her bright dark eyes and warm skin were attractive with the simple, animal attraction of youth and health. The dress of faded red suited her, giving her a sort of dark, gentle glow that was very different from the electric sparkle of the urban expatriate Greeks I had met. She looked about seventeen.

My attempt to greet her undammed a flood of delighted Greek which my sister, laughing, managed at length to stem.

"She doesn't understand, Miranda, she only knows two words. Speak English. Will you show her the way down to the beach when you've cleared away, please?"

"Of course! I shall be pleased!"

She looked more than pleased, she looked so delighted that I smiled to myself, presuming cynically that it was probably only pleasure at having an outing in the middle of a working morning. As it happened, I was wrong. Coming so recently from the grey depressions of London and the backstage bad tempers of failure, I wasn't able as yet to grasp the Greek's simple delight in doing anyone a service.

She began to pile the breakfast dishes on her tray with clattering vigour. "I shall not be long. A minute, only a minute . . ."

"And that means half an hour," said my sister placidly, as the girl bustled out. "Anyway, what's the hurry? You've all the time in the world."

"So I have," I said, in deep contentment.

The way to the beach was a shady path quilted with pine needles. It twisted through the trees, to lead out suddenly into a small clearing where a stream, trickling down to the sea, was trapped in a sunny pool under a bank of honeysuckle.

Here the path forked, one track going uphill, deeper into the woods, the other turning down steeply through pines and golden oaks towards the sea.

Miranda paused and pointed downhill. "That is the way you go. The other is to the Castello, and it is private. Nobody goes that way, it is only to the house, you understand?"

"Whereabouts is the other villa, Mr. Manning's?"

"On the other side of the bay, at the top of the cliff. You cannot see it from the beach because the trees are in the way, but there is a path going like this"—she sketched a steep zigzag—"from the boathouse up the cliff. My brother works there, my brother Spiro. It is a fine house, very beautiful, like the Signora's, though of course not so wonderful as the Castello. *That* is like a palace."

"So I believe. Does your father work on the estate, too?"

The query was no more than idle; I had completely forgotten Phyllida's nonsense, and hadn't believed it anyway, but to my intense embarrassment the girl hesitated, and I wondered for one horrified second if Phyllida had been right. I did not know, then, that the Greek takes the most intensely personal questions serenely for granted, just as he asks them himself, and I had begun to stammer something, but Miranda was already answering:

"Many years ago my father left us. He went over there."

"Over there" was at the moment a wall of trees laced with shrubs of myrtle, but I knew what lay beyond them: the grim, shut land of Communist Albania.

"You mean as a prisoner?" I asked, horrified.

She shook her head. "No. He was a Communist. We lived then in Argyrathes, in the south of Corfu, and in that part of the island there are many such." She hesitated. "I do not know why this is. It is different in the north, where my mother comes from." She spoke as if the island were four hundred miles long instead of nearly forty, but I believed her. Where two Greeks are gathered together, there will be at least three political parties represented, and possibly more.

"You've never heard from him?"

"Never. In the old days my mother still hoped, but now, of course, the frontiers are shut to all, and no one can pass in or out. If he is still alive, he must stay there. But we do not know this either."

"D'you mean that no one can travel to Albania?"

"No one." The black eyes suddenly glittered to life, as if something had sparked behind their placid orbs. "Except those who break the law."

"Not a law I'd care to break myself." Those alien snows had looked high and cold and cruel. I said awkwardly, "I'm sorry, Miranda. It must be an unhappy business for your mother."

She shrugged. "It is a long time ago. Fourteen years. I do not even know if I remember him. And we have Spiro to look after us." The sparkle again. "He works for Mr. Manning, I told you this—with the boat, and with the car, a wonderful car, very expensive!—and also with the photographs that Mr. Manning is taking for a book. He has said that when the book is finished—a real book that is sold in the shops—

he will put Spiro's name in it, in print. Imagine! Oh, there is nothing that Spiro cannot do! He is my twin, you understand."

"Is he like you?"

She looked surprised. "Like me? Why, no, he is a man, and have I not just told you that he is clever? Me, I am not clever, but then I am a woman, and there is no need. With men it is different. Yes?"

"So the men say." I laughed. "Well, thanks very much for showing me the way. Will you tell my sister that I'll be back in good time for lunch?"

I turned down the steep path under the pines. As I reached the first bend something made me glance back towards the clearing.

Miranda had gone. But I thought I saw a whisk of faded scarlet, not from the direction of the Villa Forli, but higher up in the woods, on the forbidden path to the Castello.

CHAPTER

TWO

ई

Sir, I am vex'd . . .

Act IV, Scene 1

The bay was small and sheltered, a sickle of pure white sand holding back the aquamarine sea, and held in its turn by the towering backdrop of cliff and pine and golden-green trees. My path led me steeply down past a knot of young oaks, straight on to the sand. I changed quickly in a sheltered corner, and walked out into the white blaze of the sun.

The bay was deserted and very quiet. To either side of it the wooded promontories thrust out into the calm, glittering water. Beyond them the sea deepened through peacock shades to a rich, dark blue, where the mountains of Epirus floated in the clear distance, less substantial than a bank of mist. The far snows of Albania seemed to drift like cloud.

After the heat of the sand, the water felt cool and silky. I let myself down into the milky calm, and began to swim idly along parallel to the shore, towards the southern arm of the bay. There was the faintest breeze blowing off the land, its heady mixture of orange blossom and pine, sweet and sharp, coming in warm puffs through the salt smell of the sea. Soon I was nearing the promontory, where white rocks came down to the water, and a grove of pines hung out, shadowing a deep green pool. I stayed in the sun, turning lazily on my back to float, eyes shut against the brilliance of the sky.

The pines breathed and whispered; the tranquil water made no sound at all. . . .

A ripple rocked me, nearly turning me over. As I floundered, trying to right myself, another came, a wash like that of a small boat passing, rolling me in its wake. But I had heard neither oars nor engine; could hear nothing now except the slap of the exhausted ripples against the rock.

Treading water, I looked around me, puzzled and a little alarmed. Nothing. The sea shimmered, empty and calm, to the turquoise and blue of its horizon. I felt downwards with my feet, to find that I had drifted a little farther out from shore, and could barely touch bottom with the tips of my toes. I turned back towards the shallows.

This time the wash lifted me clear off my feet, and as I plunged clumsily forward another followed it, tumbling me over, so that I struggled helplessly for a minute, swallowing water, before striking out, thoroughly alarmed now, for shore.

Beside me, suddenly, the water swirled and hissed. Something touched me—a cold, momentary graze along the thigh—as a body drove past me under water. . . .

I gave a gasp of sheer fright, and the only reason I didn't scream was because I gasped myself full of water, and went under. Fighting back, terrified, to the surface, I shook the salt out of my eyes and looked wildly round—to see the bay as empty as before, but with its surface marked now by the arrowing ripples of whatever sea creature had brushed by me. The arrow's point was moving fast away, its wake as clear as a vapour trail across the flat water of the bay. It tore on its way, straight for the open sea . . . then curved in a long arc, heading back. . . .

I didn't wait to see what it was. My ignorant mind, panic-stricken, screamed "*Sharks!*" and I struck out madly for the rocks of the promontory.

It was coming fast. Thirty yards off, the surface of the water bulged, swelled, and broke to the curved thrust of a huge, silver-black back. The water parted, and poured off its sides like liquid glass. There was a gasping puff of breath; I caught the glimpse of a dark bright eye, and a dorsal fin cusped like a crescent moon, then the creature submerged again, its wash lifting me a couple of yards forward towards my rock. I found a handhold, clung, and scrambled out, gasping, and thoroughly scared.

It surely wasn't a shark. Hundreds of adventure stories had told me that one knew a shark by the great triangular fin, and I had seen pictures of the terrible jaws and tiny, brutal eye. This creature had breathed air, and the eye had been big and dark, like a dog's—like a seal's, perhaps? But there were no seals in these warm waters, and besides, seals didn't have dorsal fins. A porpoise, then? Too big . . .

Then I had the answer, and with it a rush of relief and delight. This was the darling of the Aegean, "the lad who lives before the wind," Apollo's beloved, "desire of the sea," the dolphin . . . the lovely names went rippling by with him as I drew myself up on to the warm rock in the shade of the pines, clasped my knees, and settled down to watch.

Here he came again, in a great curve, smooth and glistening, dark-backed and light-bellied, and as graceful as a racing yacht. This time he came right out, to lie on the surface watching me.

He was large, as dolphins go, something over eight feet long. He lay rocking gently, with the powerful shoulders waiting curved for the plunge below, and the tail—crescent-shaped, and quite unlike a fish's upright rudder—hugging the water flatly, holding the big body level. The dark-ringed eye watched me steadily, with what I could have sworn was a friendly and interested light. The smooth muzzle was curved into the perpetual dolphin smile.

Excitement and pleasure made me light-headed. "Oh, you darling!" I said foolishly, and put out a hand, rather as one puts it out to the pigeons in Trafalgar Square.

The dolphin, naturally, ignored it, but lay there placidly smiling, rocking a little closer, and watching me, entirely unafraid.

So they were true, those stories . . . I knew of the legends, of course —ancient literature was studded with stories of dolphins who had be-friended man; and while one couldn't quite accept all the miraculous dolphins of legend, there were also many more recent tales, sworn to with every kind of modern proof. There was the dolphin called Pelorus Jack, fifty years ago in New Zealand, who saw the ships through Cook Strait for twenty years; the Opononi dolphin of the fifties, who enter-tained the holiday-makers in the bay; the one more recently in Italy, who played with the children near the shore, attracting such large crowds that eventually a little group of businessmen from a nearby re-sort, whose custom was being drawn away, lay in wait for the dolphin and shot her dead as she came in to play. These, and others, gave the old legends rather more than the benefit of the doubt.

And here, indeed, was the living proof. Here was I, Lucy Waring, be-ing asked into the water for a game. The dolphin couldn't have made it clearer if he'd been carrying a placard on that lovely moon's-horn fin of his. He rocked himself, watching me, then half turned, rolled, and came up again, nearer still. . . .

A stray breeze moved the pines, and I heard a bee go past my cheek, travelling like a bullet. The dolphin arched suddenly away in a deep dive. The sea sucked, swirled, and settled, rocking, back to emptiness.

So that was that. With a disappointment so sharp that it felt like a bereavement, I turned my head to watch for him moving out to sea, when suddenly, not far from my rock, the sea burst apart as if it had been shelled and the dolphin shot upwards on a steep slant that took him out of the water in a yard-high leap and down again with a smack of the tail as loud as a cannon shot. He tore by like a torpedo, to fetch up all standing twenty yards out from my rock and fix me once again with that bright, humorous eye.

It was an enchanting piece of show-off, and it did the trick. "All right," I said softly, "I'll come in. But if you knock me over again, I'll drown you, my lad, see if I don't!"

I lowered my legs into the water, ready to slide down off the rock. Another bee shot past above me, seawards, with a curious high humming. Something—some small fish, I suppose—splashed a white jet of water just beyond the dolphin. Even as I wondered, vaguely, what it was, the humming came again, nearer . . . and then another white spurt of water, and a curious thin, curving whine, like singing wire.

I understood then. I'd heard that sound before. These were neither bees nor fish. They were bullets, presumably from a silenced rifle, and one of them had ricocheted off the surface of the sea. Someone was shooting at the dolphin from the woods above the bay.

That I was in some danger from the ricochets myself didn't at first enter my head. I was merely furious, and concerned to do something quickly. There lay the dolphin, smiling at me on the water, while some murderous "sportsman" was no doubt taking aim yet again. . . .

Presumably he hadn't yet seen me in the shadow of the pines. I shouted at the top of my voice, "Stop that shooting! Stop it at once!" and thrust myself forward into the water.

Nobody, surely, would fire at the beast when there was the chance of hitting me. I plunged straight out into the sunlight, clumsily breasting the water, hoping that my rough approach would scare the dolphin away from the danger.

It did. He allowed me to come within a few feet, but as I lunged farther, with a hand out as if to touch him, he rolled gently away from me, submerged, and vanished.

I stood breast-deep, watching the sea. Nothing. It stretched silent and empty towards the tranquil, floating hills of the mainland. The ripples ran back to the shore, and flattened, whispering. The dolphin had gone. And the magic had gone with him. This was only a small—and lonely—bathing place, above which waited an unpleasant and frustrated character with a gun.

I turned to look up at the enclosing cliffs.

The first thing I saw, high up above the bay's centre, was what must be the upper stories of the Castello dei Fiori, rearing their incongruously embattled turrets against a background of holm oak and cedar and Mediterranean cypress. The house was set well back, so that I could not see the ground-floor windows, but a wide balcony, or terrace, edged with a stone balustrade, jutted forward right to the cliff's edge over the bay. From the beach directly below nothing of this would be visible through the tangle of flowering shrubs that curtained the steep, broken cliff, but from where I stood I could see the full length of the balustrade with its moss-grown statues at the corners, a stone jar or two full of flowers showing bright against the dark background of cypress, and, a little way back from the balustrade, a table and chairs set in the shadow of a stone pine.

And a man standing, half invisible in the shade of the pine, watching me.

A moment's study convinced me that it could not be Sir Julian Gale. This man was too dark, and even from this distance looked quite unfamiliar—too casual in his bearing, perhaps, and certainly too young. The gardener, probably; the one who threw the trespassers over the cliff. Well, if Sir Julian's gardener had the habit of amusing himself with a bit of shooting practice, it was high time he was stopped.

I was out of the water before even the dolphin could have dived twice, had snatched up shoes and wrap, and was making for a dilapidated flight of steps near the cliff which, I assumed, led up to the terrace.

From above I heard a shout, and looked up. He had come forward to the balustrade, and was leaning over. I could barely see him through the thick screen of hibiscus and bramble, but he didn't look like a Greek, and as I paused he shouted in English, "That way, please!" and his arm went out in a gesture towards the southern end of the bay.

I ignored it. Whoever he was—some guest of Julian Gale's, presumably—I was going to have this out with him here and now, while I was hot with temper; not wait until I had to meet him at some polite bun fight of Phyllida's. . . . "But you really mustn't shoot at dolphins, Mr. Whosit, they do no harm. . . ." The same old polite spiel, gone through a thousand times with stupid, trigger-happy men who shot or trapped badgers, otters, kestrels—harmless creatures, killed because some man wanted a walk out with his dog on a fine day. No, this time I was white-hot, and brave with it, and I was going to say my piece.

I went up those steps like a rocket leaving the launching pad.

They were steep and crooked, and wound up through the thickest of the wood. They skirted the roots of the cliff, flicked up and round thickets of myrtle and summer jasmine, and emerged into a sloping glade full of dappled sunlight.

He was there, looking annoyed, having apparently come down from the terrace to intercept me. I only realized when I stopped to face him how very much at a disadvantage I was. He had come down some fifty feet; I had hurtled up a hundred or so. He presumably had a right to be where he was; I had not. He was also minding his own business, which was emphatically none of mine. Moreover, he was fully dressed, and I was in swimming costume, with a wet wrap flying loose round me. I clutched it to me, and fought for breath, feeling angrier than ever, but now this didn't help at all, as I couldn't get a word out.

He said, not aggressively but not politely, "This is private ground, you know. Perhaps you'd be good enough to leave by the way you came? This only takes you up to the terrace, and then more or less through the house."

I got enough breath to speak, and wasted neither time nor words. "Why were you shooting at that dolphin?"

He looked as blank as if I had suddenly slapped his face. "Why was I what?"

"That was you just now, wasn't it, shooting at the dolphin down in the bay?"

"My dear g—" He checked himself, and said, like someone dealing with a lunatic, "Just what are you talking about?"

"Don't pretend you don't know! It must have been you! If you're such death on trespassers, who else would be there?" I was panting hard, and my hands were shaking as I clutched the wrap to me clumsily. "Someone took a couple of potshots at it, just a few minutes ago. I was down there, and I saw you on the terrace."

"I certainly saw a dolphin there. I didn't see you, until you shouted and came jumping out from under the trees. But you must be mistaken. There was no shooting. I'd have been bound to hear it if there was."

"It was silenced, of course," I said impatiently. "I tell you, I was down there when the shots came! D'you think I'd have come running up here for the fun of the thing? They were bullets all right! I know a ricochet when I hear it."

His brows snapped down at that, and he stared at me frowningly, as if seeing me for the first time as a person, and not just a nuisance to be thrown down the cliff as quickly as possible.

"Then why did you jump into the water near the dolphin?"

"Well, obviously! I wanted to drive it away before it got hurt!"

"But you might have been badly hurt yourself. Don't you know that a bullet ricochets off water the way it does off rock?"

"Of course I do! But I had to do something, hadn't I?"

"Brave girl." There was a dryness in his voice that brought my cooling temper fizzing to the boil again. I said hotly:

"You don't believe me, do you? I tell you it's true! They *were* shots, and *of course* I jumped in to stop you! I knew you'd have to stop if someone was there."

"You know," he said, "you can't have it both ways. Either I did the shooting or I don't believe there was any shooting. Not both. You can take your pick. If I were you, I'd choose the second; I mean, it's simply not credible, is it? Even supposing someone wanted to shoot a dolphin, why use a silencer?"

"*I'm* asking *you*," I said.

For a moment I thought I had gone too far. His lips compressed, and his eyes looked angry. There was a short silence, while he stared at me frowningly and we measured each other.

I saw a strongly built man of about thirty, carelessly dressed in slacks and a sleeveless Sea Island shirt which exposed a chest and arms that might have belonged to any of the Greek navvies I was to see building the roads with their bare hands and very little more. Like theirs, too, his hair and eyes were very dark. But something at once sensual and sensitive about the mouth contradicted the impression of a purely physical personality; here, one felt, was a man of aggressive impulses, but one who paid for them in his own private coinage.

What impression he was getting of me I hated to think—damp hair, flushed face, half-embarrassed fury, and a damned wrap that kept slipping—but of one thing I could feel pretty sure: at this very moment he was having one of those aggressive impulses of his. Fortunately it wasn't physical . . . yet.

"Well," he said shortly, "I'm afraid you'll have to take my word for it. I did not shoot at the beast, with a rifle or a catapult or anything else. Will that do? And now if you'll excuse me, I'll be obliged if you would—"

"Go out by the way I came in? All right. I get the message. I'm sorry, perhaps I was wrong. But I certainly wasn't wrong about the shooting. I don't see any more than you do why anyone should do it, but the fact remains that they did." I hesitated, faltering now under his indifferent eye. "Look, I don't want to be any more of a nuisance, but I can't just leave it at that. . . . It might happen again. . . . Since it wasn't you, have you any idea who it could have been?"

"No."

"Not the gardener?"

"No."

"Or the tenant at the Villa Rotha?"

"Manning? On the contrary, if you want help in your protection campaign I suggest you go to the Villa Rotha straight away. Manning's been photographing that beast for weeks. It was he who tamed it in the first place, he and the Greek boy who works for him."

"Tamed it? Oh . . . I see. Well, then," I added lamely, "it wouldn't be him, obviously."

He said nothing, waiting, it seemed, with a kind of neutral patience for me to go. I bit my lip, hesitating miserably, feeling a fool. (Why did one always feel such a fool when it was a matter of kindness—what the more sophisticated saw as sentimentality?) I found that I was shivering. Anger and energy had drained out of me together. The glade was cool with shadows.

I said, "Well, I imagine I'll see Mr. Manning sometime soon, and if he can't help, I'm sure my brother-in-law will. I mean, if this is all private land, and the shore as well, then we ought to be able to stop that kind of trespasser, oughtn't we?"

He said quickly, "We?"

"The people who own the place. I'm Lucy Waring, Phyllida Forli's sister. I take it you're staying with Sir Julian?"

"I'm his son. So you're Miss Waring? I hadn't realized you were here already." He appeared to be hesitating on the brink of some apology, but asked instead, "Is Forli at home now?"

"No," I said shortly, and turned to go. There was a trail of bramble across my shoe, and I bent to disengage it.

"I'm sorry if I was a little abrupt." His voice had not noticeably softened, but that might have been due to awkwardness. "We've had rather a lot of bother with people coming around lately, and my father . . . he's been ill, and came here to convalesce, so you can imagine that he prefers to be left to himself."

"Did I look like an autograph hunter?"

For the first time there was a twitch of amusement. "Well, no. But your dolphin has been more of an attraction even than my father: the word got round somehow that it was being photographed hereabouts, and then of course the rumour started that a film was being made, so we got a few boatloads of sightseers coming round into the bay, not to mention stray parties in the woods. It's all been a bit trying. I wouldn't mind, personally, if people wanted to use the beach, if it weren't that they always come armed with transistor radios, and that I cannot stand. I'm a professional musician, and I'm here to work." He added dryly, "And if you're thinking that this gives me the best of reasons for wanting to get rid of the dolphin, I can only assure you again that it didn't occur to me."

"Well," I said, "it seems there's no more to be said, doesn't it? I'm sorry if I interrupted your work. I'll go now and let you get back to it. Good-bye, Mr. Gale."

My exit from the clearing was ruined by the fact that my wrap caught on the bramble and came clean off me. It took me some three horrible minutes to disentangle it and go.

But I needn't have worried about the threat to my dignity. He had already gone. From somewhere above, and alarmingly near, I heard voices, question and answer, so brief and idle as to be in themselves an insult. Then music, as a wireless or gramophone let loose a flood of weird atonal chords on the still air.

I could be sure I was already forgotten.

CHAPTER

THREE

෧෧

This gallant which thou seest
Was in the wreck; and, but he's something stain'd
With grief (that's beauty's canker) thou mightst call him
A goodly person.

Act I, Scene 2

By the time I had showered and dressed I felt calmer, and very ready to tell Phyllida all about it, and possibly to hear her barbed comments on the unaccommodating Mr. Gale. But when I looked on the terrace she was not to be seen, only the table half laid for lunch, with the silver thrown down, as if hastily, in the middle of the cloth. There was no sign of Miranda or her mother.

Then I heard the door from the kitchen premises swing open and shut, and the quick tap of my sister's steps crossing the hall, to enter the big living room she called the *salotto.*

"Lucy? Was that you I heard?"

"I'm out here." I made for the french windows as I spoke, but she had already hurried out to meet me, and one look at her face drove all thoughts of my morning's adventure from my head.

"Phyl! What's the matter? You look ghastly. Is it Caliban?"

She shook her hand. "Nothing so simple. There's been bad news, an awful thing. Poor Maria's boy's been drowned: Spiro, the boy I told you about at breakfast."

"*Phyl!* Oh, my dear, how frightful! But—how? When?"

"Last night. He was out with Godfrey in the boat—Godfrey Manning, that is—and there was an accident. Godfrey's just come over with the news, and I've been breaking it to Maria and Miranda. I—I've sent them home." She put a hand to her head. "Lucy, it was so awful! I simply can't tell you. If Maria had even *said* anything, but she didn't, not one single word. . . . Oh well, come on in. Godfrey's still here; you'd better come and meet him."

I drew back. "No, no, don't you bother about me: I'll go to my room, or something. Mr. Manning won't want to have to do the polite. Poor Phyl; I'm sorry. . . . Look, would you like me to take myself right away for the rest of the day? I'll go and get lunch somewhere, and then—"

"No, please, I'd rather you stayed." She dropped her voice for a moment. "He's taking it pretty hard, and quite honestly I think it might do him good to talk about it. Come on in. . . . God! I could do with a drink! Caliban'll have to lump it, for once." She smiled a bit thinly, and led the way in through the long window.

The *salotto* was a long, cool room, with three big windows opening on the terrace with its dazzling view. The sun was tempered by the wistaria that roofed the terrace, and the room was cool and airy, its duck-egg-blue walls and white paint setting off to perfection the gilt of the Italian mirrors and the pale gold polished wood of the floor. A calm room, with the kind of graceful simplicity that money and good taste can produce. Phyllida had always had excellent taste. It was a good thing, I sometimes reflected, that she, and not I, had married the rich man. My own taste—since I had outgrown the gingham-and-Chianti-bottle stage—had been heavily conditioned by the fact that I had lived for so long in a perpetual welter of junk-shop props picked up cheaply and licked into stageworthiness for the current show. At best, the effect was a kind of poor man's Cecil Beaton; at worst, a cross between sets designed by Emmett and Ronald Searle for a stage version of Samuel Beckett's *Watt*. That I enjoyed my kind of life didn't stop me from admiring my sister's undoubted talent for elegance.

There was a table at the far end of the room, laden with bottles. A man stood with his back to us, splashing soda into a glass. He turned as we came in.

My first quick impression was of a mask of rather chilly control held hard down over some strong emotion. Then the impression faded, and I saw that I was wrong: the control was not a mask; it was part of the man, and was created by the emotion itself, as a Westinghouse brake is slammed on automatically by the head of steam. Here was something very different from Mr. Gale. I looked at him with interest, and some compassion.

He was tall, and toughly built, with brown hair bleached by the sun, a narrow, clever face, and grey eyes which looked tired and dragged down at the corners, as if he had had no sleep. I put his age somewhere in the middle thirties.

Phyllida introduced us, and he acknowledged me civilly, but all his attention was on my sister. "You've told them? Was it very bad?"

"Worse than bad. Get me a drink, for heaven's sake, will you?" She sank into a chair. "What? . . . Oh, Scotch, please. What about you, Lucy?"

"If that's fruit juice in the jug, may I have that, please? Is there ice?"

"Of course." He handed the drinks. "Look, Phyl, ought I to go and talk to them now? There'll be things they'll want to ask."

She drank, sighed, and seemed to relax a little. "I'd leave it for now, if I were you. I told them they could go home, and they didn't say a word, just picked up their things. I suppose the police'll be there to see them. . . . Later on they'll want to hear every last detail from you, but just at the moment I doubt if Maria's fit to take anything in at all, except that he's dead. As a matter of fact, I don't think she even took *that* in, I don't think she believes it, yet." She looked up at him. "Godfrey, I suppose . . . I suppose there couldn't be any doubt?"

He hesitated, swirling the whisky in his glass, frowning down at it. The lines of fatigue were deep in his face, and made me wonder if he was older than I had thought.

"Well, yes. That's rather the hell of it, don't you see? That's why I didn't come over till now. . . . I've been phoning around all over the place, trying to find out if he could possibly have got ashore either here or on the mainland, or if he'd been . . . well, found. If his body had been washed ashore, that is." He looked up from the drink. "But I'm morally certain there's no chance. I mean, I saw him go."

"And how far out were you?"

He grimaced. "About dead-centre."

"From here?"

"Farther north, out from Kouloura, right in the strait. But that's still a mile each way."

I said, "What happened?"

They both started as if they had forgotten my presence completely. Godfrey Manning straightened his shoulders, and smoothed back his hair in a gesture I was to know well.

"Do you know, I'm still hardly sure. Does that sound incredibly stupid? It's no more than the truth. I've been over it so many times in my mind since it happened that I'm beginning to wonder now how much I really do remember. And of course a night without sleep doesn't help." He crossed to the table to pour himself another drink, saying over his shoulder, "The worst of it is, I can't get rid of the feeling that there must have been something I could have done to prevent it."

Phyllida cried out at that, and I said quickly, "I'm sure that's not true! I'm sorry, I shouldn't have asked. You won't want to talk about it any more."

"It's all right." He came back to a chair, but didn't sit in it, just perched rather restlessly on the arm. "I've already been through it with the police, and given Phyl a sketch of a sort. You might say the worst part is over . . . except, God help me, that I'll have to talk to the boy's mother. She'll want to know rather more than the police were concerned with. . . . As a matter of fact, it would be quite a relief to talk it out." He took a pull at the whisky as if he needed it, and looked at me straight for the first time. "You hadn't met Spiro?"

"I only came last night."

His mouth turned down at the corners. "What a start to your visit. Well, he was Miranda's twin—I take it you'll have met her and her mother?—and he works, or rather worked, for me."

"Phyl told me."

"I was lucky to have him. He was a clever mechanic, and that's something not so easy to find in these parts. In most of the villages the only 'machines' are donkeys and mules, and there's no work for a mechanically minded boy. They move to the towns. But of course Spiro wanted work near home; his father's dead, and he wanted to live with his mother and sister. I came here last year, and he's worked for me all that time. What he didn't know about boats wasn't worth knowing, and when I tell you that I even let him loose on my car, you'll realize he was pretty good." He nodded towards the window, where a big portfolio lay on a table. "I don't know if Phyl told you, but I'm working on a book, mainly photographs, and even with that Spiro was invaluable. He not only picked up enough to help me technically—with the processing, and so on—but I actually got him to model for a few of them."

"They're marvellous, too," Phyllida told me warmly.

He smiled, a tight, meaningless little smile. "They are good, aren't they? Well, that was Spiro. Not a world-beater, whatever poor Miranda says about him. What brains he had were in his hands, and he was slow, and as stubborn as a blind mule—but he was tough, and you could trust him. And he had that one extra, priceless quality which was worth the earth to me—he photographed like a dream. He was a 'natural' for the camera—you simply couldn't miss." He swallowed the last of his whisky, and stooped to set the glass down. The click of glass on wood sounded oddly final, like the full stop after the valediction. "Which brings me to last night."

There was a little pause. The tired grey eyes came back to me.

"I've been doing some experiments in night photography—fishing boats at night, moonscapes, that kind of thing—and I wanted to try my hand at the sunrise over the mainland while there's still snow on the mountains. Spiro and I took my boat out last night. There was a stiffish breeze, but it was nothing to worry about. We went up the coast. You'll know, perhaps, that Mount Pantokrator lies north of here? Well, the coast curves right out, running almost due east under the shelter of the mountain. It's only when you come to the end of this and turn north through the open strait that you get the weather. We got there within half an hour or so of dawn, and turned up about opposite Kouloura— that's the narrowest bit between here and the mainland. The sea was choppy, but nothing a sailor would call rough, though the wind was still rising from the north. . . . Well, I was in the cabin, busy with my camera, and Spiro was aft, when the engine suddenly stopped. I called to ask what was wrong, and he shouted that he thought something was fouling the screw, and he'd have it clear in a minute. So I went on with my job, only then I found he'd let the boat's head fall away, and she'd turned across the wind and was rolling rather too much for comfort. So I went out to see what was going on."

He lifted one hand in a slight, but oddly final gesture. "Then it happened. I saw Spiro in the stern, leaning over. The boat was heeling pretty steeply, and I think—I can't be sure—that I yelled to him to take care. Then a gust or a wave or something got her on the beam, and she kicked over like a mule. He'd had hold of the toe rail, but it was slippery, and he lost it. I saw him grab again as he went over, but he missed. He just disappeared. By the time I got to the stern I couldn't even see him."

"He couldn't swim?"

"Oh, yes, but it was very dark, and the boat was drifting fast, with a fair sea on by that time. The wind must have got up more than I'd realized while I was working in the cabin and we must have been driven yards apart in as many seconds. Even if he'd stayed afloat it would have been hard to find him . . . and I don't think he can have done, or he'd have shouted, and I'd surely have heard something. I yelled myself hoarse, as it was, and there was no answer. . . ."

He got up again, restlessly, and prowled over to the window. "Well, that's all. I threw a life belt out, but we were being blown away at a fair speed, and by the time I'd got the engine started, and gone back to where I thought he'd gone overboard, there wasn't a sign. I must have been somewhere near the right place, because I found the life belt. I cruised about for a couple of hours—rather stupidly, I suppose, but then one can't somehow give up and go. A fishing boat came within hail, and helped, but it was no use."

There was a pause. He stood with his back to us, looking out.

Phyllida said drearily, "It's a horrible thing to happen. Horrible."

"And was the propeller fouled after all?" I asked.

He turned. "What? No, it wasn't. At least, I saw nothing there. It was a choked jet. It only took a few seconds to put right. If he'd looked there first . . ." He lifted his shoulders, letting the sentence hang.

"Well," said Phyl, with an attempt at briskness, "I honestly don't see why you should reproach yourself at all. What could you have done more?"

"Oh, it's not that I blame myself for what happened, I know that's absurd. It's my failure to find him that I find so hard to live with. Casting round for two hours in that black windy sea, and knowing all the time that at any minute it would be too late . . . Don't misunderstand me, but it would be a lot easier if I'd had to bring the boy's body home."

"Because his mother can't believe he's gone?"

He nodded. "As it is, she'll probably hope against hope and sit waiting for him to turn up. And then when—if—his body is washed ashore, this will all be to go through again."

Phyllida said, "Then all we can do is hope the body will turn up soon."

"I doubt if it will. The wind and tide were setting the other way. And if he went ashore on the Albanian coast, we may never hear about it. She may wait for years."

"The way she did for his father," I said.

He stared at me, as if for some seconds he hardly saw me. "His father? Oh, God, yes, I forgot that."

Phyllida stirred. "Then go on forgetting it, for heaven's sake, Godfrey! You're not to flay yourself over this any more! The situation's horrible enough without your trying to blame yourself for something you couldn't help and couldn't have prevented!"

"As long as his mother and sister understand that."

"Of course they will! Once the shock's over and you can talk to them, you'll have to tell them the whole story, just as you've told us. You'll find they'll accept it, without even thinking of praise or blame—just as they'd accept anything fate chose to hand out to them. These people do. They're as strong as their own rocks, and so's their faith."

He was looking at her in some surprise. People who only see the everyday side of Phyllida—the volatile, pretty-butterfly side—are always surprised when they come up against her core of solid maternal warmth. He also looked grateful, and relieved, as if she had somehow excused him from blame, and this mattered.

She smiled at him. "Your trouble is, you've not only had a rotten experience and a bad shock, but now you're dreading having to face Maria and stand a scene; and I don't blame you one bit." Her frankness was as comfortable as it was devastating. "But you needn't worry. There'll be no scenes, and it won't even occur to them to ask you questions."

"You don't quite understand. Spiro wasn't to have gone with me last night—he had a date of some sort in the town. I persuaded him to break it. His mother didn't even know till the last minute."

"So what? No doubt you were paying him overtime of a sort, the way you always did? . . . I thought as much. . . . Oh, yes, I knew all about it, Maria told me. Believe me, they were terribly grateful for the work you gave him, *and* for the way you paid, always so generous. Spiro thought the world of you, and so does Maria. Good heavens, *you* to worry what they'll say to you?"

"Could I offer them anything, do you think?"

"Money?" She knitted her brows. "I don't know. I'll have to think. I don't know quite what they'll do now . . . But don't let's worry about that yet. I'll ask a tactful question or two, and let you know, shall I? But I'll tell you one thing, you'd better take those pictures home with you when you go. I've not looked at them properly, but it'd be a pity if Maria saw them just now."

"Oh. Yes, of course. I'll take them."

He picked up the portfolio, and stood holding it irresolutely, as if he didn't quite know what to do next. One habit my profession has taught me is to watch faces and listen to voices; and if the people concerned are under some kind of stress, so much the better. As an actress I shall never be in the top class, but I am fairly good at reading people, and I felt here, in Godfrey Manning's hesitation and hunger for reassurance, something not quite in character: the contrast between the man as one felt he should be and what shock had made of him was obscurely disquieting, like watching an actor badly miscast. It made me say hastily, and not very tactfully—almost as if any diversion were better than none:

"Are those the photographs for your book?"

"Some of them, prints I brought the other day for Phyl to look at. Would you care to see them?"

He came quickly across the room, and laid the portfolio on a low table beside my chair. I wasn't sure that I wanted, at this moment, to look at the prints, among which were presumably some of the dead boy, but Phyl made no protest, and to Godfrey Manning, quite obviously, it was some kind of a relief. So I said nothing as he pulled the big prints from between the guard sheets and began to spread them out.

The first ones he showed me were mainly of scenery: bold pieces of cliff and brilliant sea, with the bright tangled flowers splashing down over sunlit rock and pictures of peasant women with their goats and donkeys passing between hedgerows of apple blossom and purple broom, or stooping over a stone cistern with their piles of coloured washing. And the sea: this was in most of the pictures; sometimes just the corner of a pool laced with seaweed, or the inside of a curling wave, or the pattern of withdrawing foam over damp sand; and one marvellous one of a rocky inlet where, smiling and with bright intelligent eye, the dolphin lay watching the camera.

"Oh, look, the dolphin!" I cried, for the first time remembering my morning's adventure. Godfrey Manning looked curiously at me, but before I could say anything further Phyllida had lifted the print aside and I found myself staring down at a picture of the dead boy.

He was very like his sister: there were the round face and wide smile, the sunburned skin, the thick black hair as springy as heather. I saw at once what Godfrey had meant when he called the boy a "natural model": the sturdy body and thick neck which gave Miranda her heavy, peasant look were translated in the boy into a kind of classical strength, the familiar, deliberately thickened lines of sculpture. He fitted into the background of rock and sea as inevitably as the pillars of the temple at Sunium.

Just as I was wondering how to break the silence, my sister broke it quite easily.

"You know, Godfrey, I'm quite sure that later on, when things ease off a bit, Maria would love to have one of these. Why don't you do one for her?"

"If you think she would . . . It might be an idea. Yes, and I could frame it for her." He began to put the prints back into the portfolio. "Sometime, perhaps, you'd help me choose the one you think she'd like?"

"Oh, there's no question," said Phyllida, and pulled one out of the pile. "This. It's the best I've seen in years, and exactly like him."

He gave it a brief glance. "Oh, yes. It was a lucky one." His voice was quite colourless.

I said nothing, but stared and stared.

There was the dolphin, arching gently out of a turquoise sea, its back streaming silver drops. Standing thigh-deep beside the animal, laughing, with one hand stretched out to touch it, was the boy, bronzed and naked, his arrow-straight body cutting the arc made by the silver dolphin at the exact point known to painters as golden section. It was one of those miracles of photography—skill and chance combining to throw colour, light, and mass into a flawless moment caught and held forever.

I said, "It's marvellous! There's no other word for it! It's a myth come true! If I hadn't seen the dolphin myself, I'd have thought it was faked!"

He had been looking down at the picture without expression. Now he smiled. "Oh, it's genuine enough. Spiro tamed the beast for me, and it would come right in to play when he went swimming. It was a most cooperative creature, with a lot of personal charm. Did you say you'd seen it?"

"Yes. I've just been down for a swim, and it came to take a look at me. What's more, I may tell you, you nearly lost your dolphin for good and all this morning."

"Lost the dolphin?" said Phyl. "What on earth d'you mean?"

"Someone was shooting at it," I said crisply. "I came panting up here to tell you about it, but then your news knocked it clean out of my head till now." I glanced up at Godfrey. "When I was down in the bay, there was somebody up in the woods above, with a rifle, taking potshots. If I hadn't been there and shooed the dolphin away, he'd probably have got it."

"But . . . this is incredible!" This, at least, had broken through his preoccupation with Spiro's death. He stared at me frowningly. "Someone up in these woods, shooting? Are you sure?"

"Quite sure. And, which makes it worse, the rifle was silenced—so it wasn't just some sportsman out after hares or something, amusing himself by sniping at the dolphin. It was a deliberate attempt to kill it. I was sitting up under the trees, and I suppose he hadn't seen me. But when I yelled and jumped in beside the dolphin, the shooting stopped."

"But, *Lucy!*" Phyllida was horrified. "You might have been hurt!"

"I didn't think," I confessed. "I was just so blazing-mad, I had to stop him somehow."

"You never do think! One of these days you *will* get hurt!" She turned, with a gesture half of exasperation, half of amusement, to Godfrey. "She's always been the same. It's the only thing I've ever seen her really fly off the handle about—animals. She even rescues drowning wasps, and spiders out of the bath, and worms that come out when it rains and get caught crossing the road. The funny thing is, they see her coming. She once put her hand down on an adder, and it didn't even bite her."

"It was probably knocked cold," I said curtly, as embarrassed under Godfrey's amused look as if I were being accused of some odd perversion. I added defiantly, "I can't stand seeing anything hurt, that's all. So from now on I'll keep my eye on it if I have to bathe there every day. That dolphin of yours has got itself a one girl guard, Mr. Manning."

"I'm delighted to hear it."

Phyl said, "I still can't believe it. Who in the world could it have been, up in those woods with a gun?"

I thought for a moment he was going to answer, but he turned back to his task of stowing away the photographs, shutting the portfolio on the last of them with a snap. "I can't imagine." Then, to me, "I suppose you didn't see anyone?"

"Oh, yes."

This produced a gratifying amount of sensation. Phyllida gave a little squeak, and clapped a hand to where, roughly, one imagined Caliban to be. Godfrey Manning said quickly, "You did? Where? I suppose you didn't get near enough to see who it was."

"I did indeed, in the wood below the Castello terrace, and he was utterly beastly!" I said warmly. "He said he was Julian Gale's son, and—"

"*Max Gale!*" This from Phyllida, incredulously. "Lucy, you're not trying to tell me that Max Gale was running round in the woods with a rifle, loosing it off at all and sundry? Don't be silly!"

"Well, he did say it wasn't him," I admitted, "and he'd got rid of the gun, so I couldn't prove it was, but I didn't believe him. He *looked* as if he'd be capable of anything, and anyway, he was quite foully rude, and it wasn't a bit necessary!"

"You were trespassing," said Godfrey dryly.

"Even so, it couldn't have been him!" said my sister positively.

"Probably not," said Godfrey.

She looked at him sharply. "What is it?"

"Nothing."

But she had obviously understood whatever it was he hadn't said. Her eyes widened. "But why in the world—" She caught her breath, and I thought she changed colour. "Oh, my God, I suppose it could be . . . ! But, Godfrey, that's frightful! If *he* got his hands on a gun—"

"Quite. And if he did, naturally Gale would cover up."

"Well, but what can we do? I mean, if there's any danger—"

"There won't be, now," he said calmly. "Look, Phyl, it'll be all right.

If Max Gale didn't know before, he does now, and he'll have the sense to keep anything like that out of the old man's hands."

"How?" she demanded. "Just tell me how? Have you ever *been* in that ghastly museum of a place?"

"No. Why? Is there a gun room or something?"

"Gun room!" said Phyllida. "Give me strength! Gun room! The Castello walls are just about *papered* with the things! Guns, daggers, spears, assegais, the lot. I'll swear there's everything there from carbines to knuckle-dusters. There's even a cannon at the front door! Good heavens, Leo's grandfather *collected* the things! Nobody's going to know if a dozen rifles or so go missing!"

"Now isn't that nice?" said Godfrey.

"Look," I said forcibly, "one minute more of this, and I shall scream. What's all the mystery? Are you two talking about Julian Gale? Because if you are I never heard anything so silly in my life. Why in the world should *he* go round getting savage with a rifle? He might pick off a few theatre critics—I can think of one who's been asking for it for years—but not that dolphin! It's just not possible."

"D'you know him?" Godfrey Manning's tone was abrupt and surprised.

"I've never met him, he's way out of my star. But I've known stacks of people who've worked with him, and they all adored him. I tell you, it's not in character. And if you ask how I know that, let me tell you I've seen every play he's been in for the last ten years, and if there's one kind of person who can't hide what sort of man he is under everything he has to do and say, it's an actor. That's a paradox, I suppose, but it's true. And that Julian Gale could kill a living creature straight out of a Greek myth—no, it simply isn't *on*. Unless he was drunk, or went raving-mad—"

I stopped. The look that had flashed between them would have wrecked a geiger counter. There was a silence that could be felt.

"Well?" I said.

Godfrey cleared his throat awkwardly. He seemed uncertain of how to begin.

"Oh, for goodness' sake, if she's going to be here for a few weeks she'd better know," said my sister. "She's almost certain to meet him sooner or later. I know he only goes to the Karithis place, and to play chess with someone in Corfu, and they never leave him alone the rest of the time, but I met him myself at the Karithises', and she may come across him any day in the grounds."

"I suppose so."

She turned to me. "You said this morning that you wondered why he disappeared like that after he'd retired. You know about the car smash three or four years ago, when his wife and daughter were killed?"

"Oh, Lord, yes. It happened just the week before he opened in *Tiger, Tiger*. I saw it after it had been running about a month. Lucky for him it was a part to tear a cat in, so he was better than ever, if possible, but he'd lost a couple of stones' weight. I know he was ill after he left the cast, and rumours started going round then that he was planning to retire, but of course nobody really believed them, and he seemed quite all right for the Stratford season; then they suddenly announced *The Tempest* as his last appearance. What happened, then? Was he ill again after that came off?"

"In a way. He finished up in a nursing home with a nervous breakdown, and he was there over a year."

I stared at her, deeply shocked. "I never knew that."

"Nobody knew," said my sister. "It's not the sort of thing one advertises, especially if one's a public person like Julian Gale. I only knew myself because Max Gale said something to Leo when they rented the house, and then a friend of mine told me the rest. He's supposed to be better, and he does go out sometimes to visit friends, but there's always someone with him."

I said flatly, "You mean he has to be watched? You're trying to tell me that Julian Gale is—" I paused. Why were all the words so awful? If they didn't conjure up grotesque images of Bedlam, they were even worse, genteel synonyms for the most tragic sickness of all. "—Unbalanced?" I finished.

"I don't know!" Phyllida looked distressed. "Heaven knows, one doesn't want to make too much of it, and the very fact that he was discharged—if that's the word—from the home must mean that he's all right, surely?"

"But he *must* be all right! Anyway, you said you'd met him. How did he seem then?"

"Perfectly normal. In fact, I fell for him like a ton of bricks. He's very charming." She looked worriedly across at Godfrey. "But I suppose these things can recur? I never thought . . . the idea wasn't even raised . . . but if I'd thought, with the children coming here for their holidays and everything—"

"Look," said Godfrey briskly, "you're making altogether too much of this, you know. The very mention of a gun seems to have blown everything up right out of proportion. The man's not a homicidal maniac or anything like it—and never has been, or he wouldn't be here at all."

"Yes, I suppose you're right. Silly of me to panic." She gave a sigh, and subsided in her chair. "In any case, Lucy probably dreamed it! If she never even *saw* a gun, and never heard it, either . . . ! Oh well, let's forget it, shall we?"

I didn't trouble to insist. It no longer mattered. What I had just learned was too fresh and too distressing. I said miserably, "I wish I'd been a bit nicer to Mr. Gale, that's all. He must have had a foul time. It's bad enough for other people, but for his son—"

"Oh, honey, don't look so stricken!" Phyl, her worry apparently gone, was back in the role of comforter. "We're all probably *quite* wrong, and there's nothing the matter at all, except that the old man needs a bit of peace and quiet to recuperate in, and Max is seeing he gets it! If it comes to that, I wouldn't be surprised if it's Max who insists on the quarantine for his own sake; he's writing the score for some film or other, so the story goes, and *he* never appears at all. Hence all the 'trespassers will be shot' stuff, and young Adonis playing bodyguard."

"Young *who?*"

"Adonis. The gardener."

"Good heavens! Can anyone get away with a name like that, even in Greece?"

She laughed. "Oh, he does, believe you me!"

She turned to Godfrey then, saying something about Adonis, who had apparently been a close friend of Spiro's. I caught Miranda's name again, and something about a dowry, and difficulties now that the brother was dead; but I wasn't really listening. I was still caught up unhappily in the news I had just heard. We do not take easily to the displacing of our idols. It was like making a long and difficult journey to see Michelangelo's David and finding nothing there but a broken pedestal.

I found I was reliving, as clearly as if it had been yesterday, that "last appearance" in *The Tempest*; the gentle, disciplined verses resigning Prospero's dark powers, and with them, if this story was true, so much more:

> . . . *This rough magic*
> *I here abjure, and, when I have requir'd*
> *Some heavenly music (which even now I do)*
> *To work mine end upon their senses that*
> *This airy charm is for, I'll break my staff,*
> *Bury it certain fathoms in the earth.*
> *And deeper than did ever plummet sound*
> *I'll drown my book.*

I stirred in my chair, pushed my own distress aside with an effort of will, and came back to the *salotto*, where Godfrey Manning was taking his leave.

"I'd better go. I meant to ask you, Phyl, when's Leo coming over?"

"He may manage this next weekend, I'm not sure. But definitely for Easter, with the children. D'you have to go? Stay to lunch if you like. Maria's done the vegetables, thank goodness—how I hate potatoes in the raw!—and the rest's cold. Won't you stay?"

"I'd like to, but I want to get back to the telephone. There may be news."

"Oh, yes, of course. You'll phone me straight away if you hear anything, won't you?"

"Certainly." He picked up the portfolio. "Let me know as soon as you think Maria would like to see me."

He said his good-byes, and went. We sat in silence till the engine of his car faded among the trees.

"Well," said my sister, "I suppose we'd better find something to eat. Poor Godfrey, he's taking it hard. A bit surprising, really, I never thought he'd be knocked endways quite like that. He must have been fonder of Spiro than he cares to admit."

"Phyl," I said abruptly.

"Mm?"

"Was that true, or was it just another of your stories, when you said Julian Gale was probably Miranda's father?"

She looked at me sideways. "Well . . . Oh, damn it, Lucy, you don't have to take everything quite so literally! Heaven knows—but there's *something* in it, only I don't know what. He christened the girl 'Miranda,' and can you imagine any Corfiote hatching up a name like that? And then Maria's husband deserted them. What's more, I'll swear Julian Gale's been supporting the family. Maria's never said a word, but Miranda's let things drop once or twice, and I'm sure he does. And why, tell me that? Not just because he happened to know the husband during the war!"

"Then if Miranda and Spiro are twins, he's Spiro's father, too?"

"The facts of life being what they are, you might even be right. Oh!" She went rigid in her chair, and turned large eyes on me. "You mean— you mean someone ought to go and break the news to *him*?" All at once she looked very uncertain and flustered. "But, Lucy, it's only a rumour, and one could hardly *assume* it, could one? I mean, think if one went over there, and—"

"I didn't mean that," I said. "In any case, it's not our job to tell him,

Maria'll tell him herself. He'll hear soon enough. Forget it. Where's this lunch you were talking about? I'm starving."

As I followed her out to the kitchen, I was reflecting that Julian Gale had almost certainly had the news already. From my chair facing the *salotto* windows, I had seen Maria and her daughter leave the house together. And not by the drive that would take them back to their own cottage. They had taken the little path that Miranda had shown me that morning, the path that led only to the empty bay, or to the Castello dei Fiori.

CHAPTER

FOUR

ह

He is drown'd
Whom thus we stray to find, and the sea mocks
Our frustrate search on land. Well, let him go.

Act III, Scene 3

Days went by; peaceful, lovely days. I kept my word, and went down daily to the bay. Sometimes the dolphin came, though never near enough for me to touch him, and, although I knew that for the animal's own sake I ought to try to frighten him and drive him away, his friendly presence delighted me so much that I couldn't bring myself to what would seem an act of betrayal.

I did keep a wary eye on the Castello terrace, but there was no further shooting incident, nor had there been any rumour that a local man might have been trespassing with a rifle. But I swam every day, and watched, and never left the bay until the dolphin had finally submerged and headed for the open sea.

There had been no news of Spiro. Maria and her daughter had come back to the Villa Forli the morning after the boy's death, and had gone stoically on with their work. Miranda had lost the plump brightness that characterized her; she looked as if she cried a lot, and her voice and movements were subdued. I saw little of Maria, who kept mostly to the kitchen, going silently about her work with the black headkerchief pulled across her face.

The weather was brilliant, and hot even in the shade. Phyllida was rather listless. Once or twice she went with me on my sightseeing trips, or into the town of Corfu, and one evening Godfrey Manning took us both to dine at the Corfu Palace Hotel, but on the whole the week slipped quietly by, while I bathed and sat on the terrace with Phyllida, or took the little car and drove myself out in the afternoons to explore.

Leo, Phyllida's husband, hadn't managed to get away for the weekend, and Palm Sunday came without a visit from him. Phyllida had advised me to go into the town that morning to watch the Palm Sunday procession, which is one of the four occasions in the year when the island Saint, Spiridion, is brought out of the church where he lies the year round in a dim shrine all smoky with taperlight, and is carried through the streets in his golden palanquin. It is not an image of the Saint, but his actual mummified body which is carried in the procession, and this, somehow, makes him a very personal and homely kind of patron saint to have: the islanders believe that he has Corfu and all its people in his personal and always benevolent care, and has nothing to do but concern himself deeply in all their affairs, however trivial—which may explain why, on the procession days, just about the whole population of the island crowds into the town to greet him.

"What's more," said my sister, "it's a *pretty* procession, not just a gaggle of top brass. And St. Spiro's golden chair is beautiful; you can see his face quite clearly through the glass. You'd think it would be creepy, but it's not, not a bit. He's so tiny, and so . . . well, he's a sort of *cozy* saint!" She laughed. "If you stay long in Corfu you'll begin to get the feeling you know him personally. He's pretty well in charge of the island, you know: looks after the fishing, raises the wind, watches the weather for the crops, brings your boys safe home from sea . . ." She stopped, then sighed. "Poor Maria. I wonder if she'll go today. She doesn't usually miss it."

"What about you?" I asked. "Are you sure you won't come with me?"

She shook her head. "I'll stay at home. You have to stand about for rather a long time while the procession goes past, and there'll be a bit of a crush. Caliban and I take up too much room. Home for lunch? . . . Good. Well, enjoy yourself."

The little town of Corfu was packed with a holiday crowd, and the air was loud with bells. Caught up in the river of people which flowed through the narrow streets, I wandered happily along under the sound of the bells, which competed with the subdued roar of voices and the occasional bursts of raucous brass from some upper window, where a village band was struggling with some last-minute practice. Shops were open, selling food and sweets and toys, their windows crammed with scarlet eggs ready for Easter, cockerels, dolls, baskets of tiny crystallized oranges, or enormous rabbits laden with Easter eggs. Someone tried to sell me a sponge the size of a football, and someone else to convince me that I must need a string of onions and a red plush donkey, but I managed to stay unburdened, and presently found my way to the Esplanade, which is Corfu's main square. Here the pavements were already packed, but when I tried to take my place at the back, the peasants—who must have come into town in the early morning and waited hours for their places—made way for me with insistent gestures, almost forcing me forward into the place of honour.

Presently, from somewhere, a big bell struck, and there came the distant sound of the bands starting up. The vast crowd fell almost silent, all eyes turned to watch the narrow mouth of Nikephoros Street, where the first banners glinted, slowly moving up into the sunlight of the square. The procession had begun.

I am not sure what I had expected—a spectacle at once quaint and interesting, because "foreign"—something to take photographs of, and then forget, till you got them out to look at, some evening at home. In fact, I found it very moving.

The bands—there were four of them, all gorgeously uniformed—played solemnly and rather badly, each a different tune. The village banners with their pious legends were crudely painted, enormous, and cruelly heavy, so that the men carrying them sweated and trembled under the weight, and the faces of the boys helping them wore expressions of fierce and dedicated gravity. There were variations in the uniforms of the schoolchildren that were distinctly unconventional, but the standard of personal beauty was so high that one hardly noticed the shabby coats of the boys, or the cheap shoes the girls wore; and the young servicemen in their reach-me-down uniforms, with their noticeable absence of pipe clay and their ragged timing, had still about them, visibly, the glamour of two Thermopylaes.

And there was never a moment's doubt that all this was done in honour of the Saint. Crowded along the pavements in the heat, the people watched in silence, neither moving nor pushing. There were no police, as there would have had to be in Athens: this was their own Spiridion, their island's patron, come out into the sunlight to bless them.

And here he came. The Archbishop, a white-bearded ninety-two, walked ahead, followed by Church dignitaries, whose robes of saffron and white and rose shone splendidly in the sun, until, as they passed nearer, you saw the rubbed and faded patches, and the darns. Then came the forest of tall white candles, each with its gilt crown and wreath of flowers, and each one fluttering its long ribbons of white and lilac and scarlet. Then finally, flanked by the four great gilded lanterns, and shaded by its canopy, the gold palanquin approached, with the Saint himself inside it, sitting up for all to see; a tiny, withered mummy, his head sagging on to his left shoulder, the dead features flattened and formless, a pattern of shadows behind the gleaming glass.

All around me, the women crossed themselves, and their lips moved.

The Saint and his party paused for prayer, and the music stopped. A gun boomed once in salute from the Old Fort, and as the echo died a flight of pigeons went over, their wings whistling in the silence.

I stood watching the coloured ribbons glinting in the sun, the wreaths of flowers fading already, and hanging crookedly from the crowned candles; the old, upraised hand of the Archbishop, and the faces of the peasant women near me, rapt and shining under the snowy coifs. To my own surprise, I felt my throat tighten, as if with tears.

A woman sobbed, in sudden, uncontrollable distress. The sound was loud in the silence, and I had glanced round before I could prevent myself. Then I saw it was Miranda. She was standing some yards from me, back among the crowd, staring with fiercely intent eyes at the palanquin, her lips moving as she crossed herself repeatedly. There were passion and grief in her face, as if she were reproaching the Saint for his negligence. There was nothing irreverent in such a thought: the Greek's religion is based on such simplicities. I suppose the old Church knew how great an emotional satisfaction there is in being able to lay the blame squarely and personally where it belongs.

The procession had passed; the crowd was breaking up. I saw Miranda duck back through it, as if ashamed of her tears, and walk quickly away. The crowds began to filter back again down the narrow main streets of the town, and I drifted with the tide, back down Nikephoros Street, towards the open space near the harbour where I had left the car.

Halfway down, the street opens into a little square. It chanced that as I passed this I saw Miranda again. She was standing under a plane tree, with her back to me and her hands up to her face. I thought she was weeping.

I hesitated, but a man who had been hovering near, watching her, now walked across and spoke. She neither moved nor gave any sign that she had heard him, but stood still with her back turned to him and her head bowed. I couldn't see his face, but he was young, with a strong and graceful build that the cheap navy blue of his Sunday best suit could not disguise.

He moved up closer behind the girl, speaking softly and, it seemed, with a sort of urgent persuasion. It appeared to me from his gestures that he was pressing her to go with him up one of the side streets away from the crowd; but at this she shook her head, and I saw her reach quickly for the corner of her kerchief and pull it across to hide her face. Her attitude was one of shy, even shrinking, dejection.

I went quickly across to them.

"Miranda? It's Miss Lucy. I have the car here, and I'm going back now. Would you like me to take you home?"

She did turn then. Above the kerchief her eyes were swollen with tears. She nodded without speaking.

I hadn't looked at the youth, assuming that he would now give up his importunities and vanish into the crowd. But he, too, swung round, exclaiming as though in relief.

"Oh, thank you! That's very kind! She ought not to have come, of course—and now there's no bus for an hour! Of course she must go home!"

I found myself staring, not at his easy assumption of responsibility for the girl, or even at the near perfect English he spoke, but simply because of his looks.

In a country where beauty among the young is a commonplace, he was still striking. He had the fine Byzantine features, with the clear skin and huge, long-lashed eyes that one sees staring down from the walls of every church in Greece; the type which El Greco himself immortalized, and which still, recognizably, walks the streets. Not that this young man conformed in anything but the brilliant eyes and the hauntingly perfect structure of the face: there was nothing to be seen here of the melancholy and weakness which (understandably) tends to afflict the saintly persons who spend their days gazing down from the plaster on the church walls—the small-lipped mouths, the meekly slanted heads, the air of resignation and surprise with which the Byzantine saint properly faces the sinful world. This youth had, indeed, the air of one who had faced the sinful world for some years now, but had obviously liked it enormously, and had cheerfully sampled a good deal of what it had to offer. No church-plaster saint, this one. And not, I judged, a day over nineteen.

The beautiful eyes were taking me in with the frank appraisal of the Greek. "You must be Miss Waring?"

"Why, yes," I said, in surprise; then suddenly saw who, inevitably, this must be. "And you're—Adonis?"

I couldn't for the life of me help bringing out the name with the kind of embarrassment one would feel in labelling one's own compatriot "Venus" or "Cupid." That in Greece one could meet any day a Pericles, an Aspasia, an Electra, or even an Alcibiades, didn't help at all. It was the looks that did it.

He grinned. He had very white teeth, and eyelashes at least an inch long. "It's a bit much, isn't it? In Greek we say 'Àdoni.'" (He pronounced it À-*thoni*.) "Perhaps you'd find that easier to say? Not quite so sissy?"

"You know too much by half!" I said involuntarily and quite naturally, and he laughed, then sobered abruptly.

"Where is your car, Miss Waring?"

"It's down near the harbour." I looked dubiously at the crowded street, then at the girl's bent head. "It's not far, but there's a dreadful crowd."

"We can go by a back way." He indicated a narrow opening at the corner of the square, where steps led up into the shadow between two tall houses.

I glanced again at the silent girl, who waited passively. "She will come," said Adoni, and spoke to her in Greek, briefly, then turned to me and began to usher me across the square and up the steps. Miranda followed, keeping a pace or so behind us.

He said in my ear, "It was a mistake for her to come, but she is very religious. She should have waited. It is barely a week since he died."

"You knew him well, didn't you?"

"He was my friend." His face shut, as if everything had been said. As, I suppose, it had.

"I'm sorry," I said.

We walked for a while in silence. The alleys were deserted, save for the thin cats, and the singing birds in cages on the walls. Here and there, where a gap in the houses laid a blazing wedge of sunlight across the stones, dusty kittens baked themselves in patches of marigolds, or very old women peered from the black doorways. The smell of charcoal-cooking hung in the warm air. Our steps echoed up the walls, while from the main streets the sound of talk and laughter surged back to us, muted like the roar of a river in a distant gorge. Eventually our way opened into a broader lane, and a long flight of shallow steps, which dropped down past a church wall straight to the harbour square where I had left Phyl's little Fiat.

There were crowds here, too, but these were broken knots of people, moving purposefully in search of transport home, or the midday meal. Nobody paid any attention to us.

Adoni, who apparently knew the car, shouldered his way purposefully through the groups of people, and held out a hand to me for the keys.

Almost as meekly as Miranda (who hadn't yet spoken a word) I handed them over, and our escort unlocked the doors and ushered her into the back seat. She got in with bent head, and sat well back in a corner. I wondered, with some amusement, if this masterful young man

intended to drive us both home—and whether Phyl would mind—but
he made no such attempt. He shut the driver's door on me and then
got in beside me.

"You are used to our traffic now?"

"Oh, yes." If he meant was I used to driving on the right-hand side,
I was. As for traffic, there was none in Corfu worth mentioning: if I met
one lorry and half a dozen donkeys on an average afternoon's excur-
sion, it was the most I had had to contend with. But today there was
the packed and teeming harbour boulevard, and possibly because of this,
Adoni said nothing more as we weaved our way through the people and
out on to the road north. We climbed a steep, badly cambered turn,
and then the road was clear between high hedges of judas trees and
asphodel. The surface was in places badly pitted by the winter's rain,
so I had to drive slowly, and the third gear was noisy. Under cover of
its noise I said quietly to Adoni:

"Will Miranda and her mother be able to keep themselves, now that
Spiro has gone?"

"They will be cared for." It was said flatly, and with complete confidence.

I was surprised, and also curious. If Godfrey Manning had made an
offer, he would surely have told Phyllida so; and besides, whatever he
chose to give Maria now, he would hardly feel that he owed this kind of
conscience money. But if it was Julian Gale who was providing for
the family, as Phyllida had alleged, it might mean that her story of the
twins' parentage was true. I would have been less than human if I
hadn't madly wanted to know.

I put out a cautious feeler. "I'm glad to hear that. I didn't realize
there was some other relative."

"Well," said Adoni, "there is Sir Gale, in a way, but I didn't mean him
or Max. I meant that I would look after them myself."

"You?"

He nodded, and I saw him throw a half glance over his shoulder at
Miranda. I could see her in the driving mirror; she was taking no notice
of our soft conversation in English, which in any case may have been
too rapid for her to follow, but was staring dully out of the window,
obviously miles away. Adoni leaned forward and put a finger on the
radio button, a gadget without which no Greek or Italian car ever seems
to take the road. "You permit?"

"Of course."

Some pop singer from Athens Radio mooed from under the dash.
Adoni said quietly, "I shall marry her. There is no dowry, but that's no

matter, Spiro was my friend, and one has obligations. He had saved to provide for her, but now that he is dead her mother must keep it; I can't take it."

I knew that in the old Greek marriage contract, the girl brought goods and land, the boy nothing but his virility, and this was considered good exchange; but families with a crop of daughters to marry off had been beggared before now, and Miranda, circumstanced as she was, would hardly have had a hope of marriage. Now here was this handsome boy calmly offering her a contract which any family would have been glad to accept, and one in which, moreover, he was providing all the capital; of the virility there could certainly be no doubt, and besides, he had a good job in a country where jobs are scarce, and, if I was any judge of character, he would keep it. The handsome Adoni would have been a bargain at any reckoning. He knew this, of course, he'd have been a fool not to; but it seemed that he felt a duty to his dead friend, and from what I had seen of him, he would fulfill it completely, efficiently, and to everyone's satisfaction—not least Miranda's. And besides (I thought prosaically), Leo would probably come through with a handsome wedding present.

"Of course," added Adoni, "Sir Gale may give her a dowry, I don't know. But it would make no difference; I shall take her. I haven't told her so yet, but later, when it's more fitting, I shall tell Sir Gale, and he will arrange it."

"I— Yes, of course. I hope you'll both be very happy."

"Thank you."

I said, "Sir Julian is— He makes himself responsible for them, then?"

"He was godfather to the twins." He glanced at me. "I think you have this in England, don't you, but it is not quite the same? Here in Greece, the godfather, the *koumbàros*, is very important in the child's life, often as important as the real father, and it is he who arranges the marriage contract."

"I see." As simple as that. "I did know Sir Julian had known the family for years, and had christened the twins, but I didn't know he—well, had a responsibility. The accident must have been a dreadful shock to him, too." I added awkwardly, "How is he?"

"He is well. Have you met him yet, Miss Waring?"

"No. I understood he didn't see anyone."

"He doesn't go out much, it's true, but since the summer he has had visitors. You've met Max, though, haven't you?"

"Yes." There had been nothing in Adoni's voice to show what he knew about that meeting, but since he called him "Max," without prefix, one might assume a relationship informal enough for Max to have told him just what had passed. Anyway, this was the faithful watchdog who threw the callers over the cliff. No doubt he had heard all about it—and might even have had orders regarding further encroachments by Miss Lucy Waring. . . .

I added woodenly, "I understood he didn't see anyone, either."

"Well, it depends," said Adoni cheerfully. He pulled a duster out from somewhere under the dashboard, and began to polish the inside of the screen. "Not that this helps much, it's all the insects that get squashed on the outside. We're nearly there, or you could stop and I'd do it for you."

"It doesn't matter, thanks."

So that was as far as I'd get. In any case, Miranda seemed to be coming back to life. The back seat creaked as she moved, and in the mirror I could see that she had put back her kerchief and was watching the back of Adoni's head. Something in her expression, still blurred though it was with tears, indicated that I had been right about the probable success of the marriage.

I said, in the brisk tone of one who changes the subject to neutral ground, "Do you ever go out shooting, Adoni?"

He laughed, undeceived. "Are you still looking for your criminal? I think you must have been mistaken—there's no Greek would shoot a dolphin. I am a sailor, too—all Corfiotes are sailors—and the dolphin is the beast of fair weather. We even call it 'dolphin weather'—the summertime, when the dolphins go with the boats. No, me, I only shoot people."

"*People?*"

"That was a joke," explained Adoni. "Here we are. Thank you very much for bringing us. I'll take Miranda to her mother now, then I've promised to go back to the Castello. Max wants to go out this afternoon. Perhaps I shall see you there soon?"

"Thank you, but I— No, I doubt if you will."

"That would be a pity. While you are here, you should see the orange orchards; they are something quite special. You have heard of the *koùm koyàts*—the miniature trees? They are very attractive." That quick, enchanting smile. "I should like to show them to you."

"Perhaps sometime."

"I hope so. Come, Miranda."

As I put the car into gear, I saw him usher the silent girl through her mother's door as if he already owned the place. Suppressing a sharp —and surely primitive—envy for a woman who could have her problems simply taken out of her hands and solved for her, willy-nilly, I put down my own independent and emancipated foot and sent the little Fiat bucketing over the ruts of the drive and down the turning to the Villa Forli.

At least, if Max Gale was to be out, I could have my afternoon swim in peace.

I went down after tea, when the heat was slackening off and the cliff cast a crescent of shade at the edge of the sand.

Afterwards I dressed, picked up my towel, and began slowly to climb the path back to the villa.

When I reached the little clearing where the pool lay, I paused to get my breath. The trickle of the falling stream was cool and lovely, and light spangled down golden through the young oak leaves. A bird sang somewhere, but only one. The woods were silent, stretching away dim-shadowed in the heat of the late afternoon. Bee orchises swarmed by the water, over a bank of daisies. A blue tit flew across the clearing, obviously in a great hurry, its beak stuffed with insects for the waiting family.

A moment later the shriek came, a bird's cry of terror, then the rapid, machine-gun swearing of the parent tit. Some other small birds joined the clamour. The shrieks of terror jagged through the peaceful woods. I dropped my towel on the grass, and ran towards the noise.

The blue tits met me, the two parent birds, fluttering and shrieking, their wings almost brushing me as I ran up a twisting path and out into the open stretch of thin grass and irises where the tragedy was taking place.

This couldn't have been easier to locate. The first thing I saw as I burst from the bushes was a magnificent white Persian cat, crouched picturesquely to spring, tail jerking to and fro in the scanty grass. Two yards from his nose, crying wildly, and unable to move an inch, was the baby blue tit. The parents, with anguished cries, darted repeatedly and ineffectually at the cat, which took not the slightest notice.

I did the only possible thing. I dived on the cat in a flying tackle, took him gently by the body, and held him fast. The tits swept past me, their wings brushing my hands. The little one sat corpse-still now, not even squeaking.

I suppose I could have been badly scratched, but the white cat had strong nerves and excellent manners. He spat furiously, which was only to be expected, and wriggled to be free, but he neither scratched nor bit. I held him down, talking soothingly till he was quiet, then lifted him and turned away, while behind me the parent birds swooped down to chivvy their baby out of sight.

I hurried my captive out of the clearing before he got a chance to see where the birds were making for, and away at random through the bushes. Far from objecting to this, the cat seemed now rather pleased at the attention than otherwise; having had to surrender to *force majeure*, he managed—in the way of his species—to let me know that he did in fact prefer to be carried. . . . And when, presently, I found myself toiling up a ferny bank which grew steeper, and steeper yet, he even began to purr.

This was too much. I stopped.

"I'll tell you something," I said to him, "you weigh a ton. You can darned well walk, Butch, as from now! And I hope you know your way home from here, because I'm not letting you go back to those birds!"

I put him down. Still purring, he stropped himself against me a couple of times, then strolled ahead of me up the bank, tail high, to where at the top the bushes thinned to show bright sunlight. There he paused, glancing back and down at me, before stalking forward out of view.

He knew his way, no doubt of that. Hoping there was a path there that would take me back clear of the tangled bushes, I clambered up in his wake, to find myself in a big clearing, full of sunshine, the hum of bees, and a blaze of flowers that pulled me up short, gaping.

After the dappled dimness of the woods, it took some moments before one could do more than blink at the dazzle of colour. Straight ahead of me an arras of wistaria hung fully fifteen feet, and below it there were roses. Somewhere to one side was a thicket of purple judas trees, and apple blossom glinting with the wings of working bees. Arum lilies grew in a damp corner, and some other lily with petals like gold parchment, transparent in the light. And everywhere, roses. Great bushes of them rampaged up the trees; a blue spruce was half smothered with sprays of vivid Persian pink, and one dense bush of frilled white roses must have been ten feet high. There were moss roses, musk roses, damask roses, roses pied and streaked, and one old pink rose straight from a mediaeval manuscript, hemispherical, as if a knife had sliced it across, its hundred petals as tightly whorled and packed as the layers of an onion. There must have been twenty or thirty varieties there, all in full bloom; old roses, planted years ago and left to run wild, as if in some secret garden whose key is lost. The place seemed hardly real.

I must have stood stock-still for some minutes, looking about me, dizzied with the scent and the sunlight. I had forgotten roses could smell like that. A spray of speckled carmine brushed my hand, and I

broke it off and held it to my face. Deep among the leaves, in the gap
I had made, I saw the edge of an old metal label, and reached gingerly
for it among the thorns. It was thick with lichen, but the stamped name
showed clearly: Belle de Crécy.

I knew where I was now. Roses: they had been another hobby of
Leo's grandfather. Phyl had some of his books up at the Villa, and I
had turned them over idly the other night, enjoying the plates and the
old names which evoked, like poetry, the old gardens of France, of
Persia, of Provence . . . Belle de Crécy, Belle Isis, Deuil du Roi de Rome,
Rosamunde, Camaïeux, Ispahan . . .

The names were all there, hidden deep in the rampant leaves, where
some predecessor of Adoni's had lovingly attached them a century
ago. The white cat, posing in front of an elegant background of dark
fern, watched benevolently as I hunted for them, my hands filling with
plundered roses. The scent was heavy as a drug. The air zoomed with
bees. The general effect was of having strayed out of the dark wood
into some fairy tale. One almost expected the cat to speak.

When the voice did come, suddenly, from somewhere above, it nearly
startled me out of my wits. It was a beautiful voice, and it enhanced,
rather than broke, the spell. It spoke, moreover, in poetry, as deliberately elegant as the white cat:

> " '*Most sure, the goddess*
> *On whom these airs attend! Vouchsafe my prayer*
> *May know if you remain upon this Island . . .*' "

I peered upwards, at first seeing no one. Then a man's head appeared
at the top of the wistaria—and only then did I realize that the curtain
of blossom hung in fact down some kind of high retaining wall, which
it had hidden. I saw, between the thick trusses of flowers, sections of
the stone balustrading. The terrace of the Castello. The rose garden
had been planted right up beside it.

I wanted to turn and run, but the voice held me. Needless to say, it
was not Max Gale's; this was a voice I had heard many times before,
spinning just such a toil of grace as this in the stuffy darkness of London theatres.

" '*My prime request,*' " added Sir Julian Gale, " '*Which I do last pro-
nounce,*' and which in fact you may think impertinent, '*is, O you wonder! If you be maid, or no?*' "

I suppose if I had met him normally, on our common ground of the
theatre, I might have been too overawed to do more than stutter. But
here at least the answer was laid down in the text, and had, besides, the

advantage of being the truth. I narrowed my eyes against the sun, and smiled up at the head.

> *"'No wonder, sir,*
> *But certainly a maid.'"*

"*My language! Heavens!*" The actor abruptly abandoned the Bard, and looked delighted. "I was right! You're Max's trespasser!"

I felt myself flushing. "I'm afraid I am, and I seem to be trespassing again. I'm terribly sorry, I didn't realize the terrace was quite so near. I wouldn't have dreamed of coming so far up, but I was rescuing a bird from Butch there."

"From whom?"

"The cat. Is he yours? I suppose he's called something terribly aristocratic, like Florizel, or Cosimo dei Fiori?"

"As a matter of fact," said Julian Gale, "I call him Nit. I'm sorry, but it's short for Nitwit, and when you get to know him, you'll see why. He's a gentleman, but he has very little brain. Now you're here, won't you come up?"

"Oh, no!" I spoke hastily, backing a little. "Thanks all the same, but I've got to get back."

"I can't believe there's all that hurry. Won't you please take pity on me and break the deadly Sabbath peace up a little? Ah!" He leaned farther over. "Not only trespass, I see, but theft as well! You've been stealing my roses!"

This statement, uttered in the voice whose least whisper was clearly audible in the back row of the gallery, had all the force of an accusation made before the High Praesidium. I started guiltily, glanced down at the forgotten blooms in my hands, and stammered:

"Well, yes, I—I have. Oh, murder . . . I never thought . . . I mean, I took it they were sort of wild. You know, planted ages ago and just left . . ." My voice faltered as I looked round me and saw what I hadn't noticed before, that the bushes, in spite of their riotous appearance, were well shaped, and that the edges of the mossed paths were tidily clipped. "I—I suppose this is your garden now, or something? I'm most terribly sorry!"

"'Or something'? By heaven, she picks an armful of my beloved Gallicas, and then thinks they come out of my garden 'or something'! That settles it, young woman! By all the rules you have to pay a forfeit. If Beauty strays into the Beast's garden, literally loaded with his roses, she's asking for trouble, isn't she? Come along, now, and no arguments! There are the steps, Nit'll bring you up. Nitwit! Show the lady the way!"

The white cat rose, blinked at me, then swarmed in an elaborately careless manner up the wistaria, straight into Julian Gale's arms. The latter straightened, smiling.

"Did I say he hadn't much brain? I traduced him. Do you think you could manage something similar?"

His charm, the charm that had made Phyllida fall for him "like a ton of bricks," was having its effect. I believe I had completely forgotten what else she had told me about him.

I laughed. "In my own plodding way, I might."

"Then come along."

The way up was a flight of shallow steps, half hidden by a bush of York and Lancaster. It curved round the base of some moss-green statue, and brought me out between two enormous cypresses, on to the terrace.

Julian Gale had set the cat down, and now advanced on me.

"Come in, Miss Lucy Waring. You see, I've heard all about you. And here's my son. But of course you've already met. . . ."

CHAPTER

FIVE

ह&

You do look, my son, in a mov'd sort,
As if you were dismay'd. Be cheerful, sir . . .

Act IV, Scene 1

Max Gale was sitting there under the stone pine, at a big table covered with papers. As he got to his feet, I stopped in my tracks.

"But I thought you weren't here!" I hadn't thought I could have blurted out anything quite so naïve. I finished the performance by blushing furiously and adding, in confusion, "Adoni said . . . I thought . . . I'm sure he said you'd be out!"

"I was, but only till teatime. How do you do?" His eyes, indifferent rather than hostile, touched mine briefly, and dropped to the roses in my hands. It was possibly only to fill the sizzling pause of embarrassment that he asked, "Was Adoni down in the garden?"

I saw Sir Julian's glance flick from one to the other of us. "He was not, or he might have stopped her pillaging the place! She's made a good selection, hasn't she? I thought she should be made to pay a forfeit, à la Beauty and the Beast. We'll let her off the kiss on such short acquaintance, but she'll have to stay and have a drink with us, at least!"

I thought I saw the younger man hesitate, and his glance went down to the littered table as if looking there for a quick excuse. There wasn't far to look; the table was spread with scribbled manuscript scores, notebooks, and papers galore, and on a chair beside it stood a tape recorder with a long flex that trailed over the flags and in through an open french window.

I said quickly, "Thank you, but I really can't—"

"You're in no position to refuse, young lady!" Sir Julian's eyes held a gleam of amusement, whether at my reluctance or his son's it was impossible to guess. "Come now, half an hour spent entertaining a recluse is a small price to pay for your loot. Have we some sherry, Max?"

"Yes, of course." The colourlessness of his voice might after all only be in comparison with his father's. "I'm afraid we've no choice, Miss Waring. Do you like it dry?"

"Well . . ." I hesitated. I would have to stay now. I could hardly snub Sir Julian, who was after all my host, and besides, I had no wish to pass up the chance to talk to a man who was at the head of my own profession, and whom I had admired and loved for as long as I could remember. "Actually, if there is one, I'd love a long drink, long and cold . . . ? I've just been swimming, and I'm genuinely thirsty. Would there be any orange juice, or something like that?"

"You ask that here? Of course." Max Gale smiled at me suddenly, and with unexpected charm, and went into the house.

As at the Villa Forli, there were long windows opening from the terrace into some big room, all of them shuttered against the sun except the one through which Max Gale had vanished. Through this dark opening I thought I could make out the shapes of a grand piano, what looked like a huge gramophone, and a revolving bookcase. The tops of the two last were stacked with books and records.

"Sun or shade?" asked Sir Julian, pulling up a gaudy camp chair for me. I chose sun, and he settled himself beside me, the sombre wall of cypresses beyond the balustrade making as effective a backcloth for him as the ferns had for the white cat. The latter, purring, jumped up on to the actor's knee, turned carefully round twice, and settled down, paws going.

The pair of them made a striking picture. Sir Julian was not—had never been—handsome, but he was a big man, of the physical type to which the years can add a sort of heavy splendour. (One remembered his Mark Antony, and how after it all other attempts at the part seemed to be variations of his; attempts, in fact, to play *him*.) He had the powerful breadth of chest and shoulder that runs to weight in middle age, and his head was what is commonly called leonine—thick grey hair, a brow and nose in the grand manner, and fine grey eyes—but with some hint of weakness about the jaw from which the charm of the wide mouth distracted you. His eyes looked pouchy and a little strained, and there were sagging lines in his face which naturally I had never seen across the footlights, lines which might be those of petulance or dissipation, or merely a result of his illness and consequent loss of weight. It was difficult to tell just where his undeniable attractiveness lay; it would, indeed, be hard to give any definite description of him: his face was too familiar for that, melting as one watched him into one character after another that he had made his own, as if the man existed only as one saw him on the stage—king, madman, insurance salesman, soldier, fop . . . as if in leaving that lighted frame, he ceased to exist. It was a disquieting idea when one remembered that he had, in fact, left his frame. If he could not be himself now, he was nothing.

He glanced up from the cat, caught me staring, and smiled. He must be very used to it. What he cannot have realized is that I was trying to find in his face and movements some evidence of nervous strain that might justify Phyllida's fears. But he seemed quite self-contained and relaxed, his hands (those betrayers) lying motionless and elegantly disposed—perhaps just a bit too elegantly disposed?—over the cat's fur.

"I'm sorry," I said, "was I staring? I've never been so close to you before. It's usually the upper circle."

"With me tastefully disguised behind several pounds of false beard, and robed and crowned at that? Well, here you see the man himself, poor, bare forked creature that he is. I won't ask you what you think of him, but you must at least give me your opinion of his setting. What do you think of our crumbling splendours?"

"The Castello? Well, since you ask . . . I'd have said it wasn't quite *you.* It would make a marvellous background for a Gothic thriller—*Frankenstein,* or *The mysteries of Udolpho,* or something."

"It would, wouldn't it? One feels it ought to be permanently shrouded in mist, with vampires crawling down the walls—not surrounded by flowers, and the peace and sunshine of this enchanted island. However, I suppose it's highly appropriate for a decayed actor to retire to, and it's certainly a haven of peace, now that Max has clamped down on the sightseers."

"I heard you'd been ill. I'm sorry. We—we miss you terribly in London."

"Do you, my dear? That's nice of you. Ah, Max, here you are. Miss Waring thinks the house is a perfect setting for Frankenstein and his monster."

"I did not! I never said—I certainly didn't put it like that!"

Max Gale laughed. "I heard what you said. You could hardly insult this kind of crazy baroque anyway. Loco rococo. This is fresh orange, is that all right for you?"

"Lovely, thank you."

He had brought the same for himself, and for his father. I noticed that the latter's hand, as he put it out for the glass, shook badly, and his son quickly lifted a small iron table within reach, set the glass down on that, and poured the iced juice in. Sir Julian dropped his hands back into the cat's fur, where they once more lay statue-still. I had been right about the self-consciousness of that pose. But it hadn't been vanity, unless it is vanity that conceals a weakness of which one is ashamed.

As Max Gale poured my drink, I made to lay the roses on the table, but he set the jug down and put out a hand.

"Give them to me. I'll put them in water for you till you go."

"So I'm to be allowed to keep them, after I've paid the forfeit?"

"My dear child," said Sir Julian, "you're welcome to the lot! I hope you don't take my teasing seriously, it was only an excuse to make you come up. I'm only glad you liked them so much."

"I love them. They look like the roses in old pictures—you know, *real* roses in old storybooks. *The Secret Garden*, and Andrew Lang's *Sleeping Beauty*, and *The Arabian Nights*."

"That's just what they are. That one was found growing on a pavilion in Persia, where Haroun-al-Raschid may have seen it. This is the one out of the *Romance of the Rose*. And this was found growing in Fair Rosamund's garden at Woodstock. And this, they say, is the oldest rose in the world." His hands were almost steady as he touched the flowers one by one. "You must come back for more when these die. I'd leave them in the music room, Max, it's reasonably cool. . . . Now, pay up, Miss Lucy Waring. I'm told you're in the business, and one of the reasons I lured you up here was to hear all you can give me of the latest gossip. The facts I can get from the periodicals, but the gossip is usually a great deal more entertaining—and quite often twice as true. Tell me . . ."

I forget now just what he asked me, or how much I was able to tell him, but though I moved in very different theatrical circles from him, I did know a good deal of what was going on in town; and I remember that in my turn I found it exciting to hear him using, casually and in passing, names which were as far above my touch as the clouds on Mount Pantokrator. He certainly gave me the impression that he found me good value as an entertainer, but how far this was due to his own charm I can't guess, even today. I know that when, finally, he turned the conversation to my affairs, you'd have thought this was the big moment towards which all the star-spangled conversation had been leading.

"And now tell me about yourself. What are you doing, and where? And why have we never met before?"

"Oh, heavens, I'm not anywhere near your league! I'd only just got to the West End as it was!"

I stopped. The last phrase had been a dead giveaway, not only of the facts, but of feelings which I had not discussed, even with Phyllida. I had my vanities, too.

"Play folded?" Where a layman's sympathy would have jarred, his matter-of-fact tone was marvellously comforting. "What was it?"

I told him, and he nodded.

"Yes, that was McAndrew's pet pigeon, wasn't it? Not a very wise venture on Mac's part, I thought. I read the play. Who were you? What's-her-name, the girl who has those unlikely hysterics all over Act Two?"

"Shirley. Yes. I was rotten."

"There was nothing there to get hold of. That sort of fantasy masquerading as working-class realism needs rigid selection and perfect timing—not merely uncontrolled verbal vomit, if you'll forgive the phrase. And he never can do women, haven't you noticed?"

"Maggie in *The Single End?*"

"Do you call her a woman?"

"Well . . . I suppose you're right."

"I'm right in telling you not to blame yourself over Shirley. What comes next?"

I hesitated.

"Like that, is it?" he said. "Well, it happens. How wise of you to cut and run for Corfu while you could! I remember . . ." And he turned neatly off into a couple of malicious and very funny stories involving a well-known agent of the thirties, and a brash young actor whom I had no difficulty in identifying as Sir Julian Gale himself. When he had finished, and we had done laughing, I found myself countering with some of my own experiences which I had certainly never expected to find funny—or even to tell anybody about. Now, for some reason, to talk about them was a kind of release, even a pleasure, while the crenellated shadow of the Castello advanced unheeded across the weedy flags, and Sir Julian Gale listened, and commented, and asked questions, as if he had "lured" me to his terrace for no other reason than to hear the life story of a mediocre young actress who would never play anything but seconds in her life.

A slight sound stopped me, and brought me sharply round. I had forgotten all about Max Gale. I hadn't heard him come out of the house again, but he was there, sitting on the balustrade, well within hearing. How long he had been there I had no idea.

It was only then that I realized how the light had faded. My forfeit was paid, and it was time to be gone, but I could hardly take my leave within seconds, as it were, of acknowledging Max Gale's presence. I had to make some motion of civility towards him first.

I looked across at him. "Did you go to watch the procession this morning, Mr. Gale?"

"I? Yes, I was there. I saw you in the town. Did you get a good place?"

"I was on the Esplanade, at the corner by the Palace."

"It's rather . . . appealing, don't you think?"

"Very." I smiled. "Being a musician, you'd appreciate the bands."

He laughed, and all at once I saw his father in him. "Very much. And when all four play at the same time, it really is something."

"The leitmotiv for your *Tempest*, Max," said his father, stroking the white cat. " 'The isle is full of noises.' "

Max grinned. "Perhaps. Though even I might fight shy of reproducing some of them."

Sir Julian turned to me. "My son is writing a score for a film version of *The Tempest*."

"Is that what it's to be? How exciting! I gather you've come to the right place to do it, too. Is that why you chose Corfu after you'd drowned your book at Stratford, Sir Julian?"

"Not really; the thing's fortuitous. I've known the island on and off for thirty years, and I've friends here. But it's a pleasant chance that brought this work to Max when we happened to be marooned here."

"Do you really think this is Prospero's island?"

"Why not?" asked Julian Gale, and Max said, "That's torn it," and laughed.

I looked at him in surprise. "What have I said?"

"Nothing. Nothing at all. But if you will invite a man to explain a theory he's been brooding over for weeks, you must be prepared for a lecture, and by the gleam in my father's eye, nothing can save you now."

"But I'd love to hear it! Besides, your father could make the Telephone Directory sound like *War and Peace* if he tried, so his private theory about *The Tempest* ought to be *something*! Don't take any notice of him, Sir Julian! Why do you think this might be Prospero's island?"

"You are a delightful young lady," said Sir Julian, "and if you wish to dig my roses out by the roots and carry them away, I shall send Adoni to help you. No, on second thought, Max can do it. It would be good for him to do a little real work, instead of floating around in the lunatic fringe where musicians seem to live. . . . Who was it who said that the really wise man isn't the man who wants a thing proved before he'll believe in it, but the man who is prepared to believe anything until it's shown to be false?"

"I don't know, but it sounds to me like somebody's definition of a visionary or a genius."

"*All* the roses," said Sir Julian warmly. "Did you hear that, Max? My theories about *The Tempest* are those of a visionary and a genius."

"Oh, sure," said his son.

He was still sitting on the balustrade, leaning back against the stone urn that stood at the corner. I had been watching his face covertly for some resemblance to his father, but, except for his build and an occasional chance expression, could see none. His eyes were dark, and more deeply set, the mouth straighter, the whole face less mobile. I thought the hint of the neurotic was there, too, in the faint lines between the brows, and somewhere in the set of the mouth. The careful under-emphasis in all he said and did might well be a deliberate attempt to control this, or merely to avoid profiting by his father's charm. Where Sir Julian seemed automatically, as it were, to make the most of his lines, Max threw his away. It seemed to me that he was even concerned not to be liked, where his father, consciously or not, had the actor's need to be loved.

"There is no evidence of any kind," Sir Julian was saying, "to connect this island with the island of the play, any more than we can prove it was the 'Scheria' of Odysseus and Nausicaä; but in both cases tradition is strong, and when traditions persist hard enough it seems only sensible to conclude that there may be something in them worth investigating."

"Schliemann and Troy," murmured Max.

"Exactly," said Sir Julian. He gave me that sudden smile that was so like his son's. "So, being like Schliemann a genius and a visionary, and being determined to believe that Corfu *is* Prospero's island, I've been looking for evidence to prove it."

"And is there any?"

"Perhaps not 'evidence.' That's a strong word. But once you start looking, you can find all sorts of fascinating parallels. Start with the easiest, the description of the natural details of the island, if you can remember them."

"I think I can, fairly well. There's rather more physical description of the setting than you usually find in Shakespeare, isn't there?"

"I'd say more than anywhere, except *Venus and Adonis*. And what description one gleans from the play fits this island well enough: the pines, tilled lands, the fertility (not so many of the Mediterranean islands are really fertile, you know), the beaches and coves, the lime groves outside Prospero's cave . . ." He lifted a hand to point where a group of trees stood golden green beside the pines on the southern promontory. "There are young limes growing all down the cliff beyond Manning's villa, and the whole coast is honeycombed with caves. You might say these things are found on any island, but one thing isn't—the brine pits that Caliban talks about, remember?"

"And there are some here?"

"Yes, down at Korissia, in the south. They've been there for centuries."

"What about the pignuts and filberts he promised to dig up? Do they grow here?"

"Filberts certainly, and pignuts, too, if he means the English soil. And if he means truffles—as I believe—yes, those too."

"And the marmosets?" I asked it diffidently, as one who puts a question in doubtful taste.

Sir Julian waved the marmosets aside. "A momentary confusion with the still vex'd Bermoothes. No doubt Ariel had been shooting a nice line in travel tales, and the poor monster was muddled."

Max said, "You can't argue with a man with an obsession. Humour him, Miss Waring."

"I'll do no such thing! If a theory's worth holding, it's worth fighting over! What about the *story*, then, Sir Julian? Take the start of it, the shipwreck. If the ship was on its way from Tunis to Naples, you'd think Corfu was just a little too far off course—"

"Ah, yes, you run up against the same thing in the Odysseus story, where they're supposed to have rowed—rowed, mark you—from Scheria to Euboea in a single night. But to my mind, that does nothing to discount Corfu's claim to be Scheria. It's poetic truth, the kind of telescoping that you find in the seven days of Creation—one assumes that the gods helped them. The same with the Neapolitan ship in *The Tempest*. The storm was a tremendous one, an historic tempest. The ship was blown right off her course, and could have driven blindly along for days before fetching up on these coastal rocks. Can't you see that what makes the story plausible is its very unlikelihood?"

"Have a heart," said his son. "Of course she can't."

"It's very simple. The fact that the ship did end up here, so fantastically off course, made it necessary later on to explain the storm as being magical, or somehow supernatural."

"Just a minute," I said quickly. " 'The fact'? Are you trying to say that the business of the shipwreck is *true*?"

"Only that like all legends it could be founded on the truth, just as there really was a Cretan labyrinth, and a Troy that burned. It's my guess—strictly as a visionary—that there was in fact some spectacular wreck here that became the basis of a legend."

"No more than a guess? You haven't found any actual Corfiote story, or any real record?"

"No."

"Then why here? Why Corfu? Your geographical details don't prove a thing. They might confirm, but they're hardly a start."

Sir Julian nodded, smoothing the cat's head with a gentle finger. "I started at the wrong end. I should have begun not with the 'facts,' but with the play—the play's kingpin, Prospero. To my mind, the conception of his character is the most remarkable thing about the play; his use as a sort of summing up of Shakespeare's essay on human power. Look at the way he's presented: a father figure, a magician in control of natural forces like the winds and the sea, a sort of benevolent and supernatural Machiavelli who controls the island and all who are in it."

He finished on a faint note of inquiry, and looked at me with raised eyebrows, waiting for my reply.

"Saint Spiridion?"

"Saint Spiridion. Exactly!" He glanced up at Max, as if showing off the cleverness of a favourite pupil. I saw Max smile faintly. "Even the name . . . you'll notice the similarity; and its abbreviation, 'Spiro,' makes it even closer." The shadow which touched his face was gone immediately. "Saint Spiridion—his body, that is—was brought here in 1489, and in no time at all he had the reputation for all sorts of magic, miracles if you like, especially weather magic. There was another saint, a female, brought with him. Her mummy is also in a church in the town, but she didn't catch the public imagination, so she doesn't get the outings. In fact, I can't even remember her name."

"I've never even heard she existed," I said.

He smiled. "It's a man's country. But she may well be the origin of the *idea* of Miranda, the magician's daughter. She would hardly survive into legend merely as a female companion, or even as a wife. Magicians don't have them, for reasons which I suppose it would be fascinating to explore, but which you might disagree with, Miss Lucy Waring."

"I know, Delilah and Co. All right, I don't resent it, it's a man's world. If it comes to that, witches don't have husbands, not the real old fairy-story witches, anyway."

"Fair enough." Sir Julian leaned back in his chair. "Well, there you have your starting point, the fabulously fertile island of Corfu, guarded by a Saint who is believed to control the weather. Now we postulate a tempest, some historic humdinger of a storm, when some important ship—perhaps even with a few Italian VIP's on board—was driven far off course and wrecked here, but with her passengers saved from drowning by some apparent miracle that would be imputed to the Saint. So a legend starts to grow. Later the Germanic elements of fairy tale are added to it—the 'magic,' the beautiful daughter, the fairy characters." He paused, with a mischievous gleam at me. "It would be nice if one could somehow equate the elementals with the facts of the island's history, wouldn't it? I've tried my hardest to see the 'foul witch Sycorax' from 'Argier,' as a sort of personification of the Moslem rulers who penned the heavenly power—Ariel—in a cloven pine till the Saint-magician released him . . . But I'm afraid I can't quite make that one stick."

"What a pity!" I said it quite without irony: I was enjoying myself vastly. "And Caliban? Paganism or something?"

"If you like. There's the brutality, the sexuality, and the superbly sensitive poetry. And he was certainly a Greek."

"How d'you work that out?" I asked, startled.

He chuckled. "He welcomed Prospero to the island with 'water with berries in it.' Haven't you come across the Greek custom of giving you berried jam in a glass of water?"

"No, I haven't. But really, you can't have that! It could even be coffee! What would that make him? French?"

"All right," he said amiably, "we'll leave poor Caliban as an 'infernal' seeking for grace. Well, that's all." Here the white cat stretched, flexed its claws, and yawned, very loudly. Sir Julian laughed. "You shouldn't have encouraged me. Nitwit has heard it all before, and so, I'm afraid, has poor Max."

"Well, I hadn't, and it's fascinating. One could have endless fun. I must read it again and look for all these things. I wish I thought my sister had a copy here."

"Take mine," he said immediately. "It should be somewhere on top of the bookcase, I think, Max. . . . Thanks very much." This as his son went to get it.

I said quickly, "But if you're working on it—"

"Working?" The word, lightly spoken as it was, sounded somehow out of tune. "You've just heard how seriously. In any case, I use a Penguin for working, one I can mark and cut up . . . Ah, thank you, Max; and here are your roses, too. That's my own copy; it's a bit ancient, and I'm afraid it's been scribbled in, but perhaps you can ignore that."

I had already seen the pencilled notes. Holding the book as if it were the original Blackfriars prompt copy, with the author's jottings in the margin, I got to my feet. Sir Julian rose with me, and the white cat, displaced, jumped down and stalked with offended dignity off the terrace and down the steps to the rose garden.

"I'll really have to go," I said. "Thank you for the book, I'll take great care of it. I—I know I've stayed far too long, but I've really loved it."

"My dear child, you've done us both a kindness. I've enjoyed your visit enormously, and I hope you'll come back soon. As you see, there's a limit to the amount of my conversation that Max and the cat will stand, and it's pleasant to have a good-mannered and captive audience again. Well, if you must . . ."

The woods were dark already with the quickly falling twilight. Mr. Gale, accompanying me politely to the edge of the rose garden, pointed out the path which led down to the clearing where the pool lay. The beautiful Nitwit was there, dreamily regarding a large moth which hovered near some honeysuckle. Max Gale picked him up, said goodbye to me, and went quickly back. A very few minutes later I heard the sound of the piano. He had lost no time in getting back to work. Then the woods closed in and I was out of hearing.

The woods were always quiet, but now, with the darkness muffling their boughs, they seemed to hold a hushed and heavy stillness that might be the herald of storm. The scent of flowers hung like musk on the air.

As I picked my way carefully down the path I was thinking of the recent interview; not of the "theory" with which Sir Julian had been beguiling his exile, but of Sir Julian himself, and what Phyl and Godfrey had said about him.

That there had been—still was—something badly wrong seemed obvious: not only was there the physical evidence that even I could see, there was also that attitude of watchful tension in the younger man. But against this could be set the recent conversation, not the normal —and even gay—tone of it, but the use of certain phrases that had struck me. Would a man who had recently emerged from a mental home talk so casually and cheerfully about the "lunatic fringe" inhabited by his son? A son had, after all, a big stake in his father's sanity. And would the son, in his turn, speak of his father's "obsession," and the need to "humour" him? Perhaps if the need was serious, this was Mr. Gale's way of passing off a potentially tricky situation? Perhaps that edgy, watchful air of his was on my behalf as much as his father's?

Here I gave up. But as for the idea of Sir Julian's roaming the countryside with a rifle to the danger of all and sundry, I could believe it no more than formerly. I would as soon suspect Phyllida, or Godfrey Manning himself.

And (I thought) I would suspect Max Gale a darned sight sooner than any.

I could hear the trickle of water now, and ahead of me was the break in the trees where the pool lay. At the same moment I became conscious of a strange noise, new to me, like nothing more or less than the clucking and chattering of a collection of hens. It seemed to come from the clearing.

Then I realized what it was: the evening chorus at the pool—the croaking of the innumerable frogs who must live there. I had stopped at the edge of the clearing to pick up my towel, and some of them must have seen me, for the croaking stopped, and then I heard the rhythmic plopping of small bodies diving into the water. Intrigued, I drew back behind the bushes, then made a silent way round the outer edge of the clearing towards the far side of the pool, where there was cover. Now I was above the bank. I gently pressed the branches aside, and peered down.

At first, in the dusk, I could see nothing but the dark gleam of the water where the sky's reflection struck it between the upper boughs, and the mat circles of the small lily leaves and some floating weed. Then I saw a frog, a big one, sitting on a lily pad, his throat distended and pulsing with his queer little song. His body was fat and freckled, like a laurel leaf by moonlight, and the light struck back from eyes bright as blackberry pips. Close by him sang another, and then another. . . .

Amused and interested, I stood very still. Growing every moment in volume, the chorus gobbled happily on.

Silence, as sudden as if a switch had been pressed. Then my frog dived. All around the lily pads the surface ringed and plopped as the whole choir took to the water. Someone was coming up the path from the bay.

For a moment I wondered if Phyllida had been down to the beach to find me; then I realized that the newcomer was a man. His steps were heavy, and his breathing, and then I heard him clear his throat softly and spit. It was a cautious sound, as if he were anxious not to make too much noise. The heavy steps were cautious, too, and the rough, hurried breathing, which he was obviously trying to control, sounded oddly disquieting in the now silent woods. I let the bushes slip back into place, and stood still where I was, to wait for him to pass.

The dimming light showed him as he emerged into the clearing; Greek, someone I hadn't seen before, a young man, thickset and broad-chested, in dark trousers and a high-necked fisherman's sweater. He carried an old jacket of some lighter colour over one arm.

He paused at the other side of the pool, but only to reach into a pocket for a cigarette, which he put between his lips. But in the very act of striking the match, he checked himself, then shrugged, and put it away again, shoving the cigarette behind his ear. He could not have indicated his need for secrecy more plainly if he had spoken.

As he turned to go on his way, I saw his face fairly clearly. There was a furtive, sweating excitement there that was disturbing, so that when he glanced round as if he had heard some noise I found myself shrinking back behind my screen of leaves, conscious of my own quickened heartbeats.

He saw nothing. He drew the back of a hand over his forehead, shifted his coat to the other arm, and trod with the same hasty caution up the steep path towards the Castello.

Above me a sudden gust of wind ran through the treetops, and chilly air blew through the trunks with the fresh, sharp smell of coming rain.

But I kept quite still until the sound of the Greek's footsteps had died away and beside me the frog had climbed out again on to his lily pad and swelled his little throat for song.

CHAPTER

SIX

ह**ू**

Methinks he hath no drowning mark upon him . . .

Act I, Scene 1

For some reason that I never paused to examine, I didn't tell my sister about my visit to the Gales, not even when next morning she decided that for once she would go down to the bay with me, and, as we passed the pool, pointed out the path that led up to the Castello.

The clearing looked very different this morning with the high clear light pouring into it. There had been a sudden little snap of storm during the night, with a strong wind that died with the dawn, and this had cleared the air and freshened the woods. Down in the bay the sand was dazzling in the morning sun, and the wake of the wind had left a ripple at the sea's edge.

I spread a rug in the shade of the pines that overhung the sand, and dumped our things on it.

"You are coming in, aren't you?"

"Sure thing. Now I'm down here, nothing will stop me from wallowing in the shallow bit, even if I do look like a mother elephant expecting twins. That's a smashing swimsuit, Lucy, where'd you get it?"

"Marks and Spencers."

"Good heavens."

"Well, *I* didn't marry a rich man," I said cheerfully, pulling up the shoulder straps.

"And a fat lot of good it does me in my condition." She looked sadly down at her figure, sighed, and dropped her smart beach coat down beside the hold-all containing all the sun lotions, magazines, Elizabeth Arden cosmetics, and other paraphernalia without which she would never dream of committing herself to the beach. "It isn't fair. Just look at me, and these things come from Fabiani."

"You poor thing," I said derisively. "Will they go in the water? And for Pete's sake, are you going to bathe with that Koh-i-noor thing on?"

"Heavens, *no!*" She slipped the enormous marquise diamond off her finger, dropped it into the plastic bag that held her cosmetics, and zipped the bag shut. "Well, let's go in. I only hope your friend doesn't mistake me for the dolphin and let fly. Much the same general shape, wouldn't you say?"

"You'll be all right. He doesn't wear yellow."

"Seriously, there *isn't* anyone watching, is there, Lucy? I'd just as soon not have an audience."

"If you keep near inshore they can't see you anyway, unless they come to the front of the terrace. I'll go and look."

The water in the shade of the pines was a deep, deep green, lighting to a dazzling pale blue where a bar of sand ran out into the bay. I walked out along this, thigh-deep, until I was about fifty yards from the shore, then turned and looked up towards the terrace of the Castello. There was no one visible, so I waved to Phyllida to follow me in. As we swam and splashed, I kept an eye open to seaward for the dolphin, but, though I thought once that I could see a gleaming wheel turning a long way out, the creature did not approach the bay. After a time we waded back to the beach, where we lay sunning ourselves and talking idly, until Phyl's remarks, which had been getting briefer and briefer, and more and more sleepy, ceased altogether.

I left her sleeping, and went back into the water.

Though I had kept a wary eye on the woods and the terrace every time I bathed, I had never seen anyone since the first day, so it was with a slight feeling of surprise that I now saw someone sitting there, at the table under the stone pine. Grey hair. Sir Julian Gale. He lifted a hand to me, and I waved back, feeling absurdly pleased that he should have bothered. He turned away immediately, his head bent over a book. I caught the flutter of its pages.

There was no one with him on the terrace, but as I turned to let myself down into the deep water beyond the bar, something else caught my eye.

In one of the upper windows, which stood open, something had flashed. And behind the flash I saw movement, as whoever stood watching there lifted the binoculars again to focus them on the bay. . . .

There is something particularly infuriating about being watched in this way. I should have dearly loved to return rudeness for rudeness by pulling a very nasty face straight at the Castello windows, but Sir Julian might have seen it and thought it was meant for him, so I merely splashed back to the sandbar, where I stood up, and, without another glance, stalked expressively (drama school exercise: Outraged Bather Driven from Water) towards the rocks at the southern edge of the bay. I would finish my swim from the rocks beyond the point, out of range of the Castello.

I hadn't reckoned on its being quite so difficult to stalk with dignity through three feet of water. By the time I reached the end of the sandbar and the deep pool near the rocks, I was furiously angry with Max Gale and wishing I had gone straight out on to the beach. But I was damned if I would be driven back now. I plunged across the deep water, and was soon scrambling out under the pines.

A path ran through the tumble of rocks at the cliff's foot, leading, I supposed, to Godfrey Manning's villa, but its surface looked stony, so I stayed on the rocks below. These, scoured white by the sea and seamed with rock pools, stretched out from the cliff in stacks and ridges, with their roots in the calm, creaming water.

I began to pick my way along between the pools. The rocks were hot, and smooth to the feet. There were crevices filled with flowering bushes, running right down to the water's edge, where the green swell lifted and sank, and here and there a jut of the living cliff thrust out into the water, with the path above it, and bushes at its rim hanging right out over the sea.

At the point I paused. Here the rocks were more broken, as if the tide was driven hard that way when there was a wind, and under the cliff was a pile of broken rock and sea wrack, some of which looked fresh enough to have come up in last night's squall. Farther round, beyond the next curve of the cliff, I could see where a cove or inlet ran in, deep and narrow and surrounded by thick trees which stretched right up the slopes of the cliff; there were pines and oaks and hollies, and among them the limes of which Sir Julian had spoken. Through the boughs of a young thicket at the cliff's foot I caught a glimpse of red tiling which must be the roof of Godfrey's boathouse.

There was nobody about. I decided to finish my bathe in the deep water off the point and then return by the path.

I made my way carefully through the piled rocks and the sea wrack. Here and there a shallow pool barred the way, and I paddled across with caution, wondering uneasily about sea urchins, which in these waters (I had read) can drive poisonous spines into your feet. "Like hedgehogs which Lie tumbling in my barefoot way and mount Their pricks at my footfall . . ." Poor Caliban. Was Julian Gale right? I wondered. I had read *The Tempest* late into the night, following up the fascinating game he had suggested, and I had even had a few ideas myself, things I must ask him when I went to the Castello again . . . if I ever went to the Castello again. . . . But of course I would have to return the Shakespeare . . . if I could find out from Miranda or Adoni or someone when Max Gale was likely to be out. . . .

I had come to the edge of a deep inlet, a miniature cove running back through the rocks. This would be as good a place as any. I paused, peering down into it, to see what the bottom was like.

The water was the colour of Imperial jade. Tiny shrimplike creatures scudded here and there among the olive and scarlet bladders, and shoals of small fish darted and nibbled. The shadows cast by the sun looked blue-black, and were alive with the movements of crabs which shuffled through the brown weed that clothed the bottom. The weed itself moved all the time, faintly and continuously, like rags in the swell. A cuttlefish bone showed white and bare. "Of his bones are coral made. Those are pearls . . ."

The body was lying half in, half out, of the largest patch of shadow. The sun, shining straight into my eyes, had hidden it till now, the hump of flesh and clothes not holding any kind of human shape, just a lump of rags rolled over and over by the swell and dumped there, jammed somehow under an overhang at the base of the pool.

Even now, with the sun directly in my eyes, I could hardly be sure. Sick and shaken, I hesitated; but of course I would have to look. I sank to my knees at the edge of the pool, and shaded my eyes to peer downwards. . . .

The rags moved in the faint swell like weed. Surely it was only weed . . . ? But then I saw the head, the face, a shape blurred and bleached under dark hair. Some sea creatures had already been at it. the tiny fish flicked to and fro, busily, in the green water.

Spiro, I thought, *Spiro.* . . . And his mother would have to see this. Surely it would be better to say nothing, to let the tide carry it away again; let the busy sea creatures purge and clean it to its sea change, like the cuttlefish bone showing white beside the dark hair . . . ?

Then reason threw its ice water on my confusion. She would have to be told. It would be crueller not to tell her. And there was no tide here. Without another storm, the thing could be held down here for days, for anyone to find.

Some freak current thrust a tentacle of movement through the pool. The water swayed, and the dead man moved his head. With the movement, I knew him. It wasn't specifically the face that I recognized; that would have been impossible: but somehow everything came together in the same moment to enforce recognition—the shape of face and head, the colours, better seen now, of the sodden lumps of rag that had been navy trousers and sweater and light grey jacket. . . .

It wasn't Spiro after all; not, that is, unless it had been Spiro in the woods last night, still alive and making his way up towards the Castello. There could be no doubt about it, no possible doubt. This was the man I had seen last night in the clearing. I found that I was sitting back on my heels, slumped to one side, with a hand out to the hot face of a boulder beside me. It was one thing to find a dead man; but to recognize him, and to know where he had been shortly before he had met his death . . .

I had my eyes shut as tightly as the fingers that gripped the hot stone. The sunlight boiled and fizzed against the closed lids. I bit my lips, and breathed slowly and hard, and concentrated on not being sick. Phyllida: the thought was as bracing as sal volatile: Phyllida mustn't see this, or even be allowed to suspect the horror that lay just round the point from her. I must steady myself decently, then go back to Phyllida, and somehow persuade her to leave the beach soon. Then get quietly to the telephone and get in touch with the police.

I opened my eyes with a silly hope that somehow I had been wrong and there was no dead man there in the water. But he still lay in his splash of inky shadow, grotesque and faintly moving and familiar. I got to my feet, held myself steady by the boulder for another full minute, then, without looking back, made my way through the tumble of rock towards the thicket that edged the cliff path. It was only when I had reached the bushes, and was wondering if I could pull myself up the eight feet or so to the path, that some sound, vaguely heard a few moments ago, and now repeated, made me pause and glance to my left, towards the boathouse. Someone had slammed a door. Something appeared to be wrong with the catch, because I heard, clearly now, an exclamation of irritation, and the slam was repeated. This time the door shut firmly, and a moment later I heard footsteps, and Godfrey Manning came briskly into view along the path.

I wasn't sure if he was coming my way, or if the path branched off above the trees somewhere for the Villa Rotha. I opened my mouth to call him, hoping that this wouldn't also bring Phyllida, but at the same moment Godfrey glanced up and saw me below him on the rocks. He lifted a hand in greeting, but before he could call out I put a finger to my lips, then beckoned urgently.

Not surprisingly, he looked startled, but his expression deepened sharply into concern as he approached and paused on the path above me.

"Lucy? Is something wrong? Are you feeling ill? The sun?" Then his voice changed. "It's not that damned lunatic again with the rifle?"

I shook my head. Infuriatingly, after I had so far controlled myself, I found I couldn't speak. I pointed.

He glanced over towards the pool, but at that distance nothing was visible. Then he swung himself lightly down through the bushes to where I stood, and his arm went round me, gently.

"You'd better sit down. . . . There. Better? . . . All right, don't try to talk any more. Something scared you, over there in the big pool? . . . Relax a minute now; I'll go and take a look, but don't you move. Just sit there quietly, and don't worry. I won't be long."

I sat with my hands jammed tightly together between my knees, and watched my feet. I heard Godfrey's steps, quick and confident, cross the rocks towards the pool. Then there was silence, prolonged. The sea murmured, and some cliff-building swallows twittered shrilly as they cut in and out above the path.

I looked up. He was standing stock-still where I had stood, staring down. He was in profile to me, and I could see that he looked considerably shaken. It was only then that it occurred to me that he, too, must in the first moment of shock have expected it to be Spiro. If I had been capable of reasoned thought or speech, I should have known this, and spared him.

I cleared my throat. "It's not . . . Spiro, is it?"

"No."

"Do you know who it is?"

I thought he hesitated, then he nodded. "His name's Yanni Zoulas."

"Oh? You *do* know him?" Somehow this shook me, too, though it was reasonable to assume that the man had been drowned locally. "Is he from near here, then?"

"Yes, from the village."

"What—what do you suppose happened?"

"God knows. Some accident at sea, that's obvious. He was a fisherman, and usually went out alone . . . You must have seen his boat; it was always plying to and fro along this bit of shore—the rather pretty blue boat, with the dark brown sail. But in last night's sea . . . I wouldn't have thought . . ."

His voice trailed away as he stared frowningly down at the pool. Then he turned and made his way back across the rock to where I sat.

"Two in a week?" I said. It came out as a query, asked quite as if

Godfrey could supply the answer. I hadn't meant even to say it aloud, and could have bitten my tongue with vexation as soon as it was out.

"Two in a week?" He spoke so blankly that it was evident my meaning hadn't registered. "Oh, I see."

"I'm sorry. It was stupid of me. I was thinking aloud. I shouldn't have reminded you. It's just one of those ghastly coincidences."

"Normally," he said, "I'd have said I didn't believe in coincidence. In fact, if I hadn't seen with my own eyes what happened to Spiro, I'd certainly be starting to wonder what was going on around here." He paused, and his eyes went back to the pool. "As it is, all that has happened is that two young men from the same district have died this week by drowning, and in a community that lives largely by the sea that's hardly surprising. Only—" He stopped.

"Only what?"

He looked at me with troubled eyes. "One doesn't expect an epidemic of it in summer weather, that's all."

"Godfrey, what is it? You look as if you thought—" I, too, checked myself, biting my lip. He watched me bleakly, saying nothing. I finished, rather hoarsely, "Are you trying to tell me that this wasn't an accident?"

"Good God, no! Just that it poses problems. But none that you need worry about. In any case, they may never arise."

None that you need worry about. . . . Heaven knew what he'd have said if he had had even the slightest inkling of the problem it had set me. . . . Why I still said nothing about last night I am not quite sure. I think now that this last incident took its place in a context of violence, felt rather than apprehended, that made it unsurprising and that forced me, through some instinct of fear, to hold my tongue. It was as if the first shot from that silenced rifle had been the signal for danger and fear to crowd in; as if by my silence I could still detach myself from them and stay inside my own bubble of security, keep my own enchanted island free of invaders from the violent world I had come here to escape.

So I said instead, "Has he any people?"

"A wife. They live with his parents. You probably know the house, it's that pink one at the crossroads."

"Yes, I do. It's very pretty. I remember thinking that the folk in it must be well off."

"They were. They're going to miss him."

I looked at him, startled, not by the words, which were trite, but by the quite undue dryness of his tone.

"You *are* getting at something. You *know* something about this, don't you? Why won't you tell me?"

He hesitated, then smiled suddenly. "I don't really know why not. It hardly concerns me, and it certainly won't touch you. It's only that when the police move in on this, something might crop up that could be awkward."

"Such as?"

He lifted his shoulders. "No plain and simple fisherman lived as well as Yanni and his family. Rumour has it that he was a smuggler, with a regular 'milk run' into Albania, and that he made a good bit on the side."

"Well, but surely . . . I'd have imagined that an awful lot of men played around with that sort of thing hereabouts? And Corfu's very well placed, just next door to the Iron Curtain. I suppose any sort of 'luxury goods' would go well there? But how could anyone like Yanni Zoulas get supplies of things like that?"

"How do I know? He'd have his contacts: someone in Corfu town, perhaps, who has connections with Athens or Italy. . . . But I'm sure that Yanni Zoulas wouldn't be in it on his own account. He wasn't exactly a mastermind. He probably did it for a salary."

I licked my lips. "Even so . . . You wouldn't suggest that there could be any connection—that he was *killed* because of this? Is that what you're getting at? That—that would make it murder, Godfrey."

"No, no. For goodness' sake, I wasn't suggesting anything like that! Good God, no! Don't upset yourself. Why, you're as white as a sheet! Look, the idea's pure nonsense. I doubt if poor Yanni would ever be important enough to get himself murdered! You can forget that. But it did occur to me to wonder if he could have run into trouble on the other side—coast guard trouble: I believe they're hot stuff over there, searchlights, machine guns, the lot. If he did, and was wounded, and then ran for home, that might account for an accident happening on a night that wasn't particularly rough. He might have fainted and gone overboard."

"I see. But even if the police do find out something about it, his family won't be in trouble, will they?"

"I doubt it. It isn't that."

"Then what's worrying *you?*"

"It might bring them closer to young Spiro than would be quite pleasant," said Godfrey frankly. "I've a strong suspicion that he'd been out with Yanni more than once. It didn't worry me, and I asked no questions; the boy had a mother and sister to keep, and how he did it was his own affair. But I don't want them to find out about it now. It would serve no purpose, and might distress his mother. According to her, Spiro was *sans peur et sans reproche*, and a good Christian into the bargain. I'm sure she'd label smuggling as immoral, however lightly you or I might regard it."

"I didn't say I regarded it lightly. I think that if you live under a country's protection you should obey its laws. I just wasn't surprised. But you know, even if the police do find out something discreditable about Spiro, I'm sure they'd never tell Maria. Police are human, when all's said and done, and the boy's dead."

"You're probably right. Ah well . . ." He stretched, and sighed. "Hell, what a wretched business. We'd better go and get it over. Do you feel as if you'd like to move now?"

"Oh, yes, I'm fine."

He took my arm, and helped me up the rough bank to the path.

"I'm going to take you up to my house now, to telephone," he said. "It's nearer, and there's no need to alarm your sister till you're feeling a bit more the thing yourself. The police will want to see you, and you can see them at my place if you like, then I'll take you home by road, in the car. . . . Now, did you have some clothes with you, or some sort of wrap and shoes? If you wait here a moment, I'll get them."

"They're back in the bay, but I'm afraid Phyl's there, too. I left her asleep on the beach. She's probably awake by now, and wondering where I am."

"Oh." He looked uncertain. "Well, that alters things, doesn't it? We'll have to tell her. I don't know much about these things, but will it—well, upset her, or anything?"

"I think she'll be okay as long as she doesn't see the body. She'll have to know soon enough. . . . Wait a minute, someone's coming. That'll be her."

A second later she appeared on the path, round the point of the cliff. She must have been awake for some time, for all traces of the sea had been removed; she was freshly made up, her hair was shining and immaculate, she had clipped a pretty beach skirt on over her bathing costume, and she wore her gay beach coat. As usual, the sight of her brought my own shortcomings immediately to mind. I was conscious for the first time of what I must look like, with the salt dried on my skin, my hair damp, and my face—I imagined—still sallow with shock.

She said gaily, "I thought I heard voices! Hullo, Godfrey! Were you on your way over to us, or did you just come down to swim?"

"Neither. I was down at the boathouse giving the boat a once-over, when I saw Lucy."

I said, "Are those my shoes you've brought? Thanks very much. How did you guess I'd be wanting them?"

"Well, dearie, knowing you," said Phyllida, "when I woke up and found you'd vanished, I knew you'd be straying along here, poking around in the rock pools, and heaven knew how far you'd get." She laughed up at Godfrey. "It wouldn't surprise me in the least to find her with a jam jar full of assorted shrimps and things to take home. I remember once—" She stopped. There was a pause, in which she looked from one to the other of us. Then her voice sharpened. "Lucy. Godfrey. Something's wrong. What is it?"

He hesitated just that second too long. "Your sister was feeling the heat a bit, and I offered to take her up to my house and give her a drink. She told me you were on the beach, so I was just coming across for you. I hope you'll come up, too?"

His tone was perfect, easy and natural, but my sister was never anybody's fool. She had seen all she needed to see in my face, and in the fact that Godfrey's hand still supported my arm.

She said, more sharply still, "Something *is* wrong. Lucy, you look awful . . . and it's not the heat, either; don't give me that; you never felt the heat in your life. What's happened? Have you hurt yourself, or something?"

"No, no. There's nothing the matter with me, honestly." I disengaged myself gently, and looked up at Godfrey. It struck me suddenly, irrelevantly, that he was better-looking than I had thought. The sunlight showed up the deep tan of his skin and the crisp hair bleached fair at the front. Against the tan his eyes looked a very clear grey.

I said, "You may as well tell her straight away."

"Very well. Phyl, I'm afraid a beastly thing's happened. One of the local fishermen's been drowned and washed ashore over there, and Lucy found the body."

"Oh, my God, how ghastly! Lucy, my dear . . . you poor kid! I suppose it looked—" Then her eyes widened and a hand went up to her face. "Did you *see?* Could you tell? I mean . . . after a week . . ."

"It's not Spiro." Godfrey spoke quickly, almost harshly.

"*It's not?*" The hand dropped, and she let out a long breath of relief. "Oh, I was so sure . . . But does that mean *two*, in just a few days? Have you any idea who it is?"

"It's a local man called Yanni Zoulas. I doubt if you know him. Look, we were just going up to telephone. Will you come with us? If I just go back now to the bay for the rest of—"

He stopped abruptly, and turned. A shadow fell across me where I sat pulling on my sandals. Max Gale's voice said, just behind me:

"Is anything the matter?"

I know I jumped as if he had hit me. The other two were caught gaping, as if in some guilty act. He must be stones heavier than Phyllida, but we had none of us heard a sound. I thought, He must move like a cat.

For seconds nobody replied. It was a queer, hair-prickling little pause, during which the men eyed each other like unfriendly dogs circling one another, and I sat with a sandal half on, watching them.

"The matter?" said Godfrey.

I knew then that he didn't want to tell Gale what had happened. The knowledge, somehow not surprising, came like a cold breath along my skin. Mr. Gale glanced from Godfrey to Phyl, then down at me, and I bent my head quickly, pulled the sandal on, and began to fasten the strap.

He said impatiently, "It's obvious there's something. I was watching the bay with glasses, and I thought I saw something odd—some debris or other floating, away out; I couldn't make it out. Then Miss Waring came this way, and I saw her on the rocks that run out from the point. She stopped and looked into one of the pools, and her reactions made it pretty obvious that there was something very wrong indeed. Then you went over and made it rather plainer. What is it? Or shall I go and see for myself?"

It was Phyllida who answered him. She must not have felt the overtones that had chilled me—but then she didn't know what I knew. She said, in a sort of rush, "It's a dead body. Drowned. In that pool, there. We were just going up to phone the police."

There was a moment in which I seemed to hear the cliff swallows, very loud and shrill, just overhead. Then Max Gale said, "Who is it? Do you know?"

Godfrey still said nothing. He had not taken his eyes off the other man's face. It was again Phyllida who answered.

"I forget the name. Godfrey says he's from the village. Yanni something."

"Yanni Zoulas," I said.

He looked down at me as if he were aware fully for the first time that I was there. But I got the strong impression that he wasn't seeing me even now. He didn't speak.

"Did you know him?" I asked.

The dark eyes focussed on me for a moment, then he looked away again, over towards the pool. "Why, yes, slightly."

Godfrey said, "You say you were watching something floating, some debris. You couldn't say what sort of thing? Could it have been flotsam from a sunk boat?"

"Eh? Well, I told you I couldn't see at that distance, but it could have been . . . My God, yes, I suppose it could!" All of a sudden Gale was fully with us; his gaze sharpened, and he spoke abruptly. "I wonder what time he went out last night. I thought I heard a boat soon after midnight, bearing northeast." He looked at Godfrey. "Did you hear it?"

"No."

"Last night?" said Phyllida. "Did it happen as recently as that? Could you tell, Godfrey?"

"I'm not an expert. I don't know. I don't think he's been there long. However, it shouldn't be hard to find out when he was last seen."

I had been watching Max Gale's face. He was looking thoughtful now, grave—anything but the way I knew he ought to be looking. "It must have happened within the last forty-eight hours. I saw his boat myself on Saturday. It went past the bay at about three in the afternoon."

If I hadn't known what I did, I'd never have known that he was lying —or rather, implying a lie. For a moment I even wondered if perhaps Yanni had not been on his way to the Castello last night, then I remembered that Mr. Gale had, in the last few minutes, given me another reason for doubting his good faith. He looked down suddenly, and caught me watching him. I bent my head again, and fiddled with the second sandal.

"Well," said Godfrey, "it'll be easy enough to check with his family, and the sooner we let the experts get on the job, the better. Shall we go? One thing, nobody need stay with the body. There's no tide to shift it . . . Where are you going?"

Max Gale didn't trouble to answer; he was already swinging himself down to the rocks below us. Godfrey made a quick, involuntary movement as if to stop him, then he shrugged, said softly to us, "Do you mind? We won't be long," and slithered in his turn down through the bushes.

Gale was bending over the pool. Like Godfrey, he stood looking down at the body for some time in silence, then he did what neither Godfrey nor I had done: he lay flat at the edge of the rock, and reached down through the water as if to touch the dead man. I saw Godfrey make another of those sharp, involuntary movements, but he must have decided that what evidence there was could hardly be damaged further by a touch, for he said nothing, merely stooping down himself to watch with close attention.

"What in the world are they doing?" asked Phyl, rather petulantly.

I was clasping my knees, hugging myself together closely. In spite of the sun, I had begun to feel cold. "I don't know and I don't care. I hope they hurry, that's all. I want to get some clothes on and get the police over and done with."

"You poor lamb, are you cold? Here, have my coat." She took it off and dropped it over my shoulders, and I hugged it gratefully round me.

"Thanks a lot. That's marvellous." I laughed a little. "At least it puts me in competition again! I wish you didn't always look as if you'd just got back from Elizabeth Arden, when I feel like a bit of Mr. Gale's debris. It was probably me he saw floating. If, that is, he saw anything."

She looked quickly down at me. "What does that mean? It sounds loaded."

"Not really."

She sat down beside me. "You don't often make remarks for nothing. What *did* you mean?"

"I'm not happy about this affair, that's all."

"Well, heavens, who is? But is it an 'affair'?"

"I don't know. There's a feeling . . . a feeling that there's something going on. I can't put it better than that, and I'm probably wrong, but I think—I *think*—Godfrey feels it, too. Why don't he and Mr. Gale like each other?"

"I didn't know they didn't. They *were* a bit wary today, weren't they? I suppose Godfrey's more upset than he lets on . . . after all, it's rather soon after the Spiro business . . . and Max Gale doesn't just put himself out to be charming, does he?"

"He has things on his mind," I said.

The remark was intended merely as an evasion, to imply only that his personal worries—over his father—made him difficult to know or like, but she took it to refer specifically to what had just happened. She nodded.

"I thought so, too. Oh, nothing special, just that he seemed to be thinking about something else. But what did *you* mean?" She shot me another look. "Something's really worrying you, isn't it?"

I hesitated. "Did it strike you as odd, the way Mr. Gale took the news?"

"Well, no, it didn't. Perhaps because I know him better than you. He's never very forthcoming. What sort of 'odd' did you mean?"

I hesitated again, then decided not to specify. "As if he weren't surprised that a body should roll up here."

"I don't suppose he was. He'd be expecting it to be Spiro."

"Oh, of course," I said. "Look, they seem to be coming back."

Mr. Gale had finished whatever grisly examination he had been conducting, and had withdrawn his hand. He rinsed it in the salt water, then stood up, drying it on a handkerchief. As far as I could make out, the two men still hadn't spoken a word. Now Godfrey said something with a gesture towards Phyl and myself, and they turned together and started over to us.

"Thank goodness," I said.

"You'll feel better when you've had a drink, old dear," said my sister.

"Coffee," I said, "as hot as love and as sweet as hell."

"Godfrey might even run to that, you never know."

The men scrambled up to the path beside us.

"Well?" said Phyl and I, together.

They exchanged a glance, which might even be said to hold complicity. Then Gale said, "It should be interesting to hear what the doctor has to say. He seems to have been knocked about the head a bit. I was wondering if the neck was broken, but I don't think so."

Godfrey's eye met mine. I stood up. "Well, when the boat's found, there may be something there to show how it happened."

"For all we know," said Godfrey, "that's been done and the hue and cry's on already. Let's go, shall we?"

"Thank goodness!" I said. "But I still want to get dressed. My things—"

"Good God, I was forgetting. Well, hang on another minute or two, I won't be long."

Max Gale said, in that abrupt, rather aggressive way of his, "You three start up the path. I'll go and pick your stuff up and bring it along."

He had so plainly not been invited to go with us, and just as plainly fully intended to hear all that was said to the police, that I thought Godfrey was going to demur. But Phyllida got eagerly to her feet.

"Yes, let's get away from here! It's giving me the grue. Mr. Gale, if you *would* be an angel . . . I've left some things, too; they're under the pine trees."

"I saw where they were. I won't be long. Don't wait for me; I'll catch you up."

He went quickly. Godfrey looked after him, the grey eyes curiously cold. Then he caught me watching him, and smiled. "Well, this way."

The path followed the cliff as far as the boathouse, then turned up a steep zigzag through the trees. We toiled up it, grateful for the shade. Godfrey walked between us, in a sort of awkwardly divided solicitude that might at any other time have been amusing; but just now all I could think of was a bit of solitude in his bathroom, then a comfortable chair, and—failing the coffee—a long, cool drink. I hoped Max Gale would hurry with the clothes. I thought he probably would: he wouldn't want to miss what was said to the police. It had surprised me that he had risked this by offering to go back.

Godfrey had paused to help Phyl negotiate a dry gully which the winter's rain had gouged across the path. I was a few paces ahead of them when I came to a corner where a sudden gap in the trees gave a view of the point below.

I might have known there would be a good reason for Max Gale's offer. He was back at the rock pool, lying flat as before, reaching down into the water. I could just see his head and shoulders. Just as I caught the glimpse of him he withdrew his arm and got quickly to his feet. As he turned, I drew back into the shade of the trees, and just in time, for he glanced up briefly before he vaulted up to the path and out of sight.

"Tired?" asked Godfrey, just behind me.

I started. "No, not a bit. Just getting my breath. But I'll be glad when it's all over."

"So shall we all. I seem to have spent the whole week with the police as it is." He added, rather bitterly, "At least they know their way here, and most of the questions to ask."

Phyllida touched his arm gently. "Poor Godfrey. But we're terribly grateful. And at least this time it doesn't touch you . . . except as a rather ghastly sort of coincidence."

His eyes met mine. They held the bleak expression I was beginning to know.

"I don't believe in coincidence," he said.

CHAPTER

SEVEN

ॐ

What have we here? A man or a fish? Dead or alive?

Act II, Scene 2

Either she had been more distressed than she had allowed us to see or else the trip down to the beach in the heat, with the bathe and the climb to the Villa Rotha, had been too much for Phyllida. Though we spent the rest of the day quietly and she lay down after lunch for a couple of hours, by evening she was tired, fidgety, and more than somewhat out of temper, and very ready to be persuaded to go to bed early.

Maria and Miranda had gone as soon as dinner was over. By ten o'clock the house was very quiet. Even the pines on the hill behind it were still, and once I had shut the windows I could hear no sound from the sea.

I felt tired myself, but restless, with sleep still a long way off, so I went along to the scrubbed and empty kitchen, made myself more coffee, then took it through to the *salotto*, put my feet on a chair, some Mozart on the gramophone, and settled myself for a quiet evening.

But things didn't quite work out that way. The calm, beautiful room, even the music, did not manage to keep at bay the thoughts that had been knocking for admission since that morning. In spite of myself, my mind went persistently back to the morning's incidents: the discovery in the pool, the two men's raw antagonism, and the long, wearying aftermath of interrogation, with the fresh problems it had brought to light.

The police from Corfu had been civil, thorough, and kind. They had arrived fairly soon after we had reached Godfrey's house, and had gone straight down with the two men to see the body. Shortly after that a boat had arrived from somewhere, and presently departed with its burden. Another came soon afterwards, and cruised off out to sea—searching, one assumed, for the "debris" which Mr. Gale insisted that he had seen. From the terrace of the Villa Rotha, Phyl and I had watched it tacking to and fro some way out from land, but with what success it had been impossible—failing Mr. Gale's binoculars—to guess.

Then the men came back. The questions had been searching, but easy enough for my part to answer, because of course nobody imagined that I had ever seen Yanni before in my life, so the only questions I was asked were those touching on my finding of the body.

And when Max Gale reiterated to the police that he had not laid eyes on Yanni Zoulas since a possible glimpse of his boat on Saturday afternoon, I had not said a word.

It was this that bore on me now, heavily, as I sat there alone in the *salotto*, with darkness thickening outside the windows and moths thumping against the lighted glass. And if I was beginning to get too clear an idea why, I didn't want to face that, either. I pushed that line of thought to one side, and concentrated firmly on the facts.

These were, in their own way, comforting. Godfrey had rung up in the late afternoon to give us the latest reports. It appeared that Yanni's boat had been found drifting, and on the boom were traces of hairs and blood where, as the boat heeled in a sudden squall, it must have struck him and sent him overboard. An almost empty bottle of ouzo, which had rolled away behind a pile of rope and tackle, seemed to provide a clue to the young fisherman's carelessness. The doctor had given it as his opinion (said Godfrey) that Yanni had been dead when he went into the water. The police did not seem inclined to press the matter further. Of the debris reported by Mr. Gale no trace had been found.

Finally—Godfrey was a little cryptic over this part of the message, as the telephone was on a party line—finally, no mention had been made of any illegal activities of the dead man. Presumably his boat had been searched, and nothing had come to light, so the police (who preferred to turn a blind eye to small offences unless action was forced on them) were satisfied that the fatal voyage had been a routine fishing trip, and that Yanni's death had been accidental. It was obvious that they had no intention of opening any further line of inquiry.

So much for Godfrey's anxiety. My own went a little further.

It had transpired, from police inquiries, that the last time Yanni's family had seen him alive was on Sunday: he had spent the day with them, they said, going with them to watch the procession and returning home in the late afternoon. Yes, he had seemed in good spirits. Yes, he had been drinking a fair amount. He had had a meal, and then had gone out. No, he had not said where he was going, why should he? They had assumed he was going fishing, as usual. He had gone down to the boat. Yes, alone; he usually went alone. That was the last time they had seen him.

It was the last time anyone had seen him, according to the police report. And I had said nothing to make them alter it. Where Godfrey had been worrying about the inquiry's leading back to Spiro, I was worrying about its involving Julian Gale. That Max Gale was somehow implicated seemed obvious, but I had my own theories about that, and they hardly justified turning the police searchlight on Yanni's activities, and so wrecking Sir Julian's precarious peace. With Yanni's death an accident—and I saw no reason to doubt this—it didn't matter if he had indeed paid a furtive visit to the Castello before going out last night. So if Max Gale chose to say nothing about it, then it was none of my business. I could stay in my enchanted bubble and keep quiet. It didn't matter one way or the other. . . .

But I knew quite well that it did, and it was this knowledge that kept me sleepless in my chair, while one record followed another, unheeded, and the clock crawled on towards midnight. For one thing, I had had information forced on me that I would rather not have owned. For another—

The record stopped. With its slow, deliberate series of robot clicks, the auto-changer dropped another on the turntable, moved a gentle arm down on it, and loosed Gervase de Peyer's clarinet into the room in a brilliant shower of gold.

I switched my own thoughts back into the groove of facts. One thing at a time. The best way of forgetting how you think you feel is to concentrate on what you know you know. . . .

Godfrey had been sure that Yanni was a smuggler, and that he must have some "contact" who was probably his boss. I was pretty sure now that the contact was Max Gale. It all tied up: it would explain that furtive visit just before Yanni's voyage, and Gale's silence on the subject. It would also account for the thing that had so much worried me this morning—Gale's reaction to the news of Yanni's death. He had not been surprised at the news that a body was on the rocks, and this was not, as Phyl had assumed, because he thought it was Spiro. To me it was obvious that Spiro had never entered his head. His first questions had been, "Who is it? Do you know?" though the obvious assumption would have been the one the rest of us had made, that this must be the body of the drowned boy.

If my guess about him was correct, then his actions were perfectly consistent. He had known Yanni was to make a trip the night before;

he must have known there was some risk involved. He would obviously not have expected Yanni to meet his death, but, once faced with a drowned body, he had had no doubts as to who it would be. His story of floating debris was nonsense, of that I was sure: what had happened was that he had seen me, and then Godfrey, at the rock pool, had jumped to conclusions, and had made an excuse to come down to see for himself. There had been that sharp "Who is it?" and then the next, immediate, reaction—to examine the body as closely as he dared, presumably for any evidence of violence. No doubt if such evidence had been there, he would have had to come out with the truth, or part of it. As it was, he had held his tongue, and no doubt shared Godfrey's relief that the matter need not be brought into the open.

Yes, it all tied up, even Gale's surreptitious return to the pool, presumably to examine the body more closely than he had dared with Godfrey there, and to remove anything Yanni might have been carrying which might link him with his "contact." And it was Gale's luck that the boat had proved innocent: either poor Yanni had been on his way home when the accident happened or last night's trip had, in fact, merely been a routine one to the fishing grounds. Even the attack on the dolphin took its place with the rest. I was certain, now, that Gale had shot at the creature because he was afraid it would attract the tourist crowds and destroy his badly needed privacy. But the anger that this action had roused in me didn't give me the right, I decided, to open up a field of inquiry that would probably hurt Spiro's people, and would certainly hurt Yanni's. The two bereaved families had already quite enough to bear. No, I would hold my tongue, and be thankful that I had been allowed to stay inside my enchanted bubble with a quiet conscience. And as for Max Gale—

The Clarinet Concerto came to an end, the bright pomp ascending, jubilant, into a triumph of golden chords. The player switched itself off. In the silence that followed I heard sounds from Phyllida's room. She was up and busy.

I glanced at the clock. Twenty past twelve. She should have been asleep long ago. I went across the hallway to her door.

"Phyllida?"

"Oh, come in, come in!"

She sounded thoroughly edgy and upset. I went in, to find her out of bed and rummaging through a drawer, dragging the contents out anyhow and strewing them on the floor. She was looking enchantingly pretty in some voluminous affair of yellow nylon, with her hair down and her eyes wide and dark-shadowed. She also looked as if she were on the verge of tears.

"What's up? Are you looking for something?"

"Oh, God!" She jerked open another drawer and rummaged in it, and slammed it shut again. "Not that it'll be *there*. . . . I would do a damn-fool thing like that, wouldn't I?"

I looked at her in some alarm. Phyllida hardly ever swears. "Like what? Lost something?"

"My ring. The diamond. The goddamned Forli blasted diamond. When we were down at the bay. I've only just this moment remembered it, what with everything. I had it on, didn't I? *Didn't* I?"

"Oh, my heaven, yes, you did! But don't you remember, you took it off before we went in the water? Look, stop fussing, Phyl, it's not lost. You put it in your make-up bag, that little zip thing covered with roses. I saw you."

She was at the wardrobe now, feeling in the pockets of the beach coat. "Did I or did I not put it on again after I'd left the water?"

"I don't think so. I don't remember . . . No, I'm sure you didn't. I'd have noticed it on your hand. You didn't have it on when we were having coffee up at Godfrey's. But, honey, it'll be in the little bag. I know you put it there."

She shoved the coat back, and slammed the wardrobe shut. "That's the whole blasted point! The beastly bag's still down on the beach!"

"Oh, no!"

"It must be! I tell you, it's not here, I've looked everywhere." The bathroom was ajar, and on the floor her beach bag lay in a heap with slippers and towel. She picked up the bag for what was obviously the umpteenth time, turned it upside down, shook it, and let it fall. She kicked over the towel with her foot, then turned to face me, eyes tragic, hands spread like a mourning angel invoking a blessing. "You see? I bloody *left* the thing, on the bloody *beach!*"

"Yes, but listen a minute. . . ." I thought back rapidly. "Perhaps you did put it back on. After all, you used the zip bag when you did your face. Did you put the ring on then, and take it off again when you washed at Godfrey's? Perhaps you left it in his bathroom."

"I'm sure I didn't. I can't remember a thing about it, and I know that if I *had* the thing on when I washed at Godfrey's, I'd have known it. You can't help knowing," she said ingenuously, "when you're flashing a thing like that about on your hand. Oh, what a *fool* I am! I didn't mean to bring it here at all, but I forgot to put it in the bank, and it's safer on my hand than off it. . . . Or so I thought! Oh, hell, hell, *hell!*"

"Well, look," I said soothingly, "don't start to worry yet. If you didn't put it back on, it's still in the little bag. Where was that when you last saw it?"

"Just where we were sitting. It must have got pushed to one side under the trees or something, and when Max Gale went back for our things he just wouldn't see it. He'd just grab the things and chase after us."

"Probably. He'd be in a hurry."

"That's what I mean." She noticed nothing in my tone, but spoke quite simply, staring at me with those wide, scared eyes. "The wretched thing's just *sitting* there on the sand, and—"

"Well, for heaven's sake, don't look like that! It'll be as safe as a house! Nobody'll be there, and if they were, who'd pick up a scruffy plastic bag with make-up in?"

"It's not scruffy, and Leo gave it to me." She began to cry. "If it comes to that, he gave me the beastly ring, and it belongs to his beastly family, and if I lose it—"

"You haven't lost it."

"The tide'll wash it away."

"There's no tide."

"Your foul dolphin'll eat it. *Something'll* happen to it, I know it will." She had cast reason to the winds now, and was crying quite hard. "Leo had no *business* to give me anything like that and expect me to watch it *all the time!* Diamonds are hell anyway—if they're not in the bank you feel as miserable as sin, and if they *are* in the bank you're all frustrated, so you simply can't *win;* they're not worth having, and that ring cost thousands and thousands, and it's worse in lire, *millions* of lire," wept Phyl unreasonably, "and there'll be his mother to face, not to mention that ghastly collection of aunts, and did I tell you his uncle's probably going to be a C-Cardinal—"

"Well, honey, this won't exactly wreck his chances, so take a pull at yourself, will you, and—Hey! Just what do you think you're doing?"

She had yanked the wardrobe door open again, and was pulling out a coat. "If you think I'll get a wink, a *single wink* of sleep while that ring's lying out there—"

"Oh, no, you don't!" I said with great firmness, taking the coat from her and putting it back. "Now, don't be a nit! Of course you're worried stiff—who wouldn't be?—but you're certainly not going down there tonight!"

"But I've got to!" Her voice thinned and rose, and she grabbed for the coat again. She was very near to real hysteria.

I said quickly, "You have not. I'll go myself."

"You can't! You can't go alone. It's after midnight!"

I laughed. "So what? It's a nice night, and I'd a darned sight rather take a walk out than see you work yourself into a fit of the screaming abdabs. I don't blame you, I'd be climbing the walls myself! Serves you right for flashing that kind of ice around, my girl!"

"But, Lucy—"

"I mean it. I'll go straight away and get the wretched thing, so for sweet pete's sake, dry your eyes or you'll be fretting yourself into a miscarriage or something, and then Leo *will* have something to say, not to mention his mother and the aunts."

"I'll come with you."

"You'll do no such thing. Don't argue. Get back into bed. Go on . . . I know exactly where we were sitting, and I'll take a torch. Now mop up, and I'll make you some Ovaltine or something, and then go. Hurry up now, get *in!*"

I don't often get tough with Phyllida, but she is surprisingly meek when I do. She got in, and smiled shakily.

"You're an angel, you really are. I feel so ashamed of myself, but it's no use, I shan't rest till I've got it. . . . Look, I've had an idea, couldn't we just ring Godfrey and ask him to go? Oh, no, he said he was going to be out late, didn't he? Well, what about Max Gale? It's his fault, in a way, for not seeing the thing. . . . We could ring him up to ask if he'd noticed it, and then he'd *have* to offer to go down—"

"I'm not asking favours of Max Gale."

This time she did notice my tone. I added hastily, "I'd rather go myself. I honestly don't mind."

"You won't be scared?"

"What's there to be scared of? I don't believe in ghosts. Anyway, it's not so dark as it looks from in here; the sky's thick with stars. I suppose you've got a torch?"

"There's one in the kitchen, on the shelf beside the door. Oh, Lucy, you *are* a saint! I shouldn't have slept a wink without that beastly thing safe in its box!"

I laughed at her. "You should be like me, and get your jewellery you-know-where. Then you could lose the lot down on the beach and not worry about Leo's beating you."

"If that was all I thought would happen," said Phyllida, with a spice of her usual self, "I'd probably enjoy it. But it's his mother."

"I know. And the aunts. And the Cardinal. Don't come that one over me, my girl, I know darned well they all spoil you to death. Now, stop worrying. I'll bring you the Ovaltine, and you shall have the Grand Cham's diamond safe under your pillow 'or ere your pulse twice beat.' See you."

The woods were still and silent, the clearing full of starlight. The frogs had dived at my approach; the only sound now from the pool was the lap and stir of the lily pads as the rings of water shimmered through them and set them rocking.

I paused for a moment. I had told Phyllida that I didn't believe in ghosts, and I knew I had no reason to be afraid, but for the life of me I couldn't help glancing towards the place where Yanni had appeared last night, while just for a moment I felt my skin prickle and brush up like a cat's fur.

Next moment, very faintly, I heard the piano. I tilted my head to listen to the thin, falling melodic line that crept down through the trees. I recognized phrases that I had heard last night. It was this, no doubt, that had unconsciously given me pause and called up poor Yanni for me.

The ghost had gone. The pathway to the beach was just a pathway. But I didn't follow it yet: slowly, rather as if I were breasting water instead of air, I climbed the path to the Castello.

I paused at the edge of the rose garden, hanging back in shadow. The roses smelled heavy and sweet. The music was clear now, but muted, so that I guessed it came from the house rather than the terrace. I recognized another passage, a simple, almost lyrical line that suddenly broke and stumbled in the middle, like a step missed in the dark. I found it disquieting. After a while the pianist stopped, started again, played for another half minute before he broke off to go back a few bars; then the same long phrase was played over several times before being allowed to flow on unchecked.

The next time he stopped I heard the murmur of voices. Julian Gale's tones carried beautifully; Max replied indistinguishably. Then the piano began again.

He was there, and working. They were both there. As if I had had something proved to me—whatever it was I had come for—I turned away and, with the help of the torch, followed the Castello's own path downhill, through the clearing where I had met Max Gale, and on down the broken steps to the bay.

After the heavy shade of the path, the open beach seemed as light as day. The white crescent of sand was firm and easy walking. As I left the woods I switched off the torch, and went rapidly across the bay to where we had been sitting that morning. The pines, overhanging, made a black pool of shadow, so black that for a moment it looked as if something were lying there. Another body.

But this time I didn't pause. I knew it for a trick of the shadows, no more; just another ghost to fur the skin with gooseflesh; an image painted on the memory, not of the living Yanni this time, but of the dead.

The music sounded faintly from above. I kept the torch switched off in case the flash attracted the Gales' attention, and approached the trees.

Something *was* lying there. Not shadows; it was solid, a long, dark bundle shape, like the thing in the rock pool. And it was real.

This time the shock really did hit me. I still remember the kick over the heart, the sharp, frightening pain that knocked all the blood in my body into hammering motion, the way a kick starts a motorcycle engine. The blood slammed in heavy, painful strokes in my head, my fingers, my throat. My hand tightened so convulsively on the torch that the switch went down and the light came on, pinpointing whatever it was that lay there under the pines.

It wasn't a body. It was a long, smoothly wrapped bundle of something, longer than a man. It was lying just where we had been sitting that morning.

I had my free hand clamped tightly against my ribs, under the left breast. It is a theatrical gesture, but, like all the theatre's clichés, it is based soundly on truth. I believe I felt I must hold my terrified heart from battering its way out of the rib cage. I must have stood there for several minutes, rigid, unable either to move forward or to run away.

The thing didn't move. There was no sound other than the distant notes of the piano and the soft hushing of the sea.

My terror slowly faded. Body or no body, it obviously wasn't going to hurt me, and, I thought grimly, I'd be better facing a dozen bodies than going back to Phyllida without the Forli diamond.

I pointed the torchlight straight at the thing under the trees, and approached it bravely.

The bundle stirred. As my breath whistled sharply in, I saw, in the torchlight, the gleam of a living eye. But then in the split half second that prevented me from screaming, I saw what—not who—this was. It was the dolphin.

Apollo's child. Amphitrite's darling. The sea magician. High and dry.

The eye moved, watching me. The tail stirred again, as if trying to beat movement out of the hard earth as it would from water. It struck the edge of the crisping ripples with a splash that seemed to echo right up the rocks.

I tiptoed closer, under the blackness of the pines. "Darling?" I said softly. "What's the matter? Are you hurt?"

The creature lay still, unblinking, the eye liquid and watchful. It was silly to look, as I did, for recognition, but at least I could see no fear of me. I shone the torch carefully over the big body. There seemed to be no wound, or mark of any kind. I examined the sand round about. There was no blood, only a wide, dragged wake where the animal had been hauled or thrown out of the water. Near a pine root the torchlight caught the pale gleam of Phyllida's make-up bag. I snatched this up; I didn't even look inside, but rammed it into my pocket and then forgot it. Presumably the diamond was safe inside it, but more important now than any diamond was the dolphin, stranded and helpless, a prey for anyone who wanted to hurt him. And that someone did want to hurt him, I very well knew. . . . Moreover, unless he could be got back into the water, he would die as soon as the sun got up and dried his body out.

I straightened up, trying to force my thoughts into order, and to recall everything I had ever read or known about dolphins. It was little enough. I knew that, like whales, they sometimes stranded themselves for no obvious reason, but that if they were unhurt and could be refloated fairly soon, they would suffer no ill effects. I knew, too, that they must be kept wet, or the skin cracked and went septic; and that they breathed through an air hole on the top of the head, and that this must be kept clear.

I shone the torch again. Yes, there was the air hole, a crescent-shaped, glistening nostril on top of the head. It was open, but half clotted with sand thrown up as the creature had ploughed ashore. I fixed the torch as best I could in the crotch of a pine bough, dipped my hands in the sea, and gently wiped the sand from the hole.

The dolphin's breath was warm on my hands, and this was somehow surprising: the creature was all at once less alien, his friendliness and intelligence at the same time were less magical and more touching. It was unthinkable that I might have to watch him die.

I ran my hands over his skin, noticing with fear how rough this was; the breeze was drying it out. I tried to judge the distance I would have to drag him. Now and again a ripple, driven by that same breeze, washed right up to the dolphin's tail, but this was the thinnest film of water licking up from the shallows four yards away. Another few feet out, as I knew, the sand shelved sharply to deeper water beside the rocks. Once get him even half floating, and I should be able easily to manage his weight.

I switched off the torch, then put my arms round the dolphin as far as I could and tried to pull him. But I couldn't get hold of him; my hands slipped over the faultless streamlining of his body. Nor could I grasp the dorsal fin, and when I tried tugging at his flippers he fidgeted for the first time, and I thought he was going to struggle and work himself farther up the shore. Finally, kneeling, I got my shoulder right against his and tried to thrust him backwards with all the strength I could muster. But he never moved an inch.

I stood back at length, panting, sweating, and almost in tears. "I can't do it. Sweetie, I can't even *budge* you!" The bright liquid eye watched me silently. Behind him, four yards away, the sea heaved and whispered under the tail of the wind. Four yards: life or death.

I reached the torch down from the tree. "I'll go and get a rope. If I tie it around you, I could *pull* you. Get a leverage round a tree—anything!" I stooped to caress his shoulder, whispering, "I'll hurry, love; I'll run all the way."

But the feel of the dolphin's skin, dry and roughening, made me hesitate. It might take some time to find a rope or get help. No good going for Godfrey: if he was still up, it would be time lost. And I couldn't go to the Castello. I would have to go all the way home. I had better throw some seawater over the animal's skin before I left him, to keep him safe while I was away.

I kicked off my sandals and ran into the shallows. But the spray I splashed up barely reached beyond his tail, and (so shallow was the water here) came up full of sand and grit that would dry on him even more disastrously than before.

Then I remembered the plastic bag, stupidly small, but better than nothing. I ran out of the water, dragged the bag from my pocket, shone the torch down, and tipped Phyllida's make-up out on the sand. The Forli diamond fell into the torchlight with a flash and a shimmer. I snatched it up and pushed it on my finger, and dropped the rest of the things back into my pocket, along with the torch. Then I ran back to the sea's edge and scooped up my pathetic pint of water to throw over the dolphin.

It seemed to take an age. Stooping, straightening, running, tipping, stooping, running, tipping . . . When I reached the beast's shoulders I put a hand over the air hole and poured the water carefully round it; unbelievably, dolphins could drown, and under the circumstances, one couldn't expect the right reflexes to be working. When I poured water over his face the first time he blinked, which startled me a little, but after that he watched me steadily, the nearer eye swivelling as I moved to and fro.

At last he seemed wet enough to be safe. I dropped the dripping bag, wiped my hands on my coat, which was probably already ruined beyond repair, pulled on my sandals, and petted the damp shoulder again.

"I'll be back, sweetie; don't worry. I'll be as quick as I can. Keep breathing. And let's pray no one comes."

This was the nearest I had got to admitting, even to myself, why I had been whispering, and why, as soon as I no longer needed the light, I had snapped the torch out.

I ran back across the sand. The piano had stopped, but I could still see the faint glow of light from the open terrace window. Nothing moved on the terrace itself. Then I was in the shadow of the woods, where the path to the Villa Forli went up steeply. Using the torch once more, I clambered breathlessly. The breeze, steady now, had filled the woods with a rustling that drowned my steps.

And now the starlit clearing. The frogs plopped into the pool. The stream glittered in the flying edge of my torchlight. I switched off as I emerged from the trees, and crossed the open space quietly, pausing at the far side of it to get my breath, leaning up against a young oak that stood where the path tunnelled afresh into the black burrow of the woods.

As I came out from under the oak, something moved on the path.

I checked, fingers fumbling clumsily with the torch. It flashed on, catching the edge of a side-stepping figure. A man, only a yard or so away. I would have run straight into him.

The bushes rustled just beside me. Someone jumped. The torch was struck out of my hand. I whipped round, and I think I would have screamed to wake the dead, only he grabbed me, pulled me to him brutally, and his hand came down hard over my mouth.

CHAPTER

EIGHT

ॐ

Pray you, tread softly, that the blind mole may not
Hear a foot fall; we now are near his cell.

Act IV, Scene 1

He was very strong. I struggled and fought, necessarily in silence, but I couldn't do a thing. I must have hurt him, though, in clawing at his hand, for he flinched, and I heard his breath go in sharply. He took the hand away with a hissed *"Keep quiet, will you?"* in English, and then made it certain by jamming my head hard into the front of his jacket, so that I was not only dumb, but blinded, too. His coat was damp, and smelled of the sea. I got the swift impression of other movement nearby, but heard nothing above my own and my assailant's breathing, and the thudding of my heart. The pressure of his hand on the back of my head was hurting me, and a button scored my cheek. My ribs, held in the hard embrace of his other arm, felt as if they were cracking.

I stopped fighting and went slack, and straight away the cruel grip eased, but he still held me pressed to him, both arms caught now and firmly pinioned. As his hold relaxed I pulled my head free. If I screamed, they would hear me from the Castello terrace . . . they could be down here in a few seconds. . . . Surely, even Max Gale—

"Where have you been?" demanded my captor.

I gaped at him. As soon as he saw I had no intention of screaming, he let me go. *"You?"* I said.

"Where have you been?"

I had my hands to my face, rubbing the sore cheeks. "What's that got to do with you?" I asked furiously. "You go a bit far, don't you, Mr. Gale?"

"Have you been up at the Castello?"

"I have not! And if I had—"

"Then you've been to the beach. Why?"

"Is there any reason—" I began, then stopped. Fright and fury, together, had let me forget for a moment what else had happened that day. Max Gale might have no business to demand an account of my movements, but he might well have the best of reasons for wanting to know them.

Nothing was to be gained by refusing to tell him. I said, rather sulkily, "I went down to get Phyl's ring. She left it on the beach this morning. You needn't look as if you don't believe me: it was in a little bag, and you missed it. There, see?" I flashed the diamond at him, then pushed the hand deep into my coat pocket, almost as if I expected him to grab it from me, and glared up at him. "And now perhaps you'll tell me what *you're* playing at? This game of yours is way beyond a joke, let me tell you! It'll be man-traps next, I suppose. You hurt me."

"I'm sorry. I didn't mean to. I thought you were going to scream."

"Good heavens, of course I was! But why should you have minded if I had?"

"Well, I—" He hesitated. "Anyone might have heard . . . My father . . . It might have startled him."

"Thoughtful of you!" I said tartly. "It didn't matter, did it, if you scared *me* half out of my wits? What a model son you are, aren't you? I'm surprised you could bring yourself to go out so late and leave your father alone! If it comes to that, where've *you* been that you don't want anyone to know about?"

"Fishing."

"Oh?" The heavily ironic retort that jumped to my lips withered there and died. I said slowly, "But you were up there at the Castello half an hour ago."

"What do you mean? I thought you said you hadn't been near the Castello."

"The noise *you* make with that piano," I said nastily, "you could hear it from the mainland. I heard you from the beach."

"That's impossible." He spoke abruptly, but with a note of puzzlement.

"I tell you I did! You were playing the piano, and then talking to your father. I know your voices. It *was* you."

He was silent for a moment. Then he said slowly, "It sounds to me as if you heard a working session on tape being played through, comments and all. But I still don't see how that could be. My father isn't there. He's away, staying the night at a friend's house."

"How far away?"

"If it's anything to do with you, Corfu."

"You must think I've a scream like a steam whistle," I said dryly.

"What? Oh, I . . ." He had the grace to stammer slightly. "I'm afraid I did rather say the first thing that came into my head. But it's true that he's not at home."

"And neither were you?" I said. "Well, whoever was playing the tape, it certainly made a wonderful alibi."

"Don't be silly." His laugh was excellently done. He must have some of his father's talent, after all. Possibly only someone as experienced with actors' voices as I could have told that the easy amusement was assumed over some urgent preoccupation. "Your imagination's working overtime, Miss Waring! Please don't go making a mystery out of this. All that'll have happened is that my father's decided for some reason to come home, and he was amusing himself with the tape recorder. As for myself, I've been out fishing with Adoni. . . . And if it's any satisfaction to you, *you* frightened *me* half out of my wits. I'm afraid my reactions were a bit rough. I'm sorry for that. But if someone suddenly breaks out of the dark and runs straight into you, you—well, you act according."

"According to what? Jungle law?" I was still smarting. "I wouldn't have said those reactions were exactly normal, unless you were expecting— Just what *were* you expecting, Mr. Gale?"

"I'm not sure." This, at any rate, sounded like the truth. "I thought I heard someone coming up from the beach, fast, and trying not to be heard, but the breeze was covering most of the sounds, and I couldn't be certain. Then the sounds stopped, as if whoever it was, was hiding and waiting. Naturally that made me begin to wonder what they might be up to, so I waited, too."

"I only stopped to get my breath. Your imagination's working overtime, Mr. Gale."

"Very probably." I wasn't sure if he had even noticed the gibe. His head was bent, and he seemed to be studying one of his hands, turning it this way and that. "Well, just as I decided I'd been mistaken, you erupted from the trees like a deer on the run. I grabbed you. Pure reflex."

"I see. And I suppose it was pure reflex that you knocked the torch out of my hand before I could see anything?"

"Of course," he said woodenly.

"And that even when you saw who it was you acted like a—a Gestapo?" No reply to that. I can only suppose that excitement and the moment's fright had pumped too much adrenalin into my bloodstream;

I think I was a bit "high" with it. I remember feeling vaguely surprised that I was not in the least afraid of him. At some level, I suppose, I was reasoning that the man (in spite of his dubious bit of adventuring in what Godfrey had called the "milk run") was hardly a dangerous criminal, and that he obviously intended me no harm: on the conscious level I was damned if I went tamely home now without finding exactly what was going on around here. It had already touched me far too closely to be ignored. The enchanted bubble had never really existed. I was beginning to suspect that there was no such thing.

So I asked, as if it were a matter of purely academic interest, "I still want to know why it should have mattered to you where I'd been. Or that I might recognize you. Or was it the others I wasn't supposed to see?"

I thought for a moment that he wasn't going to answer. From somewhere farther up in the woods, an owl called breathily once, and then again. In the pool, a frog tried his voice tentatively for a moment, lost his nerve, and dived again. Max Gale said quietly, "Others?"

"The men who went past while you were holding me."

"You're mistaken."

"Oh, no, I'm not. There was somebody else there. I saw him beside the path, just as you jumped on me."

"Then you probably recognized him as well. That was Adoni, our gardener. You've met him, I believe?"

You wouldn't have thought he was admitting another lie, or even conceding a slight point. The tone was that of a cool social brush-off. I felt the adrenalin soaring dangerously again as he added calmly, "He usually comes with me when I go fishing. What's the matter? Don't you believe me?"

I managed to say, quite pleasantly, "I was just wondering why you didn't beach the boat in your own bay. This seems a funny way to come—if you've just been fishing."

"The wind was getting up, and it was easier to come in the other side of the point. And now, if you'll excuse me—"

"You mean," I said, "that you left your boat on *our* side of the point? Tied to our jetty, even? Now, isn't that too bad? I think you'd better go straight down again and move it, Mr. Gale. We don't like trespassers at the Villa Forli."

There was a short, sharp pause. Then, unexpectedly, he laughed. "All right. One to you. But not tonight. It's late, and I've got things to do."

"I suppose you ought to be helping Adoni to carry home the fish? Or would it be more correct to call it 'the catch'?"

That got through. You'd have thought I'd hit him. He made a sudden movement, not towards me, but I felt my muscles tighten, and I think I even backed a pace. I wondered why I had ever thought him a subdued edition of his father. And, quite suddenly, I was scared.

I spoke quickly. "You needn't worry. I don't mean to give you away! Why should I? It's nothing to me, but you must see it's awful to be in the middle of something and not know just what's going on! Oh, yes, I know about it, it was obvious enough. But I'll not say anything—I think too much of Miranda and her mother, and, if it comes to that, of your father, to drag the police back here with a lot more questions. Why should I care what you've got yourself into? But I *do* care about Adoni. . . . Did you know he's going to marry Miranda? Why did you have to involve him in this? Hasn't there been enough trouble?"

After that first, uncontrollable start, he had listened without movement or comment, but I could see his eyes on me, narrow and intent in the dim light. Now he said, very quietly, "Just what are you talking about?"

"You know quite well. I suppose poor Yanni never got the job done last night, so you've been across there tonight, to the Albanian coast, to do it yourself. Am I right?"

"Where did you get this . . . fantasy?"

"Fantasy, nothing," I said roundly. "Godfrey Manning told me this morning."

"*What?*" If I had got through before, this was straight between the joints of the harness. The word alone sent me back another pace, and this time he followed. I felt my back come up against a tree, and turned aside blindly—I think to run away—but his hand shot out and took my wrist, not hard, but in a grip I couldn't have broken without struggling, and probably not even then. "Manning? *He* told you?"

"Let me go!"

"No, wait a minute. I'm not going to hurt you, don't be scared . . . but you've got to tell me. What did Manning say to you?"

"Let me go, please!"

He dropped the wrist immediately. I rubbed it, though it was not in the least hurt. But I was shaking now. Something had happened that had changed the whole pitch of the scene; in place of the slightly pleasurable bitchiness of the previous exchange, there was now something urgent, hard, and yes, threatening. And it was Godfrey's name that had done it.

Gale repeated, "What did he tell you?"

"About Yanni? That he was a smuggler, and that he would probably have a 'contact,' or whatever you call it, who'd get his supplies for him, and that he hoped the police wouldn't tumble to it, because Spiro had been in it, too, and it would hurt Maria if it came out."

"That was all?"

"Yes."

"When did he tell you all this?"

"This morning, at the point, before you came down."

"Ah." I heard his breath go out. "Then you weren't up at Manning's house just now?"

"Of course I wasn't! Have you any idea what time it is?"

"I—of course. I'm sorry. I didn't think. I wasn't trying to be offensive. Did Manning tell you that I was Yanni's 'contact'?"

"No. I worked that out for myself."

"You did? How?"

I hesitated. The feeling of fear had gone, and common sense had come back to tell me that I was in no danger. Smuggler or not, he would hardly murder me for this. I said, "I saw Yanni coming up to the Castello last night."

"I . . . see." I could almost feel the amazement, the rapid reassessment of the situation. "But you said nothing to the police."

"No."

"Why not?"

I said carefully, "I'm not quite sure. To begin with, I kept quiet because I thought I might be mistaken, and Yanni possibly hadn't been going up to the Castello at all. If I'd thought you'd had anything to do with his death, I'd have told straight away. Then later I realized that there *was* some connection between you and Yanni, and that you'd known he was going out last night."

"How?"

"Because you weren't surprised when you heard he'd been drowned—"

"You noticed that, did you? My mistake. Go on."

"But you *were* shocked. I saw that."

"You see a darned sight too much." He sounded grim. "Was that what made you decide I hadn't killed him?"

"Good heavens, no! It wouldn't have occurred to me that you'd killed him! If I'd thought it was anything but an accident, I'd have told the whole thing straight away! It—it wasn't, was it?"

"Not that I'm aware of. Go on. What else did you see?"

"I saw you go back to the body and have another look at it."

"Did you, by God? From the path? Careless of me. I thought I was out of view. Who else saw that?"

"Nobody."

"You're sure of that?"

"Pretty well."

"And you said nothing about that, either? Well, well. So it was entirely your own idea that I was smuggling along with Yanni?"

"Yes."

"And now you've found out for certain. Do you still propose to say nothing?"

I said, without challenge, but out of simple curiosity, "How would you make sure of it?"

He said, equally simply, "My dear, I couldn't begin to try. I can only tell you that it's urgent that nobody should know I've been out tonight, nobody at all, and beg you to keep quiet."

"Then don't worry. I will."

There was a short pause. "As easy as that?" he said in an odd tone.

"I told you—for your father's sake," I said, perhaps a little too quickly, "and for Maria's. The only thing is—"

"Yes?"

"Things go in threes, they say, and if anything should happen to Adoni—"

He laughed. "Nothing shall, I promise you! I couldn't take the responsibility for damaging a work of art like Adoni! We-ell . . ." There was a whole world of relief in the long-drawn syllable. Then his voice changed; it was brisk, easy, normal. "I mustn't keep you any more. Heaven knows what the time is, and you must get home with that treasure trove of yours. I'm sorry I missed it this morning and gave your sister a bad half hour . . . And I'm sorry I frightened you just now. To say that I'm grateful is the understatement of the year. You'll let me see you home?"

"There's no need, really, thank you. In any case, hadn't you better get up there to help Adoni?"

"He's all right. Didn't you hear the signal?"

"Signal? But there hasn't been—" I stopped as I saw him smile. "Not the owls? No, really, how corny can you get! Was that really Adoni?"

He laughed. "It was. The robber's mate is home and dry, complete with 'catch.' So come along now, I'll take you home."

"No, really, I—"

"Please. After all, these woods are pretty dark and you were nervous, weren't you?"

"Nervous? No, of course not!"

He looked down in surprise. "Then what in the world were you racing back like that for?"

"Because I—" I stopped dead. The dolphin. I had forgotten the dolphin. The breeze, riffling the treetops, breathed gooseflesh along my skin. I thought of the dolphin, drying in it, back there on the beach. I said quickly, "It was so late, and Phyl was worrying. Don't bother, please, I'll go alone. Good night."

But as I reached the tunnel of trees, he caught me up. "I'd sooner see you safely home. Besides, you were quite right about shifting the boat; I'd rather have her nearer to hand in the morning. I'll take her across into the lee of the pines."

For the life of me, I couldn't suppress a jerk of apprehension. He felt it, and stopped.

"Just a minute."

His hand was on my arm. I turned. It was very dark under the trees.

He said, "You've found out more about me than is quite comfortable. It's time you were a little bit honest about yourself, I think. Did you meet anyone down in the bay?"

"No."

"See anyone?"

"N-no."

"Quite sure? This is important."

"Yes."

"Then why don't you want me to go down there?"

I said nothing. My throat was stiff and dry as cardboard. Tears of strain, fear, and exhaustion were not very far away.

"Look," he said urgently and not unkindly, "I have to know. Someday I'll tell you why. Damn it, I've got to trust you; what about your trusting me for a change? Something did happen down there to scare you, didn't it? It sent you running up here like a hare in front of a gun. Now, what was it? Either you tell me what it was or I go down and look for myself. Well?"

I threw in my cards. I said shakily, "It was the dolphin."

"The dolphin?" he echoed blankly.

"It's in the bay."

There was a pause, then he said, with a sharpness that was part exasperation, part relief, "And am I supposed to be going down there to shoot it in the middle of the night? I told you before that I'd never touched the beast!" He added, more kindly, "Look, you've had a grim sort of day, and you're frightened and upset. Nobody's going to hurt your dolphin, so dry your eyes, and I'll take you back home now. He can look after himself, you know."

"He can't. He's on the beach."

"He's what?"

"He's stranded. He can't get away."

"Well, my God, you don't *still* think I'd do him any harm—" He stopped, and seemed for the first time to take in what I had been telling him. "*Stranded?* You mean the creature's actually beached?"

"Yes. High and dry. He'll die. I've been trying and trying to move him, and I can't. I was running just now to get a rope, that's why I was hurrying. If he's out of water too long, the wind'll dry him and he'll die. And all this time we've been wasting—"

"Where is he?"

"The other side, under the pines. What are you— Oh!" This was an involuntary cry as his hand tightened on my arm and swung me round. "What are you doing?"

"Don't worry, this isn't another assault. Now listen, there's a rope in my boat. I'll go down and get it, and I'll be with you as soon as I can. Get away back to your dolphin now, and wait for me. Can you keep him going another twenty minutes? . . . Good. We'll manage him between us, don't worry. But"—a slight pause—"be very quiet, do you mind?"

Before I could reply, he was gone, and I heard him making a swift but still stealthy course back the way he had come.

CHAPTER

NINE

ટ੭

> . . . To the elements
> Be free, and fare thou well!
>
> Act v, Scene 1

There was no time for doubt or questioning. That could come later. I obeyed him, flying back down the path to the beach, back across the pale sand to where the big bulk still lay motionless.

The dark eye watched. He was alive. I whispered, "It's all right now, he's coming," and went straight back to my scooping and tipping of seawater. If I noticed that I hadn't bothered, even in my thoughts, to specify the "he," that was another question that could wait till later.

He came, sooner than I had expected. A small motorboat came nosing round the bay, without her engine, just with a dip and splash of oars as she was poled gently along. The breeze and the lapping of the sea on the rocks covered all sound until the boat was a rocking shadow within yards of me. I saw him stand up then, and lever it nearer the shore. Timber grated gently on rock, and he stepped out, making fast to a young pine, and then he was beside me on the sand, with a coil of rope over his arm.

"Good God! How did he get out here?"

"They do," I said. "I've read about it. Sometimes a storm blows them in, but sometimes they get their radar beams fogged up, or something, and they come in at a fast lick, and before they know where they are they're high and dry. We're lucky there's only a foot or so of tide, or the water might have been miles away from him by now. Can you move him, d'you think?"

"I can try." He stooped over the animal. "Trouble is, you can't really get a hold. Didn't you have a torch?"

"I dropped it when you savaged me up in the woods."

"So you did. There's one in the boat—no, perhaps not, we'll do without. Now, can you get to his other side?"

Together we fought to grasp and lift the dolphin, and with some success, for we did drag and shove him a foot or so downshore. But the dolphin himself defeated us; frightened, possibly, of the man's presence, or hurt by our tugging and by the friction of sand and pebbles, he began to struggle, spasmodically but violently; and at the end of the first strenuous minutes we had gained only a foot. I was exhausted, and Max Gale was breathing very hard.

"No good." He stood back. "He weighs a ton, and it's like trying to get hold of an outsize greased bomb. It'll have to be the rope. Won't it hurt him?"

"I don't know, but we'll have to try it. He'll die if he stays here."

"True enough. All right, help me get it round the narrow bit above the tail."

The dolphin lay like a log, his eye turning slowly back to watch us as we bent to tackle the tail rope. Without the torch it was impossible to tell, but I had begun to imagine that the eye wasn't so bright or watchful now. The tail felt heavy and cold, like something already dead. He never flickered a muscle as we fought to lift and put a loop round it.

"He's dying," I said, on a sort of gulp. "That fight must have finished him." I dashed the back of my hand over my eyes, and bent to the job. The rope was damp and horrible to handle, and the dolphin's tail was covered with coarse sand.

"You do tear yourself up rather, don't you?"

I looked up at him as he worked over the loop. His tone was not ungentle, but I got the impression from it that half his mind was elsewhere: he cared nothing for the dolphin, but wanted merely to get this over, and get back himself to whatever his own queer and shady night's work had been.

Well, fair enough. It was good of him to have come at all. But some old instinct of defensiveness made me say a little bitterly:

"It seems to me you can be awfully happy in this life if you stand aside and watch and mind your own business, and let other people do as they like about damaging themselves and one another. You go on kidding yourself that you're impartial and tolerant and all that, then all of a sudden you realize you're dead, and you've never been alive at all. Being alive hurts."

"So you have to break your heart over an animal who wouldn't even know you, and who doesn't even recognize you?"

"Someone has to bother," I said feebly. "Besides, he does recognize me, he knows me perfectly well."

He let that one pass, straightening up from the rope. "Well, there it is, that's the best we can do, and I'm hoping to heaven we can get it off again before he takes off at sixty knots or so. . . . Well, here goes. Ready?"

I dropped my coat on the sand, kicked off my sandals, and splashed into the shallows beside him. We took the strain of the rope together. It didn't even strike me as odd that we should be there, hands touching, working together as naturally as if we had done it every day of our lives. But I was very conscious of the touch of his hand against mine on the rope.

The dolphin moved an inch or two; another inch; slid smoothly for a foot; stuck fast. This way he seemed even heavier to haul, a dead weight on a rope that bit our hands and must surely be hurting him abominably, perhaps even cutting the skin. . . .

"Easy, now," said Max Gale in my ear.

We relaxed. I let go the rope, and splashed shorewards. "I'll go and take a look at him. I'm so afraid he's—"

"*Blast!*" This from Gale as the dolphin heaved forward suddenly, beating with his tail, slapping up water and sand. I heard the rope creak through Gale's hands, and another sharp curse from him as he plunged to keep his footing.

I ran back. "I'm sorry— Oh! What is it?" He had twisted the rope round his right hand and wrist, and I saw how he held his left arm up, taut, the fingers half clenched as if it had hurt him. I remembered how he had examined it, up in the glade. This must be why he had made such heavy weather of fixing the rope, and had been unable to shift the dolphin.

"Your hand?" I said sharply. "Is it hurt?"

"No. Sorry, but I nearly went in then. Well, at least the beast's still alive. Come on, we'll have another go before he really does take fright."

He laid hold once more, and we tried again. This time the dolphin lay still, dead weight again, moving slowly, slowly, till the lost ground was regained; but then he stuck once more, apparently immovable.

"There must be a ridge or something, he sticks every time." Gale paused to brush the sweat out of his eyes. I saw him drop his left hand from the rope and let it hang.

"Look," I said tentatively, "this'll take all night. Couldn't we possibly —I mean, could the *boat* tow him out . . . with the engine?"

He was silent for so long that I lost my nerve, and said hurriedly,

"It's all right, I do understand. I—I just thought, if Adoni really had got safe in, it wouldn't matter. Forget it. It was marvellous of you to bother at all, with your hand and everything. Perhaps . . . if I just stay here all night and keep him damp, and if you could . . . *do* you think you could ring Phyl for me and tell her? You could say you saw me from the terrace, and came down? And if you could come back in the morning, when it doesn't matter, with the boat, or with Adoni . . ." He had turned and was looking down at me. I couldn't see him except as a shadow against the stars. "If you wouldn't mind?" I finished.

"We'll use the boat now," he said abruptly. "What do we do—make the rope fast to the bows, and then back her out slowly?"

I nodded eagerly. "I'll stay beside him till he's floated. I'll probably have to hold him upright in the water till he recovers. If he rolls, he'll drown. The air hole gets covered, and they have to breathe terribly often."

"You'll be soaked."

"I'm soaked now."

"Well, you'd better have my knife. Here. If you have to cut the rope, cut it as near his tail as you can."

I stuck the knife in my belt, piratewise, then splashed back to where the dolphin lay. It wasn't my imagination, the lovely dark eye was duller, and the skin felt harsh and dry again. I put a hand on him, and bent down.

"Only a minute now, sweetheart. Don't be frightened. Only a minute."

"Okay?" called Max softly, from the boat, which was bobbing a few yards from shore. He had fixed the rope; it trailed through the water from the dolphin's tail to a ring on the bows.

"Okay," I said.

The engine started with a splutter and then a throbbing that seemed to fill the night. My hand was on the dolphin's body still. . . . Not even a tremor; boats' engines held no terrors for him. Then the motor steadied down to a mutter and the boat began to back quietly out from shore.

The rope lifted, vibrated, with the water flying from it in shining spray; then it tightened. The engine's note quickened; the rope stretched, the starlight running and dripping along it. The loop, fastened just where the great bow of the tail springs out horizontally from the spine, seemed to bite into the beast's flesh. It was very tight; the skin was straining; it must be hurting vilely.

The dolphin made a convulsive movement, and my hand clenched on the knife, but I kept still. My lip bled where I was biting on it, and I was sweating as if I were being hurt myself. The boat's engine beat gently, steadily; the starlight ran and dripped along the rope. . . .

The dolphin moved. Softly, smoothly, the huge body began to slide backwards down the sand towards the water. With my hand still on the loop of the tail rope, I went with it.

"It's working!" I said breathlessly. "Can you keep it very slow?"

"Right. That okay? Sing out as soon as he's afloat, and I'll cast off here."

The dolphin slithered slowly backwards, like a vessel beginning its run down the launching ramp. The grating of sand and broken shells under his body sounded as loud to me as the throbbing engine a few yards out to sea. Now, at last, he touched water . . . was drawn through the crisping ripples . . . was slowly, slowly, gaining the sea. I followed him as he slid deeper. The ripples washed over my feet, my ankles, my knees; the hand that I kept on the loop of rope was under water to the wrist.

And now we had reached the place where the bottom shelved more steeply. All in a moment I found myself standing nearly breast-deep, gasping as the water rose round me in the night chill. The dolphin, moving with me, rocked as the water began to take his weight. Another few seconds, and he would be afloat. He only moved once, a convulsive, flapping heave that twanged the rope like a bowstring and hurt my hand abominably, so that I cried out, and the engine shut to a murmur as Max said sharply:

"Are you hurt?"

"No. Go on. It held him."

"How far now?"

"Nearly deep enough. He's quiet now, I think he's— Oh, God, I think he's dead! Oh, Max . . ."

"Steady, my dear, I'll come. Hold him, we'll float him first. Say when."

"Nearly . . . *Right! Stop!*"

The engine shut off, as suddenly as if a soundproof door had slammed. The dolphin's body floated past me, bumping and wallowing. I braced myself to hold him. Max had paid out the rope, and was swiftly poling the boat back to her mooring under the pines. I heard the rattle of a chain as he made fast, and in another few moments he was beside me in the water, with the slack of the rope looped over his arm.

"How goes it? Is he dead?"

"I don't know. I don't know. I'll hold him up while you get the rope off."

"Turn his head to seaward first, just in case. . . . Come along, old chap, round you come. . . . There. Fine. Now hang on, my dear; I'll be as quick as I can."

The dolphin lay motionless in my arms, the air hole flaccid and wide open, just out of water, his body rolling heavily, like a leaky boat about to founder. "You're all right now," I told him in an agonized whisper that he certainly couldn't hear, "you're in the sea . . . the *sea*. You can't die now . . . you can't. . . ."

"Stop worrying." Max's voice came, cheerfully brisk, from the other end of the dolphin. "St. Spiridion looks after his own. He is a bit sub, poor beast, isn't he? However, heaven keep him so till I've got this damned rope off him. Are you cold?"

"Not very," I said, teeth chattering.

As he bent over the rope again, I thought I felt the dolphin stir against me. Next moment I was sure. The muscles flexed under the skin, a slow ripple of strength ran along the powerful back, a flipper stirred, feeling the water, using it, taking his weight. . . .

"He's moving!" I said excitedly. "He's all right! Oh, Max—quick— if he takes off now—"

"If he takes off now, we'll go with him. The rope's wet, I can't do a thing, I'll have to cut it. Knife, please."

As he slid the blade in under the rope and started to saw at it, the dolphin came to life. The huge muscles flexed smoothly once, twice, against me, then I saw the big shoulders ripple and bunch. The air hole closed.

I said urgently, "Quick! He's going!"

The dolphin pulled out of my arms. There was a sudden surge of cold water that soaked me to the breast as the great body went by in a splendid diving roll, heading straight out to sea. I heard Max swear sharply, and there was a nearer, secondary splash and swell as he disappeared in his turn, completely under the water. The double wash swept over me, so that I staggered, almost losing my footing, and for one ghastly moment I thought that Max, hanging grimly on to the rope, had been towed straight out to sea in the dolphin's wake, like a minnow on a line. But as I regained my own balance, staggering back towards shallower water, he surfaced beside me, waist-deep and dripping, with the cut loop in his hand, and the rope trailing.

I gripped his arm, almost crying with relief and excitement. "Oh, Max!" I staggered again, and his soaking arm came round me. I hardly noticed. I was watching the dark, starry sea where, far out, a trail of sea fire burned and burst in long, joyous leaps and curves, and vanished into the blackness. . . .

"Oh, Max . . . look, there he goes; d'you see the light? There . . . he's gone. He's gone. Oh, wasn't it *marvellous?*"

For the second time that night I felt myself gripped, and roughly silenced, but this time by his mouth. It was cold, and tasted of salt, and the kiss seemed to last forever. We were both soaked to the skin, and chilled, but where our bodies met and clung I could feel the quick heat of his skin and the blood beating warm against mine. We might as well have been naked.

He let me go, and we stood there staring at each other.

I pulled myself together with an effort. "What was that, the forfeit for the roses?"

"Hardly. Call it the climax of a hell of a night." He pushed the soaking hair back off his forehead, and I saw him grin. "The recreation of the warrior, Miss Waring. Do you mind?"

"You're welcome." *Take it lightly, I thought, take it lightly.* "You and Adoni must have had yourselves quite a time out fishing."

"Quite a time." He was not trying to take it any way at all; he merely sounded cheerful, and decidedly pleased with himself. "As a matter of fact, that was the pent-up feelings of a hell of a week. Didn't you see it coming? My father did."

"Your father? After that first meeting? I don't believe you. You looked as if you'd have liked to lynch me."

"My feelings," he said carefully, "could best be described as mixed. And damn it, if you will persist in being half naked every time you come near me—"

"Max Gale!"

He laughed at me. "Didn't they ever tell you that men were only human, Lucy Waring? And some a bit more human than others?"

"If you call it human. You flatter yourself."

"All right, darling, we'll call it the forfeit for the roses. You took a fair number, didn't you? Splendid. Come here."

"Max, you're impossible . . . Of all the complacent— This is ridiculous! What a time to *choose.* . . ."

"Well, my love, since you spark like a cat every time I come near you, what can I do but duck you first?"

"Shows what a lot you know about electricity."

"Uh-huh. No, keep still a minute. You pack a pretty lethal charge, don't you?"

"You could blow a few fuses yourself, if it comes to that. . . . For pity's sake, we must be mad." I pushed him away. "Come on out. I'd love to die with you and be buried in one grave, but not of pneumonia, it's not romantic. . . . No, Max! I admit I owe you anything you like, but let's reckon it up on dry land! Come on *out*, for goodness' sake."

He laughed, and let me go. "All right. Come on. Oh, God, I've dropped the rope . . . No, here it is. And that's to pay for, too, let me tell you; a brand-new sisal rope, sixty feet of it—"

"You're not the only one. This frock cost five guineas, and the sandals were three pounds ten, and I don't suppose they'll ever be quite the same again."

"I'm perfectly willing to pay for them," said Max cheerfully, stopping in eighteen inches of water.

"I'm sure you are, but it's not your bill. Oh, darling, don't be *crazy*, come *out!*"

"Pity. Who do you suppose settles the dolphin's accounts? Apollo, or the Saint? I think I'd opt for Apollo if I were you. Of course, if you've lost your sister's diamond it'll step the bill up quite a lot."

"*Murder!* Oh, no, here it is." The great marquise flashed blue in the starlight. "Oh, Max, seriously, thank you most awfully—you were so wonderful . . . I've been such a fool! As if you could ever—"

His hand tightened warningly on my arm, and in the same moment I saw a light, a small dancing light, like that of an electric torch, coming round the point along the path from the Villa Rotha. It skipped along the rocks, paused on the moored boat, so that for the first time I saw her name, *Ariel*; then it glanced over the water and caught us, dripping and bedraggled, splashing out of the shallows. We were also, by the time it caught us, at least four feet apart.

"Great God in heaven!" said Godfrey's voice. "What goes on? Gale—Lucy . . . you're soaked, both of you! Is this another accident, for heaven's sake?"

"No," said Max. "What brought you down?"

His tone was about as informative, and as welcoming, as a blank wall with broken glass on the top. But Godfrey seemed not to have noticed. He had already jumped lightly down from the rocks to the sand beneath the pines. I saw the torchlight pause again, then rake the place where the dolphin had lain, and the wide, gouged track where he had been dragged down to the sea. My coat lay there in a huddle, with the sandals kicked off anyhow.

"For pity's sake, what gives?" Godfrey sounded distinctly alarmed, and very curious. "Lucy, you haven't had trouble, have you? Did you get the diamond?"

"How did you know that?" I asked blankly.

"Good God, Phyl rang up, of course. She said you'd come down hours ago, and she was worried. I said I'd come and look for you. I'd only just got in." The torchlight fingered us both again, and rested on Max. "What's happened?"

"Don't flash that thing in my face," said Max irritably. "Nothing's happened, at least not in the sense you mean. That dolphin of yours got itself stranded. Miss Waring was trying to heave it back into the water, and couldn't manage, so I brought the boat along and towed the beast out to sea. We got drenched in the process."

"You mean to tell me"—Godfrey sounded frankly incredulous—"that you brought your boat out at this time of night to rescue *a dolphin?*"

"Wasn't it good of him?" I put in eagerly.

"Very," said Godfrey. He hadn't taken his eyes off Max. "I could have sworn I heard you go out some time ago."

"I thought you were out yourself," said Max. "And had only just come in."

Here we were again, I thought, the stiff-backed dogs warily circling. But it might be that Max's tone was repressive only because he was talking through clenched teeth—owing to cold, rather than emotion—because he added, civilly enough, "I said 'along,' not 'out.' We went out, as it happened, sometime after ten. We got in a few minutes ago. Adoni had just gone up when Miss Waring came running. I was still in the boat."

Godfrey laughed. "I'm sorry, I didn't mean to belittle the good deed! What a piece of luck for Lucy and the dolphin!"

"Yes, wasn't it?" I said. "I was just wondering what on earth to do, when I heard Mr. Gale. I'd have come for you, but Phyl had said you wouldn't be there."

"I wasn't." I thought he was going to say something further, but he changed it to: "I went out about ten thirty, and I'd only just got into the house when the telephone rang. *Did* you find the ring?"

"Yes, thank you. Oh, it's been quite a saga, you've no idea!"

"I'm sorry I missed it," he said. "I'd have enjoyed the party."

"I enjoyed it myself," said Max. "Now, look, to hell with the civilities, you'll have to hear it all some other time. If we're not to die of pneumonia, we've got to go. Where are your shoes, Miss Waring? . . . Oh, thanks." This as Godfrey's torch picked them out and he handed them to me. "Get them on quickly, will you?"

"What's this?" Godfrey's voice altered sharply.

"My coat." I paid very little attention to his tone; I was shivering freely now, and engaged in the very unpleasant struggle to get my sandals on over wet and sandy feet. "Oh, and there's Phyl's bag. Mr. Gale, would you mind—"

"That's blood!" said Godfrey. He was holding the coat up, and his torch shone, powerful as a head lamp, on the sleeve. I looked up, startled.

It was indeed blood. One sleeve of the coat was streaked with it.

I felt, rather than saw, Max stiffen beside me. The torch beam started its swing towards him. I said sharply, "*Please* put the torch out, Godfrey! I don't feel decent in this sopping dress. Give me the coat, please. Yes, it's blood . . . The dolphin had got a cut from a stone, or something; it bled all over me before I saw it. I'll be lucky if I ever get the stain out."

"Hurry up," said Max brusquely, "you're shivering. Put this round you. Come on, we'll have to go."

He slung the coat round my shoulders. My teeth were chattering now like a typewriter; the coat was no comfort at all over the soaked and clinging dress. "Y-yes," I said, "I'm coming. I'll tell you about it when I see you, Godfrey. Th-thanks for coming down."

"Good night," said Godfrey. "I'll come over tomorrow and see how you are."

He turned back into the shadow of the pines. I saw the torchlight move slowly over the ground where the dolphin had lain before it dodged once again up on to the rocks.

Max and I went briskly across the sand. The wind blew cold on our wet clothing.

"The coat cost nine pounds fifteen," I said, "and *that* bill's yours. That dolphin wasn't bleeding. What have you done to your hand?"

"Nothing that won't mend. Here, this way."

We were at the foot of the Castello steps and I would have gone past, but he put out a hand and checked me.

"You can't go all the way home in those things. Come on up."

"Oh, no, I think I'd better—"

"Don't be silly, why not? Manning'll telephone your sister. So can you, if it comes to that. And I'm not going to escort you all the way over there and then tramp back myself in these. What's more, these blasted boots are full of water."

"You might have drowned."

"So I might. And how much would that have been to Apollo's account?"

"You know how much," I said, not lightly at all, but not for him to hear.

CHAPTER

TEN

ह

He is drunk now. Where had he wine?

Act v, Scene 1

The terrace was empty, but one of the long windows stood open, and Max led the way in through this.

The room was lit only by one small shaded lamp on a low table, and looked enormous and mysterious, a cave full of shadows. The piano showed its teeth vaguely near a darkened window, and the unlit stove and the huge gramophone loomed like sarcophagi in some dim museum.

Sir Julian sat in an armchair beside the lamp, which cast an almost melodramatic slant of light on the silver hair and emphatic brow. The white cat on his knee, and the elegant hand that stroked it, completed the picture. The effect was stagy in the extreme. Poe's "Raven," I thought appreciatively; all it needs is the purple drapes, and the croaking from the shadows over the door. . . .

In the same moment I became aware of other, even less comfortable stage effects than these. On the table at his elbow, under the lamp, stood a bottle of Turkish gin, two thirds empty, a jug of water, and two glasses. And Sir Julian was talking to himself. He was reciting from *The Tempest,* the speech where Prospero drowns his book; he was saying it softly, an old magician talking half to himself, half to the heavenly powers from whose kingdom he was abdicating. I had never heard him do it better. And if anyone had wanted to know how much sheer technique—as opposed to nightly sweat and blood in front of the lights— was worth, here was the answer. It was doubtful if Sir Julian Gale even knew what he was saying. He was very drunk indeed.

Max had stopped dead just inside the window, with me close behind him, and I heard him make some sort of sound under his breath. Then I saw that Sir Julian was not alone. Adoni detached himself from the thicker darkness beyond the lamp, and came forward. He was dressed, like Max, in a fisherman's sweater and boots, rough clothing which only served to emphasize his startling good looks. But his face was sharp with anxiety.

"Max—" he began, then stopped abruptly as he saw me and the state we were both in. "It was *you?* What's happened?"

"Nothing that matters," said Max shortly.

This wasn't the time to choose words, or, certainly, to resent them. So much was made more than ever obvious as he advanced into the light, and I saw him clearly for the first time that night. Whatever aggressive high spirits had prompted the little interlude there in the sea had vanished abruptly; he looked not only worried now, but angry and ashamed, and also very tired indeed. His left hand was thrust deep into his trouser pocket, and there was some rag—a handkerchief, perhaps —twisted round the wrist, and blotched with blood.

Sir Julian had turned his head at the same time.

"Ah, Max . . ." Then he, too, saw me, and the hand which had been stroking the cat lifted in a graceful, practiced gesture that looked as natural as breathing. "'Most sure, the goddess, On whom'— No, we had that before, didn't we? But how delightful to see you again, Miss Lucy . . . Forgive me for not getting up; the cat, as you see . . ." His voice trailed away uncertainly. It seemed he was dimly realizing that there was need of more excuse than the cat would provide. A smile, loose enough to be disturbing, slackened his mouth. "I was having some music. If you'd care to listen . . ."

The hand moved, not very steadily, to the switch of the tape recorder which stood on a chair beside him, but Adoni stooped quickly and laid a hand over it, with a gentle phrase in Greek. Sir Julian gave up the attempt, and sank back in his chair, nodding and smiling. I saw with horrified compassion that the nod had changed to a tremor which it cost him an effort to check.

"Who's been here, Father?" asked Max.

The actor glanced up at him, then away, with a look that might, in a less distinguished face, have been called shifty. "Been here? Who should have been here?"

"Do you know, Adoni?"

The young man lifted his shoulders. "No. He was like this when I got in. I didn't know there was any in the house."

"There wasn't. I suppose he was alone when you got in? You'd hardly have given me the 'all clear' otherwise." He glanced down at his father, who was taking not the slightest notice of the conversation, but had retreated once more into some private world of his own, some gin-fumed distance apparently lit by strong ambers and swimming in a haze of poetry. "Why did he come back? I wonder. He hasn't told you that?"

"He said something about Michael Andiakis being taken ill, but I haven't had time to get anything more out of him. He's not been talking sense . . . he keeps trying to switch that thing on again. It was going when I got up to the house. I got a fright; I thought someone was here with him."

"Someone certainly has been." Max's voice was tight and grim. "He didn't say how he got back from town?"

Adoni shook his head. "I did think of telephoning Andiakis' house to ask, but at this time of night—"

"No, you can't do that." He bent over his father's chair and spoke gently and clearly. "Father. Who's been here?"

Sir Julian, starting out of his dreams, glanced up, focussed, and said, with dignity, "There were matters to discuss."

His enunciation was as faultless as ever; the only thing was, you could hear him working to keep it so. His hands lay motionless now on the cat's fur, and there, again, you could see the controls being switched on. The same with Max, who had himself well in hand now, but I could hear the effort that the patient tone was costing him. Watching them, I felt myself so shaken with compassion and love that it seemed it was that, and not my wet clothes, which made me shiver.

"Naturally," said Julian clearly, "I had to ask him in when he had driven me home. It was very good of him."

Max and Adoni exchanged glances. "Who had?"

No reply. Adoni said, "He won't answer anything straight. It's no use."

"It's got to be. We've got to know who this was and what he's told him."

"I doubt if he told him much. He wouldn't say anything to me, only tried to turn the tape on, and talked on and on about the story you are writing the music for, you know, the old story of the island that he was telling Miranda and Spiro."

Max pushed the damp hair off his brow with a gesture almost of desperation. "We've got to find out—now, before he passes out. He knew perfectly well where we were going. He agreed to stay out of the way. My God, I was sure he could be trusted now. I thought he'd be safe with Michael. Why the *hell* did he come home?"

"Home is where the heart is," said Sir Julian. "When my wife died, the house was empty as a lord's great kitchen without a fire in it. Lucy knows, don't you, my dear?"

"Yes," I said. "Shall I go, Max?"

"No, please . . . if you don't mind. If you'll please stay . . . Look, Father, it's all right now. There's only me and Adoni and Lucy. You can tell us about it. Why didn't you stay at Michael's?"

"Poor Michael was playing a very interesting game, Steinitz gambit, and I lost a rook in the first few minutes. Do you play chess, my dear?"

"I know the moves," I said.

"Five moves would have done it. White to play, and mate in five moves. A foregone conclusion. But then he had the attack."

"What sort of attack?" asked Max.

"I had no idea that his heart wasn't all it should be, for all he never drinks. I am quite aware that this is one reason why you like me to visit Michael, but a drink occasionally, for purely social reasons, never does the least harm. My heart is as strong as a bell. As strong as a bell. One's heart," added Sir Julian, with the air of one dismissing the subject, "is where the home is. Good night."

"Just a minute. You mean Michael Andiakis has died of a heart attack? I *see*. I'm sorry, Father. No wonder you felt you needed—"

"No, *no!* Who said he had died? Of course he didn't, I was there. They have no telephone, so it was a good thing, the doctor said so, a very good thing. But then if I hadn't been there, I doubt if Michael would have had the attack at all. He always did get too excitable over our little game. Poor Michael."

"You went to fetch the doctor?"

"I told you," said his father impatiently. "Why can't you listen? I think I'd like to go to bed."

"What happened when the doctor came?"

"He put Michael to bed, and I helped him." It was the first direct answer he had given, and he seemed to feel obscurely that something was wrong, for he gave that sidelong look at his son before going on. "It's as well that I'm as sound as a bell myself, though I have never understood why bells should be particularly—particularly sound. Sweet bells jangled, out of tune and harsh. Then I went to get the doctor." He paused. "I mean the daughter. Yes, the daughter."

Adoni said, "There's a married daughter who lives in Capodistrias Street. She has three children. If she had to bring them with her, there would be no room for Sir Gale to stay."

"I see. How did you get the lift back, Father?"

"Well, I went to Karamanlis' garage, of course." Sir Julian suddenly sounded sober, and very irritable. "Really, Max, I don't know why you talk as if I'm incapable of looking after myself! Please try to remember that I lived here before you were born! I thought Leander might oblige me, but he was away. There was only one boy on duty, but he offered to get his brother to take me. We had a very interesting chat, very interesting indeed. I knew his uncle, Manoulis was the name. I remember once, when I was at Avra—"

"Was it Manoulis who brought you home?"

Sir Julian focussed. "Home?"

"Back here?" amended Max quickly.

The older man hesitated. "The thing was, I had to ask him in. When he came in for petrol and saw me there, you might say he had to offer the lift, but all the same, one has to be civil. I'm sorry, Max."

"It's all right, I understand. Of course one must. He brought you home, and you felt you'd have to ask him in, so you bought the gin?"

"Gin?" Sir Julian was drifting again. I thought I could see something struggling in his face, some intelligence half drowned with gin and sleep, holding on by a gleam of cunning. "That's Turkish gin, too, terrible stuff. God knows what they put in it. It was what he said he liked. . . . We stopped at that taverna—Constantinos' it used to be, but I forget the name now—two miles out of Ipsos. I think he must have guessed there wouldn't be any in the house."

Max was silent. I couldn't see his face.

Adoni broke the pause. "Max, look." I had seen him stoop to pick something up, and now he held out a hand, with some small object on the palm: a cigarette stub. "It was down there, by the stove. It's not one of yours, is it?"

"No." Max picked the thing up, and held it closer to the light.

Adoni said, "It is, isn't it?"

"Obviously." Their eyes met again, over the old man's head. There was a silence, in which the cat suddenly purred. " '*Things to discuss*' " Max quoted it softly, but with a new note in his voice that I found frightening. "What the sweet hell can *he* have wanted to discuss with my father?"

"This meeting," said Adoni, "could it be accidental?"

"It must have been. He was driving by, and picked my father up. Pure chance. Who could have foreseen that? Damn and damn and damn."

"And getting him . . . like this?"

"Letting him get like this. There's a difference. That can't have been deliberate. Nobody knew he was like this except us, and Michael and the Karithises."

Adoni said, "Maybe he's been talking this sort of nonsense all evening. Maybe *he* couldn't get any sense out of him, either."

"He couldn't get any sense out of me," said Sir Julian, with intense satisfaction.

"Oh, my God," said Max, "let's hope he's right." He flicked the cigarette butt back towards the stove, and straightened his shoulders. "Well, I'll get him to bed. Be a good chap and look after Miss Lucy, will you? Show her the bathroom—the one my father uses is the least repulsive, I think. Find her a towel and show her a spare bedroom—the one Michael sleeps in. There's an electric fire there."

"All right, but what about your hand? Haven't you seen to it at all?"

"Not yet, but I will in a moment. Go on, man, don't fuss. Believe me, I'd fuss plenty if I thought it was serious; I'm a pianist of a sort, don't forget! Lucy, I'm sorry about this. Will you go with him now?"

"Of course."

"This way," said Adoni.

The massive door swung shut behind us, and our steps rattled across the chequerboard marble of the hall floor.

It would have taken Dali and Ronald Searle, working overtime on alternate jags of mescal and Benzedrine, to design the interior of the Castello dei Fiori. At one end of a hall was a massive curved staircase, with a wrought-iron banister and bare stone treads. The walls were panelled in the darkest possible oak, and what small rugs lay islanded on the marble sea were done (as far as I could judge in the gloom) in uniform shades of drab and olive green. A colossal open fireplace, built for roasting oxen whole, by men who had never roasted, and would never roast, an ox whole in their lives, half filled one wall. The hearth of this bristled with spits and dogs and tongs and cauldrons and a hundred other mediaeval kitchen gadgets whose functions I couldn't even guess at; they looked like—and probably were—instruments of torture. For the rest, the hall was cluttered like a bargain basement: the Gales must have thrown most of the furniture out of their big living room to clear the acoustics—or perhaps merely in the interests of sane living—and as a result the hall was crammed full of enormous overstuffed furniture in various shades of mud, with innumerable extras in the way of bamboo tables, Chinese screens, and whatnots in spindly and very shiny wood. I thought I glimpsed a harmonium, but might have been wrong, because there was a full-sized organ, pipes and all, in the darkness beyond a fretwork dresser and a coatrack made of stags' antlers. There was cer-

tainly a harp, and a small forest of pampas grass stuck in what I am sure
was the severed foot of an elephant. These riches were lit with a merciful dimness by a single weak bulb in a torch held by a fully armed Java-
nese warrior who looked a bit like a gila monster in rut.

Adoni ran gracefully up the wide stairs in front of me. I followed
more slowly, hampered by my icily clinging clothes, my sandals leaving
horrible wet marks on the treads. He paused to wait for me, eying me
curiously.

"What happened to you and Max?"

"The dolphin—Spiro's dolphin—was stranded on the beach, and he
helped me to float it again. It pulled us both in."

"No, did it really?" He laughed. "I'd like to have seen that!"

"I'm sure you would." At least his spirits didn't seem to have been
damped by the recent scene in the music room. I wondered if he was
used to it.

"When you ran into Max, then you were coming for help? I see! But
why were you out on the beach in the dark?"

"Now don't *you* start!" I said warmly. "I had plenty of that from Max!
I was down there picking up a ring—this ring—that my sister had left
this morning."

His eyes and mouth rounded at the sight of the diamond. "*Po po po!*
That must be worth a few drachs, that one! No wonder you didn't mind
making a journey in the dark!"

"Worth more than your journey?" I asked innocently.

The beautiful eyes danced. "I wouldn't say that."

"No?" I regarded him uneasily. What on earth—what in heaven—
could they have been up to? Drugs? Surely not! Arms? Ridiculous! But
then, what did I know about Max, after all? And his worry in case his father might have "talked" hadn't just been worry; it had been fear. As for
Adoni—I had few illusions as to what my young Byzantine saint would
be capable of. . . .

He asked, "When you first went out through the woods, you saw nobody?"

"Max asked me that. I heard Sir Julian playing the tape recorder, but
I've no idea if his visitor was still there. I gather you know who it was?"

"I think so. It's a guess, but I think so. Sir Gale may tell Max when
they are alone, I don't know."

"Max doesn't normally have drink in the house at all?"

"None that his—none that can be found."

"I see."

I did indeed see. I saw how the rumours had arisen, and just how false Phyl's picture of the situation had been. Except in so far as this sort of periodic "bender" was a symptom of mental strain, Sir Julian Gale was sane enough. And now that I thought even further back, there had been whispers in the theatre world, possibly strong ones among those who knew him, but on my level the merest breath . . . rumours scotched once and for all by Sir Julian's faultless performances right up to the moment of retirement. Well, I had had a personal demonstration tonight of how it had been done.

"We thought he was better," said Adoni. "He has not done this for, oh, a long time. This will make Max very . . ." He searched for a word and came up with one that was, I felt, not quite adequate. ". . . unhappy."

"I'm sorry. But he does seem to have been pushed into it this time."

"Pushed in? Oh, yes, I understand. That is true. Well, Max will deal with it." He gave a little laugh. "Poor Max, he gets everything to deal with. Look, we had better hurry, or you will get cold, and then Max will deal with *me!*"

"Could he?"

"Easily. He pays my wages."

He paused, and pressed a switch in the panelling, invisible except to its intimates. Another dim light faltered into life, this time held aloft by a startling figure in flesh-pink marble, carved by some robust Victorian with a mind above fig leaves. A wide corridor now stretched ahead of us, lined on one side by massive iron studded doors, and on the other by what would, in daylight, be stained-glass windows of a peculiarly repulsive design.

"This way."

He led the way quickly along the corridor. To either side the light glimmered yellow on the pathetic heads of deer and ibexes, and case after case where stuffed birds stood enthroned and moth-eaten. Every other available foot of wall space was filled with weapons—axes, swords, daggers, and ancient firearms which I (who had furnished a few period plays in my time) identified as flintlocks and muskets, probably dating from the Greek War of Independence. It was to be hoped that Sir Julian and his son were as blind to the murderous décor as Adoni appeared to be.

"Your bathroom is along there." He pointed ahead to a vast door, opposite which hung a tasteful design in crossed whips and spurs. "I'll just show you where everything is, then I must go and dress his wrist."

"How badly is he hurt? He wouldn't say."

"Not badly at all. I think it's only a graze, for all it bled a lot. Don't worry, Max is sensible, he'll take all the care he should."

"And you?" I said.

He looked surprised. "I?"

"Will you take care of yourself as well? Oh, I know it's nothing to do with me, Adoni, but . . . well, be careful. For Miranda's sake, if not for your own."

He laughed at me, and touched a thin silver chain at his neck which must have held a cross or some sort of medal. "Don't you worry about me, either, Miss Lucy. The Saint looks after his own." A vivid look. "Believe me, he does."

"I take it you did well tonight?" I said, a little dryly.

"I think so. Here we are." He shoved the door wide, and found another switch. I glimpsed the splendours of marble and mahogany beyond him. "The bedroom is the next one, through there. I'll find you a towel, and later I shall make you something hot to drink. You can find the way down?"

"Yes, thank you."

He rummaged in a cupboard the size of a small garage, and emerged with a couple of towels. "Here you are. You have everything now?"

"I think so. The only thing is—do I have to touch that thing?"

"That thing" was a fearsome contraption which, apparently, heated the water. It looked like a stranded mine, and sat on a panel of dials and switches that might have come straight off the flight deck of an airliner designed by Emmett.

"You are as bad as Sir Gale," said Adoni indulgently. "He calls it Lolita, and refuses to touch it. It's perfectly safe, Spiro made it."

"Oh."

"It did go on fire once, but it's all right now. We rewired it only last month, Spiro and I."

Another dazzling smile, and the door shut gently. I was alone with Lolita.

You had to climb three steps to the bath, which was about the size of a swimming pool, and fairly bristling with gadgets in blackened brass. But I forgave the Castello everything when I turned the tap marked C and the water rushed out in a boiling cloud of steam. I hoped poor Max wouldn't be long before he achieved a similiar state of bliss—it was to be assumed there was another bathroom, and another Lolita as efficient as mine—but just at the moment I spared Max no more than the most passing of thoughts, and none whatever for the rest of the night's adventures. All I wanted was to be out of those dreadful, sodden clothes and into that glorious bath. . . .

By the time I was languidly drying a body broiled all over to a glowing pink, my underclothing, which was mostly nylon, was dry. The dress and coat were still wet, so I left them spread over the hot pipes, put on the dressing gown which hung behind the door, then padded through into the bedroom to attend to my face and hair.

I had what I had salvaged of Phyl's make-up, which included a comb, so I did the best I could with the inevitable dim light and a cheval-glass swinging between two mahogany pillars, which seemed designed to hang perpetually facing the carpet, until I found on the floor and re-placed the wedge of newspaper that had held it in position since, apparently, July 20, 1917.

In the greenish glass my reflection swam like something that might well have startled the Lady of Shalott out of her few wits. The dressing gown was obviously one of Sir Julian's stagier efforts; it was long, of thick, dark red silk, and made one think of Coward comedies. With Phyl's lipstick, and my short, damply curling hair, and the enormous diamond on my hand, it made a pretty high camp effect.

Well, it was no odder than the other guises he had seen me in up to now. I wondered if this, too, would qualify as "half naked." Not that it mattered, just now he would have other things very much on his mind.

I grimaced briefly at the image in the glass, then went out, back along Murder Alley, and down the stairs.

CHAPTER

ELEVEN

ह*

*The very instant that I saw you, did
My heart fly to your service; there resides,
To make me slave to it . . .*

Act III, Scene 1

The music-room door was standing open, but, though the lamp still burned, there was no one there. The gin had vanished, too, and in its place was something that looked like the remains of a stiff Alka-Seltzer, and a cup that had probably contained coffee.

As I hesitated in the doorway, I heard a quick step, and the service door under the stairway opened with a swish of chilly air.

"Lucy? Ah, I thought I heard you. You're all right? Warm now?"

"Lovely, thank you." He himself looked a different person. I noticed that there was a fresh white bandage on his wrist, and that his dry clothes—another thick sweater and dark trousers—made him look as tough as before, but younger, rather nearer Adoni's league. So did the look in his face: he looked tired still, but with a tautness that now seemed to have some sort of affinity with Adoni's dark glow of excitement. A worthwhile trip, indeed. . . .

I said quickly, "Your clothes . . . You're surely not planning to go out again?"

"Only to drive you home, don't worry. Come along to the kitchen, will you? It's warm there, and there's coffee. Adoni and I have been having something to eat."

"I'd adore some coffee. But I don't know if I ought to stay—my sister really will have the wind up by now."

"I rang her up and told her what had happened . . . more or less." He grinned, a boy's grin. "Actually, Godfrey Manning had already called up and told her about the dolphin, and that her ring was safe, so she's quite happy, and says she'll expect you when she sees you. So come along."

I followed him through the service door and down a bare, echoing passage. It seemed that the Castello servants could not be allowed to share the glories which fell to their betters, for "below stairs" the Castello was unadorned by dead animals and lethal weapons. Personally I'd have traded the whole building, organ pipes and all, for the kitchen, a wonderful, huge cavern of a place, with a smaller cave for fireplace, where big logs burned merrily in their iron basket, adding their sweet, pungent smells to the smells of food and coffee, and lighting the big room with a living, beating glow. Hanging from the rafters, among the high, flickering shadows, bunches of dried herbs and strings of onions stirred and glimmered in the updraught of warm air.

In the centre of the kitchen was about an acre of scrubbed wooden table, and in a corner of the room Adoni was frying something on an electric cooker which had probably been built, or at any rate wired, by himself and Spiro. There was a wonderful smell of bacon and coffee.

"You can eat some bacon and eggs, surely?" asked Max.

"She will have to," said Adoni briefly, over his shoulder. "I have done them already."

"Well . . ." I said, and Max pulled out a chair for me at the end of the table nearest to the fire, where a rather peculiar assortment of plates and cutlery were set in a space comprising about a fiftieth of the table's total area. Adoni put a plate down in front of me, and I realized that I was suddenly, marvellously hungry. "Have you had yours?" I asked.

"Adoni has, and I've just reached the coffee stage," said Max. "Shall I pour some for you straight away?"

"Yes, please." I wondered whether it would be tactful to ask after Sir Julian, and this made me remember my borrowed finery. "My things were still wet, so I borrowed your father's dressing gown. Will he mind, do you think? It's a terribly grand one."

"*Present Laughter*," said Max. "Of course he won't. He'll be delighted. Sugar?"

"Yes, please."

"There. If you can get outside that lot, I doubt if the pneumonia bugs will stand a chance. Adoni's a good cook, when pushed to it."

"It's marvellous," I said, with my mouth full, and Adoni gave me that heart-shaking smile of his, said, "It's a pleasure," and then, to Max, something that I recognized (from a week's painful study of a phrase book) as "Does she speak Greek?"

Max jerked his head in that curious gesture—like a refractory camel snorting—that the Greeks use for "No," and the boy plunged forthwith into a long and earnest speech of which I caught no intelligible word at all. It was, I guessed, urgent and excited rather than apprehensive. Max listened, frowning, and without comment, except that twice he interrupted with a Greek phrase—the same one each time—that checked the flow and sent Adoni back to speak more slowly and clearly. I ate placidly through my bacon and eggs, trying not to notice the deepening frown on Max's face or the steadily heightened excitement of Adoni's narrative.

At length the latter straightened up, glancing at my empty plate. "Would you like some more? Or cheese, perhaps?"

"Oh, no, thank you. That was wonderful."

"Some more coffee, then?"

"Is there some?"

"Of course." Max poured it, and pushed the sugar nearer. "Cigarette?"

"No, thanks."

He was returning the pack to his pocket when Adoni, who had been removing my plate, said something quickly and softly in Greek, and Max held the pack out to him. Adoni took three cigarettes, with the glimmer of a smile at me when he saw that I was watching, then he said something else in Greek to Max, added "Good night, Miss Lucy," and went out through a door I hadn't noticed before, in a far corner of the kitchen.

Max said easily, "Forgive the mystery. We've been putting my father to bed."

"Is he all right?"

"He will be." He threw me a look. "I suppose you knew about his —difficulty?"

"No, how could I? I'd no idea."

"But if you're in the business . . . I thought it must surely have got round."

"It didn't get to me," I said. "I suppose there must have been rumours, but all I ever knew was that he wasn't well. I thought it was heart or something. And honestly, nobody knew here—at least, Phyl didn't, and if there's been any talk you can bet she'd be the first to hear it. She just knew what you told Leo, that he'd been ill, and in a nursing home. Does it happen often?"

"If you'd asked me that yesterday," he said, a little bitterly, "I'd have said it probably wouldn't happen again."

"Did he talk when you took him upstairs?"

"A little."

"Tell you who it was?"

"Yes."

"And what they'd talked about?"

"Not really, no. He just kept repeating that he 'hadn't got anything out of him.' That, with variations. He seemed rather more pleased and amused than anything else. Then he went to sleep."

I said, "You know, I think you can stop worrying. I'd be willing to bet that your father's said nothing whatever."

He looked at me with surprise. I hadn't realized before how dark his eyes were. "What makes you so sure?"

"Well . . ." I hesitated. "You were a bit upset in there, but I had nothing to do but notice things. I'll tell you how it struck me. He was certainly drunk, but I think he was hanging on to something he knew . . . he'd forgotten *why*, but just knew he had to. He knew he hadn't to say anything about—about whatever you and Adoni were doing. He was so fuddled that he couldn't sort out who was safe and who wasn't, but he wasn't parting with anything: he even kept stalling you and Adoni because I was there, and even about things that didn't matter, like what happened at Mr. Andiakis'." I smiled. "And then the way he was reciting, and fiddling with the tape recorder . . . You can't tell me he normally gives private renderings of Shakespeare in his own drawing room. Actors don't. They may go on acting their heads off offstage, but they aren't usually bores. It struck me— Look, I'm sorry, am I speaking out of turn? Perhaps you'd rather I didn't—"

"God, no. Go on."

"It struck me that he was reciting because he knew that once he'd got himself—or the tape—safely switched into a groove, he could just go on and on without any danger of being jumped into saying the wrong thing. When I heard it, he was probably playing the tape to his visitor."

His mouth twitched in momentary amusement. "Serve him right. What's more, I'm certain that the meeting at the garage was an accident. If Adoni and I had been suspected, we'd have been watched, and perhaps followed . . . or intercepted on our way home."

"Well, there you are; and it stands to reason that if your father had told him anything, or even dropped a hint where you both were, there's been masses of time to have the police along, or . . . or anything."

"Of course." The look he gave me was not quite easy, for all that.

I hesitated. "Worrying about your father, though—that's a different thing. I don't know about these things. Do you think it may have, well, started him drinking again?"

"One can't tell. He's not an alcoholic, you know; it wasn't chronic, or approaching it. It's just that he started to go on these periodic drunks to get out of his jags of depression. We can only wait and see."

I said no more, but turned my chair away from the table to face the fire and drank my coffee. The logs purred and hissed, and the resin came bubbling out of one of them, in little opal globes that popped and swelled against the charring bark. The big airy room was filled with the companionable noises of the night: the bubbling of the resin, the spurt and flutter of flames, the creak of some ancient wooden floor settling for the night, the clang of the old hot-water system. As I stretched Sir Julian's bedroom slippers nearer the fire a cricket chirped, suddenly and clearly, about a yard away. I jumped, then, looking up, caught Max watching me, and we smiled at each other. Neither of us moved or spoke, but a kind of wordless conversation seemed to take place, and I was filled with a sudden, heart-swelling elation and happiness, as if the sun had come out on my birthday morning and I had been given the world.

Then he had turned away, and was looking into the fire again. He said, as if he were simply going on from where we had left off:

"It started just over four years ago. Father was rehearsing at the time for that rather spectacular thing that Hayward wrote for him, *Tiger, Tiger*. You'll remember it; it ran forever. Just eight days before the play was due to open, my mother and sister were both killed together in a motor accident. My sister was driving the car when it happened; it wasn't her fault, but that was no comfort. My mother was killed instantly; my sister regained consciousness and lived for a day—long enough to guess what had happened, though they tried to keep it from her. I was away at the time in the States, and, as bad luck would have it, was in hospital there with appendicitis, and couldn't get home. Well, I told you, it was only eight days before *Tiger, Tiger* was due to open, and it did open. I don't have to tell you what a situation like that would do to someone like my father. It would damage anybody, and it half killed him."

"I can imagine." I was also imagining Max himself, chained to his alien hospital bed, getting it all by telephone, by cable, through the mail. . . .

"That was when he started drinking. It was nearly two months before I got home, and a lot of the damage had been done. Of course, I had realized how it would hit him, but it took the shock of actually coming home to make me realize . . ." He paused. "You can imagine that, too; the house empty, and looking lost, almost as if it hadn't even been dusted for weeks, though that was silly, of course it had. But it felt deserted—echoing, almost. Sally—my sister—had always been a bit of a live wire. And there was Father, as thin as a telegraph post, with his hair three shades whiter, drifting about that damned great place like a dead leaf in a draughty barn. Not sleeping, of course, and drinking." He shifted in his chair. "What was that he said about the house being like a lord's kitchen without a fire?"

"It's from a play, Tourneur's *Revenger's Tragedy*. 'Hell would look like a lord's great kitchen without fire in't.'"

"'Hell'?" he quoted. "Yes, I see."

I said quickly, "It wasn't even relevant. It only occurred to him as a sort of image."

"Of emptiness?" He smiled suddenly. "Sweet of you, but don't worry, things pass." He paused. "That was the start. It got better, of course; shock wears off, and with me at home he didn't drink so much, but now and again, when he was tired or overstrained, or just in one of those damned abysmal depressions that his sort of person suffers—they're as real as the measles, I don't have to tell you that—he would drink himself blind, 'just this once.' Unhappily, it takes remarkably little to do it. Well, if you remember, the play ran for a long time, and he stayed in it eighteen months. In all that time I only got him away for three weeks, then back he'd go to London, and after a while the house would get him down, and 'just this once' he'd go on another drunk."

"You couldn't get him to sell the house and move?"

"No. He'd been born there, and his father. It was something he wouldn't even begin to think about. Well, a couple of years of that, and he was going downhill like something on the Cresta Run. Then the 'breakdowns' started, still, thanks to his friends, attributed publicly to strain and overwork. He had the sense to know what was happening to him, and the integrity and pride to get out while he could still do it with his legend intact. He did what he could . . . went into a 'home' and was 'cured.' Then I got him to come away here, to make quite sure he was all right, and to rest. Now he's breaking his heart to get back, but I know he won't do it while there's any danger of its starting again." He gave a quick sigh. "I thought he was through with it, but now I don't know. It isn't just a question of willpower, you know. Don't despise him."

"I know that. And how could I despise him? I love him."

"Lucy Waring's specialty. Given away regardless and for no known reason. No, I'm not laughing at you, heaven forbid. . . . Will you tell me something?"

"What?"

"Did you mean what you said down there on the beach?"

The abrupt, almost casual question threw me for a moment. "On the beach? When? What did I say?"

"I realize I wasn't meant to hear it. We were just starting up the steps."

There was a pause. A log fell in with a soft crash and a jet of hissing light.

I said, with some difficulty, "You don't ask much, do you?"

"I'm sorry, that was stupid of me. Skip it. My God, I choose my moments, as you say."

He leaned down, picked a poker up from the hearthstone, and busied himself with rearranging the pieces of burning wood. I stared at his averted face, while a straitjacket of shyness gripped me, and with it a sort of anger at his obtuseness in asking this. I couldn't have spoken if I'd tried.

A jet of flame, stirred by the poker, leaped up and caught the other log. It lit his face, briefly highlighting the traces of the night's excitement and pain and tension, the frowning brows so like his father's, the hard, exciting line of his cheek; his mouth. And the same brief flash lit something else for me. I was the one who was stupid. If one asks a question, it is because one wants to know the answer. Why should he have to wait and wrap it up some other way when the "moment" suited me?

I said it quite easily after all. "If you'd asked me a thing like that three hours ago, I think I'd have said I didn't even like you, and I . . . I think I'd have believed it . . . I think. . . . And now there you sit looking at me, and all you do is look—like that—and my damned bones turn to water, and it isn't fair, it's never happened to me before, and I'd do anything in the world for you, and you know it, or if you don't you ought to— No, look, I—I didn't mean . . . you *asked* me . . ."

It was a better kiss this time, no less breathless, but at least we were dry and warm, and had known each other nearly two hours longer. . . .

From somewhere in the shadows came a sharp click and a whirring sound. Instantly, we were a yard apart.

A small, fluting voice said, "*Cuckoo, cuckoo, cuckoo, cuckoo,*" and clicked back into silence.

"That damned clock!" said Max explosively, then began to laugh. "It always frightens me out of my wits. It sounds like someone sneaking in with a tommy gun. I'm sorry, did I drop you too hard?"

"Right down to earth," I said shakily. "Four o'clock, I'll have to go."

"Wait just a little longer, can't you? No, listen, there's something you've got to know. I'll try not to take too long, if you'll just sit down again . . . ? Don't take any notice of that clock, it's always fast." He cocked an eyebrow. "What are you looking at me like that for?"

"For a start," I said, "men don't usually jump sky-high when they hear a noise like a tommy gun. Unless they could be expecting one, that is. Were you?"

"Could be," he said cheerfully.

"Goodness me! Then I'll certainly stay to hear all about it!" I sat down, folding my silk skirts demurely about me. "Go on."

"A moment. I'll put another log on the fire. Are you warm enough?"

"Yes, thank you."

"You won't smoke? You never do? Wise girl. Well . . ."

He leaned his elbows on his knees, and stared once more at the fire.

". . . I'm not quite sure where to start, but I'll try to make it short. You can have the details later, those you can't fill in for yourself. I want to tell you what's happened tonight, and especially what's going to happen tomorrow—today, I mean—because I want you to help me, if you will. But to make it clear I'll have to go back to the start of the story. I suppose you could say that it starts with Yanni Zoulas; at any rate, that's where I'll begin."

"It was true, then? He was a smuggler?"

"Yes, indeed. Yanni carried stuff regularly—all kinds of goods in short supply—over to the Albanian coast. Your guess was right about the 'contacts': he had his 'contact' on the other side, a man called Milo, and he had people over here who supplied the stuff and paid him. But not me. Your guess was wrong there. Now, how much d'you know about Albania?"

"Hardly a thing. I did try to read it up before I came here, but there's so little to read. I know it's Communist, of course, and at daggers drawn with Tito's Yugoslavia, *and* with Greece on the other border. I gather that it's a poor country, without much workable land and no industries, just peasant villages perched on the edge of starvation, like some of the Greek ones. I don't know any of the towns except Durrës, on the coast, and Tirana, the capital. I gathered that they were still pretty Stone Age at the end of the war, but trying hard and looking round for help. That was when the U.S.S.R. stepped in, wasn't it?"

"Yes. She supplied Albania with tools and tractors and seeds, and so forth, all it needed to get its agriculture going again after the war. But it wasn't all plain sailing. I won't go into it now—in fact, I'm not at all sure that I've got it straight myself—but a few years ago Albania quarrelled with Russia, and broke with the Cominform, but because it still badly needed help (and possible support against Russia) it applied to

Communist China; and China, which was then at loggerheads with Russia, jumped happily in to play fairy godmother to Albania as Russia had done before—and presumably to get one foot wedged in Europe's back door. The situation's still roughly that, and now Albania's closed its frontiers completely, except to China. You can't get in, and by heaven, you certainly can't get out."

"Like Spiro's father?"

"I suspect he didn't want to. But you might say he brings us to the next point in the story, which is Spiro. I suppose you've heard about our connection with Maria and her family?"

"In a way. Adoni told me."

"My father was here in Corfu during the war, and he was working in with Spiro's father for a time—a wild type, I gather, but rather picturesque and appealing. He appealed to the romantic in my father, anyway." Max grinned. "One gathers they had some pretty tearing times together. When the twins were born, Father stood godfather to them. You won't know this, but over here it's a relationship that's taken very seriously. The godfather really does take responsibility—he has as much say in the kids' future as their father does, sometimes more."

"I gathered that from Adoni. It was obvious he had a say in the christening, anyway!"

He laughed. "It certainly was. The isle of Corfu went to his head even in those days. Thank God I was born in London, or I've a feeling nothing could have saved me from Ferdinand. Would you have minded?"

"Terribly. Ferdinand makes me think of a rather pansy kind of bull. What is your name, anyway? Maximilian?"

"Praise heaven, no. Maxwell. It was my mother's name."

"I take it you had a godfather with no obsessions."

He grinned. "Too right. In the correct English manner, he gave me a silver teaspoon, then vanished from my life. But you can't do that in Corfu. When Spiro's own father did actually vanish, the godfather was almost literally left holding the babies."

"He was still over here when that happened?"

"Yes. He was here for a bit after the European War was finished, and during that time he felt himself more or less responsible for the family. He would have been if he'd been a Greek, since Maria had no relatives and they were as poor as mice, so he took the family on, and even after he'd gone home sent money to them every month."

"Good heavens! But surely, with children of his own—"

"He managed." Max's voice was suddenly grave. "We're not rich,

heaven knows . . . and an actor's life's a darned uncertain one at best
. . . but it's rather frightening how little a Greek family can manage
on quite cheerfully. He kept them completely till Maria went out to
work, and even after that he more or less kept them until the children
could work, too." He stretched out a foot and shoved the log deeper on
its bed of burning ash. "We came over here for holidays most years;
that's where I learned my Greek and the kids their English. We had a
whale of a time, and Father always loved it. I was thankful I had somewhere like this to bring him when the crash came . . . it was like having
another family ready-made. It's helped him more than anything else
could have done. Being wanted does."

"Good heavens, the thousands that want him! But I know it's different. So he came back here for peace to recover in, and then Spiro was
killed. It must have hit him terribly."

"The trouble was," said Max, "that Maria wouldn't believe the boy
could be dead. She never stopped begging and praying my father to find
out what really happened to him, and to bring him back. Apparently
she'd made a special petition to St. Spiridion for him, so she simply
wouldn't believe he could have drowned. She got some sort of idea that
he'd gone after his father and must be brought home."

The second cigarette stub went after the first. It hit a bar of the fire,
and fell back on the hearthstone. He got up, picked it up and dropped
it on the fire, then stayed on his feet with a shoulder propped against
the high mantel.

"I know it wasn't reasonable, not after Manning had told her what
had happened, but mothers don't always listen to reason, and there
was always the faint chance that the boy *had* survived. My father didn't
feel equal to handling it, and I knew that neither he nor Maria would
have any peace of mind till they found what had become of his body,
so I took it on. I've been having inquiries made wherever I could, here
and on the mainland, to find out in the first place if he'd been washed
ashore, dead or alive. I've also had someone in Athens trying to get information from the Albanian side. Where Spiro went in, the current
sets dead towards the Albanian coast. Well, I did manage to get
through in the end, but with no results. He hadn't been seen, either
on the Greek coast or the Albanian."

I said, "And I read you a lesson on helping other people. I'm sorry."

"You couldn't know it was any concern of mine."

"Well, no, it did rather seem to be Godfrey's."

"I suppose so, but the local Greeks at any rate assumed that it was
my father's job—or mine—to do it. So the police kept in touch with us,

and we knew we'd get any information that was going. And when Yanni Zoulas went across on his routine smuggling trip on Saturday night and did actually get some news of Spiro through his Albanian 'contact,' he came straight to us. Or rather, as straight as he could. You saw him on his way up to see us, on Sunday evening."

I was bolt-upright in my chair. "*News of Spiro?* Good news?"

I knew the answer before he spoke. The gleam in his eyes reminded me suddenly, vividly, of the way Adoni had looked at me on the staircase, glowing.

"Oh, yes. He came to tell us Spiro was alive."

"*Max!*"

"Yes, I know. You can guess how we felt. He'd been washed ashore on the Albanian side, with a broken leg, and in the last stages of exhaustion, but he'd survived. The people who found him were simple coast folk, shepherds, who didn't see any reason to report things to the People's Police, or whatever it's called over there. Most people know about the smuggling that goes on, and I gather that these folk assumed that Spiro was mixed up in something of the sort, so they kept quiet about him. What's more, they informed the local smuggler, who—naturally—knew Milo, Yanni's 'contact,' who in turn passed the news along to Yanni on Saturday."

"Oh, Max, this is marvellous! It really is! Did Yanni actually see him?"

"No. It all came at rather third hand. Milo hasn't much Greek, so all that Yanni got from him was the bare facts, and an urgent message that Spiro somehow managed to convey that no one, no one at all—not even Maria—was to be told that he was still alive, except myself, my father, and Adoni . . . the people who'd presumably get him out somehow." He paused briefly. "Well, obviously we couldn't go to the police and get him out by normal channels, or the people who'd rescued him would be in trouble, not to mention Yanni and Milo. So Yanni fixed up a rendezvous to bring the boy off by night."

"And he went back last night after he'd seen you, and ran into the coastguards and got hurt?"

But he was shaking his head. "He couldn't have gone back alone; getting that boy off wasn't one man's job—don't forget he was strapped to a stretcher. No, when Yanni came up on Sunday night, he came to ask me to go across with him. The rendezvous was fixed for tonight; Milo and his friend were to have Spiro there, and Yanni and I were to take him off. So you see . . ."

I didn't hear what he was going to say. It had all come together at last, and I could only wonder at my slowness in not seeing it all before. My eyes flew to his bandaged wrist as the events of the night came rushing back: the secrecy of his journey through the woods, the impression I had had of more than one man passing me there, the owl's call, Adoni's vivid face . . .

I was on my feet. "The catch! Adoni and the catch! You took Adoni, and went over there yourself tonight! You mean it's *done?* You've actually *brought Spiro home?*"

His eyes were dancing. "We have indeed. He's here at this moment, a bit tired, but alive and well. I told you our night's work had been worthwhile."

I sat down again, rather heavily. "I can hardly take it in. This is . . . wonderful. Oh, Maria will be able to light herself a lovely candle this Easter! Think of it, Maria, Miranda, Sir Julian, Godfrey, Phyl . . . how happy everyone's going to be! I can hardly wait till daylight, to see the news go round!"

The glow faded abruptly from his face. It must have been only imagination, but the gay firelight seemed dimmer, too.

He said sombrely, "I'm afraid it mustn't go round yet, not any further."

"But"—I stared, bewildered—"not to his mother or sister? Why on earth not, if he's safely home? Surely, once he's out of Albania he has nothing to fear. And Milo needn't be involved at all—no one need even know Spiro was ever on Albanian soil. We could invent some story—"

"I'd thought of that. The story will be that he was thrown ashore on one of the islands in the strait, the Peristeroi Islands, and that he managed to attract our attention when we were out fishing. It won't fool the Greek police, or the doctor, but it'll do for general release, as it were. But that's not the point."

"Then what is?"

He hesitated, then said slowly, "Spiro may still be in danger . . . not from the other side, but here. What touched him touched Yanni, too. And Yanni died."

Something in his face—his very reluctance to speak—frightened me. I found myself protesting violently, too violently, as if by protesting I could push the unwanted knowledge further away. "But we *know* what happened to Spiro! He went overboard from Godfrey's boat! How *can* he be in any danger now? And Yanni's death was an accident! You *said* so!"

I stopped. The silence was so intense that you could hear the crazy ticking of the cuckoo clock and the scrape of silk on flesh as my hands gripped together in my lap.

I said quietly, "Go on. Say it straight out, you may as well. You're insinuating that Godfrey Manning—"

"I'm insinuating nothing." His voice was curt, even to rudeness. "I'm telling you. Here it is. Godfrey Manning threw Spiro overboard, and left him to drown."

Silence again, a different kind of silence.

"Max, I—I can't accept that. I'm sorry, but it isn't possible."

"It's fact, no more nor less. Spiro says so. Yes, I thought you were forgetting that I've talked to him. He says so, and I believe him. He has no reason to lie."

Seconds were out with a vengeance. Now that he had decided he must tell me, he hurled his facts like stones. And they hit like stones.

"But—*why?*"

"I don't know. Neither does the boy, which, when you come to think about it, makes it the more likely that he's telling the truth. It's something he'd have no reason to invent. He's as stunned by it as you are." He added, more gently, "I'm sorry, Lucy, but I'm afraid it's true."

I sat in silence for a minute or two, not thinking, but looking down at my hands, twisting and turning the great diamond, and watching the firelight break and dazzle among its facets. Slowly the stunned feeling faded, and I began to think. . . .

"Did you suspect Godfrey before?"

"No," he said, "why should I? But when I got that message from Yanni, I did wonder why Godfrey hadn't to be told. After all, it seemed reasonable to keep the news from Spiro's mother and sister, because they'd be so elated that they might give everything away before Yanni had done the job; but Godfrey was a different matter. He would presumably be worrying about Spiro, and he has by far the best boat. What's more, he's an experienced seaman, and I'm not. I'd have expected him to be asked in on the rescue, rather than me and Adoni. It wasn't much, but it did make me wonder. Then when Yanni was found dead next day, on top of Spiro's odd warning, I wondered still more."

I said, "You're not suggesting now—you *can't* be suggesting that Godfrey killed Yanni Zoulas? Max—"

"What I've told you about Spiro is fact: what happened to Yanni is guesswork. But to my mind the one murder follows the other as the night the day."

Murder . . . I don't think I said it aloud, but he nodded as if I had.

"I'm pretty sure of it. Same method, too. He'd been hit hard on the head and thrown into the sea. The bottle of ouzo was a nice touch, I thought."

"He was hit by the boom. The police said there were hairs—"

"He could also have been hit *with* the boom. Anyone can crack an unconscious man's head on a handy chunk of wood like that, hard enough to kill him before you throw him overboard—and hard enough to hide the crack you knocked him out with. I'm not bringing this out as a theory; I'm only saying it could have been done."

"Why did you go back to the body after we'd left?"

"After Yanni left us on Sunday night I heard his boat go out, and I did wonder if he'd been stupid enough to go back on his own and had run into trouble with the coastguards. From all that we'd been able to see, he might have had a bullet hole in him somewhere, or some other evidence that would start a serious investigation. I was pretty anxious in case they started patrolling local waters before I'd got Spiro safely home."

"I see. And your own wrist—was that the coastguards?"

"Yes, a stray bullet, and a spent one at that. It's honestly only a graze; I'll get it looked at when I get Spiro's leg seen to. They must have heard something, and fired blind. We were just about out of range, and well beyond their lights."

I said, rather wearily, "I suppose you do know what you're saying, but it all seems so . . . so impossible to me. And I don't understand even the start of it."

"My God, who does? But I told you, it's all guesswork about Yanni, and there's no future in discussing that now. The first thing is to talk to Spiro again. I've only had time to get the barest statement from him, and I want to hear the rest before I decide what's best to do. He should be fit enough by now to tell us exactly what happened; and whether he knows it or not, he may have some clue as to why Manning tried to kill him. If he has, it may be a pointer to Yanni's death. And whatever it is that makes two murders necessary." He straightened abruptly, his shoulder coming away from the mantel. "Well, you can see that we have to get the boy safely into the hands of the authorities with his story before Godfrey Manning has even a suspicion that he's not as dead as Yanni. Will you come with me now and see him?"

I looked up in surprise. "Me? You want me to?"

"If you will. I told you I wanted you to help me, and—if you'll agree —you'd better know as much as we do about it."

"Of course, whatever I can."

"Darling. Come here. Now, stop looking like that, and stop worrying.

It's all impossible, as you say, but then this sort of situation is bound to be when one gets mixed up in it oneself. All we can do is play for safety, and that means, for the moment, believing Spiro. All right?"

I nodded as best I could with my head comfortably against his shoulder.

"Then listen. What I've got to do, as I see it, is get the boy straight off to Athens in the morning, to the hospital, then to the police. Once he's told his story there, he'll be safe to come home." He loosed me. "Well, shall we go?"

"Where is he?"

He laughed. "Right below our feet, in a very Gothic but reasonably safe dungeon, with Adoni standing guard over him with the one efficient rifle in this damned great arsenal of Leo's. Come along, then. Straight under the cuckoo clock, and fork right for the dungeons!"

CHAPTER

TWELVE

જ

My cellar is in a rock by th' seaside where my wine is hid.

Act II, Scene 2

A wide flight of stone steps led downwards from just beyond the door.
Max touched a switch, and a weak yellow light came on to show us the
way. He shut the ponderous door, and I heard a key grate in the lock
behind us.

"I'll go first, shall I?"

I followed him, curiously looking about me. The rest of the building
had led me to expect goodness knew what horrors down here: it would
hardly have come as a surprise to have found mouldering skeletons
dangling in chains from the walls. But the underground corridor into
which the stairs led us was innocent of anything except racks for wine
—largely empty—which lined the wide passageway. The floor was clean,
and the walls surprisingly free of the dust and webs which would have
accumulated in a similar place in England. The air smelled fresh, and
slightly damp.

I said as much to Max, who nodded. "You'll see why in a minute.
This is the official wine cellar, but it leads off into a natural cave farther
along. I don't know where the opening is—it's probably no bigger than
a chimney—but the air's always fresh, and you can smell the sea. There
are more wine racks down there. In the last century, when one drank
one's four bottles a day, rather a lot of room was needed. Anyway, it
must have seemed a natural to use the caves in the cliff when they built
the Castello."

"It's rather exciting. I suppose these are the caves your father was
talking about."

"Yes. Most of the cliffs along this coast have caves in them, but as
you can imagine, he'd love to think the Castello cave was the original

Prospero's cell. When I point out that it doesn't look as if it had ever been open to the outside air, he says that doesn't matter. I gather it's more 'poetic truth,' like the marmosets."

"Well, it's a lovely romantic theory, and I'm all for it! After all, what are facts? We get those every day. . . . Whereabouts are we now in relation to 'outside'?"

"At present we're still moving along under the foundations of the house. The cave itself is in the southern headland, fairly deep down. We go down more steps in a moment, and then there's a natural passage through to the cave. Wait, here we are."

He had stopped two thirds of the way along the corridor, and put a hand up to the empty racks. I watched him, puzzled. He laid hold of what looked like part of the wall of racks, and pulled. Ponderously, and by no means silently, a narrow section swung out into the corridor. Beyond where it had been was a gap in the wall, opening on blackness.

"Goodness me!" I exclaimed, and Max laughed.

"Marvellous, isn't it? I tell you, the Castello's got everything! As a matter of fact, I have a suspicion that old Forli kept the better vintages down here, out of the butler's reach. . . . Careful, now, there's no light from here on. I've brought a torch—here, take it for a moment, will you, while I shut this behind us. Don't look so scared!"

"It won't stay shut and trap us here forever, till our bones bleach?"

"Not even till morning, I'm sorry to say. There. The torch, please. I'll go ahead."

The second flight sloped more steeply down, and, instead of being made of smooth slabs, seemed to be hacked out of solid rock. At the foot of the flight a rock-hewn passage curved away into darkness, still descending. Max went ahead, shining the beam for me. Here and there the walls showed a glint of damp, and the fresh smell was stronger, and perceptibly salty, while the hollow rock seemed—perhaps only in imagination—to hold a faint, echoing hum like the shushing of the sea through the curves of a shell. A moment I thought I heard it, then it was gone, and there was only the still, cold air, and the sound of our footsteps on the rock.

The yellow torchlight flung sharp lights and shadows on Max's face as he turned to guide me, sketching in, momentarily, the face of a stranger. His shadow moved distorted and huge on the rough walls.

"Is it much farther?" My voice sounded unfamiliar, like a whisper in an echo chamber.

"Round this corner," said Max, "and down five, no, six steps—and there's the watchdog."

A flash of the torch showed the pale blur of a face upturned, and a gun barrel gleaming blue.

"Adoni? It's Max, and I've brought Miss Lucy along. Is he all right?"

"He's fine now. He's awake."

Behind Adoni hung a rough curtain of some material like sacking, from beyond which came a dim, warm glow. Adoni drew the curtain aside for me and stood back. Max put the torch out and motioned me past him. I went into the cave.

This was large, with a great arched roof lost in shadows where stalactites hung like icicles; but the walls had been whitewashed to a height of six feet or so, and were lined with wine racks and crates and the comfortable, bulging shapes of barrels. On one of these, upturned to make a table, stood an old-fashioned lantern, a coach lamp of about 1830 vintage, probably borrowed from the museum upstairs, which dispensed a soft orange light and the cheerful twinkle of brass. The air was warmed by a paraffin stove which stood in the middle of the floor, with a pan of coffee on it. Somewhere in the shadows a drip of water fell regularly—some stalactite dripping fresh water into a pocket of rock; the sound was as homely as a dripping tap. The unexpected effect of coziness was enhanced by the smell of cigarettes and coffee and the faint fumes of the paraffin stove.

The injured boy lay at the far side of the cave, on a bed pushed up against a row of crates. The bed was a makeshift affair which nevertheless looked extremely comfortable—a couple of spring mattresses laid one above the other, with blankets galore, and feather pillows, and a vast eiderdown. Some sort of cage had been rigged up under the bedclothes to keep their weight off the injured leg.

Spiro, lying there in what looked like a pair of Sir Julian's pyjamas (pale blue silk with crimson piping), looked comfortable enough, and not at the moment particularly ill. He was propped up on his pillows, drinking coffee.

He looked up across the cup, a little startled at the sight of me, and threw a quick question at Max, who answered in English:

"It's Kyria Forli's sister. She's my friend, and yours. She's going to help us, and I want her to hear your story."

Spiro regarded me steadily, without noticeable welcome, the round dark eyes, so like his sister's, wary and appraising. I could recognize the boy in the photographs, but only just; there was the thick, springing hair and the stocky body, with obvious strength in the shoulders and thick neck; but the bloom of health and sunlight—and happiness—was gone. He looked pale, and—in the pyjamas—young and unprotected-looking.

Max pulled a box forward for me to sit on. "How do you feel?" he asked the boy. "Is it hurting?"

"No," said Spiro. That this was a lie was quite obvious, but it was not said with any sort of bravado. It was simply that one did not admit to weakness, and pain was weakness.

"He has slept," said Adoni.

"Good." Max perched himself half sitting against the cask which held the lantern. His shadow, thrown hugely up the walls, arched brooding and gigantic across the cave. He studied the younger boy for a minute or two, then said briskly:

"If you're feeling better, I want you to tell us exactly what happened to you. All the details this time, please."

"All the what?"

"Everything you can remember," said Max, and Adoni, from the head of the bed, added a soft gloss in Greek.

"All right." Spiro drained the coffee cup and handed it up, without looking, to Adoni. The latter took it, set it quietly aside, then crossed back to the bed and sat down, curling up gracefully, naturally, like a cat, near the head of the bed, away from the injured leg. He reached into a pocket for two of the cigarettes he had got from Max, stuck them in his mouth, lit them both, and handed one to Spiro. Spiro took it without word or glance, but there was no suggestion, as there had been with me, of anything withdrawn or unfriendly. It was obvious that these two young men knew each other almost too well to need words. They sat there side by side against the pillows, Adoni relaxed and graceful, Spiro square and watchful and smoking jerkily, with his hand cupped working-class fashion round the cigarette.

He sent one more wary glance at me, then took no more notice of me: all his attention was on Max, almost as if the latter were judging him—at once judge and saviour and final court of appeal. Max listened without moving, the huge, curved shadow thrown right up the wall and over half the ceiling of the cave.

The boy spoke slowly, with the signs of fatigue deepening in his face. I have no recollection now of what language he spoke; whether his English was good, or whether Max and Adoni eked it out with translation: the latter, I suspect; but whatever the case, the story came over vividly and sharply in that darkened cellar cave, with the lantern light, and the smell of the cigarettes, and the two boys curled in the welter of bedclothes, and the faint tangy scent from the silk of Julian Gale's dressing gown.

I suppose that the strange, secret surroundings, the time of night, my own weariness and recent emotional encounter with Max, had edged the scene somehow; but it seemed real now only as a dream is real. In the dream I found I had already accepted Godfrey's guilt; I only waited now to hear how he had done it. Perhaps in the light of morning things would take a different dimension; but now it seemed as if any tale could be true, even the old man's romantic theory that this was Prospero's cave, and that here on this rough floor the Neapolitan lords had waited to hear the story from the long-drowned Duke, as I now waited to hear Spiro's.

There had been nothing, he said, that had struck him as unusual about the trip that night. The only thing that had surprised him was that the sky was none too clear, and from what the wireless had said, it might well be stormy at dawn. He had pointed this out to Godfrey, but Godfrey had said, a little abruptly, that it would clear. They had got the boat out, and gone shortly before midnight. As Spiro had anticipated, the night was black and thick, but he had said nothing more to Godfrey, who had stayed in the cabin, allegedly busying himself with his camera and equipment.

"He seemed much as usual?" asked Max.

Spiro frowned, considering this. "I cannot say," he replied at length. "He was quiet, and perhaps a bit sharp with me when I protested about the weather, but all day he had been the same. I thought he was still angry with me because I had gone into the boathouse that morning on my own to service the engine, so I said nothing, and thought nothing. He pays me, and that is that."

"All the same, that might be interesting," said Max slowly. "But go on now. You were out in the strait, and the night was black."

Spiro took a quick drag on the cigarette, and reached awkwardly, hampered by the leg, to tap the ash onto the floor. Adoni slipped the saucer from under the empty coffee cup, and slid it within his reach.

"I reckoned we were about halfway over," said Spiro, "in the strait between Kouloura and the mainland. We had gone close to the Peristeroi Islands; there was enough of a sea running to see the white foam quite distinctly. I asked Mr. Manning if we should lie up a little in the lee of them and wait for the cloud to clear; there were gaps under the wind, where you could see stars; but he said no, we would go farther across. We went on for a time, till I reckoned we were about two miles out. He came out of the cabin then, and sent me in to make some cof-fee." The boy glanced up under his thick brows at Max. "The camera was there, on the table, but I did not think he could have been looking at it, because he had had no light on, only a storm lantern hardly lit. At the time I did not think of these things; while we took pictures at night, we always—naturally—ran without lights. But afterwards, when I had all that time lying in bed, and nothing to do but think, and won-der . . . then I remembered all the things that seemed strange. It was strange that we were going at all on that dark night to take pictures, it was strange that he lied to me about the camera, and the next thing that happened was more strange still."

Adoni grinned. "I know, the engine failed. And what was so strange about that, when you'd been taking it to bits that morning, my little genius?"

Spiro smiled for the first time, and said something in Greek which nobody bothered to translate for me. "If that had happened," he added, with fine simplicity, "it would indeed have been strange. But it did not."

"But you told us before—"

"I told you the engine stopped. I did not say that it failed. There was nothing wrong with the engine."

Max stirred. "You're sure, naturally."

The boy nodded. "And it didn't need a genius with engines to know there was nothing wrong. Even you"—a glint at Adoni—"even you would have known, my pretty one." He ducked aside from Adoni's feint, and laughed. "Go on, hit me, no doubt you could do it now."

"I'll wait," said Adoni.

Spiro turned back to Max. "No, the engine was all right. Listen. I heard it stop, then Mr. Manning called me. I put my head out of the door and shouted that I would take a look—the engine hatch is under the cabin steps, you understand. But he said, 'I don't think it's there, Spiro, I think something's fouled the screw and stalled it. Can you take a look?' I went to the stern. He was standing there, at the tiller. He said, 'Steady as you go, boy, she's pitching a bit. Here, I'll hold the torch for you.' I gave him the torch, and then I leaned over to see if the shaft was fouled. The boat was pitching, and the toe rail was wet, but I was holding on tightly. I should have been quite safe."

He paused, and stirred in the bed, as if the leg were hurting him. Adoni slipped to the floor and padded across to where a bottle stood on a box beside two empty glasses. He slopped some of the wine—it looked like the dark, sweet stuff they called *demèstica*—into one of the glasses and took it to the other boy, then glanced inquiringly at Max, who shook his head. Adoni set the bottle down, and returned to his place on the bed, adjusting his body, catlike, to the new position of the injured boy.

"It all happened very fast. The boat gave a lurch, very sharp, as if Mr. Manning had turned her across the wind too quickly. I was thrown against the rail, but still safe enough, because I had a good grip, but then something hits me from behind, on the head. It does not stun me, but I think I try to turn and put an arm up, then the boat pitches again, and before I know what has happened, I am falling. I try to grip the rail, but it slips from me. Something hits me across the hand—here—and I let go. Then I am in the water. When I come up, the boat is still near, and I see Mr. Manning in the stern, peering out for me in the darkness. I shout—not loudly, you understand, because I am full of water and too cold, gasping for air. But he must have heard me."

He shot a look up at Max, all of a sudden vivid, alive with pure hatred.

"And if he did not hear me, then he saw me. He put the torch on, and shone it on me in the sea."

"Yes?" said Max. His voice was expressionless, but I got the impression of a cold wind stirring in the cellar. Adoni felt it, too. He glanced fleetingly up at Max before his eyes went back to Spiro.

"I was not afraid, you understand," said Spiro, "not of him. It did not occur to me that it was he who had hit me, I thought it had been some accident. No, I was not afraid. I am a good swimmer, and though he had no engine, the boat was drifting down towards me, and he could see me. In a moment he could pick me up again. I called out again and swam towards him. I saw he had the starting handle in his hand, but I still did not imagine what this was for. Then as I came within reach, he leaned down and hit me again. But the boat was pitching and he had to hold the rail, so he could not point the torch properly. The blow touched me, but this time I saw it coming, and I ducked away, and he hit my arm and not my head. I think he felt the blow, but did not see, because the torch went out and a big wave swept me away from the boat's stern and out of his sight. You can imagine that this time I let it take me. I saw the light go on again, but I made no sound, and let myself be carried away into the dark. Then I heard the engine start." He drained the glass, and looked up at Max. "He looked for me for a little while, but the current took me away fast and the waves hid me. Then he turned the boat away and left me there in the sea."

There was silence. Nobody moved. For me, the dreamlike feeling persisted. The cave seemed darker, echoing with the sounds of the sea, the mutter of the receding boat, the empty hissing of waves running under the night wind.

"But the Saint was with you," said Adoni, and the deep human satisfaction in his voice sent the shadows scurrying. The cave was warm again, and full of the soft light from the English Victorian lantern.

Spiro handed the empty glass to Adoni, pulled the bedclothes more comfortably round him, and nodded. "Yes, he was with me. Do you want the rest, Kyrie Max? You know what happened."

"I want Miss Lucy to hear it. Go on, but make it short. You're tired, and it's very late."

The rest of the story was pure classic, made predictable and credible by half a hundred stories from Odysseus to St. Paul.

It was the murderer's bad luck that the wind that night had set a fast current in to the Albanian coast. Spiro was a fair swimmer, and the Ionian Sea is very salt, but even so he would have been hard put to it to survive if he had not gone overboard into the stream of the current. Between that, the buoyancy of the water, and his stubborn efforts, he managed to keep afloat long enough for the sea race to throw him ashore sometime just before dawn.

By the time he neared the shore he was almost exhausted, all his energy taken by the mere effort of keeping afloat, and at the mercy of the tide. He was not even aware that he had come to shore, but when a driving swell flung him against the cruel coastal rocks, he found just enough strength to cling there, resisting the backward drag once, twice, three times, before he could pull himself clear of it and crawl farther up the slimy rock.

And here the luck turned. St. Spiridion, having seen him ashore, and out of his own territory, abandoned him abruptly. Spiro slipped, fell back across a jut of sharp rock with a broken leg twisted under him, and at last fainted.

He had no recollection of being found—by an old shepherd who had clambered down a section of cliff after a crag-fast ewe. When Spiro woke he was bedded down, roughly but dry and warm, in the shepherd's cottage, and it appeared that the shepherd had some rough surgical skill, for the leg had been set and strapped up. The old woman produced a drink that sent him to sleep again, and when he woke for the second time, the pain was a good deal easier, and he was able to remember, and think. . . .

"And the rest you know." He yawned suddenly, tremendously, like an animal, and lay back among the blankets.

"Yes, the rest we know." Max got to his feet, stretching. "Well, you'd better get some sleep. In the morning—my God, in about three hours! —I'm going to get you out of here; don't ask me how, but I'll do it somehow, with Mr. Manning none the wiser. I want to get that leg of yours properly seen to, and then you've got to tell your story to the right authorities."

The boy glanced up, weariness and puzzlement lending his face a sullen, heavy look. "Authorities? Police? You mean you are going to accuse Kyrios Manning of trying to drown me? On my word alone? They will laugh at you."

"It's not just a question of accusing Mr. Manning of throwing you overboard. What I want to know is why? There's something here that must be investigated, Spiro. You'll have to trust me. Now, just for a few minutes longer, I want you to think back. You must have thought about it a lot yourself while you were lying in bed. . . . Why do you think he did it? Have you any idea at all? You surely don't imagine it was because he was irritated with you for overhauling the engine without being told."

"Of course not."

"There was nothing else—nothing had happened at any other time?"

"No. I have thought. Of course I have thought. No."

"Then we come back to the morning of the trip. When one has nothing to go on, one looks for anything, however slight, that's out of pattern—out of the ordinary. Did you usually overhaul that boat by yourself?"

"No, but I have done so before." Spiro stirred as if his leg hurt him. "And I have been alone on it before."

"You have always asked him first?"

"Of course."

"But this time you didn't. Why did you go to work on the boat this time without asking him?"

"Because he had told me that he meant to go out and he wanted the engine serviced. I was to go that morning after breakfast, and work on it. But I had got up very early, to swim, and when I had done, I thought I would go straight along and start work. I knew where he kept the extra key, so I let myself in and made some coffee in the galley, then opened the big doors for the light and started work. It was a good morning, with the summer coming, and I felt good. I worked well. When Mr. Manning had finished his breakfast and came down, I was half finished already. I thought he would be pleased, but he was very angry and asked how I got in, and then I didn't like to tell him that I had seen where he hid the key, so I said the door was not locked properly, and he believed this, because the catch is stiff sometimes. But he was still very angry, and said he would have the lock changed, and then I was angry also, and asked if he thought I was a thief, and if he thought so he had better count the money in his wallet which he had left in the galley. As if I would touch it! I was very angry!" Spiro remembered this with some satisfaction. "I told him also that I would mend his lock for him myself, and that I would never come to his house again. After that he was pleasant, and said he was sorry, and it was all right."

Max was frowning. "It was then that he asked you to go out that night?"

"I think . . . Yes, it must have been. He had said before that he did not want me with him, but he changed his mind . . . I thought because he was sorry he had spoken to me like that." He added naïvely, "It was a way to give me extra money without offence."

"Then it looks as if that was when he decided to take you and get rid of you. You can see that it only makes sense if he thought you'd seen something you shouldn't have seen . . . And that means in the boat, or the boathouse. Now, think hard, Spiro. Was there anything unusual about the boat? Or the boathouse? Or about anything that Mr. Manning said, or did . . . or carried with him?"

"No." The boy repeated himself with a kind of weary emphasis. "I have thought. Nothing."

"The wallet. You say he'd left his wallet lying. Where did you find it?"

"Down beside the stove in the galley. It had slipped there and he had not noticed. I put it on the cabin table."

"Were there papers in it? Money?"

"How should I know?" Spiro ruffled up again, like a young turkey cock, then subsided under Max's look with a grin. "Well, I did take a look, a very small one. There was money, but I don't know how much, I only saw the corners. It wasn't Greek money, anyway, so what use did he think it would have been to me? But if it had been a million drachmas, I would not have taken it! You know that, Kyrie Max!"

"Of course I know it. Did he leave you alone in the boat after this?"

"No. When I had finished there, he asked me to go up to the house and help him with some photographs. I worked there all day. He telephoned to the Forli house to tell my mother that I was to go with him that night."

"In fact, he made sure that you saw nobody all that day. Did you ever have any suspicion that he did anything illegal on these expeditions?"

"No—and why should it matter? I would not have told the police."
Spiro's eyes glinted up at him. "He would not be the only one."

Max declined the gambit, merely nodding. "All right, Spiro, I'll not
bother you any more now. Adoni, I'm going to lock the pair of you in
while I take Miss Lucy home. I'll be back within the half hour. You
have the gun."

"Yes."

"And this." Spiro searched under his pillow and produced, with as
much drama as if it had been a handkerchief, a commando knife
sharpened to a murderous glitter.

"That's the stuff," said Max cheerfully. "Now, you go to sleep, and
very soon I'll get you away." He stooped, and dropped a hand for a moment on the boy's shoulder. "All will be well, *Spiro mou.*"

Adoni followed us to the door.

"And Sir Gale?" he asked softly.

"I'll look in on him," promised Max. "He'll sleep soundly enough, you
can be sure of that. He's in no danger, so stop worrying and get some
sleep yourself. When I get back I'll spend the rest of the night in the
kitchen. If you need me, you've only to come to the upper door and
call me. Good night."

"Good night, Adoni," I said.

"Good night." Adoni gave me that smile again, perhaps a little frayed
at the edges, then let the curtain fall into place across the cave entrance, lopping off the warm glow and shutting Max and me out into
the darkness of the rocky passage.

He switched on the torch, and we started up the steps. The rough
walls, the curving passageway, the hewn flight of stairs, swam past in
a sort of dream of fatigue, but a corner of my brain still felt awake and
restless, alert to what he was saying.

"You can see now why I'm hiding that boy away till I can smuggle
him out to Athens? It's not so much that he's in actual danger still—
though he may well be—as simply that we stand a far better chance of
finding out what Manning's up to if he has no idea that we suspect
him. It's something big—that seems obvious . . . And I'm pretty sure
in my own mind where to start looking for it."

"The boat?"

"Either that or the boathouse. He's up to something involving that
boat, and the damned good 'cover' that his photography gives him.
If you accept Spiro's story, which I do, his little quarrel with Manning
that morning provides the only faint clue . . . the only deviation from
pattern that I can see . . . and it could tie in with Yanni's death as

well. I've been thinking about that. When Yanni brought Spiro's message here on Sunday night we discussed it pretty freely, and I let it be seen that I thought it very odd that Manning hadn't to be told. Yanni then said that he'd seen Manning's boat out at odd times and in odd places and that he'd thought for some time he was up to no good, and when I mentioned the photographs he just shrugged and looked cynical. Well, that's nothing to go by—a man like Yanni would think that photography was a pretty queer occupation for anyone; but he could have very well been suspicious and curious enough after our conversation to go down that night and snoop around the boathouse, or somewhere else he had no right to be, and so got himself murdered. It's my guess he was taken by surprise and knocked out from behind, then bundled into his own boat, with Manning's dinghy attached, taken out to sea, had his head smashed on the boom, and was dumped overboard. Manning then set the boom loose, emptied a bottle of ouzo around, turned the boat adrift, and rowed himself silently home. Oh, yes, it could have been done. He couldn't take him a great distance, since he'd have to row himself home, and then there was the squall which washed the body straight back—but it worked; he got away with it. An impulsive chap, our Godfrey . . . and with one hell of a lot at stake, that's for sure. Yes, I could bear to know just what it is."

I said, in quick apprehension, "You've got to promise me something."

"What's that?"

"You're not going there tonight. You wouldn't be so silly!"

He laughed. "You're dead-right I would not, my love! I've got to see Spiro safe where he belongs before I go arguing with anyone with Manning's peculiar ideas on life and death. He must have shot at the dolphin, you'd realized that?" He nodded at my exclamation. "Who else? There's only one plausible reason, the one you imputed to me, that the word had gone round, and people were beginning to come to this piece of coast to see the creature. When Manning first saw you there in the bay, he may have thought you were one of them—a stranger, getting too close to whatever he was trying to keep secret. As Spiro and Yanni did."

"But . . . those beautiful pictures! They really are beautiful, Max! He *couldn't* destroy it when he'd worked with it like that! He must have been fond of it!"

His smile was crooked. "And of Spiro, too?" I was silent. "Well, here we are. A moment while I push the racks back."

"What do you want me to do?"

"Something I know will be safe, and I hope will be easy. Cover my trip back from Athens with Spiro."

"Of course, if I can. How?"

"By keeping Manning away from Corfu harbour tomorrow at the time when I'm likely to be there. It would be quicker to go by plane, but I can't take the boy that way without the whole island knowing, so I'll have to take him in my car, hidden under a rug or something, across by the *Igoumenitsa*."

"The what?"

"The ferry to the mainland. I'll drive to Jannina and get the Athens plane from there. It means we can't get there and back in the one day, but I'll try to get home tomorrow, and I'll ring up this evening to let you know which ferry we'll get. The late one doesn't get in till a quarter to eleven; it's pitch-dark then, and I doubt if he'd be around. But I'd like to get the earlier one if I can, and that gets in at five fifteen. So if you could bear to be having tea with him or something till after six, to give me time to drive home . . . ?"

"Just at the moment I feel it would choke me, but I'll do my best," I said.

We were back in the kitchen. Its light and warmth and comfortable food smells closed round us like memories from a real but distant world, something safe and bright beyond the tossing straits of the night's dream. He pulled the great door shut behind us, and I heard the key drive the lock shut with a grating snap.

"There. Now you must go home. Come upstairs and get your things, and I'll look along to see if my father's safely asleep."

"Let's hope Phyl is, too, or heaven knows what story I'll have to cook up! Anything but the truth, I suppose!" I stared up at him. "I can't believe it. You realize that, don't you? I know it's true, but I can't believe it. And in the morning, in daylight, it'll be quite impossible."

"I know. Don't think about it now. You've had yourself quite an evening, as they say; but you'll feel different when you've had some sleep."

"My watch has stopped. Oh, hell, I suppose I got water in it. What's the time, Max?"

He glanced at his wrist. "So has mine. Blast. That little sea bathe doesn't seem to have done either of us much good, does it?"

I laughed. "Things that might have been better expressed, Mr. Gale?"

He reached out, and pulled me to him. "Things that might have been better done," he said, and did them.

CHAPTER

THIRTEEN

&

While you here do snoring lie,
Open-ey'd Conspiracy
His time doth take.

Act II, Scene 1

I slept very late that day. The first thing I remember is the sound of shutters being folded back, and then the sudden hot blaze of sunlight striking across the pillow into my eyes.

Phyllida's voice said, "And high time, too, Rip Van Winkle!"

As I murmured something, dragging myself up out of the depths of sleep, she added, "Godfrey rang you up."

"Oh?" I blinked into the sunlight. "Rang *me* up? What did he want —did you say *Godfrey?*" The jerk of recollection brought me awake, and up off the pillow so sharply that I saw her look of surprise, and it helped me to pull myself together.

"I was dreaming," I said, rubbing my eyes. "What on earth's the time?"

"High noon, my child."

"Goodness! What was he ringing about?"

"To know if you'd got safely home with the ring, of course."

"Did he expect Mr. Gale to steal it en route?"

Too late, I heard the tartness in my voice, and my sister looked at me curiously, but all she said was, "I woke you up too suddenly. Never mind, I brought some coffee. Here."

"Angel . . . Thank you. Heavens, I must have slept like the dead. . . . Your ring's over there on the dressing table. Oh, you've got it."

"You bet your sweet life I have. I came in a couple of hours ago and took it, but I couldn't bear to wake you, you were flat out, you poor kid." She turned her hand in the sunlight, and the diamond flashed.

"Thank heaven for that! Bless you, Lucy, I'm really terribly grateful! I'd have gone stark ravers if I'd had to sit there all night, wondering if someone had wandered by and picked it up. And I wouldn't have dared go down myself! What on earth time did you get in?"

"I hardly know," I said truthfully. "My watch stopped. I thought I'd got water in it, but I'd only forgotten to wind it up. Some ghastly hour of the morning." I laughed. "There were complications, actually. Didn't Godfrey tell you about them?"

"I didn't quite get that bit. Something about the dolphin being up on the beach and you and Max Gale wrestling about with it in the water. I must say it all sounded highly unlikely. What did happen?"

"More or less that." I gave her a rapid—and suitably expurgated— version of the dolphin's rescue, finishing with Godfrey's arrival on the beach. "And you'll find the wreck of your precious plastic bag in the bathroom, I'm afraid. I'm fearfully sorry, but I had to use something."

"Good heavens, that old thing! It couldn't matter less!"

"I'm relieved. The way you were talking last night, I thought it was practically a holy relic."

She shot me a look as she disappeared through the bathroom door. "I was not myself last night, and you know it."

"Well, no." I reached for the coffeepot which she had put down beside the bed, and poured myself more coffee.

She emerged from the bathroom, holding the bag between thumb and forefinger. " 'Wreck' was the word, wasn't it? I suppose you don't even know what happened to my Lizzie Arden lipstick?"

"Lord, I suppose that was a holy relic, too?"

"Well, it was gold."

I drank coffee. "You'll find it in Sir Julian Gale's dressing-gown pocket. I forgot it. I'm sorry again. You might say I was not myself last night either."

"Julian Gale's dressing gown? This gets better and better! What happened?" She sat down on the edge of the bed. "I tried like mad to stay awake till you got in, but those beastly pills put me right out, once Godfrey'd phoned and I stopped worrying. Go on. I want to know what I've missed."

"Oh, nothing, really. We were both soaked, so I had to go up to the Castello to get dry, and they gave me coffee, and I had a bath. . . . Phyl, the bathroom! You'd hardly *believe* the ghastly— Oh, sorry; I forgot, it's the Forli ancestral palace. Well, then you'll know the bathroom."

"There are two," said Phyl. "Don't forget there are twenty bedrooms. One must have one's comforts. I'll say I know the bathrooms. Was it the one with the alabaster bath, or the porphyry?"

"You make it sound like the New Jerusalem. I don't know, I don't live at those levels. It was a rather nasty dark red with white spots, exactly like stale salami."

"Porphyry," said my sister. "Was the water hot?"

"Boiling."

"*Was* it? They must have done something, then. It never used to get more than warm, and in fact I seem to remember a tap for *sea*water, which was pumped up in some weird way from the caves. There are caves under the Castello."

"Are there?"

"They used to use them to keep the wine in."

"Really. How exciting."

"Only, shrimps and things kept coming in, which was discouraging, and once a baby squid."

"It must have been."

"So Leo stopped it. It was supposed to be terribly health-giving, but there are limits."

"I'm sure there are," I said. "Shrimps in the wine would be one of them."

"Shrimps in the *wine*? What on earth are you talking about?"

I put down my empty cup. "I'm not quite sure. I thought it was the wine cellars."

"The seawater baths, idiot! Leo stopped them. Oh, I see, you're laughing at me. Well, go on, anyway. You had a bath. But I still don't see how you got hot water; they *can't* have got the furnaces to work. They used to burn about a ton of coal a day, and it practically needed three slaves to stoke all round the clock."

"Adoni and Spiro invented a geyser."

"Dear God," said Phyl devoutly, "does it work?"

"Yes, I told you, the water was marvellous. What's more, there were hot pipes to dry my things on, *and* an electric fire in the bedroom next door. Well, while my things dried I wore Sir Julian's dressing gown—which is why I left all your make-up in the pockets—and had coffee and bacon and eggs in the kitchen. Then Max Gale brought me home with the diamond, and that's the end of the saga." I leaned back and grinned at her. "As a matter of fact, it was rather fun."

"It sounds it! Was Max Gale civil?"

"Oh, yes. Very."

"I must say I'm surprised he helped you. I thought he was supposed to be trying to get rid of the dolphin."

"It can't have been him after all. He helped me as soon as I asked him. And it wasn't his father, either, I'm certain of that. I think it must just have been some beastly local lad out for a bit of fun." I sat up and pushed back the coverlet. "I'd better get up."

My sister glanced at her wrist, and stood up with an exclamation. "Heavens, yes, I'll have to run if I'm to be ready."

"Where are you going?"

"To get my hair done, and I've got some shopping to do, so I thought I'd have lunch in town. I ought to have waked you before to ask if you'd like to come, but you looked so tired. . . . There's cold meat and a fruit flan if you stay home, but you're welcome to come if you like. Can you make it? I'll have to leave in about twenty minutes."

I hesitated. "Did Godfrey expect me to ring him back or anything?"

"Oh, heavens, yes, I'd forgotten. He's pining to hear all about last night at first hand, I gather. I told him I'd be out to lunch, or I'd have asked him over, but I think he was going to ask you to lunch with him." She paused, a hand on the door. "There's the phone now, that'll be him. What shall I tell him?"

I reached for my stockings, and sat down to pull them on. The action covered some rapid thinking.

Godfrey would obviously be very curious to know what had passed at the Castello last night—what Sir Julian had told us, and what Max's reactions had been. If I could put him off till tomorrow, I might use this curiosity to keep him out of Max's way.

I said, "Say I'm in the bathroom or something, and can't come to the phone now, and tell him I'm going out with you, and I don't know when I'll be in, but I'll ring him . . . No, he can ring me. Sometime tonight."

Phyl raised an eyebrow. "Hard to get, huh? All right. Then you are coming with me?"

"No, I'll never make it, thanks all the same. I'll laze around and go down to the beach later."

"Okay," said my sister amiably, and went to silence the telephone.

I had no intention of going down to the beach, as it happened, it being more than likely that Godfrey would see me there and come down. But I did want to go over to the Castello to find out if Max and Spiro had got safely away. I hesitated to use the party telephone, and in any case, I doubted if Sir Julian would want to talk to me this morn-

ing, but I had hopes of finding Adoni about in the garden, and of seeing
him alone.

So I ate my cold luncheon early, and rather hurriedly, then, telling
Miranda that I was going down to the beach for the afternoon, went
to my room for my things.

But she was waiting for me in the hall as I came out, with a small
package in her hand.

"For me?" I said. "What is it?"

"Adoni just brought it. It's some things you left there last night."

I took it from her. Through the paper I could feel the small hard
shapes of Phyl's lipstick and powder box. "Oh, that's good of him. I was
thinking I'd have to go across to collect them. Is he still here?"

"No, miss, he wouldn't stay. But I was to say to you that all was
well."

There was just the faintest lift of curiosity in her voice. I noticed
then how bright her eyes were, and that the flush was back in her cheeks,
and for a moment I wondered if Adoni had given her some hint of the
truth.

"I'm glad of that. Did he tell you about the adventure we had last
night?"

"The dolphin? Yes, he told me. It must have been strange." The
strangest thing to her Greek mind was, I could see, that anyone should
have gone to that amount of trouble. "But your coat, Miss Lucy! I don't
know if it will ever come right!"

I laughed. "It did get rather a beating, didn't it? I thought you'd be
wondering what I'd been doing."

"I knew you must have fallen in the sea, because of your dress and
coat . . . and the bathroom, *po po po*. I have washed the dress, but the
coat must go to a proper cleaner."

"Oh, goodness, yes, you mustn't bother with it. Thanks very much
for doing the dress, Miranda. Well, when you see Adoni, will you thank
him for bringing these things? And for the message. That was all, that
all was well?"

"Yes."

"That's fine," I said heartily. "I did wonder. Sir Julian wasn't feeling
well last night, and I was worried."

She nodded. "He will be all right this morning."

I stared for a moment, then realized that she knew exactly what my
careful meiosis meant, and was untroubled by it. The Greek mind
again: if a man chose to get drunk now and again, what did it matter
except to himself? His women would accept it as they accepted all else.
Life here had its shining simplicities.

"I'm very glad," I said, and went out towards the pine woods.

As soon as I was out of sight of the house I left the path and climbed higher through the woods, where the trees thinned and a few scattered pines stood on top of the promontory. I spread my rug in the shade, and lay down. The ground was felted with pine needles, and here and there grew soft furry leaves of ground ivy, and the pretty, dull pink orchids, and lilac irises flecked with white. The Castello was hidden from view by its trees, but from this height I could just see, on the southern headland, the roof of the Villa Rotha. The Forli house was visible below me. In the distance, beyond the sparkling sea, lay the mountains of Epirus. Their snow had almost gone, but farther north the Albanian peaks still gleamed white. There, beneath them, would be the rocks where Spiro had gone ashore, and where Max had brought him off under the coastguards' guns. And there, a coloured cluster under the violet hills of Epirus, was Igoumenitsa, where the ferry ran. . . .

I had brought a book, but couldn't read, and it was not long before I saw what I had been expecting: Godfrey, coming with an air of purpose along the path round the headland. He didn't descend into the bay; just stood there, as if looking for someone who might have been on the beach or in the sea. He waited a little while, and I thought at one point that he was going to cross the sand and climb to the Forli house, but he didn't. He hung around for a few minutes more, then turned and went back.

Some time later my eye was caught by a glimpse of moving white, a glint beyond the treetops that rimmed the sea; and presently a boat stole out under sail from beyond the farther headland, cutting a curved path of white through the glittering blue.

I lay, chin on hand, watching her.

She was not unlike a boat that Leo had owned some years back, and on which I had spent a holiday one summer, the year I had left school. She was a powered sloop, perhaps thirty feet overall, Bermuda-rigged, with—as far as I could make out—a mast that could be lowered. That this was so seemed probable, since from something Godfrey had said I assumed she was Dutch-built, so might presumably be adapted for canal cruising and negotiating low bridges. In any case, I had gathered last night that she was customarily moored not in the bay, but in the boathouse; and even if this was built on the same lavish scale as the Castello and designed to house several craft, it would have to be a vast place indeed to take the sloop's forty-odd-foot mast. Her hull was sea grey, with a white line at the bows. She was a lovely craft, and at any other time I would have lain dreamily admiring her sleek lines and the

beauty of her canvas, but today I merely wondered about her speed—
seven or eight knots, I supposed—and narrowed my eyes to watch the
small black figure at the tiller, which was Godfrey.

The sea raced glittering along the grey hull (grey for camouflage?);
the white wake creamed; she turned, beautiful, between me and the
sun, and I could see no more of her except as a winged shape heading
in a long tack out to sea, and then south, towards Corfu town.

"Lucy?" said the telephone.

"Yes. Hullo. You're very faint."

"Did you get the message from Adoni?"

"Yes. Just that all was well, so I assumed you'd got away safely. I
hope it still is?"

"So far, a bit discouraging, but I'm still hoping. What about you?"

"I'm fine, thank you, and all's well here. Calm and normal, as far as
I can see. Don't worry about this end."

"Ah." A slight pause. Though I knew there was no one else in the
house, I found myself glancing quickly around me. Max's voice said,
distant in my ear, "You know this libretto I came over here to discuss
with that friend of mine? We've been talking over the story all afternoon now, and he's not very keen on it. Says it's not plausible. I'm not
sure if I'm going to be able to persuade him to do much about it."

"I get it," I said, "but look, this line's all right. My sister's out, and
so is the other party on the line; I saw his boat go out, with him in it,
quite a bit ago, and it's not back yet. I've been watching till now. You
can say what you like."

"Well, I'm not sure how good their English is at the Corfu Exchange," said Max, "but you'll have gathered it's not very good news in
any language. We've been with the police all afternoon, and they've
listened civilly enough, but they're not inclined to take it all that seriously—certainly not to take action against our friend without some solid
proof."

"If he were to be watched—"

"They're inclined to think it's not worth it. The general idea is that
it's only another spot of illegal trading, and no one's prepared to take
it seriously enough to spend money on investigating."

"Don't they believe the boy's story, then?"

He hesitated. "I can't quite make that out. I don't think they do.
They think he may be mistaken, and they're favouring the idea of an
accident."

"A nice, trouble-free verdict," I said dryly. "And was Y.'s death an accident, too?"

"They're inclined to stick to the first verdict there as well. The trouble is, you see, they're furious with me over last night's little effort, which I've had to tell them about, and which might have started some trouble. The Greek-Albanian frontier's always like a train of dynamite with a slow fuse crawling up to it. Oh, they did admit in the end that I could hardly have called the police in on a rendezvous with Milo and his pal, but I did also withhold evidence in the inquiry on Y.Z., after they'd been so helpful to Father and myself over Spiro. . . . I must say I rather see their point, but my name's mud for the moment, and they're simply not prepared to take action on my say-so, especially if it means coming in over the heads of the local coppers. You see, there's no possible motive."

"But if it was . . . 'illegal trading'?"

"That would hardly have led to murder. As we know, it's barely even taken seriously from this side of the border."

"I see."

"So they look like accepting accident on both counts. And of course, damn it, we can't prove a thing. I simply don't know what's going to happen."

"Can you bring him back—the boy?"

"I don't know that either. As far as the hospital's concerned, it's all right, but as to whether it's safe for him . . . If only one could find even some shred of an idea why it happened, let alone proof that it did . . . If I didn't know the boy so well, and if it weren't for Y.'s death, I'd take the same attitude as the police, I can tell you that. You were right last night when you said it was incredible. In the cold light of day the idea's fantastic—but still my bones tell me it's true. . . . Ah, well. I'm going to talk to them again later tonight, and there's still tomorrow. We may get something done yet."

"When will you come back?"

"Tomorrow. I'll try to manage the earlier time I gave you."

"All right. I'm fairly sure I can have that under control. You won't be met."

"Well, that's one load off my mind." I heard him laugh. "We managed fine on the way out, but the hospital's fitted a wonderful new cast that won't go in the boot, so it's the back seat and a rug—and a damned awkward situation if anyone is hanging about. Will it be hard to arrange?"

"Dead-easy—I think. I'm not sure which is the spider and which is the fly, but I don't think I'll even have to try."

"Well, for pity's sake, watch your step."

"Don't worry, he'll get nothing out of me. I may be a darned bad actress on the stage, but off it I'm terrific."

He laughed again. "Who's telling whom? But that's not what I meant."

"I know. It's all right, I'll be careful."

I heard him take a long breath. "I feel better now. I'll go and tackle this bunch of very nice but all too sensible policemen again. I must go. Bless you. Take care of yourself."

"And you," I said.

The receiver at the other end was cradled, and through the wire washed the crackling hiss of the miles of sea and air that lay between us. As I put my own receiver down gently, I found that I was staring out of the long glass pane of the door that led to the terrace. It framed an oblong of the empty evening sky, dusk, with one burning planet among a trail of dusty stars. I sat for a few minutes without moving, one hand still on the receiver, not thinking of anything, just watching that bright planet and feeling in me all tensions stilled at once, as if someone had laid a finger across a thrumming string.

When the telephone rang again, right under my hand, I hardly even jumped. I sat back in the chair and put the receiver to my ear.

"Yes?" I said. "Oh, hullo, Godfrey. Yes, it's Lucy. In Corfu, are you? No, I've been home a little while. I was wondering when you'd ring. . . ."

CHAPTER

FOURTEEN

౾

He's safe for these three hours.

Act iii, Scene 1

He called for me next day immediately after lunch. He had suggested that I lunch with him, and certainly he had sounded flatteringly anxious for my company, but since I didn't imagine he really wanted anything from me but information, and I had no idea how long I could hold him, I pleaded an engagement for lunch, but allowed myself to be suitably eager for a drive in the afternoon.

I even managed to suggest the route. Not that there was much choice in the matter: the road north was barely navigable by a car one cared about, so I could hardly suggest that Godfrey take it. We would have to go south on the road by which Max and Spiro would eventually be driving home, but there was, happily, a road leading off this to Palaiokastritsa, a famous beauty spot on the western coast which I could be legitimately anxious to visit. It was in fact true that I had looked the place up on the map, but had put off going there because the road seemed mountainous and I had been slightly nervous of tackling it in Phyl's little car. With me driving (I told Godfrey) it would be nerve-racking, and with Phyl driving it would be suicide. But if Godfrey would drive me, and if he had a car that would manage the gradients . . .

He had laughed, sounding pleased, and had professed himself delighted to brave any gradients I wished, and yes, he had a car that would manage it quite easily. . . .

He certainly had. It was a black XK 150, blunt-nosed, powerful, and about as accommodating on the narrow roads as a bull seal on his own bit of beach. It nosed its way impatiently along the drive, humming like a hive of killer bees, bucked on to the rutted sweep of the Castello's private road, and turned to swoop down to the gate where Maria's cottage stood.

Maria was outside, bending over a rusty tin with a stick, stirring what seemed to be hen food. When she heard the car she straightened up with the tin clutched to her breast and the hens clucking and chattering round her feet. Godfrey, slowing down for the turn into the main road, raised a hand and called out a greeting, to which she returned a look of pleasure mingled with respect, as warm a look as I had seen on her face in the last week or so. I had noticed the same look, shy but pleased, in Miranda's face as she had showed him into the *salotto* earlier, as if the two women were grateful to Spiro's employer for his continued kindness to them in their bereavement.

I stole a look at him as the car swerved—rather too fast, and with a blare of its twin horns that sent Maria's hens up in a squawking cloud —on to the main road. I don't know quite what I had expected to see this afternoon—some smooth-skinned monster, perhaps, with hoofs, horns, and tail all visible to the eye of knowledge—but he was just the same, an undeniably attractive man, who handled his exciting car with skill and obvious enjoyment.

And this man, I thought, was supposed to have brushed the boy—the beloved son and brother—off the stern of his boat as if he were a jelly-fish, and then sailed on, leaving him to drown. . . .

He must have felt me watching him, for he flicked me a glance and smiled, and I found myself smiling back spontaneously, and quite without guile. In spite of myself, in spite of Max, and Spiro's story, I could not believe it. The thing was, as I had said to Max, impossible in daylight.

Which was just as well. If I was to spend the next few hours with him, I would have to shut my mind to all that I had learned, to blot out the scene in the cellar, drop Spiro out of existence as if he were indeed dead. And, harder than all, drop Max. There was a curiously strong and secret pleasure, I had found, in speaking of him as "Mr. Gale" in the offhand tones that Godfrey and Phyllida commonly used, as one might of a stranger to whom one is under an obligation, but whom one hardly considers enough to like or dislike. Once, as I had mentioned his name in passing, my eye, downcast, caught the faint mark of a bruise on my arm. The secret thrill of pleasure that ran up my spine startled me a little; I slipped my other hand over the mark to hide it, and found it cupping the flesh as if it were his, and not my own. I looked away, out of the car, and made some random remark about the scenery.

It was a very pretty road. To our left was the sea, blue and smooth, broken only by a tiny white crescent of sail thin as a nail paring and almost lost in the heat haze. On the right was a high hedge of apple blossom and judas trees, their feet deep in a vivid bank of meadow flowers, yellow and purple and white. Two little girls, in patched and faded dresses of scarlet, stood barefoot in the dust to watch us go by, one of them holding a bough of oranges as an English child might hold a stick of balloons, the fruit bulging and glowing among the green leaves.

The road straightened, and the XK 150 surged forward with a smooth burst of speed. My spirits lifted. This was going to be easy; in fact, there was no reason why I shouldn't simply relax and enjoy it, too. I sat back and chatted on—I hoped naturally—about nothings: the view, the people Phyl had met yesterday in Corfu, the prospect of Leo's coming with the children for Easter. . . .

We flashed by a fork in the road.

I sat up sharply. "That was the turning, wasn't it? I'm sure the sign post said Palaiokastritsa!"

"Oh, yes, it was. I'm sorry, I wasn't thinking; I meant to have told you, I'm not taking you there today. It's a long way, and we've hardly time. We'll go another day if you like, when we don't have to be back early."

"*Do* we have to be back early?"

The question slipped out before I thought, ingenuous in its dismay. I saw the faint shadow of gratified surprise in his face, and reflected that after my evasions over the telephone he had every right to find provocation in it.

"I'm afraid so. I'm going out tonight. I don't say we couldn't do it, but it's a shame to go all the way for a short time; it's a lovely place, and there's a lot to see. Besides which, it's a damned waste to go there and not have lunch; there's a restaurant right on the beach where they keep crayfish alive in pots in the sea, and you choose your own and they take them out fresh to cook." A sideways look at me and a teasing smile. "I suppose you disapprove, but I can tell you, they're wonderful. I'll take you there soon if you promise not to stand me up for lunch next time."

"I didn't—that would be lovely."

We flicked through a tiny village, one narrow street of houses and a baked white church with a red roof. The snarl of the engine echoed back in a quick blast from the hot walls, and we were through, nose down through a scatter of goats, children, a scraggy puppy, and a donkey trailing a frayed end of rope. The children stared after us, admiring and unresentful.

"One thing," said Godfrey cheerfully, "one doesn't have to plan one's outings here according to the weather. The sun's always on call in this blessed isle, and one day's as good as another."

That's what you think, I said savagely to myself. My hands were tight together in my lap now, as much because of his driving as in a panic-stricken attempt to think of the map. How to get him off this road, head him away from Corfu?

I said aloud, "I'll hold you to that one day, *and* I'll eat the crayfish! I can't feel strongly about fish, I'm afraid! Where are we going then, Pellekas?" For Pellekas one turned off just at the north end of Corfu —the only other turning before the town.

"No, the Achilleion."

"Oh? That's a wonderful idea!"

It was a bloody awful idea, as well I knew. To get there one went right through Corfu—not quite to the harbour, but near enough—and of course the whole way home we would be using the same road as Max. Well, I'd just have to see that we didn't head for home around five thirty, and I could only hope there was plenty of scope for sightseeing to the south of Corfu town. I reached for my handbag and fished in it for the guide I had brought, adding with great enthusiasm, "I'd planned to visit it one day, but there was the same objection—Phyl told me it was on top of a hill with the most ghastly zigzag going up to it! Yes, here it is: 'The villa of Achilleion, erected for the Empress Elizabeth of Austria. . . . The villa, which is in Italian Renaissance style, was purchased in 1907 by the German Emperor. The gardens are open to visitors (admission one drachma, applied to charitable purposes).'"

"What? What on earth's that?"

"An ancient Baedeker I found on Phyl's shelves. It was my grandfather's—date 1909. It's really rather sweet. Listen to the bit at the beginning about the history of the island. He says 'it came into the possession of' the Romans, then 'fell to the share of' the Venetians, then 'was occupied by' the French, then 'was under Turkish, then Russian sway,' but—notice the *but*—from 1815 to 1863 it 'came under the protection of' the British. Rule Brittania. Those were the days."

"They certainly were." He laughed. "Well, you can see the whole palace as well, today, and it will cost a damned sight more than a drachma, and I imagine the gate money'll go straight to the Greek Government. As usual, charity begins at home. . . . I wish there'd been some classical relics to take you to—Phyl told me you were interested —but I don't know any, apart from some temple or other inside the Mon Repos park, which is private. However, you might say Achilles is the patron saint of the Achilleion, so perhaps it'll do! There's some talk of turning it into a casino, so this may be the last chance of seeing it more or less in the original state. And the drive up there is very pretty, you'll enjoy it."

"You're very kind," I said. It was all I could do not to stare. He spoke so easily and charmingly, sitting there relaxed and handsome at the wheel, the sun throwing up fair highlights in his hair, and a dusting of freckles along the bare brown arms. He was wearing an open-necked shirt, with a yellow silk scarf tucked in at the neck—Top People summer uniform—which suited him very well. He looked calm and contented, and perfectly normal.

Well, why not? When a felon's not engaged in his employment, he has to look as ordinary as possible for his own skin's sake. I supposed it was perfectly possible for a man to drown two young men one week and enjoy a pleasant day out with a girl the next, take a lot of trouble to plan an outing for her and even enjoy the view himself. . . .

"And there's a marvellous view," he said. "The palace is set on a steep wooded hill over the sea. From the belvedere you can see practically the whole way from Vutrinto, in Albania, to Perdika, along the Greek coast. On a clear day the harbour at Igoumenitsa's quite plain."

"How splendid."

"And now supposing you tell me exactly what happened last night at the Castello?"

It took every scrap of discipline and technique I had not to jump like a shot rabbit. "What happened? Well . . . nothing much—what should? I got home with the diamond, you know that."

"Oh, to hell with the diamond, you know quite well what I mean." He sent me another sideways, amused look. "Did you see Julian Gale?"

"Oh. Yes, I did. Adoni was with him when we got up there."

"Ah, yes, the faithful watch-pup. He would be. How was Sir Julian?"

"He went to bed pretty soon," I said cautiously. I kept my eyes on the road, and in the windscreen I saw Godfrey glance at me again. "He was—tired," I said.

"Say what you mean," said Godfrey. "He was stoned."

"How do you know?" The question came out flatly and even accusingly, but since he himself had hit the ball into the open with the last phrase there was no reason why I shouldn't keep it there.

"Come off it, they knew who'd been with him, didn't they?"

"We-ll, it was mentioned." I leaned back in my seat and let a spice of mischievous amusement creep into my voice. It sounded so like Phyl as to be startling. "Mr. Gale wasn't awfully pleased with you, Godfrey."

"Damn it all, what's it got to do with me if he wants to get plastered? By the time I saw which way the land lay, he was halfway there. Do they imagine it was up to me to stop him?"

"I wouldn't know. But I'd watch out for Mr. Gale if I were you."

"So?" His mouth curved. "Pistols for two and coffee for one, or just a horsewhip? Well, maybe he does owe it me, after all."

I knew then. I'm not sure what it was, something in his voice, or the infinitesimal degree of satisfaction at the corners of his mouth; something at once cruel and gay and quite terrifying. All the daylight doubts fled, once forever. Of course he was a murderer. The man was a natural destroyer. "Evil, be thou my good. . . ." And the instinct that had allowed him to create those pictures wasn't even incongruous: no doubt it had given him much the same pleasure to destroy Spiro as it had to photograph him. Destroying Sir Julian would hardly have cost him a moment's thought.

I dragged my eyes and thoughts away from the evil sitting beside me in the car, and concentrated on the idyll of silver olive and black cypress through which the XK 150 slashed its way in a train of dust.

"What a lovely road."

"I wish they'd do something about these potholes, that's all. Don't sidetrack, Lucy. Was it really horsewhips?"

"I wouldn't be surprised. I mean, Mr. Gale had had a trying evening. I'd had hysterics all over him and dragged him out to help with the dolphin, and he fell slap in the sea, and then on top of it all when we got up to the house we found his father drunk . . . in front of me, too. You can't blame him if he's out for your blood."

"I suppose not." He didn't sound as if it worried him vastly. "Where is he today?"

"I believe he said he was going to Athens. It was just some remark to Adoni—I didn't take much notice. But you're probably safe for to-day."

He laughed. "I breathe again. Just look at the colour of that girl's frock, the one picking up olives over there, that dusty red against the rather acid green."

"Don't *you* sidetrack. I want to know what happened."

He raised his brows. "Heavens, nothing, really. I saw the old man at the garage on the harbour, and he was looking for a lift, so I took him home. I was rather pleased to have the chance to talk to him, as it happened—you can never get near him alone, and it was too good a chance to miss."

"What on earth did you want to get him alone for? Don't tell me you're looking for a walk-on in the next Gale play!"

He grinned. "That'll be the day—always providing there is one. No, there were things I wanted to know, and I thought he'd be the softest touch. Max Gale and I aren't just the best of friends, and the watch-pup dislikes me, I can't think why."

"Godfrey! Are you telling me you got him drunk on purpose?"

"Good God, no. Why should I? I wasn't trying to get state secrets out of him. But by the time he'd had a couple there was no stopping him, and it wasn't my business to stop him, was it? I admit I didn't try." That fleeting smile again, gone in an instant; a flash of satisfaction, no more. "It was quite entertaining up to a point."

"What on earth *were* you wanting to get out of him?"

"Only what the police were up to."

"Police?"

He glanced at me with a lifted eyebrow. "Don't sound so startled. What have you been doing? No, it's only that on this island everything gets to the Gales' ears and to no one else's. I had a hell of a job finding anything out about the Spiro affair—nobody seemed to think it was my business, but I'm damned sure they tell the Gales everything that turns up."

"Well, I gather there's some sort of family connection."

"So I'm told. But I don't see why that gives them an 'exclusive' on a police inquiry that involved me as closely as Spiro's death did."

"I do so agree," I said sympathetically. "It must have been a terribly nerve-racking time for you."

"It still is." Certainly if I hadn't known what I knew, I'd have heard nothing in the grave rejoinder but what should properly be there. But, keyed as I was, the two brief syllables hid a whole world of secret amusement. I found that the hand in my lap was clenched tightly, and deliberately relaxed it.

"Did Sir Julian have any news? What has turned up about Spiro?"

"Search me. He wouldn't say a word. We had a couple of drinks at the taverna, and I thought his manner was a bit odd; I thought at first he was being cagey and there was something he didn't want to tell me, but after a bit I realized that he was merely feeling his corn and trying to hide it. It's my guess the poor old chap hasn't had anything stronger than half a mild sherry for a year." His mouth twitched. "Well, after that I'm afraid I did rather give the party a push along the right lines. . . . I wanted to lay in a few bottles for myself—I was out of ouzo, for one thing, and there was a new *koùm koyàt* liqueur I was wanting to try, so I bought them, but when I suggested we should go along to my place the old man wouldn't have it. He was mellowing a bit by that time, and insisted on taking me to the Castello and buying a bottle of gin to treat me to. It didn't take much of that stuff to get him good and lit, but I'm afraid it finished any hope I'd had of getting sense out of him. He'd got it fixed in his head that the only reason I'd gone to the Castello was to hear the recording of their blasted film music." He gave a short laugh where the exasperation still lingered. "Believe you me, I got the lot, words and all."

"Oh, I believe you! Hunks of *The Tempest?*"

"Did he do that for you, too?"

I laughed. "He was reciting when Mr. Gale and I got up to the house. As a matter of fact, I enjoyed it. He did it marvellously, gin or no gin."

"He's had plenty of practice."

The cruel words were lightly spoken, but I think it was at that moment that I began to hate Godfrey Manning. I remembered Max's face, strained and tired; Sir Julian's, blurred and drowning, holding on to heaven knew what straw of integrity; the two boys curled close together on the makeshift bed; Maria's grateful humility. Until this moment I had been content to think that I was helping Max: this had franked a piece of deception whose end I had not let myself explore. But now I explored it, and with relish. If Godfrey Manning was to be proved a murderer, then presumably he was going to be punished for it; and I was going to help with everything I had. Something settled in me, cold and hard. I sat down in the saddle and prepared to ride him down.

I felt him glance at me, and got my face into order.

"What actually happened when you got to the house?" he asked. "What did he tell them, Max and the model-boy?"

"Nothing, while I was there. No honestly, Godfrey!" I was pleased to hear how very honest I sounded. "They only guessed it was you who'd been with him because you'd thrown a Sobranie butt into the stove."

He gave a crack of laughter. "Detectives Unlimited! You did have an exciting night, didn't you? Did they let anything drop in front of you—about Spiro, I mean?"

"Not a thing."

"Or Yanni Zoulas?"

I turned wide, surprised eyes on him. "Yanni— Oh, the fisherman who was drowned. No, why?"

"I wondered. Pure curiosity."

I said nothing, letting the silence hang. Now we were getting somewhere. . . . It was obvious that he was still uncertain whether the police really had accepted "accident" as the verdict on Spiro and Yanni; and I thought it was obvious, too, that he badly wanted to know. And since he wasn't the man to sweat about what he had done, it must be what he still had to do that was occupying him: he needed a clear field, and no watchers. His efforts with Sir Julian, and now with me, showed that he had no suspicion that he was being watched, just that he badly needed a green light, and soon.

Well, I thought cheerfully, leaning back in my seat, let him sweat a bit longer. He'd get no green light from me.

The road was climbing now, zigzagging steeply up a wooded hill clothed with vineyards and olive groves, and the fields of green corn with their shifting grape bloom shadows.

He said suddenly, "Didn't you see him go back to the body after we'd left it?"

"What? See who?"

"Gale, of course."

"Oh, yes . . . sorry, I was looking at the view. Yes, I did. Why?"

"Didn't you wonder why he did that?"

"I can't say I did. I supposed he just wanted another look." I gave a little shiver. "Better him than me. Why, did you think he saw something we didn't?"

He shrugged. "Nothing was said to you?"

"Nothing at all. Anyway, I hardly know the Gales; they wouldn't tell me things any more than you. You aren't beginning to think there was more in Yanni's death than met the eye?"

"Oh, no. Let's just say it's curiosity, and a little natural human resentment at having things taken out of my hands. The man was drowned on my doorstep—as Spiro was from my boat—and I think I should have been kept in the picture. That's all."

"Well," I said, "if anything had turned up about Spiro, Maria would know, and she'd tell my sister and me straight away. If there is anything, I'll let you know. I realize how you must be feeling."

"I'm sure you do. And here we are. Shall we see if they'll let us in for one drachma?"

The gates were open, rusting on their seedy pillars. Huge trees, heavy already with summer, hung over the walls. A sleepy janitor relieved us of twenty drachmas or so and nodded us through.

The house was very near the gate, set among thick trees. The doors were open. I had vaguely expected a museum of some kind, a carefully kept relic of the past, but this was merely an empty house, a summer residence from which the owners had moved out, leaving doors and windows unlocked, so that dead leaves and insects had drifted year by year into the deserted rooms, floorboards had rotted, paintwork had decayed, metal had rusted. . . . The place was a derelict, set in the derelict remains of formal gardens and terraces, and beyond the garden boundaries crowded the trees and bushes of a park run wild.

I remember very little now of my tour of the Achilleion. I am sure Godfrey was a good guide: I recollect that he talked charmingly and informatively all the time, and I must have made the right responses; but I was obsessed with my new hatred of him, which I felt must be bound to show as plainly as a stain; in consequence I was possibly even a little too charming back again. I know that as the afternoon went on his manner warmed perceptibly. It was a relief to escape at length from the dusty rooms on to the terrace.

Here at least the air was fresh, and it wasn't quite as hard to linger admiringly as it had been in the dusty rooms of the palace, with their unkempt and shabby grandeurs. The terrace was floored with horrible liver-coloured tiles, and the crowding trees below it obscured any view there might have been, but I did my best with the hideous metal statues at the corners and the row of dim-looking marble "Muses" posing sadly along a loggia. I was a model sightseer. I stopped at every one. You'd have thought they were Michelangelos. Three fifteen . . . three twenty . . . Even at three minutes per Muse it would keep us there only till three forty-seven. . . .

There remained the garden. We went in detail round it; arum lilies deep in the weeds at the foot of palm trees; a few unhappy peonies struggling up in the dank shade; a dreadful statue of Achilles triumphant (six minutes) and a worse one of Achilles dying (four); some Teutonic warriors mercifully cutting one another's throats in a riot of brambles (one and a half). I would even have braved the thorny tangle of the wood to admire a statue of Heine sitting in a chair if the gate hadn't been secured with barbed wire, and if I hadn't been afraid that I would wear out even Godfrey's patience.

I needn't have worried. It was unassailable. He had to put the time in somehow, and I am certain that it never once crossed his mind that a day out with him could be anything but a thrill for me from first to last.

Which, to be fair, it certainly was. The thrill that I got, quite literally, when he took me by the elbow to lead me gently back towards the gate and the waiting Jaguar went through my bone marrow as if the bones had been electrically wired. It was only twenty past four. If we left for home now, and if Godfrey, as seemed likely, suggested tea in Corfu, we should just be in nice time to meet the ferry.

There was one more statue near the gate, a small one of a fisher boy sitting on the fragment of a boat, bare-legged, chubby, smiling down at something, and wearing a dreadful hat. It was on about the same level of genius as the Muses, but of course I stopped in front of it, rapt, with Baedeker at the ready and my eyes madly searching the tiny print to see if there were any other "sights" between here and Corfu which I could use to delay my blessedly complacent guide.

"Do you like it?" Godfrey's tone was amused and indulgent. He laid the back of a finger against the childish cheek. "Do you notice? If this had been done seven years ago instead of seventy it might have been Spiro. One wonders if the model wasn't a grandfather or something. It's very like, don't you think?"

"I never knew Spiro."

"Of course not, I forgot. Well, Miranda, then."

"Yes, perhaps I do see it. I was just thinking it was charming."

"The face is warm," said Godfrey, running a light hand down the line of the cheek. I turned away quickly, feeling my face too naked. Half past four.

He dropped his hand. "You keep looking at your watch. I suppose you're like Phyl, always gasping for tea at this time? Shall we go and look for some in Corfu?"

"What's the other way? The coast looked so lovely from the belvedere."

"Nothing much, the usual pretty road, and a fishing village called Benitses."

"There'll be a *kafenéion* there, surely? That would be more fun for a change. Wouldn't there be tea there?"

He laughed. "The usual wide choice, Nescafé or lemonade. There might even be some of those slices of bread, cut thick and dried in the oven. I've never yet discovered who eats them or even how. I can't even break them. Well, on your head be it. Jump in."

We got tea after all at Benitses, at a plain, clean little hotel set right on the sea. It couldn't have been better placed—for me, that is. There were tables outside, and I chose one right on the dusty shore, under a pepper tree, and sat down facing the sea. Just beside us a whole stable of coloured boats dozed at their moorings, vermilion and turquoise and peacock, their masts swaying gently with the breathing of the sea; but beyond them I saw nothing but one red sail dancing alone on the empty and glittering acres.

Godfrey glanced over his shoulder. "What's going on there that's so interesting?"

"Nothing, really, but I could watch the sea by the hour, couldn't you? Those boats are so pretty. Your own is a real beauty."

"When did you see her?"

"Yesterday afternoon. I saw you go out."

"Oh? Where were you? I'd been looking for you down on the beach."

"What a pity! No, I didn't go down after all, I stayed up in the woods and slept." I laughed. "I rather needed the sleep."

"You'd certainly had a strenuous time. I wish I'd seen your rescue act with the dolphin. Some pictures by flash would have been interesting." He stirred the pale tea, squashing the lemon slice against the side of the cup. "I read somewhere—I think it was Norman Douglas—that while dolphins are dying they change colour. I believe it can be a remarkable display. Fascinating if one could get that, don't you think?"

"Marvellous. Did you say you were going out tonight?"

"Yes."

"I suppose you couldn't do with a crew? I'd adore to come."

"Brave of you, under the circumstances. You'd not be afraid to crew for me?"

"Not in the least, I'd love it. You mean I may? What time are you going?"

If he had accepted the offer I'm not sure what I'd have done; broken an ankle at least, I expect. But he said:

"Of course you may, someday soon, but you've got me wrong, I didn't mean I was going out with the boat tonight. Actually, I'm going by car to visit friends."

"Oh, I'm sorry, I must have got hold of the wrong end of the stick. A pity, I was getting all excited."

He smiled. "I tell you what: I'll take you sailing soon—Friday, perhaps? Or Saturday? We'll go round to Lake Kalikiopoulos and look for the place—one of the places, I should say—where Odysseus is supposed to have stepped ashore into the arms of Nausicaä. Would that be classical enough for you?"

"It would be marvellous."

"Then I'll look forward to it. . . . Look, there's the ferry."

"Ferry?" It came out in a startled croak, and I cleared my throat. "What ferry?"

"The mainland boat. She crosses to Igoumenitsa and back. There, see? It's not easy to see her against the glitter. She'll be in in about twenty minutes." He looked at his watch, and pushed back his chair. "Hm, she's late. Well, shall we go?"

"I'd like to go upstairs, please, if they have one."

The owner of the hotel, who was at Godfrey's elbow with the check, interpreted this remark with no difficulty, and led me up an outside stair and along a scrubbed corridor to an enormous room which had been made into a bathroom. It was spotlessly clean, and furnished, apart from the usual offices, with a whole gallery of devotional pictures. Perhaps others before me had fled to this sanctuary to think. . . .

But it was Baedeker I had come to study. I whipped it open and ran a finger down the page. The print was hideously small, and danced under my eyes. "One drachma a day for the dragoman is ample . . . valets-de-place, 5 dr. per day, may be dispensed with. . . ."

Ah, here was something that might be expected to appeal to an avid classicist like myself. "*The Tomb of Menecrates, dating from the 6th or 7th century B.C.* . . ." And bang on the way home, at that. Now, if only I could persuade Godfrey that my day would be blighted if I didn't visit this tomb, whatever it was . . .

I could; and it was a winner, for the simple reason that nobody knew where it was. We asked everybody we met, and were directed in turn, with the utmost eagerness and goodwill, to a prison, a football ground, the site of a Venetian fort, and a pond; and I could have felt sorry for Godfrey if I hadn't seen quite clearly that he thought that I was trying desperately to spin out my afternoon with him. The man's armour was complete. In his vocabulary, God was short for Godfrey.

I was paid out when we did finally run Menecrates to earth in the garden of the police station, and the custodian, welcoming us as if the last tourist to visit it had been Herr Karl Baedeker himself in 1909, pressed on me a faded document to read, and thereafter solemnly walked me round the thing three times, while Godfrey sat on the wall and smoked, and the lovely dusk fell, and the hands of my watch slid imperceptibly round, and into the clear. . . .

"After six o'clock," said Godfrey, rising. "Well, I hope you've time to have a drink with me before I take you home. The Astir has a very nice terrace overlooking the harbour."

"That would be wonderful," I said.

CHAPTER

FIFTEEN

ह*

I prithee now, lead the way without any more talking.

Act II, Scene 2

It was quite dark when Godfrey finally drove me back to the Villa Forli. I said good-bye at the front door, waited till the car had vanished among the trees, then turned and hurried indoors.

A light from the kitchen showed that either Miranda or her mother was there; but the *salotto* was empty in its cool, grey dusk and no light showed from Phyl's bedroom door. In a moment I knew why: I had made straight for the telephone, and just before I lifted the receiver I saw the pale oblong of a note left on the table beside it. I switched on the table lamp, to find a note from Phyl.

Lucy dear, [it ran] *got a wire this afternoon to say that Leo and the kids are coming on Saturday, and he can stay two whole weeks. Calloo, callay! Anyway, I've gone into Corfu to lay in a few things. Don't wait for me if you're hungry. There's plenty for G., too, if he wants to stay. Love, Phyl.*

As I finished reading this, Miranda came into the hall.

"Oh, it's you, Miss Lucy! I thought I heard a car. Did you see the letter from the Signora?"

"Yes, thank you. Look, Miranda, there's no need for you to stay. Mr. Manning's gone home and my sister may be late, so if there's something cold I can get—"

"I came to tell you. She telephoned just a few minutes ago. She has met friends in Corfu—Italian friends who are spending one night only —and is having dinner with them. She said if you wanted to go, to get a taxi and join them at the Corfu Palace, but"—a dimple showed—

"none of them speaks any English, so she thinks you would rather stay here, yes?"

I laughed. "But definitely yes. Well, in that case, I'll have a bath, and then have supper as soon as you like. But I can easily look after myself, you know. If you'll tell me what there is, you can go home if you want to."

"No, no, I shall stay. There is a cold lobster, and salad, but I am making soup." She gave her wide, flashing smile. "I make good soup, Miss Lucy. You will like it."

"I'm sure I shall. Thank you."

She didn't go, but lingered at the edge of the light thrown by the little lamp, her hands busily, almost nervously, pleating the skirt of the red dress. I realized then, suddenly, what my preoccupation hadn't let me notice till now: this was not the subdued and tear-bleached Miranda of the last week. Some of the gloss was back on her, and there was a sort of eagerness in her face, as if she were on the edge of speech.

But all she said was, "Of course I will stay. I had a day off this afternoon. A day off? Is that what the Signora calls it?"

"Yes, that's right. The afternoon off. What do you do when you get an afternoon off?"

She hesitated again, and I saw her skin darken and glow. "Sometimes also Adoni has the afternoon off."

"I see." I couldn't quite keep the uneasiness out of my voice. So she had spent the afternoon with Adoni. It might be that fact alone which had set her shining again, but I wondered if anyone as young as Adoni could possibly be trusted not to have told her about Spiro. Even for myself, the temptation to break the news to the girl and her mother had been very strong, while for the nineteen-year-old Adoni, longing, like anyone of his age, to boast of his own share in last night's exploits, the urge must have been overwhelming. I added, "No, don't go for a moment, Miranda; I want to make a phone call in rather a hurry, and I don't know how to ask for the number. The Castello, please; Mr. Max."

"But he is not there, he is away."

"I know, but he was to be back before six."

She shook her head. "He will not be here till late. Adoni told me so. Mr. Max rang up at five o'clock. He said he would be home tonight, but late, and not to expect him to dinner."

"Oh." I found that I had sat down rather heavily in the chair beside the telephone, as if the news was in actual physical fact a letdown. I did not think then of the effort that had been wasted, but simply of

the empty spaces of the evening that stretched ahead, without news
. . . and without him. "Did he say anything else?"

"Only that 'nothing had changed.'" She gave the words quotation
marks, and there was something puzzled and inquiring in her look that
told me what I had wanted to know. Adoni had after all kept his word:
the girl had no idea that there was anything afoot.

Meanwhile I must make do with what crumbs I had. "Nothing had
changed." We could presumably expect him on the late ferry, but if
nothing had changed it didn't sound as if a police escort was likely, so
he might not bring Spiro back with him, either. More I could not guess,
but my part in the affair was decidedly over for the day: I couldn't have
kept Godfrey any longer, and it didn't seem now as if it was going to
matter.

"Where was Mr. Max speaking from?"

"I don't know. From Athens, I suppose."

"From *Athens*? At five o'clock? But if he was planning to come back
tonight—"

"I forgot. It couldn't have been Athens, could it? Adoni didn't say,
just that it was the mainland." She waved a hand largely. "Somewhere
over there, that's all." And, her tone implied, it didn't matter much
one way or the other; outside Corfu all places were the same, and not
worth visiting anyway.

I laughed, and she laughed with me, the first spontaneous sound of
pleasure that I had heard from her since the news of her brother's loss.
I said, "What is it, Miranda? You seem excited tonight. Has something
nice happened?"

She was opening her lips to answer, when some sound from the
kitchen made her whisk round. "The soup! I must go! Excuse me!"
And she vanished towards the kitchen door.

I went to have my bath, then made my way to the dining room,
where Miranda was just setting the contents of a large tray out in lonely
state at one end of the table. She showed no desire to leave me, but
hovered anxiously as I tasted the soup, and glowed again at my praise.
We talked cooking all through the soup, and while I helped myself to
the lobster salad. I asked no more questions, but ate, and listened, and
wondered again what magic the "afternoon off" with young Adoni had
done for her. (I should say here that Miranda's English, unlike Adoni's,
was not nearly as good as I have reported it; but it was rapid enough,
and perfectly understandable, so for the sake of clarity I have translated
it fairly freely.)

"This is a dressing from the Signora's book," she told me, handing a dish. "She does not like the Greek dressing, so I have tried it from the French book. Is it good? You had a nice day, Miss Lucy?"

"Lovely, thanks. We went to the Achilleion."

"I have been there once. It is very wonderful, is it not?"

"Very. Then we had tea at Benitses."

"Benitses? Why did you go there? There is nothing at Benitses! In Corfu it is better."

"I wanted to see it, and to drive back along the sea. Besides, I was longing for some tea, and Corfu was too far, and I wanted to look at some antiquities on the way home."

She knitted her brows. "Antiquities? Oh, you mean statues, like the ones on the Esplanade, the fine English ones."

"In a way, though those aren't old enough. It really means things many hundreds of years old, like the things in the museum in Corfu."

"Are they valuable, these antiquities?"

"Very. I don't know if you could say what they were worth in terms of money, but I'd say they're beyond price. Have you seen them?"

She shook her head. She said nothing, but that was because she was biting her lips together as if forcibly to prevent speech. Her eyes were brilliant.

I stopped with my glass halfway to my mouth. "Miranda, what is it? Something *has* happened—you can't pretend—you look as if you'd been given a present. Can't you tell me?"

She took in her breath with something of a gulp. Her fingers were once again pleating and unpleating a fold of her skirt. "It is something . . . something Adoni has found."

I put down the glass. It clattered against the table. I waited.

A silence, then she said, with a rush, "Adoni and I, we found it together, this afternoon. When I got the afternoon off I went over to the Castello." She sent me a sideways glance. "Sometimes, you see, Adoni works in the garden while Sir Gale sleeps, and then we talk. But today Mr. Karithis was visiting with Sir Gale, and they told me Adoni had gone to swim. So I went down to the bay."

"Yes?" She had my attention now, every scrap of it.

"I could not find him, so after a bit I walked along the path, round the rocks towards the Villa Rotha. Then I saw him. He was up the cliff, coming out of a bush."

"Coming out of a *bush?*"

"It was really a cave," explained Miranda. "Everybody knows that there are caves in the rock under the Castello, they used to use them for wine; and Adoni told me that he had seen down through a crack, and heard water, so he knew that there must be more caves below. This island is full of caves. Why, over near Ermones—"

"Adoni had found a new cave?"

She nodded. "He had not been on that part of the cliff before. I did not know he was interested in—I don't know the word—exploring? . . . Thank you. But today he said he wanted to find out where the water was that lay under the Castello, and he knew that Mr. Manning was away with you, so it was all right. I think"—here she dimpled—"that he was not very pleased to see me. I think he had heard me, and thought it was Mr. Manning come back. He looked quite frightened."

And well he might, I thought. My heart was bumping a bit. "Go on, what had he found?"

Her face went all at once solemn, and lighted. "He had found proof."

I jumped. *"Proof?"*

"That is what he said. Myself, I do not think that proof is needed, but that is what he said."

"Miranda!" I heard my voice rise sharply on the word, and controlled it. "Please explain. I have no idea what you're talking about. What proof had Adoni found?"

"Proof of St. Spiridion and his miracles."

I sat back in my chair. She stared at me solemnly, and as the silence drew out I felt my heartbeats slowing down to normal. I had a near-hysterical desire to laugh, but managed to stop myself. After a while I said gently, "Well, go on. Tell me— No, don't hover there, I've finished, thank you. Look, would you like to bring the coffee, and then sit down here and have some with me and tell me all about it?"

She hurried out, but when she came back with the coffee she refused to take any with me, or to sit down, but stood gripping a chair back, obviously bursting to get on with her story.

I poured coffee. "Go on. What's this about the Saint?"

"You were at the procession on Palm Sunday."

"Yes."

"Then perhaps you know about the Saint, the patron of this island?"

"Yes, I know about him. I read a lot about the island before I came here. He was Bishop of Cyprus, wasn't he, who was tortured by the Romans, and after he died his body was embalmed, and carried from place to place until it came to Corfu. We have a Saint like that in England, too, called Cuthbert. There are lots of stories about him, and about the miracles his body did."

"In England also?" It was plain that she had never credited that cold and misty land with anything as heart-warming as a real saint. "Then you understand that we of Corfu are taught all about our Saint as children, and many stories of the miracles and marvels. And they are true. I know this."

"Of course."

She swallowed. "But there are other stories—stories that Sir Gale has told me of the Saint, that I have never heard before. He—my *koumbàros* —told us many tales when we were children, Spiro and me. He is a very learned man, as learned as the *papàs*—the priest—and he knows very many stories about Greece, the stories of our history that we learn in school, Pericles and Alexander and Odysseus and Agamemnon, and also stories of our Saint, things that happened long, long ago, in this very place, things that the *papàs* never told us, and that I have not heard before."

She paused. I said, "Yes?" but I knew what was coming now.

"He has told us how the Saint lived here, in a cave, and had his daughter with him, a princess she was, very beautiful. He had angels and devils to do his bidding, and worked much magic, raising storms and stilling them, and saving the shipwrecked sailors."

She paused doubtfully. "I don't believe, me, about the daughter. The Saint was a bishop, and they do not have daughters. Perhaps she was a holy nun. . . . It is possible that Sir Gale has got the story a little bit wrong?"

"Very possible," I said. "Was the daughter called Miranda?"

"Yes! It was after this holy woman, a Corfiote, that I was called! Then you know this story, too?"

"In a way." I was wondering, in some apprehension, what rich and strange confusion Sir Julian's Shakespearean theories might have created. "In the English story we call him Prospero, and he was a magician—but he wasn't a bishop; he was a duke, and he came from Milan, in Italy. So you see, it's only a—"

"He lived in a cave behind the grove of lime trees along the cliff." She waved northwards, and I recognized Sir Julian's cheerfully arbitrary placing of the scene of *The Tempest*. "And there he did all his magic, but when he became old he turned to God, and drowned his books and his magic staff."

"But, Miranda . . ." I began, then stopped. This wasn't the time to try to point out the discrepancies between this story and that of the Bishop of Cyprus, who (for one thing) had already been with God for some thousand years when his body arrived at the island. I hoped there was some way of explaining how legends grew round some central figure like alum crystals round a thread. "Yes?" I said again.

She leaned forward over the chair back. "Well, Adoni says that Mr. Max is making a play out of this story, like . . . like . . ." She searched her mind, and then, being a Greek, came up with the best there is. ". . . like *Oedipus* (that is a play of the old gods; they do it in Athens). I asked Sir Gale about this play, and when he told me the story I said that the priests should know of this, because I had not heard it, and the *papàs* in my village has not heard it either, and he must be told, so that he can ask the Bishop. Why do you smile, Miss Lucy?"

"Nothing." I was thinking that I need hardly have worried. The Greeks invented cynicism, after all; and every Greek is born with an inquiring mind, just as every foxhound is born with a nose. "Go on; what did Sir Julian say?"

"He laughed, and said that his story—of the magic and the books—is not true, or perhaps it is only a little true, and changed with time, and that the poet who wrote the story added things from other stories and from his own mind, to make it more beautiful." She looked earnestly at me. "This happens. My *koumbàros* said it was like the story of Odysseus—that is another story of this island that we have in our schools, but you will not know it."

"I do know the story."

She stared. "You know this, too? Are all English so learned, Miss Lucy?"

I laughed. "It's a very famous story. We have it in our schools, too."

She gaped. This was fame indeed.

"We learn all your Greek stories," I said. "Well, Sir Julian's story of the magician may have some tiny fragment of truth in it, like the legends about Odysseus, but I honestly think not much more. I'm sure he didn't mean you to believe it word for word. The story he told you, that Mr. Max is making a film play out of, *is* just something that a poet invented, and probably has nothing to do with the real St. Spiridion at all. And you must see for yourself that the bit about the cave and the princess can't possibly be true—"

"But it is!"

"But look, Miranda, when the Saint was brought here in 1489, he was already—"

"Dead many years, I know that! But there is *something* that is true in Sir Gale's story, and the priests must be told of it. We can prove it, Adoni and I! I told you, we found the proof today!"

"Proof that *The Tempest* is true?" It was my turn to stare blankly.

Somehow, after the mounting excitement of Miranda's narrative, this came as a climax of the most stunning irrelevance.

"I don't know about any tempest, but today we found them, in the cave behind the lime trees. There's a passage, and a cave, very deep in the cliff, with water, and that is where he drowned his books." She leaned forward over the chair back. "That is what Adoni found today, and he took me in and showed me. They are there in the water, plain to see, in the very same place where Sir Gale told us—the magic books of the Saint!"

Her voice rose to a dramatic stop that Edith Evans might have envied. Her face was shining, lighted, and full of awe. For a full half minute all I could do was sit there, gazing blankly back at her, framing kind little sentences which might explain and question without too cruel a disillusionment. Adoni had been with her, I thought impatiently; what in the world had Adoni been thinking about to allow this fantasy to go on breeding? Certainly he would not share her beliefs, and she would have accepted an explanation from him, whereas from me, now . . .

Adoni. The name stabbed through the haze in my mind like a spearpoint going through butter muslin. What Adoni did, he usually had a good reason for. I sat up, demanding sharply, "Adoni found these—things—in a cave in the cliff? Where's the entrance?"

"Round the point, halfway up the cliff, above the boathouse."

"Ah. Could it be seen from the bay—our bay?"

She shook her head. "You go halfway up the path to the Villa Rotha. Then it is above the path, in the rocks, behind bushes."

"I see." My heart was bumping again. "Now, when Adoni saw it was you, what did he say? Try to remember exactly."

"I told you, he was angry at first, and would have hurried me away, because we should not have been there. Then he stopped and thought, and said no, I must come into the cave and see what he had found. He took me in; it was a steep passage, and long, going right down, but he had a torch, and it was dry. At the bottom was a big cave, full of water, very deep, but clear. Under a ledge, hidden with pebbles, we saw the books."

"A moment. What made you think they were books?"

"They looked like books," said Miranda reasonably. "Old, old books, coloured. The corners showed from under the pebbles. You could see the writing on them."

"Writing?"

She nodded. "Yes, in a foreign tongue, and pictures and magical signs."

"But, my dear girl, *books?* In seawater? They'd be pulp in a couple of hours!"

She said simply, "You forget. They are holy books. They would not perish."

I let that one pass. "Didn't Adoni try to get at them?"

"It was too deep, and very cold, and besides, there was an eel." She shivered. "And he said they must not be disturbed; he would tell Sir Gale, he said, and Mr. Max, and they would come. He said that I was his witness that he had found them there, and that I was to tell nobody about them, except you, Miss Lucy."

I put my hands flat on the table and held them there, hard. I could feel the blood pumping in the fingertips.

"He told you to tell me?"

"Yes."

"Miranda. You told me earlier that Adoni had said these books were 'proof.' Did he say proof of what?"

She knitted her brows. "What could he have meant, but proof of the story?"

"I see," I said. "Well, that's marvellous, and thank you for telling me. I can hardly wait to see them, but you won't tell anyone else, will you, anyone at all, even your mother? If—if it turns out to be a mistake, it would be dreadful to have raised people's hopes."

"I won't tell. I promised Adoni. It is our secret, his and mine."

"Of course. But I'd love to ask him about it. I think I'll go over to the Castello now. D'you think you could get him on the phone for me?"

She glanced at the clock. "There will be nobody there now. Sir Gale was going back to Corfu with Mr. Karithis for dinner, and Adoni went with them."

"But Max has the car. Adoni didn't have to drive them, surely?"

"No, Mr. Karithis brought his car. But Adoni wanted to go into Corfu, so he went with them, and he said he would come back with Mr. Max later."

Of course he would. Whatever he had found in the cave by the Villa Rotha, whatever "proof" he had now got, Adoni would get it to Max at the first possible moment, and if he was right about his discovery—and I had no doubt he was—then tonight the hounds would close in, and the end I had wanted this afternoon to hasten would come.

I glanced at my watch. If the ferry docked at ten forty-five . . . give

Max an hour at most to hear Adoni's story and possibly collect police help in Corfu . . . half an hour more for the drive . . . at the outside that made it a quarter past midnight. Even if Godfrey had got back from his date, whatever it was, he might be in bed by that time, not where he would hear or see explorers probing the secrets of the cliff. . . .

My hands moved of their own accord to the edge of the table, and gripped it. My thoughts, till now formlessly spinning, settled and stood.

Godfrey had said he was going out tonight, and there was the impression I had had of urgent business to be done and a clear field needed to do it in. Was it not conceivable that the objects so mysteriously hidden under his house were part of this same night's business? That in fact by the time Max and the police were led to the cave in the small hours the "proof" would have gone? And even with Adoni's word and that of his witness there would be nothing to show what had been there, or where it had gone? We would be back where we were, possibly with Godfrey's business finished, and himself in the clear. . . .

Reluctantly, I worked it out. Reluctantly, I reached the obvious, the only conclusion. I stood up.

"Will you show me this cave and the books? Now?"

She had started to stack the supper things back on the tray. She paused, startled. "Now, miss?"

"Yes, now. It may be important. I'd like to see them myself."

"But—it's so dark. You wouldn't want to go along there in the dark. In the morning, when Adoni's back ”

"Don't ask me to explain, Miranda, but I must go now, it might be important. If you'll just show me the cave, the entrance, that's all."

"Well, of course, miss." But the words dragged doubtfully. "What would happen if Mr. Manning came down?"

"He won't. He's out, away somewhere in his car, he told me so, so he's not likely to be using the cliff path. But we'll make sure he's out, we'll ring up the house . . . I can pretend I left something in the car. Will you get me the number, please?"

Somewhere in Godfrey's empty house the telephone bell shrilled on and on, while I waited and Miranda hung over me, uneasy, but obviously flattered by my interest in her story.

At length I put the receiver back. "That's that. He's out, so it's all right." I looked at her. "Will you, Miranda? Please? Just show me where the cave is, and you can come straight back."

"Well, of course, if you really want to. . . . If Kyrios Manning is away I don't mind at all. Shall I get the torch, Miss Lucy?"

"Yes, please. Give me five minutes to get a coat, and some other shoes," I said, "and have you got a coat here, or something extra to put on?" I didn't bother to ask if it was something dark; by the Saint's mercy the Corfiote peasants never wore anything else.

Three minutes later I was dressed in light rubber-soled shoes and a dark coat, and was rummaging through Leo's dressing-table drawer for the gun I knew he kept there.

CHAPTER

SIXTEEN

ह≫

This is the mouth o' th' cell. No noise, and enter . . .

Act IV, Scene 1

The bay was dark and silent: no sound, no point of light. It was easy enough to see our way across the pale sand without using the torch we had brought; and once we had scrambled up under the shadow of the pines where the dolphin had lain and gained the rocky path along the foot of the southern headland, we found that we could again make our way without a betraying light.

We turned off the track into the bushes some way before reaching the zigzag path that led up towards the Villa Rotha. Miranda led the way, plunging steeply uphill, apparently straight into the thickest tangle of bushes that masked the cliff. Above us the limes leaned out, densely black and silent. Not a leaf stirred. You could hardly hear the sea. Even after we had switched the torch on to help us, our stealthy progress through the bushes sounded like the charge of a couple of healthy buffaloes.

Fortunately it wasn't far. Miranda stopped where a clump of evergreens—junipers, by the scent—lay back, apparently right against the cliff.

"Here," she whispered, and pulled the bushes back. I shone the torchlight through.

It showed a narrow gap, scarcely more than a fissure, giving on a passage that sloped sharply downwards for perhaps four yards, to be apparently blocked by a wall of rock. The floor of the passage looked smooth, and the walls were dry.

I hesitated. A puff of breeze brought a murmur from the trees, and the bushes rustled. I could feel the same breeze—or was it the same?—run cold along my skin.

"The passage goes to the left there"—Miranda's whisper betrayed nothing but pleased excitement—"and then down again, quite a long way, but it is easy. Will you go first, or shall I?"

I had originally intended merely to stay hidden where I could watch the cave's entrance until Adoni brought the men down, and to send Miranda home, out of harm's way. But now it occurred to me that if Godfrey did come to remove the "books" before Max arrived I, too, should need a witness. This was to put it at its highest. To put it at its lowest, I wanted company. And even if Godfrey found us (which seemed unlikely in this tangle of darkness), there was no risk of our meeting with Yanni's fate. I was prepared, and there was the gun—the gun, and the simple fact that two people were more than twice as hard to dispose of as one.

But still I hesitated. Now that we were here, in the quiet dark, with the sounds and gentle airs of the night so normal around us, I wanted nothing so much as to see for myself what it was Adoni had found. If Godfrey did come tonight to remove it, if I should be unable to get a look at it, or to follow him, then we were back at the post, and no better off than before. . . .

Three parts bravado, three parts revenge for these people I had come so quickly to love and admire, and three parts sheer blazing human curiosity—it was no very creditable mixture of emotions that made me say with a briskness that might pass for bravery in the dark, "Is there anywhere to hide once you get inside the cave?"

I saw the glint of her eyes, but she answered simply, "Yes, a lot of places, other caves, with fallen rocks, and passages—"

"Fair enough. Let's go. You lead the way."

Behind us the juniper rustled back into its place across the gap.

The passage led steadily downwards, as sharply right-angled as a maze; I guessed that the mass of rock had weathered into great rectangular blocks, and that the passage led down the cracks between them. Here and there side cracks led off, but the main route was as unmistakable as a highway running through a labyrinth of country lanes.

Miranda led the way without faltering; left, then right, then straight on for thirty feet or so, then right again, and along . . . well into the heart of the promontory, I supposed. At the end of the last stretch it looked as if the floor of the passage dropped sheer away into black depths.

She paused, pointing. "The cave is down there. You can climb down quite easily, it is like steps."

A few moments later we were at the edge of the drop, with before us a sort of subterranean Giants' Staircase—a vast natural stairway of weathered rock leading down block by block on to a ledge that ran the length of a long, lozenge-shaped cave floored with black water, overhanging the smooth, scooped-out sides of the pool.

We clambered down the stairway, and I shone the light forward into the cave.

This was large, but not awesomely so. At the end where we stood the roof was not so very high—perhaps twenty feet; but as the torchlight travelled farther, it was lost in the shadows where the roof arched upwards into darkness. There, I suppose, would be the funnelled cracks or chimneys which carried the fresh air into the upper caves, and through which Adoni had first detected the existence of the one where we now stood. Farther along the ledge there were recesses and tunnels leading off the main cave, which promised a good choice of bolt hole should the need arise. The walls were of pale limestone, scoured and damp, so that I guessed that with the wind on shore the sea must find its way in through more of the cracks and crevices. Now the deep vat of seawater at our feet lay still and dead, and the place smelled of salt and wet stone.

Miranda gripped my arm. "Down there! Shine the light. Down there!"

I turned the torch downwards. At first I could see nothing but the rich dazzle as the water threw back the beam, then the light seemed to soak down through the water like a stain through silk, and I saw the bottom, a jumble of smooth, round pebbles, their colours all drained by the torchlight to bone white and washed green and pearl. Something moved across them, a whip of shadow flicking out of sight into a crevice.

"See?" Miranda crouched, pointing. "In under the ledge, where the stones have been moved. There!"

I saw it then, a corner like the corner of a big book, or box, jutting out from among the pebbles. It looked as if the object, whatever it was, had been thrust well under the ledge where we stood and the stones piled roughly over it.

I kneeled beside Miranda, peering intently down. Some stray movement of the sea outside had communicated itself to the pool, and the water shifted, shadows and reflections breaking and coalescing through the rocking torch beam. The thing was coloured, I thought, and smooth-surfaced; a simple mind conditioned by Sir Julian's stories might well have thought it was a book; myself, I took it for the corner of a box with some sort of a label. Vaguely, I could see what might be lettering.

"You see?" Miranda's whisper echoed in the cave.

"Yes, I see." Any thoughts I might have had of braving the eel and the icy water to get at the object died a natural and unregretted death. Even if I could have dived for the thing and lifted it, I couldn't have climbed the four smooth feet of overhang out of the pool without a rope.

"It is a book, yes?"

"It could be. But if it is, I don't think you'll find it's a very old one. The only way it could be kept down there is if it was wrapped in poly-thene or something, and that means—"

I broke off. Something had made a noise, some new noise that wasn't part of the cave's echo, or the faint whispers of the night that reached us through the invisible fissures in the cliff. I switched the light out, and the darkness came down like a candle-snuffer, thick as black wool. I put a hand on the girl's arm.

"Keep very still. I heard something. Listen."

Through the drip of water on limestone it came again: the sound of a careful footstep somewhere in the passage above.

Here he came. Dear God, here he came.

Miranda stirred. "Something coming. It must be Adoni back already. Perhaps—"

I stopped her with a touch, my lips at her ear. "That won't be Adoni. We mustn't be found here, we've got to hide. Quickly. . . ."

I took her arm, pulling her deeper into the cave. She came without question. We kept close to the wall, feeling our way inch by inch till we came to a corner, and rounded it safely.

"Wait." I dared a single brief flash of the torch, and breathed relief. We were in a deep recess or blocked tunnel, low-roofed, and filled with long-since-fallen debris that burrowed its way back into the cliff above the water level.

I put the light out. Slowly, carefully, and almost without a sound, we slithered our way into cover, deep into a crevice under a wedged block of limestone, flattening ourselves back into it like starfish hiding from the pronged hooks of the bait-fishers.

Not a moment too soon. Light spread, and warmed the cave. I was too deeply tucked back into the cleft to be able to see more than a curved section of the roof and far side of the main cave, but of course I could hear very clearly, as the cave and the water magnified every sound: the tread of boots on rock; the chink as the powerful torch was put down somewhere and the light steadied; the man's breathing. Then the splash of something—whether his body or something else I couldn't tell —that was let down into the pool.

A pause, while the water lapped and sucked, and the breathing sounded loud and urgent with some sort of effort. Then a different splashing noise, a sucking and slapping of water, as if something had been withdrawn from the pool. Another pause, filled now with the sounds of dripping, streaming water. Then at last the light moved, the slow footsteps retreated, and the sea sounds of the disturbed pool, slowly diminishing, held the cave.

I felt Miranda stir beside me.

"He has taken the book. *Could* it not be Adoni, Miss Lucy? Perhaps he has come back to get the book for Sir Gale? Who else would know? Shall I go—"

"No!" My whisper was as urgent as I could make it. "It's not Adoni, I'm sure of that. This is something else, Miranda. I can't tell you now, but trust me, please. Stay here. Don't move. I'm going to take a look."

I slid out of the cleft and switched on the torch, but kept a hand over the glass, so that the light came in dimmed slits between my fingers. I caught the gleam of her eyes watching me, but she neither moved again nor spoke. I inched my cautious way forward to the main cave, to pause at the corner of the ledge, switch off the torch, and listen yet again. There was no sound but the steady drip of water and the faint residual murmur from the pool.

Flashing the light full on, I knelt at the edge and looked down.

As I expected, the pile of stones had been rudely disturbed, and, as far as I could judge, had dwindled in height. But there must have been more than one of the rectangular objects there, for I could see another corner jutting from the cobbles at a different angle from the one that had been visible before. And there on the ledge, leaning against the wall as if waiting for him to come back, was an iron grapple, a long hooked shaft which dripped sluggishly on to the limestone.

I stood up, thinking furiously. So much for that. Adoni had been right: here was the key we were wanting, the clue to Godfrey's murderous business. And it was surely simple enough to see what I ought to do next. I had no means of telling what proportion of his cache Godfrey had taken, or if he would come back tonight for the rest; but in either case, nothing would be gained by taking the appalling risk of following him now. If he came back, we might meet in the passage. If he didn't— well, the rest of the "proof" would still be safely there for Max when he arrived at last.

And so, let's face it, would I . . .

I was hardly back in my niche before we heard him coming back, the light growing and brightening before him up the limestone walls. The performance was repeated almost exactly: the plunge of the grapple, the grating haul through the pebbles, the withdrawal, the pause while the water drained . . . then once more the light retreated, and we were left in blackness, with the hollow sucking of the troubled pool.

"Wait," I whispered again.

As soon as I got to the main cave I saw that the grapple was gone. I crouched once more on the streaming rock and peered down. As I expected, the pile of pebbles had settled lower, spreading level as what it had hidden had been dragged away. The pool was empty of its treasure.

No need, this time, to stop and think. The decision was, unhappily, as clear as before. I would have to follow him now. And I had better hurry.

In a matter of seconds I was back beside Miranda. "You can come out now. Quick!"

She materialized beside me. Her breathing was fast and shallow, and she was shivering. She was still taut and bright-eyed, but the quality of her excitement had changed. She looked scared.

"What is it, miss? What is it?"

I tried to sound calm and sure. "The 'books' have gone, and it was Mr. Manning who took them, I'm sure it was. I have to see where he puts them, but he mustn't see us. D'you understand, *he mustn't see us*. . . . I'll explain it all later, but we'll have to hurry now. Come on."

We heaved ourselves up the last of the Giants' Staircase, and crept from angle to angle of the passage, lighting the way warily and stopping at each corner to listen ahead. But nothing disturbed us, and soon we were at the mouth of the cleft, cautiously parting the junipers. The air smelled warm and sweet after the cave, full of flower scents and the tang of bruised herbs; and a breeze had got up and was moving the bushes, ready to mask what sounds we made.

We edged down, feeling our way, through the tangle of bushes and young trees. Although no moon was visible, the sky was alight with stars, and we went quickly enough. I dared not make for the path, but pushed a cautious way, bent double, above one arm of the zigzag from which I thought we should be able to see the boathouse, and at length we came to the end of the ridge where honeysuckle and (less happily) brambles made thick cover between the young limes.

We were just above the boathouse. Its roof was silhouetted like a black wedge against the paler sea beyond. I thought, but could not quite make out, that the landward door stood open.

Next moment it shut softly, but with the definite *chunk* of a spring-locking door. A shadow moved along the boathouse wall, and then he came quietly up the path. We lay mouse-still, hardly breathing. He rounded the corner below us, and came on up, with a quick, stealthy stride whose grace I recognized, and next moment, as he passed within feet of us, I saw him clearly. He had changed from the light clothes of the afternoon, and now wore dark trousers and a heavy dark jersey. He carried nothing in his hands. He went straight on past us, and his light tread was lost in the movements of the breeze.

In the heavy shadow where we lay I couldn't see Miranda, but I felt her turn to look at me, and presently she put out a hand and touched my arm. The hand was trembling.

"Miss—miss, what *is* it?"

I put a hand over hers, and held it, "You're quite right, it's not just a case of being caught trespassing, it's something much more serious, and it might be dangerous. I'm sorry you're in it, too, but I want your help."

She said nothing. I took a breath, and tightened my hand over hers.

"Listen. I can't tell you it all now, but there have been . . . things have been happening, and we think . . . Mr. Max and I . . . that they have something to do with your brother's accident. Adoni thinks so, too. We want to find out. Will you just trust me and do as I say?"

There was a pause. Still she didn't speak, but this time the air between us was so charged that I felt it vibrate like a bowstring after the shaft has gone.

"Yes."

"You saw who it was?"

"Of course. It was Mr. Manning."

"Good. You may be asked— What is it?"

"Look there." She had moved sharply, pointing past me up the cliff to where, above the black trees, a light had just flashed on. The Villa Rotha.

I felt my breath go out. "Then he's safe there for a bit, thank God. I wish I knew the time."

"We dare not shine the torch?"

"No. I should have looked before. Never mind. It looks as if he's put those things in the boathouse; I wish to heaven I dared go down and take a look at them . . . he did say he was going out tonight, and *not* with the boat, but he might only have been putting me off so that he'd be able to go to the cave. He may hang around here all night . . . or he may have been lying, and he'll come down again and take the boat, and that will be that." I stirred restlessly, watching that steady square of light with hatred. "In any case, the damned thing's locked. Even if—"

"I know where the key is."

I jerked round to peer at her. "*You do?*"

"Spiro told me. There was an extra key which was kept underneath the floor, where the house reaches the water. I know the place; he showed me."

I swallowed. "It's probably not there now, and in any case—"

I stopped abruptly. The light had gone out.

Minutes later we heard the car. That it was Godfrey's car there could be no manner of doubt: he switched on her lights, and they swept round in a wide curve, lancing through the trees and out into space, to move on and vanish in the blackness over the headland as the engine's note receded through the woods. There was a brief, distant stutter as he accelerated, then the sound died and there was darkness.

"He's gone," said Miranda unnecessarily.

I sat up. I was furious to find that my teeth were chattering, and clenched them hard, pushing a hand down into the pocket where Leo's gun hung heavy and awkward against my thigh. Two things were quite certain: I did not want to go anywhere near Godfrey Manning's boathouse; and if I didn't, I should despise myself for a coward as long as I lived. I had a gun. There was probably a key. I had at least to try it.

"Come on, then," I said, and pushed my way out of cover and dropped to the path, Miranda behind me. As we ran downhill I gasped out instructions. "You must get straight back to the house. Can you get into the Castello?"

"Yes."

"Then go there. That way, you'll see them as soon as they get home. But try to telephone Adoni first. Do you know where he might be?"

"Sometimes he eats at Chrisomalis', or the Corfu Bar."

"Then try them. If he's not there, some of his friends may know where he'll be. He may have gone down to the harbour to wait, or even to the police. . . . Try, anyway."

We had reached the boathouse. I stopped at the door, trying it . . . futilely, of course: it was fast locked. Miranda thrust past me, and I heard her fumbling in the shadows round the side of the building, then she was beside me, pushing the cold shape of a Yale key into my hand.

"Here. What shall I tell Adoni?"

"Don't tell him what's happened. Mr. Manning may get back to the house and pick the phone up, you never know. Just say he must come straight back here, it's urgent, Miss Lucy says so. He'll understand. If he doesn't, tell him anything you like—tell him I'm ill and you have to have help—anything to get him back here. He's not to tell Sir Julian. Then you wait for him. Don't leave the Castello, and don't open the door to anyone else except Max or the police . . . or me. If I'm not back by the time he comes, tell him everything that's happened, and that I'm down here. Okay?"

"Yes." She was an ally in a million. Confused and frightened though she must have been, she obeyed as unquestioningly as before. I heard her say, "The Saint be with you, miss," and then she was gone, running at a fair speed along the shore path to the Castello's bay.

With one more glance up at the lightless headland and a prayer on my own account, I prodded around the lock with a shamefully shaky key until at last I got it home.

The catch gave, stiffly, and I slipped inside.

CHAPTER

SEVENTEEN

ॐ

No tongue! all eyes! Be silent.

The boathouse was a vast structure with a high roof lost in shadows, where the sea sounds echoed hollowly, as in a cave. Running round the three walls was a narrow platform of planks set above the water, and along the near side of this lay the sloop. The rapidly dimming light of my torch showed me the lovely, powerful lines, and the name painted along the bows: *Aleister*. It also showed me, propped against the wall by the door, the grapple from the cave.

There was no hiding place in the boathouse other than the boat itself. I clicked the lock shut behind me, then stepped in over the cockpit coaming to try the cabin door.

It was unlocked, but I didn't go straight in. There was a window in the back of the boathouse, facing the cliff, which showed a section of the path, then the black looming mass of cliff and tree, and—at the top—a paler section of sky where stars burned. With eyes now adjusted to the darkness, I could just make out the sharp angle of some part of the Villa Rotha's roof. So far, excellent. If Godfrey did come back too soon, I should have the warning of the car or house lights.

Inside the cabin, I let the torchlight move round once, twice. . . .

The layout was much as I remembered in Leo's boat. Big curtained windows to either side, under which were settee berths with cushions in bright chintz; between these a fixed drop-leaf table above which swung a lamp. A curtain was drawn over the doorway in the forward bulkhead, but no doubt beyond it I would find another berth, the w.c., and the usual sail bags, ropes, and spare anchor stowed in the bows. Immediately to my right, just inside the door, was the galley, and opposite this the quarter berth—a space-saving berth with half its length in the cabin and the other half burrowing, as it were, into the space beyond the after bulkhead, under the port cockpit seat. The quarter berth was heaped with blankets, and was separated from the settee berth by a small table with a cupboard underneath.

And everywhere, lockers and cupboards. . . .

I started, methodically, along the starboard side.

Nothing in the galley: the oven empty, the cupboards stocked with cooking equipment so compact as to leave no hiding place. In the lockers, crockery, photographic stuff, tins of food, cardboard boxes full of an innocent miscellany of gear. In the wardrobe cupboards, coats, oilskins, sweaters, and a shelf holding sea boots, and shoes neatly racked, all as well polished and slick as Godfrey himself.

It was the same everywhere: everything was open to the searcher, all the contents normal and innocent—clothing, spare blankets, photographic equipment, tools. The only place not open to the prying eye was the cupboard at the end of the quarter berth, which was locked. But—from its shallow shape and my memory of Leo's boat—I imagined that this was only because it held the liquor; there was none elsewhere, and it was hardly big enough to store the packages I was looking for. I left it, and went on, even prodding the mattresses and feeling under the piled blankets, but all that came to light was a paperback copy of *Tropic of Cancer*, which I pushed back, rearranging the blankets as they had been before. Then I started on the floor.

Here there would be, I knew, a couple of "traps," or sections of the flooring which were made to lift out and give access to the bilges. Sure enough, under the table, and set in the boards, my eye caught the gleam of a sunken ring which, when pulled, lifted an eighteen-inch square of the planking, like a small trap door. But there was no treasure cave below, only the gleam of bilge water shifting between the frames with the boat's motion, and a faint smell of gas. And the same with the trap in the fo'c'sle.

The engine hatchway under the cabin steps was hardly a likely place for a cache; all the same, I looked there, and even lifted the inspection cover off the fresh-water tank, to see nothing but the ghostly reflection of the torchlight and my own shadow shivering on the surface of the full forty-gallon complement of water. Not here. . . .

I screwed the cover down with hands that sweated now, and shook, then I put the torch out and fled up the steps and on to the deck.

The window first. . . . No light showed outside, but I had to make sure. I ran aft, ducked under the boom, and climbed on the stern seat to peer anxiously out.

All was dark and still. I could—I must—allow myself a little longer.

I started over the cockpit, using the torch again, but keeping a wary eye on the boathouse window. Here, too, all seemed innocent. Under the starboard seat was the space occupied by the Calor gas cylinders, and nothing else. Under the stern seat was nothing but folded tarpaulins and skin-diving equipment. The port seat merely hid the end of the quarter berth. Nothing. Nor were there any strange objects fastened overside, or trailing under the *Aleister* in the sea; that bright idea was disposed of in a very few seconds. I straightened up finally from my inspection, and stood there, hovering, miserably undecided, and trying hard to think through the tension that gripped me.

He must have brought the packages here. He had not had time to take them up to his house, and he would hardly have cached them somewhere outside when he had the *Aleister* handy, and, moreover, no idea that he was even suspected. He might, of course, have handed them to some accomplice there and then, and merely have been returning the grapple to the boathouse, but the accomplice would have had to have some means of transport, which meant either a donkey or a boat; if a donkey, Miranda and I must surely have heard it; we might not have heard a rowing boat, but why should Godfrey use one when the *Aleister* and her dinghy lay ready to his own hand? No, it was obvious that there could be no innocent explanation of his use of the hidden cave.

But I had looked everywhere. They were not in the boat, or tied under the boat; they were not on the platform, or on the single shelf above it. Where in the world could he, in this scoured-out space, have hidden those bulky and dripping objects so quickly and effectively?

An answer came then—so obvious as to be insulting. In the water. He had moved them merely from the bottom of the cave to the bottom of the bay. They must be under the *Aleister*, right under, and if I could only see them there was the grapple ready to hand, with the water still dripping off it to make a pool on the boards.

I was actually up on the cockpit coaming, making for the grapple, when I saw the real answer, the obvious, easy answer which I should have seen straight away; which would have saved me all those precious minutes, and how much more besides; the trail of drops leading in through the boathouse door and along the platform; the trail left by the dripping packages, as obvious to the intelligent eye as footprints in fresh snow. I had no excuse, except fear and haste, and (I thought bitterly) Nemesis armed with a nice, heavy gun had no business to be afraid at all.

And the trail was already drying. I was calling myself names that I hadn't even known I knew, as I shone the yellow and flickering torch-light over the boards of the platform.

Yes, there they were, the footprints in the snow: the two faint, ir-regular trails, interweaving like the track of bicycle wheels, leading in through the door, along the platform, over the edge . . .

But not into the water after all. They went in over the side of the *Aleister* and across her deck and straight in through the cabin door.

I was in after them in a flash. Down the steps, to the table. . . . I had never even glanced at the bare table top, but now I saw on the formica surface the still damp square where he had laid the packages down.

And there the trail stopped. But this time there was only one an-swer. The trail had stopped simply because all Godfrey had had to do from there was to open the trap door under the table and lift the things straight down.

I had the trap open again in seconds. I laid it aside. The square hole gaped.

I ran back to the steps and peered up at the window. No light showed. I dropped on my knees beside the trap, clicked on the torch, and sent the small yellow eye which was all it had left skidding over the greasy water in the *Aleister's* bilges.

Nothing. No sign. But now I knew they had to be there . . . and they were there. I had gone flat down on the floor, and was hanging half inside the trap door before I saw them, but they were there; not in the bottom, but tucked, as neatly as could be, right up under the floorboards, in what were obviously racks made specially to carry them. They were clear of the water, and well back from the edges of the hatch, so that you would have had—like me—to be half in the bilges yourself before you saw them.

I ducked back, checked on the window again, then dived once more into the bilges.

Two sweating minutes, and I had it, a big, heavy square package wrapped in polythene. I heaved it out on deck, spreading the skirts of my coat for it so that I in my turn would leave no trail, then turned the light on it.

The torch was shaking now in my hand. The yellow glowworm crawled and prodded over the surface to the package, but the glossy wrapping almost defeated the miserable light, and all I got, in the three seconds' look I allowed myself, was the impression of a jumble of faint colours, something looking like a picture, a badge, even (Miranda had been right) a couple of words . . . LEKE, I read, and in front of this something that could be—but surely wasn't—NJEMIJE.

Somewhere something slammed, nearly frightening me out of what wits I still had. The torch dropped with a rattle, rolling in a wide semi-circle that missed the trap by millimetres. I grabbed it back again, and whirled to look. There was nothing there. Only darkness.

Which was just as well, I thought, recovering my senses rather wryly. Even if I had reacted properly, and grabbed for the gun instead of the torch, I couldn't have got it. Prospero's damned book, or whatever the package was, was sitting right on top of it, on the skirts of my coat. I had a long way to go, I reflected bitterly, before I got into the James Bond class.

The wind must be rising fast. The big seaward doors shook again, as if someone were pulling at the padlock, and the other door bumped and rattled. The water ran hissing and lapping along the walls, and shadows, thrown by some faint reflection of starlight, shivered up into the rafters.

The window was still dark, but I had had my warning, and enough was enough. The trap door went snugly back into place, my torch dropped into my other pocket, and, clasping the package to me with both hands, I clambered carefully out of the *Aleister*.

At the same instant as I gained the platform, I saw the movement on the path outside the window. Only a shadow, but as before there was no mistaking the way he moved. No light, no nothing, but here he was, just above the boathouse, and coming fast.

And here was I, stuck with my arms full of his precious package, for which he had almost certainly tried to do double murder. And I couldn't get out of the place if I tried.

The first thing was to get rid of the package.

I crouched and let the thing slide down between the platform and the boat. The boat was moored close, and for a panic-stricken moment I thought there wasn't enough room there; the package was tangled in my coat, then it jammed in the gap, and I couldn't move it either way, and when I tried to grab it back I couldn't, it was slippery and I couldn't get a grip on it again. . . .

I flung myself down, got a shoulder to the *Aleister*, and shoved. She moved the inch or so I needed, and with a brief, sharp struggle I managed to ram the package through and down.

It vanished with a faint splash. And then, like an echo, came the fainter but quite final splash of Leo's gun slipping from the pocket of my coat, to vanish in its turn under the water.

For one wild, crazy moment of fear I thought of swinging myself down to follow gun and package and hide under the platform, but I couldn't get down here, and there was no time to run the length of the boat. In any case, he would have heard me. He was at the door. His key scraped the lock.

There was only one place big enough to hide, and that was right bang in the target area. The boat itself. It did cross my mind that I could stand still and try to bluff it out, but even had the *Aleister* been innocent and Godfrey found me here at this hour, inside a locked door, no bluff would have worked. With the boat literally loaded, I hadn't a hope. It was the cabin or nothing.

I was already over the side, and letting myself as quietly as a ghost into the cabin, as his key went home in the lock and turned with a click. I didn't hear the door open. I was already, like a hunted mouse, holed up in the covered end of the quarter berth, with the pile of blankets pulled up as best I could to hide me.

The blankets smelled of dust and carbolic soap. They covered me with a thick, stuffy darkness that at least felt a bit like security. The trouble was that they deprived me of my hearing, the only sense that was left to tell what Godfrey was up to. Strain as I might through the thudding of my own heartbeats, I could only get the vaguest impression of where he was and what he was doing. All I could do was lie still and pray he wouldn't come into the cabin.

The boat rocked sharply, and for a moment I thought he was already in her, but again it was only the wind. This seemed to be rising still, in sharper gusts which sent little waves slapping hard along the hull, and sucking up and down the piles on which the platform stood. I could feel the jerking motion as the *Aleister* tugged at her rope, then she bucked, sharply and unmistakably: Godfrey had jumped into her.

Minutes passed, filled with the muffled night noises, but I could feel, rather than hear, his weight moving about the boat, and strained my senses, trying to judge where he was and what he was doing. The boat was steadier now, swaying gently to the small ripples passing under her keel. A draught moved through the cabin, smelling freshly of the sea wind, so that I guessed he must have left the boathouse door open, and this might mean he didn't mean to stay long. . . .

The wind must be quite strong now. The boat swayed under me, and a hissing wave ran right along beside my head. The *Aleister* lifted to it with a creak of timber, and I heard the unmistakable sound of straining rope and the rattle of metal.

Then I knew what had happened. There was no mistaking it, rope and metal and timber active and moving—the boat was alive, and out in the living sea. He must have swung the big doors open without my hearing him, then poled her gently out, and now she was alive, under sail, slipping silently along shore, away from the bay.

I couldn't move. I simply lay there, shivering under my load of blankets, every muscle knotted and tense with the effort of keeping my head, and trying to think. . . .

Max would surely be back by now; and even if he was still in Corfu, Adoni was probably already on his way home . . . and he would have left Miranda's message for Max, so Max wouldn't linger in Corfu, but would come straight here, and probably bring the police. When they got down to the boathouse and found the boat gone, and me with it, they would guess what had happened. There wasn't—I knew this—much hope of their finding the *Aleister* in the darkness, but at least I might have a card or two I could play if Godfrey found me. Under the circumstances, he could hardly expect to get away with my disappearance as well.

Or so I hoped. I knew that if he discovered about the missing package he would probably search the sloop and find me. But since there was nothing I could do about that, my only course was to stay hidden here and pray for a choppy sea that would keep him on deck looking after the *Aleister*. Why, he might not even come below at all. . . .

Just three minutes later he opened the cabin door.

CHAPTER

EIGHTEEN

&

What shall I do? say what. What shall I do?

Act 1, Scene 2

I heard the click, and felt the sudden swirl of fresh air, cut off as the door shut again.

There was the rasp of a match; the sharp tang of it pierced right up into my hidden corner, and with it the first smoke of a newly lighted cigarette. He must have come in out of the wind for this, and now he would go . . .

But he didn't. No movement followed. He must be very near me; I could feel, like an animal in the presence of danger, the hair brushing up along my skin. Now I was thankful for the chop and hiss of water, and for the hundred creaking, straining noises of the *Aleister* scudding on her way through the darkness. Without them, I thought he would have heard my heartbeats.

He can only have stood there for a few seconds, though for me it was a pause prolonged almost to screaming point. But it seemed he had only waited to get his cigarette properly alight: he struck another match, dropped it and the box after it on the table, and then went out and shut the door behind him.

Relief left me weak and sweating. The closed end of the berth seemed like an oven, so I pushed the blanket folds back a little, to let the air in, and cautiously peered over them, out into the cabin.

A weapon; that was the first thing. . . . I had the torch, but it was not a heavy one, and would hardly count as adequate armament against a murderer. Not that it was easy in the circumstances to think of anything (short of Leo's gun) that would have been "adequate," though I would have settled for a good, loaded bottle, if only the damned cupboard had been open. But bottles there were none. I cast my mind furiously back over the cabin's contents. . . . The galley? Surely the galley must be packed with implements? Pans were too clumsy; it must be something I could conceal. . . . A knife? I hadn't opened the shallow drawers during my search, but one of them was bound to hold a knife. Or there was the starting handle for the engine, if I could get the engine hatch opened silently, and then station myself on the galley side, behind the door, and wait for him. . . .

Cautiously, one eye on the door, I reached down to push the blanket aside, ready to slide out of the quarter berth.

Then froze, staring with horror at the foot of the berth.

Even in the almost-darkness I could see it, and Godfrey, in the matchlight, must have seen it quite clearly—my toe, clad in a light yellow canvas shoe, protruding from the huddle of blankets. I was about as well hidden as an ostrich beak deep in sand.

Now I knew what had happened. He had come in quickly out of the wind to light his cigarette, had seen what he thought was a foot, had struck another match to make sure—and, having made sure, had done what?

I was answered immediately. The boat had levelled and steadied, as if she were losing way. Now, seemingly just beside me, the engine fired with a jerk and a brief, coughing roar that nearly sent me straight through the bulkhead; then it was throttled quickly back to a murmur, the merest throb and quiver of the boards, as the *Aleister* moved sedately forward on an even keel. He had merely turned the boat head to wind without taking in the mainsail, and started the engine, so that she would hold herself steady without attention. I didn't have to guess why. His quick step was already at the cabin door.

I whisked off the berth, dropped my wet coat, and straightened my dress. There wasn't even time to dive across the cabin and open the knife drawer. As Godfrey opened the door I was heading for the table and the box of matches, apparently intent on nothing more deadly than lighting the lamp.

I threw a gay greeting at him over my shoulder.

"Hullo, there. I hope you don't mind a stowaway?"

The wick caught, and the light spread. I got the globe fitted back at the third try, but perhaps he hadn't noticed my shaking hands. He had moved to draw the curtains.

"Naturally I'm delighted. How did you know I'd decided to come out after all?"

"Oh, I didn't, but I was hoping!" I added, with what I'm sure was a

ghastly archness, "You saw me, didn't you? You were coming in to un-
mask me. What's the penalty for stowing away in these seas?"

"We'll arrange that later," said Godfrey.

His voice and manner were pleasant as ever, but after that first bright
glance I didn't dare let him see my eyes; not yet. There was a mirror
set in a cupboard door. I turned to this and made the gestures of tidying
my hair.

"What brought you down?" he asked.

"Well, I wanted a walk after supper, and— *Have* you a comb, Godfrey? I look like a mouse's nest!"

Without a word he took one from a pocket and handed it to me. I
began, rather elaborately, to fuss with my hair.

"I went down to the beach; I had a sort of vague idea the dolphin
might come back—they do, I believe. Anyway, I went to look, but it
wasn't there. I walked along the path a bit, listening to the sea and
wishing you *had* been going out. Then I heard you—I knew it must be
you—over at the boathouse, so I hurried. You know, just hoping."

He had moved so that he was directly behind me. He stood very close,
watching my face in the glass. I smiled at him, but got no response; the
light eyes were like stones.

"You heard me at the boathouse?"

"Yes. I heard the door."

"When was this?"

"Oh, goodness knows, half an hour ago? Less? I'm no good over
times. I'd have called out, but you seemed to be in a hurry, so—"

"You saw me?"

His breath on the back of my neck brought panic, just a flash of it,
like a heart spasm. I turned away quickly, handed him his comb, and
sat down on the settee berth, curling my legs up under me with an assumption of ease.

"I did. You were just coming out of the boathouse, and you went
rushing off up the path to the house."

I saw the slightest relaxation as he registered that I hadn't seen him
coming down from the cave with the packages. He drew on his cigarette,
blowing out a long jet of grey smoke into a haze round the lamp. "And
then?"

I smiled up at him—I hoped provocatively. "Oh, I was going to call
after you, but then I saw you had a sweater and things on, so you probably *were* going out after all. I thought if I just stuck around you'd be
back and I could ask you."

"Why didn't you?"

"Why didn't I what?"

"Ask me."

I looked embarrassed and fidgeted with a bit of blanket. "Well, I'm sorry, I know I should have, but you were quite a time, and I got bored and tried the door, and it was open, so—"

"The door was open?"

"Yes."

"That's not possible. I locked it."

I nodded. "I know. I heard you. But it hadn't quite caught, or something, you know how those spring locks are. I'd only tried it for something to do—you know how one fidgets about—and when it opened I was quite surprised."

There was no way of knowing whether he believed me or not, but according to Spiro, the catch had been stiff, and Godfrey had no idea I could have known that. I didn't think he could have changed the lock as he had threatened, for I had heard him myself wrestling with it on Monday; but that was a chance I had to take.

He tapped ash into a bowl on the liquor cupboard, and waited. He looked very tall; the slightly swaying lamp was on a level with his eyes. I toyed with the idea of giving it a sudden shove that would knock his head in, but doubted if I could get there quickly enough. Later, perhaps. Now I smiled at him instead, letting a touch of uncertainty, even of distress, appear.

"I—I'm sorry. I suppose it was awful of me, and I should have waited, but I was *sure* you wouldn't mind my looking at the boat—"

"Then why did you hide when I came down?"

"I don't know!" The note of exasperated honesty came out exactly right. "I honestly don't know! But I was *in* the boat, you see, in here, actually, poking about in the cupboards and the ga— kitchen and everything—"

"What for?"

"What *for*?" Every bit of technique I'd ever had went into it. "Well, what does a woman usually poke around in other people's houses for? And a boat's so much more fun than a house; I wanted to see how it was fitted, and the cooking arrangements, and—well, everything!" I laughed, wooing him back to good temper with all I had, playing the ignorant: it might be as well not to let him know how much I knew about the sloop's layout. "And it really is smashing, Godfrey! I'd no idea!" I faltered then, biting my lip. "You're annoyed with me. You *do* mind. I—I suppose it *was* the hell of a nerve. In fact, I *knew* it was, and I suppose that's why I hid when I heard you at the door. . . . I suddenly thought how it must look, and you might be furious, so I got in a panic and hid. I had a vague idea that if you weren't going sailing after all I could slip out after you had gone. That's all."

I sat back, wondering if tears at this point would be too much, and deciding that they probably would. Instead, I looked at him meltingly through my lashes—at least, that's what I tried to do, but I shall never believe the romantic novelists again; it's a physical impossibility. Godfrey, at any rate, remained unmelted, so I abandoned the attempt and made do with a quivering little smile, and a hand, genuinely none too steady, brushing my eyes. "I'm sorry," I said, "I truly am. Please don't be angry."

"I'm not angry." For the first time he took his eyes off me. He mounted a step to pull the door open, and looked out into the blackness. What he saw appeared to satisfy him, but when he turned back he didn't shut the door.

"Well, now you are here you might as well enjoy it. I can't leave the tiller much longer, so come along out. That's not a very thick coat, is it? Try this." And he pulled open the cupboard and produced a heavy navy duffel coat, which he held for me.

"Don't bother, mine will do." I stood up and reached for my own coat, with the torch in the pocket, then remembered how wet it was. For the life of me I couldn't think offhand of any reason for the soaked skirt where I had knelt in the puddles of water. I dropped the coat back on the bunk. "Well, thanks awfully, yours'll be warmer, I suppose. It sounds like quite a windy night now."

As he held it for me to put on, I smiled up at him over my shoulder. "Have you forgiven me? It was a silly thing to do, and you've a right to be furious."

"I wasn't furious," said Godfrey, and smiled. Then he turned me round and kissed me.

Well, I had asked for it, and now I was getting it. I shut my eyes. If I pretended it was Max . . . No, that wasn't possible. Well, then, someone who didn't matter—for instance, that rather nice boy I'd once had an abortive affair with but hadn't cared about when it came to the push . . . But that wouldn't work either. Whatever Godfrey was or wasn't, he didn't kiss like a rather nice boy. . . .

I opened my eyes and watched, over his shoulder, the lovely heavy lamp swinging about a foot away from his head. If I could manoeuvre him into its orbit . . . I supposed there were circumstances in which it was correct, even praiseworthy, for a girl to bash a man's head in with a lamp while he was kissing her. . . .

The *Aleister* gave a sudden lurch, and yawed sharply. Godfrey dropped me as if I had bitten him.

"Put the lamp out, will you?"

"Of course."

He ran up the steps. I blew the lamp out, and had the glass back in a matter of seconds, but already the *Aleister* was steady again, and Godfrey paused in the doorway without leaving the cabin, and turned back to hold a hand down to me.

"Come out and see the stars."

"Just a moment."

His voice sharpened a fraction. He wasn't as calm as he made out. "What is it?"

"My hankie. It's in my own coat pocket." I was fumbling in the dimness of the quarter berth among the folds of coat and blanket. The torch dropped sweetly into the pocket of the duffel coat; I snatched the handkerchief, then ran up the steps and put a hand into his.

Outside was a lovely windswept night, stars and spray, and black sea glinting as it rushed up to burst in great fans of spindrift. Dimly on our left I could see the coast outlined black against the sky, a mass of high land blocking out the stars. Low down there were lights, small and few, and seemingly not too far away.

"Where are we?"

"About half a mile out from Glyfa."

"Where's that?"

"You know how the coast curves eastwards here along the foot of Mount Pantokrator, towards the mainland? We're about halfway along the curve . . ."

"So we're running east?"

"For the moment. Off Kouloura we turn up into the strait."

("I reckoned we were about halfway over," Spiro had said, "in the strait between Kouloura and the mainland.")

"You'll feel the wind a bit more when we get out of the lee of Pantokrator," said Godfrey. "It's rising quite strongly now." He slipped an arm round me, friendly, inexorable. "Come and sit by me. She won't look after herself forever. Do you know anything about sailing?"

"Not a thing." As he urged me towards the stern seat, my eyes were busily searching the dimly seen cockpit. Only too well did I know there was no handy weapon lying about, even if that loverlike arm would have allowed me to reach for it. But I looked all the same. It had occurred to me that he probably carried a gun, and I had already found out that there was nothing in the pocket nearest me, the left; if he got amorous again it might be possible to find out if it was in the other pocket. . . . As he drew me down beside him on the stern seat I pulled the duffel coat round me for protection against his hands, at the same time relaxing right into the curve of his shoulder. I was thinking that if he wore a shoulder holster he would hardly have cuddled me so blithely to his left side, and I was right. There was no gun there. I leaned cozily back, and set myself to show him how little I knew about sailing. "How fast will it go?"

"About eight knots."

"Oh?" I let it be heard that I had no idea what a knot was, but didn't want to expose my ignorance. He didn't enlighten me. He settled the arm round me, threw his cigarette overside, and added:

"Under sail, that is. Six or seven under power."

"Oh?" I had another shot at the same intonation, and was apparently successful, because he laughed indulgently as he turned to kiss me again.

The *Aleister* tilted and swung up to a cross-sea, and the boom came over above us with the mainsail cracking like a rifle shot. It supplied me with an excuse for the instinctive recoil I gave as his mouth fastened on mine, but next moment I had hold of myself, and responded with a sort of guarded enthusiasm while my open eyes watched the boom's pendulum movements above our heads and I tried to detach my mind from Godfrey and think.

What he was doing was obvious enough: not being sure yet of my innocence, he hadn't wanted to risk leaving me unguarded while he got the mainsail in and took the *Aleister* along under power. All he could do was hold her as she was, head to the wind, the engine ticking over, the idle mainsail weathercocking her along, until he had decided what to do with me. It was just my luck, I thought sourly, stroking his cheek with a caressing hand, that the wind was more or less in the direction he wanted. If he was aiming (as I supposed he was) for the same place as on the night he had tried to drown Spiro, then he must still be pretty well on course.

A sudden gust on the beam sent the *Aleister's* bows rearing up at an angle that brought the boom back again overhead with a creak and a thud, and Godfrey released me abruptly, his right hand going to the tiller. And as he moved, leaning forward momentarily, I saw my weapon.

Just beyond him, hanging on its hooks behind the stern cockpit seat, was the sloop's life belt, and attached to this by a length of rope was the smoke flare . . . a metal tube about a foot long, with a drum-shaped float of hollow metal about two thirds of the way up its length. It was heavy enough, and deadly enough in shape, to make a formidable weapon if I could only manage to reach it down from the hook where it hung a foot to my side of the life belt. The rope attaching it was coiled lightly over the hook, and would be some ten or fifteen feet long —ample play for such a weapon. It only remained to get hold of it. I could hardly reach past him for it, and would certainly get no chance to use it if I did. If I could only get him to his feet for a moment, away from me . . .

"Why do you leave the sail up?" I asked. "I'd have thought it ought to come down if the engine was going."

"Not necessarily. I'll want to take her in under sail soon, and in the meantime she'll take care of herself this way."

"I see." It was all I could do, this time, to sound as if I didn't. I saw, all right. He would take her in under sail for the same reason that he had taken her out: for silence. And it was pretty obvious where we were heading. We were making for the Albanian coast with our cargo; and "in the meantime" I, no doubt, would be shed as Spiro had been shed. After I had gone he could spare both hands for the *Aleister.*

I took a deep breath of the salt air, and leaned my head confidingly against his shoulder. "Heavenly, isn't it? I'm so glad I stowed away, and that you're not really angry with me about it. Look at those stars . . . that's a thing one misses terribly in London now: no night sky; only that horrible dirty glare from five million sodium lamps. Oughtn't you to have a light, Godfrey?"

"I ought, but I don't. As long as I don't meet anyone else breaking the law, *we* see *them*, so there's no harm done."

"Breaking the law?"

I thought he was smiling. "Running without lights."

"Oh. You're taking photographs, then? Of the dawn?" I giggled. "What'll Phyl say *this* time, I wonder, when I land home with the milk?"

"Where is she tonight? Did she know you'd come out?"

"She's out with friends at the Corfu Palace. I got a note from her when I got in, and it was too late to join them, so I just stayed home. I . . . felt kind of blue. We'd had such a lovely day, you and I, I just couldn't stay in the house, somehow."

"Poor Lucy. And then I was foul to you, I'm so sorry. Anybody know where you are?"

The question was casual, almost caressing, and it went off like a fire alarm. I hesitated perhaps a second too long. "Miranda was in the house. I told her I was coming out."

"To the boathouse?"

"Well, no. I didn't know that myself, did I?"

He did not reply. I had no way of knowing whether my wretched bluff had worked. The cool uncommitted tone—pleasant enough—and the cold sensuality of his love-making, gave no clue at all to what he felt, or planned to do. It was a personality from which normal human guesses simply glanced off. But whether or not he had accepted my innocence, I had reckoned that nothing I could say would make any difference to my fate. The only weapon I held so far against him was the knowledge I possessed: that Spiro was alive, that Godfrey might be accused of Yanni's murder, that Adoni and Miranda had seen the packages, and that Miranda had watched him carrying them to the boathouse, and must know where I was now. And finally, that Godfrey on his return would certainly be met by Max, Adoni, and (by now) the police, who this time would not be prepared to accept easily any story he might dream up. In plain words, whether he killed me or not, his game was up.

The trouble was, it worked both ways. If it made no difference what he did with me, then obviously his best course would be to kill me, and make his getaway (surely already planned for) without going back at all into the waiting hands of Max and the Greek police.

So silence was the only course. It was faintly possible, that, if he believed me innocent, he might abandon his mission and take me home, or that I might be able to persuade him to relax his watch on me for long enough to let me get hold of the more tangible weapon that hung beyond his right shoulder.

I said quickly, "Listen. What's the matter with the engine? Did you hear that?"

He turned his head. "What? It sounds all right to me."

"I don't know . . . I thought it made a queer noise, a sort of knocking."

He listened for a moment, while the engine purred smoothly on, then shook his head. "You must be hearing that other boat—there's one over there, see, northeast of us, out from Kentroma. You can hear it in the gusts of the wind." His arm tightened as I twisted to look, pulling away as if to get to my feet. "It's nothing. Some clapped-out old scow from Kentroma with a prewar engine. Sit still."

I strained my eyes over the black and tossing water to where the light, dim and rocking, appeared and disappeared with the heaving sea. Upwind of us, I was thinking: they'd never hear anything; and if they did, they'd never catch the *Aleister* with her lovely lines and silken engine.

Suddenly, only a short way from us, a flash caught my eye, a curve and splash of light where some big fish cut a phosphorescent track like a line of green fire.

"Godfrey! Look!"

He glanced across sharply. "What?"

I was half out of my seat. "Light, lovely green light, just there in the sea! Honestly, it was just *there* . . ."

"A school of fish or some such thing." His tone was barely patient, and I realized with a jerk of fear that his mind was moving towards some goal of its own. "You often see phosphorescence at night hereabouts."

"There it is again! Could it be photographed? Oh, look! Let me go a moment, Godfrey, please, I—"

"No. Stay here." The arm was like an iron bar. "I want to ask you something."

"What?"

"I've had the answer to one question already. But that leaves me with another. Why did you come?"

"I told you—"

"I know what you told me. Do you expect me to believe you?"

"I don't understand what you—"

"I've kissed women before. Don't ask me to believe you came along because you wanted to be with me."

"Well," I said, "I admit I wasn't expecting it to be quite like that."

"Like what?"

"You know quite well."

"I believe I do. But if you follow a man round and hide in his bed and play Cleopatra wrapped in a rug you can hardly expect him to say it with lace-edged Valentines."

It was like acid spilling over a polished surface, to show the stripped wood, coarse and ugly. There had been splashes of the same corrosive this afternoon. If there had been light enough to see by, he would have caught me staring.

"Do you have to be so offensive? I know you were annoyed, but I thought you'd got over that, and if you want the truth I can't see why you should mind so damned much if someone *does* have a look at your boat. I've told you exactly what happened, and if you don't believe me, or if you think I should fall straight into bed with you here and now, you can just think again. It's not a habit of mine."

"Then why did you behave as if it were?"

"Now, look!" I broke off, and then laughed. At all costs I mustn't let him force a showdown on me yet. I would have to let anger go, and try a bit more sweet apology. "Look, Godfrey, forget it! I'm sorry, it's silly to blame you, I did ask for it . . . and I *was* putting on a bit of an act in the cabin, I admit it. That was silly, too. But when a woman gets in a jam, and finds herself faced with an angry male, it's an instinct to use her sex to get her out of it. I haven't shown up a bit well tonight, have I? But I never thought you would be quite so furious, or quite so . . . well, quick off the mark."

"Sexually? How little you know."

"Well, you've had your revenge. I haven't felt so idiotic and miserable since I remember. And you needn't worry that I'll follow you around again . . . I'll never face you by daylight again as long as I live!"

He did not answer, but to my stretching senses it was as if he had laughed aloud. I could feel the irony of my words ring and bite in the windy air. A little way to starboard the trail of green fire curved and flashed again, and was gone. I said, "Well, after that, I suppose I must ask you to ruin your trip finally and completely, and take me home."

"No use, my dear." The words were brisk, the tone quite different. I felt a quiver run through me. "Here you are, and here you stay. You're coming the whole way."

"But you can't want me—"

"I don't. You came because you wanted to—or so you say—and now you'll stay because I say you have to. I've no time to take you back, even if I wished to. You've wasted too much of my time as it is. I'm on an urgent trip tonight and I'm running to schedule—"

"Godfrey—"

"—Taking a load of forged currency across to the Albanian coast. It's under the cabin floor. Seven hundred thousand leks, slightly used, in small denominations; and damned good ones, too. If I'm caught, I'll be shot. Get it?"

"I . . . don't believe you, you're ribbing me."

"Far from it. Want to see them?"

"No. No. I'll believe you if you like, but I don't understand. Why? What would you do a thing like that for?"

Kentroma was abeam of us now, about the same distance away. I thought I saw the faint outline of ghostly foam very near, and the loom of land, and my heart leaped; but it vanished. A small rocky islet at most, lightless, and scoured by the wind. As we ran clear of it I felt the sudden freshening kick of the wind, no longer steady from the east but veering and gusting as the mountains to either side of the strait caught and volleyed the currents of air.

And there, not so far off now, were the lights of Kouloura, where the land ended and the strait began. . . .

I dragged my mind back to what he was saying.

". . . And at the moment the situation in Albania is that anything could happen, and it's to certain interests—I'm sure you follow me?—to see that it does. The Balkan pot can always be made to boil, if you apply heat in the right place. You've got Yugoslavia, and Greece, and Bulgaria, all at daggers drawn, all sitting round on the Albanian frontier, prepared for trouble, but none of them daring to make it."

"Or wanting to," I said sharply. "Don't give me that! The last thing Greece wants is any sort of frontier trouble that she can be blamed for . . . Oh!"

"Yes, I thought you might see it. Dead-easy, isn't it? A lovely setup. Communist China sitting pretty in Albania, with a nice little base in Europe, the sort of foothold that Big Brother over there'd give his eye teeth to have. And if the present pro-Chinese government fell, and the fall was attributed to Greece, there'd be a nice almighty Balkan blowup, and the Chinese would be out and the Russians in. And maybe into Greece as well. Get it now?"

"Oh, God, yes. It's an old dodge. Hitler tried it in the last war. Flood a country with forged currency and down goes the government like a house of cards. How long has this been going on?"

"Ferrying the currency? For some time now. This is the last load. D Day is Good Friday; it's to filter as from then, and believe you me, after that the bang comes in a matter of days." He laughed. "They'll see the mushroom cloud right from Washington."

"And you? Where will you see it from?"

"Oh, I'll have a ringside seat, don't worry—but it won't be the Villa Rotha. 'G. Manning, Esquire,' will be vanishing almost immediately. You wouldn't have got your trip out with me on Saturday after all, my dear. A pity, I thought so at the time. I enjoyed our day out; we've a lot in common."

"Do you have to be so insulting?"

It didn't even register. He was staring into the darkness to the north. "The thing I really regret is that I'll never be able to use the photographs. Poor Spiro won't even get that memorial. We'll soon be reaching the place where I threw him in."

There had been no change of tone. He was still holding me, his arm about as personal as a steel fetter; which was just as well; the touch of his body jammed against mine was making my skin crawl. The cracking of the sail as the boom moved overhead made me jump as if he had laid a whip to me.

"Nervy, aren't you?" said Godfrey, and laughed.

"Who's paying you?"

"Shall we just leave it that it isn't Greece?"

"I hardly supposed that it was. Who is it?"

"What would you say if I told you I was being paid twice?"

"I'd say it was a pity you couldn't be shot twice."

"Sweet girl." The smooth voice mocked. "That's the least of what the Greeks would do to me if they caught me!"

"Where's the currency made? I can't believe anyone in Corfu—"

"Oh, God, no. There's a clever little chap who lives out near Ciampino . . . I've been getting my photographic supplies from him for a long time now. He used to work in the local branch of Leo's bank. It was through him I was brought in on this . . . and, of course, because I knew Leo."

I must have gone white: I felt the blood leave my face, and the skin round my mouth was cold and rigid. "*Leo?* I will not believe that Leo even *begins to know* about this!"

He hesitated fractionally. I could almost feel the cruel impulse to lie; then he must have decided it would be more amusing after all to keep the credit. "No, no. Pure as the driven snow, our Leo. I only meant because I had an 'in' with him to get the house, a perfect situation for this job, and of course with that boathouse, which is ideal. And then there's my own cover, being next door to the Forlis themselves. If anything had gone wrong and inquiries had been made, where do you suppose the official eye would have gone first? Where but the Villa Forli, where the director of the bank lived? And by the time they got round to the Villa Rotha, it would be empty of evidence, and possibly—if things were really bad—of me."

"And when the 'mushroom cloud' goes up? I take it that part of the plan is to have the currency traceable to Greece?"

"Of course. Eventually, as far back as Corfu, but with luck, no farther."

"I see. I suppose Spiro had found out?"

He lifted his shoulders. "I doubt it. But there was a chance he'd seen a sample I was carrying in my wallet."

"So you murdered him on the off chance." I drew in my breath. "And you don't even care, do you? It's almost funny to think what fuss I made about the dolphin . . . you must have shot at him for sheer jolly fun, since you were leaving in a few days anyway." I peered at him in the darkness. "How do people *get* like you? You simply don't care who or what you wreck, do you? You're a traitor to your own country, and the one you're a guest in, and not only that, you wreck God knows how many people into the bargain. I don't only mean Spiro, I mean Phyl and Leo and the children. You know what it will do to them."

"Don't be sentimental. There's no room for that sort of talk in a man's world."

"Funny, isn't it, how often that so-called 'man's world' works out as a sort of juvenile delinquents' playground? Bombs and lies and cloak-and-dagger nonsense and uniforms and loud voices. All right, have it your own way, but remember I'm an actress, and I'm interested in how people work, even sawn-off morons like you. Just tell me *why?*"

I felt it at last, the movement of anger through his body. His arm had slackened.

"Do you do it for the money?" My voice nagged sharply at him. "But surely you've got money. And you've got a talent of a sort with a camera, so it can't be frustration—unless that turn-of-the-century technique of yours can't get you any sex that's willing. And you can't be committed politically, since you bragged you were working for two sides. Why, then? I'd love to know, just for the record, what makes a horro-comic like you tick over."

"You've got a poisonous tongue, haven't you?"

"It's the company I keep. Well? Just a wrecker, is that it? You do it for kicks?"

I heard his breath go in, then he laughed, an ugly little sound. I suppose he could afford to. He must have found, back there in the cabin, that I had no weapon on me, and he knew I couldn't escape him now. His hold was loose on me, but he could still have grabbed me if I had moved. I sat still.

"Just exactly that," he said.

"I thought as much. It measures up. Is that why you called your boat *Aleister?*"

"What a well-read little girl it is, to be sure! Of course. His motto was the same as mine, *'Fais ce que veult.'* "

" 'Do what thou wilt'?" I said. "Well, Rabelais had it first. I doubt if you'll ever be anything but thirdhand, Godfrey. Throwing people overboard hardly gets you into the master class."

He made no reply. The lights of Kouloura were coming abeam of us. The wind backed in a sudden squall, leaping the black waves from the north. His hand moved on the tiller, and the *Aleister* bucked and rose to meet it. The stars swung behind the mast, tilted. The wind sang in the ropes. The deck heeled steeply as the starboard rail lifted against the rush of stars. The boom crashed over.

"Is that what you're going to do with me?" I asked. "Throw me overboard?"

The *Aleister* came back head to wind, and steadied sweetly. Godfrey's hand left the tiller.

"By the time I do, by God," he said, "you'll be glad to go."

Then he was out of his seat, and swinging round on me, his hands reaching for my throat.

I flinched back as far as I could from the brutal hands, dragging the torch from my pocket as I went. My back came up hard against the port coaming. Then he was on me. The boat lurched; the boom thudded to starboard with the sail cracking like a whip; a glistening fan of water burst over the rail so that his foot slipped and the wet hands slithered, missing their grip on my throat.

The *Aleister* was turning into the seas; the boom was coming back. His hands had found their hold, the thumbs digging in. I braced my back against the coaming, wrenched my left hand free, and smashed a blow with the torch at his face.

It wasn't much of a blow. He didn't let go, but he jerked back from it instinctively, straightening his body, dragging me with him. . . .

I kicked upwards with my right foot past his body, jammed the foot against the tiller with all my strength, and shoved it hard over.

The *Aleister*, already starting the swing, came round like a boomerang, heeling so steeply into the starboard tack that the rail went under.

And the boom slammed over with the force of a ramjet, straight at Godfrey's head.

CHAPTER

NINETEEN

ह‍

*Swam ashore, man, like a duck. I can
swim like a duck, I'll be sworn.*

Act II, Scene 2

If I had been able to take him completely by surprise, it would have
ended the business then and there. But he had felt my foot go lashing
past his body, and the sudden heeling of the *Aleister* gave him a split
second's warning of what must happen. His yachtsman's instinct did
the rest.

He ducked forward over me, one arm flying up to protect his head—
but I was in his way, hitting at his face, struggling to thrust him back
and up into the path of the boom as it came over with a whistle and a
crash that could have felled a bull.

It struck him with appalling force, but a glancing blow, the upflung
arm taking the force of the smash. He was flung sprawling right across
me, a dead weight bearing me back helplessly against the seat.

I had no idea if he was still conscious, or even alive. The seat was wet
and slippery; my hands scrabbled for a hold to drag myself free, but
before I could do this the *Aleister*, caught now with the wind on her
beam, swung hard into the other tack. Godfrey's body was flung back
off mine. He went to the deck all anyhow, and I with him, helplessly
tangled in the loose folds of the duffel coat. The two of us slithered together across the streaming boards, to fetch up hard against the starboard side of the cockpit.

The *Aleister* kicked her way upwards, shuddered, hung posed for the
next perilous swing. I tore myself free of the tangling coat and managed
somehow to claw my way to my feet, bent double to avoid the murderous boom, staggering and sprawling as the deck went up like a lift, and
the boom came back again to port with a force that threatened to take

the whole mast overside. I threw myself at the wildly swinging tiller, grabbed it somehow and clung there, fighting to steady the sloop and trying, through the bursting fans of spray, to see.

At first I thought he was dead. His body sprawled in a slack heap where it had been thrown back to the port side by the last violent tack. His head rolled, and I could see the blur of his face, not the pale oval that had been visible before, but half an oval . . . half his face must be black with blood. Then the *Aleister* shipped another wave, and the cold salt must have brought him sharply to his senses, for the head moved, lifting this time from the deck, and a hand went with terrifying precision to the edge of the cockpit seat, groping for a hold to pull his body up.

I thrust the tiller hard to starboard again and laid the sloop right over. His hand slipped, and he was thrown violently back across the deck. It was now or never. I let go the tiller and tore the smoke flare down from its hook behind me. I could only pray that its rope was long enough to let me reach Godfrey where he lay against the side, his left hand now strongly grasping the seat, his right dragging at something in his pocket.

I lifted the metal flare and lurched forward.

Too late: the gun was in his hand. He was shouting something: words that were lost in the noise of wind and cracking spars and the hammering of the boom. But the message was unmistakable. I dropped the smoke flare, and leaped back for the stern seat.

The pale half face turned with me. The gun's eye lifted.

I yanked wildly at the life belt hanging there on its hooks. It came free suddenly, and I went staggering against the side with it clutched to me like a shield. As I gripped the coaming and hauled myself up, the engine controls were just beside my feet. I kicked the throttle full open, and jumped for the rail.

The *Aleister* surged forward with a roar. I saw Godfrey let go his hold, dash the blood from his eyes with his free hand, jerk the muzzle of the gun after me, and fire.

I heard no shot. I saw the tiny jet of smoke spurt and vanish in the wind. I put a hand to my stomach, doubled up and pitched headlong into the sea.

I was coughing, swallowing salt water, gasping with lungs that hurt vilely, fighting the black weight of the sea with a wild instinct that brought me at last to the surface. My eyes opened wide, stinging, on pitch blackness. My arms flailed the water; my legs kicked like those of a hanging man; then I went out of control, lurching forward again and down, down. . . .

The cold water closing over me for the second time struck me back to full consciousness. Godfrey. The shot which—fired at a dim target on a wildly bucking boat—had missed me completely. The life belt which had been torn from me as I fell, its rope pulled tight on the hooks by my own hasty action with the smoke flare. The *Aleister*, which I had sent swerving away fast at full throttle from the place where I went in, but whose master would have her under control again, searching for me to make sure. . . .

I fought my panic down, as I had fought the sea. I surfaced easily enough, and this time the thick blackness was reassuring. I felt a shoe go, and even this little load lightened me. I trod water, retching and gasping, and tried to look about me.

Darkness. Nothing but darkness, and the noises of wind and sea. Then I heard the engine, I couldn't judge how far from me, but in the pauses of the wind it seemed to be coming nearer. He would come back to look for me; of course he would. I hoped he would think I had been hit and couldn't possibly survive, but he could hardly take the risk. He would stay here, beating the sea between me and the land, until he found me.

A mounting hill of a wave caught and lifted me. As I reached its crest I saw him; he had a light on, and the *Aleister*, now bare of canvas, was slipping along at half throttle, searching the waves. She was still a good way off, and moving away from me at a slant, but she would be back.

What was more, she was between me and the land. I saw this now, dimly, a black mass studded with faint points of light. It seemed a lot farther away than it had from the deck of the *Aleister*.

Half a mile, he had said. I could never swim half a mile; not in this sea. The water was very buoyant, and I was lightly clad, but I wasn't in Spiro's class as a swimmer, and could hardly hope for his luck. I dared do no other than swim straight towards the nearest land, and if Godfrey hunted about long enough he would be bound to see me.

He had turned, and was beating back on a long tack, still between me and the shore. All around me the crests of the seas were creaming and blowing. I was carried up climbing slopes of glass, their tops streaming off against the black sky till the whole night seemed a windy race of wet stars. Foam blew into my eyes, my mouth. My body was no longer mine, but a thing of unfamiliar action, cold and buoyant. I could do little more than stay afloat, try to swim in the right direction, and let the seas take me.

As I swam up the next mounting wave I caught, clearly, the reek of petrol in the wind, and saw a light not two hundred yards away. The engine was throttled back to the merest throb, and the boat circled slowly round the beam, which was directed downwards into the water. I even thought I saw him stooping over the side, reaching for something —my shoe, perhaps, kept floating by its rubber sole. He might take it as evidence that I was drowned; on the other hand, he might beat in widening circles round the place until he found me. . . .

Then not far away I saw another light, dimmer than the *Aleister's* and riding high. The *Aleister's* light went out. I heard the beat of another engine, and the second light bobbed closer. Faintly, a hail sounded. The clapped-out old scow from Kentroma was coming to take a look at the odd light on her fishing pitch. . . .

The *Aleister's* throttle opened with a roar, and I heard it dwindling away until the wind took all sound.

Then I shouted.

The sound came out as little more than a gasping cry, a feeble yell that was picked up by the wind and thrown away like the cry of a gull. The Kentroma boat may have attempted to go in the track of the *Aleister*, I do not know, but I had lost sight of her yellow light, and the sound of her engine, long before I gave up from sheer exhaustion, and concentrated on swimming rather than merely keeping afloat.

It was then that I realized that the sea was dropping. I was well into the lee of the great curve of Corfu, where Pantokrator broke the winds and held the gulf quiet. And the lights of Kouloura were a long way to my right. I had been drifting westwards, far faster than I could have swum.

The discovery was like a shot of Benzedrine. My brain cleared. Of course. We had been still some distance from the eastbound current that had carried Spiro to the Albanian coast. And tonight it was an east wind. Where I had gone in the drift must be strongly to the southwest. He had thrown Yanni's body in the gulf, and Yanni's body had fetched up at the Villa Rotha. I doubted if St. Spiridion would take me quite so neatly home, but at least, if I could stay afloat and make some progress, I might hope to stay alive.

So I swam and prayed, and if St. Spiridion got muddled up in my wordless prayers with Poseidon and Prospero, and even Max, no doubt it would come to the right ears in the end.

Twenty minutes later, in a sea that was little more than choppy, and with the roar of the rocky shore barely a hundred yards ahead, I knew I couldn't make it. What had been chance for Spiro was none at all for me. Under the lee of the cliff some freak current was setting hard off shore, probably only the backwash of the main stream that had brought me here, striking the coast at an angle and being volleyed back to the open water; but where I had till now been able to keep afloat and even angle my course slightly north across the current, I no longer had strength to fight any sea that wasn't going my way: my arms felt like cotton wool, my body like lead; I gulped and floundered as the cross-waves met me, and every little slapping crest threatened to submerge me.

Eventually one did. I swallowed more water, and in my panic began to struggle again. I burst free of the water, my eyes wide and sore, arms flapping feebly now, failing to drive me on or even to keep me above water. The roar of the breakers came to me oddly muffled, as if they were far away, or as if their noise came only through the water that was filling my ears. . . . I was being carried back, down, down, like a sackful of lead, like a body already drowned, to be tumbled with the other sea wrack on the rocks in the bright morning. . . .

It was bright morning now. It was silly to struggle and fight my way up into darkness when I could just let myself drift down like this, when in a moment or two if I put my feet down I would find sand, golden sand, and sweet air, sweet airs that give delight and hurt not . . . no, that was music, and this was a dream . . . how silly of me to panic so about a dream . . . I had had a thousand dreams like this, floating and flying away in darkness. In a few moments I would wake, and the sun would be out, and Max would be here. . . .

He was here now. He was lifting me. He thrust and shoved at me, up, up, out of the nightmare of choking blackness, into the air.

I could breathe. I was at the surface, thrown there by a strength I hadn't believed a man could command outside his own element. As I floundered forward, spewing the sea from burning lungs, his body turned beside me in a rolling dive that half lifted, half threw me across the current; then before the sea could lay hold on me again to whirl me back and away, I was struck and batted forward, brutally, right into the white surge and confusion of the breakers, rolling over slack and joint-less as a rag in the wind.

A huge wave lifted me forward, tumbled me over helpless in its break-ing foam, then dropped me hard in its wake. I went down like a stone, hit something, and went flat on the bottom . . . pancaked on the sand of a sloping beach, with the sea recoiling past me, my hands already driven into the land, like hooks to hold me there against the drag and suck of the retreating wave. The sea tore and pulled and streamed back past me. Sobbing and retching, I crawled and humped myself up the slope, while wave after wave, diminishing, broke over me and then drew back, combing the sand where I clung. And then I was crawling through the creaming shallows, on to the firm dry beach.

I have a half memory, just as I collapsed, of looking back for my rescuer and of seeing him rear up from the waves as if to see me safe home, his body gleaming black through the phosphorescence, the witches' oils of his track burning green and white on the water. The starlight caught the cusp of the dorsal fin, glittered there briefly, then he was gone, with a triumphant smack of the tail that echoed right up the rocks.

Then I went out flat on the sand, barely a foot above the edge of the sea.

CHAPTER

TWENTY

ह♥

Though the seas threaten, they are merciful,
I have curs'd them without cause.

Act v, Scene 1

There was a light, hanging seemingly in the sky far above me.

When this resolved itself into a lamp set in a cottage window, high up near the head of the cliffs, it still seemed as remote as the moon. I cannot even remember now what it cost me to drag myself in my dripping, icy clothes up the path that clung to the rock face, but I suppose I was lucky that there was a path at all. Eventually I made it, stopping to lean—collapse—against the trunk of an ancient olive that stood where a stream cut through the path to fall sharply seawards under a rough bridge.

Here a shallow valley ran back through a gap in the cliff. Dimly I could see the stretches of smoothed ground between the olive trees, painfully cultivated with beans and corn. Here and there among the trees were the scattered lights of the cottages, each with its own grove and its grazing for goats and sheep. The groves were old; the immense heads of the trees stirred and whispered even in that sheltered spot, and the small hard fruit pattered to the ground like rain. The twisted boughs stood out black against the light from the nearest window.

I forced my shivering, lead-weight limbs to move. Under my feet the rubbery olives rolled and squashed. The stems of camomile caught between my bare toes, and I stubbed my foot on a stone and cried out. Immediately there was a volley of barking, and a dog—one of the vicious, half-wild dogs that are a hazard of the Greek countryside—hurled itself towards me through the trees. I took no notice of it, except to speak as I limped forward, and the dog, every hair on end, circled behind me, growling. I felt the touch of his nose, cold on the cold flesh of my leg, but he didn't snap. Next moment the cottage door opened, loosing a shaft of light across the grass. A man, in thickset silhouette, peered out.

I stumbled into the light. "Please," I said breathlessly, in English, "please . . . can you help me?"

There was a startled moment of silence while he stared at me, coming ghostlike out of the night, soaked and filthy with sand and dust, with the dog circling at my heels. Then he shouted something at the dog which sent it swerving away, and fired some sharp question at me. I didn't know what it was; didn't even recognize the language, but in any case I doubt if I could have spoken again. I just went forward blindly towards the light and the human warmth of the house, my hand stretched out like those of the traditional suppliant, and came heavily to my knees over the threshold, right at his feet.

The blackout cannot have lasted more than a couple of seconds. I heard him call out, then there came a woman's voice, questioning shrilly, and hands were on me, half lifting, half dragging me in to the light and warmth of a room where the embers of a wood fire still burned red. The man said something rough and urgent to his wife, and then went quickly out, slamming the door. For a dazed, frightened moment I wondered where he had gone, then as the woman, chattering in some undistinguishable gutturals, began to fumble with my soaked and clinging clothes, I realized that her husband had merely left the cottage's single room while I undressed.

I struggled out of the sopping clothes. I suppose the old woman was asking questions, but I couldn't understand, and in fact hardly heard. My brain was as numb as my body with the dreadful cold and shivering of exhaustion and shock. But presently I was stripped and dried on a fine linen towel so stiff and yellowed that I imagine it must have been part of the woman's dowry, never used till now, and then a rough blanket was wrapped round me, I was pushed gently into a wooden chair near the fire, logs were thrown on, a pot shoved down into the leaping flames, and only when my discarded clothes were carefully hung up above the fireplace—with much interested fingering of the nylon—did the old woman go to the door and call her man back.

He came in, an elderly, villainous-looking peasant, with a ferocious moustache, and a dirty homemade cigarette drooping from his lips. He was followed, inevitably, by two others, shortish, tough-bodied men out of the same mould, with dark, fierce faces. They came into the light, staring at me. My host asked a question.

I shook my head, but the thing that mattered most to me at that moment was easy enough. I put an arm out of my blanket to make a gesture embracing my surroundings. "Kerkyra?" I asked. "This—Kerkyra?"

The storm of nods and assenting "*ne's*" that this provoked broke over me with a physical sense of relief. To open human communications, to know where one was on the map . . . of such is sanity. Heaven knows what I had expected the answer to be: I suppose that shreds of nightmare still clung to me, and it needed the spoken assurance to bring me finally out of the bad dream—the isolated near death of the sea, the prison of the *Aleister* with Godfrey, the unknown black cliff I had been climbing. This was Corfu, and these were Greeks. I was safe.

I said, "I'm English. Do you speak English?"

This time the heads were shaken, but I heard the word go round, "Anglìtha," so they had understood.

I tried again. "Villa Forli? Castello dei Fiori?"

Again they understood. Another fire of talk where I caught a word I knew, "*thàlassa*," which means the sea.

I nodded, with another gesture. "Me," I said, indicating my swaddled person, "*thàlassa* . . . boat . . ." A pantomime, rather hampered by the blanket. "Swim . . . drown."

Exclamations, while the woman thrust a bowl into my hands, with words of invitation and sympathy. It was soup of some kind—beans, I think—and rather thick and tasteless, but it was hot and filling, and under the circumstances, delicious. The men looked the other way politely while I ate, talking in quick-fire undertones among themselves.

As I finished, and gave the bowl back to the woman, one of them—not my host—came forward a pace, clearing his throat. He spoke in very bad German.

"You are from the Castello dei Fiori?"

"*Ja.*" My German was very little better than his, but even a smattering might see us through. I said slowly, picking the words, "To go to Castello, how far?"

More muttering. "Ten." He held up his fingers. "*Ja*, ten."

"Ten kilometres?"

"*Ja.*"

"Is—a road?"

"*Ja, ja.*"

"Is—a car?"

"No." He was too polite to say so, but the impression that the single syllable gave was that of course there was no car. There never had been a car. What would they want with a car? They had the donkeys and the women.

I swallowed. So I wasn't yet free of the nightmare; I still had the long frustrations of the impossible journey ahead of me. I tried, not very coherently, to think what Godfrey would do.

He was bound to discover at his rendezvous that the package was missing, and would know that I must have taken it, and where I must have hidden it. But I hoped he would decide that as yet no one else could have reason to suspect him: he might well reckon that if there had been any suspicion of him his journey would have been intercepted. No, it was to be hoped that he would think I had made a chance discovery—possibly that I had seen him carrying the packages, had hunted for them out of curiosity, and having seen them, had realized that something big was afoot, and had been frightened into hiding and carrying out the elaborate pantomime of innocence on the *Aleister* to save my skin. I was sure that he wouldn't even give Miranda a thought.

Well, he had got rid of me. My disappearance would provoke a hue and cry which he might well find embarrassing after what had happened to Spiro and Yanni, and this might decide him to cut his losses here and now, but the sudden absence of "G. Manning, Esquire," would naturally focus official attention on his house, and the boathouse, so (since it was unlikely that any official alarm had been raised for me yet) I felt sure that he would have to risk going back tonight to find and remove the last package of forged currency.

And this was where I had to come in. Even if Max were there to receive him, it would take evidence to hold him—hard evidence, not just the hearsay of Adoni and Miranda, or even Spiro, which I was sure Godfrey could cut his way through without much trouble. Once they had taken their hands off him for five minutes, "G. Manning, Esquire," with his prepared getaway, could vanish without trace, for good and all.

I looked up at the ring of men.

"Is—a telephone?" I asked it without much hope, but they all brightened. Yes, of course there was a telephone, up in the village, farther up the hill, where the road started. (This came in Greek from everybody at once, with gestures, and was surprisingly easy to understand.) Did I want the telephone now? They would take me there.

I nodded and smiled and thanked them, and then, indicating my clothes, turned an inquiring look on the woman. In a moment the men had melted from the room, and she began to take my things off the line. The nylon was dry, but the cotton dress was still damp and unpleasant. I threw the blanket off thankfully—it smelled of what I tried charitably to imagine was goat—and began to dress. But when I tried to put on my frock the old woman restrained me.

"No, no, no, *this* . . . it is an honour for me. You are welcome. . . ."

The words couldn't have been plainer if she had said them in English. "*This*" was a blouse of white lawn, beautifully embroidered in scarlet and green and gold, and with it a full black skirt, gay with the same colours at the hem—the Corfiote national dress, worn for high days and holidays. Either this also had been part of her trousseau as a young bride, or else it was her daughter's. I put it on. It fitted, too. The skirt was of thick, hand-woven stuff, and there was a warm jacket to go over the blouse. She hovered round me, delighted, stroking and praising, and then called the men in to see.

They were all waiting outside, not three now, but—I counted—sixteen. On an impulse I stooped and kissed the wrinkled cheek of the old woman, and she caught my hand in both of hers. There were tears in her eyes.

"You are welcome," she said. "English. You are welcome."

Then I was outside, swept up by the band of men and escorted royally up the stony track through the groves to the tiny village, to rouse the sleeping owner of the shop where stood the telephone.

No reply from the Castello. I hesitated, then tried the Villa Forli. The bell had hardly sounded before Phyl was on the line, alert and anxious.

"*Lucy*. Where in the world—"

"It's all right, Phyl, don't worry. I'm sorry I couldn't ring you up before, but I'm quite okay."

"Where *are* you? I tried Godfrey, but—"

"When?"

"An hour ago—three quarters, perhaps. He wasn't in, so I thought you might be out with him. Are you?"

"No. Listen, Phyl, will you do something for me?"

"What? What *is* all this?"

"I'll tell you when I see you, but there's no time now. Just don't ask any questions, but will you ring up Godfrey's house again now? If he answers, tell him I'm not home yet, and ask if I'm still with him—just as you would if you hadn't heard from me and were worried. It's terribly important not to let him know I rang up. Will you do that? It's *terribly* important, Phyl."

"Yes, but—"

"Then please do it, there's an angel. I promise you I'll be home soon and tell you all about it. But I must know if he's got home. As soon as you've rung him, ring me back here." I gave her the number.

"How in the world did you get *there*? Did you go out with him again?

I know you were in to supper, because it wasn't washed up; Miranda seems to have just walked out and left everything."

"That was my fault. I sent her on a message."

"You did? Look, just what *is* going on? What with all the supper things just left lying, and you halfway up Pantokrator in the middle of the night—"

"You might say Godfrey ditched me. You know, the long walk home."

"*Lucy!* You mean he tried something on?"

"You might say so," I said. "I don't like your Godfrey, Phyl, but just in case he's home by now, I'll ring off and wait to hear from you. But please do just as I say, it's important."

"My God, I will. Let him worry," said Phyl viciously. "Okay, sweetie, hang on, I'll ring you back. D'you want me to come for you?"

"I might at that."

"Stinking twerp," said my sister, but presumably not to me, and rang off.

There were twenty-three men now in the village shop, and something had happened. There were smiles all round. As I put down the receiver, my German-speaking friend was at my elbow.

"*Fräulein*, come and see." He gestured proudly to the door of the shop. "For you, at your service."

Outside in the starlight stood a motorcycle, a magnificent, almost new two-stroke affair, straddled proudly but shyly by a youth of about twenty. Round this now crowded the men, delighted that they had been able to help.

"He comes from Spartylas," said my friend, pointing behind the shop up the towering side of Pantokrator, where, a few miles away, I could see a couple of vague lights which must mark another village. "He has been visiting in Kouloura, at the house of his uncle, and we heard him coming, and stopped him. See? It is a very good machine, as good as a car. You cannot stay here, this village is not good enough for a foreigner. But he will take you home."

I felt the tears of emotion, brought on by anxiety and sheer exhaustion, sting my eyes. "You are too good. You are too good. Thank you, thank you all."

It was all I could say, and it seemed to be all they could desire. The kindness and goodwill that surrounded me were as palpable as light and fire; they warmed the night.

Someone was bringing a cushion; it looked like the best one his house could offer. Someone else strapped it on. A third man thrust the bundle containing my damp frock into a carrier behind the saddle. The youth stood smiling, eying me sideways, curiously.

The telephone rang once, briefly, and I ran back.

"Yes?"

"Lucy. I got the Villa Rotha, but he's not there."

"No reply?"

"Well, of course not. Look, can't you tell me what all this is about?"

"Darling, I can't, not just now . . . I'll be home soon. Don't worry. But don't tell anyone I rang you up. *Anyone*. Not even Max."

"Not *even* Max? Since when did—"

"And don't bother to come for me, I've got transport. Be seeing you."

The shopkeeper refused to take money for the telephone. It was a pleasure, I gathered, a pleasure to be roused from his bed in the middle of the night by a half-drowned, incoherent stranger. And the men who had helped me would not even take my thanks; it was a privilege to help me, indeed it was. They sat me on the pillion, showed me where to put my feet and how to hang on to the young man's waist, wished me God-speed, and stood back as my new friend kicked the engine into an un-silenced roar that slashed through the village like Pandemonium itself. It must have woken every sleeper within miles. No doubt they would count this, also, as a privilege. . . .

We roared off with a jerk and a cloud of smoke. The road was rutted, surfaced with loose gravel, and twisted like a snake through the olive groves that skirted the steep cliffs, some three hundred feet above the sea. Not a fast road, one would have said—but we took it fast, heeling over on the bends as the *Aleister* had heeled to the seas, with gravel spurting out under our front wheel like a bow wave, and behind us a wake of dust half a mile long. I didn't care. The feel of the wind in my hair and the bouncing, roaring speed between my thighs were at once exciting and satisfying after the terrors and frustrations of the night. And I couldn't be afraid. This was—quite literally—the "god in the ma-chine" who had come to the rescue, and he couldn't fail me. I clung grimly to his leather-clad back as we roared along, the shadowy groves flicking past us in a blur of speed, and down—way down—on our left the hollow darkness of the sea.

The god turned his curly head and shouted something cheerfully. We shot round a bend, through a small stream, up something remarkably like a rough flight of steps, and met the blessed smooth camber of a metalled road.

Not that this was really an improvement: it swooped clean down the side of Pantokrator in a series of tight-packed hairpin bends which I suppose were steep and dangerous, but which we took at a speed that carried us each time to the very verge, where a tuft or so of daisies or a small stone would catch us and cannon us back on to the metal. The tires screeched, the god shouted gaily, the smell of burning rubber filled the night, and down we went, in a series of birdlike swoops which carried us at last to the foot of the mountain and the level of the sea.

The road straightened. I saw the god's hand move hopefully to the throttle.

"Okay?" he yelled over his shoulder.

"Okay!" I screamed, clinging like a monkey in a hurricane.

The hand moved. The night, the flying trees, the hedgerows ghostly with apple blossom, accelerated past us into a streaming blur. . . .

All at once we were running through a village I knew, and he was slowing down. We ran gently between walls of black cypress, past the cottage in the lemon grove, past the little tea garden with its deserted tables, under the pine, and up to the Castello gate, to stop almost between the pillars.

The youth put his feet down and turned inquiringly, jerking a thumb towards the drive, but I shook my head. It was a long walk up through the grounds of the Castello, but until I knew what was going on I certainly wasn't going to advertise my homecoming by roaring right up to the front door.

So I loosed my limpet catch from the leather jacket, and got rather stiffly off my perch, shaking out the pretty embroidered skirt and pulling my own bedraggled cotton dress from the carrier.

When I tried to thank my rescuer, he smiled and shook his head, wheeling the machine back to face the way we had come and shouting something, which, of course, must mean, "It was a pleasure."

As his hand moved on the controls I put mine out quickly to touch it.

"Your name?" I knew the Greek for that. "Your name, please?"

I saw him grin and bob his head. "Spiridion," he said. "God with you."

Next second he was nothing but a receding roar in the darkness and a cloud of dust swirling to settle in the road.

CHAPTER

TWENTY-ONE

ဒ&

Thou does here usurp
The name thou ow'st not; and hast put thyself
Upon this island, as a spy . . .

Act 1, Scene 2

There was no light in the Castello. The house loomed huge in the star-light, turreted and embattled and almost as romantic-looking as its builder had intended. I walked round it to the terrace, treading softly on the mossed tiles. No light there either, no movement, nothing. The long windows were blank and curtained, and—when I tried them—locked.

Keeping to the deepest shadows, I skirted the terrace till I reached the balustrade overhanging the cliff and the bay. The invisible sea whispered, and all round me was the dark, peppery smell of the cypresses. I could smell the roses, too, and there were bats about, cutting the silence with their thin, knife-edge cries. A movement caught my eye and made me turn quickly—a small slither of pale colour vanishing like ectoplasm through the stone balustrade and drifting downhill. The white cat, out on his wild lone.

Then I caught a glimpse of light. This came from somewhere beyond the trees to the right, where the Villa Rotha must lie. As softly as the white cat, and almost as silently as the ghost from the sea that I was, I crept off the terrace and padded down through the woods towards the light.

I nearly fell over the XK 150, parked among the trees. He must simply have driven her away from the house, so that a chance caller would assume he was out with the car and look no farther.

A few minutes later I was edging my way through the thicket of myrtle that overhung the bungalow.

This was, as I have said before, the twin of the Forli house. The main door, facing the woods, had a cleared sweep of driveway in front of it, and from this a paved path led round the house to the wide terrace overlooking the sea. A light burned over the door. I parted the leaves and peered through.

Two cars stood on the sweep, Max's big, shabby black Buick and a small car I didn't know.

So he was back, and it was battle stations. I wondered if the other car was the police.

My borrowed rope soles made no sound as I crept round towards the terrace, hugging the house wall.

The terrace, too, was the twin of Phyllida's, except that the pergola was covered with a vine instead of wistaria and there was no dining table, only a couple of large chairs and a low table which held a tray with bottles and glasses. I bypassed these quietly, making for the french windows.

All three were shut and curtained, but the centre one showed a gap between the curtains some three inches wide through which I could see the room; and as I reached it I realized that I would be able to hear as well. . . . In the glass beside the window catch gaped a big, starred hole where someone had smashed a way in. . . .

The first person I saw was Godfrey, near the window and to one side of it, sitting very much at his ease in a chair beside the big elmwood desk, with a glass of whisky in his hand. He was still dressed in the jersey and dark trousers, and over the back of his chair hung the navy duffel coat which I had torn free of before I went into the sea. I was delighted to see that one side of his face bore a really classic bruise, smeared liberally with dried blood, and that the good-looking mouth appeared to hurt him when he drank. He was dabbing at a swollen lip with his handkerchief.

The room had seemed at that first glance full of people, but the crowd now resolved itself into a fairly simple pattern. A couple of yards from Godfrey, in the middle of the floor and half turned away from me, stood Max. I couldn't see his face. Adoni was over beside the door, facing towards the windows, but with his attention also riveted on Godfrey. Near me and just to one side of my window was Spiro, sitting rather on the edge of a low chair, with the injured leg in its new white cast thrust out awkwardly in front of him, and Miranda crouched on the floor beside his chair, hugging its arm against her breast as (it seemed) she would have liked to hug Spiro's. The two faces were amazingly alike, even allowing for the difference of male from female; and at the moment the likeness was made more striking still by the expression that both faces shared: a pure, uncomplicated hatred, directed unwinkingly at Godfrey. On the floor beside the boy's chair lay a rifle, and from the way his hand hung near it, twitching from time to time, I guessed that only a forcible order from the police had made him lay it down.

For the police were here. Across the width of the room from Godfrey, and near the door, sat a man I recognized as the Inspector (I didn't know the Greek equivalent) from Corfu who had been in charge of the inquiry into Yanni's death. This was a stoutish, grey-haired man with a thick moustache and black, intelligent eyes. His clothes were untidy, and had obviously been hastily put on, and in spite of the deadpan face and calm, steady stare I sensed that he was not quite sure of his ground, even ill at ease.

Godfrey was speaking in that light, cool voice that I knew so well, so very well.

"As you wish, Mr. Papadopoulos. But I warn you that I'm not prepared to overlook what happened down in my boathouse, or the fact that these two men have apparently broken into my house. As for the girl, I'm not quite sure what it is that I'm supposed to have done with her, but I have given you a complete account of our movements this afternoon, and I'm sure you can find any number of people who will bear me out."

"It's your movements tonight that we're interested in." Max's voice was rough, and only precariously controlled. "For a start, what happened to your face?"

"An accident with the main boom," said Godfrey shortly.

"Another? Rather too common, these accidents, wouldn't you say? How did it happen?"

"Are you a yachtsman?"

"No."

"Then don't ask stupid questions." Godfrey gave him a brief, cold look. "You've had your turn, damn you. Back down. You've no more right to question me than you had to manhandle me or break in here to ransack the place. If you hadn't telephoned for the police, you can be very sure I'd have done so myself. We'll talk about your methods later."

Papadopoulos said heavily, "If you please, Max. Now, Mr. Manning, you have told us that you have not seen Miss Lucy Waring since shortly after seven this last evening, when you took her home?"

"That is so." To the Inspector his tone was one of tired but patient courtesy. He was playing his part to perfection. All his dislike of Max was there, patent through tonight's more immediate outrage, with weariness and puzzlement and a nice touch of worry about me. "I took her home before dinner. I myself had to go out again."

"And you have not seen her since?"

"How often must I—I'm sorry, Inspector, I'm a little tired. No, I have not seen her since."

"You have given us an account of your movements after you took Miss Waring home. Now, when you finally went down to take out your boat you found the boathouse still locked, and as far as you are aware, there was nobody there?"

"That is so."

"There was nothing to indicate that anyone—Miss Waring or anyone else—had been there, and gone again?"

I thought Godfrey hesitated, but it was barely perceptible. He must be very sure that he had sunk me without trace. "No."

"You heard what this girl had to say?"

"Miranda?" Godfrey's tone was not even contemptuous, merely lightly dismissive. "She'd say anything. She's got some bee in her bonnet over her brother, and she'd invent any tale to see me in trouble. Heaven knows why, or where the boy's got this incredible idea of his from. I've never been happier about anything in my life than I was to see him here tonight."

Spiro said something in Greek, one short, vicious-sounding phrase whose import there was no mistaking, and which drew a shocked glance from his sister. He made it clear. "I spit," he said, and did so.

"Spiro," said Max sharply, and Godfrey raised an eyebrow—a very civilized eyebrow—at the Inspector, and laughed.

"Satan rebuking sin? Always an amusing sight, don't you think?"

"I'm sorry," said Papadopoulos. "You will control yourself, Spiro, or you will go. Let us go back, Mr. Manning. You must excuse me, my English is not so very good; I do not follow this about Satan, and bees, was it? Bees in the bonnet?" He glanced up at Max, who hesitated, and Adoni snapped out some phrase in Greek. "I see." The stout man sat back. "You were saying?" This to Godfrey.

"I was saying that whatever Miranda accuses me of, the fact remains that she did not see Lucy Waring enter my boathouse or go near my boat. There is nothing to show that she did either."

"No. Well, Mr. Manning, we'll leave that for the moment. . . . Yes, Max, I know, but there is nothing more we can do until Petros gets up here from the boathouse and reports on his search there. He will be here before long. Meanwhile, Mr. Manning, with your permission, there are a few other questions I want to ask you."

"Well?"

"Forgetting about Miss Waring's movements for the moment, I should like to hear about yours . . . after you went down to your boat-house. When Mr. Gale met you on your return, and accused you—"

"Attacked me, you mean."

"As you wish. When he asked you where you had been, you told him this was a 'normal trip.' What do you mean by a 'normal trip,' Mr. Manning? Fishing, perhaps?"

Adoni said, without expression, "His cameras were in the cabin."

"So you were out taking photographs, Mr. Manning? May one know where?"

There was a short silence. Godfrey took a sip of whisky, then sat for a moment staring down at the glass, swirling the spirit round gently. Then he looked up, meeting the policeman's eyes, and gave a faint smile that had the effect of a shrug.

"I can see that I'll have to make a clean breast of it. I never thought you'd get on to me. If it hadn't been for this misunderstanding about the girl, I doubt if you would have. Or were you tipped off?"

There was no change in the Inspector's expression, but I saw Max stiffen, and Adoni was staring. Capitulation, when they hadn't even brought up a gun?

"If you please," said Papadopoulos courteously, "I do not understand. If you would use simpler English—"

"More idioms," said Adoni. "He means that he knows you've been told about him, so he's going to confess."

"I meant no such thing. Keep your pretty mouth shut, if you can. This is between men." Godfrey flung it at him without even a glance, indifferently, as one might swat a midge. Adoni's eyes went back to him, and his expression did not change, but I thought, with a queer jump of the heart, Your mistake, Godfrey. . . .

"Please," said Papadopoulos. "Let us not waste time. Well, Mr. Manning?"

Godfrey leaned back in his chair, regarding him coolly. You'd have thought there was nobody else in the room. "With your man down there searching my boat it's not much use pretending I have been taking photographs, is it? You have only to look at the cameras . . . No, as a matter of cold truth, I had business over the other side."

If the room had been still before, it was stiller now. I thought dazedly, He can't just confess like that. . . . Why? Why? Then I saw.

Miranda had told the police what she knew, and Godfrey realized now that she had been with me on the shore. I did not think that the cave or the packages had been mentioned yet in front of him, but he could guess that she had seen as much as I, and must have told the police about the packages. Moreover, a police constable was now searching the *Aleister*, and if he was even half good at his job he would find the cache under the cabin floor. I guessed that Godfrey was intent on getting some relatively harmless explanation in before the inevitable discovery was made.

"Whereabouts on the other side?" asked Papadopoulos.

"Albania."

"And the business?"

"Shall we call it 'importing'?"

"What you call it does not matter. This I understand perfectly." The Greek regarded him for a moment in silence. "So you admit this?"

Godfrey moved impatiently. "I have admitted it. Surely you aren't going to pretend you didn't know that this went on? I know you've shut your eyes to the way Yanni Zoulas was killed, but between ourselves—"

"Yanni Zoulas?" I saw Papadopoulos flash a glance at Max. Godfrey was taking the wind out of this sail, too, before it had even been hoisted.

"Ah," said Godfrey, "I see you understand me. I thought you would."

"You know something about Zoulas' death that you didn't tell the police?"

"Not a thing. I'm only guessing, from my own experiences with the coast guard system the other side. It's quite remarkably efficient."

"So you think he ran into trouble there?"

"I think nothing. I was only guessing. But guesses aren't evidence, are they?" The grey eyes touched Max's briefly. "I only mean that if one runs the gauntlet of those coasts often enough, it's not surprising if one gets hurt. What was surprising was that the police made so little of it. You must have known what he was doing."

"What was Zoulas' connection with you?"

"With me? None at all. I didn't know the man."

"Then how do you know this about him?"

Godfrey smiled. "In the trade, word goes round."

"He was not connected with you?"

"I've answered that. Not in any way."

Papadopoulos said, "It has been suggested that Spiro here, and after him Yanni Zoulas, discovered something about your business . . ."

I missed the rest. From somewhere behind me, below the terrace, came the moving flicker of a torch and the sound of footsteps. This would be the constable coming up from his search of the boathouse. I drew away from the lighted window, wondering if I should approach him now and tell him about the package I had sunk in the boathouse; then I remembered that he probably spoke no English. He passed below the end of the terrace, and trod gently round the house.

I tiptoed back to the window. It was just possible that the man had found the package, and if so, I might as well wait a little longer and hear what Godfrey's defence would be before I went in to blow it apart.

He had changed his ground, and was now giving a fine rendering of an angry man who has got himself in hand, but only just. He said, with controlled violence, "And perhaps you will tell me what in hell's name I could be doing that would drive me to wholesale murder?"

"I cannot," said Papadopoulos regretfully. "From what you are telling me of the type of goods you 'trade in,' I cannot. Radio parts, tobacco, antibiotics? And so on, and so on. The usual list, Mr. Manning. One wonders merely why it should have paid you. . . . The rent of this house, your boat, the trouble to make the contacts, the risks . . . You are not a poor man. Why do you do it?"

"Is it so hard to understand?" said Godfrey. "I was stuck here working on my damned book, and I was bored. Of course I don't need the money. But I was bored, and there was the boat, and the promise of a bit of fun with her . . ." He broke off, turning up a hand. "But do you really want all that tonight? Say I do it for kicks, and leave it at that. Apollo will translate."

Adoni said gently, "He means that he likes risks and violence for their own sakes. It is a phrase that irresponsible criminals use, and adolescents."

Max laughed. Godfrey's hand whitened on his glass. "Why, you little—"

"Markos!" Max broke across it, swinging round on the Greek. I saw his face for the first time. "None of this matters just now! I'm sorry, I realize that if this man's smuggling across the border it's very much your affair, but all that really matters here and now is the girl. If he insists that—"

"A moment," said Papadopoulos, and turned his head. Adoni put a hand to the door beside him and pulled it open, and the constable came into the room.

He had obviously not found the package, and apparently nothing else either, for when his superior barked a question at him he spread empty hands and shrugged, answering with a swift spate of Greek. Max asked another question in Greek, and the man turned to him, speaking volubly and with many gestures. But I no longer paid him any heed. As I had craned forward to see if the package was in his hands, I must have made some movement that caught Adoni's attention. I found myself meeting his eyes, clear across the room.

Nobody was looking at him; all eyes were for the newcomer, except Spiro's, whose flick-knife gaze never left Godfrey. Nobody seemed to notice as Adoni slipped quietly out through the open door, pulling it shut behind him.

I backed quickly away from the window, out of the fringe of light, and soft-footed my way back round the corner of the house.

A light step beside me in the darkness, and a whisper:

"*Miss Lucy!* Miss Lucy! I thought—I could not be sure—in those clothes. . . . But it is you! We thought you must be dead!" Somehow his arms were round me, quite unself-consciously hugging me to him. It was amazingly comforting. "Oh, Miss Lucy, we thought you had gone with that devil in his boat and been killed!"

I found myself clinging to him. "I did. I did go with him . . . and he did try to kill me, but I got away. I went overboard, like Spiro, and he left me to drown, but—*Adoni!* You mustn't say things like that! Where *did* you learn them? . . . No, hush, they'll hear you. . . ."

"We've got to get him now. We've got to make sure of him."

"We will, I promise you we will. I know all about it now, Adoni. It's not just Spiro and Yanni and me—he's a traitor and a paid spy, and I can prove it."

"So?" He let me go. "Come in now, Miss Lucy, there's no need to be afraid of him. Come in straight away. Max is half crazy, I thought he would kill him."

"Not for a minute. . . . No, wait, I *must* know what's happened. Can you tell me, very quickly? Those are the Corfu police, aren't they? Didn't anyone come from Athens?"

"No. The Athens people said that Max must bring Spiro home and go to the Corfu police in the morning. They said they would look into it, but I don't think they were much interested—they had their hands full after that Communist demonstration on Tuesday, and this is the affair of the Corfu people anyway. So Max and Spiro came back alone, and I met the ferry. I told Max about the cave and the boxes that were hidden there, and he was afraid to waste more time by going to the police then—it was eleven o'clock, and only the night man was on duty—so he decided to drive home quickly and go to the cave himself."

"Then you hadn't had my message from Miranda?"

"No. She telephoned the Corfu Bar, but I hadn't been in there. I'd gone to Dionysios' house, a friend of mine, and had supper there, and then we went to the Mimosa on the harbour, to wait for the ferry. They sent a boy running to look for me from the Corfu Bar, but he didn't find me. When we got to the Castello, Miranda was waiting for us, and after a time she remembered, and told us about you."

" 'After a time?' "

I heard the smile even through the whisper. "There was Spiro."

"Oh, Lord, yes, of course! She'd forget everything else. Well, I don't blame her. . . . Go on. She told you about me."

"Yes. I have never seen Max like that before. We ran down to the boathouse, he and I, but the boat was gone, and you. We searched there, and along the shore, and then went up to the Villa Rotha. It was locked, so Max broke the window, and we looked for you, but found nothing. So he got to the telephone, and got Mr. Papadopoulos at his home, and told him everything very quickly, and told him to bring Spiro and Miranda from the Castello as he came. Then Max and I went back to the boathouse to wait for Mr. Manning."

"Yes?"

"We waited for some time. Then we saw him coming, no engine, just the sail, very quiet. We stood in the shadow, just inside the doors, waiting. He did not come in through the doors, but just to the end of the jetty, and he berthed the boat facing the sea, then got out very quietly and tied her up, so we knew he meant to leave again soon. Then he came back along the jetty and into the boathouse." He stirred. "We took him, Max and I. He fought, but we had him. Then Max sent me to look in the boat for you, and when I got back Mr. Manning was pretending to be surprised and very angry, but Max just said, 'Where is she? Where's my girl?' and had him by the throat, and I thought he was going to kill him, and when Mr. Manning said he knew nothing Max said to me, 'Hurry up, Adoni, before the police get here. They won't like it.' "

"Won't like what?"

"What we would have done to make him talk," said Adoni simply. "But the police came then. Mr. Manning was very angry, and complained, and one could see that Mr. Papadopoulos was uncomfortable. We had to come up to the house. The other man stayed to search the boat. You saw him come back just now? He hasn't found anything, only the place under the deck where Mr. Manning had hidden the boxes. But you heard all that, didn't you?"

"Guessed it. It was in Greek."

"Of course. I forget. Well, that was all. Wait a moment." He vanished round the house wall, and in a few seconds materialized again beside me. A glass was pushed into my hand. "Drink this. There was some whisky on the terrace. You're cold?"

"No. Excited. But thanks all the same." I drank the spirit, and handed back the glass. I saw him stoop to put it down somewhere, then he straightened, and his hand closed over my arm. "What now, Miss Lucy? You said we could get him. Is this true?"

"Quite true. There's not time enough to tell you it all now, but I must tell you some of it—enough—just in case anything happens to me. . . . Listen." In a few brief sentences I gave him the gist of what Godfrey had told me. "So that's it. Athens can follow up his contacts, I suppose, and it should be possible to work out roughly where he'd go ashore, in the time it took him. They'll have to get on to Tirana straight away and find some way of stopping the stuff circulating. But that's not our concern. What we have to do now is to get the police to hold him, and hold him good and hard."

"What's your proof you said you had? Enough to make them listen?"

"Yes. I've got one of the boxes of currency. Yes, really. I dumped it off the platform in the boathouse, about halfway along the left side. I want you to go down and get it."

"Of course. But I'll go in with you first."

"There's no need. I'd rather you got the box safe. He knows I took it —he must know—and he'll have a good idea where I hid it. He's a dangerous man, Adoni, and if this should go wrong . . . I don't want to run any risks at all of his getting down there somehow and getting away, or of his having another shot at killing me if he thinks I'm the only one who knows where the box is. So we'd better not both be exposed to him at once. You must go and get it straight away."

"All right. Be careful of yourself."

"I'll do that. The swine had a gun. I suppose you took it?"

"Yes. And the police took it from us."

"Well, here we go." I took a shaky little breath. "Oh, Adoni . . ."

"You are afraid?"

"Afraid?" I said. "It'll be the entrance of my life. Come on."

The scene was unchanged except that the constable now stood in Adoni's place by the door. Godfrey had lit a cigarette, and looked once more at his ease, but still ruffled and irritated, like a man who has been caught out in some misdemeanour for which he will now have to pay a stiff fine. They had apparently got to the cave and the packages, which were, according to Godfrey, radio sets. He was explaining, wearily yet civilly, how the "sets" had been packed and stored.

I put a cautious hand in through the broken pane, and began to ease the window catch open. It moved stiffly, but without noise.

". . . But surely this can wait till morning? I've admitted to an offence, and I'm perfectly willing to tell you more, but not now—and certainly not in front of a bunch of amateurs and children who seem to be trying to pin a mass murder on me." He paused, adding in a reasonable voice, "Look, Inspector, if you insist, I'll come in to Corfu with you now, but if Miss Waring is genuinely missing, I really do think you should concentrate on her and leave my small sins till morning."

The Inspector and Max started to speak together, the former stolidly, the latter with passion and anger, but Miranda cried out suddenly for the first time, on a piercing note that drowned them both.

"He knows where she is! He has killed her! Do not listen to him! He has killed her! I know she went to the boat! He took her and killed her, as he tried to kill Spiro, my brother!"

"It is true," said Spiro violently. "As God watches me now, it is true."

"Oh, for God's sake," said Godfrey. He got abruptly to his feet, a man whose patience has suddenly given way. "I think this has gone on long enough. I've answered your questions civilly, Papadopoulos, but it's time this scene came to an end! This is my house, and I'll put up with you and your man if I have to, but I'm damned if I sit here any longer being yapped at by the local peasants. I suggest you clear them out of here, now, please, this minute, and Gale with them."

The catch was off. As the window yielded softly to my hand, I heard Max say, in a voice I hardly knew was his:

"Markos, I beg of you. The girl . . . there's no time. Give me five minutes alone with him. Just five minutes. You'll not regret it."

Papadopoulos' reply was cut off by a crash as Godfrey slammed the flat of his hand down on the desk and exploded.

"This is beyond anything! It's more, it's a criminal conspiracy! By God, Inspector, you'll have to answer for this! What the hell are you trying to do, the lot of you? Papadopoulos, you'll clear these people out of my house immediately, do you hear me? I've told you all I'm going to tell you tonight, and as for Lucy Waring, how often do I have to repeat that I took the damned girl home at seven and I haven't seen her since? That's the truth, I swear to God!"

No actress ever had a better cue. I pulled the window open, and went in.

CHAPTER TWENTY-TWO

Let us not burthen our remembrances with
A heaviness that's gone.

Act v, Scene 1

For a moment no one moved. I was watching Godfrey, and Godfrey alone, so I was conscious only of that moment's desperate stillness, then of exclamations and confused movement as Max started forward and Papadopoulos jerked out a restraining hand and gripped his sleeve.

I said, "I suppose you weren't expecting me, Godfrey?"

He didn't speak. His face had drained, visibly, of colour, and he took a step backwards, his hand seeking the edge of the desk. Down beside me I caught the flutter of a hand as Miranda crossed herself.

"Lucy," said Max hoarsely, "Lucy—my dear . . ."

The Inspector had recovered from his surprise. He sat back. "It is Miss Waring, is not? I did not know you for the moment. We have been wondering where you were." I noticed suddenly that Petros, the constable, had a gun in his hand.

I said, "I know. I'm afraid I've been listening, but I wanted to hear what Mr. Manning had to say; and I wanted to know what had happened since I left him an hour or so ago."

"By God," said Max, "we were right. Markos—"

"An hour ago, Miss Waring? He was out in his boat an hour ago."

"Oh, yes. I was with him. I must have gone overboard some way to the east of Kouloura, beyond the island."

"Ah . . ." said Spiro, his face blazing with excitement and satisfaction. There were exclamations, and I saw Petros move forward from the door, gun in hand. Godfrey hadn't spoken or moved. He was leaning on the desk now as if for support. He was very pale, and the bruised side of his face stood out blacker as the blood ebbed from the rest.

"Are we to understand—" began Papadopoulos.

Max said, "Look at his face. He tried to kill you?"

I nodded.

"*Max!*" cried Papadopoulas warningly. "Petros? Ah . . . Now, Miss Waring, your story, please, and quickly."

"Yes, of course, but there's something—something urgent—that I've got to tell you first."

"Well?" demanded the Inspector.

I opened my mouth to answer, but what I had to say was drowned by the sudden, strident ringing of the telephone. The sound seemed to rip the quiet room. I know I jumped, and I suppose everyone's attention flicked to the instrument for a split second. The constable, who held the gun, made an automatic move towards it as if to answer it.

It was enough. I hardly even saw Godfrey move, but in one lightning movement the hand that leaned on the edge of the desk had flashed an inch lower, flicked open a drawer, jerked a gun up, and fired, all in one movement as swift and fluid as the rake of a cat's paw. Like an echo, Petros' gun answered, but fractionally too late. His bullet smacked into the wall behind the desk, and then his gun spun smoking to the floor and skidded, scoring the polish, out of sight under the desk. Petros made some sound, clapped a hand to his right arm, and reeled back a pace, right into Max's path as the latter jumped forward.

Simultaneously with the crack of the gun Godfrey had leaped for the open window where I stood, two paces from him. I felt my arm seized and twisted up behind my back in a brutal grip as he dragged my body back against him as a shield. And a hostage. The gun was digging into my side.

"*Keep back!*"

Max, who was halfway across the room, stopped dead. Papadopoulos froze in the act of rising, his hands clamped to the arms of his chair. The constable leaned against the wall where Max's thrust had sent him, blood oozing between his fingers. The twins never moved, but I heard a little sobbing moan from Miranda.

I felt myself sway as my knees loosened, and the gun jabbed cruelly. "Keep on your feet, bitch-eyes," said Godfrey, "or I'll shoot you here and now. The rest of you listen. I'm going now, and the girl with me. If I'm followed, I don't have to tell you what'll happen to her. You've shown me how little I've got to lose . . . Oh, no, I'm not taking her with me . . . She's a damned uncomfortable companion on a boat. You can come down for her as soon as you hear me leave—not before. Understand? Do it before, and . . ." A movement with the gun completed the sentence, so that I cried out, and Max moved uncontrollably. "Keep your distance!" snapped Godfrey.

He had been slowly pulling me backwards toward the window as he spoke. I didn't dare fight, but I tried to hang against him like a dead weight.

Max said hoarsely, "He won't leave her alive, Markos. He'll kill her."

"It won't help him." I managed to gasp it somehow. "I told . . . everything . . . to Adoni. Adoni knows—"

"Shut your goddamned mouth," said Godfrey.

"You heard that?" said Max. "Let her go, blast your soul. You don't imagine you can get away with this, do you? Let her go!"

Papadopoulos said quickly, "If you do not hurt the girl, perhaps we will—"

"It will give me great pleasure," said Godfrey, "to hurt her very much." He jerked hard on my arm, and took a step towards the window. "Come along, you. Where's the pretty boy, eh? Where did he go?"

He stopped. We were full in the window. For a moment I felt his body grow still and rigid against mine, then he pulled me out of the shaft of light, backing up sharply against the window frame, with me swung round to cover him, and the gun thrust forward now beside my waist and nosing round in a half circle. Behind us, out on the dark terrace, something had moved.

Adoni . . . It was Adoni with the package, delivering it and himself neatly into the muzzle of Godfrey's gun.

The next second I knew I was wrong. There was the tinkle of glass, the splashing of liquid, and the sound of someone humming a tune. "'Come where the booze is cheaper,'" sang Sir Julian happily, helping himself to Godfrey's whisky. Then he saw us. The slurred and beautiful voice said cheerfully, "Hullo, Manning. Hope you don't mind my coming over? Saw the light . . . thought Max might be here. Why, Lucy, m'dear . . ."

I think I must have been half fainting. I have only the haziest recollection of the next minute or so. Sir Julian came forward, blinking amiably, with a slopping glass in one hand and the bottle still grasped in the other. His face had the gentle, foolish smile of someone already very drunk, and he waved the bottle at Godfrey.

"Helped myself, my dear Manning. Hope you don't mind?"

"You're welcome," said Godfrey shortly, and jerked his head. "Into the room."

Sir Julian seemed to have noticed nothing amiss. I tried to speak, and couldn't. Dimly I wondered why Max had made no sound. Then his father saw him. "Why, Max . . ." He paused as if a vague sense of something wrong was filtering through the fog of alcohol. His eyes came uncertainly back to Godfrey, peering through the shaft of light thrown by the window. "There's the telephone. Someone's ringing up." He frowned. "Can't be me. I thought of it, but came instead."

"Inside, you drunken old fool," said Godfrey, and dragged at my arm to pull me out past him.

Sir Julian merely smiled stupidly, raised the bottle in a wavering salute, and then hurled it straight at the light.

It missed, but only just. It caught the flex, and the light careened wildly up to the ceiling and swung down again, sending wild shadows lurching and flying up the walls, so that the ensuing maelstrom of action seemed like something from an old film, flickering drunkenly, and far too fast. . . .

Something white scraped along the floor . . . Spiro's cast, thrust hard against Godfrey's legs. Godfrey staggered, recovered as his shoulder met the window frame, and with an obscene little grunt in my ear, fired down at the boy. I felt the jerk of the gun against my waist and smelled the acrid tang of singeing cloth. He may have been aiming at Spiro, but the light still reeled as if in an earthquake, and off balance as I was, I spoiled his aim. The bullet hit the cast, which shattered. It must have been like a blow right across the broken leg. The boy screamed, rolling aside, with Miranda shrieking something as she threw herself down beside him.

I don't know whether I tore myself away, or whether Godfrey flung me aside, but suddenly I was free, my arm dropping, half broken, to my side. As I fell he fired again, and then something hit me, hurling me down and to the floor. Max, going past me in a silent, murderous dive for Godfrey's gun hand.

I went down heavily into the wreckage of the plaster cast. The place stank of whisky and cordite. The telephone still screeched. I was deafened, blinded, sobbing with pain. The two men hurtled backwards out on to the terrace, locked together in a struggle of grunting breaths and stamping feet. One of them trod on my hand as he passed. Papadopoulos thudded past and out, and Petros was on his knees nearby, cursing and groping under the desk for his gun.

Then someone's arms came round me, and held me tightly. Sir Julian reeked of whisky, but his voice was quite sober. "Are you all right, dear child?"

I nodded. I couldn't speak. I clung to him, flinching and shaking as the sound of the fight crashed round the terrace. It was impossible, in that diffused and rocking light, to see which man was which. I saw Papadopoulos standing near me, legs apart, the gun in his hand moving irresolutely as the locked bodies stamped and wrestled past him. Godfrey's gun spat again, and the metal table whanged. Papadopoulos yelled something, and the injured constable lurched to his feet and ran to the windows, dragging the curtains wide, so that the light poured out.

But already they were beyond the reach of it, hurtling back against the balustrade that edged the steep and tree-hung cliff. I saw them, dimly silhouetted against the sky. One of them had the other rammed back across the stone. There was a crack, a sound of pain. Sir Julian's breath whistled in my ear and he said "*Lord Almighty*," and I saw that the man over the stone was Max.

Beside us was a scraping sound and a harshly drawn breath. Spiro's voice said urgently, "*Koumbàre . . .*" and a hand thrust Sir Julian aside. The boy had dragged himself through the welter of broken plaster to the window, and lay on his belly, with the levelled rifle hugged to his cheek. I cried out, and Sir Julian shot a hand down and thrust the barrel lower. "*No! Wait!*"

From the locked and straining bodies over the balustrade came a curse, a sudden flurry of movement, a grunt. Max kicked up savagely, twisted with surprising force, and tore sideways and free. He lost his grip of Godfrey's gun hand, but before the latter could collect himself to use it Max smashed a blow at the bad side of his face, a cruel blow which sent Godfrey spinning back, to lose his balance and fall in his turn violently against the stone.

For two long seconds the men were feet apart. Beside me, Spiro jerked the rifle up and fired. I heard the bullet chip stone. Max, flinching back, checked for a vital instant, and in that instant Godfrey had rolled over the wide stone parapet in a sideways, kicking vault, and had dropped down into the bushes out of sight.

By all the laws he should have broken his back, or at least a leg, but he must have been unhurt. There was a series of slithering crashes as he hurled himself downhill, and then a thud as he jumped to the track.

I don't even remember moving, but I beat Papadopoulos and Miranda to Max's side as he hung, gasping, over the parapet.

"Are you hurt?"

"No." It was hardly a word. He had already thrust himself upright and was making for the shallow steps that led down from the terrace to the zigzag path.

Godfrey was visible below, a shadow racing from patch to patch of starlight downhill between the trees. Papadopoulos levelled his pistol across the parapet, then put it up again with an exclamation. For a moment I couldn't see why, then I realized that Adoni was on the branch of the zigzag path below Godfrey, and more or less in line with him. Godfrey hadn't seen him for the bushes in between.

But the boy must have heard the shots and the fracas up above, and now the thudding of Godfrey's racing steps must have warned him what was happening. He stopped. One moment he was there in the path, standing rigid, head up, listening, then the next he had melted into the shadow of the trees. Godfrey, unaware or uncaring, ran on and down.

Beside me, Miranda caught her breath. Papadopoulos was craning to see. Max had stopped dead at the head of the steps.

Godfrey turned the corner and ran down past the place where Adoni stood waiting.

Ran down . . . and past . . . and was lost to sight beyond the lower thicket of lime trees.

Miranda cried out shrilly, and Papadopoulos said incredulously, "He let him go."

I said quickly, "He has the evidence I sent him for. He had to keep it safely."

"He is a coward!" cried Miranda passionately, and ran for the steps.

Next moment Adoni emerged from the trees. I couldn't see if he had the package, but he was coming fast uphill. Max had started down the steps in what was now obviously a futile attempt to catch the fugitive, but Miranda flew past him, shrieking, and met Adoni head on, her fists beating furiously against his chest.

"Coward! Coward! Coward! To be afraid of that Bulgar swine! After what he did to your brother, to let him go? Coward! Woman! I spit on you, I spit! If I were a man I would eat his heart out!"

She tried with the last words to tear away and past him, but he caught and held her with one arm, whirling her aside with an almost absent-minded ease as he stepped full into Max's way and thrust the other arm across his chest, barring his path. As I ran down the steps and came up to them I heard, through Miranda's breathless and sobbing abuse, Adoni saying, quick and low, "No. No, Max. Wait. Wait and see."

Where there had been pandemonium before, now quite suddenly there was stillness. Max, at the boy's words, had stopped dead. The three of them looked like some group of statuary, the two men still, staring into each other's eyes, Adoni full in Max's path, looking in the starlight like Michael barring the gates of Paradise: the girl collapsed now and weeping against his side. At some time the telephone must have stopped ringing. Papadopoulos had run back to it and could be heard shouting urgently into it. Sir Julian must have gone to Spiro. The constable was starting down the steps, but slowly, because of his wound, and because it was so obviously too late. . . .

The last of the wind had died, and the air was still with the hush before dawn. We heard it all quite clearly, the slam of the boathouse door and the quick thud of running feet along the wooden platform. The pause as he reached the *Aleister* and tore her loose from her rope. He would be thrusting her hard away from the jetty. . . .

The sudden stutter of her motor was as loud as gunfire. There was a brief, racing crescendo as the *Aleister* leaped towards the open sea and freedom.

Then the sound was swallowed, shattered, blanked out in the great sheeted roar of flame as the sloop exploded. The blast hit us where we stood. The flames licked and flared over the water, and were gone. The echo of the blast ran up the cliff and beat from rock to rock, humming, before it died into the rustle of the trees.

Sir Julian was saying, "What happened? What happened?" and I heard a flood of breathless Greek from Spiro.

Papadopoulos had dropped the telephone and ran forward above us to the parapet.

"Max? What in hell's name happened?"

Max tore his eyes from Adoni. He cleared his throat, hesitating. I said shakenly, "I think I know. When I was on board I smelled gas. It's a terribly easy thing to do . . . leave a gas tap on by mistake in the galley, and then the gas leaks down and builds up under the deck boards. You don't notice it, but as soon as the engine fires, up she goes. I—I once saw it happen on the Norfolk Broads."

"Spiro was saying something about gas." He mopped his face. "My God, what a night. My God. I suppose it must have been . . . Had he been using the galley?"

"Not on the way out. It stands to reason, anyway, he'd have noticed the smell when he took the boxes out from under the deck if it had been really bad. No, he must have used it on the way home. When I took a box out myself the smell was pretty faint. Did you get the box, Adoni?"

"Yes."

"You got a box?" The Inspector's attention sharpened, diverted for a moment. "This is what you were going to tell us, eh? Is it a radio set?"

"It is not. It's a batch of forged currency, Inspector Papadopoulos, part of a cargo of seven hundred thousand Albanian leks that he took across tonight. I managed to steal one package and hide it in the boat-house before he—he took me. That's where Adoni's been. I sent him to collect it." I added, "I think that you may find that this—accident —has saved everybody a lot of trouble. I mean, if the Greeks had had to shoot him . . ."

I let the sentence hang. Beside me, Max and Adoni stood very still. The Inspector surveyed us for a moment, then he nodded.

"You may be right. Well, Miss Waring, I'll be with you again in a minute or two, and I'll be very glad to listen to you then. You have the box safe, young Adoni? . . . Good. Bring it up, will you? Now we'd better get down there and see if there's anything to pick up. Are you still on your feet, Petros?"

The two police vanished down the track. There was another silence. Everyone turned, as if impelled, and looked at Adoni. He met our eyes levelly, and smiled. He looked very beautiful. Miranda said, on a long, whispered note, "It was you. It was you," and sank down to the ground beside him, with her hand to her cheek and a face of shining worship lifted to his.

He looked down at her, and said something in Greek, a sentence spoken very tenderly. I heard Max take in a sharp little breath, and then he came to me and took me in his arms and kissed me.

Sir Julian was waiting for us on the terrace. We need not have been afraid that he would comment on what had just passed between his son and me. He was basking in a warm bath of self-congratulation.

"The performance of my life," he said complacently.

"It certainly was. It fooled me. Did you know he wasn't drunk?" I asked Max.

"Yes, I wasn't quite sure what he'd try on, but I thought it might break the situation our way. Which it did—but only just. You're a lousy shot, Father."

"It was the waste of good whisky. It put me off my stroke," said his father. "However, there was enough left in the glass to put Spiro under; I've got the poor child strapped up again, and flat out on the sofa in there. That'll be another trip to hospital as soon as it's light, I'm afraid. Oh, and I telephoned your sister, Lucy. I reassured her quite suc-cessfully. It's been quite a night, as they say."

"And not over yet by a damned long way," said Max, a little grimly. "I shan't get any rest till I've heard Lucy's story . . . No, it's all right, darling, we'll leave it till Markos gets back. You won't want to go through it all again for him. You must be exhausted."

"I think I've gone beyond that. I feel more or less all right . . . floating a bit, that's all." I went slowly to the parapet, and leaned there, gazing out over the dark sea. The dawn was coming: the faintest glimmer touched the far Albanian snows. "Do you suppose there'll be—anything —for them to find?"

"I'm sure there won't." He came to my side and slipped an arm round me. "Forget it. Don't let it haunt you. It was better this way."

"I know."

Sir Julian, at my other side, quoted: " 'Let us not burthen our remembrances with the heaviness that's gone.' And I may say, Max, that I have come to the conclusion that Prospero is not for me. A waste of talent. I shall set my sights at Trinculo for this film of ours. I shall write and tell Sandy so today."

"Then you're coming back to us?" I said.

"I shall hate it," said Sir Julian, "but I shall do it. Who wants to leave an enchanted island for the icy, damp, roaring, garish, glorious lights of London?"

Max said nothing, but I felt his arm tighten. Adoni and Miranda came softly up the terrace steps, heads bent, whispering, and vanished in through the french windows.

"Beatrice and Benedick," said Sir Julian softly. "I never thought to hear that magnificently Shakespearean outburst actually in the flesh, as it were. 'O God, that I were a man! I would eat his heart in the market-place.' Did you catch it, Lucy?"

"I didn't understand the Greek. Was that it? What did she actually say?" When he told me, I asked, "And Adoni? What was it he said when she was kissing his hand?"

"I didn't hear that."

Max glanced down at me, hesitated, and then quoted, rather dryly: " 'You wanted to eat his heart, little sister. I have cooked it for you.' "

"Dear heaven," I said.

Sir Julian smiled. "You've seen the other face of the enchanted isle tonight, haven't you, my poor child? It's a rough sort of magic for such as we are—a mere musician, and a couple of players."

"Much as I adore being bracketed with you," I said, "it's putting me too high."

"Then could you bear to be bracketed with me instead?" asked Max.

"Well, that is rather going to the other end of the scale," said his father, "but I'd be delighted if she'd give the matter some thought. Do you think, my dear, that you could ever consider dwindling as far as a musician's wife?"

I laughed. "I'm not at all sure who this proposal's coming from," I said, "but to either, or to both of you, yes."

Far out in the bay a curve of blue fire melted, rolled in a silver wheel, and was lost under the light of day.

THE IVY TREE

A north country maid up to London had stray'd,
  Although with her nature it did not agree;
She wept, and she sighed, and she bitterly cried:
  "I wish once again in the North I could be!
Oh! the oak and the ash, and the bonny ivy tree,
  They flourish at home in the North Country.

"No doubt, did I please, I could marry with ease;
  Where maidens are fair many lovers will come:
But he whom I wed must be North Country bred,
  And carry me back to my North Country home.
Oh! the oak and the ash, and the bonny ivy tree,
  They flourished at home in my own country."

                    Seventeenth Century Traditional.

CHAPTER

ONE

"Come you not from Newcastle?
    Come you not there away?
  Oh, met you not my true love?"

Traditional.

I might have been alone in a painted landscape. The sky was still and blue, and the high cauliflower clouds over towards the south seemed to hang without movement. Against their curded bases the fells curved and folded, blue foothills of the Pennines giving way to the misty green of pasture, where, small in the distance as hedge-parsley, trees showed in the folded valleys, symbols, perhaps, of houses and farms. But in all that windless, wide landscape, I could see no sign of man's hand, except the lines—as old as the ridge and furrow of the pasture below me —of the dry stone walls, and the arrogant stride of the great Wall which Hadrian had driven across Northumberland, nearly two thousand years ago.

The blocks of the Roman-cut stone were warm against my back. Where I sat, the Wall ran high along a ridge. To the right, the cliff fell sheer away to water, the long reach of Crag Lough, now quiet as glass in the sun. To the left, the sweeping, magnificent view to the Pennines. Ahead of me, ridge after ridge running west, with the Wall cresting each curve like a stallion's mane.

There was a sycamore in the gully just below me. Some stray current of air rustled its leaves, momentarily, with a sound like rain. Two lambs, their mother astray somewhere not far away, were sleeping, closely cuddled together, in the warm May sunshine. They had watched me for a time, but I sat there without moving, except for the hand that lifted the cigarette to my mouth, and after a while the two heads went down again to the warm grass, and they slept.

I sat in the sun, and thought. Nothing definite, but if I had been asked to define my thoughts they would all have come to one word.

England. This turf, this sky, the heartsease in the grass; the old lines of ridge and furrow, and the still older ghosts of Roman road and Wall; the ordered, spare beauty of the northern fells; this, in front of me now, was England. *This other Eden, demi-paradise. This dear, dear land.*

It was lonely enough, certainly. We had it to ourselves, I and the lambs, and the curlew away up above, and the fritillaries that flickered like amber sparks over the spring grasses. I might have been the first and only woman in it; Eve, sitting there in the sunlight and dreaming of Adam. . . .

"Annabel!"

He spoke from behind me. I hadn't heard him approach. He must have come quietly along the turf to the south of the Wall, with his dog trotting gently at heel. He was less than four yards from me when I whirled round, my cigarette flying from startled fingers down among the wild thyme and yellow cinquefoil that furred the lower courses of the Roman stones.

Dimly I was aware that the lambs had bolted, crying.

The man who had shattered the dream had stopped two yards from me. Not Adam; just a young man in shabby, serviceable country tweeds. He was tall, and slenderly built, with that whippy look to him that told you he would be an ugly customer in a fight—and with something else about him that made it sufficiently obvious that he would not need much excuse to join any fight that was going. Possibly it is a look that is inbred with the Irish, for there could be no doubt about this young man's ancestry. He had the almost excessive good looks of a certain type of Irishman, black hair, eyes of startling blue, and charm in the long, mobile mouth. His skin was fair, but had acquired that hard tan which is the result of weathering rather than of sunburn, and which would, in another twenty years, carve his face into a handsome mask of oak. He had a stick in one hand, and a collie hung watchfully at his heels, a beautiful creature with the same kind of springy, rapier grace as the master, and the same air of self-confident good breeding.

Not Adam, no, this intruder into my demi-Eden. But quite possibly the serpent. He was looking just about as friendly and as safe as a black mamba.

He took in his breath in a long sound that might even have been described as a hiss.

"So it is you! I thought I couldn't be mistaken! *It is you.* . . . The old man always insisted you couldn't be dead, and that you'd come back one day . . . and by God, who'd have thought he was right?"

He was speaking quite softly, but just what was underlying that very pleasant voice I can't quite describe. The dog heard it, too. It would be too much to say that its hackles lifted, but I saw its ears flatten momentarily, as it rolled him an upward, white-eyed look, and the thick collie-ruff stirred on its neck.

I hadn't moved. I must have sat there, dumb and stiff as the stones themselves, gaping up at the man. I did open my mouth to say something, but the quiet, angry voice swept on, edged now with what sounded (fantastic though it should have seemed on that lovely afternoon) like danger.

"And what have you come back for? Tell me that! Just what do you propose to do? Walk straight home and hang up your hat? Because if that's the idea, my girl, you can think again, and fast! It's not your grandfather you'll be dealing with now, you know, it's me . . . I'm in charge, sweetheart, and I'm staying that way. So be warned."

I did manage to speak then. In face of whatever strong emotion was burning the air between us, anything that I could think of to say could hardly fail to sound absurd. What I achieved at last, in a feeble sort of croak that sounded half paralyzed with fright, was merely, "I—I beg your pardon?"

"I saw you get off the bus at Chollerford." He was breathing hard, and the fine nostrils were white and pinched-looking. "I don't know where you'd been—I suppose you'd been down at Whitescar, blast you. You got on the Housesteads bus, and I followed you. I didn't want you to recognize me coming up through the field, so I waited to let you get right up here, because I wanted to talk to you. Alone."

At the final word, with its deliberately lingering emphasis, something must have shown in my face. I saw a flash of satisfaction pass over his. I was scared, and the fact pleased him.

Something, some prick of humiliation perhaps, passing for courage, helped me to pull myself together.

I said, abruptly, and a good deal too loudly, "Look, you're making a mistake! I don't—"

"*Mistake?* Don't try and give me that!" He made a slight movement that managed to convey—his body was as eloquent as his face—a menace as genuine and as startling as his next words. "You've got a nerve, you bitch, haven't you? After all these years . . . walking back as calm as you please, and in broad daylight! Well, here am I, too. . . ." His teeth showed. "It doesn't necessarily have to be midnight, does it, when you and I go walking at the edge of a cliff with water at the bottom? Remember? You'd never have come mooning up here alone, would you, darling, if you'd known I was coming too?"

This brought me to my feet, really frightened now. It was no longer imagination to think that he looked thoroughly dangerous. His astounding good looks, oddly enough, helped the impression. They gave him a touch of the theatrical which made violence and even tragedy part of the acceptable pattern of action.

I remember how steep, suddenly, the cliff looked, dropping sharply away within feet of me. At its foot Crag Lough stirred and gleamed under some stray breeze, like a sheet of blown nylon. It looked a long way down.

He took a step towards me. I saw his knuckles whiten round the heavy stick. For a mad moment I thought I would turn and run; but there was the steep broken slope behind me, and the Wall at my right, and, on the left, the sheer cliff to the water. And there was the dog.

He was saying sharply, and I knew the question mattered, "Had you been down to the farm already? To Whitescar? *Had* you?"

This was absurd. It had to be stopped. Somehow I managed to grab at the fraying edges of panic. I found my senses, and my voice. I said flatly, and still too loudly, "I don't know what you're talking about! *I don't know you!* I told you you'd made a mistake, and as far as I'm concerned you're also behaving like a dangerous lunatic! I've no idea who you think you're talking to, but I never saw you before in my life!"

He hadn't been moving, but the effect was as if I'd stopped him with a charge of shot. Where I had been sitting I had been half turned away from him. As I rose I had turned to face him, and was standing now only two paces from him. I saw his eyes widen in startled disbelief, then, at the sound of my voice, a sort of flicker of uncertainty went across his face, taking the anger out of it, and with the anger, the menace.

I followed up my advantage. I said, rudely, because I had been frightened, and so felt foolish, "And now will you please go away and leave me alone?"

He didn't move. He stood there staring, then said, still in that edged, angry tone that was somehow smudged by doubt, "Are you trying to pretend that you don't recognize me? I'm your cousin Con."

"I told you I didn't. I never saw you in my life. And I never had a cousin Con." I took a deep, steadying breath. "It seems I'm lucky in that. You must be a very happy and united family. But you'll excuse me if I don't stay to get to know you better. Good-bye."

"Look, just a minute—no, please don't go! I'm most terribly sorry if I've made a mistake! But, really—" He was still standing squarely in the path which would take me back to the farm track, and the main road. The cliff was still sheer to one side, and the water, far below us, smooth once more, glassed the unruffled sky. But what had seemed to be a dramatic symbol of menace towering between me and freedom had dwindled now simply into a nice-looking young man standing in the sunshine, with doubt melting on his face into horrified apology.

"I really am most desperately sorry! I must have frightened you. Good God, what on earth can you think of me? You must have thought I was crazy or something. I can't tell you how sorry I am. I, well, I thought you were someone I used to know."

I said, very drily, "I rather gathered that."

"Look, please don't be angry. I admit you've every right, but really— I mean, it's pretty remarkable. You could be her, you really could. Even now that I see you closely . . . oh, perhaps there are differences, when one comes to look for them, but—well, I could still swear—"

He stopped abruptly. He was still breathing rather fast. It was plain that he had indeed suffered a considerable shock. And, for all his apology, he was still staring at me as though he found it difficult to believe me against the evidence of his eyes.

I said, "And I'll swear too, if you like. I don't know you. I never did. My name isn't Arabella, it's Mary. Mary Grey. And I've never even been to this part of the world before."

"You're an American, aren't you? Your voice. It's very slight, but—"

"Canadian."

He said slowly, "*She* went to the States. . . ."

I said violently and angrily, "Now, look here—"

"No, please, I'm sorry. I didn't mean it!" He smiled then, for the first time. The charm was beginning to surface, now, through what I realized had been still a faint filming of disbelief. "I believe you, truly I do, though it gets more fantastic every minute I look at you, even with the foreign accent! You might be her twin. . . ." With an effort, it seemed, he dragged his uncomfortably intent stare from my face, and bent to caress the dog's ears. "Please forgive me!" The swift upward glance held nothing now but a charming apology. "I must have scared you, charging up like that and looming over you like a threat from the past."

"My past," I retorted, "never produced anything quite like this! That was some welcome your poor Prodigal was going to get, wasn't it? I—er, I did gather you weren't exactly going to kill the fatted calf for Arabella? You did say Arabella?"

"Annabel. Well, no, perhaps I wasn't." He looked away from me, down at the stretch of gleaming water. He seemed to be intent on a pair of swans sailing along near the reeds of the further shore. "You'd gather I was trying to frighten her, with all that talk."

It was a statement, not a question, but it had a curiously tentative effect. I said, "I did, rather."

"You didn't imagine I meant any of that nonsense, I hope?"

I said calmly, "Not knowing the circumstances, I have no idea. But I definitely formed the impression that this cliff was a great deal too high, and the road was a great deal too far away."

"Did you now?" There, at last, was the faintest undercurrent of an Irish lilt. He turned his head, and our eyes met.

I was angry to find that I was slightly breathless again, though it was obvious that, if this excessively dramatic young man really had intended murder five minutes ago, he had abandoned the intention. He was smiling at me now, Irish charm turned full on, looking, I thought irritably, so like the traditional answer to the maiden's prayer that it couldn't possibly be true. He was offering me his cigarette case, and saying, with a beautifully calculated lift of one eyebrow, "You've forgiven me? You're not going to bolt straight away?"

I ought, of course, to have turned and gone then and there. But the situation was no longer—if, indeed, it had ever been—dangerous. I had already looked, and felt, fool enough for one day: it would look infinitely more foolish now to turn and hurry off, quite apart from its being difficult to do with dignity. Besides, as my fright had subsided, my curiosity had taken over. There were things I wanted to know. It isn't every day that one is recognized—and attacked—for a "double" apparently some years dead.

So I stayed where I was, returned his smile of amused apology, and accepted the cigarette.

I sat down again where I had been before, and he sat on the Wall a yard away, with the collie at his feet. He was half turned to face me, one knee up, and his hands clasping it. His cigarette hung in the corner of his mouth, the smoke wisping up past his narrowed eyes.

"Are you staying near by? No, I suppose you can't be, or everyone would be talking. . . . You've a face well known in these parts. You're just up here for the day, then? Over here on holiday?"

"In a way. Actually I work in Newcastle, in a café. This is my day off."

"In *Newcastle?*" He repeated it in a tone of the blankest surprise. "You?"

"Yes. Why on earth not? It's a nice town."

"Of course. It's only that . . . well, all things considered, it seems odd that you should have come to this part of the world. What brought you up here?"

A little pause. I said abruptly, "You know, you still don't quite believe me. Do you?"

For a moment he didn't reply, that narrow gaze still intent through the smoke of the cigarette. I met it squarely. Then he unclasped his hands slowly, and took the cigarette out of his mouth. He tapped ash off it, watching the small gout of grey feathering away in the air to nothing.

"Yes. I believe you. But you mustn't blame me too much for being rude, and staring. It's a queer experience, running into the double of someone you knew."

"Believe me, it's even queerer learning that one *has* a double," I said. "Funnily enough, it's a thing one's inclined to resent."

"Do you know, I hadn't thought of that, but I believe you're right! I should hate like hell to think there were two of me."

I thought: and I believe *you*; though I didn't say it aloud. I smiled. "It's a violation of one's individuality, I suppose. A survival of a primitive feeling of—what can one call it—identity? Self-hood? You want to be *you*, and nobody else. And it's uncomfortably like magic. You feel like a savage with a looking glass, or Shelley seeing his *Doppelgänger* one morning before breakfast."

"Did he?"

"He said so. It was supposed to be a presage of evil, probably death." He grinned. "I'll risk it."

"Oh lord, not your death. The one that meets the image is the one who dies."

"Well, that is me. You're the image, aren't you?"

"There you are," I said, "that's just the core of the matter. That's just what one resents. We none of us want to be 'the image.' We're the thing itself."

"Fair enough. You're the thing itself, and Annabel's the ghost. After all, she's dead."

It wasn't so much the casual phrasing that was shocking, as the lack of something in his voice that ought to have been there. The effect was as startling and as definite as if he had used an obscene word.

I said, uncomfortably, "You know, I didn't mean to . . . I should have realized that talking like this can't be pleasant for you, even if you, well, didn't get on with Annabel. After all, she was a relative; your cousin, didn't you say?"

"I was going to marry her."

I was just drawing on my cigarette as he spoke. I almost choked over the smoke. I must have stared with my mouth open for quite five seconds. Then I said feebly, "Really?"

His mouth curved. It was odd that the lineaments of beauty could lend themselves to something quite different. "You're thinking, maybe, that there'd have been very little love lost? Well, you might be right. Or you might not. She ran away, sooner than marry me. Disappeared into the blue eight years ago with nothing but a note from the States to her grandfather to say she was safe, and we none of us need expect to hear from her again. Oh, I admit there'd been a quarrel, and I might have been—" a pause, and a little shrug—"well, anyway, she went, and never a word to me since that day. How easily do you expect a man to forgive that?"

You? Never, I thought. There it was once more, the touch of something dark and clouded that altered his whole face; something lost and uncertain moving like a stranger behind the smooth façade of assurance that physical beauty gives. No, a rebuff was the one thing he would never forgive.

I said, "Eight years is a long time, though, to nurse a grudge. After all, you've probably been happily married to someone else for most of that time."

"I'm not married."

"No?" I must have sounded surprised. He would be all of thirty, and with that exterior, he must, to say the least of it, have had opportunities.

He grinned at my tone, the assurance back in his face, as smoothly armoured as if there had never been a flaw. "My sister keeps house at Whitescar; my half-sister, I should say. She's a wonderful cook, and she thinks a lot of me. With Lisa around, I don't need a wife."

"Whitescar, that's your farm, you said?" There was a tuft of sea-pink growing in a crevice beside me. I ran a finger over its springy cushion of green, watching how the tiny rosettes sprang back into place as the finger was withdrawn. "You're the owner? You and your sister?"

"I am." The words sounded curt, almost snapped off. He must have felt this himself, for he went on to explain in some detail.

"It's more than a farm; it's 'the Winslow place.' We've been there for donkey's ages . . . longer than the local gentry who've built their park round us, and tried to shift us, time out of mind. Whitescar's a kind of enclave, older than the oldest tree in the park—about a quarter the age of that wall you're sitting on. It gets its name, they say, from an old quarry up near the road, and nobody knows how old those workings are. Anyway, you can't shift Whitescar. The Hall tried hard enough in the old days, and now the Hall's gone, but we're still there— You're not listening."

"I am. Go on. What happened to the Hall?"

But he was off at a tangent, still obviously dwelling on my likeness to his cousin. "Have *you* ever lived on a farm?"

"Yes. In Canada. But it's not my thing, I'm afraid."

"What is?"

"Lord, I don't know; that's my trouble. Country life, certainly, but not farming. A house, gardening, cooking—I've spent the last few years living with a friend who had a house near Montreal, and looking after her. She'd had polio, and was crippled. I was very happy there, but she died six months ago. That was when I decided to come over here. But I've no training for anything, if that's what you mean." I smiled. "I stayed at home too long. I know that's not fashionable any more, but that's the way it happened."

"You ought to have married."

"Perhaps."

"Horses, now. Do you ride?"

The question was so sudden and seemingly irrelevant that I must have looked and sounded almost startled. "Horses? Good heavens, no! Why?"

"Oh, just a hangover from your looking so like Annabel. That was her thing. She was a wizard, a witch I should say, with horses. She could whisper them."

"She could *what*?"

"You know, whisper to them like a gipsy, and then they'd do any blessed thing for her. If she'd been dark like me, instead of blonde, she'd have been taken for a horse-thieving gipsy's changeling."

"Well," I said, "I do know one end of a horse from the other, and on principle I keep clear of both. . . . You know, I wish you'd stop staring."

"I'm sorry. But I—well, I can't leave it alone, this likeness of yours to Annabel. It's uncanny. I *know* you're not her; it was absurd anyway ever to think she might have come back . . . if she'd been alive she'd have been here long since, she had too much to lose by staying away. But what was I to think, seeing you sitting here, in the same place, with not a stone of it changed, and you only changed a little? It was like seeing the pages of a book turned back, or a film flashing back to where it was eight years ago."

"Eight years is a long time."

"Yes. She was nineteen when she ran away."

A pause. He looked at me, so obviously expectant that I laughed. "All right. You didn't ask . . . quite. I'm twenty-seven. Nearly twenty-eight."

I heard him take in his breath. "I told you it was uncanny. Even sitting as close to you as this, and talking to you; even with that accent of yours . . . it's not really an accent, just a sort of slur . . . rather nice. And she'd have changed, too, in eight years."

"She might even have acquired the accent," I said cheerfully.

"Yes. She might." Some quality in his voice made me look quickly at him. He said, "Am I still staring? I'm sorry. I was thinking. I—it's something one feels one ought not to let pass. As if it was . . . meant."

"What *do* you mean?"

"Nothing. Skip it. Tell me about yourself. You were just going to. Forget Annabel; I want to hear about you. You've told me you're Mary Grey, from Canada, with a job in Newcastle. I still want to know what brought you there, and then up here to the Wall, and why you were on that bus from Bellingham to Chollerford today, going within a stone's throw of the Winslow land." He threw the butt of his cigarette over the cliff, and clasped both hands round the uplifted knee. All his movements had a grace that seemed a perfectly normal part of his physical beauty. "I'm not pretending I've any right to ask you. But you must see that it's an odd thing to accept, to say the least. I refuse to believe that such a likeness is pure chance. Or the fact that you came here. I think, under the circumstances, I'm entitled to be curious—" that swift and charming smile again—"if nothing else."

"Yes, of course I see that." I paused for a moment. "You know, you may be right; about this likeness not being chance, I mean. I don't know. My people did come from hereabouts, so my grandmother told me."

"Did they now? From Whitescar?"

I shook my head. "I never heard the name, that I remember. I was very little when Granny died, and she only knew what my great-grandmother told her, anyway. My own mother was never much interested in the past. I know my family did originally come from somewhere in Northumberland, though I've never heard Granny mention the name Winslow. Hers was Armstrong."

"It's a common name along the borders."

"So she said, and not with a very savoury history, some of them! Wasn't there an Armstrong once who actually lived just here, in the Roman Fort at Housesteads? Wasn't he a horse thief? If I could only 'whisper' horses like your cousin Annabel, you might suppose—"

"Do you know when your people left England?" he asked, not so much ignoring my red herring as oblivious of it. He seemed to be pursuing some very definite line of his own.

"I suppose in my great-grandfather's time. Would that be somewhere about the middle of the last century? About then, anyway. The family settled first at a place called Antigonish, in Nova Scotia, but after my father married, he—"

"What brought you back to England?" The singleness of purpose that seemed to be prompting his questions robbed the interruption of rudeness. Like an examiner, I thought, bringing the candidate back to the point. . . . Certainly his questions seemed to be directed towards some definite end. They had never been quite idle, and now they were sharp with purpose.

I said, perhaps a little warily, "What brings anyone over? My people are dead, and there was nothing to keep me at home, and I'd always wanted to see England. When I was little, Granny used to talk and talk about England. She'd never seen it, but she'd been brought up on her own mother's stories of 'home.' Oh yes, I heard all about 'bonny Northumberland,' and what an exciting city Newcastle was—I almost expected to see the sailing ships lying along the wharves, and the horse trams in the streets, she'd made it all so vivid for me. And Hexham, and Sundays in the Abbey, and the market there on Tuesdays, and the road along the Tyne to Corbridge, and the Roman Wall with all those lovely names—Castle Nick and Borcovicium and Aesica and the Nine Nicks of Thirlwall . . . I read about it all, too. I've always liked history. I'd always promised myself that some day I'd come over, maybe to visit, maybe—if I liked it—to stay."

"To stay?"

I laughed. "That's what I'd told myself. But I hadn't seen myself coming back quite like this, I'm afraid. I—well, I was left pretty badly off. I got my fare together, and enough to tide me over till I got a job, and that's my situation now. It sounds like the opposite of the usual story, doesn't it? Usually the lone wolf sets out to the New World to make his way, but I—well, I wanted to come over here. The New World can be a bit wearing when you're on your own, and—don't laugh—but I thought I might fit in better here."

"Because your roots are here?" He smiled at my look. "They are, you know. I'm sure I'm right. There must have been someone, some Winslow, way back in the last century, who went to Canada from here. Probably more than one, you know how it was then; in the days when everybody had thirteen children, and *they* all had thirteen children, I'm pretty sure that one or two Winslows went abroad to stay. Whitescar wouldn't have been big enough, anyway, and nobody would have got a look-in except the eldest son. . . . Yes, that's it, that explains it. Some Winslow went to Canada, and one of his daughters—your great-grandmother, would it be?—married an Armstrong there. Or something like that. There'll be records at Whitescar, surely? I don't know, I wasn't brought up there. But that must be it."

"Perhaps."

"Well," he said, with that charmingly quizzical lift of the eyebrow that was perhaps just a little too well practiced, "that does make us cousins, doesn't it?"

"Does it?"

"Of course it does. It's as plain as a pikestaff that you must be a Winslow. Nothing else would account for the likeness; I refuse to believe in pure chance. You're a type, the Winslow type, it's unmistakable —that fair hair, and your eyes that queer colour between green and grey, and those lovely dark eyelashes. . . ."

"Carefully darkened," I said calmly. "After all, why go through life with light lashes if you don't have to?"

"Then Annabel's must have been darkened, too. By heaven, yes, they were! I remember now, when I first came to Whitescar she'd be only fifteen, and I suppose she hadn't started using that sort of thing. Yes, they were light. I don't even remember when the change took place! I was only nineteen when I came, you know, and straight from the back of beyond. I just took her for granted as the most beautiful girl I'd ever seen."

He spoke, for once, quite simply. I felt myself going scarlet, as if the tribute had been aimed at me. As, in a way, it was.

I said, to cover my embarrassment, "You talk of me as being a 'Winslow type.' Where do you come in? You don't seem to conform."

"Oh, I'm a sport." The white teeth showed. "Pure Irish, like my mother."

"Then you are Irish? I thought you looked it. Is Con short for Connor?"

"Sure. She was from Galway. I've her colouring. But the good looks come from the Winslows. We're all beauties."

"Well, well," I said drily, "it's a pity I haven't a better claim, isn't it?" I stubbed out my cigarette on the stone beside me, then flicked the butt out over the cliff's edge. I watched the place where it had vanished for a moment. "There is . . . one thing. Something I do remember, I think. It came back as we were talking. I don't know if it means anything. . . ."

"Yes?"

"It was just—I'm sure I remember Granny talking about a forest, some forest near Bellingham. Is there something near your 'Winslow place,' perhaps, that—?"

"Forrest!" He looked excited. "Indeed there is! You remember I told you that Whitescar was a kind of enclave in the park belonging to the local bigwigs? That's Forrest Park; the Park's really a big tract of land enclosed in a loop of the river, almost an island. The whole place is usually just spoken of as 'Forrest'—and the Forrests, the family, were there for generations. It was all theirs, except the one piece by the river, in the centre of the loop; that's Whitescar. I told you how they tried to winkle us out of it. The big house was Forrest Hall."

"Was? Oh, yes, you said the Hall had 'gone.' What happened? Who were they? This does sound as if my great-grandmother, at any rate, may have come from hereabouts, doesn't it?"

"It certainly does. I knew it couldn't be sheer chance, that likeness. Why, this means—"

"Who were the Forrests? Could she have known the family? What happened to them?"

"She'd certainly have known them if she lived at Whitescar. The family wasn't an especially old one, merchant adventurers who made a fortune trading with the East India Company in the seventeenth century, then built the Hall and settled down as landed gentry. By the middle of the nineteenth, they'd made another fortune out of railway shares. They extended their gardens, and did a spot of landscaping in the park, and built some rather extravagant stables, the last owner ran it as a stud at one time, and did their damnedest to buy the Winslows out of Whitescar. They couldn't, of course. Another cigarette?"

"No, thank you."

He talked on for a few minutes more about Whitescar and Forrest; there had been in no sense, he said, a feud between the families, it was only that the Winslows had held their small parcel of excellent land for generations, and were fiercely proud of it, and of their position as yeomen farmers independent of the family at the Hall, which, in its palmy days, had managed to acquire all the countryside from Darkwater Bank to Greenside, with the single exception of Whitescar, entrenched on its very doorstep.

"Then, of course, with the mid-twentieth century, came the end, the tragic Fall of the House of Forrest." He grinned. It was very evident that, whatever tragedy had touched the Hall, it didn't matter a damn if it hadn't also touched Whitescar. "Even if the Hall hadn't been burned down, they'd have had to give it up. Old Mr. Forrest had lost a packet during the slump, and then after his death, what with taxes and death duties—"

"It was burned down? What happened? When you said 'tragic,' you didn't mean that anyone was *killed?*"

"Oh, lord, no. Everyone got out all right. There were only the Forrests themselves in the house, and the couple who ran the garden and house between them, Johnny Rudd and his wife, and old Miss Wragg who looked after Mrs. Forrest. But it was quite a night, believe me. You could see the flames from Bellingham."

"I suppose you were there? It must have been awful."

"There wasn't much anyone could do. By the time the fire brigade could get there the place was well away." He talked about the scene for a little longer, describing it quite graphically, then went on: "It had started in Mrs. Forrest's bedroom, apparently, in the small hours. Her poodle raised the place, and Forrest went along. The bed was alight by that time. He managed to drag the bedclothes off her—she was unconscious—and carry her downstairs." A sideways look. "They were damned lucky to get the insurance paid up, if you ask me. There was talk of an empty brandy bottle in her room, and sleeping pills, and of how there'd been a small fire once before in her bedroom, and Forrest had forbidden Miss Wragg to let her have cigarettes in her room at night. But there's always talk when these things happen—and heaven knows there'd been enough gossip about the Forrests . . . of every sort. There always is, when a couple doesn't get on. I always liked him, so did everybody else for that matter, but the old woman, Miss Wragg, used to blackguard him right and left to anyone who'd listen. She'd been Crystal Forrest's nurse, and had come to look after her when she decided to be a chronic invalid, and she had a tongue like poison."

"Decided to be—that's an odd way of putting it."

"Believe me, Crystal Forrest was a damned odd sort of woman. How any man ever—oh, well, they say he married her for her money anyway. Must have, if you ask me. If it was true, he certainly paid for every penny of it that he'd put into that stud of his, poor devil. There can't have been much money, actually, because I know for a fact that when they left England after the fire they lived pretty much on the insurance, and on what he'd got for the horses. They went to live in Florence—bought a small villa there, but then she got worse, went right round the bend, one gathers, and he took her off to some man in Vienna. Till she died, two years ago, she'd been in one psychiatric clinic after another—or whatever is the fashionable name for the more expensive loony bins—in Vienna, and that had taken everything. When Forrest got back from Austria eventually, to finish selling up here, there was nothing left."

"He's back, then?"

"No, he's not here now. He only came over to sell the place. The Forestry Commission have the park land, and they've planted the lot, blast them. That's the whole point. If I'd been able to lay my hands on a bit—" He broke off.

"The whole point?"

"Skip it. Where was I? Oh, yes. The Hall's gone completely, of course, and the gardens are running wild. But the Rudds—they were the couple who used to work at the Hall—the Rudds have moved across to the other side of the Park, where the West Lodge and the stables are. Johnny Rudd runs the place now as a sort of small holding, and when Forrest was over here last year, he and Johnny got the old gardens going again, as a market garden, and I believe it's doing quite well. Johnny's running it now, with a couple of local boys."

He was gazing away from me as he talked, almost dreamily, as if his attention was not fully on what he was saying. His profile was as handsome as the rest of him, and something about the way he lifted his chin and blew out a long jet of smoke told me that he knew it, and knew I was watching him, too.

"And Mr. Forrest?" I asked, idly. "Does he live permanently in Italy now?"

"Mm? Italy? Yes, I told you, he has this place near Florence. He's there now, and the place is abandoned to Johnny Rudd, and the Forestry Commission . . . and Whitescar." He turned his head. The long mouth curved with satisfaction. "Well? How's that for a dramatic story of your homeland, Mary Grey? The Fall of the House of Forrest!" Then, accusingly, as I was silent, "You weren't even listening!"

"Oh, I was. I was, really. You made a good story of it."

I didn't add what I had been thinking while I watched him; that he had told the dreary, sad little tale—about a man he liked—with rather less feeling and sympathy than there would have been in a newspaper report; had told it, in fact, as if he were rounding off a thoroughly satisfactory episode. Except, that is, for that one curious remark about the Forestry Commission's planting programme.

He had also told it as if he had had no doubt of my own absorbed interest in every detail. I wondered why.

If I had some suspicion of the answer, I wasn't prepared to wait and see if I was right. I looked round me for my handbag.

He said quickly, "What is it?"

The bag was on the ground at the foot of the Wall. I picked it up. "I'll have to go now. I'd forgotten the time. My bus—"

"But you can't go yet! This was just getting exciting! If your great-grandmother knew about Forrest, it might mean—"

"Yes, I suppose it might. But I'll still have to go. We work Sunday evenings at my café." I got to my feet. "I'm sorry, but there it is. Well, Mr. Winslow, it's been interesting meeting you, and I—"

"Look, you can't just go like this!" He had risen too. He made a sudden little movement almost as if he would have detained me, but he didn't touch me. The rather conscious charm had gone from his face. He spoke quickly, with a kind of urgency. "I'm serious. Don't go yet. My car's here. I can run you back."

"I wouldn't think of letting you. No, really, it's been—"

"Don't tell me again that it's been 'interesting.' It's been a hell of a lot more than that. It's been important."

I stared at him. "What *do* you mean?"

"I told you. This sort of thing isn't pure chance. I tell you, it was meant."

"Meant?"

"Ordained. Destined. Kismet."

"Don't be absurd."

"It's not absurd. This thing that's happened, it's more than just queer. We can't simply walk away in opposite directions now and forget it."

"Why not?"

"*Why not?*" He said it almost explosively. "Because—oh, hell, I can't explain, because I haven't had time to think, but at any rate tell me the address of this place where you work." He was searching his pockets while he spoke, and eventually produced a used envelope and a pencil. When I didn't answer, he looked up sharply. "Well?"

I said slowly, "Forgive me, I can't explain either. But . . . I'd rather not."

"What d'you mean?"

"Just that I would rather—what did you say?—that we walked away in opposite directions now, and forgot all about it. I'm sorry. Please try to understand."

"I don't even begin to understand! It's perfectly obvious to me that this likeness of yours to Annabel Winslow *isn't* pure chance. Your people came from hereabouts. I wasn't only joking when I said we were long-lost cousins."

"Possibly we are. But can't you grasp this? Let me be blunt. Whitescar and Winslows and all the rest may mean a lot to you, but why should they mean anything to me? I've been on my own a good long time now, and I like it that way."

"A job in a café? Doing what? Waiting on tables? Cash desk? Washing up? *You*? Don't be a fool!"

"You take this imaginary cousinship a bit too much for granted, don't you?"

"All right. I'm sorry I was rude. But I meant it. You can't just walk away and—after all, you told me you were nearly broke."

I said, after a pause, "You—you take your family responsibilities very seriously, don't you, Mr. Winslow? Am I to take it you were thinking of offering me a job?"

He said slowly, "Do you know, I might, at that. I . . . might." He laughed suddenly, and added, very lightly, "Blood being thicker than water, Mary Grey."

I must have sounded as much at a loss as I felt. "Well it's very nice of you, but really . . . you can hardly expect me to take you up on it, can you, even if our families *might* just possibly have been connected a hundred years or so ago? No, thanks very much, Mr. Winslow, but I meant what I said." I smiled. "You know, you can't have thought. Just what sort of a sensation would there be if I did turn up at Whitescar with you? Had you thought of *that?*"

He said, in a very strange voice, "Oddly enough, I had."

For a moment our eyes met, and held. I had the oddest feeling that for just those few seconds each knew what the other was thinking.

I said abruptly, "I must go. Really. Please, let's leave it at that. I won't annoy you by telling you again that it's been interesting. It's been—quite an experience. But forgive me if I say it's one I don't want to take any further. I mean that. Thank you for your offer of help. It was kind of you. And now this really is good-bye."

I held out my hand. The formal gesture seemed, in these surroundings, and after what had passed, faintly absurd, but it would, I hoped, give the touch of finality to the interview, and provide the cue on which I could turn my back and leave him standing there.

To my relief, after a moment's hesitation, he made no further protest. He took the hand quite simply, in a sort of courteous recognition of defeat.

"Good-bye, then, Mary Grey. I'm sorry. All the best."

As I left him I was very conscious of him standing there and staring after me.

CHAPTER

TWO

"Or take me by the body so meek,
  Follow, my love, come over the strand—
And throw me in the water so deep,
  For I darena go back to Northumberland."
                    Ballad: *The Fair Flower of Northumberland.*

When the knock came at my bedroom door, I knew who it was, even before I looked up from my packing.

My landlady, Mrs. Smithson, was out; but even without this knowledge I could never have mistaken the tentative, even nervous quality of this knock, for Mrs. Smithson's forthright rapping. As clearly as if the thick, shiningly varnished door were made of glass, I could see who stood there; the stodgy, brown-clad woman who, for the past three evenings, had haunted the Kasbah Coffee House, staring at me as if her life depended on memorizing everything about me—"as if," one of the girls at the Espresso counter had said, "she was a talent scout looking for a new film star." Or as if (I said to myself) she thought that perhaps she recognized me, and was trying to nerve herself to speak. . . .

With the recent encounter on the Roman Wall still fresh in my mind, I had, in my turn, watched her a little wearily. Though I had never, to my knowledge, seen her before, there was about her something that was faintly familiar, and also (though I had no idea why) disturbing.

Outwardly, there was nothing in her appearance to alarm anyone. She could have been anything between thirty-five and forty. She wore goodish, but badly chosen country clothes and a minimum of make-up —powder, I guessed, and a touch of lipstick which did little to lighten the dull, rather heavy features. The general effect of dullness was not helped by the browns and fawns of the colour scheme she affected. Her hair under the slightly out-of-date felt hat was dark, and worn plainly in a bun. Her eyebrows were thick and well-marked, but untidy looking over badly set eyes. The outer corners of brows, eyes and mouth were pulled down slightly, giving the face its heavy, almost discontented expression. One got the curious impression that the woman only just missed being good-looking; that the features were somehow blurred and ill-defined, as if they had been drawn conventionally enough, and then the artist had smoothed a light, dry hand carelessly down over the drawing, dragging it just that fraction out of focus. She could have been a bad copy of a portrait I already knew; a print blotted off some dramatically sharp sketch that was vaguely familiar.

But even as I tried to place the impression, it slid away from me. I had never, to my recollection, seen her before. If I had, I would scarcely have noticed her, I thought. She was the kind of woman whom, normally, one wouldn't have looked at twice, being at first sight devoid of any of the positive qualities that go to make up that curious thing called charm. Charm presupposes some sort of vivacity and spark, at least what one might call some gesture of advance towards life. This woman merely sat there, heavily, apparently content to wait while life went on around her.

Except for the tireless stare of those toffee-brown eyes . . .

She had left the café at last, without speaking, and I had dismissed her with a mental shrug. But the next day, Tuesday, she was there again. And the next, still watching me steadily and disconcertingly from under the brim of the brown hat, until finally, in a moment of exasperation, I had gone over towards her table, intending to speak to her.

She had watched me coming, without moving, but in her heavy face a sudden spark of animation showed, momentarily lighting the plain features. . . .

I saw it then, the likeness that had troubled me; the poorish copy of that dramatically handsome face, the sepia print of Connor Winslow's Glorious Technicolour. "*My half-sister keeps house at Whitescar,*" he had said. "*With Lisa around, I don't need a wife*" . . . She would be some half-dozen years older than he, with the different colouring she had probably got from her Irish father, and none of the good looks that his Winslow blood had given Connor; but the likeness, ill-defined, shadowy, a characterless travesty of his vivid charm, was there.

I had walked straight by her table without pausing, out through the swing doors into the café kitchen, and had handed in my notice then and there.

And now, the same evening, here she was, at my door. It could be no one else. How she had found me out, why she had followed me, I could only guess. I hadn't heard her come upstairs, though the bare and echoing linoleum of the two flights to my room was a more than sufficient herald of approach. She must have come up very softly.

I hesitated. She must know I was here. I had seen no reason for silence, and the light would be showing under my door.

As the soft, insistent rapping came again, I threw a swift look round the room.

The ash tray by the bed, almost full . . . the bed itself, disordered, evidence of the time spent smoking and staring at the fly-spotted ceiling and wondering at myself and the impulse of panic which had driven me from the café, and even to consider leaving my lodgings. My cases stood, half-filled, in the middle of the floor.

Well, it was too late to do anything about them now. But there, on the table near the window, was a still more cogent witness to the impact that my meeting with Connor Winslow had had on me. The telephone directory, borrowed from downstairs, lay open at the page headed: "Wilson—Winthorpe. . . ."

I went silently across the room, and shut it. Then I turned back to the dresser and pulled open a drawer.

I said, on a note of inquiry, "Yes? Come in."

When the door opened, I had my back to it, lifting clothes out of the drawer. "Oh, Mrs. Smithson," I began, as I turned, then stopped short, my brows lifted, my face registering, I hoped, nothing but surprise.

She said, standing squarely in the doorway, "Miss Grey?"

"Yes? I'm afraid—" I paused, and let recognition dawn, and with it puzzlement. "Wait a moment. I think—don't I know your face? You were in the Kasbah this afternoon, the café where I work, weren't you? I remember noticing you in the corner."

"That's right. My name's Dermott, Lisa Dermott." She pronounced the name Continental-fashion, *Leeza*. She paused to let it register, then added, "From Whitescar."

I said, still on that puzzled note, "How do you do, Miss—Mrs.?— Dermott. Is there something I can do for you?"

She came into the room unasked, her eyes watchful on my face. She shut the door behind her, and began to pull off her plain, good hogskin gloves. I stood there without moving, my hands full of clothes, plainly intending, I hoped, not to invite her to sit down.

She sat down. She said flatly, "My brother met you up on the Roman Wall beyond Housesteads on Sunday."

"On the Ro—oh, yes, of course I remember. A man spoke to me.

Winslow, he was called, from somewhere near Bellingham." *Careful now, Mary Grey; don't overplay it; she'll know you'd not be likely to forget a thing like that.* I added slowly, "Whitescar. Yes. That's where he said he came from. We had a rather—odd conversation."

I put the things I was holding back into the drawer, and then turned to face her. There was a packet of Players in my handbag lying beside me on the dresser. I shook one loose. "Do you smoke?"

"No, thank you."

"D'you mind if I do?"

"It's your own room."

"Yes." If she noticed the irony she gave no sign of it. She sat there solidly, uninvited, in the only chair my wretched little room boasted, and set her handbag down on the table beside her. She hadn't taken her eyes off me. "I'm Miss Dermott," she said. "I'm not married. Con Winslow's my half-brother."

"Yes, I believe he mentioned you. I remember now."

"He told me all about *you*," she said. "I didn't believe him, but he was right. It's amazing. Even given the eight years, it's amazing. I'd have known you anywhere."

I said, carefully, "He told me I was exactly like a young cousin of his who'd left home some eight years ago. She had an odd name, Annabel. Is that right?"

"Quite right."

"And you see the same resemblance?"

"Certainly. I didn't actually know Annabel herself. I came to Whitescar after she'd gone. But the old man used to keep her photographs in his room, a regular gallery of them, and I dusted them every day, till I suppose I knew every expression she had. I'm sure that anyone who knew her would make the same mistake as Con. It's uncanny, believe me."

"It seems I must believe you." I drew deeply on my cigarette. "The 'old man' you spoke of . . . would that be Mr. Winslow's father?"

"His great-uncle. He was Annabel's grandfather."

I had been standing by the table. I sat down on the edge of it. I didn't look at her; I was watching the end of my cigarette. Then I said, so abruptly that it sounded rude, "So what, Miss Dermott?"

"I beg your pardon?"

"It's an expression we have on our side of the Atlantic. It means, roughly, all right, you've made your point, now where is it supposed to get us? You say I'm the image of this Annabel of yours. Granted, I'll accept that. You and Mr. Winslow have gone to a lot of trouble to tell me so. I repeat: so what?"

"You must admit—" she seemed to be choosing her words—"that we were bound to be interested, terribly interested?"

I said bluntly, "You've gone a little beyond 'interest,' haven't you? Unless, of course, you give the word its other meaning."

"I don't follow you."

"No? I think you do. Tell me something frankly, please. Does your brother still persist in thinking that I might *actually be* Annabel Winslow?"

"No. Oh, no."

"Very well. Then you have to admit that this 'interest' of yours does go far beyond mere curiosity, Miss Dermott. He might have sent you to take a look at me, Annabel's double, once, but not more than—" I caught myself in time—"not more than that. I mean, you'd have hardly followed me home. No, you're 'interested' in quite another sense, aren't you?" I paused, tapped ash into the wastebasket, and added, " 'Interested parties,' shall we say? In other words, you've something at stake."

She sounded as calm as ever. "I suppose it's natural for you to be so hostile." There was the faintest glimmer of a smile on her face: perhaps not so much a smile, as a lightening of the stolidity of her expression. "I don't imagine that Con was exactly, well, tactful, to start with . . . He upset you, didn't he?"

"He frightened me out of my wits," I said frankly. I got up from the table, and moved restlessly to the window. The curtains were undrawn. Outside, the lights and clamour of the street made a pattern two stories below, as remote as that of a coastal town seen from a passing ship. I turned my back on it.

"Look, Miss Dermott, let me be plain, please. Certain things are obvious to me, and I don't see any advantage in playing stupid about them. For one thing, I don't want to prolong this interview. As you see, I'm busy. Now, your brother was interested in me because I look like this Annabel Winslow. He told you about me. All right. That's natural enough. But it isn't just pure coincidence that brought you to the Kasbah, and I know darned well I never told him where I worked. It sticks out a mile that he followed me home on Sunday, and either he came here and asked someone where I worked, or he saw me go on for the late Sunday shift at the café, and then went back and told you. And you came next day to have a look at me . . . yes, I admit I did see you before today. How could I help noticing you, the way you stared?

Well, no doubt he and you had a talk about it, and today you've followed me home. Am I right?"

"More or less."

"I told you I was being frank, Miss Dermott. I don't like it. I didn't like the way your brother talked to me on Sunday, and I don't like being watched, and I'm damned if I like being followed."

She nodded calmly, as if I had said something a little pettish, but fairly reasonable. "Of course you don't. But if you'll just be a little patient with me, I'll explain. And I'm sure you'll be interested then. . . ."

All this time she had been watching me, and there was some quality about her steady gaze that I associated with something I couldn't place. It made me feel uncomfortable, and I wanted to look away from her. Con Winslow had had the same look, only his had held a frankly male appraisal that made it more understandable, and easier to face.

She looked away at last. Her gaze shifted from me to the appointments of the shabby little room; the iron bedstead, the garish linoleum, the varnished fireplace with its elaborately ugly overmantel, the gas ring on the cracked tiles of the hearth. She looked further, as if wondering, now, whether something of me, personally, was anywhere superimposed on the room's characterless ugliness. But there were no photographs, and what books I had had with me were packed. The questing look came to rest, defeated, on the clothes untidily hanging from the drawer I had been emptying, on the handbag I had pulled open to get my cigarettes, from which had spilled a lipstick, a pocket comb, and a small gold cigarette lighter whose convoluted initials caught the light quite clearly: M.G.

Her eyes came back to my face. I suppressed a desire to say tartly, "Satisfied?" and said instead, "Are you sure you won't smoke?" I was already lighting another for myself.

"I think I might, after all." She took cigarette and light with the slight awkwardness that betrayed it as an unaccustomed action. She took a rapid puff at the cigarette, looked down at it as if she wondered what it was there for, then said in that flat voice of hers,

"I'll come to the main point first, and explain afterwards. You were right in saying that our interest in you was more than the normal curiosity you'd expect the likeness to arouse. You were even right—terribly right—when you said we had 'something at stake.'"

She paused, laid her cigarette carefully down in the ash tray I had placed near her on the table. She put her hands flat down on her thighs and leaned forward slightly. "What we want," she said, "is Annabel, back at Whitescar. It's important. I can't tell you how important. She must come back."

The voice was undramatic; the words, in their impact, absurdly sensational. I felt my heart give a little painful twist of nervous excitement. Though I had suspected some nonsense of this kind—and of course it *was* nonsense—all along, the knowledge did nothing to prevent my blood jerking unevenly through my veins as if driven by a faulty pump. I said nothing.

The brown eyes held mine. She seemed to think everything had been said. I wondered, with a spasm of genuine anger, why people with some obsessive trouble of their own always thought that others should be nerve-end conscious of it, too. A cruel impulse made me say, obtusely, "But Annabel's dead."

Something flickered behind the woman's eyes. "Yes, she's dead. She can't come back, Miss Grey, she can't come back . . . to spoil anything for you . . . or for us."

I watched the ash from my cigarette float and fall towards the wastebasket. I didn't look at her. I said at length, with no expression at all, "You want me to go to Whitescar. As Annabel Winslow."

She leaned back. The basket chair gave a long, gasping creak like a gigantic breath of relief. It was obvious that she had taken my apparent calmness for compliance.

"Yes," she said, "that's it. We want you to come to Whitescar . . . Annabel."

I laughed then. I couldn't help it. Possibly the laughter was as much the result of taut nerves as of the obvious absurdity of her proposal, but if there was a suggestion of hysteria in it, she took no notice. She sat quite still, watching me with that expression which, suddenly, I recognized. It was the look of someone who, themselves uninvolved, coolly assesses a theatrical performance. She had all this time been weighing my looks, my voice, my movements, my reactions, against those of the Annabel Winslow of whom she knew so much, and whom she and her brother must have spent the greater part of the last three days discussing.

I felt some nerve tighten somewhere inside me again, and deliberately relaxed it. My laughter died. I said, "Forgive me, but it sounded so absurd when it finally got put into words. Why on earth should Annabel come back? It—it's so theatrical and romantic and impossible. Impersonation—that old stuff? Look, Miss Dermott, I'm sorry, but it's crazy! You can't be serious!"

She said calmly, "It's been done."

"Oh, yes, in stories. It's an old favourite, we know that, from the *Comedy of Errors* on. And that's a point, too: it may be all right in books, but on the stage, where one can *see*, and still one's supposed to be deceived, it's absurd. Unless you do really have identical twins . . . or one person plays both parts."

"That," said Miss Dermott, "is the whole point, isn't it? We *have* got identical twins. It could be done."

"Look at it this way," I said. "It's something, you say, that has been done. But, surely, in much simpler times than these? I mean, think of the lawyers, handwriting, written records, photographs, and, if it came to the point, police . . . oh, no, they're all too efficient nowadays. The risks are too great. No, it belongs in stories, and I doubt if it's even readily acceptable there any more. Too many coincidences required, too much luck."

She nodded. Arguing with her was like battering a feather pillow. You got tired, and the pillow stayed just the same. "Yes, of course. There has to be luck, certainly, and there has to be careful planning. But it's like murder, isn't it?"

I stared at her. "Murder?"

"Yes. You only know about the ones that are found out. Nobody ever hears about the ones that get away with it. All the counting's on the negative side."

"I suppose so. But—"

"The point is that you'd not be *claiming* anything from anybody; there'd be nobody to fight you. The only person who'd lose by your reappearance is Julie, and she has enough of her own. Besides, she adored Annabel; she'll be so pleased to see you, that she'll hardly stop to think what it'll mean in terms of money. . . ."

"Julie?"

"Annabel's young cousin. She's not at Whitescar now, but she'll be coming some time this summer. You needn't worry about her, she was only ten or eleven when Annabel went away, and she'll hardly remember enough about her to suspect you. Besides, why should she? I tell you, it's not a risk, it's a certainty. Take it from me, Con and I wouldn't dare take risks, either! We've everything to lose. You wouldn't even find it nerve-racking. Apart from the daily help, and the farm hands you need hardly see, you'll be mostly with Con and myself, and we'll help you all we can."

"I don't understand. If Julie isn't there, who are you trying to—?"

"And the point about the old man is that he's never believed Annabel was dead. He simply won't have it. He'll never even question you, believe me. You can just walk in."

I was staring at her, my cigarette arrested halfway to my mouth. "The old man? Who? Who are you talking about?"

"Old Mr. Winslow, her grandfather. I spoke of him before. He thought the world of her. He kept half a dozen pictures of her in his room—"

"But surely . . . I understood he was dead."

She looked up in surprise. "Where did you get that idea? No, he's very much alive." Her mouth twisted suddenly, incongruously, into a likeness of that not-so-pleasant smile of Con's. "You might say that's the whole cause of this—situation. What made you think he was dead?"

"I didn't think. But I somehow got the impression. . . . When you spoke of 'the old man' before, you used the past tense. You said '*he was* Annabel's grandfather.'"

"Did I? Possibly. But, of course, the past tense," she said softly, "would be for Annabel."

"I see that now. Yes. But it was added somehow to an impression I got on Sunday . . . your brother said something, I forget what. . . . Yes, of course, he said—implied, I suppose, would be more accurate— that he owned the farm. No, he stated it flatly. I'm sure he did."

She smiled then, genuinely, and for the first time I saw the warmth of real feeling in her face. She looked amused, indulgent, affectionate, as a mother might look when watching the pranks of a naughty but attractive child. "Yes, he would. Poor Con." She didn't take it further, merely adding, "No, he doesn't own Whitescar. He's old Mr. Winslow's manager. He's . . . not even Mr. Winslow's heir."

"I *see*. Oh lord, yes, I see it now."

I got up abruptly, and went over again to the window. Opposite, in one of the tall, drab houses, someone came into a bedroom and switched on the light. I caught a too-familiar glimpse of yellow wallpaper with a writhing pattern of green and brown, a pink plastic lampshade, the gleam of a highly polished radio, before the curtains were twitched across the window. The radio was switched on, and some comedian clacked into the night. Somewhere a child wailed, drearily. In the street below, a woman was shouting a child's name in a wailing northern cadence.

"What do you see?"

I said, slowly, still staring out at the dark, "Not much, really. Just that Mr. Winslow—Con—wants Whitescar, and that somehow he thinks he can fix it, if I go back there as Annabel. I take it that Julie must be the heir now, if he isn't. But how on earth it's going to help Con to bring back Annabel, and put two people in the way instead of one. . . ." I finished heavily, "Oh lord, the whole thing's fantastic anyway. I can't think why I've bothered to listen."

"Extraordinary, perhaps, but not fantastic." The colourless voice behind me might have been discussing a knitting pattern. I didn't turn. I leaned my forehead against the glass and watched, without seeing them, the moving lights of the traffic in the street below. "But then, families are extraordinary, don't you think? And with all their faults, the Winslows have never been exactly dull . . . Listen for a little while longer, and you'll understand what Con and I are getting at."

I let her talk. I just leaned my head against the glass and watched the traffic, and let the soft, unemphatic voice flow on and on. I felt, suddenly, too tired even to try and stop her.

She told me the recent family history very briefly. Old Matthew Winslow (she said) had had two sons: the elder had one daughter, Annabel, who had lived with her parents at Whitescar. When the girl was fourteen, her father was killed in an accident with a tractor, and her mother died soon afterwards, within the year, of pneumonia, leaving her an orphan in her grandfather's care. The latter was then only in his early sixties, but had been for some time handicapped by arthritis, and found it heavy work to manage the place on his own. His younger son had been killed some years previously in the Battle of Britain, leaving a widow, and a month-old daughter, Julie. Matthew Winslow had immediately invited his daughter-in-law to Whitescar, but she had chosen to remain in London. She had eventually remarried, and gone out, with her small daughter, to live in Kenya. Later, when Julie was some seven years old, she had been sent back to England to school; she spent the winter vacations with her parents in Africa, but her spring and summer holidays had been passed with her grandfather at Whitescar, which she regarded as her English home.

It had not been for some time after his elder son's death that Mr. Winslow thought of offering a home and a job to Connor Winslow, his only surviving male relative. Matthew Winslow had had a nephew, who had gone to Ireland to work in a big training stable in Galway, where he had met and married a young Irish widow, a Mrs. Dermott, who had a five-year-old daughter, Lisa. A year later, Connor was born, to become the spoiled darling of his parents, and also, surprisingly, of his half-sister, who had adored him, and had never dreamed of resenting her mother's preference for the good-looking only son. But this apparently safe and happy circle had been rudely shattered when Connor was thirteen. His father broke his neck one day over a big Irish in-and-out, and exactly ten months later the inconsolable widow cheerfully married for the third time.

The young Connor found himself all at once relegated to the background of his mother's life, and kept there by an unsympathetic stepfather and (very soon) by the even stronger claims of a new young family. Con's father had left no money, and it became increasingly obvious that his step father, and now his mother, were not prepared to spare either time, or material help, on the son of the earlier marriage. So when Matthew Winslow, the great-uncle whose existence he had half forgotten, wrote out of the blue to ask Connor, then aged nineteen, to make his home at Whitescar and be trained for farm management, the boy had gone like an arrow from a bow, and with very little in the nature of a by-your-leave. If Lisa wept after he had gone, nobody knew; there was plenty for Lisa to do at home, anyway. . . .

Small wonder that Con arrived at Whitescar with the determination to make a place for himself, and stay; a determination that, very soon, hardened into a definite ambition. Security. The Winslow property. Whitescar itself. There was only Annabel in the way, and Con came very quickly to think that she had no business to be in the way at all. It didn't take him long to find out that the place, backed by Matthew Winslow's not inconsiderable private income, could be willed any way that the old man wished.

So Connor Winslow had set to work. He had learned his job, he made himself very quickly indispensable, he had worked like a navvy at anything and everything that came along, earning the respect and even the admiration of the slow, conservative local farmers, who at first had been rather inclined to regard the good-looking lad from Ireland as an extravagant whim of Matthew's; showy, perhaps, but bound to be a poor stayer. He had proved them wrong.

Matthew himself, though he had never publicly admitted it, had had the same doubts, but Con defeated his prejudices first, then proceeded to charm his great-uncle "like a bird off a tree," (so said Lisa, surprisingly). But charm he never so wisely, Con couldn't quite charm Whitescar from him, away from Annabel. "Because Con tried, he admits it," said Lisa. "The old man thought the world of him, and still does, but he's like the rest of the English Winslows, as stubborn as the devil and

as sticky as a limpet. What he has, he hangs on to. He wanted her to
have it after him, and what he wants, goes. The fact that she's dead,"
added Lisa bitterly, "doesn't make a bit of difference. If the old man
said black was white, he'd believe it was true. He can't be wrong, you
see; he once said she'd come back, and he won't change. He'll die
sooner. Literally. *And* he'll leave everything to Annabel in his will, and
the mess'll take years to clear up, and the odds are that Julie's the
residuary beneficiary. The point is, we just don't know. He won't say
a word. But it does seem unfair."

She paused for a moment. I had half turned back from the window,
and was standing leaning against the shutter. But I still didn't look at
her, or make any comment on the story. I felt her eyes on me for a
few moments, then she went on.

There wasn't much more. Con's next move had been the obvious
one. If Annabel and Whitescar were to go together, then he would
try to take both. Indeed, he was genuinely (so Lisa told me) in love
with her, and an understanding between them was such an obvious and
satisfactory thing to happen that the old man, who was fond of them
both, was delighted.

"But," said Lisa, hesitating now and appearing to choose her words,
"it went wrong, somehow. I won't go into details now—in any case,
I don't know a great deal, because I wasn't there, and Con hasn't said
much—but they quarrelled terribly, and she used to try and make him
jealous, he says, and, well, that's only too easy with Con, and he has a
terrible temper. They had a dreadful quarrel one night. I don't know
what happened, but I think Con may have said something to frighten
her, and she threw him over once and for all, said she couldn't stay at
Whitescar while he was there, and all that sort of thing. Then she ran
off to see her grandfather. Con doesn't know what happened between
them, or if he does, he won't tell me. But of course the old man was
bound to be furious, and disappointed, and *he* never was one to mince
his words, either. The result was another dreadful row, and she left that
night, without a word to anyone. There was a note for her grandfather,
that was all. Nothing for Con. She just said she wasn't coming back.
Of course the old man was too stubborn and furious even to try and
find her, and persuade her, and he forbade Con to try either. Con did
what he could, quietly, but there was no trace. Then, a month later,
her grandfather got a note, postmarked New York. It just said she was
quite safe, had got a job with friends, and she wasn't ever coming back
to England again. After that there was nothing, until three years later

someone sent Mr. Winslow a cutting from a Los Angeles paper describing an accident in which an express train had run into a bus at some country crossing, and a lot of people had been killed. One of them was a 'Miss Anna Winslow' of no given address, who'd been staying at some boarding house in the city, and who was thought to be English. We made inquiries, and they were all negative. It could have been Annabel. It would certainly be enough, with the long absence, to allow us to presume her dead. After all this time, she must be; or else she really isn't ever coming back, which amounts to the same thing, in the end." She paused. "That's all."

I turned my head. "And you? Where do you come in?"

"After she'd gone," said Lisa Dermott, "Con remembered me."

She said it quite simply. There was no hint of self-pity or complaint in the soft, flattened voice. I looked down at her, sitting stolid and unattractive in the old basket chair, and said gently, "He got Mr. Winslow to send for you?"

She nodded. "Someone had to run the house, and it seemed too good a chance to miss. But even with the two of us there, doing all that we do, it's not the slightest use."

The impulse of pity that had stirred in me, died without a pang. I had a sudden vivid picture of the two of them, camped there at Whitescar, hammering home their claims, Con with his charm and industry, Lisa with her polish and her apple pies. . . . She had called it "unfair," and perhaps it was; certainly one must admit they had a right to a point of view. But then so had Matthew Winslow.

"You see," she said, "how unjust it all is? You do see that, don't you?"

"Yes, I see. But I still don't see what you think I can do about it! You want me to go to Whitescar, and somehow or other *that* is going to help Con to become the heir, and owner. How?"

I had left the window as I spoke, and come forward to the table again. She leaned towards me, looking up under the brim of the brown hat. There was a gleam in her eyes that might have been excitement.

"You're interested now, aren't you? I thought you would be, when you heard a bit more."

"I'm not. You've got me wrong. I was interested in your story, I admit, but that was because I think your brother may be right when he says I must come originally from some branch of the same family. But I never said I was interested in your proposition! I'm not! I told you what I thought about it! It's a crazy idea straight out of nineteenth-century romance, long-lost heirs and missing wills and—and all that drivel!" I found that I was speaking roughly, almost angrily, and made myself smile at her, adding, mildly enough, "You'll be telling me next that Annabel had a strawberry mark—"

I stopped. Her hand had moved, quickly, to the telephone directory on the table beside her. I saw, then, that I had shut it over a pencil which still lay between the leaves.

The book fell open under her hand, at the page headed *Wilson— Winthorpe*. She looked at it without expression. Then her blunt, well-kept finger moved down towards the foot of the second column, and stopped there.

Winslow, Matthew. Frmr. Whitescar. . . . Bellingham 248.

The entry was marked, faintly, in pencil.

I said, trying to keep my voice flat, and only succeeding in making it sound sulky, "Yes, I looked it up. It puzzled me, because your brother had said he owned the farm. It isn't an old directory, so when you first spoke of 'the old man,' I assumed he must have died quite recently."

She didn't answer. She shut the book, then leaned back in her chair and looked up at me, with that calm, appraising look. I met it almost defiantly.

"All right, I was interested before. Who wouldn't be? After that business on Sunday . . . oh, well, skip it. Call it curiosity if you like, I'm only human. But my heaven, there's no reason why it should go further than curiosity! This—proposition you appear to be suggesting takes my breath away. No, no, I don't want to hear any more about it. I can't even believe you're serious. *Are* you?"

"Quite."

"Very well. But can you give me any conceivable reason why *I* should be?"

She looked at me almost blankly. There it was again; that merciless all-excluding obsession with their personal problems. "I don't understand."

I found that I was reaching, automatically, for another cigarette. I let it slip back into the packet. I had smoked too much that evening already; my eyes and throat felt hot and aching, and my brain stupid. I said, "Look, you approach me out of the blue with your family history, which may be intriguing, but which can really mean very little to me. You propose, let's face it, that somehow or other I should help you to perpetrate a fraud. It may mean everything to you; I don't see how, but we'll grant it for argument's sake. But why should it mean a thing to me? You tell me it'll be 'easy.' Why should I care? Why should I involve myself? In plain words, why on earth should I go out of my way to help you and your brother Con to anything?"

I didn't add, "when I don't much like you, and I don't trust him," but to my horror the words seemed to repeat themselves into the air of the room as clearly as if I, and not the tone of my voice, had said them.

If she heard them, she may have been too unwilling to antagonize me to resent them. Nor did she appear to mind my actual rudeness. She said, simply, "Why, for money, of course. What other reason is there?"

"For *money?*"

She gave a slight, summing, eloquent glance round the room. "If you'll forgive me, you appear to need it. You said so, in fact, to my brother; that was one of the reasons why we felt we could approach you. You have so much to gain. You will forgive my speaking so plainly on such a short acquaintance?"

"Do," I said ironically.

"You are a gentlewoman," said Miss Dermott, the outmoded word sounding perfectly normal on her lips. "And this room . . . and your job at that dreadful café . . . You've been over here from Canada for how long?"

"Just a few days."

"And this has been all you could find?"

"As far as I looked. It took all I had to get me here. I'm marking time while I get my bearings. I took the first thing that came. You don't have to worry about me, Miss Dermott. I'll make out. I don't have to work in the Kasbah for life, you know."

"All the same," she said, "it's worth your while to listen to me. In plain terms, I'm offering you a job, a good one, the job of coming back to Whitescar as Annabel Winslow, and persuading the old man that that is who you are. You will have a home and every comfort, a position, everything; and eventually a small assured income for life. You call it a fraud: of course it is, but it's not a cruel one. The old man wants you there, and your coming will make him very happy."

"Why did he remove the photographs?"

"I beg your pardon?"

"You said earlier that he used to keep a 'whole gallery' of this girl's photographs in his room. Doesn't he still?"

"You're very quick." She sounded appreciative, as of a favourite horse who was showing a pretty turn of speed. "He didn't get rid of them, don't worry; he keeps them in a drawer in his office, and he still has one in his bedroom. He moved the others last year, when he had one done of Julie." She eyed me for a moment. "She'll be coming up for her summer holiday before very long. You see?"

"I see why you and your brother might want to work quickly, yes."

"Of course. You must come home before Julie persuades him to be reasonable about Annabel's death . . . and to put Julie herself in Annabel's place. Whatever happens, it'll happen soon. It's doubtful if the old man'll see the year out, and I think he's beginning to realize it."

I looked up quickly. "Is he ill?"

"He had a slight stroke three months ago, and he refuses to take very much care. He's always been strong, and still, in spite of the arthritis, pretty active, and he seems to resent any suggestion that he should do less. He takes it as an encroachment. . . ." Her lips tightened over whatever she had been going to say, then she added, "The doctor has warned him. He may live for some time, but he may, if he does anything silly, have another stroke at almost any moment, and this time it might be fatal. So you see why this is so urgent? Why meeting you like that seemed, to Con, like a gift from heaven?"

I said, after a pause, "And when he's gone?"

She said patiently, "It's all thought out. We can go into details later. Briefly, all you have to do is establish yourself at Whitescar, *be* Annabel Winslow, and inherit the property (and her share of the capital) when the old man dies. I tell you, there'll be no question. Don't you see, you'll not actually be coming back to *claim* anything, simply coming home to live? With luck you'll be able to settle quietly in and establish yourself, long before there's any sort of a crisis, and by the time the old man does die, you'll have been accepted without question. Then, after a decent interval, when things seem settled, you'll turn your legacy over to Con. You'll get your cut, don't worry. Annabel's mother left her some money, which she could have claimed when she was twenty-one; it brings in a nice little independent income. You'll have that—in any case, it would look absurd if you attempted to hand *that* over. As for the main transaction, the handing over of Whitescar, that can be arranged to look normal enough. You can say you want to live elsewhere . . . abroad, perhaps . . . whatever you'd planned for yourself. In fact, you'll be able to lead your own life again, but with a nice little assured income behind you. And if 'Annabel' decided to live away from Whitescar again, leaving the place to her cousin, who's run it for years anyway, there's no reason why anyone should question it."

"The young cousin? Julie?"

"I tell you, you needn't be afraid of her. Her step-father has money, there's no other child, and she'll certainly also get a share of Mr. Winslow's capital. You'll rob her of Whitescar, yes, but she's never given the slightest hint that she cares anything about it, except as a place to spend a holiday in. Since she left school last year, she's taken a job in London, in the Drama Department at the B.B.C., and she's only been up here once, for the inside of a fortnight. All she could do, if the place was hers, would be to sell it, or pay Con to manage it. You needn't have Julie on your conscience."

"But surely—" it was absurd, I thought, to feel as if one was being backed against a wall by this steady pressure of will—"but surely, if the old man realized that he was ill, and still Annabel *hadn't* come back, he *would* leave things to Con? Or if he left them to Julie, and she was content to let Con go on as manager, wouldn't that be all right?"

Her lips folded in that soft obstinate line. "That wouldn't answer. Can't you see how impossible—ah, well, take it from me that it wouldn't work out like that. No, my dear, this is the best way, and you're the gift straight from the gods. Con believes he'll never get control of Whitescar and the capital except this way. When you've said you'll help, I'll explain more fully, and you'll see what a chance it is for all of us, and no harm done, least of all to that stubborn old man sitting at Whitescar waiting for her to come home. . . ."

Somehow, without wanting it, I had taken the cigarette, my hands fidgeting with package and lighter in spite of myself. I stood silently while she talked, looking about me through the first, blue, sharp-scented cloud of smoke . . . the sagging bed, the purplish wallpaper, the wardrobe and dresser of yellow deal, the table cloth with the geometric flowers of Prussian blue and carmine, and the stain on the ceiling that was the shape of the map of Ireland. I thought of the high moors and the curlews calling and the beeches coming into leaf in the windbreaks. And of the collie waving his tail, and the straight blue stare of Connor Winslow. . . .

It was disconcerting to feel the faint prickle of nervous excitement along the skin, the ever-so-slightly quickened heartbeat, the catch in the breath. Because of course the thing *was* crazy. Dangerous and crazy and impossible. This silly, stolid pudding of a woman couldn't possibly have realized how crazy it was. . . .

No, I thought. No. Go while the going's good. Don't touch it.

"Well?" said Lisa Dermott.

I went to the window and dragged the curtains shut across it. I turned abruptly back to her. The action was somehow symbolic; it shut us in together, storybook conspirators in the solitary, sleazy upstairs room that smelt of too much cigarette smoke.

"Well?" I echoed her, sharply. "All right. I am interested. And I'll come, if you can persuade me that it can possibly work . . . Go on. I'll really listen now."

CHAPTER

THREE

Oh, the oak, and the ash, and the bonny ivy tree,
They are all growing green in the North Country.

Traditional.

It took three weeks. At the end of that time Lisa Dermott vowed that I would do. There was nothing, she said, that she or Con knew about Whitescar and Annabel that I, too, didn't now know.

My handwriting, even, passed muster. The problem of the signature had been one of Lisa's worst worries, but she had brought me some old letters, written before Annabel's disappearance, and when I showed her the sheets that I had covered with carefully practised writing, she eventually admitted that they would pass.

It was on the Thursday of the second week that Lisa appeared unexpectedly. I had moved to another boarding house immediately after our first meeting, and was using the name of Winslow—this to avoid the possibility of some later inquiry turning up a connection between Con and Lisa, and one Mary Grey. When I opened the door and showed her into my room, I thought that something was ruffling her usually stolid calm, but she took off her gloves and coat with her customary deliberation, and sat down by the fire.

"I didn't expect you," I said. "Has something happened?"

She sent me a half-glance upwards, in which I thought I could read uneasiness, and even anger. "Julie's coming, that's what happened. Some time next week."

I sat on the table's edge, and reached for a cigarette. "Oh?"

She said sourly, "You take it very calmly."

"Well, you said you expected her some time during the summer."

"Yes, but she's taking her holiday much earlier than we'd expected, and I've a feeling that the old man's asked her to come, and she's getting special leave. He doesn't say so; but I know she *had* originally planned to come in August. . . . You see what it means?"

I lit the cigarette deliberately, then pitched the dead match into the fire. (The gold lighter, with its betraying monogram, lay concealed at the bottom of a suitcase.) "I see what it might mean."

"It means that if we don't get moving straight away, Julie'll have wormed her way into Whitescar, and he'll leave her every penny."

I didn't answer for a moment. I was thinking that Con, even at his most direct, was never coarse.

"So you see, this is it," said Lisa.

"Yes."

"Con says it must mean the old man's a bit more nervous about his health than he's admitted. Apparently Julie wrote to him once or twice while he was ill, and he has written back, I know. I'm sure he must have asked her to come up early, for some reason, and he certainly seems as pleased as Punch that she can get away so soon. She said she'd be here next week, some time, but would ring up and let us know. Normally we'd have had till July or August, and anything," said Lisa, bitterly, "could have happened before then. As it is—"

"Look," I said mildly, "you don't have to hunt round for motives to frighten yourselves with. Perhaps he does just want to see Julie, and perhaps she does just want to see him. It could be as simple as that. Don't look so disbelieving. People are straightforward enough, on the whole, till one starts to look for crooked motives, and then, oh boy, how crooked can they be!"

Lisa gave that small, tight-lipped smile that was more a concession to my tone than any evidence of amusement. "Well, we can't take risks. It'll have to be this week end. You can ring up on Sunday, as we arranged. If you ring up at three, the old man'll be resting, and I'll take the call. You'd better come on Monday. Con says we can't wait any longer; you'll have to come straight away, before Julie gets here, or heaven knows what Mr. Winslow'll do."

"But, look, Lisa—"

"You'll be all right, won't you? I'd have liked another week, just to make certain."

"I'm all right. It isn't that. I was going to say that surely Con's barking up the wrong tree with Julie. I don't see how she can possibly be a danger to him, whether she's at Whitescar or not."

"All I know is," said Lisa, a little grimly, "that she's as like Annabel as two peas in a pod, and the old man's getting more difficult every day . . . Heaven knows what he might take it into his head to do. Can't you see what Con's afraid of? He's pretty sure Julie's the residuary beneficiary now, but if Mr. Winslow alters his will before Annabel gets home, and makes Julie the principal. . . ."

"Oh yes, I see. In that case, I might as well not trouble to go any further. But is it likely, Lisa? If Grandfather abandons Annabel at last, and remakes his will at all, surely now, it will be in Con's favour? You said Julie's only been to Whitescar for holidays, and she's London bred. What possible prospect—?"

"That's just the point. Last year, when she was here, she was seeing a lot of one of the Fenwick boys from Nether Shields. It all seemed to blow up out of nothing, and before anyone even noticed it, he was coming over every day, getting on like a house on fire with Mr. Winslow, and Julie . . . well, *she* did nothing to discourage him."

I laughed. "Well, but Lisa, what was she? Eighteen?"

"I know. It's all speculation, and I hope it's nonsense, but you know what a razor's edge Con's living on, and anything could happen to the old man. Once you're there, things should be safe enough: he'll certainly never leave anything to Julie over *your* head, but as it is—well, she's his son's child, and Con's only a distant relative . . . and he likes Bill Fenwick."

I regarded the end of my cigarette. "And did Con never think to set up as a rival to this Bill Fenwick? An obvious move, one imagines. He tried it with Annabel."

Lisa stirred, and dropped her eyes, but not before I had seen, quite clearly, the look which had now and then showed in those unexpressive features, and which I now recognized for jealousy; jealousy, still alive and potent, of an unhappy girl whom she had believed dead for years. And now—of Julie? "I told you," she said, "it never occurred to anyone that she was even adult! She'd just left school! Con never looked at her—I think he thought of her as a schoolgirl. Mr. Winslow certainly did; the Fenwick affair amused him enormously."

"And now she's had a year in London. She'll have probably got further than the boy-next-door stage," I said cheerfully. "You'll find you're worrying about nothing."

"I hope so. But once you're there at Whitescar, things will be safe enough for Con. Julie won't be seriously in the way."

I looked at her for a moment. "No?" I got up then, and went over to the window, where I stood looking out. There was a short silence.

"What's the matter?" asked Lisa, at length. "Nerves? You'll be all right, you know. Don't worry."

I turned back into the room. I didn't feel it necessary to explain that I hadn't even been thinking about the hazards of the proposed masquerade. I had been thinking of Julie; Julie, the unknown quantity, who might have been "seriously in the way." And for some reason the phrase had made me think of Con, and the water gleaming below us, and the smooth voice saying, "*It doesn't necessarily have to be midnight, does it, when you and I go walking at the edge of a cliff with water at the bottom?*"

I smiled at Lisa, and threw the stub of my cigarette into the fire. "And don't *you* worry," I said. "Monday, was it? I'll be there."

The approach to Whitescar was down a narrow gravelled track edged with hawthorns. There was no gate. On the right of the gap where the track left the main road stood a dilapidated signpost which had once said, *Private Road to Forrest Hall.* On the left was a new and solid-looking stand for milk-churns, which bore a beautifully painted legend, WHITESCAR. Between these symbols the lane curled off between its high hawthorns, and out of sight.

I had come an hour too early, and no one was there to meet the bus. I had only two cases with me, and carrying these I set off down the lane.

Round the first bend there was a quarry, disused now and overgrown, and here, behind a thicket of brambles, I left my cases. They would be safe enough, and could be collected later. Meanwhile I was anxious to make my first reconnaissance alone.

The lane skirted the quarry, leading downhill for perhaps another two hundred yards before the hedges gave way on the one side to a high wall, and on the other—the left—to a fence which allowed a view across the territory that Lisa had been at such pains to picture for me.

I stood, leaning on the top bar of the fence, and looked at the scene below me.

Whitescar was about eight miles, as the crow flies, from Bellingham. There the river, meandering down its valley, doubles round leisurely on itself in a great loop, all but enclosing the rolling, well-timbered lands of Forrest Park. At the narrow part of the loop the bends of the river are barely two hundred yards apart, forming a sort of narrow isthmus through which ran the track on which I stood. This was the only road to the Hall, and it divided at the gate-house for Whitescar and the West Lodge which lay the other side of the park.

The main road, along which my bus had come, lay some way above the level of the river, and the drop past the quarry to the Hall gates was fairly steep. From where I stood you could see the whole near-island laid out below you in the circling arm of the river, with its woods and its water meadows and the chimneys glimpsed among the green.

To the east lay Forrest Hall itself, set in what remained of its once formal gardens and timbered walks, the grounds girdled on two sides by the curving river, and on two by a mile-long wall and a belt of thick trees. Except for a wooded path along the river, the only entrance was through the big pillared gates where the gate-house had stood. This, I knew, had long since been allowed to crumble gently into ruin. I couldn't see it from where I was, but the tracks to Whitescar and West Lodge branched off there, and I could see the latter clearly, cutting across the park from east to west, between the orderly rows of planted conifers. At the distant edge of the river, I caught a glimpse of roofs and chimneys, and the quick glitter of glass that marked the hothouses in the old walled garden that had belonged to the Hall. There, too, lay the stables, and the house called West Lodge, and a footbridge spanning the river to serve a track which climbed through the far trees and across the moors to Nether Shields farm, and, eventually, to Bellingham.

The Whitescar property, lying along the river bank at the very centre of its loop, and stretching back to the junction of the roads at the Hall gates, was like a healthy bite taken out of the circle of Forrest territory. Lying neatly between the Hall and West Lodge, it was screened now from my sight by a rise in the land that only allowed me to see its chimneys, and the tops of its trees.

I left my viewpoint, and went on down the track, not hurrying. Behind the wall to my right now loomed the Forrest woods, the huge trees full out, except for the late, lacy boughs of ash. The ditch at the wall's foot was frilled with cow-parsley. The wall was in poor repair; I saw a blackbird's nest stuffed into a hole in the coping, and there were tangles of campion and toadflax bunching from gaps between the stones.

At the Hall entrance, the lane ended in a kind of cul-de-sac, bounded by three gateways. On the left, a brand-new oak gate guarded the Forestry Commission's fir plantations and the road to West Lodge. To the right lay the pillars of the Hall entrance. Ahead was a solid, five-barred gate, painted white, with the familiar WHITESCAR blazoning the top bar. Beyond this, the track lifted itself up a gentle rise of pasture, and vanished over a ridge. From here, not even the chimney tops of White-scar were visible; only the smooth sunny prospect of green pasture and dry-stone walling sharp with blue shadows, and, in a hollow beyond the rise somewhere, the tops of some tall trees.

But the gateway to the right might have been the entrance to an-other sort of world.

Where the big gates of the Hall should have hung between their massive pillars, there was simply a gap giving onto a driveway, green and mossy, its twin tracks no longer worn by wheels, but matted over by the discs of plantain and hawkweed, rings of weed spreading and overlapping like the rings that grow and ripple over each other when a handful of gravel is thrown into water. At the edges of the drive the taller weeds began, hedge-parsley and campion, and forget-me-not gone wild, all frothing under the ranks of the rhododendrons, whose flowers showed like pale, symmetrical lamps above their splayed leaves. Overhead hung the shadowy, enormous trees.

There had been a gate-house once, tucked deep in the trees beside the entrance. A damp, dismal place it must have been to live in; the walls were almost roofless now, and half drifted over with nettles. The chimney stacks stuck up like bones from a broken limb. All that had survived of the little garden was a rank plantation of rhubarb, and the old blush rambler that ran riot through the gaping windows.

There was no legend here of FORREST to guide the visitor. For those wise in the right lores there were some heraldic beasts on top of the pillars, rampant, and holding shields where some carving made cushions under the moss. From the pillars, to either side, stretched the high wall that had once marked the boundaries. This was cracked and crumbling in many places, and the copings were off, but it was still a barrier, save in one place not far from the entrance. Here a giant oak stood. It had been originally on the inside of the wall, but with the years it had grown and spread, pressing closer and ever closer to the masonry, until its vast flank had bent and finally broken the wall, which here lay in a mere pile of tumbled and weedy stone. But the power of the oak would be its undoing, for the wall had been clothed in ivy, and the ivy had reached for the tree, crept up it, engulfed it, till now the trunk was one towering mass of the dark gleaming leaves, and only the tree's upper branches managed to thrust the young gold leaves of early summer through the strangling curtain. Eventually the ivy would kill it.

Already, through the tracery of the ivy stems, some of the oak boughs showed dead, and one great lower limb, long since broken off, had left a gap where rotten wood yawned, in holes deep enough for owls to nest in.

I looked up at it for a long time, and then along the neat sunny track that led out of the shadow of the trees towards Whitescar.

Somewhere a ringdove purred and intoned, and a wood warbler stuttered into its long trill, and fell silent. I found that I had moved, without realizing it, through the gateway, and a yard or two up the drive into the wood. I stood there in the shade, looking out at the wide fields and the cupped valley, and the white-painted gate gleaming in the sun. I realized that I was braced as if for the start of a race, my mouth dry, and the muscles of my throat taut and aching.

I swallowed a couple of times, breathed deeply and slowly to calm myself, repeating the now often-used formula of *what was there to go wrong, after all?* I was Annabel. I was coming home. I had never been anyone else. All that must be forgotten. Mary Grey need never appear again, except, perhaps, to Con and Lisa. Meanwhile, I would forget her, even in my thoughts. I was Annabel Winslow, coming home.

I walked quickly out between the crumbling pillars, and pushed open the white gate.

It didn't even creak. It swung quietly open on sleek, well-oiled hinges, and came to behind me with a smooth click that said *money*.

Well, that was what had brought me, wasn't it?

I walked quickly out of the shade of the Forrest trees, and up the sunny track towards Whitescar.

In the bright afternoon stillness the farm looked clean in its orderly whitewash, like a toy. From the top of the rise I could see it all laid out, in plan exactly like the maps that Lisa Dermott had drawn for me so carefully, and led me through in imagination so many times.

The house was long and low, two-storied, with big modern windows cut into the old thick walls. Unlike the rest of the group of buildings, it was not whitewashed, but built of sandstone, green-gold with age. The lichen on the roof showed, even at that distance, like patens of copper laid along the soft blue slates.

It faced onto a strip of garden—grass and flower borders and a lilac tree—whose lower wall edged the river. From the garden, a white wicket gate gave on a wooden footbridge. The river was fairly wide here, lying under the low, tree-hung cliffs of its further bank with that still gleam that means depth. It reflected the bridge, the trees, and the banked tangles of elder and honeysuckle, in layers of deepening colour as rich as a Flemish painter's palette.

On the nearer side of house and garden lay the farm; a courtyard— even at this distance I could see its clean baked concrete, and the freshness of the paint on doors and gates—surrounded by byres and stables and sheds, with the red roof of the big Dutch barn conspicuous beside the remains of last year's straw stacks, and a dark knot of Scotch pines.

I had been so absorbed in the picture laid out before me, that I hadn't noticed the man approaching, some thirty yards away, until the clang of his nailed boots on the iron of the cattle grid startled me.

He was a burly, middle-aged man in rough farm clothes, and he was staring at me in undisguised interest as he approached. He came at a pace that, without seeming to, carried him over the distance between us at a speed that left me no time to think at all.

I did have time to wonder briefly if my venture alone into the Winslow den was going to prove my undoing, but at least there was no possibility now of turning tail. It was with a sense of having the issue taken out of my hands that I saw the red face split into a beaming smile, and heard him say, in a broad country voice, "Why, Miss Annabel!"

There was the ruddy face, the blue eyes, the huge forearm bared to the elbow, and marked with the scar where the bull had caught him. Bates, head cattleman at Whitescar. *You'll know him straight away,* Con had said. But I didn't venture the name. The lessons of the past three weeks hummed in my head like a hive of bees: *Take it slowly. Don't rush your fences. Never be too sure. . . .*

And here was the first fence. *Tell the truth wherever possible.* I told it. I said, with genuine pleasure, "You knew me! How wonderful! It makes me feel as if I were really coming home!"

I put out both hands and he took them as if the gesture, from me, was a natural one. His grip nearly lifted me from the ground. The merle collie running at his heels circled round us, lifting a lip and sniffing the back of my legs in a disconcerting manner.

"Knew you?" His voice was gruff with pleasure. "That I did, the minute you came over the top there. Even if Miss Dermott hadn't tell't us you were coming, I'd a known you a mile off across the field, lass! We're all uncommon glad to have you back, and that's a fact."

"It's marvellous to be here. How are you? You look fine, I don't think you can be a day older! Not eight years, anyway!"

"I'm grand, and Mrs. Bates, too. You'd know I married Betsy, now? They'd tell you, maybe? Aye. . . . Well, she's in a rare taking with your coming home, spent all morning baking, and turning the place upside down, and Miss Dermott along with her. You'll likely find there's tea cakes and singin' hinnies for your tea."

"Singin' hinnies?"

"Nay, don't tell me you've forgotten! That I'll not believe. You used to tease for them every day when you was a bairn."

"No, I hadn't forgotten. It was just—hearing the name again. So— so like home." I swallowed. "How sweet of her to remember. I'm longing to see her again. How's Grandfather, Mr. Bates?"

"Why, he's champion, for his age. He's always well enough, mind you, in the dry weather; it's the damp that gets at his back. It's arthritis —you knew that?—and there's times when he can hardly get about at all. And now they say there's this other trouble forby. But you'll have heard about that, too, likely? Miss Dermott said you'd telephoned yesterday and asked them to break it gentle-like to your Granda. They'd tell you all the news?"

"Yes. I—I didn't quite know what to do. I thought of writing, but then I thought, if I telephoned Con, it might be easier. Miss Dermott answered; the others were out, and, well—we had a long talk. She told me how things were, and she said she'd get Con to break it to Grandfather. I hadn't known about Grandfather's stroke, so it's just as well I didn't just write to him out of the blue. And anyway, I wouldn't have dared just walk right in here and give everyone a shock."

His voice was rough. "There's not many dies of that sort of shock, Miss Annabel."

"That's . . . sweet of you. Well, Miss Dermott told me quite a lot of the news . . . I'm glad Grandfather keeps so well, on the whole."

"Aye, he's well enough." A quick glance under puckered eyelids. "Reckon you'll see a change, though."

"I'm afraid I probably shall. It's been a long time."

"It has that. It was a poor day's work you did, Miss Annabel, when you left us."

"I know," I said. "Don't blame me too much."

"I've no call to blame you, lass. I know naught about it, but that you and your Granda fell out." He grinned, sourly. "I know what he's like, none better, I've known him these thirty years. I never take no notice of him, rain or shine, and him and me gets on, but you're too like your dad to sit still and hold your tongue. Winslows is all the same,

I reckon. Maybe if you'd been a mite older, you'd 'a known his bark was always worse than his bite, but you were nobbut a bit lass at the time, and I reckon you'd troubles of your own, at that."

A short, breathless pause. "Troubles—of my own?"

He looked a little embarrassed, and stabbed at the ground with his stick. "Maybe I didn't ought to 'a said that. I only meant as everyone knew it wasn't all plain sailing with you and Mr. Con. Happen one takes these things too hard at nineteen."

I smiled. "Happen one does. Well, it's all over now. Let's forget it, shall we? And you mustn't blame Con or Grandfather either, you know. I was young and silly, and I suppose I thought I'd like to get away on my own for a bit. I didn't want to be tied down to Whitescar or—or anything, not just then, not yet; so when the time came, I just went without thinking. One doesn't think very straight, at nineteen. But now I'm back, and I'm going to try and forget I've ever been away."

I looked away from him, down towards the farm. I could see white hens ruffling in the straw of the stackyard, and there were pigeons on the roof. The smoke from the chimneys went straight up into the clear air. I said, "It looks just the same. Better, if anything. Or is that absence, making the heart grow fonder?"

"Nay, I'll not deny it's well looked after. As well every way, nearly, as in your Granda's time."

I stared at him. "As in—you talk as if that was past."

He was prodding at the earth again with his stick. "Happen it is."

"What d'you mean?"

That quick, almost surly glance upwards again. "You'll see, Miss Annabel. I don't doubt but what you'll see. Times change."

I didn't pursue it, and he turned the subject abruptly. He nodded past me, the way I had come, towards the towering woods that surrounded the site of Forrest Hall. "Now, there's the biggest change you'll find, and none of it for the better. Did she tell you about Forrests?"

"Yes." I looked back to where the crest of the ivied oak reared above the skyline, the glinting darkness of the ivy making it stand up like a ruined tower against the young summer green of the woods. "Yes, Miss Dermott told me. Four years ago, wasn't it? I thought the old gatehouse looked even more dilapidated than it should. I never remember anyone living there, but at least the drive looked reasonable, and the gates were on."

"They went for scrap, after the fire. Aye, we miss the Hall, though it's not all gone, you mind. They're using some of the stable buildings over at West Lodge for poultry, and the old garden's going strong. Mr. Forrest got that going himself, with Johnny Rudd—you'll mind Johnny? He's working there still, though there's nobbut one horse in the stables. Mr. Forrest kept that one when the stud went; he's one of the old 'Mountain' lot, and I reckon Mr. Forrest couldn't bear to part, but I doubt he'll have to be sold now. He's just running wild there, and eating his head off, and there's no one can hardly get near him." He grinned at me. "You'll have to work on him yourself, now you're back."

"Me? Not on your—I mean, not any more. Those days are past, Mr. Bates."

"How's that?"

The story that Lisa and I had concocted came glibly enough. "I had a bad fall in the States, and hurt my back—nothing drastic, you know, but not a thing I'd dare risk doing again."

"That's a shame, now! I reckoned Johnny'd be rare pleased when he heard you were back. He hasn't the time to bother on wi' horses now, not at this time of year; and the colt's spoiling. Mr. Con's been along to take a hand to him, now and then, but the youngster's taken a rare scunner at him, seemingly. Won't let him near. There's naught else fit for a ride at Whitescar."

"I expect I've lost my touch, anyway."

"Eh, well," he said, "it's like we said. Things change, more's the pity. Every time I walk up this road I think on the way it was. It's sad to see the old places falling down, and the families gone, but there it is."

"Yes." Beyond the ivy-clad oak, behind a sunny tracery of treetops, I could see a chimney. The sun glinted warm on the mellow stone. There was the glimpse of a tiled roof through the boughs. A wisp of cloud, moving slowly, gave the illusion of smoke, rising from a homely fire. Then it moved on, and I saw that the roof was broken.

Bates said, beside me, so suddenly that I jumped, "You've changed. I was wrong, maybe, I didn't think you had, not that much, but now I can see."

"What can you see?"

"I dunno. It's not only that you're older. You're different, Miss Annabel, no offence." The kindly blue eyes surveyed me. "Happen you'll have had a hard time of it, out there?"

He made it sound as if the Atlantic were the water of Styx, and the lands beyond it the Outer Darkness. I smiled. "Happen I have."

"You didn't marry?"

"No. Too busy earning my keep."

"Aye. That's where it is. You'd 'a done better to stay here at home, lass, where your place was."

I thought of Con, of the lonely crumbling ruin in the Forrest woods. "You think so?" I laughed a little without amusement. "Well, I'm back, anyway. I've come back to my place now, and I expect I'll have the sense to stick to it."

"You do that." The words had an emphasis that was far from idle. He was staring at me fixedly, his eyes almost fierce in the rubicund face. "Well, I'll not keep you here talking. They'll be looking for you down yonder. But you stay here, Miss Annabel, close by your Granda—and don't leave us again."

He nodded abruptly, whistled up the collie, and strode past me up the track without looking back.

I turned down towards Whitescar.

The end of the barn threw a slanting shadow half across the yard gate. Not until I was within twenty paces of it did I see that a man leaned there, unmoving, watching my approach. Con.

If Bates had been the first fence, this was the water jump. A little embarrassment was permitted, surely, to a girl meeting, after eight years, the man from whom she'd run away.

He straightened up with the lazy grace that was so typical of him, and gave me a brilliant smile that held no trace of embarrassment whatsoever. His hand went out to the latch of the gate.

"Why, Annabel," he said, and swung the gate open with a sort of ceremony of invitation. "Welcome home!"

I said feebly, "Hullo." I was trying to see, without looking too obviously round me, if there was anyone else within earshot. The yard was apparently deserted, but I didn't dare risk it. I said, feeling perilously foolish, "It—it's nice to be back."

"You're earlier than we expected. I intended to meet you with the car. Where's your luggage?"

"I left it in the quarry. Could someone fetch it later?"

"I'll go myself. You know, you really should have let me come into Newcastle for you."

"No. I—I wanted to come alone. Thanks all the same." I found to my fury that I was stammering like a schoolgirl. I did manage to reflect that if anyone happened to be watching us, they would see merely that there was something stilted and constrained about our greeting.

I still hadn't met his eyes. He had shut the gate behind me, but I stayed standing by it, talking, still feebly and rather madly, about luggage. "Of course, you know, my main baggage is in Liverpool. I can get it sent—"

"Of course." I heard the laugh in his voice, then, and looked up. Outrageously, he was looking amused. Before I could speak again he had put out both hands and taken mine in them, smiling delightfully down at me. His voice was warm and, one might have sworn, genuinely moved. "This is wonderful . . . to see you here again after all this time. We never thought . . ." He appeared to struggle for a moment with his emotions, and added, deeply, "This is a pretty shattering moment, my dear." "*You're telling me, blast you.*" I didn't dare say it aloud, but he read it in my eyes quite easily. His own were dancing. He gave me that deliberately dazzling smile of his, then pulled me towards him, and kissed me. He must have felt my startled and instinctive resistance, because he slackened his hold straight away, saying quickly under his breath, "There are windows looking this way, Mary, my dear. I think, under the circumstances, that I'd have kissed her, don't you? Strictly cousinly and affectionate, of course?"

He was still holding my hands. I said equally softly, and through shut teeth, "And don't you think, dear cousin Connor, that she might even have hauled off and slapped your face, hard? Strictly cousinly and affectionate, of course."

I felt him shake with laughter, and pulled my hands away. "*Is* there someone watching then? Can they hear us?"

"Not that I'm aware of."

"Well, *really*—!"

"Ssh, not so loudly. You never know." He had his back to the house, and was looking down at me. "Are you really as mad as blazes at me?"

"Of course I am!"

"The occasion kind of went to my head. Forgive me."

"It's all right."

Suddenly, it seemed, we were over the water jump and moving easily into the straight. I relaxed, leaning back against the gate. We smiled at one another with a certain amount of understanding. To an observer the scene would still be perfectly in character. Even from the house, I thought, the scarlet in my cheeks could be seen quite easily; and Con stood in front of me in an attitude that might have suggested hesitation, and even humility, if one hadn't been able to see his eyes.

I said, "You should have known that I'd no intention of playing this as though I'd come back ready to fall at your feet and make it up, Con Winslow."

He grinned. "No. That would be asking a bit too much, I can see that."

"You might have thought of it before you kissed me." I leaned back against the gate and added, coolly, "Do you really want to find yourself waiting for me at the altar steps some fine morning?"

There was a startled silence. It was something, I thought, not without satisfaction, to have shaken that amused assurance. I tilted my head and smiled up at him. "Yes, it's a wonder you and Lisa didn't think of that one. It's just possible that Grandfather might think it's never too late to mend. And I might accept you this time."

Silence again, two long beats of it.

"Why, you little *devil!*" It was the first genuine feeling he had shown during the interview. "Who'd have thought—?" He broke off, and the long mouth curved. "And what if I call your bluff, girl dear? It might be the perfect ending to our little game, after all, and it's just a marvel that I never thought of it before. Sweet saints alive, I can think of a lot worse fates than ending up on the altar steps with you!" He laughed at my expression. "You see? Don't pull too many bluffs with me, acushla, or you might find them called."

"And don't get too clever with me, Con, or you'll cut yourself. I could always quarrel with you again, couldn't I? And this time, who knows, Grandfather might even throw *you* out instead of me."

"All right," said Con easily, "we've called each other's bluff, and that's that." His eyes were brilliant under the long lashes: it was obvious that, however the game went, Con was going to enjoy it to the full. The eight-years'-old tragedy was now nothing more than a counter in that same game. If it had ever touched him, it did so no longer. "We'll play it your way," he said. "I'll watch my step, really I will. I didn't mean to upset you."

"It's the only way to play it."

He still had his back to the house windows, which was just as well. His face, expressive as ever, was alight with uncomplicated excitement. "Whatever the terms—and you can set them—this is going to be the hell of a partnership, Mary Grey! You're a wonderful girl! You know, you and I have got a lot in common."

I said, just a little drily, "Why, thank you. Praise indeed."

He ignored that, or perhaps he didn't see it. "A hell of a partnership! I told you, you'll call the tune. You'll have to, if it comes to that: you'll know better than I would what a girl's reactions would be, after—well, coming back like this. I'll play it any way you say. But we'll have to play it together: it's a duet, not a duel. A duet for you and me, with Lisa turning the pages."

I wondered, fleetingly, what Lisa would have thought of the rôle so lightly assigned to her. "Very well. And to start with, kisses, cousinly or not, are out. Did you ever read *Count Hannibal?*"

"Certainly I did. And I know what you're thinking of, the bit where the hero says: 'Is it to be a kiss or a blow between us, madame?' "

"That's it. And she says: 'A thousand times a blow!' Well, that's the way it is, monsieur."

"Yes, all right. But then, if you remember what happened next—"

"He slapped her face. Yes, so he did. But that's going a bit too far, don't you think? If we just keep it calm and cousinly—"

"You're enjoying this, aren't you?"

"What?" The abruptness of the question had startled me out of laughter. I must have gaped at him quite blankly. "Enjoying it?"

"Yes. Don't pretend you're not. You're as excited as I am."

"I—I don't know. I'm certainly a bit tensed up, who wouldn't be? Hang it, I'm only human." His hand moved up to cover my wrist where it lay along the top bar of the gate. "All right, my pulse is racing. Wouldn't yours be?" I pulled the hand away from under his. "Now, we've talked long enough. When will Grandfather be around?"

"He won't be expecting you quite yet. Don't worry. Lisa says he'll wait upstairs and see you in his room after he's had his rest. Shall I show you round now, before you see him?"

"Good heavens, no. I wouldn't want to look round first, you know. People first, places later. You'd better take me in and introduce me to Lisa, and I'll see Mrs. Bates."

"You keep your head, don't you?"

"Why not? I've taken the first hurdle, anyway."

"Was I a hurdle?"

I laughed. "You? You were the water jump. No, I meant that I'd met Bates when I was on my way down from the road."

"Oh, God, yes, I'd forgotten. I saw him go up, but of course I'd no idea you were coming so early. I take it you got away with it? Good for you, you see how easy it's going to be. . . . Did you greet him by name?"

"Not till he mentioned his wife. Better safe than sorry, though I felt pretty sure, and of course the scarred arm made it a certainty."

"Where did you meet him?"

"Crossing High Riggs."

I saw his eyes widen, and laughed a little. "My dear Con, you'll have to learn not to look startled. Give Lisa some credit. Why shouldn't I recognize High Riggs? It's been called that, time out of mind."

He drew a long breath. "Fair enough. I'm learning. But it's—even more disconcerting, now that I see you actually here . . . in this setting."

"We'd better go in."

"Yes. Lisa'll be in the kitchen, and Mrs. Bates with her."

"I can smell baking, even from here. Do you suppose she'll have made singin' hinnies for my tea?"

I had spoken quite naturally, as I turned to go, but the naked shock in his face stopped me short. He was staring at me as if he'd never seen me before.

His lips opened, and his tongue came out to wet them. "You can't —I never—how did you—?"

He stopped. Behind the taut mask of shock I thought I glimpsed again what I had seen in his face at our first meeting.

I lifted my brows at him. "My dear Con, if you're beginning to have doubts about me yourself, after all this time, I *must* be good!"

The strain slackened perceptibly, as if invisible guys had been loosened. "It's only, it sounded so natural, the sort of little thing she might have said . . . And you standing there, by the yard gate. It's as if it were yesterday." He took a breath; it seemed to be the first for minutes. Then he shook his head sharply, like a dog coming out of water. "I'm sorry, stupid of me. As you say, I'll have to learn. But how in the world did you know a silly little thing like that? I hadn't remembered it myself, and Lisa wouldn't know, and it's ten to one Mrs. Bates never mentioned it to her till today, if she has even now."

"Yes, she has. Bates told me she'd be making them for my tea. He nearly caught me right out. What the dickens are they, anyway?"

"Oh, a special kind of girdle-cake." He laughed, and the sound was at once elated, and half-relieved. "So you just learned it ten minutes ago, and you come out with it as to the manner born! You're wonderful! A hell of a partnership, did I call it? My God, Mary Grey—and it's the last time I'll ever call you that—you're the girl for my money! You're a winner, and didn't I know it the minute I clapped eyes on you, up there on the Wall? If it wouldn't look kind of excessive, besides going back on our pact and making you as mad as fire, I'm damned if

I wouldn't kiss you again! No, no, it's all right, don't look at me like that; I said I'd behave, and I will."

"I'm glad to hear it. And now we've been out here quite long enough. Shall we go in?"

"Sure . . . Annabel. Come along. Headed straight for the next fence; Becher's Brook this time, wouldn't you say?" His hand slid under my arm. Physical contact seemed to come as naturally to Con Winslow as breathing. "No, not that way. You ought to know they never use the front door on a farm."

"I'm sorry." I gave a quick glance round the deserted yard, and up at the empty windows. "No harm done."

"Not scared at all?"

"No. Edgy, but not scared."

The hand squeezed my arm. "That's my girl."

I withdrew it. "No. Remember?"

He was looking down at me speculatively, charmingly, still with that glint of teasing amusement, but I got the feeling that it was no longer something pleasant that amused him. He said, "Girl dear, if you only knew. . . ."

"Look," I said, "if I only knew, as you put it, I imagine I wouldn't be here at all. And we agreed to drop it all, didn't we? It's going to be quite embarrassing enough having to face you in front of Grandfather, without your amusing yourself by teasing me when we're alone."

"I only said—"

"I know what you said. And I'm saying that we'll drop the subject as from now. If I were Annabel, would you want to be reminding me of past . . . differences? Or, for that matter would you want *me* to be reminding Grandfather?"

There was a tiny pause.

"Well, well," said Con, and laughed. "All right, Annabel, my dear. A thousand times a blow. Come along into the lion's den."

CHAPTER

FOUR

She can make an Irish Stew,
  Aye, and singin' hinnies, too . . .

North Country Song: *Billy Boy*.

When Con showed me along the flagged passage, and into the kitchen, Lisa was just lifting a fresh batch of baking out of the oven. The air was full of the delectable smell of new bread.

The kitchen was a big, pleasant room, with a high ceiling, a new cream-coloured Aga stove, and long windows made gay with potted geraniums and chintz curtains that stirred in the June breeze. The floor was of red tiles, covered with those bright rugs of hooked rag that make Northern kitchens so attractive. In front of the Aga was an old-fashioned fender of polished steel, and inside it, from a basket covered with flannel, came the soft cheepings of newly hatched chickens. The black and white cat asleep in the rocking chair took no notice of the sounds, or of the tempting heavings and buttings of small heads and bodies against the covering flannel.

I stopped short, just inside the door.

At that moment, more, I think, than at any other in the whole affair, I bitterly regretted the imposture I was undertaking. For two pins I'd have bolted then and there. What had seemed exciting and even reasonable in Newcastle, simple in High Riggs, and intriguing just now in the yard outside, seemed, in this cheerful, lovely room smelling of home, to be no less than an outrage. This wasn't, any more, just a house I had come to claim for Con, or a counter in a game I was playing; it was home, a place breathing with a life of its own, fostered by generations of people who had belonged here. In the shabby Newcastle boarding house, with my lonely and prospectless Canadian life behind me, and a dreary part-time job doing nothing but stave off the future, things had looked very different: but here, in Whitescar itself, the world of second-class intrigue seemed preposterously out of place. Things should be simple in a place like this, simple and good; sunshine through flowered curtains, the smell of new bread, and chickens cheeping on the hearth; not a complicated imposture, a fantastic Oppenheim plot hatched out in a shabby bedroom with this Irish adventurer and this stolid woman with the soft, grasping hands, who, having put down the baking tray, was moving now to greet me.

They must have noticed my hesitation, but there was no one else to see it. Through a half-shut door that led to the scullery came the sounds of water running, and the chink of crockery. Mrs. Bates, I supposed. Perhaps, with instinctive tact, she had retired to let me meet the current mistress of Whitescar.

It seemed it was just as well she had, for to my surprise the stolid, ever-reliable Lisa seemed, now it had come to the point, to be the least composed of the three of us. Her normally sallow cheeks were flushed, though this may only have been from the heat of the oven. She came forward, and then hesitated, as if at a loss for words.

Con was saying, easily, at my elbow, "Here she is, Lisa. She came early, and I met her at the gate. I've been trying to tell her how welcome she is, but perhaps you'll do it better than me. She's finding it all a bit of a trial so far, I'm afraid." This with his charming smile down at me, and a little brotherly pat on the arm. "Annabel, this is my half-sister, Lisa Dermott. She's been looking after us all, you knew that."

"We've already had a long talk over the telephone," I said. "How do you do, Miss Dermott? I'm very glad to meet you. It—it's lovely to be back. I suppose I needn't tell you that."

She took my hand. She was smiling, but her eyes were anxious, and the soft hand was trembling.

She spoke quite naturally, however. "You're welcome indeed, Miss Winslow. I dare say it seems odd to you to have me greet you like this in your own home, but after all this time it's come to feel like home to me as well. So perhaps you'll let me tell you how glad everybody is to see you back. We'd—you must know, I told you yesterday—we'd all thought you must be dead. You can imagine that this is a great occasion."

"Why, Miss Dermott, how nice of you."

"I hope," she said, rather more easily, "that you'll call me Lisa."

"Of course. Thank you. And you must please drop the 'Miss Winslow,' too. We're cousins, surely, or is it half-cousins, I wouldn't know?" I smiled at her. The chink of crockery from the scullery had stopped as soon as I spoke. Through the half-shut door there came a sort of listening silence. I wondered if our conversation were sounding too impossibly stilted. If this had genuinely been my first introduction to Lisa, no doubt the situation would have been every bit as awkward. There would have been, literally, nothing to say.

I went on saying just that, in a voice that sounded, to myself, too high, too quick, too light altogether. "After all, I'm the stranger here, or so it feels, after all this time, and I'm sure you've given me a better welcome than I deserve! Of course it's your home—" I looked about me—"more than mine, now, surely! I never remember it looking half as pretty! How lovely you've got it . . . new curtains . . . new paint . . . the same old chickens, I'll swear, they were always part of the furniture . . . oh, there's the old tea caddy, I'm so glad you didn't throw it out!"

Lisa had certainly never thought fit to mention the battered old tin on the mantelpiece, but, since it was decorated with a picture of George V's Coronation, they would recognize it as a safe bet. "And the Aga! That's terrific! When was that put in?"

"Five years ago." Lisa spoke shortly, almost repressively. Con was watching me with what seemed to be amused respect, but Lisa, I could see, thought I was jumping a bit too fast into that attentive silence from the scullery.

I grinned at her, with a spice of mischief, and moved over to the hearth. "Oh lord, the old rocking chair . . . and it still creaks. . . ." I creaked it again, and the sleeping cat opened slitted green eyes, looked balefully at me, and shut them again. I laughed, almost naturally, and stooped to stroke him. "My welcome home. He looks a tough egg, this chap. What happened to Tibby?"

"He died of old age," said Con. "I buried him under your lilac tree."

"He'd have died of middle-age long before that, if I'd had my way." Lisa was back at the table, scooping hot rolls off the tin on to the baking sieve. She seemed relieved to be back in action. She didn't look at Con or me. "The place for cats is in the buildings, and they know it."

"You didn't try and keep *Tibby* outside?"

"Tibby," said Con cheerfully, "was so hedged about with the sanctity of having been your cat, that he was practically allowed to live in your bedroom. Don't worry about Tibby. He got even Lisa down in the end, and lived his life out in the greatest possible honour and luxury."

I smiled and stroked the cat's ears. "Not like Flush?"

"Flush?" This was Lisa. I caught the sudden quick overtone of apprehension, as if she had caught me speaking without the book.

Con grinned at her. "Elizabeth Barrett's dog. When Elizabeth bolted, early one morning, just like Annabel, her father is said to have wanted to destroy her little dog, as a sort of revenge."

"O—oh . . . I see."

He looked at me. "No, Annabel, not like Flush. Revenge wasn't . . . our first reaction."

I let it pass. "And this one?" I said. "What's his claim to the best chair in the kitchen?"

"Tommy? That fat, lazy brute?" Lisa was patently feeling the strain. A conversation about cats at this juncture was, obviously, the last straw in irrelevance. Lisa's Teutonic thoroughness wanted to get on with the task in hand, lay the next brick or so, and slap a few more solid lies in to mortar the brand-new structure together. She said, almost snappily, "Heaven knows I throw him out often enough, but he will come in, and I haven't had the time today to shift him."

Con said lazily, "His personality's stronger than yours, Lisa my dear." He, apparently, shared my belief that the bricks of deception could be perfectly well made with the smallest straws of irrelevance. He took a roll off the rack and bit into it. "Mmm. Not bad. They're eatable today, Lisa. I suppose that means Mrs. Bates made them?"

His sister's forbidding expression broke up into that sudden affectionate smile that was kept only for him.

"Oh, have some butter with it, Con, do. Or wait until tea time. Won't you ever grow up?"

"Isn't Mrs. Bates here?" I asked.

Lisa shot me a look, three parts relief to one of apprehension. "Yes. She's through in the scullery. Would you like—?"

But before she could finish the sentence the door was pushed open and, as if on a cue, a woman appeared in the doorway, a round squat figure of the same general shape as the Mrs. Noah from a toy ark, who stood on the threshold with arms in the traditional 'akimbo' position, surveying me with ferocious little boot-button eyes.

Lisa led in hastily, "Oh, Mrs. Bates, here's Miss Annabel."

"I can see that. I ain't blind, nor yet I ain't deaf." Mrs. Bates' thin lips shut like a trap. The fierce little eyes regarded me. "And where do *you* think you've been all this time, may I ask? And what have you been a-doing of to yourself? You look terrible. You're as thin as a rail, and if you're not careful you'll have lost all your looks, what's left of 'em, by the time you're thirty. America, indeed! Ain't your own home good enough for you?"

She was nodding while she spoke, little sharp jerking movements like one of those mandarin toys one used to see; and each nod was a condemnation. I saw Con flick an apprehensive look at me, and then at his sister. But he needn't have worried; Lisa's briefing had been thorough. *She adored Annabel, cursed her up hill and down dale, wouldn't hear anyone say a word against her; had a frightful set-to with Mr. Winslow after she ran away, and called him every tyrant under the sun. . . . She's frightfully rude—plain spoken she calls it—and she resents me, but I had to keep her; Bates is the best cattleman in the county, and she's a marvellous worker. . . .*

"A fine thing it's been for us, let me tell you," said Mrs. Bates sharply, "thinking all this time as you was lost and gone beyond recall, but now as you *is* back, there's a few things I'd like to be telling you, and that's a fact. There's none can say I'm one to flatter and mince me words, plain-spoken I may be, but I speak as I find, and for anyone to do what you gone and did, and run off without a word in the middle of the night—"

I laughed at her. "It wasn't the middle of the night, and you know it." I went up to her, took her by the shoulders and gave her a quick hug, then bent and kissed the hard round cheek. I said gently, "Make me welcome, Betsy. Don't make it harder to come home. Goodness knows I feel bad enough about it, I don't need you to tell me. I'm sorry if it distressed you all, but I—well, I was terribly unhappy, and when one's very young and very unhappy, one doesn't always stop to think, does one?"

I kissed the other cheek quickly, and straightened up. The little black eyes glared up at me, but her mouth was working. I smiled, and said lightly, "And you must admit I did the thing properly, dreadful quarrel, note left on the pincushion and everything."

"Pincushion? What did you ever want with a pincushion? Never did a decent day's work in your life, always traipsing around after horses and dogs and tractors, or that there garden of yours, let alone the house and the jobs a girl ought to take an interest in. Pincushion!" She snorted. "Where would you be finding one of them?"

"Well," I said mildly, "where did I leave it?"

"On that mantelpiece as ever was, *which* well you remember!" She nodded across the kitchen. "And when I come down that morning I was the one found it there, and I stood there fair pussystruck for five mortal minutes, I did, afore I dared pick it up. I knew what it was, you see. I'd heard you and your Granda having words the night before, *and* I heard you go to your room just after, which well you know I did. I didn't never think to have the chance to tell you this, but I folleyed you along, Miss Annabel, an' I listened outside your door."

I was very conscious of Con just at my shoulder. I said quickly, "Betsy, dear—"

I saw Con make a slight, involuntary movement, and thought: he doesn't want me to stop her; he thinks I'll learn something from all this.

He needn't have worried, she had no intention of being stopped until I had heard it all.

"But there wasn't a sound, not of crying. Just as if you was moving about the room quiet-like, getting ready for your bed. So I thought to meself, it's only a fight, I thought, the old man'll be sorry in the morning, and Miss Annabel'll tell him she won't do it again, whatever she done, riding that Everest horse of Mr. Forrest's maybe, or maybe even staying out too late, the way she has been lately, and the old man not liking it, him being old-fashioned that way. But I thinks to meself, it'll be all right in the morning, the way it always has been, so I just coughs to let you know I'm there, and I taps on the door and says: 'I'm away to bed now, Miss Annabel,' and you stopped moving about, as if I'd frightened you, and then you come over to the door and stopped inside it for a minute, but when you opened it you still had all your things on, and you said 'Good night, Betsy dear, and thank you,' and you kissed me, you remember, and you looked so terrible, white and ill, and I says, 'Don't take on so, Miss Annabel,' I says, 'there's nought that doesn't come right in the end, not if it was ever so,' and you smiled at that and said 'No.' And then I went off to bed, and I never heard no sound, and if anyone had tell't me that next morning early you'd up and go, and stay away all these years, and your Granda fretting his heart out after you, for all he's had Mr. Con here, and Julie as is coming this week, *which* she's the spitting image of you, I might say—"

"I know. Lisa told me. I'm longing to meet her." I touched her hand again. "Don't upset yourself any more. Let's leave it, shall we? I—I've come back, and I'm not going again, and don't be too angry with me for doing what I did."

Lisa rescued me, still, I gathered, trying to bring the straying runner back on course. "Your grandfather'll be awake by now. You'd better

go up, he'll want to see you straight away." She was reaching for her
apron strings. "I'll take you up. Just give me time to wash my hands."

I saw Mrs. Bates bridle, and said, smoothly enough, "Don't trouble,
Lisa. I—I'd sooner go up by myself. I'm sure you'll understand."

Lisa had stopped halfway to the sink, looking irresolute, and rather
too surprised.

Mrs. Bates was nodding again, with a kind of triumph in the tight
compression of her mouth. Con took another new roll, and saluted me
with a tiny lift of the eyebrow as he turned to go. "Of course you
would," he said. "Don't treat Annabel as a stranger, Lisa my dear. And
don't worry, Annabel. He'll be so pleased to see you that he's not likely
to rake up anything painful out of the past."

Another lift of the eyebrow on this masterly *double-entendre* of reassurance, and he was gone.

Lisa relaxed, and seemed to recollect something of her lost poise.
"I'm sorry." Her voice was once more even and colourless. "Of course
you'll want to go alone. I was forgetting. It isn't every day one gets a
—an occasion like this. Go on up now, my dear. Tea'll be ready in half
an hour. . . . Mrs. Bates, I wonder if you would help me with the tea
cakes? You're a much better hand at them than I am."

"Which is not to be wondered at, seeing as how I'm north country
bred and born, *which* no foreigner ever had a good hand with a tea
cake yet," said that lady tartly, but moving smartly towards the table.

Lisa had stooped again to the oven. Her back was towards us. I
had to say it, and this was as good a moment as any. "Betsy, bless
you, singin' hinnies! They look as good as ever!"

Lisa dropped the oven shelf with a clatter against its runners. I heard
her say, "Sorry. Clumsy," in a muffled voice. "It's all right, I didn't
spill anything."

"You don't think," said Mrs. Bates crisply, "that them singin' hinnies
is for you? Get along with you now, to your Granda."

But the nod which went along with the briskly snapping voice said,
quite plainly, "Don't be frightened. Go on. It'll be all right."

I left the kitchen door open behind me.

It was obvious that no questions of identity were going to rouse
themselves in the minds of Mrs. Bates and her husband; but the real
ordeal was still ahead of me, and if there were ever going to be questions asked, my every movement on this first day was going to be
important.

So I left the door open, and was conscious of Lisa and Mrs. Bates watching me as I crossed the flagged back lobby, pushed open the green baize door which gave on the front hall, and turned unhesitatingly to the right before the door swung shut behind me.

"It's a very simple house," Lisa had said. "It's shaped like an L, with the wing shorter than the stem of the L. The wing's where the kitchens are, and the scullery, and what used to be the dairy, but all the dairy work's done in the buildings now, so it's a laundry house with a Bendix and an electric ironing machine. There's a baize door that cuts the kitchen wing off from the main body of the house.

"It's not the original farmhouse, you know, it's what you might call a small manor. It was built about a hundred and fifty years ago, on the site of the old house that was pulled down. You'll find a print of the original farmhouse in Bewick's *Northumberland*; that was a square, grim-looking sort of building, but the new one's quite different, like a small country house, plain and sturdy, certainly, but graceful too . . . The main hall's square, almost an extra room . . . a wide staircase opposite the front door . . . drawing room to one side, dining room to the other with the library behind; that's used as an office . . . your grandfather's bedroom is the big room at the front, over the drawing room. . . ."

As the baize door shut, I leaned back against it for a moment, and let myself pause. It could not have been more than three-quarters of an hour since I had met Bates in High Riggs, but already I felt exhausted with sustained effort. I must have a minute or two alone, to collect myself, before I went upstairs. . . .

I looked about me. The hall had certainly never been built for an ordinary farmhouse. The floor was oak parquet, and the old blanket chest against the wall was carved oak, too, and beautiful. A couple of Bockhara rugs looked very rich against the honey-coloured wood of the floor. The walls were plain ivory, and there was a painting of a jar of marigolds, a copy of the Sartorius aquatint of the Darley Arabian, and an old coloured map of the North Tyne, with *Forrest Hall* clearly marked, and, in smaller letters on a neat segment of the circle labelled *Forrest Park*, I identified *Whitescar*.

Below the map, on the oak chest, stood a blue ironstone jug, and an old copper dairy pan, polished till its hammered surface gleamed like silk. It was full of blue and purple pansies and wild yellow heartsease.

Whitescar had certainly not suffered from Lisa's stewardship. I reflected, in passing, that Lisa had been wrong about Mrs. Bates. Mrs.

Bates by no means disliked her; her attitude of armed neutrality was a
faint reflection of the ferocious affection she had hurled at me. Anyone who could keep a house as Lisa had had almost certainly won Mrs.
Bates' loyalty, along with as lively a respect as a Northumbrian would
care to accord a "foreigner."

I went slowly up the wide oak staircase. The carpet was moss-green
and thick; my feet made no sound. I turned along the landing which
made a gallery to one side of the hall. At the end of it a window looked
over the garden.

Here was the door. Oak, too, with shallow panels sunk in their bev-
elled frames. I put out a finger and ran it silently down the bevel.

The landing was full of sunlight. A bee was trapped, and blundering,
with a deep hum, against the window. The sound was soporific, dreamy,
drowning time. It belonged to a thousand summer afternoons, all the
same, long, sun-drenched, lazily full of sleep. . . .

Time ran down to nothing; stood still; ran back. . . .

The moment snapped. I turned, with a sharp little movement, and
thrust open the casement beside me. The bee bumbled foolishly about
for a moment or two, then shot off into the sunlight like a pebble from
a sling. I latched the window quietly behind it, then turned and
knocked at the door.

Matthew Winslow was wide awake, and watching the door.

He lay, not on the bed, but on a broad, old-fashioned sofa near the
window. The big bed, covered with a white honeycomb quilt, stood
against the further wall. The room was large, with the massive shiny
mahogany furniture dear to the generation before last, and a thick In-
dian carpet. The windows were charming, long and latticed, and wide
open to the sun and the sound of the river at the foot of the garden.
A spray of early Albertine roses hung just outside the casement, and
bees were busy there. For all its thick carpet, cluttered ornaments, and
heavy old furniture, the room smelt fresh, of sunshine and roses on the
wall.

On a small table beside the bed were three photographs. One was of
Con, looking dramatically handsome in an open-necked shirt, with
some clever lighting throwing the planes of his face into relief. Another,
I guessed, was Julie; a young, eager face with vivid eyes and a tumble
of fair, fine hair. I couldn't see the third from where I stood.

But all this was for the moment no more than a fleeting impression.

What caught and held the eye was the figure of the old man reclining against the cushions on the sofa with a plaid rug across his knees.

Matthew Winslow was a tall, gaunt old man with a thick mane of white hair, which had once been fair. His eyes, puckered now and sunken under the prominent brows, were grey-green; now the edges of the iris had faded, but the eyes still looked bright and hard as a young man's. His mouth, too, was hard, a thin line between the deep parallels that drove from nostril to jaw line. It would have been, for all its craggy good looks, a forbidding face, had it not been for a gleam of humour that lurked somewhere near the corners of mouth and eyes. One would certainly not, at first glance, take Matthew Winslow for a man who needed to be guarded from anything. He looked as tough as pemmican, and nobody's fool.

In response to his gruff summons I had entered the room, and shut the door quietly behind me. There was a pause of complete stillness, in which the buzzing of the bees among the pink roses sounded as loud as a flight of aircraft.

I said, "Grandfather?" on a note of painful hesitation.

His voice was harsh when he spoke, and the words uncompromising, but I had seen him wet his lips and make the attempt twice. "Well, Annabel?"

There was surely, I thought confusedly, some sort of precedent for this, the prodigal's return? *He ran, and fell on his neck, and kissed him. . . .*

Well, Matthew Winslow couldn't run. That left me.

I went quickly across the room and knelt down beside the sofa, and put my hands on his lap, on top of the plaid rug. His thin hand, with its prominent, blue-knotted veins, came down hard over mine, surprisingly strong and warm.

In the end it was easy to know what to say. I said quite simply, "I'm sorry, Grandfather. Will you have me back?"

The hand moved, holding mine together even more tightly. "If I said no," said Grandfather crisply, "it would be no more than you deserve." He cleared his throat violently. "We thought you were dead."

"I'm sorry."

His other hand reached forward and lifted my chin. He studied my face, turning it towards the light of the window. I bit my lip and waited, not meeting his gaze. He said nothing for a long time, then, as harshly as before, "You've been unhappy. Haven't you?"

I nodded. He let me go, and at last I was able to put my forehead down on the rug, so that he couldn't see my face. He said, "So have we," and fell silent again, patting my hand.

Out of the corner of my eye I could see Con's portrait, the fine mouth just moving into that smile of his, full of challenge, and something that was more than mischief; an exciting, and, yes, a dangerous face. Well, Con, it was done now, all behind me, the burned boats, the Rubicons. We were over Becher's Brook, the Canal Turn, the lot, and into the straight. Home.

Con's eyes watched. What good would it do now to lift my head and say, "Your beloved Con's betraying you. He's paying me to come and pretend I'm your grand-daughter, because he thinks you'll die soon, and he wants your money, and your place." And something in me, some little voice I'd never listened to before, added, "And once he's made certain of that, I wouldn't give twopence for your life, Grandfather, I wouldn't really. . . ."

I stayed where I was, not speaking.

The old man said nothing. The bees had gone. A small bird flew into the roses by the open window; I heard the flirt of its wings, and the tap and swish of the twigs as it alighted.

At length I lifted my head, and smiled at him. He removed his hands, and looked at me under the thrust of his brows. If there had been any sign of emotion in his face, it had been banished now.

"Get a chair." He spoke abruptly. "And sit where I can see you."

I obeyed him. I chose an upright chair, and sat correctly and rather primly on it, knees and feet together, back straight, hands in lap, like a small girl about to recite her catechism.

I thought I saw a glimmer of appreciation in his eyes. "Well?" he said. Without moving, he seemed all at once to sit up straighter, even to tower over me. "You've got a lot of talking to do, girl. Supposing you start."

CHAPTER

FIVE

Some men has plenty money and no brains, and
some men has plenty brains and no money. Surely
men with plenty money and no brains were made
for men with plenty brains and no money.
                    —From the Notebook of the Tichborne claimant.

"Well?" said Lisa softly, like an echo.

She was waiting at the foot of the stairs. A shaft of sunlight through
the hall window dazzled along the edge of the copper bowl of pansies.
She had her back to the light, and I couldn't see her expression, but
even in the one softly uttered word I could hear some of the trembling
uncertainty she had showed in the kitchen. "How did it go off?"

I had paused when I saw her waiting, and now came reluctantly
down the stairs.

"All right. Far better than I'd have expected."

She gave her withdrawn, close-lipped smile. It was as if, with this
quiet lying-in-wait, these careful whispers, she was deliberately putting
me back where I belonged; inside a dusty little cell of conspiracy, able
to share my thoughts and hopes only with herself and Con, bound to
them in a reluctant but unbreakable intimacy.

She said, "I told you there was nothing to be afraid of."

"I know. But I suppose conscience makes cowards of us all."

"What?"

"Nothing. A quotation. Shakespeare."

She looked faintly resentful, as she had in the kitchen when Con
and I had seemed to be moving too fast for her. Perhaps the quotation
irked her, or the realization that I hadn't come from Grandfather's
room bursting with confidences; or perhaps she didn't like to be reminded that I had once had a conscience. At any rate she slammed the
door of the conspirators' cell hard on me once again. "You're very literary today. You want to be careful. It isn't in character."

I smiled. "I've had plenty of time to settle down and improve my mind abroad."

"Hm. He didn't—he wasn't suspicious at all?"

"No." I spoke a little wearily. "It's exactly as you and Con foretold. There's no reason why he should be. It never even entered his head."

She pursed her lips with satisfaction. "Well, what did happen?"

My mind went back to the scene upstairs. Well, they couldn't buy everything.

I said slowly, "You can have the main outlines, if you like. I told him where I'd been since I left here, and how I'd been living. You know we'd arranged to tell the simple truth about that, as much as possible."

"Did he say much about . . . the trouble? The reason why you went?"

"Nothing that need concern you. I just tried to make it clear that, whatever had happened in the past, nothing in the world would persuade me to—well, to take up with Con again." I saw the look in her face, and added smoothly, "That, of course, was to protect Con and myself. It was quite possible, you know, that Grandfather was nursing some hopes of a reconciliation. I had to insist that there could never be anything between Con and myself except—" I hesitated—"you might call it armed neutrality."

"I see. Yes, that would have been—" she stopped. That conspirators' look again. "I'm sure you're right. There was nothing more? Nothing about the—the future?"

"Nothing at all."

She looked about her. "Well, you can't say much more just now, that's obvious. He'll be coming down soon. Later tonight, when we're alone, you can tell me all that was said."

"Make my report? No," I said gently.

Her mouth opened, with as much surprise as if I had struck her. "What d'you mean? You surely don't think that you can—"

"You probably wouldn't understand what I mean. But let's put it like this. I've a difficult rôle to play, and the only way to play it is to *be* it, to live in it, breathe it, think it, try to dream it. In other words, not to have to keep stepping out of Annabel's skin to remember that I'm just someone pretending to be Annabel. I can't act this thing in a series of little scenes, Lisa, with commentaries to you and Con in the intervals. If there's anything vital, or if I should want your help, believe me, I won't hesitate to come to you. But the biggest help you can both give me is simply to forget all that's happened in the last three weeks, and think of me, if you can, just as Annabel, come back to take my accustomed place in my own home. If you keep asking me questions, jerking me back out of my part into the part of Mary Grey, impostor . . . Well, then, Lisa, some day I may get my parts mixed up, and go wrong. And I could go very wrong indeed, very easily."

I paused, and added, lightly enough, "Well, there it is. Forget Mary Grey. Forget she ever existed. Believe me, I'm right. This is the only way to take it."

She said doubtfully, "Well, yes, but . . ."

I laughed. "Oh, Lisa, stop looking at me as if you were Frankenstein, and the monster had just got away from you! I'm only talking common sense! And you've only to remember that Con and I are mutually committed, even to the extent of signing those deadly little 'confessions' for each other to keep, just in case. I've no doubt Con keeps mine next to his skin, day and night. Call it remote control if you like, but it's there! Even if Annabel Winslow *is* home again, at least you know that she's got to bat on Con's side this time!"

"I—well, yes, of course. Forgive me, I didn't really doubt you, but this afternoon has been disconcerting, to say the least. You . . . you're so very *good* at this. I've been the one to be nervous."

"I assure you, I'm quaking inside! It's all right. I won't doublecross you, you know, Lisa, even if I dared."

"Dared?"

I didn't answer, and after a moment her eyes dropped. "Well, that's that, then. And you're quite right. I'll try and do as you say, and forget it all, unless there's anything urgent. But it certainly doesn't look as if you're going to need much help, my dear. If you got away with that—" A movement of her head towards the upper landing completed the sentence for her.

"Well, I did. Now let's forget it. Did you say something about tea?"

"I was just going to make it."

"Do you want any help?"

"Not on your first day home."

"Then I think I'll go upstairs for a little. Am I in my old room?"

She smiled. "Yes. D'you mind using the nursery bathroom? You'll be sharing it with Julie."

"Of course not. Does she know about me?"

"Yes. She rang up last night, to say she'd be here on Wednesday, and Mr. Winslow told her about you. That's all I know."

"Wednesday . . ." I paused with a foot on the lowest stair. "Ah well, that gives us two more days. Oh, Lisa, I forgot, my cases—"

"Con brought them in just now, and took them up."

"Oh? It was good of him to get them so quickly. I'll see you at tea, then. Where d'you have it?"

"When I'm alone, in the kitchen as often as not. But for today, the drawing-room. Your grandfather'll be down, I expect. Did he say?"

"Yes. He—he wants to show me round the place himself after tea."

The brown eyes held mine just a moment longer than was necessary.

"Of course," said Lisa, abandoning comment with what looked like an effort, "he would want to do that. Naturally. Well—I'll see you later."

I turned and went back upstairs. I could see her watching me as, unhesitatingly, I took the left-hand passage past the head of the gallery.

Yours is the second door. . . . It was a pleasant room, with a long latticed window like Grandfather's, and the same Albertine rose nodding outside it. There was a wide window seat, covered with chintz in a pretty, Persian-looking pattern of birds and flowers and trellis work, done in deliberately faded colours. The same chintz appeared for curtains and bedspread. The furniture was plain deal, white-painted; originally it would speak of "nursery," but now a new coat of paint made it merely cottage and very charming. The floor was of polished boards with a couple of rugs, and the walls and ceiling were plain ivory white.

Con had dumped my baggage on the floor near the foot of the bed. He had also thoughtfully brought up my handbag, which I must have left in the kitchen, and this lay on the bed.

I wasn't prepared to cope with unpacking yet. I picked up the handbag and carried it across to the window seat. I sat down, opened the bag, and took out my cigarettes.

As I shook one loose from the pack, I glanced at the door. There was a key in the lock. So far, so good. I had a feeling that I was going to need frequent doses of privacy to recover from the rounds of a game which, though so far it had proved a walk-over, might well get stickier as time went on.

I put the cigarette in my mouth, and felt in the little mirror-pocket in my bag where I had carried a flat book of matches. It wasn't there. My fingers met merely a slip of paper. Surely, I thought, irritably, I had had one? I had been smoking in the bus coming from Newcastle . . . I pulled the bag wider to look for it. I saw it immediately, then, a little scarlet book labelled *Café Kasbah,* tucked deep in the pocket on

the other side of my bag, where I kept bills and shopping lists and odd-
ments of that sort.

I lit the cigarette slowly, and sat contemplating the bag, open on
my lap. Now that I had noticed it, there were other signs. The top
had come loose on one of my lipsticks; the few papers that I carried
were shuffled hastily back into their places as I didn't think I had put
them; the slip of paper where I had scribbled down the Whitescar telephone number, which had been among the other papers, was pushed
into the mirror compartment where normally the matches were kept.
Whoever had scrabbled hastily through my handbag had taken few
pains to cover his tracks.

Con? Lisa? I grinned to myself. What was it they called this kind of
thing? Counter-espionage? That, I was sure, was how it would rank in
Lisa's mind. Whatever you called it, it was surely a little late, now, for
them to be checking on my *bona fides*.

I went quickly through what was there. The telephone number; it
was natural enough that I should have scribbled that down; numbers
change in eight years. A bus time table, acquired that day on my way
here. The receipt for my lodgings near the Haymarket, also received
that morning. That was all right; it was addressed to "Miss A.
Winslow."

Then I hesitated, with it in my hand. Was it all right, after all? It
was admittedly unlikely that Grandfather would ever see it, or check on
it if he did, but both Con and Lisa had visited me there. It was better
out of the way. I crumpled the paper up, and threw it into the empty
fireplace. I would burn it before I went downstairs.

I turned over the other papers. A few shopping chits; a couple of used
bus tickets; a folded paper of pale green. . . .

I picked it out from among the others, and unfolded it. "*Passenger
Motor Vehicle Permit . . . Mary Grey . . .*" and the address near Montreal. There it lay, clear as a curse, the Canadian car permit; the owner's
licence that you carry daily, yearly, and never even see, except when the
time comes round to renew it. . . .

Well, I thought, as I crumpled it in my hand, Con and Lisa must
realize what an easy mistake this had been to make. I wondered, not
without amusement, how on earth they would manage to warn me
about it, without having to confess that they had searched my belong-
ings. At least they could not also have searched my cases; the key hung
on a chain round my neck, and there it was going to stay. . . .

From somewhere outside I heard Lisa calling, and Con's voice in reply. I heard him cross the yard towards the house. There was a low-voiced colloquy, then he went back towards the buildings.

I got up, and set a match to the crumpled bill in the fireplace, then carefully fed the car permit into the flames. I picked up the poker, and stirred the burned fragments of paper till they flaked and fell away to nothing, through the bars of the grate. Then I went back to the sunny window, picked up my half-smoked cigarette, and sat for some minutes longer, trying to relax.

The window looked out over the small front garden. This was a simple square bounded by low sandstone walls, and sloping slightly towards the river. From the front door a gravel path, weedy and unraked, led straight to the white wicket gate that gave on the river bank and the bridge that spanned the water. The path was bordered by ragged hedges of lavender, under which sprawled a few hardy pansies and marigolds. Behind these borders, to either side, the unkempt grass reached back to what had once been the flower beds.

Here was confusion indeed. Lupins had run wild, all the gay colours faded back to their pristine blue; peonies crouched sullenly under the strangling bushes of fuchsia and flowering currant, and everywhere ivy, bindweed, and rose-bay willow herb were joyously completing their deadly work. At first glance, the riot of colour might deceive the eye into thinking that here was a pretty garden still, but then one saw the dandelions, the rampant rose bushes, the docks in the rank grass under the double white lilac tree. . . .

Beyond the far wall, and the white wicket, was a verge of sheep-bitten grass, and the wooden bridge that was Whitescar's short cut to town. From the other end of the bridge the track wound up through the trees that crowded the far bank, and vanished eventually into their shadow.

My eye came back, momentarily, to the tangled garden. Two blackbirds had flown into the lilac tree, quarrelling furiously. The great heads of milky blossom shook and swayed. I could smell lilac from where I sat.

(*Annabel's garden. She planted it all. Remember to ask Con what's in it . . . if he knows.*)

He had not known.

I leaned to stub out my cigarette on the stone sill outside the window frame.

It was time to go down. Act Two. Back into the conspirators' cell with Con and Lisa.

I found myself hoping passionately that Con wouldn't be in to tea.

He wasn't, and it was still, it seemed, going to be easy. Grandfather came down a little late, opening the drawing-room door on me discussing amiably with Lisa what had happened to various neighbours during my long absence, and thereafter acted more or less as though the eight years' gap had never been.

After tea he took me outside, and led the way towards the farm buildings. He walked fairly rapidly, and held his gaunt body upright apparently without effort. With the westering sun behind him, shadowing the thinned, bony face, and making the grey hair look blond as it must once have been, it wasn't difficult to see once more the active, opinionated, quick-tempered man who had done so much through his long life to make Whitescar the prosperous concern it now was. I could see, too, why Con—in spite of the old man's favour—walked warily.

Grandfather paused at the yard gate. "Changed much?"

"The farm? I—it's hard to tell."

A quick look under the jutting white brows. "What d'you mean?"

I said slowly, "Oh, some things, yes. The new paint, and—that wall's new, isn't it? And the concrete, and all that drainage. But I meant— well, I've been gone a long time, and I suppose I've lived so long on a memory of Whitescar, that now it's bound to look strange to me. My picture of it my imagined picture, I mean—has become almost more real than the thing itself. For one thing," I laughed a little, "I remember it as being always in sunshine. One does, you know."

"So they say. I'd have thought you'd be more likely to remember it the way you left it. It was a vile day."

"Yes. I went before it was fully light, and you can imagine what it looked like. Rain and wind, and the fields all grey and flattened. I remember how awful that one looked—at least, was it in corn that year? I—I forget."

"Turnips. But you're quite right. The corn was badly laid everywhere that year."

"The odd thing is," I said, "that I hardly really remember that at all. Perhaps the psychologists would say that the rain and wind, and that grey early morning, were all mixed up in my mind with the misery of leaving home, and that I've allowed myself to forget it." I laughed. "I wouldn't know. But all the years I was away, I remembered nothing

but sunshine . . . fine, lovely days, and all the things we used to do
. . . childhood memories, mostly." I paused for a little. "I suppose you
could say that my actual memories of home got overlaid, in time, with
dream-pictures. I know that, after a few years, I'd have been hard put
to it to give a really accurate description of . . . this, for instance."

I gestured to the tidy yard, the shadowy cave of the barn, the double
stable doors with the tops latched back to the wall.

"If you'd even asked me what sort of stone it was built of, I couldn't
have told you. And yet, now that I'm back, I notice everything. Tiny
things that I must have taken for granted all my life, and never really
seen before."

"Hm." He was staring at me fixedly. There was neither gentleness
nor affection, that I could see, in the clear grey-green gaze. He said
abruptly, "Con's a good lad."

I must have sounded slightly startled. "Yes, of course."

He misunderstood the wariness of my manner, for his voice had a
harsher note as he said, with equal abruptness, "Don't worry. I'm not
harking back to that business eight years back. You've told me you had
your reasons, and I've accepted that."

I said nothing. I saw him glance sideways at me, then he added
testily, as if I had been arguing, "All right, all right. We've said all there
is to say. We'll drop it now. But apart from things that are over and
forgotten, Con's a good lad, and he's been a son to me these last eight
years."

"Yes."

Another of those bright, almost inimical glances. "I mean that. I'd
have done badly without him for a long time now, and this last year or
two, it'd have been impossible. He's more than made up for what's past.
He's put everything he knows into the place."

"Yes. I know."

The white brows jutted at me. "Well? Well?"

I smiled at him. "What do you expect me to say, Grandfather? It's
quite true. I left you, and Con stayed. If you're making something of it,
go right ahead, I'm listening."

There was a little silence. Then he gave a short bark of laughter. "You
don't change," he said. "So you've come back to quarrel with me, have
you?"

"Grandfather darling," I said, "no. But I don't quite see what you're
getting at. You're trying to tell me how wonderful Con is. All right; I'll
give you that. He's been telling me himself. But you can't blame me for

being a bit wary. Eight years ago, all this would have been leading up to a spot of match-making. I hoped I'd made it clear that that was impossible."

"Mm. So you said, but one never knows how much one can believe a woman, especially when she starts talking all that claptrap about love turning to hate, and so forth."

"I said nothing of the sort. I don't hate Con. If I felt strongly about him at all, I couldn't have come back while he was still here, could I? I told you how I felt; indifferent, and more than a bit embarrassed. I'd give quite a lot not to have had to meet him again, but since he's here, and not likely to go . . ." I smiled a little. "All right, Grandfather, let it pass. I had to see you, and it'd take more than Con to keep me away. Now, you don't usually hand out compliments for the fun of the thing. You're leading up to something. What is it?"

He chuckled. "All right. It's this. You always knew Whitescar would be yours when I died, didn't you? Should have been your father's, and then it would have been yours."

"Yes. I knew that."

"And had it occurred to you that I might have made other arrangements during the time you were away?"

"Well, of course."

"And now that you've come back?"

I turned half to face him, leaning against the gate, just as I had leaned to talk to Con earlier that day. "Come to the point, Grandfather dear."

The old eyes peered down at me, bright, amused, almost malicious. For some reason I was suddenly reminded of Con, though there was no outward resemblance whatever. "I will. It's this. They'll have told you I'm not expected to live a great while—no," as I made some movement of protest, "don't bother. We all know what this confounded condition of mine means. Now, you cleared out eight years ago, and, for all we knew, you were dead. Well, you've come back." He paused. He seemed to be waiting for a reply.

I said steadily, "Are you accusing me of coming back for what I think I can get?"

He gave his sharp crack of laughter. "Don't be a fool, girl. I know you better than that. But you *would* be a fool if you hadn't thought about it, and wondered where you'd stand. Have you?"

"Of course."

He gave a nod, as if pleased. "That's a straight answer, anyway. And I'll be straight with you. Look at it this way. You walked out eight years ago; Con stayed. Do *you* think it right that you should just walk back like this, after the work that Con's put into this place meantime—and that fool Lisa Dermott for that matter—and just scoop it all up from under his very nose? Would you call that fair? I'm hanged if I would." His head thrust forward suddenly. "What in thunder are you laughing at?"

"Nothing. Nothing at all. Are you trying to tell me that you've left everything to Con and Lisa?"

Again that glint of mischief, that could have been malice. "I didn't say that. And don't you go letting them think it, either. I'm not dead yet. But is there any reason that you can think of why I shouldn't?"

"None at all."

He looked almost disconcerted, staring at me under his white brows. I realized then what the fleeting likeness had been between him and Con; it was a matter of expression, nothing else; an impression of arrogance, of deliberately enjoying a moment of power. Matthew Winslow was enjoying the situation just as much as Con, and for allied reasons. He liked the power that it gave him.

He said testily, "I wish I knew what the devil there was in all this to laugh at."

"I'm sorry," I said. "I was thinking of Con. 'The engineer hoist with his own petar.'"

"What? What are you talking about, girl?"

"It was a quotation," I said, helplessly. "I'm sorry, Grandfather. I'm serious, really I am."

"You'd better be. Quotation, indeed. You've been wasting your time abroad, I can see that. Some modern rubbish, by the sound of it. Well, what were you thinking about Con?"

"Nothing, really. Aren't you going to tell him that you've made a will in his favour?"

"I didn't say I had. And I forbid you to speak to him about it. What I want is to get things straight with you. Perhaps I should have left it till you'd been home a bit longer, but as it happens, I've been thinking a good deal about it lately. You knew Julie was coming up here?"

"Yes. Lisa told me."

"I wrote and asked her to come as soon as she could, and the child tells me she can get leave straight away. When she comes, I want to get things fixed up. Isaacs—do you remember Isaacs?"

"I—I'm not sure."

"The lawyer. Nice chap. I'm sure you met him."

"Oh, yes, of course. I remember now."

"He's coming on Friday, and then again next week. I suggested the twenty-second."

"The twenty-second? That's your birthday, isn't it?"

"Good God, fancy your remembering." He looked pleased.

"Lisa's planning a party, she told me, since we'll all be here, Julie too."

"Yes. A family gathering. Appropriate." He gave that dry, mischievous chuckle again.

I tilted my head and looked up at him, all amusement gone. "Grandfather—"

"Well?"

"At this—appropriate—family gathering—" I paused—"do you intend to tell us all where we stand?"

"A nice, old-fashioned gathering of the vultures round the old man's bones? How do you think I like all this talk of what's to happen after I'm dead?"

I grinned at him. "You started it, and you told me to be a realist. But, look, Grandfather—" I fought not to let my voice sound too urgent —"if you do intend to—to make Con your heir . . . would you tell him so? Please?"

"Why the devil should I?"

"It—it would make things easier for me."

"Easier for *you?* What d'you mean?"

"Only that he—well, he'd resent me less. You can't blame Con for being a realist, too, can you? You must know he'll have had expectations."

"If he has," said Grandfather drily, "then he's an optimist." He caught my expression, and laughed. "What I do with my property's my own affair, Annabel, and if I choose to allow people to confuse themselves, that's their funeral. Do I make myself clear?"

"Very clear."

"Good. You'll gather that I intend to keep my affairs to myself."

"Yes. Well, you've a perfect right to."

There was a pause. He seemed to be choosing his words, but when he spoke, it was bluntly enough, "You know I always wanted you to marry Connor."

"Yes, I know. I'm sorry, Grandfather."

"It always seemed to me the best answer."

"For Whitescar; yes, I see that; but not for me. And not really for Con, Grandfather. Honestly, it wouldn't work. Ever." I smiled. "And it does take two to make a match, you know. I don't think you'll find Con in the same mind as he was eight years ago."

The old eyes were suddenly very sharp and shrewd. "Not even if Whitescar went with you?"

"Of course not!" But I was disconcerted, and showed it. "Don't be so mediaeval, Grandfather!"

He still peered down at me, bright-eyed. "And if it went with Connor?"

"Is that a threat, or a bribe?"

"Neither. You've shown me how little effect it would have. I'm thinking about your future, if the place were Con's. Would you stay?"

"How could I?"

"Is that meant to be a pistol at my heart?"

"Good heavens, no. You don't have to worry about me. I'd have Mother's money."

"And Whitescar?"

I was silent.

"Wouldn't you care?"

"I—I don't know. You've just pointed out that I can hardly expect to walk straight home after eight years."

"Well, that's true enough. I'm glad you seem to have faced it. I shan't be here for ever, you know."

"I know. But at least I can be here as long as you are."

He snorted. "Soft soap, child. That'll get you nowhere. And don't glare at me like that, it cuts no ice! So you expect me to cut you right out, do you, leave Julie to her own devices, and hand the place lock, stock and barrel, to young Connor? That it?"

I pushed myself upright, away from the gate.

I said, "Grandfather, you always were insufferable, and you were never fair in all your born days. How the devil do you expect me to know what you plan to do? You'll do as the mood takes you, fair or no, and Con and I can take what comes, charm we never so wisely." I added, "That was another quotation. And don't say I've been wasting my time again, because that's from the Psalms."

Grandfather's face never changed, but something came behind the eyes that might have been a grin. He said mildly, "Don't swear at me, Annabel my girl, or old as you are, I'll soap your mouth out."

"Sorry." We smiled at one another. There was a pause.

"It's good to have you back, child. You don't know how good." He put a hand to the latch of the gate. "Come down to the river meadows. There's a yearling there you'll like to see."

We went down a lane between hedgerows whispering with budding meadowsweet. The hawthorn was rusted thickly over with bunches of dried flowers hardening to fruit.

At the end of the lane a gate opened on a field deep with buttercups and cuckoo-flowers. A grey mare moved towards us, swishing her tail, her sides sleek and heavy. From the shade of a big beech a yearling watched us with eyes as soft and wary as a deer.

"He's a beauty."

"Isn't he?" There was satisfaction and love in the old man's voice. "Best foal she ever dropped. Forrest kept a three-year-old out of her by the same sire, but they'll make nothing of him. Yes, she's a grand mare; I bought her from Forrest three years ago, when the stud was sold up. Give over, Blondie, give over, now." This to the mare, who was pushing at his chest with her muzzle as he opened the gate and held it for me. "Come through. The grass is dry enough. You'll have to find some better shoes for this tomorrow."

I followed him into the field. "What's wrong with the three-year-old?"

"What? Oh, Forrest's horse? Nothing, except that nobody had time to do anything about him. Only kept him out of sentiment, I suppose, as he's one of the old 'Mountain' lot. Everest got him; you'll remember Everest? He's gone to the Chollerford stud now; getting long in the tooth, the old devil, but his get's as good as it ever was; look at that yearling. And Forrest's colt could be a winner, too, if they'd time to school him. Rowan, they called him." He chuckled, and clapped the mare's neck. "By Everest, out of Ash Blonde here."

"Rowan? Another name for Mountain Ash?"

"That's it. Sort of nonsense Forrest always went in for with his names. You knew the stud was gone?"

"Oh, yes. What have you called this one? You said he was the same breeding."

"We haven't named him yet. That'll be for his owners."

The mare threw her head up to avoid his caressing hand, and swerved a little, flicking her tail pettishly. She pricked her ears at me, and reached out an inquiring muzzle.

I said, ignoring it, "He's sold, then?"

"Yes. I'm afraid you'll find nothing here to ride now. Blondie's heavy at foot, as you can see, and the youngster'll be away next month." He laughed. "Unless you try your hand with Forrest's three-year-old. I've no doubt he'd let you if you asked him."

The mare was pushing close to me. The yearling, looking interested, was coming to join her. From behind me, some way along the lane, I heard footsteps approaching. I backed away from the mare's advance until I was right up against the gate. She pushed her head at me again, and breathed gustily down the front of my dress.

I said breathlessly, "Asked who?"

"Forrest, of course. What the devil's the matter with you, Annabel?"

"Nothing. What should be the matter?" The footsteps were nearer.

Grandfather was regarding me curiously. "You're as white as a sheet! Anyone'd think you were afraid of the mare!"

I managed a little laugh. "Afraid of her? How absurd! Here, Blondie. . . ." I put out a hand to her. I hoped he wouldn't see how unsteady it was. The mare was nibbling the buckle of my belt. The yearling had come right up to her shoulder, and stood staring. Any minute now he would close in too. . . .

I looked away from Grandfather's curious, puzzled stare, and said quickly, "I thought Mr. Forrest was in Italy."

"He's coming back some time this week, so Johnny Rudd tells me. They didn't expect him quite yet, but I imagine the sale of the place in Italy went through quicker than he'd expected."

I gave the mare's head a shove away from me. I might as well have shoved an elephant. I said, unsteadily, "I—I understood he'd left for good. I mean, with the Hall gone, and—and everything—"

"No, no. He's planning to settle at West Lodge now, Johnny tells me, with the Rudds to look after him. He came back last year to clear up the rest of the estate, and he and Johnny set to work and got the old gardens going; I believe that's what he plans to do now."

"Yes, Con did say—"

Con's voice, from beyond the bend in the lane, called, "Uncle Matthew? Annabel?"

"Here!" called Grandfather.

The mare was nibbling at my frock, and, retreating from her advance, I was pressed so hard against the gate, that the bars bit into my back. Grandfather gave a quick little frown. "Annabel—"

"I thought as much!" Con said it, mercifully, from just behind me. "I might have known you'd bring her straight down here!"

He must have summed up the situation at a glance as he rounded the bend in the lane: Grandfather, his attention divided between the year-ling and my own odd behaviour; myself, backed against the gate, chat-tering breathlessly, and trying, with patently unsteady hands, to stop the mare from blowing lovingly down the breast of my frock.

I saw the flash of amusement in Con's eyes, and then he had leaned over the gate beside me, handed off the importunate mare with one strong thrust and a "Give over, now," that sent her swerving straight away, ears flattened and tail switching. The yearling threw up his lovely head and veered after her. As I relaxed, Con pushed open the gate and came through.

Grandfather, fortunately, was watching the yearling as it cantered away into the shade of the trees. "Moves well, doesn't he?" he said fondly.

"He's a little beauty," agreed Con.

"Little?" I said shakily. "He looks enormous!"

A flicker in Con's eyes showed me the ineptitude of this remark for someone who was supposed to have lived and breathed horses for most of her life. Then he covered up as smoothly as a practised actor, the amusement warming his voice so faintly that only I would hear it. "Yes, he's pretty well-grown, isn't he, seeing he's barely a year old. . . ." And he plunged easily off into technicalities with Mr. Winslow, no doubt to give me time to recover my poise.

Presently Grandfather said, "I was telling Annabel that she'll have to see Forrest about some riding if she wants it."

"Forrest? Oh, is he back?"

"Not yet. Some time this week. Johnny Rudd told me they didn't look for him before autumn at the soonest, but apparently he's sold the villa, and he's coming back to live at West Lodge."

Con was leaning on the gate beside me. He sent a slanting look down at me, with a lurking smile behind it. "That's a bit of luck, Annabel. He'll let you ride the Mountain colt."

I was still shaken, but I had no intention of letting Con amuse him-self further at my expense. I said immediately, with every evidence of enthusiasm, "Do you really think he would? That's wonderful!"

Con's eyes widened. Grandfather said shortly, "Of course he would, unless you've lost your touch completely! Want to come across and look at him now?"

"I'd love to."

"Can't it wait?" said Con. "You look tired."

I looked at him, slightly surprised. "I'm all right."

Con straightened up with that lazy grace of his that looked deliberate, but was in reality as natural as breathing. At the movement, slow
though it was, the mare, who was grazing near, rolled a white-rimmed
eye and moved away.

"Doesn't like you, does she?" said Matthew Winslow. "Come along
then, my dear. Coming, Con?"

Con shook his head. "No, I've a lot to do. I really only came down to
see if you'd come up into the seventeen-acre and take a look at the cutter for me. She's been running rough, and I don't seem to be able to
get to the bottom of the trouble. I could take you up in the car."

"The cutter? Good God, can't you put that right without running to
me?" But the old man had stopped and turned, looking far from dis-
pleased. "Well, in that case—" He looked at me. "Some other time, perhaps? Unless you go along there yourself? He's at grass, two fields along
from the bridge, you know the place, beyond the wood."

"Yes," I said, "I know it. I'll go now."

My one desire was to get away, to be alone, not even to have to walk
back to the house in their company. But even as I spoke, half-turning
to go, I saw a shade of what looked like genuine anxiety on Con's face.

I realized then, suddenly, that his timely appearance on the scene had
not been a matter of chance. He had not come down to see about the
repair of the cutter, and then stayed to tease me; his coming had been a
deliberate rescue bid. He had guessed that I had been brought down to
the paddock; guessed, too, what might be happening there, and that the
prolonged interview with Grandfather might be too much of a strain.
He had come down solely to get me out of it, to draw Mr. Winslow off.
In all probability there was nothing wrong with the cutter at all. . . .

And if, once here, he had been unable to resist teasing me a little, it
was no more than he was entitled to, under the circumstances. He was
standing now with grave patience, listening to a crisp lecture on the
incompetence of a young man who could not, in twenty seconds, diag-
nose and correct every fault in every piece of machinery in use on the
estate.

Well, fair was fair. I wouldn't worry him further. I interrupted the
lecture. "I don't think I will go, after all. I'll go back to the house. I—
I've done enough for today."

Matthew Winslow looked at me, still with that crinkle of puzzlement
round his eyes. "Something *has* upset you, child. What is it?"

Suddenly, absurdly, I wanted to cry. "Nothing truly. Nothing. Con's
right. I'm tired." I made a little gesture. "It's been wonderful playing

the prodigal returning, and everyone's been so kind . . . too kind. But, you know, it's terribly exhausting. I feel as if I'd been back a year already, things have crowded in so fast."

We were back in the lane. As Con pulled the gate shut behind me, he took my arm as if in reassurance.

"Of course it's a strain. We all understand that. You should go in now, and rest till supper."

He spoke, as before, gently. I saw Grandfather glance quickly from his face to mine, and back again. It must be obvious to anyone that Con's solicitude was quite genuine, and I knew the reason for it, but I wasn't going to have Matthew Winslow leaping to the wrong conclusion. I withdrew my arm and said quickly,

"I think I will." Then I turned to the old man. "Have you still got the cribbage board?"

His face lightened to a grin. "Of course. You remember how to play?"

"How could I forget?" (*She used to play with him often: it's an old-fashioned game; you know it? Good. . . .*") I added, "I also remember that you owe me a vast sum of money, Grandfather."

"Nonsense. I always beat you."

"Ah, well," I said cheerfully, "I've improved, in eight years. I'll win your house and lands off you yet, so watch your step!"

At his dry little chuckle I felt Con stiffen beside me. He said abruptly, "Well, you'll not be playing tonight, at all events, I hope?"

"No, no. The child will want an early night. Besides, I'll probably stay up in the seventeen-acre with you. How are you getting on there?"

Con answered him, and the two of them talked across me as we walked slowly back towards the yard where the car stood. Con's manner with his great-uncle was charming; relaxed and easy and familiar, but with just the hint of a deference which obviously flattered the old man, coming from someone as vital and as capable as Con, to a man who, for all his deceptive appearance of power, was a frail husk that the first chill wind might blow away.

Grandfather was saying, "Nonsense! I can give you a hand when we've got the cutter running properly."

Con gave him that flashing, affectionate smile. "You'll do no such thing. Come along, by all means, and bully us, but I'm afraid that's all we'll let you do!"

"You coddle me. I'm not senile yet, and I won't be treated like a girl."

Con grinned. "Hardly that. In any case, the girl's going to work, once she's got herself run in again! Can you drive a tractor—still, Annabel?"

"I dare say I might manage, even if I have rather lost my touch with horses," I said evenly.

We had reached the gate of the main courtyard. Grandfather climbed, a little stiffly, into the big Ford that stood waiting there. Con shut the car door on him.

In the distance, from the fields beyond High Riggs, came the steady, smooth whirr of the grass cutter. Unless I was very much mistaken, there was nothing wrong with it at all. As Con shut the car door and turned, his eyes met mine. There was a smile in them. He said, "Over to me," very softly, and then, "*Do* you drive a tractor, by the way?"

"I have done."

"And," said Con, "a car?"

I studied him for a moment, then I smiled. He had earned it, after all. I said, "I had a car in Canada; I've just burned the permit, and I don't know where my licence is, but that doesn't mean a thing. I dare say I'd qualify for a British one, if I needed to."

"Ah," said Con. "And now, if you wouldn't mind shutting the gate behind us . . . ?"

CHAPTER
SIX

" 'Tis down in yonder garden green,
    Love, where we used to walk,
The finest flower that ere was seen
    Is wither'd to a stalk."

                    Ballad: *The Unquiet Grave.*

Supper with Lisa and Grandfather was not the ordeal I had feared it might be. The old man was in excellent spirits, and, though he was in something of a "do you remember" vein, and Lisa's eyes, under their lowered lids, watched us both overanxiously, it went off smoothly enough, with no hitch that I could see. Con wasn't there. It was light late, and he was at work long hours in the hayfield while the weather lasted.

Shortly after supper Grandfather went into the office to write letters, and I helped Lisa wash up. Mrs. Bates went off at five, and the girl who helped in the kitchen and dairy had gone home when the milking was over. Lisa and I worked in silence. I was tired and preoccupied, and she must have realized that I didn't want to talk. She had made no further attempt to force a tête-à-tête on me, and she didn't try to detain me when, soon after nine o'clock, I went up to my room.

I sat there by the open window, with the scent from the climbing roses unbearably sweet in the dusk, and my mind went round and round over the events of the day like some small creature padding its cage.

The light was fading rapidly. The long flushed clouds of sunset had darkened and grown cool. Below them the sky lay still and clear, for a few moments rinsed to a pale eggshell green, fragile as blown glass. The dusk leaned down slowly, as soft as a bird coming in to brood. Later, there would be a moon.

It was very still. Close overhead I heard the scratch and rustle of small feet on the sloping roof tiles, then the throaty murmur as the pigeons settled back again to sleep. From the garden below came the smell of lilac. A moth fluttered past my cheek, and a bat cut the clear sky like a knife. Down in the neglected garden-grass the black and white cat crouched, tail whipping, then sprang. Something screamed in the grass.

I brushed the back of a hand impatiently across my cheeks, and reached for a cigarette. Round the side of the house, in the still evening, came the sharp sounds of a door opening and shutting. A man's footsteps receded across the yard, and were silenced on turf somewhere. Con had been in for a late meal, and was going out again.

I got up quickly, and reached a light coat down from the hook behind the door. I dropped the packet of cigarettes into the pocket, and went downstairs.

Lisa was clearing up after Con's meal in the kitchen. I said quickly, "I'm going out for a walk. I—I thought I'd take a look round on my own."

She nodded, incuriously. I went out into the gathering dusk.

I caught him up in the lane that led down to the river meadow. He was carrying a coil of wire, and hammer and pliers. He turned at the sound of my hurrying steps, and waited. The smile with which he greeted me faded when he saw my expression.

I said breathlessly, "Con. I had to see you."

"Yes." His voice was guarded. "What is it? Trouble?"

"No—at least, not the kind you mean. But there's something I have to say. I—I had to see you straight away, tonight."

I was close to him now. His face, still readable in the thickening dusk, had stiffened almost into hostility, arming itself against whatever was coming. So much, I thought, for Con's co-operation; it was fine as long as you stayed in line with him, but the moment he suspected you of deviating. . . .

"Well?" he said.

I had meant to start reasonably, quietly, at the right end of the argument I had prepared, but somehow the abrupt, even threatening, sound of the monosyllable shook my resolution into flinders. Womanlike, I forgot reason and argument together, and began at the end.

"This can't go on. You must see that. It can't go on!"

He stood very still. "What do you mean?"

"What I say! It'll have to stop! We were mad, anyway, even to have thought of starting it!" Once begun, it seemed I couldn't check myself. I had had more of a shaking that day than I cared to admit, even to myself. I stumbled on anyhow, growing even less coherent in the face of his unresponding silence.

"We—we'll have to think of some other way—something to tell Grandfather—I'm sure we can think something up! You must see there's no point in my staying, now, you must see! Even if I could have got away with it—"

I heard him breathe in sharply. "*Could have* got away with it? Do you mean he's found you out?"

"No, no, *no!*" I heard my voice rising, and checked it on a sort of gulp. We were near the gate where we had been that afternoon. I took a step away from him, and put out a hand to the gate, gripping it hard, as if that might steady me. I said, shakily, "Con . . . look, I'm sorry—"

His voice said coldly, behind me, "You're hysterical."

Since this was undoubtedly true, I said nothing. He put the tools and wire down beside the hedge, then came up to the gate beside me. He said, as unpleasantly as I had ever heard him speak, "Getting scruples, my dear, is that it? A little late, one feels."

His tone, even more than what his words implied, was all the cure my nerves needed. I turned my head sharply. "Does one? I think not!"

"No? Think again, my pretty."

I stared at him. "Are you trying to threaten me, Connor Winslow? And if so, with what?"

It was almost dark now, and he was standing with his back to what light there was. He had turned so that he was leaning his shoulders against the gate, seemingly quite relaxed. I felt, rather than saw, his look still on me, watchful, intent, hostile. But he spoke lightly.

"Threaten you? Not the least in the world, my love. But we're in this together, you know, and we work together. I can't have you forgetting our . . . bargain . . . quite so soon. You're doing splendidly, so far; things have gone even better than I dared to hope . . . *and* they're going to go on that way, darling, till I—and you, of course—get what we want. Fair enough?"

"Oh, quite."

The moon must be rising now beyond the thick trees. I could see the first faint glimmer on the river. The sky behind the black damask of leaf and bough was the colour of polished steel. The mare, grazing thirty yards away, had lifted her head and was staring towards us, ears pricked. Under the eclipsing shadow of hedgerow and tree she gleamed faintly, like some palladic metal, cool and smooth. The yearling was beside her, staring too.

I regarded Con curiously, straining my eyes against the dark. "I wonder . . ."

"Yes?"

I said slowly, "I wonder just how far you would go, to get what you wanted?"

"I've sometimes wondered that myself." He sounded amused. "You'd maybe be surprised what you can bring yourself to do, little cousin, when you've never had a damned thing in your life but what you could make—or take—with your own two hands. And what's wrong with that, anyway? A man who knows he can—" He broke off, and I thought I saw the gleam of a smile. "Well, there it is, girl dear. I'm not going to be sent on my travels again . . . fair means if I can, but by God, I'll see foul ones if I have to!"

"I see. Well, we know where we are, don't we?" I brought the packet of cigarettes out of my coat pocket. "Smoke?"

"Thanks. You smoke too much, don't you?"

"I suppose I do."

"I knew you'd more sense than to panic at the first hint of something you didn't like. What is the trouble, anyway? I've a light. Here."

In the momentary flare of the match I saw his face clearly. In spite of the light words, and the endearments with which he was so lavish, I could see no trace of liking, or even of any human feeling, in his expression. It was the face of a man concentrating on a job; something tricky, even dangerous, that called for every ounce of concentration. Me. I had to be got back into line.

The match went out. I thought I must have been mistaken, for his voice when he spoke was not ungentle. "Supposing you tell me exactly what's upset you? Something has, hasn't it? What was it? The horses this afternoon? You looked like seven sorts of death when I came down."

"Did I?"

"You know, you don't have to go near Forrest's horse if you don't want to."

"I know I don't—and incidentally, thank you for coming to my rescue." I leaned back against the gate beside him, and drew deeply on my cigarette. "I'm sorry I started this at the wrong end, and scared you. I don't have to tell you, I hope, that I'm not planning to let you down. I—I've had a hell of a day, that's all, and I was letting it ride me. I'll try and explain now, like a reasonable human being, which means not like a woman."

"You said it, honey, not me. Go ahead; I'm listening."

"It's true, though, that I did want to talk to you about altering our plans. No, wait, Con; the point is, things have changed."

"Changed? How? Since when?"

"Since I had my talk with Grandfather down here this evening."

"I . . . thought there had been something." I heard his breath go out. "I told you, you looked like death. I thought it was that fool of a mare."

"The point is, Con, that all this may have been for nothing. It shook me, rather. I—I think he's going to leave Whitescar to you anyway."

"*What?*"

"That's what he said."

"*He said so?*"

"Almost. I'll swear that's what he meant. Did you know that his lawyer, his name's Isaacs, isn't it?—is coming down here on Friday?"

"No, I didn't know." He sounded dazed. His voice was blurred at the edges.

"Well, he is. Julie gets here on Wednesday, and Mr. Isaacs comes on Friday. Grandfather didn't say anything definite, but he hinted like mad. I've a feeling he wants to have some sort of family gathering on his birthday, and he's asked the lawyer here before that, so it's a fairly reasonable guess that it's to be about his will. He said 'I want to get things fixed up.'"

He moved sharply, and the gate creaked. "Yes, but this *is* only a guess! What about Whitescar? What did he actually say?"

"Not very much, but—Con, it's all right. I wouldn't have mentioned it to you, if I wasn't sure. I'll swear that's what he means to do. Oh, no, he didn't quite commit himself, not in so many words, even to me. But he was as definite as he'd ever be."

"How?"

"Well, he reminded me first of all that Whitescar had always been promised to Annabel. 'It should have been your father's, and then it would have been yours.'"

"'Would have been?'" he asked, sharply.

"Yes. Then he began to praise you. You'd been a son to him, he couldn't have done without you—oh, all sorts of things. He really does recognize your place here, Con. Then he said, would it be right if I were allowed simply to walk back home, and claim Whitescar over your head. Yes, over your head. 'Would you call that fair? I'm hanged if I would!' Those were his very words."

"My God, if you're right!" he breathed. "And Julie? Did he say anything about her?"

"Nothing you could be clear about. He wouldn't even say definitely that he intended to tell us all on the twenty-second, and when I tried to pin him down—asked flat out if he was remaking his will in your favour—he just wouldn't give a straight answer. I couldn't press it, you know what he's like. He seems to like to keep people guessing, doesn't he?"

"He does, damn him!"

He spoke with such sudden, concentrated viciousness, that I stopped with my cigarette halfway to my lips. I was reminded sharply, shockingly, of the charming way he had talked to the old man that afternoon. Oddly enough, I thought that both attitudes were equally genuine.

I said gently, "The thing is, Con, don't you see, he's old? I think he *minds* not being able to do things the way he used to. He's always been —well, I've gathered he's a pretty dominating type, and now his property and his money's the only kind of power he's got left. That's why he won't commit himself; I don't think he realizes just how unfair he's being to younger people . . . to you, anyway. He just thinks—quite rightly—that it's his property, and he'll play Old Harry with it if he wants to. But he's made up his mind now. He must have, since he's sent for Mr. Isaacs."

I could see Con's cigarette smouldering unheeded between his fingers. He hadn't stirred. I got the impression that only the essentials of what I'd been saying had got through.

He said painfully, as if the readjustment of ideas was somehow a physical effort, "If he's made a decision, it's happened since you got here . . . or rather, since he knew you were coming back. He went to the telephone soon after Lisa broke the news to him. I remember her telling me so. It must have been to get hold of Isaacs." He lifted his head. "My God, but you must have got this the wrong way round! Why should he send for him now, *except to cut me out and include you in?*"

"He isn't doing that. Be sure of that. I tell you, he kept asking me, harping on it almost, if I thought it was fair for me to walk straight home after eight years and expect to take up as I left off. That was almost the very phrase he used. Yes, he asked flat out if I thought I ought to be allowed to walk straight home and scoop Whitescar from under your nose, after all the work you'd put into it."

"Did he, by God?" A long breath, then he laughed, a sharp exultant crack of sound. "And what did you say?"

"Well, I thought it would be less trouble if I just said no. I may say he seemed surprised."

"And well he might! Annabel would never have parted with a penny piece to me, and what's more, she'd have seen that he didn't, either!"

"Well," I said, "she could have learned sense in eight years, couldn't she? Found out what really mattered most?"

"You call that sense? Letting her rights go, for want of a fight?"

"'Rights?' Annabel's? What about Mr. Winslow's? Hasn't he as much 'right' to leave his own property any way he pleases?"

"No."

"Oh? Well, I'm not breaking any lances with you over Annabel. You've staked a claim of your own, and I won't argue with that, either. In any case, it looks very much as if you're going to get what you want."

"Do you know something?" said Con slowly. "You're a very much nicer person than Annabel ever was."

"Good heavens, why on earth? Because I encouraged Grandfather to give you the poor girl's property?"

"No. Because I honestly believe you want me to have it. And not just for the 'cut' you'll stand to get, either."

"Don't you believe it. I'm as mercenary as hell," I said cheerfully.

He ignored that. "You said she 'might have learned sense in eight years,' and found out what really mattered. What really does—to you?"

I knew he couldn't see my face, but all the same, I looked away. I said shortly, "I'm a woman. That should answer it."

Through the ensuing silence I heard a horse's steady cropping, now quite close at hand. At the bottom of the pasture the river glimmered. Something drifted across like a shadow, shimmering at the edges, shapeless and quiet as a ghost. The yearling, moving up nearer, beside his mother.

I had just had time to realize how Con could have interpreted my last remark, when he spoke again, mercifully ignoring it, and coming sharply back to the matter in hand.

"And there really was nothing more about Julie?"

"Nothing." I dropped my cigarette, and trod it out. "Well, there it is. I think it's true. For one thing, he told me not to tell you anything about it."

I caught the gleam of a grin. "Did he now?"

I said tartly, "And don't just accept it as if you expected me to let him down automatically. I wouldn't have told you if—if I hadn't wanted to ask you to change our . . . plans."

He didn't follow this up. He seemed to have a truly remarkable power of only attending to what he wanted to. He was saying thoughtfully, "I can't quite understand it, if it's true. Ironic, isn't it, how our little conspiracy has turned out? I find you, import you into Whitescar at great trouble and some risk, expose myself and my ambitions to your uneasy female conscience . . . and all for nothing. He'd have left it to me all along." His cigarette went fizzing down into the damp grass. "Funny, you'd have expected it to act the other way. I mean, it seems absurd to have kept you in his will all these years, in spite of me, only to cut you out when you actually do turn up. I—well, I don't get it. I wish I understood."

"I think I do. I think—how shall I put it?—he's been keeping a sort of dream alive all these years, almost in spite of what he suspected to be the truth. You've all insisted that Annabel was dead, and, being who he is, and also because he must know you wanted Whitescar, he simply got stubborn about it. He's hung on to his dream and his belief out of sheer obstinacy, even though probably in his heart he's known it wasn't true . . . and perhaps, partly, to keep some sort of hold over you, too. Yes, I think that might have come into it. . . ." I paused. "Well, now I've come back; he finds he was right all along. But also, mark you, he finds himself facing the *reality* of the dream that he's been using as a threat to stop you getting too sure of yourself. He's kept telling you that he'll leave the place to Annabel, come what may. Well, now she's here, having pretty well demonstrated that she doesn't give much of a damn for Whitescar, disappearing for eight years without a trace. You, on the other hand, have proved yourself the obvious legatee. So he's had to make his mind up in a hurry; and he's going to do, at last, what he knows he ought to have done all along."

"You may be right. It's illogical enough to be likely."

"What's more," I said, "there's one thing I'm pretty sure of."

"What's that?"

"I think you've been a residuary beneficiary all along. Maybe with Julie, maybe not. I think that, underneath it all, he's believed Annabel was dead. He's obstinate enough to have left her name as his heir, but it's my belief he's expected you to inherit any time these last few years. But my coming home has given him a jolt. He's realized he's got to do something quickly, and make it stick."

"You might be right. My God, you might be right."

"I don't see why not."

"If only we knew where Julie comes in."

"Yes, Julie's the unknown quantity. Did you hear when I told you he sent for her? He did invite her, as Lisa thought. He wrote to her. Did you know?"

"No." I heard the twist to his voice. "You see? You've been back here —twelve hours, is it? and, claim or no claim, he tells you more than he'd tell me in twelve months."

"Con, please. Don't tear yourself up so."

I spoke quite without thinking. Unexpectedly, he laughed, and his voice lightened. "All right, darling, what the hell. We'll wait and see, and pray you're right. And irony or no, I still say you're my lucky star!"

"I don't know about that. If I'd never come, your luck would have still been in. You'd have got what you wanted the way you've got everything else; just as you said, with your two hands." I half turned towards him. In spite of myself, my voice tightened. "Con . . . you still haven't heard what I came to say."

"What else? Oh lord, you're still upset, and now you feel it's all been for nothing. Is that it? Or are you beginning to worry in case I get what I want without you, and don't keep my side of the bargain? Relax, honey. I'll keep it, never fear. You'll get your cut, just the same." I heard the smile in his voice. "I'd not trust you else, sweetie, you could do me too much damage."

"No, I'm not worried about that. I'd do you no harm. I only want to go. I told you, didn't I?"

"Go?"

"Yes. Cut right out. Leave. Straight away."

He said blankly, "You're—crazy!"

"No. It's obvious that I'm not needed any more, so—"

"Now look—"

"No, Con, listen to me, please! It's true that you *might* have got all this without my coming at all, or, on the other hand, my coming may have forced the decision on Grandfather. We weren't to know which way he'd decide. The game was worth playing, as far as it went. But now it isn't necessary. We've seen that. And since I'm not needed here any more, I really would rather go. No, please don't be angry; you know I'd never have let you down if I'd been needed, but I'm not. I—I want to go. Don't ask me to explain any more, I can't, you'd only laugh at me for—for scruples or something, and I couldn't take it, not tonight. Won't you just accept the fact—?"

"I'll accept nothing!" We were back where we had been, with enmity sharp and open between us. "If it's your conscience that's bothering you, for heaven's sake forget it! You've just found out that you're not robbing anyone after all—you're not even going to have to hand Annabel's share of Whitescar over to me! You came into this with your eyes wide open, and if this is the way you intend to react after one day, then I can only say it's turned out better for you than you deserve!" He paused, and added, more pleasantly, "Now relax, for pity's sake. You're hurting nobody, and the old man's as pleased as a dog with two tails to have you here."

"I know, but—"

"And how could you walk out now? Tell me that. What d'you think people—let alone Mr. Winslow—would say? What possible excuse could there be, short of the truth?"

"It's simple enough. I've only to go to Grandfather tonight and tell him that I came back to see him, but that on second thoughts I can see how silly it was of me to come . . . because of you, I mean. After all, Con, he can't expect me to find it easy to be with you again, can he? He'll accept that; he might even think I'm sulking because of his decision to leave Whitescar to you."

I waited a moment, but he didn't speak. I turned to face the gate, gripping the top bar hard with both hands. "Con, it's best, really it is. It'll work. The luck's running our way; today's proved it. We'll think up what to say to Grandfather, then I'll go, tomorrow. I can stay in Newcastle till Wednesday—it'd look queer if I didn't stay to meet Julie —and I can come for Grandfather's birthday. Then I'll go to London. I can always come back if—if he's ill or anything." My voice was going out of control again. I stopped and took a steadying little breath that caught somehow in my throat, and must have sounded like a sob. "You —you can't want me here, Con. Can't you see, if I go, it'll do you nothing but *good*? If I go straight away again, now, that'll clinch it as far as Grandfather's concerned, surely? He'd never leave me anything at all, not even money. You'd get the lot, you and Julie."

He had made a quick movement in the dark. His hand came down over mine in a kind of pounce, and gripped it hard against the bar. "Stop this!" He spoke sharply. "You're hysterical. Think, can't you? What the hell's the matter with you tonight? You know quite well this is nonsense. If you go now, what sort of questions d'you think will be asked? Then heaven help us both, and Lisa too."

"I don't see how they could find out—"

"Another thing. There's no possible excuse you could give for going now. You'd see that, if you'd behave like a reasonable human being instead of a hysterical girl."

"I told you—"

"Oh, don't be a fool." He sounded exasperated, and thoroughly angry. "When you came back here—you, Annabel, I mean—you must have known you'd have to face me. If, after twenty-four hours, you decide you can't 'take' me any more, what's Mr. Winslow going to think? He's no fool. He's going to assume that I've made myself objectionable—made another pass at you . . . raked up the past and upset you . . . something, anyway—and this time he mightn't be prepared to forgive me. No."

"Oh. Yes. Yes, I do see that. Well, we could think of something else—"

"I tell you, *no!* For one thing, we still don't know for certain about the terms of this will, or even if there *is* to be a new will. Even if you're right, do you think I want him cutting you right out, as he certainly would if you left tomorrow?"

I stared painfully at the shadow beside me. "What do you mean?"

"My dear little conscience-stricken nitwit, do you think I want to see him splitting his capital two ways instead of three? If you stay, I get your share as well as my own. If you go, I go halves, if I'm lucky, with Julie . . . I'm talking about money now. I need the money to run the place. It's as simple as that." His hand moved over mine, holding it hard down on the bar. "So, darling, you'll stay. You'll go on playing the sweet repentant prodigal. And you'll play it till you collect at least Annabel's rightful share of what money's going. Is that clear?"

"No."

"Girl dear, do I have to give it to you in a children's comic strip? I can't put it any clearer. And in any case, it doesn't matter. You'll do as I say."

"No."

Silence.

I said shakily, "I didn't mean I didn't understand. I just meant no."

For a moment I thought his stillness would explode into violent anger. I could feel it running through his wrist and hand into mine. Then the tension changed in quality. He was peering at me, as if he would pierce the dusk to read my face.

He said slowly, "You still haven't told me the reason for all this. Now, supposing you do. . . . Well? Something's scared you, and badly, hasn't it? No . . . not the horses; something important. . . . And I'd give a lot to know just what. . . ."

His voice had altered completely. The anger had vanished, and in its place was only a kind of curiosity; no, more than that; a kind of speculation.

Where his anger had failed to frighten me, it was absurd, now, suddenly, to be afraid. I said hurriedly, "Nothing's scared me. It's just . . . I told you, I've had a rather ghastly day . . . I'm sorry, I—oh, don't ask me any more questions, *please!* I—I've done quite a lot for you today. Do this for me. We *can* think of some way, I know, if you'll only help. . . ."

For the first time, I touched him of my own volition. I reached my free hand and laid it over his, where it held mine over the bar of the gate.

Then, suddenly, the moon was there, swimming up behind the treetops into a milky sky, and the shadows of the trees bored toward us, blue and hard as steel, across grass awash with silver.

I could see his face clearly, bent to mine. The expression of his eyes was hidden; the moonlight threw back a glint from their curved, brilliant surfaces, hiding everything but an impression of blackness behind. I was again sharply aware of that terrifying single-track concentration of his. The bright, blank eyes watched me.

Then he said, quite gently, "You mean this? You really want to give it up, and go?"

"Yes."

"Very well, my dear. Have it your own way."

I must have jumped. He smiled. I said, incredulously, "You mean, you'll help me? You'll let me go—give it up, and you'll just wait and see . . . fair means?"

"If that's the way you want it." He paused, and added, very kindly, "We'll go straight in now, and tell your grandfather that you're not Annabel at all. We'll tell him that you're Mary Grey of Montreal, an enterprising tramp on the make, who wanted a peaceful niche in life in the Old Country, and a spot of assured income. We'll tell him that the three of us, Lisa, myself and you—all of whom he trusts—have plotted this thing against him, and that we've been laughing at him all day. I don't know what passed between you in his bedroom this afternoon, but I imagine that he might be quite sensitive about it, don't you? . . . Yes, I thought so. And when we've assured him, at the end of this long, happy day, that Annabel's as dead as mutton for all we know, and has been this last five years. . . . Do you see?"

The horses moved nearer, cropping the long grass. Through the hanging trees the river glittered in the growing moonlight. Across it a heron lumbered up on to its wings, and flapped ponderously downriver.

Eventually I said, "Yes. I see."

"I thought you would."

"I should never have started it."

"But you did. With your eyes open, sweetie."

"It would kill him, wouldn't it? Whatever sort of scene . . . I mean, if we told him, now?"

"Almost certainly. Any shock, any sudden strong emotional reaction, such as anger, or fear. . . . Oh yes, I think you can be sure it would kill him. And we don't want him dead—yet—do we?"

"Con!"

He laughed. "Don't worry, sweetheart, that's not the plan at all. I only said it to wake you up to the, er, realities of the situation."

"To frighten me, you mean?"

"If you like. If I want something badly enough, you know, I get it. I don't count small change."

I said, before I thought, "I know that. Don't think I haven't grasped the fact that you once tried to murder Annabel."

A long, breathless pause. Then he straightened up from the gate. "Well, well. You *have* put two and two together and made five, haven't you? Well, go on believing that; it'll keep you in line. . . . That's settled, then. We carry on as planned, and you, my lovely, will do as you're told. Won't you?"

"I suppose so."

His hand was still over mine. The other hand came up under my chin, and lifted my face to the moonlight. He was still smiling. He looked like every schoolgirl's dream of romance come true.

I moved my head away. "Don't, Con. Let me go."

He took no notice. "Don't hold this against me, honey, will you? I've said some pretty hard things to you, but—well, you know as well as I do what's at stake, and it seemed the only way. I'm not worrying really that you'll let me down when it comes to the push. . . . This was bound to happen; I was expecting it. It's reaction, that's all. It's a highly emotional set-up, and you've taken more than enough for one day. So we'll forget it, shall we? You'll feel fine in the morning." His hand touched my cheek, and he gave a little laugh. "You see how right I was to choose a nice girl? That conscience of yours does give me the slightest advantage in this mutual blackmail pact of ours, doesn't it?"

"All right. You've made your point. You're unscrupulous and I'm not. 'Vantage to you. Now let me go. I'm tired."

"Just a minute. Do you think the blackmail would run to just one kiss?"

"No. I told you this afternoon—"

"Please."

"Con, I've had enough drama for one day. I'm not going to gratify you by struggling in your arms, or whatever. Now let me go, and let's call the scene off."

He didn't. He pulled me nearer to him, saying, in a voice nicely calculated to turn any normal woman's bones to pulp, "Why do we waste our time quarrelling? Don't you know yet that I'm crazy about you? Just crazy?"

"I've gathered," I said drily, "that you've your very own way of showing it, as a rule."

His grip slackened. I thought, with satisfaction: that's spoiled your routine, anyway. But it hadn't quite thrown him out of gear. He gave a little laugh that managed to make what I had said an intimate joke between us, and drew me closer once more. His voice sank to a murmur, somewhere near my left ear. "Your hair looks like melted silver in this light. Sure, and I'm—"

"Oh, Con, don't!" How, short of cruelty, could one get through? I added, a little desperately, "Con, I'm tired—"

Then, even as Con himself had rescued me that afternoon, rescue came. The grey mare, who had been browsing her way, unnoticed, steadily nearer and nearer the gate, suddenly lifted her beautiful head, and thrust it between us, blowing gustily, and still chewing. A froth of grass stains went blubbering down the front of Con's white shirt.

He swore lamentably, and let me go.

The mare rubbed her head hard against me. Trying not to laugh, I ran a hand up to her forelock, and with the other hand held her gently by the muzzle, keeping her head away from Con. I said, shakily, "Don't be angry! She—she must have been jealous."

He didn't answer. He had taken a pace away from me, to pick up the tools and the coil of wire.

I said quickly, "Please don't be angry, Con. I'm sorry I've been a fool tonight, but I was upset."

He straightened, and turned. He wasn't looking angry. His face held no expression whatever, as he regarded me and the mare.

"So it appears. But not, apparently, by the horses."

"The—oh, well," I said, pushing the mare's head to one side, and coming away from the gate, "I told you it wasn't that, didn't I? And she's awfully gentle really, isn't she?"

He stood there, looking at me. After a moment or two he said in a curiously dry, abrupt tone, "Well, so long as you know just where you are."

"Oh yes," I said wearily, "I know just where I am."

I turned away and left him standing there in the lane, with the fencing wire in his hand.

The path to Forrest Hall looked as if nobody had been that way for a hundred years.

I don't remember consciously deciding to take it: I only wanted to get away from Con, and not to have to encounter Lisa for a little while longer. I found myself, with no clear idea why I had come this way, walking rapidly away from the house, along the river path that led towards the Hall.

The moss was silent underfoot. To my left, the sliding sparkle of the water lit the way. Big trees edged the path, lining the river bank. The track was ribbed with the shadows of their trunks, thrown slanting by the moon. Now last year's beech-mast crackled under my feet, and I thought I could smell lime blossom, until the path led me up to the high wall that girdled Forrest, and there the neglected overgrowth crowded in, with its stronger scents of ivy and rotting wood and wild garlic and elder flowers.

Set deep in the tangle was the gate leading through into the Hall grounds. The elder bushes, and the ivy cascading over the wall, had almost hidden it from sight. It creaked as I pushed it, and opened crookedly on one hinge.

It was darker in the wood, but here and there, in some chance patch of moonlit sky framed by the branches, burned a star, sparkling blue-white, like frost. The air was still, and the vast trees kept quiet their tangled boughs. The river made all the sound there was.

You could easily have missed the summerhouse if you didn't know where it was. It stood a little back from the path, under the trees, and rhododendrons had run wild up the bank in front of it, until its entrance showed only as a gaping square of blackness behind the other shadows. I had gone straight by it when an owl, sweeping past me low down, like the shadow of a flying cloud, startled me into turning. Then I saw the hard edge of the moonlight on the tiles of the roof. A flight of shallow steps, blurred by moss, led up through the bushes.

I paused for a moment, looking at it. Then I left the path, and made my way up the steps, pushing aside the sharp leaves of the rhododendrons. They were as stiff as leather, and smelt bitter and narcotic, of autumn and black water.

The summerhouse was one of those once-charming "follies" built by some eighteenth-century Forrest with a taste for romance. It was a small, square pavilion, open in front, and pillared with slender Ionic columns of peeling plaster. The floor was marble, and round the three sides ran a broad seat. A heavy, rustic-seeming table still stood in the centre of the floor. I touched it with an exploratory finger. It felt dry, but thick with dust, and, I suspected, birds' droppings. In the sunlight of high summer, with the bushes trimmed back, and the view of the river, and cushions on the benches, the place would be charming. Now it was a home not even for ghosts. Pigeons would nest there, and perhaps a blackbird or two, and the owl in the roof. I left it and went down the steps to regain the path.

There I hesitated, half inclined, now, to go back. But the events of the day still pressed on me, and the woods were quiet and fresh. If they were not full of comfort, at least they offered solitude, and a vast indifference.

I would go on, I thought, a little further; as far as the house. The moonlight was strong, and even when the path turned (as it soon did) away from the river, I could see my way fairly easily.

Presently the timber thinned again, and the path shook itself free of the engulfing rhododendrons, to skirt a knoll where an enormous cedar climbed, layer upon layer, into the night sky. I came abruptly out of the cedar's shadow into a great open space of moonlight, and there at the other side of it, backed against the far wall of trees, was the house.

The clearing where I stood had been a formal garden, enclosed by artificial banks where azaleas and berberis grew in a wild tangle. Here and there, remains of formal planting could be seen, groups of bushes and small ornamental trees, their roots deep in the rough grass that covered lawns and flower beds alike. Sheep had grazed the turf down to a close, tufted mat, but underneath this, the formal patterning of path and lawn (traced by their moon-slanted shadows) showed clear.

At the centre of the pattern stood a sundial, knee-deep in a riot of low-growing bushes. At the far side of the garden, a flight of steps mounted between urns and stone balustrading to the terrace of the house.

I paused beside the sundial. The scent of the small, frilled roses came up thick and sweet, and mixed with honeysuckle. The petals were wet, and the dew was heavy on the grass where I stood.

The shell of the house gaped. Behind it, the big trees made a horizon, against which the moon sketched in the shapes of the broken walls and windows. One end of the house, still roofed and chimneyed, thrust up looking almost intact, till you saw the forest through the window frames.

I crossed the damp, springy grass towards the terrace steps. Somewhere an owl hooted, and a moment later I saw it drift past the blind windows, to be lost in the woods beyond. I hesitated, then slowly climbed the steps. Perhaps it was here that I would find the ghosts. . . .

But they were not there. Nothing, not even a wisp of the past, stirred in the empty rooms. Peering in through the long windows, I made out the shapes of yesterday. . . . The drawing-room—a section of charred panelling, and the wreck of a door, and what remained of a once lovely fireplace. The library, with shelves still ranked against the two standing walls, and a damaged chimney-piece mounted with what looked like a coat of arms. The long dining room, where a young ash sapling had thrust its way up between broken floor boards, and where ferns hung in the cracks of the wall. . . . On an upper landing, one tall window had its lancet frames intact, standing sharply against the moonlight. For a moment it seemed as if the leaded tracery was there still, then you could see how the ferns grew in the empty sockets, with a plant of what might in daylight show to be wild campanula, its leaves and tight buds as formal as a design in metal.

No, there was nothing here. I turned away. The weedy gravel made very little sound under my feet. I paused for a moment at the head of the terrace steps, looking back at the dead house. The Fall of the House of Forrest. Con's mocking words came back to me, cruelly, and, hard after them, other words, something once read and long forgotten. . . .

Time hath his revolutions, there must be a period and an end of all temporal things, finis rerum, an end of names and dignities, and whatsoever is terrene, and why not of De Vere? For where is Bohun? Where's Mowbray? Where's Mortimer? Nay, which is more and most

of all, where is Plantagenet? they are intombed in the urnes and sepul-
chres of mortality . . .

Magnificent words; far too magnificent for this. This was no noble house ruined, no Bohun or Mowbray or Mortimer; only the home of a line of successful merchant adventurers, with a purchased coat of arms, that had never led a battle charge; but they had built something here of beauty and dignity, and cared for it, and now it had gone; and beauty and dignity had gone with it, from a world that was content to let such things run through its fingers like water.

There was a movement from the bushes at the edge of the clearing; the rustle of dead leaves underfoot, the sound of a heavy body pushing through the thicket of shrubs. There was no reason why I should have been frightened, but I jerked round to face it, my heart thudding, and my hand on the stone balustrade grown suddenly rigid. . . .

Only a ewe with a fat lamb nearly as big as herself, shoving her way between the azaleas. She saw me, and stopped dead, head up, with the moon reflecting back from her eyes and from the dew on her clipped fleece. The lamb gave a startled cry that seemed to echo back into the woods and hang there for ever, striking the sounding board of their emptiness. Then the two of them vanished like clumsy ghosts.

I found that I was shivering. I walked quickly down the steps and across the clearing. As I hurried under the layered blackness of the cedar, my foot struck a cone as solid as a clock weight, and sent it rolling among the azaleas. A roosting blackbird fled out of the bushes with a clatter of alarm notes that set every nerve jumping, and jangled on and on through the trees like a bell that has been pulled and left swinging.

It brought me up short for the second time. I was just at the entrance to the river path, where it plunged out of the moonlight into the wood.

I took half a step forward towards those shadows, then paused. I had had my hour of solitude; enough was enough. I had a home of a sort, and it was time I went back to it.

I turned aside to where the main drive entered the clearing, then hurried down its wide avenue, past the banked rhododendrons, past the ruined gate-house and the ivy tree, till I reached the painted gate marked WHITESCAR, and the well-kept road beyond it.

CHAPTER

SEVEN

Alang the Roman Wall,
Alang the Roman Wall,
The Roman ways in bygone days were terrible to recall . . .
                              Norman Turnbull: *Northumbrian Song.*

Julie arrived just before tea on a drowsy afternoon. Everywhere was the
smell of hay, and the meadowsweet was frothing out along the ditches.
The sound of the distant tractor was as much a part of the hot afternoon as the hum of the bees in the roses. It made the sound of the
approaching car unnoticeable, till Lisa looked up from the table where
she and I had been slicing and buttering scones for the men's tea, and
said, "There's a car just stopped at the gate. It must be Julie." She bit
at her lower lip. "I wonder who can be bringing her? She must have got
Bill Fenwick to meet her train."

I set down my knife rather too carefully. She gave me one of her
thoughtful, measuring looks. "I shouldn't worry. This'll be nothing,
after the rest."

"I'm not worrying."

She regarded me a moment longer, then nodded, with that little
close-lipped smile of hers. In my two-days' sojourn at Whitescar, Lisa
seemed to have got over her odd fit of nerves. Indeed, she had taken my
advice to her so much to heart that sometimes I had found myself wondering, but only momentarily, if she really had managed to persuade
herself that I was Annabel. At any rate she seemed to have adopted me
as genuine; it was a sort of protective colouration for herself.

"I'll go out and meet her," she said. "Are you coming?"

"I'll let you meet her first. Go ahead."

I followed her down the flagged passage to the back door, and waited
there, just in the door's shadow, while she went out into the sunlight.

Julie was at the wheel of an open car, a battered relic almost as old
as she was, carefully hand-enamelled a slightly smeared black, and in-

congruously decorated in dazzling chrome—at least, that was the
impression one got—with gadgets of blatant newness and dubious func-
tion. Julie dragged ineffectually at the hand brake, allowing the car to
slide to a stop at least four yards further on, then hurled herself out of
the door without even troubling to switch off the engine.

"Lisa! What heaven! We've had the most *sweltering* run! Thank God
to be here, and I can smell new scones. How's Grandfather? Has she
come? My dear, you don't mind Donald, I hope? It's his car and he
wouldn't let me drive because he says I'm the world's *ghastliest driver*,
but he had to at the end because I wouldn't get out and open the
gates. I asked him to stay—I hope you don't mind? He can have the old
nursery and I'll do every *stroke* of the work myself. *Has* she come?"

She had on a white blouse, and a blue skirt belted tightly to a slim
waist with a big leather belt the colour of new horse chestnuts. Their
simplicity did nothing to disguise the fact that they were expensive.
Her hair, which was fair and fine, shone in the sun almost as pale as
cotton floss, and her eyes were grey-green, and very clear, like water.
Her face was tanned golden, and her arms and legs, which were bare,
showed the same smooth, amber tan. A heavy gold bracelet gave emphasis to one slim wrist.

She was holding Lisa's hands, and laughing. She hadn't kissed her,
I noticed. The ecstasy of welcome was not personally for Lisa, but was
so much a part of Julie's own personality that it sprang, as it were,
unbidden. Fountains overflow. If people are near enough, the drops
fall on them, sparkling.

She dropped Lisa's hands then, and turned, with a swirl of her blue
skirt, towards the man whom I now noticed for the first time. He had
been shutting the yard gate behind the car. Now, before responding to
Julie's hail of "Donald! Come and meet Lisa!" he walked quietly across
to where the car stood, with her chrome glittering in the sun as she
shook to the vibrations of the engine. He switched the engine off, took
out the key, put it carefully into his pocket, and then approached, with
a slightly diffident air that was in startling contrast to Julie's ebullience.

I found later that Donald Seton was twenty-seven, but he looked
older, having that rather solemn, withdrawn look that scholarship sometimes imposes on the natural reserve of the Scot. He had a long face,
with high cheekbones, and eyes set well under indecisively marked
brows. The eyes were of indeterminate hazel, which could look shallow
or brilliant according to mood. They were, indeed, almost the only indication that Donald Seton ever varied his moods. His face seldom

changed from its rather watchful solemnity, except to let in, like a door opening on to bright light, his rare and extremely attractive smile. He had fine, straight hair that refused discipline, but tumbled forward in a thick mouse-brown thatch that showed reddish lights in the sun. His clothes were ancient and deplorable, and had never, even in their fairly remote past, been "good." They reminded me somehow of his car, except that his person was not ornamented to a similar extent. He was the kind of man who would, one felt, have stigmatized even the most modest band of Fair Isle as "a bit gaudy." He looked clever, gentle, and about as mercurial as the Rock of Gibraltar. He made a most remarkable foil for Julie.

She was saying, with that same air of delighted improvisation, "Lisa, this is Donald. Donald Seton. Darling, this is Lisa Dermott; I told you, she's a kind of cousin, and she's the most *dreamy* cook, you've no idea! Lisa, he can stay, can't he? Where have you put *her?*"

"Well, of course he may," said Lisa, but looking faintly taken aback. "How do you do? Have you really driven Julie all the way up from London? You must both be tired, but you're just in time for tea. Now, Mr.—Seton, was it?—"

"Didn't Grandfather *tell* you?" cried Julie. "Well, really, and he's always jumping on me for being scatterbrained! I *told* him on the phone that Donald was bringing me! Why, it was the whole *point* of my coming now, instead of August, or almost, anyway. Donald's the most terrific big bug in Roman Remains, or whatever you call it, and he's come to work up at West Woodburn where there's a Roman camp—"

"Fort," said Mr. Seton.

"Fort, then, isn't it the same thing? Anyway," said Julie eagerly, "I thought if I came *now*, I'd be up here when he was, *and* be here for the birthday party Grandfather's talking about, and anyway, June's a heavenly month and it always rains in August. *Has* she come?"

For once, Lisa's not very expressive face showed as a battleground of emotions. I could see relief at Julie's gay insouciance about her reasons for coming to Whitescar and the birthday party; avid curiosity and speculation about Donald; apprehension over the coming meeting between Julie and myself; pure social embarrassment at having another visitor foisted on her without notice, and a swift, house-proud calculation that she would manage this, as she managed everything. Besides —I could see her assessing the smile Julie flung at Donald—it might be worth it.

"Of course we can put you up, easily," she said, warmly, for her. "No, no, it doesn't matter a bit, there's always room, and any friend of Julie's—"

"It's very good of you, but I really wouldn't dream of putting you to the trouble." Mr. Seton spoke with a quiet lack of emphasis that was as definite as a full stop. "I've explained to Julie that I'll have to stay near my work. I'll be camping up there on the site, when the students come, but for a night or two, at any rate, the hotel expects me."

"Ah, well," said Lisa, "if that's what you've arranged. But of course you'll stay and have tea?"

"Thank you very much. I should like to."

"That's *absurd!*" cried Julie. "Donald, I *told* you, it would be *much* nicer staying here. You don't have to do the polite and refuse just because Grandfather forgot to tell Lisa you were coming, for goodness' sake! As a matter of fact I may have forgotten to tell Grandfather, but then I was so excited about Annabel and then it was three minutes and it's a call box in my digs and you know Grandfather's always been as mean as stink about reversing the charges. Anyway, Donald, darling, you can't *possibly* camp at West Woodburn, it's the *last* place, and I've seen that site of yours; there are *cows*. And you've got to escape your dreary old Romans sometimes, so obviously you'll stay here. That's settled, then. Lisa I can't bear it another moment. Where *is* she?"

I hadn't moved from the shadows of the passage. But the fraction before Julie turned, Donald, looking past her shoulder, saw me standing there. I had been prepared for surprise, shock, even, in the recognition of everyone who had known Annabel before, but the startled amazement in Donald Seton's eyes jolted me, until I realized that, to him, I was a ghost of Julie. The look went, banished from his eyes immediately, but I wondered just what he had seen; a Julie grown older, thinner; not greyer, that would have been absurd, but somehow greyed? The eight years were dry in my throat, like dust.

Julie had seen me. I saw her eyes widen, then the same look spring in them.

I came out into the sunlight.

"*Annabel!*"

For a moment she stayed poised, as it seemed, between welcome and something else. The moment hung suspended for ever, like the wave before it breaks. I thought, Lisa was wrong, this is the worst thing yet: I can't bear it if she hates me, and God knows, she may be the one to have the right.

"Annabel *darling!*" said Julie, and dived straight into my arms and kissed me. The broken wave washed over me; the salt drops tingled and smarted in my eyes. She was laughing and hugging me and holding me away from her and talking, and the moment slid past with all the other moments, and was gone.

"Annabel, you *devil*, how *could* you, it's been such *hell*, and we were so unhappy. Oh, I could kill you for it, I really could. And I'm so thankful you're not dead because now I can *tell* you. That's the worst of people dying, they get away. . . . Oh lord, I'm not crying—these must be those tears of joy they always shed like *mad* in books, only I've never believed them. . . . Oh, it's terrific, it really is! You've come back!" She gave me a little shake. "Only *say* something, darling, for pity's sake, or I *will* think you're a ghost!"

I noticed that Donald had turned away, tactfully, to examine the side of the Dutch barn. Since this was made of corrugated iron, it could hardly be said to provide an absorbing study for an archaeologist; but he seemed to be finding it quite fascinating. Lisa had withdrawn a little behind Julie, but she was watching unashamedly.

I looked at Julie, feeling suddenly helpless. What was there to say, after all?

I cleared my throat, smiled uncertainly, and said the only thing that came into my head. "You—you've grown."

"I suppose I have," said Julie blankly.

Then we both laughed, the laughter perhaps a little high and over-pitched. I could see Lisa looking at me with her mouth slightly open. It came to me suddenly that she was staggered and dismayed at the ineptitude with which I was playing this scene; all the more feeble since she had seen the way I dealt with Grandfather. As far as it was possible for me to do so at that moment, I felt amused. Of course there was nothing to say. Here, at least, Lisa was a bad psychologist. What did she expect me to do? Make a charmingly social occasion out of this? My part in the scene had been far more convincing than she knew.

The next second, uncannily, Julie was echoing my thought. "You know, isn't it silly? I've noticed it before, about meeting anyone one hasn't seen for a long time. You long and long for the moment, like mad, and then, when it comes, and you've got the first hullos said, there's nothing whatever to say. All that comes later, all the *where have you been and how did you get on* stuff. For the moment, it's quite enough to have you here. You do understand, don't you?"

"Of course. I'm just thanking heaven you do. I—I can't think of much in the way of conversation, myself." I smiled at her, and then at Donald, now gravely waiting on the outskirts of the conversation. "I'm still English enough to regard tea as a sort of remedy for any crisis. Shall we go in and have it? How do you do, Mr. Seton?"

"Oh lord, I'm sorry," said Julie, and hastily made the introduction. "Only for pity's sake call him Donald, everybody does, at least, everybody he *likes*, and if he doesn't like them, he never speaks to them at all, which comes to the same thing."

I laughed as I shook hands with him. "It sounds a marvellous way of getting along."

"It works," said Donald.

"Oh," said Julie, at my elbow, "Donald has his very own way of getting through life with the minimum of trouble to himself."

I glanced at her quickly. Nothing in Donald's expression showed me whether this was intended to have a sharp edge to it, or anything in Julie's, for that matter. She looked very lovely and gay, and she was laughing at him.

She thrust an arm into mine. "Where's Grandfather? Surely he's not up in the field in this weather? It's far too hot."

"He's lying down. He does every afternoon now."

"*Does* he? I mean, does he *have* to?"

Lisa had gathered Donald up, so to speak, and, with the usual polite murmur about washing his hands before tea, was shepherding him ahead of us towards the house.

I said, "It's only a precaution. He has to be careful. He might be risking another stroke if he did anything too energetic, or had any sort of upset. So, gently with him, Julie. I think my coming back has been a bit of a strain, but he's taken it remarkably well."

"And Con?" The sideways glance was disconcertingly shrewd.

I said lightly, "He's taken it very well, too." I wondered, by no means for the first time, how much the eleven-year-old Julie had known about her cousin's disappearance. "You'll see him later. I imagine he'll take his tea up in the field with the men."

"Are you going to take it up? I'll help if you like, or we can make Donald come and carry everything—you don't exactly look as if you ought to be hiking loads around in this heat, if I may say so. What on earth have you been doing to yourself, you look so thin, and your figure used to be heaven, at least *I* thought so, which might mean anything, because when I was eleven my ideal was the Angel Gabriel and they're not supposed to have figures anyway, are they?"

"Julie! At least you didn't piffle on at that rate when you were eleven, or if you did, I don't remember it! Where on earth did you learn?"

Julie laughed. "Donald."

"That I don't believe."

"Well, he never speaks at all unless it's necessary, so I have to do enough for two on one person's wits. Result, half my talk is piffle, whereas Donald's silence is a hundred per cent solid worth. Or would it be two hundred per cent? I never know."

"I see."

"And there was you."

"I?"

"Yes. Nobody could piffle quite so well. The stories you used to make up. I can still remember them, and the funny thing is, a lot of them seemed somehow more real than you, or at any rate they seemed the realest part of you."

"Perhaps they were."

She gave me a swift look as we went into the house, and squeezed my arm. "When you look like that you break my heart."

"I don't see why."

"You look unhappy, that's why. Whenever you're not actually smiling. It's just a look you have. It's not like you . . . I mean, you weren't like that before."

"I meant, I don't see why you should worry over the way I feel."

"Don't you?"

"No. Why should you care what happened to me? I lighted out regardless, didn't I? And now I come back, like a ghost to trouble sleep. Why should you care?"

The grey-green eyes were open and candid as a child's. "Because I love you, of course," said Julie, quite simply.

The passage was dim after the glare of the sun. I was glad of this. In a moment I said, lightly, "Better than the Angel Gabriel?"

She laughed. "Oh, he stopped being top hit years ago. Much better."

In a way, Julie's homecoming was as exacting as my own.

Mrs. Bates was, inevitably, lying in wait in the kitchen: "And very nice it is to see you, Julie, and very smart you're looking, quite London, I'm sure. A real shame I call it, the way they make you work at the B.B.C.—not a chance to come up and see your poor Granda, *not* to mention others as I could name what would have liked a sight of you any time this past year. And was that your young man that went through with Miss Dermott? 'Not official?' And what does that mean, may I ask?"

Then there was Con, who came down unexpectedly from the hay-field, ostensibly impatient to welcome Julie, but curious, I knew, to see who had driven her down.

It was amusing to watch the meeting between him and Donald. We were quietly settled, waiting for Mrs. Bates and the tea cart, when Con walked in. He had presumably conformed by washing his hands, but he was still in his working clothes—old breeches, and a white shirt, short-sleeved and open at the neck. He brought with him, into the rather charmingly old-fashioned room, the smell of sunshine and hay, and—it must be confessed—a faint tang of horses and outdoor, sunbaked sweat. He looked magnificent.

He greeted Donald with none of the curiosity that I knew he was feeling. If he had been wondering about Julie's new escort as a potential threat to his own position, the worry, I could see, was dispelled as soon as he entered the room, and saw the unobtrusive figure sitting quietly in the old-fashioned chintz-covered chair by the fireplace. I could also see, quite well, that he was pleased—as Donald rose to greet him—to find himself the taller of the two by at least three inches. The contrast between the two men was certainly remarkable, and I saw an odd ex-pression in Julie's eyes as she watched them. Lisa's face, for once, was much more transparent; one almost expected to hear from her the proud, contented clucking with which the mother hen regards the swan that she has just personally hatched. The only person in the room who seemed unconscious of Con's overwhelming physical splendour was Donald. He greeted the other man serenely, and then turned back to resume his conversation with me.

Grandfather came in then, followed immediately by Mrs. Bates with the tea. The old man was using a stick, which I hadn't seen him do be-fore, and I thought he looked more finely drawn than usual, with a waxy tinge to the skin.

"Grandfather, it's lovely to see you!" Julie, as she rose to greet him, gave him a fond, anxious look. "How are you?"

"Hm. You've controlled your anxiety remarkably well, haven't you? How long is it since you were here? Twelve months?"

"Only ten," said Julie. "Grandfather, this is Donald Seton. He's a London friend of mine who drove me up, such luck, and he's going to be up here all summer, working at West Woodburn."

"How d'ye do? Good of you to bring the child. Glad you could stay to tea. Working at West Woodburn, eh? What sort of work?"

As Donald answered, I noticed that Con, ostensibly talking to Julie, was listening carefully. Mrs. Bates, lingering beside Lisa, hadn't taken her eyes off Donald.

"Thank you, Mrs. Bates," said Lisa, pouring tea. "That's everything, I think . . . Annabel, I wonder if you'd help hand the cups?"

"Let me, please," said Donald quickly, getting to his feet. Con slanted a lazy look up at him, and stayed where he was.

Lisa—with great restraint—poured tea for Julie and Grandfather before she attended to Con, but when she did come to Con's cup, I noticed that she not only put sugar in, but even stirred it, before giving it to Donald to hand to him. Donald carried it across with no change of expression, and Con took it without even looking away from Julie, who was telling some story or other which involved a lot of laughter.

Mrs. Bates had made no move to go, but busied herself rather ostentatiously, handing scones. The little black eyes had never left Donald.

"London, eh?" This came as soon as he left his chair, and was detached, so to speak, from Grandfather's orbit. "So you've come up north for the summer, from what I hear?"

"Yes."

"And what d'you think of the North?" This in the tone of a champion throwing down a rather well-worn glove. "I suppose you Londoners think we've not even got electric light in these parts yet?"

"Haven't you?" said Donald, startled into a vague glance at the ceiling.

I said quickly, "Mrs. Bates regards all Londoners as ignorant southerners who think the Arctic Circle begins at Leeds, or something."

"One wonders," put in Julie from the sofa, "if they mayn't be right, sometimes. Not this year, it's been heaven *everywhere*."

"Even here?" said Grandfather, rather drily.

I saw a glance pass, like a spark across points, between Con and Lisa.

I said quickly, "Betsy, dear, Mr. Seton isn't a southerner, really; he's from Scotland."

"Oh?" She appeared only slightly mollified. "I've never been up in them parts. But you *live* in London, like?"

"Yes, I've got rooms there. But I usually spend the summer somewhere out on a—well, in the country. This year I'm at West Woodburn."

"For the whole summer?" I hoped the calculating glance that Mrs.

Bates shot at Julie wasn't as obvious to him as it was to me. But she underlined it. "How long are *you* staying, Julie?"

"Mm?" Julie had been laughing at some remark of Con's. "Who, me? As long as I can. I've got three weeks."

"Mrs. Bates," said Lisa, "there's the telephone, I think. Do you mind? . . . I'm sorry, Mr. Seton, but she's been a member of the family for so long, and of course she's known Julie since she was very small . . . I think she puts all Julie's friends into the same age group."

"And that," said Julie cheerfully, "stays at about thirteen plus. Donald doesn't mind, do you, darling?"

"Not in the least." Mr. Seton, who had, during the cross-examination, been handing sandwiches and scones round with unruffled good humour, now sat down, and took one himself. Somehow, I noticed, the stand of sandwiches and cakes had finished up in a position midway between his chair and mine, and within easy reach of both. No mean strategist, I thought, watching him finish his sandwich, and quietly take another. They were very good; I had made them myself.

"Now," said Grandfather, who, being a Winslow male, obviously thought it was time he was back in the centre of the stage, "about this Roman camp at West Woodburn. . . ."

"Fort, actually," said Donald.

"Fort, then. Habitancium, isn't that the Roman name for it?"

"Habitancum." Donald took another sandwich in an absent sort of way, while managing to keep a keenly interested gaze fixed on his questioner. "That's the name on the various inscriptions that have been uncovered. There are no other references, and the place is named solely from the inscriptions, so, in fact," that sudden, charming smile, "your guess is as good as mine, sir."

"Oh. Ah. Well, what I want to know is this—"

But Mrs. Bates, laden with more scones, and big with news, re-entered the room briskly.

"The way things gets around in these parts is like magic, it is that. Here's Julie only been at home five minutes before her young man's ringing her up on the phone. He's waiting." She slapped the plate of scones down on the tea cart, and stared pointedly at Julie.

The latter looked blank for a moment, then I saw the faintest tinge of pink slide up under her skin. "My—young man?"

"Aye," said Mrs. Bates a little sourly. "Young Bill Fenwick from Nether Shields. Saw you pass, he says, when they was working up near the road."

"Young Fenwick?" said Grandfather. "Nether Shields? What's this? What's this?"

"I've no idea." Julie spoke airily, setting down her cup. "Did he say it was for me?"

"He did, and well you know it. Never talked about anyone else since last time you were here, and if you ask me—"

"Oh, Mrs. Bates, *please!*" Julie, scarlet now, almost ran out of the drawing-room. Mrs. Bates gave a ferocious nod that was aimed somewhere between Grandfather and Donald. "He's a nice lad, Bill Fenwick is, but he's not for the likes of her, and *that's* the truth and no lie!"

"Mrs. Bates, you really mustn't—" began Lisa.

"I speak as I find," said that lady tartly.

"Hm," said Grandfather. "Pity you find such a lot. That'll do, now, Betsy. Go away."

"I'm going. Enjoy your teas, now, I made those scones meself. You'll not get the likes of *them* in London," with a nod at Donald, "*nor* in Scotland, neither, let me tell you. Now, did I see that cat come in or did I not?"

"Cat?" said Lisa. "Tommy? Oh no, surely not, he's never allowed in here."

"I thought I seed him run past when I opened the door."

"Nonsense, Betsy, you're imagining things." Grandfather was poking about testily under the sofa with his stick. "There's no cat in here. Don't make excuses, now, just go away, do. The scones are excellent. Perhaps you'll get Julie to bring the hot water in, when she's finished her telephone call?"

"All right," said Mrs. Bates, unoffended. "There's nobody can say I can't take a hint as well as anyone." But, pausing at the door, she fired her last shot. "Mr. Forrest, too, did I tell you? He's back already. Didn't expect *him* till Friday, but he's flown. Maybe *he'll* be on the phone soon." And, with a chuckle, she disappeared.

There was a pause.

"Ah, well," said Con, reaching out a lazy hand, "the scones are worth it."

"Hm," said Grandfather, "she's all right. Trust Betsy with my last halfpenny, and that's a thing you can't say of many, nowadays. Now, Seton, where were we?"

"Habitancum," said Con, "just about to start digging."

"Ah, yes. Well, what are you going to find? Tell me that? If there's anything worth finding round here, I wish you digging Johnnies would find it at Whitescar. No likelihood of *that*, I suppose?"

I saw a sudden look of surprise flicker over Donald's face, to be followed by what looked like rather furtive embarrassment. Grandfather, drinking tea, hadn't noticed, but Con had. I saw his eyes narrow momentarily in a speculative look. Then I saw what was hidden from anyone else in the room. Donald's hand, with a portion of ham sandwich, had been hanging down over the arm of his chair while he talked. The skirts of his armchair almost touched the ground. From under the edge of this crept a stealthy, black and white paw, which once again patted the edge of the ham sandwich.

"There's nothing marked hereabouts on any existing map," said Donald, now serenely ignoring this phenomenon, "but that's not to say there *was* nothing here, of course. If you start turning up Roman coins with the plough, sir, I hope you'll send straight for me." As he spoke, he had returned the sandwich to the plate, and then his hand went, oh, so idly, over the arm of the chair, holding a substantial portion broken off. The paw flashed out and took it, not too gently. Tommy, it appeared, had had to learn to snatch what bits he got.

"And how long are you to be here?"

"Possibly until August, on this particular job."

"I doubt," said Con with a grin, "if we'll be doing much ploughing before you go, then."

"No?" said Donald, adding, apologetically, "I'm afraid I'm very ignorant. Your, er, Mrs. Bates was perhaps not so far out in her judgment of Londoners."

"Well," said Grandfather, "if you can tell wheat and barley apart, which I've no doubt you can, then you'll be one up on me and Connor —I wouldn't know a Roman inscription from a whisky advertisement, and neither would he."

Con's protest, and my "Are you sure?" came simultaneously, and everyone laughed. Into the laughter came Julie, so blandly unconcerned, and so fussily careful of the hot-water jug she was carrying, that the attention of everyone in the room switched straight to her with an almost audible click. It was all Con could do, I knew, not to ask her outright what Bill Fenwick had had to say.

"Julie?" Old Mr. Winslow had no such inhibitions. "What did the boy want?"

"Oh, nothing much," said Julie airily, "just how was I, and how long was I here for, and—and all that."

"Hm. Well, now, let's have a look at you, child. Come and sit by me. Now, about this job of yours. . . ."

Conversation began to flow again, Con and Lisa both listening with some interest to Julie's account of her first year's work at Broadcasting House. Beside me, the skirts of Donald's chair began to shake in a frustrated fashion. I said gently, "Won't you have another sandwich, Mr. Seton? These are crab. They—er, they go down rather well."

I saw the glimmer in his eyes as he took one. Half a minute later I saw the paw field a piece, very smartly, and, in a matter of three-quarters of a second, come out for more. Tommy, flown with good living, was getting reckless.

"You're not eating anything," said Lisa to me. "Have another sandwich. There's one left—"

Even as she turned to look, the paw shot out, and the last of the crab sandwiches vanished, whole, from the plate on the bottom tier of the cart.

"I'm so sorry," said Donald, blandly, to me. "I took it myself. Have a macaroon."

CHAPTER

EIGHT

"O wherefore should I tell my grief,
  Since lax I canna find?
 I'm stown frae a' my kin and friends,
  And my love I left behind."

Ballad: *Baby Livingston.*

Julie and I went out together that evening. Lisa's eyes followed us to
the door, but she said nothing. Donald, not to be moved from his decision, had driven off to West Woodburn soon after tea. Grandfather,
whom the heat was tiring, I thought, more than he would admit, had
gone early to bed. Con had not come in again. No doubt he would
come back at dusk for a late supper. The sound of the tractor wound on
and on through the soft evening into the dusk.

Though it would have seemed the natural pilgrimage to take her to
see the mare, I had had enough of the lane. We went the other way,
through the garden towards the wicket gate and the river path that led
towards West Lodge. In the half-light the rank borders looked and
smelled heavy with flowers. The swifts were out, and flying high. Their
screaming was thin and ecstatic, and exciting, like all the sounds that
one feels one is not meant to hear: the singing of the grey seal and the
squeak of a bat and the moaning of shearwaters under the ground at
night on the wild sea's edge.

Now that we were alone together there still seemed curiously little
to say. She had told the truth when she said that the major things of
life had no need to be talked over. I supposed that for her the return
of the idolized cousin from the dead was one of these. Never by word
or look had she betrayed any consciousness that my advent might make
the least difference to her future. It might not even have occurred to
her . . . but it soon would; it must. If it didn't occur to her, it might
occur to Donald.

We had been filling up the eight years' gap—I with completely truth-
ful reminiscences of my life in Canada, and Julie with a lively and (it

is to be hoped) libelous account of the year she had spent in the Drama Department at Broadcasting House.

". . . no, *honestly*, Annabel, it's gospel truth!"

"I don't believe it. It sounds as if you wouldn't even know what 'gospel' means."

"'Good tidings.'"

"Heavens!"

"I thought that'd shake you," said Julie complacently.

"I suppose you got that from Donald too?"

"'All good things—?' I expect so." Her voice had abruptly lost its sparkle.

I looked at her. "He's very nice," I said, tentatively.

"Yes, I know." She spoke without enthusiasm. She had picked a dead dry stalk of last year's hedge-parsley, and switched it idly through the buttercups that lined the river path where we walked.

"You mustn't mind Mrs. Bates, Julie. Marrying and burying are meat and drink to her."

"I know. I don't mind. I suppose I did let her jump to conclusions, rather."

"Here's the boundary. Shall we go on?"

"No. Let's find somewhere to sit."

"The stile will do. It's quite dry."

We climbed the two steps of the stile and sat side by side on the broad cross-bar, facing away from the house. It was another quiet evening, and the trees that edged the meadows were still in the dusky air. The path had left the river some way to our right; along it, here, the willows streamed untrimmed, their long hair trailing in the water.

I said, "You know, I'm afraid I jumped to conclusions about Donald. I was hoping they were correct."

"Were you?"

I laughed. "I fell for your Donald, from a great height."

Her face came alight for a moment. "One does. That's how it happened, with me. He's such a—a poppet. Even when I'm a bit foul to him, like today, he's just the same. He's—oh, he's so *safe* . . . !" She finished on a note that sounded more despondent than anything else, "And I do adore him, I do, really."

"Then what's wrong?"

"I don't know."

I waited.

She extended a sandalled foot, and regarded it. "It's true; I do want to marry him. And most times I want nothing better than to marry him *soon*. And then, sometimes, suddenly . . ." A little pause. "He hasn't asked me, actually."

I smiled. "Well, you've got three weeks."

"Yes." She dimpled, then sighed. "Oh, Annabel, it's all such *hell*, isn't it? If only one could *tell!* Like *that*, the way they do in books, but when it comes to the real thing it's actually quite *different*. I mean—"

"I wouldn't have thought you need worry quite so hard. You've loads of time, after all. You're only nineteen."

"I know." Another sigh, and a despondent silence.

I said, after a minute, "Would you rather talk about something else? You don't need to tell me anything you don't want to."

"Oh, but I do. In a way it was one of the things I was so longing to see you again for. I thought you'd know, you see."

"My dear," I said helplessly.

"Oh, I know you don't know him yet. But when you do—"

"That wasn't what I meant. I meant why the blazes should you imagine I could be of any help to you? I—I made a pretty fair mess of my own life, you know."

I half expected the routine and automatic response of kindness and reassurance, but it didn't come. She said immediately, "That's why. It isn't the people who've had things their own way who—well, who get wisdom. And they haven't the time to think about what life does to other people, either. But if you've been hurt yourself, you can imagine it. You come alive to it. It's the only use I can ever see that pain has. All that stuff about welcoming suffering because it lifts up the soul is rot. People ought to avoid pain if they can, like disease . . . but if they have to stand it, its best use might be that it makes them kinder. Being kind's the main thing, isn't it?"

"Julie, I wouldn't know. I've never got these things straight with myself yet. And on a rainy day I find I believe quite different things from on a fine one. But you might be right. Being cruel's the worst thing, after all, so kindness might be the best. When you come to think about it, it covers nearly everything, doesn't it? One's whole duty to one's neighbour."

"And the other whole duty?"

"My dear, I don't even pretend to know what that duty is. My duty to my neighbour will have to do. Maybe it'll count."

She had reached out an idle hand to the bush beside her, and broken off a small spray of hawthorn blossom, not yet dead. The milky heads hung bunched; I could smell their thick, sleepy scent. She twisted the stem between her fingers, so that the flowerheads swung out and whirled like a tiny roundabout. She seemed all at once very young and uncertain as she hesitated, apparently on the brink of some confidence.

I spoke almost nervously. "Julie."

"Mm?" She seemed absorbed in the twirling flowers.

"Julie—don't ask me about it now, but . . . well, just keep quiet for the moment about the state of affairs between you and Donald, will you? I mean, if people want to jump to conclusions, like Betsy, let them."

The flowers stopped twirling. She turned her head, her eyes wide and surprised. "Heavens, why?"

"I'm sorry. I can't explain. But if you've really made up your mind to have Donald when he asks you—and if you can't make him do so in the next three weeks, I wash my hands of you—well, quarrel with him all you like in private, but don't let other people see you having too many doubts."

"Honey!" To my relief she sounded amused. "Is this Aunt Agatha's advice to young girls, or do you really mean anyone special when you say 'other people'?"

I hesitated. I believe that at that moment I very nearly told Julie the whole story. But I said, merely, "You might say I meant Grandfather. I think this stroke he's had has frightened him, rather, and he's fretting a bit about the future—our future."

She sent me a glance that was all at once adult and wise. "*My* future, do you mean, now that you've come home?"

"Yes. You know what men of his generation are like, they think there's really nothing but marriage . . . I know you're still very young, but I—I know he'd like to think of your being settled with someone like Donald. I'm sure he liked him, too. So—don't rock the boat too much, Julie, at any rate not while you're here."

"The boat? Mr. Isaacs and all?" She laughed suddenly. "I *thought* there was something in the wind! Don't you start worrying about that, Annabel, good heavens, all *I* want is to get on with my own life in my own way, and I think—I *think*—that includes Donald!" She dropped a hand over mine where it lay on the bar. "But don't you ever go away again. Promise?"

I said nothing, but she took this for assent, for her hand squeezed mine softly, and then withdrew. She added, cheerfully now, "All right,

I won't rock any boats. All the storms of my lovelife shall be—passed? blown? raged? waged?—up at the Roman camp."

"Fort."

"Oh lord, yes. I *must* learn to be accurate about the more important things of life. Fort. Look, there's Mr. Forrest's horse, over there, like a shadow. He looks awfully quiet. Don't you love the way everyone shakes their heads over him and says 'He won't be easy to school'?"

"I do rather. But I expect it's true. Blondie's foals do have that reputation."

"Do they?"

"Didn't you know? And Grandfather tells me this one is by Everest."

"By Everest? Oh, I see, you mean that's the name of the father?"

"The sire, yes. Don't you remember him? He was a bit of a handful, too, like all the old 'Mountain' lot." I glanced at her, amused. It seemed that Con had been right; this was not Julie's *métier*. She had shown the same cheerful ignorance in the drawing-room over tea, when the talk had turned on the affairs of Whitescar. Grandfather had noticed; I had seen him eyeing her; and Con had noticed, too. And now she had made it obvious that she realized my return would deprive her of her place here; she had also made it apparent that she didn't care. She wasn't only making things easy for me: I was sure it was true. For Julie, this place was a holiday, no more. I felt a real rush of relief, not only for my conscience' sake, but because Con could now bear no grudge against her. What sort of grudge, or what shape that grudge would take, I hadn't yet allowed myself to guess at.

She was holding the flowers close to her face, watching Rowan with the uncritical admiration of complete ignorance.

"He's lovely, isn't he?" she said dreamily. "Like something in a book. And the field smells like heaven. Pegasus, in the Elysian fields. He ought to have a manger of chalcedony and a bridle of pearl."

"Have you the faintest idea what chalcedony is?"

"Not the faintest. It sounds wonderful. Have you? It ought to be like marble shot with fire and gold. What is it?"

"Something looking a bit like soap, the healthy kind. As big a letdown as jasper, anyway. The gates of Paradise are made of that, according to Revelation, but really it's the most—"

"Don't tell me! Let me keep my gates of jasper just as I've always seen them! Is this what the New World does to you? Have a heart, won't you? And admit that he *ought* to have a manger made of fire and gold and cedar wood and turquoises at *least!*"

"Oh, yes," I said. "I'll give him that."

The horse was grazing steadily along the hedge where a tall guelder rose broke the yard-high barrier of hawthorn. His shoulders brushed the pale saucers of bloom, and, through the leaves, the growing moonlight touched him here and there, a dapple of light shifting over moving muscle; then a sudden liquid flash from the eye as he raised his head to stare.

I heard him blow a soft greeting through whickering nostrils. He seemed to eye us uncertainly for a moment, as if he might come forward, then he lowered his head again to the grass. "I thought he was coming," said Julie breathlessly. "They all used to, to you, didn't they? Will you help school him? Johnny Rudd says he'll be the very devil, he won't let anyone near him in the stable, and he's next to impossible to catch in the field."

"He sounds a useful sort of beast," I said drily.

She laughed. "What a way to speak of Pegasus! You can't deny he's a beauty."

"No, he's that all right. What colour is he in daylight?"

"Red chestnut, with a pale mane and tail. His name's Rowan. Aren't you going in to speak to him?"

"I am not. This isn't my night for charming wild stallions."

"It seems a dreadful pity that all the horses had to go. It must have been a dreadful wrench for Mr. Forrest—though I suppose it would only come as a sort of last straw, considering everything else that had happened."

"Yes."

There was a little pause. Then Julie said, with a curious soft abruptness, her eyes still on the horse, "You know, you don't have to pretend with me. I know all about it."

The dusky trees, the shapes of hawthorn, the ghost of the grazing horse, all seemed to blur together for a moment. I didn't speak.

"I—I just thought I'd let you know I knew," said Julie. "I've known all along. Have you . . . have you spoken to him yet?"

The confusion in my mind blurred again, swung into another shape. I said, "Have I—what do you mean? Spoken to whom?"

"Mr. Forrest, of course."

Silence again. I couldn't have spoken if I'd tried. Before I could grope for words, she looked at me again, fleetingly, sideways, and said, like a nice child who confesses to something that she may be punished for,

"I'm sorry. But I did want to tell you that I knew all the time. I knew that you and Mr. Forrest were lovers."

I said, "Oh dear sweet *heaven.*"

"I'm sorry." She repeated the words with a kind of desperation. "Perhaps I shouldn't have told you I knew. But I wanted you to know. In case it was difficult or—or anything. You see, I'm on your side. I always was."

"Julie—"

"I didn't spy on you, don't think that. But I saw you together sometimes, and people don't always notice a kid of eleven hanging about. I was always around, all that spring and summer, during the holidays and I knew you used to leave letters in the ivy tree at the old Hall gate. I thought it wonderfully romantic. But I can see now that it must have been pretty awful. For you, I mean. You were younger than I am now."

My hands were pressing down hard to either side of me on the bar of the stile. "Julie . . . you . . . we . . . I didn't . . ."

"Oh, I know there wouldn't ever be anything *wrong*. I mean, really wrong. . . ."

Let her talk, I thought, let her tell me just what she saw, what she knew. At worst she might only remember having drifted like a shadow round the edges of romance. Romance? Adam Forrest? *Con*? The two names burned in front of me, as if they had been branded in the bars of the stile. . . .

"You couldn't help it. One can't help who one falls in love with." Julie was offering this shabby cliché as if it were the panacea still sealed all glittering in its virgin polythene. "It's what one does about it that matters. That's what I meant when I said I knew you'd had a bad time; I mean, if one falls in love with a married man there *is* nothing to do, is there?" It seemed that, to Julie, falling in love was an act as definable and as little controlled by the will, as catching a disease in an epidemic. That there came a moment when the will deliberately sat back and franked the desire was as foreign to her as the knowledge that, had the will not retreated, desire would have turned aside and life, in the end, have gone as quietly on.

"One can only go away," said Julie. "It's all there is to do. I knew why you'd gone, and I thought it marvellous of you. Do you know, I used to cry about it?"

I said, in a very hard, dry voice, "You needn't have done that."

She gave a little laugh. "Oh, it wasn't all tragedy to me at that age.

It was sad, yes, but beautiful too, like a fairy tale. I used to try and make up happy endings to myself in bed, but they could never really work, because they meant that she—his wife, I mean—would have to die. And even if she *was* awful, it's always cheating, in a story, to kill off the person who prevents the happy ending. And I suppose I did see it more as a story, in those days, than as something that was really happening to people I knew. Was it so very dreadful, that time?"

"Yes."

"I've sometimes wondered, since," said Julie, "if life isn't just a little too much for all of us. Sometimes one thinks . . . oh well, never mind. You don't mind my having told you? I rather wanted you to know I knew. That was all. We won't speak of it again if you like."

"It doesn't matter. It's over."

She looked almost shocked. "Over?"

"My God, Julie, what d'you expect? One can't tear a great hole in one's life pattern and expect the picture to be unspoiled till one chooses to come back and finish it. One can't fit straight back into the space one left. Nor does one want to. Of course it's over!"

"But I thought—"

I said, and I could hear myself how nerves had sharpened my voice, "Do you seriously think I'd have *dreamed* of coming back if I'd known he was still here?"

"*Didn't* you know?"

"Of course I didn't! I thought I'd made very sure he wasn't, or I'd never have come, except perhaps just a flying visit to see Grandfather again, and make things up with him. But as for coming here to stay . . . No."

"But—" her voice sounded all at once as frankly disappointed as a child's—"but it's not the same now, is it? I mean, now that you *have* come, and he *is* here, and . . ." The sentence trailed off.

"You mean because Crystal Forrest's dead?" I said flatly.

I heard her give a little gasp. "Well . . . yes."

I laughed. "Poor Julie. Your happy ending at last. I'm sorry."

"Annabel—"

"Forget it, darling. Oblige me by forgetting it. And remind me one day to thank you for forgetting it as far as Con and the rest are concerned. I'd have rather hated them to know. Con has his own—theories —as to why I left."

Her voice was suddenly mature, and curious. "You dislike Con. Why?"

"Heaven knows. And 'dislike's' the wrong word. Say I distrust him. Julie . . ."

"Mm?"

"Just what, exactly, did you know about me and—about me and Adam?"

"Only what I told you. I knew you met, and I knew you wrote quite regularly, and put the notes in the hole in the ivy tree. And I think I knew that it—it was a hopeless passion—what are you laughing at?"

"I'm sorry. Your vocabulary. Go on, it was a hopeless passion . . ."

"All right," she said without rancour. "I suppose I do read all the wrong books. But *you're* taking this the wrong way. I believe you really don't care any more."

"No."

"Ah, well." It was a sigh almost of disappointment. "I'd hoped it would come right in the end. You see, everybody knew they were unhappy, him and his wife, I mean. You couldn't ever tell what *he* was thinking, but she didn't try very hard to pretend, did she? I mean, it got sort of painful when they were anywhere together in public. Even I noticed, though I was only a kid. It's true, isn't it?"

"Yes."

"But there wasn't ever any talk of their separating. Everybody used to say they ought to divorce, but that he wouldn't divorce her money."

"They would."

"Yes. And of course I thought it was so obvious that he would fall in love with you. Anybody would."

"Julie, my love, you and I ought to be fairly careful how we compliment one another on our looks in public."

She grinned. "True enough. All the same, between ourselves, you were pretty smashing at nineteen. Confess!"

She was laughing at me in the light of the rising moon. I looked at her appraisingly. "I'm beginning to think I must have been."

"You're nice, aren't you?" she said naïvely. "Well . . . I still can't help having the feeling that I oughtn't to talk to you about it, for fear of making you unhappy, but still . . . I've wondered since, money or no money, why he didn't divorce her. She wasn't an R.C., so it can't have been that. *Could* it have been the money, Annabel? I'm not being foul, but after all, he couldn't ever have kept Forrest going—"

"I doubt if he cares that much about Forrest." I realized as soon as I had spoken how oddly my reply was framed, but she didn't notice.

"Then why? Why did they stay together? Why was she so filthy to him, almost as if he'd done something dreadful? It wasn't you, because it was going on for years before that. Why?"

"How could I know? He—he never discussed it." Then, out of nowhere, came a guess like a certainty, "She had no child."

"I—see," said Julie, slowly. "And he . . . ?"

"Some men take life itself as a responsibility. Maybe that was it. Maybe he took her unhappiness as his. How could he leave her? You can't leave people who have nothing else."

"You know," she said, "you talk about it all as if it was sort of remote, just a story about someone else."

"That's what it feels like," I said. "Look, why don't we go in? Come along, you're yawning like a baby. You've had a long journey today, and you must be tired. There'll be plenty of time to talk. Is Donald coming down tomorrow?"

"I expect so."

"I'm looking forward to meeting him again. Tell me all about him tomorrow. I seem to have kept you on my affairs tonight, but we'll forget them, as from now, shall we?"

"If that's the way you want it."

"That's the way I want it."

"Okay." She yawned again, suddenly and unashamedly, like an animal or a child. "Oh lord, I *am* sleepy. No need to drink mandragora to sleep out the great gap of time my Donald is away." She giggled. "Funny how he simply will not fit into any romantic context."

"Maybe you're safer that way, considering the kind of thing you appear to read."

"Maybe. Oh Annabel, it *is* so good to have you here. Did I say?"

"Yes. Thank you, Julie. Sleep well."

"Oh, I shall. But this ghastly hush is *devastating* after London, and if that blasted owl starts up I shall shoot it, I swear I will, even if it *is* a mother with seven starving babies in the ivy tree."

"That sort of owl has three."

She unlatched the garden gate and pushed it open. "You always did know everything about everything."

"Oh no, Julie! You make me sound like some ghastly Nature Girl hobnobbing with the owls, and charming wild horses, and flitting about the woods at night—" I stopped.

If Julie had noticed she made no sign. "Aren't you coming in?"

"Not yet. It's a lovely night, and I'm not tired. Nature Girl on the prowl. Good night."

"Good night," said Julie.

CHAPTER

NINE

The wind doth blow to-day, my love,
    And a few small drops of rain;
I never had but one true-love;
    In cold grave she was lain.

                                        Ballad: *The Unquiet Grave*.

If you stood on the low piece of crumbling wall that enclosed the trunk, you could just reach your hand into the hole. I held on to the writhen stems of the ivy with one hand and felt above my head into the hollow left by some long-decayed and fallen bough.

I put my hand in slowly, nervously almost, as I might have done had I known that Julie's owl and seven mythical young were inside, and ready to defend it, or as I might have invaded a private drawer in someone's desk. The secret tryst; Ninus' tomb; the lovers' tree; what right had a ghost there, prying?

In any case there was nothing to pry into. Whatever secrets the ivy tree had held in the past, it was now only a tree, and the post box was an empty hole, the bottom cracked and split, its fissures filled with crumbling touchwood as dry as tinder. Some twigs and rotting straw seemed to indicate that a starling had once nested there. The ivy, brushing my face, smelt dark and bitter, like forgotten dusty things.

I climbed down from the wall and wiped my hands on my handkerchief.

Beside me, skirting the ruins of the gate-house, the neglected avenue curled away into the shadows. I turned my head to look where, in the strong moonlight beyond the blackness cast by the trees, the white gate glimmered. I could almost make out the neat black letters on the top bar. WHITESCAR. I made a half-movement in that direction, then checked myself. *If it be now, 'tis not to come.* Well, let it be now.

I put away my handkerchief, and walked quickly past the ruined gate-house, up the silent mosses of the drive, towards Forrest Hall.

The moon was fuller tonight, and it was later. The skeleton of the house stood up sharply, with the dramatic backcloth of trees cutting its lines and angles, and throwing into relief the tracery of the bare windows. One or two sheep grazed among the azaleas. The little tearing sounds they made, as they cropped the grass, sounded loud in the windless air.

I could smell the roses and honeysuckle that smothered the sundial. I went slowly down the moss-furred steps, and over the grass towards it. The dial was covered with a thick mat of leaves and tendrils. I picked one of the tiny chandeliers of the honeysuckle and held it to my face. The long stamens tickled, and the scent was thick and maddeningly sweet, like a dream of summer nights. I dropped it into the grass.

I sat down on the lowest step where the pediment jutted into the encroaching grass, and pushed aside the trailing honeysuckle with gentle hands, till the shaft of the sundial lay bare. The moonlight struck it slantingly, showing the faint shadows of carving under the soft rosettes of lichen.

I scratched a little of the moss away, and traced the letters with a slow, exploratory finger.

TIME IS.   TIME WAS. . . .

Another line below it. No need to trace that out.

TIME IS PAST. . . .

It didn't need the startled swerve of a ewe ten yards away, or the rustle and patter of small hoofs retreating, to tell me that I had been right. He had come, as I had guessed he would.

My hands were pressed flat on the dry mosses. I could feel the blood in them jump and beat against the chill of the stone. I waited for a moment, without moving, crouched there on the step of the sundial, my hands hard against the stone.

Well, let it come. Get it over with. Learn just where you stand. *If it be not now, yet it will come.*

I turned slowly round, and, as stiffly as a puppet on strings, got to my feet.

He was standing not twenty yards away, at the edge of the wood. He was just a shadow under the trees, but it could be no one else. He had come, not by the drive, but up the path from the summer-house.

I stood without moving, with the moon behind my shoulder, and my back to the sundial. I think that I had a hand on it still, as if for support, but oddly enough, the emotion that struck at me most vividly at the sight of him was that of relief. This was the worst thing that had happened, and I had had no time to be ready for it; but now it had come, and it would get over. Somehow, I would find the right things to say. . . .

It seemed a very long time before he moved. The moonlight fell strongly on him as he came forward, and even at that distance I could see that he was staring as if he had seen a ghost. His features were blanched and dramatized by the white slanting light, but even so it was apparent that some violent emotion had drained his face to a mask where the flesh seemed to have been planed from the strong-looking bones, leaving it a convention, as it were, of planes and angles, lights and shadows. The eyes looked very dark, and the brows made a bar of black across them. I could see the deeply incised lines down his cheeks, and the thin line of a mouth schooled to reserve or patience. But when his lips parted to speak, one saw all at once how thin the defences were. His voice sounded vulnerable, too, half hesitating. This was a man who was by no means sure of his reception. And why should he be? Why indeed?

He spoke at last, in a half-whisper that carried no expression. "Annabel?"

"Adam?" Even as I said it, I thought the name sounded exploratory, tentative, as if I'd never used it before.

He had stopped a yard or so away. There was a pause, painfully long. Then he said, "I came as soon as I knew."

"Did you expect to find me here?"

"I didn't know. I thought . . . I don't know what I thought. Does it matter? You came."

"Yes," I said, "I—I had to see you."

I found that I had braced myself for his response to this, but he made none. His voice was so flattened and expressionless that it sounded barely interested. "Why did you come home?"

"Grandfather's ill. He—he may not have long to live. I had to see him again."

"I see." Another pause. That flat, empty voice again. "You never told me you were coming."

He might have been talking to a stranger. Between lovers there are such situations, so highly charged that words are absurd; but then lovers have their own language. We had none. Adam Forrest's love was dead, and there was nothing to say.

I answered him in the same way. "I didn't know you were still here. I only heard it by chance, the other night, from something Grandfather said. I'd understood you lived permanently in Italy now. In fact, when I came back to England, I'd no idea that your—" I stopped, swallowed, and finished stupidly on a complete *non sequitur*, "I didn't even know that Forrest Hall had gone."

"You never did have much regard for logic, did you? What you started to say was that you didn't know that Crystal had died."

"I—"

"Wasn't it?"

"Yes. I—I hadn't heard. I'm sorry."

He acknowledged this with a slight movement of the head, and let it go. He was standing perhaps six feet away. The moonlight fell between us, slantingly, from behind my left shoulder. The angled shadows it cast made his expression difficult to read. They also, which was more important, made it impossible for him to see me clearly. But he was watching me steadily, without moving, and the close unwavering regard was discomforting.

He said slowly, "Are you trying to tell me that if you had known —that I was here at Forrest, I mean, and free—you would not have come back?"

Behind me the edge of the sundial, rough with dried lichen, bit into my hands. Was this, after all, easier than I had imagined, or was it worse? His voice and face gave nothing away. There was nothing to indicate that he cared, any more than I did. Why should he? Eight years was a long time. I said, almost with relief, "Yes. Just that."

"I see." For the first time the steady gaze dropped, momentarily, then came back to me with a jerk. "But you came tonight to meet me?"

"I told you. I came, hoping you'd come along. I had to see you. After I found out last night that you were coming back from Italy, that you still lived here, I knew I—well, I couldn't just wait around and meet you in public."

"That was nice of you." The flat voice held no irony.

I looked away. Beyond the massed shadows of the forsaken garden, the house stood up, raw-edged and broken. "Your home," I said, not very evenly, ". . . I'm sorry about that, too, Adam. That sounds a bit inadequate, but what can one say? It's been a bad time all round, hasn't it? You must have been very unhappy."

For the first time his face changed. I saw the ghost of a smile. "You say that?"

I stirred. Easy? This was intolerable. Heaven knew I had dreaded the interview, and heaven knew I could hardly have expected to get through it more smoothly than this. I had expected questions, recriminations, anger even . . . anything but this calm, dead voice and steady stare that (since the moment when I had turned momentarily into the moonlight to glance up at the house) had narrowed sharply as if he were only just bringing me into focus.

I stood away from the sundial and began to rub my scored palms together.

"I must go." I spoke hurriedly, nervously, looking down at my hands. "It's late. I—I can't think that we have anything more to say. I—"

"Why did you go?"

The question came so suddenly that, although it was softly spoken, I looked up at him, startled. He was still watching me with that steady, unreadable stare. "You know," he said, "you can't simply walk out like this. I would have thought we had a very great deal to say. And I'd like to go right back to the beginning. Why did you go like that?"

"You know why I went!" I could hear how my voice shook, edged with nerves, but I couldn't control it. I tried to thrust him back again, off the dangerous ground. "Don't let's go back over it, please! I—I couldn't stand it! That's all over, you know that as well as I do. It was over eight years ago, and it—it's best forgotten. *Everything's* best forgotten . . ." I swallowed. "I've forgotten it, I truly have. It's as if it had happened to someone else. It—it doesn't seem to mean anything to me any more. People change, you know. In all that time, people change. You've changed yourself. Can't we . . . just *leave* it, Adam? I didn't come to see you tonight because I hoped . . . because I wanted—" I floundered desperately for words—"I knew you'd feel just the same as I do, now. I only came tonight so that we could—we could—"

"Agree that it was forgotten? I know, my dear." His voice was very gentle. There was no reason why I should have to bite my lips to keep the tears back, or why I should have to turn sharply aside and jerk a spray from the yellow rose, and be twisting it round and round in my fingers. This was nothing to me, after all. "You don't have to worry," he said. "I shan't torment you. There's someone else, isn't there?"

"No!" I hadn't meant to say it quite like that. I saw his brows lift a fraction.

"Or has been?"

I shook my head.

"In eight years?"

I looked down at the bruised rose in my fingers. "No. It's not that. It's only—"

"That people change. Yes. I understand. You've changed a good deal, Annabel."

I lifted my head. "Have I?"

His mouth twisted. "So it would seem. Tell me; do you—or perhaps I should say *did* you—intend to stay at Whitescar, now that you're back?"

At least here was a safe and easy path. I scuttled down it breathlessly, talking too fast. "I hadn't really made any firm plans. I told you I only came to see Grandfather. Until I got here, up North, I mean, I had no idea he was so frail. You knew he'd had a stroke? Actually, I'd decided to come back and see him before I knew of that. I hadn't been sure if he—if they'd want me back at Whitescar, but I wanted to see him if he'd let me. I didn't know what the situation would be, but he's been very kind." I hesitated. "They all have. I'm glad I came back. I'd like to stay till . . . as long as Grandfather's here. But afterwards . . ." I stopped.

"Afterwards?"

"I don't think I'll stay afterwards."

A pause. "And the place? Whitescar?"

"There'll be Con."

I was unwinding the split and twisted rose stem with great care. A thorn had drawn blood on my thumb. I stared unseeingly at the tiny black gout of blood that blobbed and split glossily over the flesh. I didn't know he had moved until his shadow slithered forward a pace, slantingly, and fell across the grass beside me.

"You'd leave Whitescar to Connor Winslow?"

I smiled. "I may have to."

"Don't beg the question. You know what I mean. If the place were yours, would you stay?"

"No."

"Has that decision anything to do with me?"

I swallowed. "You know it has."

Quite suddenly, his voice came alive, the way flesh does after frostbite. He said, "You came back because you thought I had gone. When you found I was still here, you decided to go again. You make things very clear, Annabel."

I said, as steadily as I could, "I try to. I'm sorry."

There was a pause. He spoke almost as if he were reasoning quietly with me about something that didn't matter very greatly. "You know, I've regretted everything I said and did that night, far more bitterly than you could have done. I doubt if I'll ever quite forgive myself. Not only for losing my head and saying all that I said to you that last time we met, but for ever having allowed things to . . . get to the stage they did. You were very young, after all; it was I who should have known better. The sort of life I led with Crystal was no excuse for— for losing my head over you, when I could do nothing but hurt you."

"Don't, please, there's no need—"

"Don't think I'm trying to excuse myself for the way I spoke and acted that last night. I'd just about come to the end—or so I thought; except that, of course, one never does." He took in his breath. "So I finally lost my head, and begged you—bullied you—to go away with me, away from Whitescar and Forrest, and to hell with everybody, including my wife. And you refused."

"What else could I do? Look, there's no need to go back over this. I've told you it's best forgotten. It should never even have started. We should have realized where it would take us."

"That's what you said then, that night, isn't it? True enough, of course, but as far as I was concerned, much too late. I remember that you even promised to keep out of my way." He gave a brief smile that was more like a grimace. "So then," he said, "I told you that, if you weren't prepared to do as I asked, I never wanted to see you again. Oh no," at my involuntary movement, "I suppose I didn't put it quite so crudely, but I dimly remember a good many wild and whirling words, to the effect that either you would have to leave the neighbourhood, or I would, and since I was tied to Forrest and to my wife . . ." He drew in his breath. "But heaven help me, Annabel, I never dreamed you'd go."

"It was better. You must see it was better."

"Perhaps. Though I wonder, looking back. No doubt, in the end, I'd have behaved like a reasonable mortal, and we could have found some . . . comfort. Fundamentally, I suppose, we're both decent human beings, and you, at least, kept your moral sense intact. Then, six years later . . ." He paused, and seemed to straighten his shoulders.

"Well, there it is. You were young, and I behaved badly, and frightened and hurt you, and you went. But you're older now, Annabel. Surely you must understand a little more than you did then, about the kind of life I led with Crystal, and the reasons why I was driven to act the way I did?"

"I do, oh, I do. It isn't that. Please don't think I—I'm bearing a grudge or—or anything. This, the way I feel now, has nothing to do with what happened then, try and believe that." I added, quietly, "Whatever was said or done, it's over, eight years over. There was nothing to forgive . . . and now, let's pretend there was nothing to remember, either. Let it go, Adam. From now. It's better not to talk about it any more. Good night."

I turned quickly away from him, but his shadow moved again across the turf, this time with something like a pounce. His hand caught at my arm, and, almost before I realized what was happening, he had pulled me round to face him.

"Wait. Listen. No, I can't let you go like this. You've got to listen to me. It's only fair."

"I don't see that—"

"If you'd rather wait till you're less upset, I'll let you go now. But I've got to see you again."

I said breathlessly, trying to pull away from him, "No!"

"What do I have to do? Grovel?"

"Adam, I've been trying to explain—"

"My God," he said, "what did I do that made you hate me so?"

"I don't, I don't! I told you."

"Then stay one minute, and listen. Look, Annabel, don't cry. It's all right. Just let me—wait just one minute, and let me tell you . . . You've told me it's all over for you; you don't love me. Very well, I'll accept that. Don't worry, I'll accept it. My God, how can I expect anything else? But you can't imagine that I'll just retire quietly to West Lodge and do nothing about it, can you?"

Somewhere, far off behind the cedar tree, the owl hooted. I said waveringly, "Do nothing about what?"

"About trying to see you again." His other hand came up now, and he had me by both arms, lightly, holding me a little away from him. "You see," he said, "there's still one thing that we haven't made plain. It isn't over for me."

I felt myself stiffen, and so must he have done, for he went on quickly, "No, all right, I've told you I'll accept the fact that you want to forget the past. But there's still the future, my dear, and you've told me there's no one else; you can't expect me to stand by and do nothing, now that you've come home." He smiled suddenly, and for the first time there was warmth and even lightness in his voice. "And I owe you a courtship, don't I? We'll have no more clandestine romance, my love! No more notes sneaked into the old ivy tree, no more damned chilly moonlit meetings in the summerhouse, with the rhododendron leaves sopping wet, and you fussing about bats getting into your hair!" He shook me gently, and his smile widened. "No, this time I'll woo you properly, by daylight, according to the book. I'll even start by calling on your grandfather—"

"*No!*" This time he must have felt the genuine shock of panic that kicked through me, jerking me rigid against the light clasp of his hands. Here was something I hadn't thought of. I had come to meet him to-night, with no very clear idea of what would be said, but only with the knowledge that the eight-years'-past love affair must, somehow, be kept from Con. Eight years was a long time, and it hadn't for a moment occurred to me that passion might be still there, smouldering, ready to flare up—into danger. It had seemed so easy: all I had had to do, after all, was to tell Adam Forrest the simple truth—that I did not care for him; that the past was dead and buried, and that I wanted it to remain so.

Then, the interview once over, the friendly, civil good-byes of long-estranged lovers given . . . I had hoped, more, known, that betrayal would not come from this direction. Yet here it was: after the days of smooth, too-easy masquerading, here, where it had been least expected, was danger.

Desperately I tried to marshal my thoughts. But the only coherent thing that came to me was that Con must not know. I had a sudden vision of his face as he had looked at me, down in the lane beside the meadowsweet . . . and behind him, Lisa's watchful, toffee-brown eyes.

"Please," I said shakily, "you mustn't do that. You mustn't come to Whitescar. Promise me that you won't come to Whitescar!"

"My dear, all right." He had dropped his hands when I spoke, and was staring at me now, the smile gone, and a deep crease gathering between his brows. "Just as you wish. Heaven knows I don't want to tease you. I'll promise anything you like, except not to try to see you again. You can't ask me to go quietly away and do nothing, knowing you're there at Whitescar. For one thing, we're bound to meet, and I—" the flicker of a smile again—"am bound to see that that happens as often as possible. But don't worry. I think I understand the way you feel, and I'll respect it . . . only you mustn't deny me the chance of trying to change it, now that we're free."

"Free?" The visions crowded in again, Con, Lisa, Grandfather, Julie . . . I said, bitterly, "Which of us is ever free?"

"My dear—"

The very quietness of his insistence was terrifying. Something that could have been panic mushroomed up inside me and burst into words I had never meant to say. "You mean, now that *you're* free! You mean you think you can dismiss me when it's convenient—forget me for eight years—and then, when I come back, just calmly expect to take up where you left off? You like to keep your mistresses in your own time, is that it? 'It isn't over for you—' " I mimicked him, cruelly. "No, I dare say not! Now that you're home for good, and your wife's dead, no doubt it'll suit you to have me around! Well, it doesn't suit me! how much plainer do I have to be? I've tried to put it kindly, but you won't take it. It's over. *Over.* So will you please, please, *please*, let me go and leave me alone?"

Even in that uncertain light, I saw the change in his face, and stopped, half afraid. Then my thoughts steadied. There was danger here; I must not forget that. Whatever happened, whatever I told him, whether or not I tried to go on with the masquerade, there was danger. Why not take the risk, and get it over now? Everything ought only to have to die once. Adam Forrest had gone through all this years ago; he mustn't be allowed to start it again, and for nothing. There was only one way to prevent that. Con had shown me how to play my cards, after all.

But for the moment I could find no way to do it. I stood silent, staring at him.

Then the decision was taken from me. He spoke so pat on my thoughts that he might have been taking a cue. "If it weren't absurd," he said, very slowly, "if it weren't something so crazy as to sound like black magic . . . I'd have said you couldn't be Annabel. Even in eight years, I wouldn't have thought you'd change so much."

I drew a sharp little breath, and choked over it, then I said quickly, and perhaps too loudly, "That's silly! Who else could I be?"

"That," he said, even more slowly, "is what I'm wondering."

I suppose the interview had got through what poor defences I had had. I simply stood there, and stared at Adam Forrest, with a curious sense of drifting, of destiny. Those dark gods who watch over the moonlit trysts of lovers had helped, cajoled, and then betrayed me to this final irony. I made no attempt to speak, just stared at Adam Forrest, and watched the thing dawning, incredulously, in his face.

Even when he took a rapid step that brought him within a foot of me, I didn't move. He said slowly, "I must be going mad. It can't be possible. It can't." He put out his hands and turned me round, quite gently, to face the moon. I didn't meet his eyes. I looked down, shutting my lips tightly to stop them trembling. There was a long pause.

Then he dropped his hands again, and turned away abruptly. He took several rapid strides away from me, and I thought he was going to leave me there and then, and wondered in a brief moment of panic where he was going, but he stopped suddenly, and stood for a few seconds with his back to me, looking at the ground.

Then he turned, churning his heel in the grass, and came back. His face looked quite impassive.

"Is this true?"

I hesitated painfully. The moment stretched like a year. Then I saw that the hesitation had answered for me. I nodded without speaking.

"You're not Annabel Winslow?"

I cleared my throat and managed to say, steadily enough, even with a kind of relief, "No, I'm not Annabel Winslow."

"You're . . . not . . . Annabel." He said it again, the sharpness of his questions blurred now into bewilderment.

This time I said nothing. The irrational feeling of escape, of relief, persisted. The flooding moonlight; the backcloth, as motionless and silent as paint, of the ruined house and towering trees; the little sundial with its sharply etched shadow thrown beside our own, these lent the scene an air of complete unreality. We were not people who ate and worked and talked through the sunlit days: we were beings from a fantasy world, creatures of a moonlit stage, living only by our passions, able to talk about love and death and pain, only in the subtle and rarefied voices of poetry. This was the world of the doomed black sail, the enchanted cup, the swallow flying through the casement with the single gold hair in his beak. We were Pervaneh and Rafi, floating like ghosts through the night-time garden, and to us the death of love would come as poetry; not fear, and quarrelling, the grimy commonplaces of the station platform, the unanswered telephone, the letter gone astray, the years of dragging loneliness. . . .

The moonlight struck the sundial as sharply as the sun. Time was.

I was still facing the light. He had come close to me again, and was scrutinizing my face. "You look like her, you move like her. But your voice is different . . . and there's something else. . . . Don't ask me what. But it's . . . extraordinary. It's beyond reason."

I said gently, "But it's true."

He gave a little laugh that had no relationship with mirth. "You've spent a lot of time tonight assuring me of various truths. At least this one is the easiest to accept." He half turned away, and thrust the tangle of tendrils aside from the dial's face. "Who are you?"

"Does that matter?"

"Probably not. But it matters a great deal why you are here, and why you're doing this—whatever it is you are doing. At least you don't seem to be trying to hedge. You might as well tell me the lot; after all, I have every right to know."

"Have you?"

He turned his head as if in exasperation. "Of course. You must know a good deal about my affairs, or you wouldn't have been here to meet me tonight. Who told you? Annabel?"

"Annabel?" I said blankly.

"Who else could it have been?" He had turned back to the sundial, and appeared to be tracing out the figures with a forefinger. His voice was abrupt. "Tell me, please. Where you met her, what happened, what she told you. What you know of her."

"It wasn't that!" I cried. "It didn't happen like that! I never met Annabel! It was Julie who told me!"

"Julie?"

"Yes. Oh, don't worry, she didn't know anything, really, about you and Annabel; but she'd seen you meet and talk in the wood, and she knew about the post box in the ivy tree. She saw Annabel put a letter in there one day, and take another out. She—she just thought it was a perfectly natural and very romantic way of conducting a love affair. She never told anyone."

"I see. And just what has she told you?"

"Only this—about the meetings and the ivy tree. She wanted me to know she knew. She—she rather imagined I'd be wanting to see you again, straight away."

"Hm." He had turned back to the sundial, and seemed absorbed in chipping a flake of moss away with a fingernail. "A bit of luck for you, wasn't it? That she knew, and told you? Otherwise you'd have been a little startled at our first meeting." A piece of moss came away, and he examined the inch or so of bronze beneath it with great care. "Are you sure that was all Julie told you? I'm not suggesting that she deliberately played the spy; she was only a child at the time, and would hardly realize what was going on. But one doesn't like to think that anyone, least of all a child—"

"Honestly, there was nothing else."

"Yet you played your part so very well." His voice, now, had an edge to it that would have engraved the bronze dial he was fingering. "I find it hard to believe that you knew so little. Perhaps Connor Winslow found out somehow—"

"No!" I said it so sharply that he glanced at me, surprised. "At least, he's said nothing to me. He hardly mentions you." I added, lightly, "I'm a very good actress, of course; you'll have guessed that. I merely played to the cues I got. It wasn't difficult. After all, it's what one expects to have to do when one's involved in this kind of game. If you think back over what was actually said, you'll find that I merely played your service back. All the *statements* were made by you."

He dropped the flake of moss on to the dial. It fell with a tiny rustling click. I saw him straighten as if with relief, but he still sounded grim. "Oh yes, you'd have to be clever. But not, it appears, quite clever enough. The sudden appearance of a lover must have been something of a shock. I grant you courage, too; you did very well. . . . And now, please, back to my question. Who are you, and what is this 'game' you say you're playing?"

"Look," I said, "I've told you the truth and played fair with you. I do assure you I needn't have let you guess. I'm not going to harm anybody, I'm only out to do myself a bit of good. Can't you let it go . . . at any rate till you *see* me harming someone? Why should it concern you, what goes on at Whitescar?"

"You ask, why should it concern me? You come back here posing as Annabel, and ask why it should concern me?"

"Nobody knows about you and her except Julie, and I've already told Julie that we're not—"

"That's not the point." The words snapped. "Don't hedge. What's your name?"

"Mary Grey."

"You're very like her, but of course you know that." A long look. "The thing doesn't seem possible. Mary Grey. My God, this sort of thing doesn't happen outside the pages of fiction! Am I seriously to believe that you have somehow got yourself into Whitescar, and are masquerading as Annabel Winslow?"

"Yes."

"Why?"

I laughed. "Why do you think?"

There was a silence. He said, not pleasantly, "Funny, you don't look venal."

"Try earning your living the hard way," I said. "You never know how you'll turn out till you've been down to half a dollar and no prospects."

His lips thinned. "That's true enough."

"Oh, yes, I forgot. You do know. You work for your living now, and hard, too, they tell me. Well, didn't you mind having to spoil your hands?"

"I—beg your pardon?" He sounded considerably startled, I couldn't imagine why.

"Wouldn't *you* perhaps have taken a chance to step into some easy money, if the chance came, and it did no harm?"

"I did once. But they'll have told you about that, too. And how can we expect to calculate what harm we do? Who's briefing you?"

The question came so sharply that I jumped. "What?"

"You couldn't do this on your own. Someone's briefed you and brought you in. Julie, I suppose, wanting to spoil Connor's chances?"

I laughed. "Hardly. Con himself, and his sister."

He stared at me unbelievingly. "Con? And Lisa Dermott? Do you really expect me to believe that?"

"It's true."

"Connor Winslow bring back 'Annabel' to cut him out of what he expects? Don't take me for a fool; he'd as soon slit his own throat."

"I'm not cutting Con Winslow out."

"No. Julie, then?" His voice hardened.

"No. Annabel herself."

"Annabel's dead." Only after he had spoken them, did he seem to hear the words, as if they had been said by someone else. He turned his head almost as if he were listening, as if he expected to hear the last heavy syllable go echoing through the woods, dropping, ripple by ripple, like a stone through silence.

"Mr. Forrest, I'm sorry. . . . If I'd known—"

"Go on." His voice was as hard and sharp as before. "Explain yourself. You say Connor has brought you in to impersonate Annabel, in order to cut Annabel out of her rights in Whitescar land. What sort of a story is that, for heaven's sake?"

"It's simple enough. Grandfather has refused to believe she's dead, and he's refused to alter his will, which leaves everything to her. As things stand now, Whitescar goes to Annabel, with reversion to Julie. I think it seems pretty obvious that in the end Grandfather would have done the sensible thing, admitted that Annabel must be dead, and willed the place to Con; in fact, I think he intends to do just that. But he's ill now, really ill; and you know him, he may play about with the idea, just to torment people, until it's too late. Con *might* have got Whitescar anyway, after some sort of legal upheaval, because I'm pretty sure Julie doesn't want it, but he'd only get a proportion of Grandfather's money along with it, not enough for what he'd want to do."

"I . . . see."

"I thought you might."

"And just what do you get out of it?"

"A home, at the moment. That's a new thing for me, and I like it. A competence."

"A competence!" he said, explosively. "Why, you lying little thief, it's a small fortune!"

I smiled. If the interview had seemed unreal at first, when the ghosts and dreams of passion had hung between us, how infinitely less real it was now, with me standing there, hands deep in pockets, looking composedly up at Adam Forrest, and talking about money. "Be realistic, won't you, Mr. Forrest? Do you really see Con Winslow bringing me in out of sweet charity, and watching me pocket all the money that goes to Annabel?"

"Of course. Stupid of me." He spoke as if he were discussing the weather. "You hand the major part to him, and are allowed to keep your 'competence.' How very neat, always assuming that there's sufficient honour among thieves . . . Where did you meet Connor Winslow?"

I said evasively, "Oh, he saw me one day. I had a job in Newcastle, and I came out to this part of the county one Sunday, for a day out, you know, a walk. He saw me, and thought, as you did, that I was his cousin come back. He followed me, and found out who I was, and we talked." I didn't feel it necessary to go into details of the three weeks' planning; nor did I bother to tell him that I had, to begin with, opposed Con's plan myself.

"And hatched this up between you?" The contempt in his voice was hardly veiled. "Well, so far, I gather, you've been completely successful . . . as why shouldn't you be? The thing's so fantastic that you'd be almost bound to get away with it, given the nerve, the information . . . and the luck."

"Well," I said, calmly enough, "it seems the luck's failed, doesn't it?"

"Indeed it does." His voice was gentle, calculating. He was watching me almost with hatred, but I could forgive him that, remembering how he had betrayed himself to me. He said slowly, "Yes, you've been clever. I don't know how easily you managed to deceive the people at White-scar, but, after Julie had talked to you, you must have realized you couldn't hope to get away with such a deception with me. You must have gone through quite a bad moment when you heard that your erstwhile lover was coming home."

"Quite a bad moment," I said steadily.

"I'm glad to hear it. But you kept your head, clever Miss Grey. You had to risk seeking me out here and talking to me; you didn't dare wait to meet me for the first time in public. So you took the chance, and came. Why didn't you go to the summerhouse?"

"The summerhouse? Do you mean that little pavilion along the other path, in the rhododendrons? I didn't realize that had been your meeting place, till you told me so yourself."

"It would hardly have been here," he said drily, with a glance at the blank and staring windows.

"I did realize that. But this seemed the obvious spot to wait. I—I thought if you came at all, you'd come this way to look."

"Yes, well, I came. So far, you've been right every way, Miss Grey. But now, what happens? You're taking this remarkably calmly, aren't you? Do you really imagine that I won't blow the whole thing sky-high on you?"

I thrust my hands down into my pockets again. I said coolly, "I have no idea what you'll do. It's quite possible that tomorrow you'll turn up at Whitescar, and tell Grandfather what you've learned tonight. You'll tell him that she's dead after all, and that all these years Con has been nursing his resentment, and planning to take Whitescar . . . and look-ing forward to Grandfather's death. And you might add for good meas-ure that Julie's thinking of marrying, and that her husband's job will take her away from Whitescar."

There was a silence. Adam Forrest said unemotionally, "You bitch."

"I thought you'd see it my way." (Con, smiling at me in the lane, his voice soft in the whisper that conspirators, and lovers, use. Yes, Con had taught me how to play it.) "It's really better for everyone the way it is, isn't it?" I finished, gently.

"Whether a thing is right or wrong doesn't depend on how many people it hurts. This is wrong."

I said suddenly, violently, "How the hell dare you sit in judgment on me, Adam Forrest?"

He jumped. I saw his eyes narrow on me suddenly, then he relaxed with a queer little sigh. "Then what about Julie? I can't see that it's 'better' for her. This criminal arrangement of yours may suit everyone else, including old Mr. Winslow, since it means keeping him in a false paradise until he dies. But what about Julie?"

"Julie has money of her own. So has this man of hers, and he's way up in his profession."

"That," said Adam Forrest gently, "is hardly the point."

"It's the point unless you do propose to—what's the phrase we crooks use?—blow the gaff."

He was giving me that appraising, narrow stare again. "I could, you know. In fact, I must."

"You'd find it very difficult to convince Grandfather. Con and Lisa did a very good job of briefing, and I'm well dug in. And Julie would just laugh at you."

There was another of those silences. He didn't stir, but I felt the hair prickle along my skin as if I had expected a blow.

When he spoke, his voice sounded quite normal, friendly, almost. "You speak like an American."

"Canadian, actually." I was surprised and wary. "It's one of my assets, of course, as an impersonator. *She* went to the States, and, according to *my* story, from there to Canada."

"To come from Canada, Miss Grey, one needs a passport." He laughed suddenly, not a nice sound. "Yes, I thought that would get through to you. Nobody else thought of it?"

I said hoarsely, "Why should they? They accepted me without question. You don't usually ask to see people's papers, unless there's some doubt."

"That," he said pleasantly, "is just what I mean. And I shouldn't destroy it, my dear. They're terribly easy to trace."

I drove my fists down, and held them steady.

"Mr. Forrest—"

"Well?"

"What are you going to do?"

"What do you think?"

"I don't think you quite understand, you know. Grandfather—"

"I understand perfectly. You and Connor are trading on his age and sickness. That's quite clear. But it's Julie I'm thinking about—Julie, and my own constitutional dislike of seeing anyone get away with this kind of damned lie. If I did agree to hold my tongue now, it would be purely for old Mr. Winslow's sake. But if he dies—"

I said violently, "How much of a fool can you be? If he dies before he remakes his will, and you throw Annabel back into her grave, what do you suppose would happen to Julie?"

This time the silence was electric. The night was so still that I heard my own heart beats, and I thought he must hear them, too. Ten miles off, a train whistled for a crossing.

As if it had been a signal to wake us both, he said, "Don't be absurd." But his voice had slackened with uncertainty.

"I meant it, oddly enough. I think I know Con Winslow a little better than you do."

"That's very probable," he spoke with (I thought) a quite undue dryness. "If this—fantasy—is true, do I take it that you expect to stay on in safety at Whitescar?"

"I'll face that when the time comes."

"You think he'll marry you? Are you playing for that, too?"

"Look here—!" I began, hotly, then stopped and bit my lip. It was an obvious conclusion, after all. "I am not," I said clearly, "anything to Con Winslow, or he to me . . . except accomplices."

"I beg your pardon." His apology was surprisingly prompt, and sounded genuine. "Then am I to take it that you are protecting Julie . . . for a 'competence'?"

"You can take it how you like. I've assured you that no one will be harmed by what I'm doing, but I don't expect you to believe me. Why should you? I can only beg you to keep out of what doesn't concern you . . . at least until you see wrong being done."

He said, all at once sounding very tired, "I don't understand you."

"Why should you? But I mean what I say, remember that. And I'm telling you the truth about this. I'm playing this game for my own advantage, that's obvious; I saw a chance to get out of poverty and hard work, to grab what they call a place in the sun, and I took it. It's wrong, I admit that; I'm unscrupulous, I admit that. But I'm not *bad*, and I wouldn't do it if anyone was going to suffer for it. Believe me, they'll have plenty, and the little I'll get will mean a lot to me, and nothing to any of them."

He said, angrily, "That's immoral nonsense. It's also quite beside the point."

"I know that." I laughed. "But all the same, you think about it, Mr. Forrest. This is one of those cases where to do the right thing will be to do nothing but harm. So let well alone, will you? Stifle your conscience, and keep away from Grandfather. It's none of your business, after all."

"If I could believe you. If I knew what you were playing at."

"Don't worry about that, or about my future. It has nothing to do with you."

He let out a breath like a sigh. "No. All right. I'll keep out of it, for a while, at least. But watch your step . . . Annabel." As I caught my breath, he added, roughly, "If I'm to play your game, or even watch from the sidelines, I can hardly call you 'Miss Winslow.'"

"Then you will . . . play my game?" I said breathlessly.

"I think so. Though heaven knows why. Let's say I'll go away and think about it, and hold a watching brief. But I promise you that if I plan to—what was it?—'blow the gaff,' I'll warn you first."

I said huskily, "I don't know why you should do this for me."

"Nor do I," he said wearily. "But . . . be careful."

"I intend to. And I—I'm sorry I said those things to you."

"What things?"

"About your dismissing Annabel and then wanting to take up your—your love affair again. It was unkind, but—well, I was scared. You must see that I'd have said anything to . . . make you let me go."

"Yes, I see."

I hesitated. "Good night . . . Adam."

He didn't answer. I turned away and left him.

Just before the dark leaves of the rhododendrons hid him from me, I thought I heard him say "Good night."

CHAPTER

TEN

"Why should not I love my love?
    Why should not my love love me?
 Why should not I speed after him,
    Since love to all is free?"

Traditional.

The days went by, warm and cloudless. Haymaking was in full swing, and the mown fields smelled Elysian, lying in ribbed gold under a blue sky. Wild roses tumbled anyhow through all the hedges, and Tommy, the fat black and white cat, startled everyone by confounding the experts and having seven kittens.

And Adam Forrest did nothing.

I had got the passport away to the bank, which made me feel a little better, but it was a day or two after that moonlit meeting before I stopped watching the road between West Lodge and Whitescar. When two days, three days, passed with no sign from him, I began to think that perhaps, having "thought it over," he had decided to take me at my word and, for Grandfather's sake, to hold his tongue and await developments. I had not seen him again, though Julie had once or twice persuaded me to walk through the river meadows to look at the horse, Rowan; and I had gone, realizing that, whatever Adam Forrest's intentions, I might as well behave as normally as possible, and naturally Julie expected my interest in the colt to be intense.

I had made no further attempt at confidence with Julie, and she had offered none, but I could not help suspecting that all was still far from well between her and Donald Seton. How far her own feelings were settled, it was impossible to guess. She was young, volatile, perhaps a trifle spoiled, but from what little she had said to me—perhaps because she *had* said so little—I believed her affections to be seriously engaged. I had, on my first sight of Donald, decided that here was a man one could both like and respect; since then he had been down to Whitescar two or three times, and I had liked him better each time, though I thought I could see the cause of the tension that appeared to exist, if not between the two of them, then in Julie's mind. I could see that his quietness, his steady reserve, might appear daunting and even formidable to a nineteen-year-old extrovert accustomed to the easy and outspoken admiration of the young men of her own London set. Still waters might run deep, but at nineteen one can hardly be expected to appreciate the fact.

The complaint she had made in jest, on that first evening, had its foundations firmly in the truth. Donald Seton would not "fit into any romantic context." And Julie, for all her gay sophistication, was young enough still to want her love affair sprinkled with stardust, and vulnerable enough to be hurt by a reserve which she must mistake for indifference, or at best a reluctance to pursue. Donald was, in other words, a disappointment. Liking, affection, comradeship, all growing steadily from the first seed of love—these were not what Julie, at nineteen, was looking for. Not happiness, but intensity, was what she craved. As a lover, the quiet Scot by no means measured up to the standards of Julie's favourite reading, or (more immediately) to those of the unhappy man who, eight years ago, had left notes for his mistress in the old ivy tree. Poor Julie, if she only knew. . . . I found myself hoping, with quite startling fervour, that Donald would emerge soon from his Roman preoccupation, and *speak*.

Meanwhile, he called at Whitescar in the evenings, after work had packed up, and, on one occasion, Julie went up to West Woodburn to see what was going on there, and even, possibly, in a genuine attempt to learn something about the job.

Although in this, it seemed, she was not successful, it did appear as if Donald had moved at least a little of the way towards her. He had brought her back in the evening, and stayed to dinner, listening silently and in apparent amusement to her lively—and malicious—account of the way he occupied his time.

"Sitting in a hole," said Julie, "my *dears*, I mean it, sitting all day at the bottom of a little pit, scraping away at *mud*, and with a thing the size of a teaspoon! Nothing but mud, *honestly!* And every spoonful preserved as if it was the Grand Cham's jewels. I never was so disillusioned in my life!"

"No gold coins? No statues?" I asked, smiling.

"My dear, I think there was a Roman bootlace."

Donald's eyes twinkled. "That was our big day. You mustn't expect excitement all the time."

She opened her lips, and then shut them again. I thought her smile was brittle. I said quickly, "Just what are you doing, anyway?"

"Only a preliminary bit of dating."

"Dating?" Grandfather looked up from his cheese.

I saw Donald glance at him, in that diffident way he had, and affirm that this was genuine interest and not mere civility, before he replied. "Yes, sir. It does consist, as Julie says, of just scratching at the earth. We've dug a trial trench through the wall and rampart of the fort, and we're going down layer by layer, examining the successive ramparts, and whatever debris—in the way of pottery shards and so on—comes to light as we work down. In that way, we can determine what building was done in the fort at different times. Eventually it sorts itself out into a picture of the general history of the place, but at present—" the glimmer of a smile at her—"Julie's quite right. It's nothing but scraping at earth, and must seem deplorably dull."

"*You* seem to find it terribly absorbing, anyway," said Julie. I don't think she had meant the words to have an edge, but they sounded almost pettish, like the retort of a piqued child.

Donald didn't appear to notice. "Well," he said, "it's like most jobs, I suppose, masses of dull routine most of the time; but the good moments, when they come, can be pretty exciting."

"Oh?" said Julie, then suddenly laughed, with an attempt at her normal sparkle of good humour. "Well, for goodness' sake tell us when that's likely to happen, and we'll all come and watch! At *least*—" this to me—"he's coming up out of the mud on Wednesday. Did I tell you? *And* so am I. We're going into Newcastle, to the Royal."

"The theatre? How lovely. But, darling, Wednesday . . . it's Grandfather's birthday, had you forgotten? We're making rather an occasion of it, since we're all here—"

"Oh yes, I know, that's why we're going to the matinée. Donald says he can usually only manage Saturdays, but there weren't any seats left, and it's John Gielgud's new play, and I simply *cannot* miss it. So Donald's sneaking off Wednesday, after lunch, and we're going. Grandfather knows, and we'll be back in good time for the party. Donald's staying for that, too."

"Very sensible of him. I know Lisa's got something wonderful laid on, but she won't tell me what it is."

Lisa smiled, but rather absently. I knew she was fidgeting until she could get out of the dining room and back to the kitchen, where she could start to prepare Con's supper. When he worked late, she gave him this in the kitchen at whatever hour he came in, and I knew that, for her, this half-hour, when she had him to herself, was the peak of her day.

"Look," Donald was saying, in that pleasant, unemphatic voice of his, "it's very nice of you to have asked me, but I hadn't realized it was a family party. I think perhaps I'd better say—"

"Now, don't go crying off," said Grandfather. "We'll be thankful to have you. Never known a family gathering yet where the presence of a stranger didn't do a lot of good. Families are usually pretty damned grim when they get together, especially Winslows. We'll have to behave ourselves if you're here."

Donald laughed. "Well, if you put it like that. . . ."

"I do indeed. Anything I have to say to the family as such can be said in three minutes precisely, on the way to bed." The fierce, faded old eyes went round the table, lingering momentarily on Con's empty chair. "And better so. There's been too much talk already, and I can't stomach post mortems before I'm dead."

The sheer unfairness of this took my breath away, and I saw Julie open her eyes wide. Donald, to whom these last remarks had been addressed, said rather faintly, "Oh, quite."

I rescued him. "Then we'll see you on Wednesday? That'll be nice. What's the play, Julie?"

Julie, her face lighting, her pique forgotten, plunged happily into an account of it, unaware of the fact (or perhaps uncaring) that she was betraying with every word how far her heart lay from Whitescar and the quiet island of Forrest Park. I saw Grandfather watching her, an odd expression on his face. Ah well, I thought, this was best. I stole a glance at Lisa, to see if this was being stored up for Con, but she was looking at her watch, and murmuring something about coffee in the drawing-room.

"Well," said Grandfather, a little drily, as he pushed back his chair, "enjoy yourselves."

"We will, be sure of that! But till then," said Julie, dimpling at Donald, "I'll let you get on with your mudlarking in peace, and put in a bit of work for Con instead. In any case, I think haymaking's more fun, and far more profitable to the human race."

"Very probably," said Donald equably.

Sure enough, Julie spent the next two or three days in the hayfield, driving the tractor for Con.

Here I watched her rather more anxiously. It was just possible that Julie (provoked, restless, and already slightly bored with the country holiday that wasn't answering its purpose), was hoping to try out the age-old romantic device of making Donald jealous. She had two strings to her bow: Bill Fenwick from Nether Shields, who came over now and again, ostensibly to "give a hand" in the hayfield when he could be spared from home, but in reality, it was obvious, for a chance to be near Julie; and Con. Bill I dismissed without a thought, except to hope that he would not be hurt; but Con was a different proposition. He was not a man who could be used in this sort of way, or in any sort of way that he didn't initiate. Besides, he was extremely attractive, and older and more sensible girls than Julie had rebounded before now into far less exciting arms. And if Con suddenly decided that three-thirds of the Winslow money was even better than two, and seriously turned his attention to Julie. . . .

I need not have worried. At any other time, I suppose, Con would have flirted with her as a matter of course, a purely automatic reaction, as instinctive as that of a cock bird displaying to the female; but, just at present, Con had more important things on his mind. Mr. Isaacs, the lawyer, had been duly summoned to see Grandfather, and had spent Friday morning closeted with him in his office. The old man had said nothing whatever about this interview, but had allowed it to be known that Mr. Isaacs would call again in a few days' time, that is, on the morning of his, Grandfather's, birthday. The inference was obvious, and, to my eyes, the effect on Con was obvious, too. The tension in him had increased perceptibly in the last few days; he was quieter than usual, and seemed edgy and strained. We saw very little of him; he rarely even ate with us, but spent all his time in the hayfield, working with an energy and fierce physical concentration that were remarkable, even for him. This was partly, I thought, due to a genuine passion for hard work, partly to work off the tension he was feeling, and partly, also, to keep out of old Mr. Winslow's way. The die was cast, one way or the other; it seemed likely that it was cast in Con's favour, and Con was taking no risks.

In this he may have been wise. Since the lawyer's visit, there had been a perceptible change, too, in Grandfather. Where Con had grown tense and wary, turning that diamond-hard concentration of his on his job, old Mr. Winslow became daily more difficult and less predictable, prone to sudden irritabilities, and even (what was new in him) fits of vagueness and absence of mind. The continued hot weather seemed to trouble him. He was very easily tired, but as he did less, so his fretfulness increased, and it seemed, wherever possible, to be directed at Con. His decision now finally made, it was as if the abdication of that will-to-power, which had been his driving force, had slackened something in him. He even seemed, physically, to have grown smaller. Where before he had been formidable, he now seemed merely fretful, and his resentful nagging at Con (over matters which previously he had been quite content to leave to the younger man) were the grumblings of a pettish old man, no longer the storms of a tyrant.

For me, it was something of a relief to find myself abruptly removed from the centre of attention. Con was, for the moment, no longer concerned with me, and Lisa had accepted me completely. What jealous thoughts she may have originally had of me, she had transferred to Julie, who (to do her justice) had done nothing to deserve them. Me, she seemed even to like; I had the odd feeling that, in her stolid, brother-centred way, she was even grateful for my presence at Whitescar, where Mr. Winslow persisted in regarding her as something of a stranger, a sort of paid-housekeeper-cum-poor-relation; Mrs. Bates with a slightly jealous Northern caution; and Con himself with a casual affection that took everything, including the most detailed personal service, completely for granted.

Meanwhile, the heat increased, charging the air with thunder, adding this threat to the other perceptible weights in the air. Day by day the great soap-sud clouds built up their slow thunder towers in the southwest. The trees hung heavily, as if themselves exhausted by the heat, and the sky was a deep, waiting blue.

And Con kept quiet, and watched the clouds, and drove himself and the men like galley slaves to clear the fields before the weather broke. . . . And with that same cold preoccupation, and for a closely analogous reason, he watched Grandfather.

Wednesday came, still without the threatened thunderstorm. The air felt a little lighter, as a small breeze had sprung up, though without shifting the towering, beautiful clouds. But the sense of oppression (or was it foreboding?) seemed to have lifted.

Mr. Isaacs came just before midday, and Grandfather took him straight into the office. I gave them ten minutes, then went to the dining room to get the sherry.

As I crossed the hall, Julie came downstairs, pulling on her gloves. I paused. "Why, hullo! Are you going now? My, my, don't you look wonderful!"

This was true. She was wearing crisp cotton, the colour of lemon ice, and her gloves were white. The pale, shining hair was brushed into an elaborate and very attractive style that had been thought up at least two hundred miles from Whitescar. Over one arm she carried a little coat of the same material as the frock.

I said: "Ve—ery nice! But why so early? I thought Donald couldn't get away till after lunch?"

She tugged the second glove into place, pushing the heavy gold bracelet higher up her wrist with a sharp little movement that looked almost savage. "Donald," she said crisply, "can't get away at all."

"What?"

"He rang up an hour ago to say that he couldn't go, after all."

"Oh, Julie, no! Why?"

Her careful composure shivered a bit, like cat ice wrinkling under the wind. Her eyes were stormy. "Because he doesn't think what *I* want to do matters a damn, that's why!"

I threw a glance towards the office door. "Come into the dining room. I was just going to take Mr. Isaacs and Grandfather some sherry. . . ." In the dining room I said, "Now come off it, honey. Why can't he come? What's happened?"

"Somebody's turned up from London, that's why. Some beastly man from the Commission, who's working with Donald, and Donald says he'll have to stay and see him. He says—oh, what's it matter, anyway? I didn't listen. It's always the same, I might have known. The one time he *did* say he'd leave his precious blasted Romans—"

"Julie, he'd come if he could. He can't help it."

"I know! Oh, it isn't *that!* It's just—oh, it's just *everything!*" cried Julie. "And he sounded so *calm* and *reasonable*—"

"He always does. He would in a fire. It's a habit men have; they think it calms us, or something."

"Well, but he seemed to think *I* ought to be reasonable, too!" said Julie, furiously. "How dumb can you get? . . . Annabel, if you laugh, I'll kill you!" She gave a reluctant grin. "Anyway, you know *exactly* what I mean."

"Yes, I know. I'm sorry. But you're not being fair to Donald, are you? The man's got a job to do, and if something crops up that has to be attended to—"

"Oh, I know, I know! I'm not as silly as all that. But he knew how *foully* disappointed I'd be. He needn't have sounded just as if he didn't even *mind* not going out with me."

"He wouldn't mean to, you know. He's just not the type to spread himself all over the carpet for you to trample on. He'd be as sorry as the next man, but he—well, he just hasn't got the gift of the gab."

"No, he hasn't, has he?" Her voice was genuinely bitter. She had turned aside to pick up the jacket from the chair where she had thrown it.

"My dear—"

"It's all right. I dare say I'm being stupid about it, but I can't help that. It would be different if he'd ever—if I knew—" she sounded all at once very young—"if I was sure he cared."

"He does care. I'm sure he does."

"Then why the hell doesn't he *say* so?" cried Julie explosively. She snatched up her coat. "Oh, what's the *use?*"

"Is he still coming to dinner tonight?"

"He said he'd try. I said he could please himself."

"Oh, Julie!"

"Oh, I didn't just say it like *that*. I was really quite nice about it." She gave me a wavering smile. "Almost reasonable . . . But if he *knew* what hellish thoughts were churning away inside me. . . ."

"It's often a good thing they don't."

"They? Who?"

I grinned. "Men."

"Oh, *men*," she said, in accents of loathing. "*Why* are men?"

"I give you three guesses."

"The most harmless answer is that there'd be nothing whatever to do if there weren't any, I suppose."

"There'd be nothing whatever, period," I said.

"Well, you've got something there," said Julie, "but don't ask me to admit it for quite some time. Oh, Annabel, you've done me good. I must go now; there's the car."

"Car?"

She gave me a little sideways look under her lashes. "I told you I wasn't going to miss this play. I'm going with Bill Fenwick."

"I see."

"And just what do you see?"

I ignored that. "But surely the play's going to open in London soon? You'll see it there?"

"That," said Julie, "is not the point."

"No, quite. Donald couldn't get away, so you rang up Bill Fenwick, and asked him to take you? That it?"

"Yes," she said, with a shade of defiance.

"And *he* dropped everything, and promptly came?"

"Yes." She eyed me. "What's wrong with that?"

"Nothing at all," I said cheerfully. "I hope they've finished leading for the day at Nether Shields, that's all."

"Annabel," said Julie, warmly, "are you trying to be a pig?"

I laughed. "I was, rather. Never mind me, honey, go and enjoy your play. We'll be seeing you at dinner. And, Julie—"

"What is it?"

"If Donald does come, don't make it too obvious that you're a bit fed up with him, will you? No—" as she made a little movement of impatience—"this isn't Advice from Aunt Annabel. What's between you and Donald is your affair. I was thinking of something quite different . . . I'll explain later. There's no time now . . . but come and see me when you get in, will you? I've something to tell you."

"Sure," said Julie.

The front door shut behind her. I found the sherry glasses, and a tray, but as I set the decanter on this, the office door opened, and Grandfather came out.

He was making for the baize door that led to the kitchen lobby, but, hearing the chink of glass, he stopped, turned, and saw me through the open door of the dining room. He seemed to hesitate for a moment, then abruptly to make up his mind. He came into the room, and shut the door quietly behind him.

"I was just going to bring you some sherry," I said. "Were you looking for me?"

"I was going to get Betsy Bates and that girl Cora to witness my signature," he said, in a dry, rather harsh voice.

"Oh." I waited. He stood just inside the door, his head bent and thrust forward, staring at me under his brows.

"Child—" He seemed not quite to know what he had come to say.

"Yes?"

"I've taken you at your word."

I tried not to let him see the relief that swept through me. "I'm glad of that."

"I believe you are."

I said earnestly, "It's right, Grandfather, you said yourself it was only right and fair. It's best for everyone—Con, me, the place, your peace of mind."

"Julie?"

"And Julie," I said steadily. "Julie loves this place, don't think she doesn't, but can you see her running it?"

He gave his little bark of laughter. "Frankly, no. Must confess I've wondered, though, with young Fenwick in the offing—"

I said quickly, "There's nothing in that. It's Donald Seton, and you know he lives in London when he's not on field work."

"Hm. Gathered there was something in the wind. Not quite senile yet. Decent sort of fellow, I thought. Gentleman, and so on. Only thing is, he doesn't look as if he's got a penny to his name."

I laughed. "His clothes and car? That's affectation, when he's out on a dig. I'll bet he's formal enough in London. He makes eighteen hundred a year, rising to two thousand five hundred, and his family's got money."

"How the devil d'you know?"

"Juile told me. She looked him up."

"Good God," said Grandfather, impressed. "Girl's got sense, after all." He gave a curious little sigh, and then smiled the tight, lipless smile of the old. "Well, that's that, isn't it? All settled. But I don't mind telling you, I haven't liked it. Boy's all right, don't think I don't know it, but not m'own flesh and blood. Not the same. Young people don't understand that nowadays, but it's true. A bit too much of the damned foreigner about Connor sometimes."

"Foreigner?" I said blankly.

"Irish," said Grandfather. I thought of Donald, and smiled to myself, but he didn't see. He was looking past me, out of the window. "If your father, or Julie's, had lived, it would have been a different matter."

"Yes," I said gently.

The old eyes came back to me. "You and Connor should have made a match of it. Should still. I'm not raking up the past, but after what's been between you—"

"I told you, it would never have worked."

"Not then, no. Too much of the Winslow in both of you, perhaps. But now . . . say what you like, the onlooker sees most of the game. I still think it would be the best thing. For the place, for Connor; yes, and for you. Never a woman born yet, that wasn't the better for a husband. Don't just stand and smile at me, child. Come here."

I went and stood in front of him. He put up a hand, and held it against my cheek. It was cool and very dry, and felt as light as a leaf. "It's made me very happy, your coming back. Don't think for a moment that you're not my favourite, because you are."

"I always did say you were never fair in your life."

"I've left you some money," he said gruffly. "A good sum, and Julie, too. I want you to know."

"Grandfather, I—"

"It's settled. We'll have neither thanks nor argument. I've done what I think fair, in spite of what you say about me. Tell you just how it stands. It's tangled up in a lot of lawyers' nonsense, but it amounts to this: Whitescar goes to Connor, with the house, stock, implements, the lot. I take it you won't contest that? Or Julie?"

"No."

A grin. "Doubt if you could, anyway. Isaacs' wrapped it all up in legal jargon, with reasons stated. Seems you have to stop anyone being able to say, later on, that you were cranky when you made the will. So there it is, all laid out: Whitescar goes as an acknowledgment of Connor's 'devoted work,' for which I've so far made 'inadequate recompense.' True enough. Well, there it is. Then we come to the recompense for you."

"For me? What have I ever done, except run away?"

"Recompense for losing Whitescar. Should have been yours. Handed over your head to Connor."

"Oh." I waited, helplessly.

"The money," said Grandfather. He had a hand on the table, and was leaning on it. He sent me a look up under the white brows, a pale counterfeit of his old, bright glance, but recognizably the same. "I've divided it into three. A third goes to Julie, outright. It's all she ever expected, and I doubt if she'll quarrel with Con over Whitescar. If she marries this man of hers, she'll be well enough found. The other two-thirds I've left in trust, to pay your income for life."

"In—trust?"

"That's what I said. Worked it all out with Isaacs as the best way. I want you repaid for losing Whitescar, and I want to see you well provided for. But I don't want the money to leave the land outright. You said you'd not stay here when I'd gone; remember? So it's left in trust for your lifetime. After your death it comes back to Connor absolutely, or to his heirs. On the other hand, if Connor should die before you, without issue, then Whitescar becomes yours, and the money along with it, absolutely. I take it, if he were gone, you'd look after the place . . . ? Good girl." His hand lifted. "No, wait, I haven't finished. There's one thing more. If you should marry Connor—"

"Grandfather—"

"If you should marry Connor, and live at Whitescar, the money becomes yours then, absolutely. Clear?"

"Y—yes."

The only really clear thing was the old man's determination to tie the money to Whitescar; and me, along with it, if he could, to Con. The wrong end of the shotgun, with a vengeance. Dazedly I tried to assess the probable results of what he had just told me. "But . . . *two*-thirds for me, and a third for Julie? What about Con? If I don't—I mean—" I floundered, and stopped. It was no use insisting; let him keep his dream.

"I've left him a little, and Lisa, too."

"But, Grandfather—"

"My good girl—" he was suddenly irritable—"anyone would think you were trying to get rid of every penny piece to Connor! Are you mad? If the place comes to him over the heads of you and Julie, he can hardly expect much more! It'll not be easy for him, with only a small capital to back him, but he'll have all the liquid assets of the place, and he'll make out."

He stopped, breathing rather hard. I noticed all at once how heavily he was leaning on his hand. He pulled a handkerchief, rather fumblingly, from his breast-pocket, and touched it to his mouth. "Con's a good lad, and a clever lad; he's not afraid of work, and the land's in good heart. I think it's fair enough, all round."

"Darling, of course it is! More than fair! And now let's stop thinking about it; it's done, let's all forget it, and you forget it, too." I grinned at him. "You know I can't stomach these post mortems."

He patted my cheek. "Dear child," he said, and went abruptly out of the room.

What it cost Con in self-command I shall never know, but he did not come in to luncheon. The lawyer left immediately afterwards, and Grandfather retired to rest. I had promised Lisa to go into Bellingham that afternoon to do some shopping. She was already busy with preparations for dinner, but had refused to allow me to help her "because," she said simply, "I enjoy special occasions, and I'm selfish; but you shall do the table if you like."

I laughed. "All right, I've no quarrel with that. If I'm to be allowed to eat your cooking without having to work for it, that's okay by me."

"Oh, you can wash up," said Lisa placidly, adding, with that spice of malice that was never far away, "Julie can help you."

The shopping did not take long, and I caught the four o'clock bus back from Bellingham, which put me down at the head of the lane. I assembled my rather awkward collection of packages and set off down-hill.

When I reached the mouth of the disused quarry where, on that first day, I had left my luggage, I saw a car standing there, an old car with too much chrome winking too brightly in the sun. Donald's car.

I picked my way in at the rutted entrance of the quarry. Donald was there, pipe in mouth, hands deep in trouser pockets, his head tilted back, apparently surveying the high wall at the back of the quarry. This was of sand-coloured stone, darkened with weathering, and here and there fissured red with iron. It was a big quarry, deep and narrow, consisting of several sections opening out of one another, partitioned off by jutting walls of rock. The cliff tops were crested with woods, whose crowding trees had sown seedlings broadcast, so that every ledge and tumble of rock was hung with green, and young oaks thrust golden frilled leaves above the brambles and foxgloves that hid the edges of the quarry floor. It must have been decades since any stone had been taken out of here.

Donald turned when he heard my footsteps, took the pipe out of his mouth, and smiled.

"Why, hullo."

"Hullo." I added, a little awkwardly, with a gesture of the basket and parcels in my hands, "I saw your car, and yielded to temptation. You were coming down to Whitescar, weren't you?"

"If I hadn't been," said Donald diplomatically, "I should be now."

I laughed. "You could hardly do anything else. I've an awful nerve, haven't I?" I hoped that my glance at his suit, which was, for once, impeccably formal, had not been too obvious. "But surely, you're coming to dinner?"

I thought he looked uncertain. I added, quickly, "Julie said you weren't quite sure if you could manage it after all, but we're hoping you will. It'll be worth it, I promise you. There were rumours about duckling."

"I'm sure it will. Miss Dermott's a wonderful cook. Well, if you're sure I haven't put things out—"

"Of course you haven't. We were all hoping you'd manage to get away. Julie'll be delighted. She's out just now; she went into Newcastle after all; but she'll be back in time for dinner."

"Did she? Then she won't miss the play. I'm glad. Did her cousin take her?"

"Con? No. Bill Fenwick. Have you met him?"

"Not yet. Would you like to put your parcels in the car?" He moved to open the door and take them from me.

"Thanks very much." I handed them over with a sigh of relief. "There. At least that's one way of ensuring that you do come to dinner. I only hope I'm not taking you down too early."

"No; I wasn't going straight there, as it happens; I want to go over and see Mr. Forrest, so I'll take you down via Whitescar, and—" he grinned—"it'll be very nice to have someone to open the gates."

"Fair enough. And there's an extra one now; one of the cattle grids is damaged, and you have to use the gate." I added, curiously, for his eyes had returned to the quarry face, "What interests you here? This is a geologist's sort of thing, not an archaeologist's, surely?"

"Oh, sure. But there is something interesting. This is the local sandstone, the building stone you'll see they've used for all the old houses hereabouts, and most of the walls, too. It's an old quarry. I've been asking about it, and I'm told it stopped working in 1910. I'd like to find out when it started, how far back there are any records of it."

"I can tell you one thing, though it may be only legend. This is supposed to be the quarry that Whitescar came out of, and I suppose Forrest too, though Whitescar's older. At any rate the first workings here must be at least four hundred years old."

"Older than that, by far." He smiled. "The quarry was here long before Whitescar was built. When you come to think about it, it is more likely that the place got its name from a quarry—a white scar—that was already a well-known landmark, *before* they took the stone out to build the house."

"It could be, I suppose. Is this a guess, or can you tell, somehow?" I looked vaguely at the overgrown rock around us.

"I can tell." I saw, suddenly, a spark of excitement in the deep hazel eyes. "Come and tell me if you see what I see. Over here, and watch your feet. There are bits of old iron and stuff lying around still. The oldest end of the quarry's along here, and it's flooded. I'll go first, shall I?"

We picked our way through the foxgloves, and the buds of ragwort, where loose stones and shards of rusting iron made going dangerous.

A rabbit bolted out of a clump of nettles, and dived out of sight down an unlikely looking crevice.

"A nice fat one," said Donald, watching it.

"Were you thinking of the cooking pot, and Lisa's arts?"

"I was not. I was thinking about myxomatosis."

"Oh. Seeing the rabbits coming back, you mean?"

"Yes, the destructive little devils. But will you ever forget seeing them hobbling about, dying and in pain, and having to kill them, and not quite knowing how, and being afraid one wouldn't manage it cleanly the first time? One got sickeningly good at it, in the end. It may be the wrong thing to say to a farmer's daughter, but I'm pleased to see them back, nice and fat and immune, and I hope they eat every blade of grass belonging to the brutes who deliberately gave them the disease. . . . But of course you won't remember it. You weren't here, I keep forgetting. You seem so much a part of the scene at Whitescar. It's a lovely place, isn't it?"

"Do you know," I said, "I'm quite aware that that was a *non sequitur*, but it was also a compliment."

He looked surprised. "Was it?" He seemed to consider. "Yes, I've got it. So it was. Well, I didn't see it, but if I had I would have meant it."

"Fair enough." I laughed. "Except that *then* you'd never have said it."

He smiled slightly. "Probably not. The curse of Scotland, the pad-locked tongue." But his eyes weren't amused.

I said, before I thought, "Maybe. But is it any worse than the curse of Ireland; the tongue without a latch, even, let alone a lock?"

He grinned then, spontaneously, and I knew he was thinking as I was, too late, about Con. But all he said was, "Or the curse of England; the double tongue?"

I laughed. "Ah well, it makes life pleasanter, doesn't it? Do you like living in the South?"

"Very much. I've good rooms in London, and my work takes me out as much as anyone could want."

"Do you think you'd want to settle permanently in London?"

We had clambered over a ridge of fallen stones, jammed by time into a bank of solid clay. Below us, round in another angle of the quarry, I could see water.

He stopped. He still had his pipe in his hand. It had gone out. He examined it carefully, but absently, as if he was not quite sure what it was. Then he stuffed it into his pocket. "You mean if I married Julie?"

I hadn't been ready for quite such direct dealing. "Yes. Yes, I did mean that. Perhaps I shouldn't have—"

"If I married Julie, I should still have to go where my work was," said Donald bluntly, "and it won't always be at West Woodburn." He looked at me. "Are you trying to tell me that she'll want to come and live here?"

"No."

"Ah. Well, I didn't altogether get the impression that she was wedded to the place."

"She's not." I hesitated, then added, equally bluntly, "Nor likely to be."

He looked at me sharply. Beside me a tuft of silvery hairgrass had fluffed into a lace of pale seeds. I ran my fingers through them, and then regarded the handful of tiny particles. I took a breath and plunged on. "You know, I wouldn't dream of saying this sort of thing to you, if it weren't important. You may think I'm speaking out of turn, and if so, I hope you'll forgive me."

He made the slight, indescribable sound that, in the North, manages to express assent, deprecation, interest, dissent, apology—anything at all that the listener cares to read into it. It sounds like "Mphm," and you can conduct whole (and perfectly intelligible) conversations with that one sound, anywhere north of the Tyne. As a contribution from Donald, it was unhelpful.

I opened my hand and let the seeds drift down on to the clay. "Have you said anything to Julie yet?"

He said quite simply, "No. It's been—so quick, you see . . . eight weeks since we met, that's all. I don't mean that I'm any the less sure, but I don't know if she . . . well, she's so young."

"She's nineteen. Nowadays girls know their own minds at nineteen."

"Do they?" I caught a slight hesitation in his manner then, and wondered if he had been suddenly reminded of another nineteen-year-old, eight years ago at Whitescar. He said, "I rather thought Julie had given every indication of not knowing."

"Bill Fenwick? He's a very nice boy, I think, but I assure you, you needn't worry about him."

"I wasn't thinking about Bill Fenwick."

"What do you mean, then?"

"Connor."

"*Con?*" I stared for a moment, then said flatly, "If you'd asked me, I'd have said she didn't even like him."

He had taken out his pipe, and was filling it again, more, I thought, for something to fidget with than because he wanted to smoke. He glanced up across it, and I thought his look sharpened. "I should have thought he was the very sort of chap a girl would be bound to fall for."

"Oh, lord, lord, he's attractive," I said impatiently. "You might say devastating. But Julie's never shown any signs of falling for him, and she's had plenty chance to . . . Goodness knows, if she wasn't susceptible to sheer blazing good looks like Con's at fifteen or sixteen, then she probably never will be. You forget, she was brought up here; she probably thinks of him like a brother . . . and not a particularly favourite one."

"You think so? I'm not very knowledgeable about these things. It just seemed to be so likely, and so . . . suitable."

"Suitable? I doubt it! Anyway, Julie's not a nitwit, and she's had plenty of time to fall for Con if she was ever going to, instead of which . . ." I paused, and brushed a finger idly over a tight purple thistle top. "Things are a little—difficult—just now at Whitescar. I can't quite describe why . . . it's a sort of emotional climate. . . ."

"I know," he said, surprisingly. "Everyone seems a little too much aware of what other people are doing."

"You've felt it? Then you know what I mean. It's partly to do with my coming back, and Grandfather's stroke, and his making a new will . . . oh, and everything. But it's rather horrid, and definitely unsettling. I know Julie's feeling it, and I'm so afraid she'll do something just plain silly. If it weren't for that, I'd be quite happy to settle back, and depend on her good sense and good taste, but just at present . . ." My voice trailed off, awkwardly.

"Do you know," said Donald, "whether you meant it or not, that was a compliment?"

I glanced at him. He looked amused, relaxed, confident, calmly pressing the tobacco down into the bowl of his pipe. I suddenly realized that I had been tempering the wind to a fully grown and completely self-possesed lamb. I had underrated Donald, and so (I thought with amused relief) had Julie.

I took a little breath of relief. Then I grinned maliciously. "Think nothing of it. That was my double tongue. How do you know I meant you?"

His eyes twinkled. "It never occurred to me that you could mean anyone else. That's one of the blessings of being a Scot, a profound and unshakable conviction of your own worth."

"Then hang on to that, and forget about Con," I said. "Heavens above, what's got into me? Donald, don't ask me why, and blame me for an interfering so-and-so if you like, but I wish to goodness that you'd simply *ask* the girl!"

He sent me that sudden, transforming grin. "It'll be a pleasure. Now, come along, and be careful down this slope, there may be loose bits. Here, take my hand. That's it."

"Goodness, that water's deep, isn't it?"

"It is that. Round here now. It's all right, you can walk on the edge, the rock's safe."

The water lay still and billiard-green in the shadow of the ledge where we stood. The edges of the pool were as sharply quarried as those of a swimming bath. On two sides the water was held in by a right angle of the high cliff; at the side where we stood, the quarry was floored with flat, bare rock, as smooth as concrete, which dropped squarely away in front of us to the water level some four feet below.

Here the water was in shadow, oil-green, slightly opaque, and somehow dangerous-looking, but where the sunlight struck it, it was lucid with grass-green colour streaked with weed, and beneath the surface the planes of quarried rock showed clearly, coloured according to their depth, green-gold and gold-jade, like peaches drowned in chartreuse.

"Look." He pointed down through the water towards one of the slanting slabs of stone that showed like a buttress shoring up the side of the pool. "Do you see that bit of rock?"

"The one that's lying on a slant? Yes. It looks as if it had been shaped, doesn't it? Such a nice, regular oblong."

"It has been shaped." Something in his voice made me look at him. He said, "Look at it again. Don't you see the marks?"

I peered down. "I . . . think so. I can't be sure. Do you mean what looks like a sort of rough scoring, diagonally across the block? That's not artificial, surely?"

"I think it was. Those marks would be sharply scored originally; chisel marks. That block's been under water a long time, and even still water will smooth out a stone surface, given time."

I stood up and looked at him. "Given time?"

"I don't know how long, because I don't know when this part of the quarry was flooded. But those stones down there were quarried about two thousand years ago."

"Two thou—" I stopped short and said, rather blankly, "You mean the *Romans?*"

"That's my guess. About two thousand years ago they opened a quarry here. Later, possibly much later, the 'white scar' among the woods was re-opened and worked again. Perhaps the Roman workings were already flooded; at any rate, new ones were started, and the original ones left to the weather. And now, this year, with this dry spring, and the drought, the water level sinks a couple of feet just when I chance to be poking about in this part of the world, and I see the stones. That's how things happen."

"Is it—is it important? Forgive me, I'm terribly ignorant, but what does it tell you, apart from the fact that they got building stone from here, for the Wall?"

"Not for the Wall. Hardly, when they were driving that along the whin sill anyway. They quarried the stone for the Wall on the spot."

"For the fort at West Woodburn, then? Habitancum, where you're working?"

"The same applies. There's stone there. They dug the local stuff whenever they could, of course, to save time and transport."

He seemed to be waiting, eyeing me in amiable expectation. It was a moment or two before the very simple conclusion presented itself.

"Oh! Yes, I get it. But, Donald, there's nothing Roman hereabouts, is there? At least, I've never heard of anything, and surely, if there were, the one-inch map would have it marked?"

"Exactly," said Donald.

I stared at him stupidly for a moment or two. "I . . . see! You think there *may* be something? Some unknown Roman work?"

He pushed his pipe down into a pocket, and turned away from the water's edge. "I've no idea," he said, "but there's nothing to stop me looking, is there? And now, if you're ready, I'll be taking you down to Whitescar, and then I'll get along and see Mr. Forrest, and ask his leave to go poking around in his policies."

CHAPTER

ELEVEN

"I cannot get to my love if I wad dee,
  The water of Tyne runs between him and me."

North Country Song.

When we got to the farm, it was to find a slightly distracted Lisa watching for me with some tale of disaster that involved a cream trifle, and Tommy, the black and white cat.

"And I'll wring his neck if he comes near the dairy again," she said, violently for her.

I said mildly, "We've got to remember he's eating for eight."

"Nonsense," said Lisa, "he had them days ago. Oh, I see what you mean. Well, even if he *is* feeding seven kittens, and let me tell you if only I can find them I'll drown the lot, that's no excuse for taking the whole top off the trifle I'd made for your grandfather's birthday dinner."

"Just a minute," said Donald, "no doubt I'm not just at my best to-day, but who has taken the trifle?"

"That beastly Tommy."

"The black and white cat? The fat one I—the one who was in to tea the other day?" Donald liked cats, and had made friends with them all, even the little half-wild tortoiseshell that lived like a wraith under the henhouse.

"That's the one. And not so fat either, now he's had his kittens, but after half the trifle and a pint of cream—"

I said helplessly, seeing Donald's expression, "It's all right. Nature has not suspended her laws, not yet. Everyone was wrong about Tommy —except that marmalade brute from West Lodge, at least I suppose it was him, because now that Tommy's unmasked he's the only tom for miles. Oh lord, I'm getting muddled too. And poor Tommy's figure wasn't due to incontinence—at least, not of the kind we'd thought; it was just kittens. Seven of them."

"And Annabel saw them in the loft, and didn't tell me till next morning, and by that time the brute had shifted them, and he's too sly to let us see him going to feed them." Lisa slapped a bucket down on the kitchen table.

"You wouldn't really drown them? All?" Donald spoke in the carefully non-committal voice of the man who would sooner die stuck full of arrows than seem to be soft-hearted over an animal.

"I certainly would, and Tommy too, if he gets in the dairy again."

"You can't change a personal pronoun overnight," I said apologetically, to Donald. "I'm afraid Tommy won't even decline to Thomasina. He'll be Tommy till the end of his days."

"Which are not," said Lisa, "so far distant, though even I have not the heart to have the brute put down, and leave those wretched kittens to starve to death somewhere. But if I find them before they're too big, they'll certainly have to drown. Did Mr. Seton say he was going over to West Lodge now? Annabel, would you be an angel and go across with him as far as the gardens, and get some strawberries? I rang up, and Johnny Rudd said he'd keep them for us. They should be ready, so hurry back, if you don't mind; we'll have them all to pick over."

Something must have shown in my face, for I saw her recollect herself for the first time for days. She must have forgotten that I had not yet been across to the gardens.

I saw her eyes flicker with a moment of calculation, and then she turned to Donald, but he spoke first. He must have seen something too; he saw more than one thought, I reflected; but of course he put my hesitation down to simple physical causes.

"Annabel's tired. Look, I can easily drop in at the market garden for you. You go past it to get to the Lodge, don't you?"

I said, "It's all right, Donald, thanks all the same. I'm not tired, and if you've to see Mr. Forrest at the Lodge, time will be getting along by the time you manage to get away, and besides, you don't want to have to hurry. I'll come along with you now, if I may, and walk straight back with the strawberries by the short cut, and then we can get on with hulling them. I'd like to see Johnny Rudd, anyway. He'll be in the garden?" This to Lisa.

"Yes." Her eyes were on me. "You haven't seen him since you came back, have you? His hair's going grey now, but he hasn't changed much. He's the only one who'll still be working there by this time; he said he'd wait if he could. The two boys go off at five. But if Mr. Forrest should be in the garden—"

"Oh, did I tell you?" I said. "I saw him the other day."

"Did you?" The question only just missed being too sharp. "To speak to?"

"For a moment. I forgot what we talked about, but I thought he'd changed, rather a lot." I picked up the basket. "I'll be as quick as I can," I said.

What had been the old walled kitchen garden of Forrest Hall lay beside the stables, about a quarter of a mile from the West Lodge, where Adam Forrest now lived.

Even here some pomp remained from the once palmy days of the Forrests. The entrance to the stableyard—now worked as a small farm —was a massive archway, with shields bearing the same heraldic beasts that flaunted their improbable attitudes on the gateposts at Forrest Hall. Over the arch stood the old clock tower, with a gilded weather vane over it. Trees crowded close on the other side of the lane, and the river glittered just beyond them. The road was rutted and green with weeds, its verges deep in wild flowers, but the cobbles of the yard, glimpsed through the archway, were sparkling clean, like the shingle on a seaswept beach. A little way off, beyond a clump of laburnum and copper beech, the chimneys of West Lodge glinted in the sunlight. Smoke was rising from one of them. Life at Forrest Park had shifted its focus.

Beyond the stableyard stretched the twelve-foot-high wall of the kitchen garden. There was a wrought-iron gate set into it.

"This one?"

"Yes."

Donald stopped the car, and I got out.

"Now, don't bother about me. It's just as quick taking the cut back across the fields. I'll go that way."

"If you're sure—"

"Quite sure. Thanks for the lift. I'll see you at dinner."

The car moved off. I pushed the gate open.

The last stretch of the lane had been deep under trees. Now, I walked through the gate, between two massive yews, and into a brilliance of sunshine that made me blink and narrow my eyes.

It wasn't only the brightness, however, that gave me pause. Here, the contrast with the moonlit derelict at Forrest was both striking and disturbing. In this garden, filled with sun and warmth and scent inside its four high walls, everything, at first sight, was as it might have been in the eighteenth-century heyday of the place.

All along one wall was the glass, and under it I could see the peaches and apricots and grapes of a more luxurious age, still carefully pruned and trained, and beneath them the homely forests of tomatoes and chrysanthemum seedlings, and the occasional splashes of colour that meant hydrangeas or begonias coming into flower for the market. Along the other three walls were the espaliered fruit trees. The fruit, small, green and shining, crowded thickly on the boughs against the warm sandstone.

Down the centre of the garden went a broad walk of turf, beautifully cut and rolled, and to either side of this was a flower border, spired and splashed and shimmering with all the colours of an English June; lupins, delphiniums, peonies, poppies, irises, Canterbury bells, all held back by lavender swags of catmint, and backed by a high rustic trellis where climbing roses held up their fountains of bright flowers. At the far end of the walk, at the focal point, as it were, of the vista, I could see the basin of some disused stone fountain, with a couple of bronze herons still on guard over what had been the pool. This was set round with flagstones, between which were clumps of lavender, rosemary, thyme and sage, in a carefully planned confusion as old as the garden itself. They must have left the old herb garden, I thought, and this one avenue of flowers. The rest was all order and usefulness—peas and beans and turnips and potatoes, and regimented fruit bushes. The only other thing that spoke of the glory that had departed was a tall circular structure in one corner of the garden, a dovehouse, *columbarium*, with honeysuckle and clematis running riot over its dilapidated walls. The pegged tiles of its roof sagged gently over the beams beneath, as canvas moulds itself to the supporting ropes. The tiles showed bronze-coloured in the sunlight, their own smoky blue overlaid and softened by the rings of that lovely lichen that spreads its amber circles, like water-lily leaves, over old and beautiful things. The dove-doors had decayed, and looked like empty eye sockets; I saw starlings fly out.

But elsewhere all was order. Not a weed. I reflected that if Adam Forrest and Johnny Rudd kept all this themselves, with the help of a couple of boys, I could hardly taunt him with not understanding the meaning of labour. The place must be killing work.

At first I couldn't see anyone about at all, and walked quickly up the grass walk, towards the greenhouses, peering through the rose trellis to right and left. Then I saw a man working among raspberry canes over near one of the walls. He had his back to me, and was stooping. He was wearing faded brown corduroys, and a blue shirt, and I could see an old brown jacket hung near him over a stake. He had dark hair with grey in it.

He didn't seem to hear my approach, being intent on fastening a bird net back securely over the canes.

I stopped on the path near him. "Johnny?"

He straightened and turned. "I'm afraid—" he began, then stopped.

"You?" For the life of me I couldn't help sounding unbelieving. This was certainly the Adam Forrest I had met and spoken with a few nights ago, but now, facing him in the broad glare of the afternoon, I could see how different he was from my remembered picture of him. What I had seen on that last, almost dreamlike meeting had been something like seeing a sequence from a film taken years ago, when he had been ten, no, fifteen years younger. Some unreality of the night had lent itself to him: I remembered the fine planes of his face, the smoothness of skin young in the moonlight, the darkness of hair and eyes dramatized in the drained light. In the moonlight he had seemed merely tallish, well enough built, and had moved easily, with that air of self-confidence that goes with strength—or with inherited wealth. Now, as he straightened in the sunlight to face me, it was as if the film had spun along swiftly, and the actor had, with skilful make-up, confirmed the passage of years. His hair, which had been very dark, was showing grey; not gracefully, at the temples, but in an untidy flecking all over, like the dimming of dust. The fine structure of strong bone couldn't be altered, but there were lines I hadn't seen by moonlight, and he was thinner than the size of his frame should have allowed. Before, he had been conventionally dressed, and I had noticed neither the cut nor the quality of his clothes; but now the light showed up a shabbiness that—so unconsciously he wore it—must have been part of every day. Some part of my mind said that of course it was only common sense to wear rough clothes for a rough job, but another part, that I had not known existed, linked the shabbiness with the lines on his face, and the greying hair, and winced away from them with a pity I knew he didn't want, and that I had no right to feel. I noticed that he was wearing gloves, and remembered my taunt about his hands, and was sorry.

He smiled at me, narrowing his eyes against the sun. They were grey-blue, and puckered at the corners. He spoke easily, as if there could be no constraint between us.

"Hullo. Were you looking for Johnny Rudd? I'm afraid he's gone."

"I came for some strawberries. The cat's been at the trifle, and it's Grandfather's birthday, so Lisa rang up with an S.O.S., and Johnny said he'd try to save some."

"Then he'll have left them up in the packing shed. Come and see."

We walked up the path together. I saw him eyeing me, as curious as I had been, no doubt, to see what the daylight showed.

I said, "Have you met Julie's young man? Donald Seton?"

"No. Why?"

"He came across with me just now, to see you about something, but he thought you'd have finished for the day, so he went along to the Lodge."

"Oh? What's it about, d'you know?"

"Yes, but I'll leave him to tell you himself." I caught his quick look, and smiled a little. "Oh, don't worry, it's nothing personal. You're still quite safe."

We had reached a door in the wall behind the greenhouses, which led to the workrooms of the place—boiler room, potting houses, co'd frames. He stopped with his hand on the knob, and turned. I noticed all at once that his eyes looked tired, as if he didn't sleep well. "Safe? I?"

"Indeed, yes. If you're not an accessory after the fact, I don't know what you are. You never came after that passport. You never came across to Whitescar, and tried to trip me up and catch me out in front of Grandfather, as no doubt you think you could easily have done. You've done nothing. Why?"

"I don't know. I honestly don't know." He hesitated, as if to say something more. Then, instead, he merely turned, and pushed the door open for me. "This way, now; leave the door, it's all right; Seton may come looking for me. Is Julie with him?"

"No. She's gone into Newcastle with Bill Fenwick."

He shot me a look. "That troubles you. Why?"

"Because Con won't like it one bit," I said crisply, "and Con is a . . . creature of impulse."

"That's absurd." He said it as he had done before, but with just a shade less conviction.

"Any situation bordering on violence is absurd—until it suddenly breaks, and then, *wham*, there you are, in the middle of something you'd thought only happened in the Sunday Press."

"What about this man who's here—Seton, was it?"

"That's different. He'll take her away from Whitescar, and they'll live in London, and spend half the year in a tent somewhere, digging. Con's all for that, as you may imagine—and the further away, the better. Uzbekistan, for instance, or the Desert of Lop, if the Romans went there, I wouldn't know."

"Does she want to go?"

"Pining to," I said cheerfully. "Don't worry, I've practically fixed it. I told you I'd look after Julie." I caught his eye, and laughed. "What is it?"

"This—crazy business; and I'm as crazy as any part of it. That's what comes of working by instinct instead of sense; I suppose women do it every day, but I'm not accustomed to it, and I dislike it. There's nothing to assure you that you're still rational. Look at the situation: I'm not sure who you are; I'm not sure what you're doing; I'm certain it's wrong; but for some reason I'm prepared to let you do it."

"I told you who I was, and what I was doing."

"Yes, you did. You were honest, as far as that went. And you've got me into a position where I seem to be condoning what you do, even though I'm damned if I do more. I suppose it's because I think rather a lot of old Mr. Winslow, and oddly enough, I'd trust you over Julie, who seems to me to be the only other person who matters. I confess I'd wondered, before you came, just what the set-up would be at Whitescar, when Mr. Winslow died. You say you're 'looking after' her interests. Well, as long as Julie comes to no harm, I don't much care how you and Connor fight it out the rest of the way. If you can get it, I shan't grudge you your 'competence.' "

"You needn't worry; you can trust me over Julie."

He sighed. "The odd thing is that I believe you, and for that alone I deserve to be behind bars as an accessory, just as soon as you are. Here's the packing shed. Come and see if Johnny's left your strawberries."

The shed was big and cool, its basic smell, of geraniums and damp peat, dizzily overlaid by that of a tank crammed full with sweet peas. It was as orderly as the garden: there were shelves of plant pots and boxes, in graded sizes; printed labels in rows (probably in alphabetical order); raffia hanging in loops that looked as if they would never dare tangle or snap; and two or three pairs of clean cotton gloves on a hook beside the window.

I watched Adam Forrest with some awe as he crossed the shed and reached down a pair of these. There were two punnets of strawberries on a bench to the left of the window. "Enough, do you think?" he asked.

"I think so."

"There may be a few more ripe, in the bed by the dovehouses. I can pick them, if you've time to wait."

"No, don't trouble. I'm sure there'll be enough, and I promised to get back quickly. Dinner's at half-past seven, and we'll have them to pick over. Look, I brought a basket. We can tip them all in together, and you can keep the punnets."

"It comes cheaper that way," agreed Adam gravely.

I gaped at him for a second, for some absurd reason more embarrassed than at any time in our too rapidly intimate relationship. Lisa hadn't mentioned money; I had none with me, and hadn't thought about it till now. I said, stammering, "I—I'm afraid I can't pay for them now."

"I'll charge them," said Adam imperturbably. He reached for a notebook, and made a jotting on a meticulously columned page headed "Winslow." He caught my eye on him, and grinned, and suddenly, in the shadowed shed, the years fell away, and there was the lover of the moonlit tryst, the actor of that early film. I caught my breath. He said, "Whitescar runs an account. They don't seem to have time to grow any vegetables there themselves . . . I doubt if anybody has even touched the garden—" he shut the book and returned it neatly to its place—"since you left. Careful! You're spilling those! What did I say to make you jump?"

"You know quite well. You did it deliberately. You . . . got under my skin."

"That makes two of us," said Adam; at least, that's what I thought he said, but he muttered it under his breath, and the words were swallowed as he turned his head quickly to the door, adding aloud, "I suppose this is Mr. Seton?"

"Oh . . . hullo, Donald. Yes, Mr. Forrest's still here. Mr. Seton, Adam. . . ."

The men exchanged greetings. Donald said, "You got your strawberries?"

"I did. Your dinner's safe. I told Mr. Forrest you wanted to see him, Donald, but I managed to keep quiet about the reason."

"You needn't have done that." He turned to Adam. "I don't know if Annabel told you, sir, but I'm an archaeologist; I'm attached to the

Commission—the Royal Commission on Historical Monuments—and just at present I'm in charge of the work being done up at West Woodburn."

"I had heard that excavating has started there," said Adam. "Just what are you hoping to do?"

"Well, the Commission's job is to list and describe all existing Roman monuments, with maps and photographs and so on. It's worked on a county basis, and I'm one of the team assigned to Northumberland. . . ."

I had got the strawberries all tipped into my basket, but lingered a little, interested to hear the outcome of what Donald had to say. He gave Adam a very brief account of the work he was engaged on, and then passed, with an admirably Scottish economy of time and words, to the business of the moment.

When he described how he had seen the "Roman stones" in the quarry, it was obvious that he had caught Adam's interest. "And you think it likely, if that quarry *was* originally Roman, that there may be some Roman buildings near by?"

"Fairly near, at any rate," said Donald. "There's nothing remarkable about the rock itself—the quarried rock—if you follow me. If it were marble, for example, you might expect it to be worked, even if it had to be carried long distances; but this kind of sandstone is the common local stone. If the Romans did start a quarry there, then they would do so for pure reasons of convenience. In other words, they were building locally."

"I see," said Adam. "And am I right in thinking that there's nothing recorded hereabouts? I've never read of anything, though I've always been interested in local history."

"Quite right. There's nothing nearer than the camp at Four Laws, and, since that's on Dere Street, the materials for building it would certainly be taken from somewhere on the road, not right across country from here. So it did occur to me that, if the quarry was started here, in the peninsula, when the same stone occurs all along the ridge above the river—and is rather more get-at-able there—it did occur to me to wonder if whatever was built was built on the peninsula itself."

"Somewhere in Forrest Park?"

"Yes. I wanted to ask your permission to have a look round, if I may."

"With the greatest of pleasure. I'm afraid the Forestry Commission acres are out of my jurisdiction, but the meadowland, and the Hall grounds, by all means. Go where you like. But what exactly will you be looking for? Surely anything there was will be deep under several feet of earth and trees by now?"

"Oh yes. But I did wonder if you could help me. Can you remember if there's anything else in the way of a quarry, anything that might be an overgrown pit, or artificial bank—you know the kind of thing?"

"Not at the moment, but I'll think it over. The only pit I can think of is the old icehouse near the Forrest gate-house. That's dug deep into the earth under the trees, but that can hardly—wait a minute!"

He broke off, his brows knitted in an effort of memory. I watched him half-excitedly, Donald with the utmost placidity. Doubtless he was very much better aware than I was that "discoveries" rarely, if ever, come out of the blue.

"The icehouse," said Adam. "Mentioning the icehouse struck a chord. Wait a minute, I can't be sure, but somewhere, some time, when I was a child, I think . . . I've seen something at Forrest. A stone . . . Roman, I'll swear." He thought a moment longer, then shook his head. "No, it's gone. Could it have been the same ones, I wonder, that I saw? The ones in the quarry?"

"Not unless there was a very dry season, and you probably wouldn't have noticed them unless they were even nearer the surface than they are now. Wouldn't you say so, Annabel?"

"Certainly. And anyway, nobody but an expert could possibly have guessed those *were* Roman. They looked quite ordinary to me, and to a child they'd mean nothing at all."

"That's true. You can't remember anything more, sir? What made you think it was Roman stone? Why the icehouse? What is the icehouse, anyway?"

"A primitive sort of refrigerator. They usually built them somewhere in the grounds of big houses, in the eighteenth century," said Adam. "They were big square pits, as a rule, dug somewhere deep in the woods where it was cool. They had curved roofs, with the eaves flush with the ground, and a door in one end, over the pit. People used to cut the ice off the lake—there's a small pool beyond the house—in winter, and store it underground in layers of straw, to bring out in summer. The one at Forrest's in the woods near the old gate-house."

"Then you may have seen this thing there, surely? It was quite usual for later builders to lay hands on any Roman stones they could, to use again. They were good blocks, well shaped and dressed. If there were a few left stacked in the old quarry, above water level, a local eighteenth-century builder may well have taken them and—"

"The cellars!" said Adam. "That was it! Not the icehouse, we weren't allowed in; it wasn't safe, and it was kept locked. We weren't allowed in the cellars, either, but that was different; they were at least accessible." He grinned. "I thought there was something surreptitious and candlelit about the memory, and it also accounts for the fact that we never mentioned it to anyone. I'd forgotten all about it until this moment. Yes, I'm fairly sure it was in the cellars at Forrest. I can't remember any more than that, except that we were rather intrigued for the moment, as children are, by the carving on the stone. It was upside down, which made it harder to make out what it said, even if we could have—"

"What it *said?*" Donald's voice was sharp, for him.

Adam looked surprised. "Yes. Didn't you say the stones were carved? There was some sort of lettering, as far as I remember, and a carving of some kind . . . an animal."

"I said 'chiselled,' not 'carved,' " said Donald. "If you're right, it sounds as if you may have seen an inscription. All I saw were the ordinary tooling marks on the stone, the marks made by dressing with chisels. Like this. . . ." He fished in his inside pocket, and came out with a thick wad of papers. There seemed to be (besides a wallet, several dozen letters and a driver's licence) an Ordnance Survey map of the North Tyne, and a thin booklet of what looked like—but surely could not be—logarithms. Donald looked at them vaguely, selected an old envelope, on which I distinctly saw a postmark two years old, and restored the rest to his pocket.

Adam handed him a pencil. "Thanks. This," said Donald, drawing with beautiful economy and accuracy on the dog-eared envelope, "is something like the stones I saw."

He handed the paper to Adam, who studied it. "I see. No, that doesn't convey anything to me; I'd never have known that was Roman . . . not even now, let alone at ten years old. Well, the obvious thing to do is to go and look, isn't it? This is really rather exciting. If it turns out to be an inscription of the Ninth Legion or something, will Forrest's fortune be remade?"

"Well," said Donald cautiously, "you might get it on to T.V. . . . The house is a ruin, isn't it? Is it still possible to get into the cellars?"

"I think you'll find you can get down. I don't have to tell you to watch yourself, I'm not sure what sort of condition the place is in. But you may certainly go just where you like. Look, I'll make you a plan."

He reached to the nearby shelf for a paper—it looked like an invoice form—and spread it on the bench. Donald handed back the pencil. I came to Adam's elbow to look. He drew a couple of lines, then, with a subdued exclamation of irritation, pulled off the cotton gloves, dropped them on the bench beside him, and picked the pencil up again. "I can't write in them. Do you mind?"

"Mind?"

Then I saw. His hands were disfigured, most horribly, it must have been by burns. The skin was white and dead-looking, glassed like polythene, and here and there were puckered scars that showed purple; the shape of his hands, like the other bone structure, had been beautiful, but the injuries had distorted even that, and made them hideous, things to shock. Things to hide, as, until now, he had hidden them. This was something else that the romantic moonlighting had not revealed.

I must have made some small sound, some little gasp of indrawn breath. Adam's pencil checked, and he looked at me.

I suppose most people stared like that, sick and shocked, for a moment or two, then looked quickly away, saying nothing, talking of something else, pretending not to have seen.

I said, "Adam, your hands, your poor hands. . . . What did that to your hands?"

"I burned them."

The fire at Forrest. His wife. The bed was alight by that time. He managed to drag the bedclothes off her, and carry her downstairs. . . .

He had reached one of those terrible hands for the discarded gloves. He hadn't taken his eyes off my face. He said gently, "I'll put them on again. I'm sorry, I forgot you wouldn't know. It's rather a shock, the first time."

"It—it doesn't matter. Don't, for me . . . I—I've got to go." I reached blindly for the basket. I could feel the tears spilling hot on to my cheeks, and couldn't stop them. I had forgotten all about Donald, till I heard him say "Here" and the basket was put into my hands. I said shakily, "I've got to hurry back. Good-bye," and, without looking at either of them, my head bent low over the basket, I turned and almost ran out of the packing shed.

I was conscious of the silence I had left behind me, and of Adam, straightening abruptly, the pencil still in his hand, staring after me.

CHAPTER

TWELVE

Go with your right to Newcastle,
  And come with your left side home;
There will you see these two lovers. . . .
                    Ballad: *Fair Margaret and Sweet William.*

As it turned out, there were more than enough strawberries for supper. Julie didn't come back.

The dinner, though delicious, could hardly be said to be festive. It
was as if all the accumulated tensions of the last days had gathered that
evening at the dining table, building slowly up like the thunderheads
that stood steadily on the horizon outside.

Con had come in early, rather quiet, with watchful eyes, and lines
from nostril to chin that I hadn't noticed before. Grandfather seemed
to have recruited his energies with his afternoon rest; his eyes were
bright and a little malicious as he glanced round the table, and marked
the taut air of waiting that hung over the meal. It was his moment of
power, and he knew it.

If it had needed anything to bring the tensions to snapping point,
Julie's absence provided it. At first it was only assumed that she was
late, but, as the meal wore on, and it became apparent that she wasn't
coming, Grandfather started making irritatingly frequent remarks
about the forgetfulness and ingratitude of young people, that were
intended to sound pathetic, but only managed to sound thoroughly
bad-tempered.

Con ate more or less in silence, but a silence so unrelaxed as to be
almost aggressive. It was apparent that Grandfather thought so, for
he kept casting bright, hard looks under his brows, and once or twice
seemed on the verge of the sort of edged and provocative remark with
which he had been prodding his great-nephew for days.

I drew what fire I could, chattering shamelessly, and had the dubious
satisfaction of attracting most of the old man's attention to myself,

some of it so obviously affectionate—pointedly so—that I saw, once or twice, Con's glance cross mine like the flicker of blue steel. Afterwards, I thought, when he knows, when that restless, torturing ambition is stilled at last, it will be all right; everything will be all right. . . .

As Grandfather had predicted, Donald's presence saved the day. He seconded my efforts with great gallantry, making several remarks at least three sentences long; but he, too, was unable to keep his eyes from the clock, while Lisa, presiding over a magnificent pair of duckling *à la Rouennaise*, and the strawberries hastily assembled into whipped cream *Chantilly*, merely sat unhelpfully silent and worried, and, in consequence, looking sour.

The end of the meal came, and the coffee, and still no Julie. We all left the dining room together. As Con pushed back his chair, he said abruptly, "I'm going to telephone Nether Shields."

"What the devil for?" asked Grandfather testily. "If the girl chooses to forget, let her be."

"She's not likely to have forgotten. I'm afraid there may have been an accident."

"Then what's the use of telephoning Nether Shields? If they knew anything, they'd have rung us up. The girl's forgotten. Don't waste your time."

"I'll ring, all the same," said Con, and left the room abruptly. Grandfather's gaze as he watched him was bright and sardonic.

To forestall what comment he might make, I said quickly, "If she did forget, she may have gone back to supper with Bill Fenwick."

"Nonsense," said Grandfather roundly, and stumped out of the dining room.

In the drawing-room Lisa poured coffee, her attention stolidly on the cups. Grandfather mercifully relapsed into silence, fidgeting with his fingers, and forgetting to drink his coffee. Donald was still watching the clock, though I suspected that his motives had altered somewhat. I'd have given a lot, myself, to go for a long, long walk, preferably several miles away from Whitescar.

"If anything has happened to that child—" began Grandfather, at length.

"Nothing will have happened," I said. "You'd have heard if there'd been an accident. She'd have rung up . . . or someone else would. Don't worry, it'll be all right. She'll turn up soon."

"If a tire burst when they were miles from anywhere—" Donald put in a comforting oar—"that could delay them."

"As long as this? It's nine o'clock."

"Mphm," said Donald.

I glanced anxiously at Grandfather. The bright malice had faded. He looked his age, and more, and the hand with which he pushed aside his untasted coffee was shaking a little.

Con came back into the room.

"Nothing," he said tersely. "Mrs. Fenwick knew Julie was due back here for dinner. Bill said he'd be home by seven. No sign."

"I told you it was no use telephoning!" Grandfather almost snapped it. "But you know best, as usual."

Con took the coffee which Lisa had stirred and handed to him. "It was a chance," he said, mildly enough. "And I thought it might save you worrying."

"You're very solicitous of others, all of a sudden, aren't you, Connor? Why so anxious? Because you want to see the family all assembled together? Lisa tell you what I said at luncheon, eh?"

It was unforgivable enough, especially in front of Donald, but normally it would hardly have worried anyone. Con's reaction was indicative, uncomfortably so, of the pressure that had been building up behind the quiet, sealed front.

He went rather pale, and put down his coffee half-drunk. He didn't even look where he was setting the cup, but put it blindly down on what would have been vacancy, if Lisa had not quietly taken it out of his hand. For a moment he and Grandfather stared at one another, and I waited, with a sort of horror, for the valves to blow.

Then Con said, "If I'm wanted, I'll be in the field," and turned his back on his great-uncle. "Good night, Seton." Quietly still, but like one escaping to a freer, purer air, he went out of the room.

Unexpectedly, Grandfather chuckled. "Good lad," he said, with a sort of fierce approval, then turned a ghost of his old, charming smile on Donald. "I warned you, didn't I? You'll have to forgive us for thrusting our family squabbles on you."

Donald returned some sort of polite reply, and, thereafter, the conversation trickled back into fairly normal channels. But half an hour went by, and still there was no sign of Julie, nor did the telephone ring. I must have shown how worried I was, and Grandfather took to saying, at shorter and shorter intervals, "Where on earth can the child have got to?" or alternatively, "Why the devil couldn't she have telephoned?" until I could see it was getting across even Donald's admirable nervous system. I wasn't surprised when, almost too soon for civility, he rose to his feet, and said he thought he had better be going.

No one made any attempt to stop him. Lisa got up with rather too patent relief, and let him carry the coffee cups out to the kitchen for her.

I followed. "I'll come back in a minute, Lisa, when I've done the gate for Donald. Leave them for me: you said you would."

It was dusk in the lee of the big barn, where Donald had parked his car. When I reached it, I couldn't see him. Puzzled, I paused beside the car, peering around me into the shadows.

Then I heard a soft step, and turned swiftly. Donald came very quietly round the end of the barn, from the direction of the stable-yard. Seeing me waiting beside the car, he stopped abruptly, and even in that light I could see he was out of countenance. I stared at him, completely at a loss for words. He looked like a man who has been caught out in a dubious act.

There was one of those ghastly pauses, then he smiled. "It's all right, I haven't been hiding the silver behind the barn. I've been visiting friends."

"Friends?" I said, blankly.

He laughed. "Come and see."

I followed him into the yard, where he pushed open the half-door of the empty stable. The interior smelled sweet and dry, of hay and horses. Opposite the door was a big loose-box, the bars down now, since Blondie had gone out to grass. Donald switched on the light, and led the way into the loose-box. There was an iron manger running the breadth of it, deep, and half full of clean straw. I supposed the hens laid there sometimes.

"Here," said Donald softly, "meet the family."

I leaned over the manger. Deep in the straw was a nest, but not of eggs. Seven kittens, some days old, still blind and boneless, all sleeping soundly, lay curled together in a tight, furry mass, black and white and ginger. Donald put down a gentle hand to touch the warm fur. As he did so, a wraith, black and white, jumped on to the iron manger at his elbow, purred softly, and slid down beside the kittens. There was a wriggling, and butting, and readjusting of fur, then Tommy settled down, eyes slitted and happy, paws steadily kneading the rustling straw.

"How on earth did you find them?" I whispered.

"Tommy showed me tonight, when I got back from West Lodge."

"Well, I'll keep your secret. Nobody'll come in here, while the horses are out. . . . Did you really have to leave so early?"

"I thought I'd better."

"Mm, yes, I see what you mean." We left the darkened stable quietly, and walked back to the car. Beside it, I hesitated for a moment, then turned quickly to him. "Look, Donald, don't worry."

"Aren't you worrying?"

"Well, one can't help it, can one? But nothing'll have happened. Depend on it, they've forgotten, and stayed out to a meal, or something."

"It seems unlikely."

"Well, perhaps the car *has* broken down."

"Mphm," said Donald.

"Why don't you wait? They really ought not to be long."

"No, thanks, but I won't. Did I remember to thank Miss Dermott for the supper?"

"You thanked her very nicely. No, I'll do the gate."

"Oh, thank you. . . ." But he lingered, a hand on the car door. He seemed about to say something, then I thought he changed his mind. What he did say, rather tentatively, was, "Nice chap, Forrest."

"Yes."

"He seems interested in this quarry. He says he'll come over himself tomorrow, and hunt up that stone in the cellar with me."

"I hope you'll find it. Does it sound to you as if it could be the real thing?"

"That's impossible to tell, but I think it may well be, if only because he's kept that strong impression, all these years, that it was Roman. He thinks there must have been at least one or two words that he and his sister would have recognized as Latin, even at the age of nine or ten." He grinned. "He reckons that an EST or a SUB would have been about their limit at the time. Let's hope he's right."

"It's terribly exciting, isn't it?"

"At best," said Donald cheerfully, "it'll probably simply say 'Vote for P. Varro as quarry foreman. Shorter hours and longer pay.'"

I laughed. "Well, good luck to it, anyway."

"Would you care to come along tomorrow afternoon and help in the hunt?"

"No, thanks, I won't. I—I have things I've got to do."

"Mphm," said Donald. This time it seemed to signify a vague agreement. He hesitated again, and suddenly I found myself wondering if Julie had told him anything about Adam.

I glanced up at him. "I'm sorry I was upset this afternoon. Did he—did he mind, d'you think?"

"He didn't seem to." Donald spoke so quickly that I realized that this was exactly what he had been wanting to say, and hadn't liked to broach the subject, even to bring me comfort. "He said nothing. I'm sure he'd understand. I shouldn't worry."

"I won't," I said. "Good night, Donald."

"Good night."

The car's engine started with a roar, and the ancient vehicle jerked forward. I saw Donald lift a hand as he passed me, then the car grumbled its way off into the dusk towards High Riggs and the top of the hill.

The washing-up was done, and we were back in the drawing-room, Lisa with some mending for Con, myself playing a rather abstracted game of cribbage with Grandfather, when at length we heard a car enter the yard. Almost before it had drawn to a halt, one of its doors slammed; there was a short pause, and, faintly, the sound of voices, then the car moved off again immediately, and high heels tapped quickly across the yard to the kitchen door. We heard Julie cross the kitchen lobby and push open the green baize door to the hall. Then the hasty steps tapped their way across the hall, and were on the carpeted stairs.

Grandfather put his cards down with a slam, and shouted, "Julie!"

The flying steps stopped. There was a pause.

"Julie!"

She came slowly down the stairs again, and crossed the hall to the drawing-room door. With another part of my mind I heard the car's engine receding over the hill.

The drawing-room door opened. Julie stood there for a moment before she came in. Her eyes went swiftly round the room, and came to rest on Grandfather. Her hair was ruffled from the ride in the open car; her colour was high, and her eyes shone brilliantly. She looked very lovely; she also looked like the conventional picture of the young girl fresh from her lover's embrace, confused by the sudden light and the watching eyes. For a moment I wondered, with a sinking heart, if I had been wrong, and her interest in Bill Fenwick was serious, but then—I'm not quite sure how, except that Julie and I were so much alike—I knew, with relieved certainty, that the confused brilliance of her glance was due, not to love and embarrassment, but to sheer temper.

I saw Lisa's plump hands check in their work, and the sock she was mending sink slowly to her lap, as she stared at Julie with what looked like speculation.

"Julie!" Grandfather sounded angry. "Where have you been? We've spent the whole evening waiting and watching for you, and worrying in case anything had happened. Heaven knows I don't expect you to remember anything as completely unimportant as your grandfather's birthday, but I do think—"

"I'm sorry, Grandfather." Her voice was tolerably composed, but I saw how white her hand was on the doorknob. "I—we meant to get back. I didn't forget—there was an accident."

"An accident?" The old man's hands had been flat on the table among the cards. I saw them twitch, like a puppet's hands pulled by strings threaded through the arms.

I looked up quickly. "I take it nobody's hurt?"

She shook her head. "No, it was a silly thing. It wasn't Bill's fault. We weren't going fast—it was in the speed limit area, and Bill really was driving quite slowly. Somebody backed out of a garage straight into us."

"Was Bill's car damaged?"

"Yes. The door panel was dented, and he'd hit the front wheel, and Bill was afraid he'd knocked it out of true, and bent the track rod, or whatever you call it, but he hadn't. Then there was all the fuss, and the police—" she swallowed—"you know how it is; and then we had to get the car back to a garage and let them see what the damage was, and Bill had to arrange to take it back later to have it done. I—we couldn't help it, really we couldn't."

"Of course you couldn't," I said. "Look, honey, have you had supper? Because—"

"You could have telephoned," said Grandfather sharply. I noticed he was breathing hard, and the thin fingers twitched among the fallen cards.

"I'm sorry," said Julie again, but with something too sharp and driven-sounding in her voice. Outside, the yard gate clashed, and I saw her jump. "I know I should have, but I didn't think of it till we were on the way home. You—you know how it is, with everything happening, and Bill's car, and the other man being foul about it, and telling all sorts of lies to the police, only they *did* believe Bill and me . . ." Her voice quavered and she stopped.

Grandfather opened his mouth to speak, but I forestalled him. "She'd be too upset to think about it, Grandfather. You know what even the smallest of accidents is like; it shakes you right to pieces. Well, it's lucky it's no worse." Then, to Julie, "We thought it might be something like this; we knew you wouldn't have skipped the party unless something *had* happened. Look, my dear—" I got to my feet—"it's obvious you've had a shaking. I think you should get yourself straight upstairs to bed. I'll bring you something to eat; there's plenty left. . . . That was a wonderful meal you missed—Aylesbury ducklings, and strawberries straight off the straw. Tommy ate the trifle."

"Did he?" said Julie uncertainly. "Lisa, really, I'm terribly sorry, but—"

Lisa said, "Donald Seton was here." It was impossible to tell, from her composed, colourless tone, whether or not she was actuated by deliberate malice.

The result was the same. Julie bit her lip, stammered, and looked ready to cry. "Here? I—I didn't think he was coming."

I said gently, "I met him when I was on my way back from Bellingham. His London colleague had left early, and he was free, so I told him we were expecting him. He'd obviously been hoping to come, anyway," I smiled. "He'd changed into a very respectable suit."

"He left some time ago," said Lisa. "We thought he would wait to see you, but he said he had to go."

Julie turned to look at her, but vaguely, as if she wasn't really seeing her. I said, as lightly as I could, "I hope this all happened *after* the play? You saw that all right?"

"Oh, yes. It—it was wonderful."

"Then I expect, when you've had a rest," I said briskly, "you'll vote it was worth it, accident or no. Now, darling, I really think—"

The baize door opened and swung shut on a *whoosh* of air. Con came quickly across the hall, to pause in the open doorway behind Julie.

He had changed back into his work clothes before he had gone up to the field, and in breeches and open-necked shirt he looked tough, and also extremely handsome. And this for the same reason as Julie. He, too, was in a flaming temper, and it didn't need much gazing in the crystal ball to guess that the pair of them had just had a monumental row.

Julie never even turned her head on his approach. She merely hunched one shoulder a little stiffly, as if he were a cold draught behind her, and said to Lisa, on a strained, high note, "Did Donald say anything?"

"What about?" asked Lisa.

"No, Julie," I said.

Grandfather's hand scuffed irritably at the cards on the table in front of him. "What's all this? What's all this? Young Seton? What's he got to do with it?"

"Nothing," said Julie. "Nothing at all!" Her voice went thin and high. "And nor has Con!" She flung him a glance over her shoulder, about as friendly as a volley of swan-shot.

"Con?" Grandfather's eyes went from one to the other. "Con?" he repeated querulously. "Where does Con come into this?"

"That's just it!" said Julie, dangerously. "He doesn't, for all he seems to think he's the master here, and I'm answerable to him! Can you *imagine*—?" She checked herself, and went on in a voice that trembled insecurely on the edge of self-control, "Just now, as we came back, Bill had to stop the car for the gate at High Riggs—you know the grid's broken, and you've to use the gate—well, Con saw fit to come over, and ask me where the hell I'd been, (I'm sorry, Grandfather, but I'm only saying what *he* said) and why was I so late, and, as if that wasn't bad enough, he started pitching into Bill! As if it had been Bill's fault! Even if it *had*, it's not *your* business—" swinging on her cousin—"to start anything like that! What put *you* in such a howling temper, for heaven's sake? Speaking to Bill like that, swearing and everything, making a fool of me . . . and I'll be very surprised if he shows his face here again! He was furious, and I don't blame him! I had to apologize for you! How do you like *that*?"

"You know, Connor," said Grandfather, mildly enough, "you ought not to have done this. Julie's explained it to us. It wasn't young Fenwick's fault that—"

"That's not the *point!*" cried Julie. "Don't you *see*? Even if it *had* been Bill's fault, or mine, it's *none of Con's business!* If I choose to stay out all *night*, that's *my* affair!"

"And mine," said Grandfather, with sudden grim humour.

"All right," said Julie, "yours! But not Con's! He takes too dashed much on himself, and always did! It's time someone said something. It's been going on for years, without anyone noticing, and now this— *this* sort of thing—is the last straw as far as I'm concerned! Being ticked off like a naughty child in front of Bill Fenwick, and all because

—" she mimicked Con's voice—"it was 'vital we should all have been here tonight, and now Great-Uncle Matthew's as mad as fire!'" She swung back on Con. "So what? I've explained to him, and that's all there is to it. Why should you make it your business? You're not the master here yet, and as far as *I'm* concerned you never will be!"

"Julie!" I said sharply. "That's enough!"

They ignored me. Grandfather thrust his head forward, his eyes intent under scowling brows. "And just what do you mean by that?"

"Just," said Julie, "that this is my home, and Con—why, Con doesn't even *belong* here! And I'm beginning to think there isn't room for both of us, not any more! If I'm to be able to go on coming here—"

Grandfather slammed the cards down on the table in front of him. "And now, perhaps you'll let me speak! What you appear to forget, all of you, is that this is *my* house . . . still! Oh, I know you think I'm old, and sick, and that I'll go at any moment; I'm not a fool, that may be true, and by heaven, from the sort of scene you've made tonight, you appear to be eager to see the last of me! No, keep quiet, you've said enough; you've had a shaking, and I'll excuse you for that reason, and we'll say no more, but let me make this clear; this is my house, and while I'm alive I'll expect civil conduct in it—or you, Julie, and you, Connor, can both of you go elsewhere! And now I'm going to bed." And he put shaky hands to the arms of his chair.

Julie said raggedly, on a sob, "I'm sorry, Grandfather. I—I am a bit shaken up, I guess. I didn't mean to upset you. I don't want any food, Annabel. I'm going upstairs."

She turned past Con as if he didn't exist, and ran out of the room.

Con hadn't moved. It wasn't until that moment, when we were all looking at him, that I realized that, since he had come in, he hadn't spoken. His face seemed to have emptied even of anger, and gone blank. His eyes looked unfocussed.

"Well?" said Grandfather, harshly. "What are you waiting for?"

Con turned on his heel without a word, and went back across the hall. The baize door whispered itself shut behind him.

I stooped over Grandfather's chair. "Darling, don't upset yourself. Julie's a bit strung-up tonight; she's more shaken than she knows . . . and Con . . . Con's been working far too hard, you know he has, and I guess he's tired. It wasn't very sensible of him to tackle Julie, but if they hadn't both been a bit edgy, it wouldn't have come to anything. I expect they'll apologize in the morning."

He looked up at me, almost vaguely, as if the effort of that last speech had exhausted him. He looked very old, and tired, and almost as if he didn't quite know who I was. He said, muttering it to himself rather than to me, "Always the same. Always the same. Too highly strung, that's what it is, your mother always said so; and Julie's the same. History repeats itself." The faded eyes focussed on me then. "Annabel. Should have married Con in the first place, as I wanted. Settled the pair of you. Settled this. I'm going to bed."

I bent to help him rise, but as soon as he was on his feet he shook me off almost pettishly. "I can manage, I can manage. No, don't come with me. I don't want a pack of women. And that goes for you, too, Lisa. Good God, d'you think I can't see myself to bed?"

He went slowly to the door. I thought, he really is old; the tallness, and the sudden flashes of energy are what deceive us. . . . Something closed round me that might have been loneliness, or fear. . . .

He went out. Lisa and I were left looking at one another.

I remember thinking, with something like a shock, one forgets she's there; she heard all that; she heard what was said to Con. . . .

She had put her work composedly away. For all she showed it, the scene might never have taken place. As she moved towards the door, I said quickly, "He meant it, you know. I wouldn't upset him by saying anything else."

"I wasn't going to. I'm going to bed. Good night."

It didn't even seem strange at the time that it was Lisa who should go unconcernedly upstairs, and I who should look for Con.

He was in the kitchen, sitting in the rocking chair by the range, pulling on his gumboots. His face still wore that blind, shuttered look that was so unlike him. He glanced up briefly, then down again.

I said, "Con, don't pay any attention. She's upset because she and Donald quarrelled, and she missed seeing him tonight. She didn't mean a thing. She doesn't really think those things, I'm sure."

"It's my experience," said Con woodenly, thrusting his foot down into the boot and dragging it on, "that when people are upset they say exactly what they do think. She was quite startlingly explicit, wasn't she?"

I said, without quite realizing what I was saying, "Don't let it hurt you."

"Hurt me?" He looked up again at that. The blue eyes held an odd expression; something puzzled, perhaps, along with a glitter I didn't like. Then he smiled, a deliberately charming smile that made goose-pimples run along my spine. "You can't know how funny that is, Annabel, my sweet."

"Well, my dear," I said calmly, "funny or not, try to see the thing in proportion. I don't know if anyone told you, but Julie and Bill Fenwick were involved in a sort of minor accident tonight. That's what made her late, and distressed her so much. Bill, too—his car was damaged, so he wouldn't be in too sweet a mood. It'll blow over."

"What makes you explain to me?" He stood up and reached for the jacket that hung on the back of the door. "It's none of my business. I don't belong here. Lisa and I are only the hired help."

"Where are you going?"

"To the buildings."

"Oh, Con, it's late. You've done enough. Aren't you tired?"

"Flaked out. But there's something wrong with the cooler, and I'll have to get it put right." That quick, glittering look again. "I suppose even Julie would be content to let that be my business? Or would it be interfering too much with the running of her home?"

"Con, for pity's sake—"

"Sweet of you to come and bind up the wounds, girl dear, but I assure you they don't go deep."

"Are you sure?" His hand was already on the door latch. I said, "Listen. I ought not to tell you, but I'm going to. You've no need to worry any more."

He stopped, as still as a lizard when a shadow falls across it. Then he turned. "What d'you mean?"

"You do belong here. You've made your place . . . the way you said . . . with your two hands; and you do belong. That's all I—ought to say. You understand me. Let it go at that."

There was a silence. The shutters were up again in his face. It was impossible to guess what he was thinking, but I should have known. He said at length, "And the money? The capital?" Silence. "Did he tell you?"

I nodded.

"Well?"

"I don't know if I ought to say any more."

"Don't be a fool. He would have told us all, himself, tonight, only that damned girl made a scene."

"I still don't think I should."

He made a movement of such violent impatience that I was startled into remembering the perilous volcano-edge of the last few days. I had gone so far; let us have peace, I thought.

He was saying, savagely, in a low voice, "Whose side are you on? By God, you've had me wondering, you're so thick with Julie and the old man! If you've started any thoughts of feathering your own nest—! How do I know I can trust you? What right have you got to keep this to yourself?"

"Very well. Here it is. It comes out much as you'd expected, except that, nominally, very little of the capital comes to you."

"How's that?" His gaze was brilliant now, fixed, penetrating.

"He's divided it between Julie and me, except for a small sum, which you get outright. He didn't say how much that was. With you inheriting the property over our heads, he thought that was only fair." I went on to tell him what Grandfather had said to me. "The major part is divided into three, as we'd expected, with two-thirds of it nominally mine. That can be passed to you, just as we planned." I smiled. "Don't forget the blackmail's mutual."

He didn't smile back. He seemed hardly to be listening. "Julie. Will she fight the will? She'll have grounds."

"I'm sure she won't. She doesn't want the place."

"No, she just thinks I should be out of it." He turned away, abruptly. "Well, since the boy's not afraid of hard work, he'd better go out and get on with it, hadn't he?"

"Con, wait a minute—"

"Good night."

He went. I stayed where I was for a moment, frowning after him. For heaven's sake, I thought, suddenly irritable, did I have to add to the tangle by feeling sorry for Con as well? Con was perfectly capable of taking care of himself; always had been; had always had to be . . . I shook myself impatiently. Con, let's face it, was a tough customer. Keep that straight, and keep out of it. . . .

I went slowly upstairs, and stood on the landing for a few moments, wondering if it would be better to see Julie now, or wait till morning.

I had tried to set Con's mind at rest, with no very conspicuous success; had I the right to give Donald's confidence away, in an attempt to do the same for Julie? More urgent still was the other problem; how much to tell her of the truth about my own situation. Something had to be told her, I knew that; I hadn't yet decided how much, but it was imperative that she should be made to realize, a little more clearly, the kind of person Con was, and of what he was capable.

I hovered there for some time, between her door and my own, before it occurred to me that, by seeing her now, I could probably kill
two birds with one stone: if her mind were cleared with regard to
Donald, she would happily leave the Whitescar field open for Con. Let
us have peace. . . .

I went to the door of her room and knocked softly. There was no
reply. No light showed under the door, or from the adjacent bathroom.

She could surely not be in bed yet? I tapped again and said softly,
"Julie; it's me, Annabel."

No answer. As I stood, irresolute, I heard a soft step in the passage
beside me. Lisa's voice said, calmly,

"She's gone."

I looked at her blankly. "What?"

She smiled. " 'History repeats itself,' he said, didn't he? She's run
out on us."

"Don't be absurd!" I was so shocked that I said it very angrily. She
only shrugged, a slight uncaring gesture of the heavy shoulders.

"I found her room empty. Look."

Reaching past me, she pushed the door open, and switched on the
light. For a second it felt like an intolerable invasion of privacy, then
I saw that, indeed, the bedroom was deserted. Julie had made no attempt to get ready for bed. Even the curtains were undrawn, and this
emphasized the vacant look of the room.

"Look," repeated Lisa. I followed her pointing finger, and saw the
pretty high-heeled sandals tossed anyhow on the floor. "You see? She's
changed into flat ones."

"But she may not have gone *out*."

"Oh yes, she has. Her door was standing wide when I came upstairs,
and then I saw her from my window. She went over the bridge."

"Over the bridge?" I went swiftly to the window. The moon was
not yet strong, and the narrow footbridge that led from the garden
gate could barely be seen in the diffused lights from the house. "But
why?" I swung round. "Lisa, you *were* joking, weren't you? She can't
possibly really have—oh, no!" This as I pulled open the wardrobe
door. "Her things are here."

"Don't worry. She won't have gone far. No such luck."

So the scene in the drawing-room had gone home. I shut the wardrobe door with a sharp little click. "But where can she have gone? If
she only wanted to escape—go for a moonlight walk—surely she'd have

gone into the river meadows where you can see your way, or along towards Forrest Hall?"

"Heaven knows. Why worry about a silly girl's nonsense? She'll have
run off to cry on her young man's shoulder, as likely as not."

"But that's ridiculous!"

She shrugged again. "Girls are fools at nineteen."

"So they are."

"In any case, I saw her go."

"But it's miles to West Woodburn!"

Something sharpened for the first time in her gaze. "West Woodburn? I was thinking of Nether Shields."

"Good heavens," I said impatiently, "Bill Fenwick never came into
it, poor chap! I thought you understood that, when you prodded her
about Donald Seton tonight."

"I didn't know. I wondered." Her voice was as composed and unin-
terested as ever.

Something I didn't yet recognize as fear shook me with a violent
irritation. "Wherever she's gone, I don't much care for the idea of her
wandering about the countryside at this time of night! If it *was* either
West Woodburn or Nether Shields, you'd think she'd have taken the
car!"

"When Con has the key in his pocket?"

"Oh. No, I see. But if she'd waited to see me—"

"And with you," said Lisa, "talking to Con in the kitchen?"

I stared at her for a moment, uncomprehendingly. Then I said, "For
goodness' sake, Julie couldn't be so stupid! Do you mean to say she
thought I was ganging up on her? With Con? Just how young and silly
can you get?"

My sharp exasperation was partly induced by the fact that I hardly
understood my own motives in following Con to the kitchen. When
Lisa laughed, suddenly and uncharacteristically, I stared at her for a moment, blankly, before I said slowly, "Yes, I see that that's funny."

"What did you say to Con?"

"Nothing much. I wanted to apologize for Julie, but he was in a
hurry."

"A hurry?"

"He was on his way out."

The toffee-brown eyes touched mine for a moment. "Oh?" said Lisa.
"Well, I shouldn't wait up. Good night."

Left to myself, I crossed again to the window. There was no sign

of movement from the garden, or the river path. I strained my eyes
for the glimpse of a light coat returning through the trees. Down to
my right I could see the reflection of the lights from the byres where
Con was working, and hear the hum of machinery. The garden below me was in darkness.

I believe I was trying to clear my mind, to think of the problem
as it now faced me—Julie and Donald, Con and Lisa—but for some
reason, standing there staring into the dark, I found I was thinking
about Adam Forrest's hands. . . . Some seconds later I traced the
thought to its cause; some memory of that first sunlit evening when
I had seen the cat pounce in the long grass, and some creature had
cried out with pain and fear.

There had been bees in the roses, then; now it was the steady hum
of machinery that filled the darkness, unaltering, unfaltering in its beat.
. . . *History repeats itself*, Lisa had said.

Something tugged at the skirts of my mind, jerked me awake. A formless, frightening idea became certainty. Julie, running to change her
shoes, seizing a coat, perhaps, creeping softly downstairs, and out . . .
Con, in the kitchen, hearing the door, seeing her pass the window
. . . Then, the girl running along the river in the dark, up the steep
path where the high bank shelved over the deep pool . . . that pool
where the rocks could stun you, and the snags hold you down. . . .

He was on his way out, I had said, and Lisa had given me that look.
Well, I shouldn't wait up.

The machinery ran smoothly from the byre. The lights were on.

I didn't wait to grab a coat. I slid out of the room, and ran like a
hare for the stairs.

CHAPTER

THIRTEEN

"O where hae ye been, my handsome young man?"

Ballad: *Lord Randal.*

I didn't even look to see if Con were in the buildings after all. The something that had taken over from my reasoning mind told me he wouldn't be. I had no time to make assurance double sure. I ran across the yard, and down the narrow river path towards the bridge. The wicket at the end of the bridge was standing open, its white paint making it insubstantial in the dusk, like a stage prop.

It was really only a few minutes since Julie had left the house. Con would hardly have had time to go up-river as far as the stepping stones at the end of the lane, where he could cross, and wait to intercept her on the path above the pool. But the impression of haste that he had given in the kitchen stayed with me as a spur. I ran.

The path sloped up steeply, runged like a ladder with the roots of trees. The ground was dry and hard. Above me the trees hung in still, black clouds, not a leaf stirring. It was very dark. I stumbled badly, stumbled again, and slowed to a walk, my outstretched hands reaching for the dimly seen, supporting stems of the trees. Julie would have had to go slowly, too; she could not have got so very far. . . .

I thought I heard a movement ahead of me, and suddenly realized what in my fear I hadn't thought of before. There was no need for silence here. If it were Con, and he knew I was coming, it might be enough.

I called shrilly, "Julie! Julie! Con!"

Then, not far ahead of me, I heard Julie cry out. It wasn't a scream, just a short, breathless cry, almost unvoiced, that broke off short as if she'd been hit in the throat.

I called her name again, my own cry echoing the same sound of fear and shock, and ran forward as fast as I dared, through the whipping boughs of alder and hazel, and out into the little clearing above the pool.

Julie was lying on the ground, at a point where the path skirted the drop to the pool. She lay half on her back, with one arm flung wide, and her head at the brink of the drop. I saw the loose fall of her hair, pale in the moonlight, and the still paler blur of her face. Con was beside her, down on one knee. He was stooping over her to take hold of her.

I cried, "Julie! No!" and ran out from under the trees, only to stop short as a shadow detached itself from the other side of the clearing, and crossed the open space in four large strides. Before Con could so much as turn his head, the newcomer's hand shot out, and dragged him back from Julie's body. There was a startled curse from Con, which was swallowed up in the sounds of a brief, sharp struggle, and the crashing of hazel bushes.

After the first moment of paralyzing shock, I had run straight to Julie. Her eyes were shut, but she seemed to be breathing normally. I tried quickly, desperately, straining my eyes in the dimness, to see if there were any bruises or marks of injury on her, but could find none. Where she had fallen, though the ground was hard, there was a thickish mat of dog's mercury, and her head lay in a spongy cushion of primrose leaves. I pushed the soft hair aside with unsteady gentle fingers, and felt over her scalp.

Her rescuer trod behind me. I said, "She's all right, Adam. I think she's only fainted."

He sounded breathless, and I realized that he, too, had heard the cries, and come running. The noise that I had made must have masked his approach from Con. "What's going on?" he demanded. "Is this your cousin Julie? Who's the man?"

I said shortly, "My cousin Con."

"Oh." The change in his voice was subtle but perceptible. "What's he done to her?"

"Nothing, as far as I know. I think you've probably jumped the gun a bit. Is there any way of getting water from the river?"

"Are you trying to tell me—?"

"Be quiet," I said, "she's coming round."

Julie stirred, and gasped a little. Her eyes fluttered and opened fully, dark and alive where her face had been a sealed blank. They turned to me. "Annabel? Oh, Annabel. . . ."

"Hush now, it's all right. I'm here."

Behind me came the crash and rustle of hazel boughs. Julie said, "Con—"

"It's all right, Julie, nothing's going to happen. Mr. Forrest's here with us. Lie quiet."

She whispered, like a child, "Con was going to kill me."

I heard Adam draw in his breath. Then Con's voice said, rather thickly, from behind us, "Forrest? What the hell was that in aid of?"

He was on his feet, not quite steady, perhaps, with his shoulder against a tree. He put the back of a hand up to his mouth. "What the bloody hell do you think you were doing? Have you gone mad?"

Adam said quietly, "Did you hear what she said?"

"I heard. And why you should choose to listen to crap of that sort, without—"

"I also heard her cry out. Don't you think that perhaps it's you who've got the explaining to do?"

Con brought his hand away from his face, and I saw him looking down as if he could feel blood on it. He said violently, "Don't be a damned fool. What sort of story's that? Kill her? Are you crazy, or just drunk?"

Adam regarded him for a moment. "Come off it. For a start, you can tell us why she fainted."

"How the devil do I know? She probably thought I was a ghost. I hadn't spoken a damned word to her, before she went flat out on the path."

I said to Julie, "Is this true?"

The scarcely perceptible movement of her head might have meant anything. She had shut her eyes again, and turned her face in to my shoulder. Con said angrily, "Why don't you tell them it's true, Julie?" He swung back to the silent Adam. "The simple truth of the matter is, Julie and I had words tonight, never mind why, but some pretty hard things were said. Afterwards I found out that she'd been involved in a car accident earlier in the evening, and I was sorry I'd made the scene with her. I'd seen her go flying out of the house, and I knew how upset she'd been when she went upstairs earlier . . . Annabel, blast it all, tell him this is true!"

Adam glanced down at me. "Apart from Con's feelings," I said, "to which I've never had a clue, it's quite true."

"So," said Con, "it occurred to me to come across and intercept her, and tell her I was sorry for what had happened, only no sooner did she see me in the path than she let out a screech like a frightened virgin, and keeled clean over. I went to see what was the matter, and the next thing was you were manhandling me into that damned bush. Don't worry, I'll take your apologies for granted, I suppose it was quite natural for you to think what you did. But *you*—" he addressed Julie on a scarcely conciliatory note—"it's to be hoped you'll see fit to stop making these damned silly accusations, Julie! I'm sorry I scared you, if that's what you want me to say, and I'm sorry if you've hurt yourself. Now for pity's sake try to get up, and I'll help Annabel take you home!"

But as he came towards us, Julie shrank a little against my shoulder. "Keep away from me!"

Con stopped. Adam was standing between him and Julie, and, though I couldn't see his expression, I realized he was at something of a loss. The situation seemed to be hovering uncertainly between melodrama and farce. Then Con said, on a note of pure exasperation, "Oh, for God's sake!" and turned on his heel and left the clearing. We could hear him, unhurrying, making his way downstream towards the bridge.

The silence in which he left the three of us was the silence of pure anticlimax. I had a strong feeling that, whatever had happened to-night, Con Winslow had walked off with the honours of war.

Adam started to say something then, I think to ask Julie a question, but I cut across it. "That can wait. I think we'd better get Julie back to the house. Con told you the truth; she's had a shock tonight, and now a bad fright, and the sooner we get her to bed the better. Can you get up, my dear?"

"I think so. Yes, I'm all right."

Between us, Adam and I helped her to her feet. She still seemed dazed, and was shivering a little. I pulled her coat close round her. "Come on, darling, can you walk? We must get you back. Where were you going, anyway?"

"To Donald, of course." This in the tone of one answering a very stupid question.

"Oh. Well, you'll see him tomorrow. Come along now, and don't worry, you're all right with Adam and me."

She responded to my urging arm, and went forward across the clearing, but so uncertainly and slowly that Adam's arm soon came round over mine to support her.

"I'd better carry you," he said. "It'd be quicker."

"I'm too heavy," protested Julie, still in that small, shaky voice quite unlike her own.

"Nonsense." He took her up into his arms, and quite unselfconsciously she put her own round his neck and held on. I went ahead of them to hold back the swinging branches, and, when we got to the bridge, opened the gate and held it. Con, even in his anger, had taken the trouble to shut and latch it.

The back door was standing open. The kitchen was dark, and the house seemed quiet. At least, I thought, snapping on the light, there was no sign of Con.

Adam paused inside the door, to say a little breathlessly, "Shall I take her straight upstairs? I can manage."

Julie lifted her head, blinking in the light. "I'm all right now. Really I am. Put me down, I'm fine."

He set her gently on her feet, but kept an arm round her. I was thankful to see that, though still pale, she didn't look anything like as drawn as she had seemed in the dead light of the moon. She managed a little smile for Adam. "Thanks very much for . . . everything. I'm sorry to be a nuisance. All right, Annabel, I'll go to bed, but may I just sit down a minute first and get warm?"

I said, "Put her in the rocking chair near the stove, Adam. I'll get some brandy. Would you like a drink?"

"Thank you. Whisky, if you have it."

When I brought the drinks in, Julie was in the rocking chair, leaning back as if exhausted, but looking every moment more like her usual self. Adam stood by the table, watching me. At the sight of his expression, my heart sank.

"Mix your own, will you, Adam?" I said. "Here you are, honey."

"I loathe brandy," said Julie, with a healthy flicker of rebellion.

"You'll take it and like it." I lifted the cover off the stove, and slid the kettle over the hot plate. "And a hot-water bottle in your bed, and some soup or something just as soon as I get you there." I glanced at Adam. "It's no wonder she fainted; the silly little ass wouldn't have any supper, and all this on top of a mishap to the car she was in, and a mad quarrel with Con. Julie, there's some of tonight's soup left over. Can you take it? It was very nice."

"As a matter of fact," said Julie, showing signs of abandoning the rôle of invalid, "I should adore it."

"Then finish your brandy while I put the soup to heat, then I'll take you up to bed."

Adam, if he heard this very palpable hint, gave no sign. As I brought the pan of soup in, he was saying to Julie, "You're beginning to look a little better. How do you feel?"

"Not a thing wrong with me, except hunger."

"You didn't hurt yourself—give yourself a knock or anything—when you fell?"

"I—I don't think I can have. I can't feel anything." She prodded herself experimentally, and then smiled up at him. "I think I'll live."

There was no answering smile on his face. "Then can you tell us now," he asked, "why you said that your cousin was going to kill you?"

I set the soup pan on the stove with a rap. "I don't think Julie's fit to talk about it now. I saw what happened, and—"

"So did I. I also heard what she said." His eyes met mine across Julie's head. They were as hard as slate, and his voice was inimical. I saw Julie look quickly from the one to the other of us, and even, in that moment, spared a flicker of pity for a child's dead romance.

"You seem uncommonly concerned," he said, "to stop her telling her story."

"You've heard what happened," I said steadily, "and there's nothing to be gained by discussing it now. If we talk much longer there's a chance we'll disturb Grandfather, and he's had more than enough upset for one night. I know that most of what Con told you was true, and almost certainly the last bit was, as well. Julie saw him, got a sudden fright, and fainted. I'm fully prepared to believe that's just what happened."

"I'm sure you are," said Adam, and I saw Julie turn her head at his tone.

"For heaven's sake!" I said crudely. "You're surely not *still* trying to make out it was attempted murder!"

I heard Julie take in a little breath. "Annabel—"

"It's all right, darling, I know you said it, but you didn't know just what you were saying. He'd half scared you to death, looming up like that through the trees. Now, if you're ready—"

"Will you please let your cousin speak for herself?" said Adam.

I looked at him for a few moments. "Very well. Julie?"

Julie looked doubtfully up at him. "Well, it's true," she said. Her voice held a puzzled uncertainty that was uncommonly convincing. "I know I *said* he was trying to kill me, and I—I think I must really have thought so, for a moment, though why, I can't quite tell you." She broke off and knitted her brows. "But actually, it happened just as Con said, and

Annabel. . . . I'm not lying, Mr. Forrest, really I'm not. He—he never touched me. I know it sounds silly, but I'm sure I'd never have fainted if it hadn't been for the car accident, and then not having anything to eat . . . and then when I saw him, suddenly, like that, in the dark—" she gave a tremulous smile—"and, let's face it, I *was* feeling a bit wary of him, because I'd said some pretty foul things to him, and . . . well, that's all I remember."

I said, "Do you want Mr. Forrest to telephone the police, and report what happened?"

"Police?" Her eyes widened. "What on earth for?"

"In case it happens to be true that Con meant to kill you."

"*Con?* Annabel, how crazy can you get? Why, you don't really think—?"

"No, honey, no. But I think that's the way Mr. Forrest's mind's working. He threw Con into a bush."

"*Did* you?" Julie sounded shocked, then, lamentably, began to giggle. "Oh dear, thank you very much, but—poor Con! Next time he really *will* try to murder me, and I don't blame him!"

I didn't dare look at Adam. I said hurriedly, to Julie, "Darling, it's time you went upstairs, and don't make a *sound*. Adam, I'm most desperately sorry you've had all this—oh, my dear sweet *heaven*, the soup!"

It was hissing gently down the sides of the pan on to the top of the spotless stove. "Oh, Lisa's stove, and you should *never* let soup boil! It just shows—" as I seized a cloth and swabbed madly at the enamel—"that you shouldn't mix cooking and high drama. All this talk of murder—Adam, I'm *sorry*—"

"Think nothing of it." His face was wooden. "I'd better go." He turned to Julie. "Good night. I hope you'll feel quite all right in the morning." Then to me, "I hope my ill-advised attempts to help haven't made the soup quite undrinkable."

The door shut very softly behind him.

"Annabel!" said Julie. "Do you think he *meant* to be nasty?"

"I'm quite certain he did," I said.

The cooler-house was clean, shining and empty. The floors had been swilled some time earlier, and were not yet dry; they gleamed under the harsh, strong light from the unshaded bulbs. Aluminum shone coldly, and enamel glared white and sterile. The machinery hummed, and this, since there was nobody in sight, gave the place an even barer, emptier appearance.

I stepped over a twist of black hosepipe, and looked through an open door into the byre. There, too, the lights glared on emptiness. "Con?"

No reply. I crossed the wet floor and threw the switch over. The machinery stopped. The silence seemed to surge in, frightening, thick, solid. Somewhere a tap dripped, an urgent rapping on metal. I went back to the door of the byre and reached for the light switch. My steps sounded incredibly, frighteningly loud, and so did the snap of the switch as I clicked it off. I turned back into the cooler-house.

Adam came quietly in and stood there, just inside the doorway. I stopped dead. My heart began to jerk. I must have looked white with fatigue, and as guilty as sin. I said nothing.

After a while he said, "Covering up?"

"What?"

"For your accomplice. You knew what I meant, didn't you?"

"I suppose I did."

"Well?"

"Look," I said, striving to sound no more than reasonable, "I know what you think, but, believe it or not, we told you the truth! For goodness' sake, don't try to take this thing any further!"

"Do you really think I can leave it there, after tonight?"

"But nothing *happened* tonight!"

"No, because I was there, and possibly because you were, too."

"You surely can't think that I—!" I checked myself. "But you heard what Julie told you."

"I heard what you persuaded her to say. I also heard her say that Con was going to kill her."

"She admitted she had nothing to go by! She was scared of him, and got a sudden fright—what's the use of going over and over it! You can see for yourself how seriously Julie's taking it now!"

"She trusts you. That's something I find particularly hard to take. She's another fool, it seems, but she at least has the excuse of being young, and knowing nothing against you."

I looked at him rather blankly.

He gave a tight little smile. "I only mean that Julie has no reason not to trust you, whereas I had, being merely a fool 'sick of an old passion.' Well, that's over. You can't expect to take any more advantage of my folly, now."

"But I've *told* you—"

"You've told me very loud and clear, you and Con. And Julie has echoed you. You showed a touching family solidarity. All right, you can tell me three more things. One, why Connor went across the river at all."

"He explained that. He was going—"

"Oh yes, I forgot. He was going to apologize to her, wasn't he?" The irony bit. "Well, we'll skip that. Now tell me why he left the machinery running while he did so? I heard it; it was going all the time, and the lights were on. Odd, wouldn't you say? A careful type like that, who shuts gates behind him even when he's just been chucked into a bush and accused of murder?"

"There's—there's nothing in that. Maybe someone else was here."

"Who else, at this time of night? No one's here now. But we'll skip that, too. The third thing is, why did you follow Julie yourself?"

"Well, obviously, I didn't like the idea of her going out alone like that when she was so upset."

"Did you know Connor had gone to intercept her?"

"No, of course not! The lights were on in the byre, anyway. I thought he was working here."

"Then why," said Adam, "did you cry out—sounding so frightened, at that—as you ran up through the wood?"

"I—I heard her scream. Of course I was frightened!"

"You called out before she made a sound."

"Did I? I must have wanted to stop her, make her wait for me."

"Why, in that case, did you call 'Julie, Julie! *Con!*'"

Silence.

"So you did expect him to be there?"

"I thought he might be."

"And you were frightened."

"Yes," I said, "yes, yes, yes! And don't ask me why, because I've told you before! It was you who said it was absurd when I told you Con might be violent."

"I know I did. I thought you were exaggerating. Which is one of the reasons I so stupidly believed you, when you said you could look after Julie. Well, now we know better."

"Listen, Adam—"

"I've done enough listening. Look at this from my point of view. You told me you're in some racket or other which will turn out right in the end. You persuaded me to keep out of it, God knows how, but you did. Now, tonight, this happens. Because I chanced to be there, no harm was done. But you admit that Connor may have intended to do harm. That he may be dangerous."

"I've always admitted that."

"Very well. But the time has come for me to stop trusting you, you must see that. In the first place, I had no reason to, except that . . . I had no reason to. Now after this—" a gesture took in the sterile, gleaming shed, and the now silent machinery—"I have less than none."

I said, after a pause, "Well? I can't stop you. What are you going to do? Telephone the police? Tell them Con tried to frighten Julie to death? Even if you had some sort of case—which you haven't; even if Julie would charge Con—which she won't; even if you had me as a witness—which you haven't, what could you prove? Nothing, because there *is* nothing to prove. All you'd achieve would be a howling scandal, and Grandfather laid out, and all for nothing."

"I might count it an achievement to have made the police take a look at you."

"At me?" For a moment I regarded him blankly. "Oh, *that.*"

It must have been obvious that I genuinely hadn't realized for a moment what he was talking about. I thought he was disconcerted, but he said steadily, "I promised I'd warn you. Here's the warning, now. I'll give you twenty-four hours, as from now, to make your break with Connor, and leave. I don't care what story you tell, or what excuse you offer, but you must break this thing up, and go. And don't imagine that, in the event of Mr. Winslow's death, you can come back. I promise you that if 'Annabel' is a legatee in his Will, and turns up to lay claim to a single penny of it, I'll have you investigated so thoroughly that you won't see the outside of Durham Gaol for ten years. And what will happen to Connor and his sister, I neither know nor care. Good night."

"Adam!"

He paused in the doorway, and looked back.

"Adam—" Rigid self-control made my voice colourless almost to stupidity. "Wait just a moment. Don't go. Listen—"

"I've done enough listening." In the harsh light his face was as hard as stone, and as strange. There was nothing in it but weariness and contempt. "I'm afraid I'm no longer in the mood to play this extraordinary game of yours. I meant what I said, Miss Grey. Good night."

In the silence after he had gone, the tap dripped, a small, maddening sound, like a reiterated note on a harpsichord, a little out of tune.

I found I was leaning against the chilly metal of the cooler. I felt cold, with a sweating, empty slackness, like someone who has just vomited. My brain felt bruised, and incapable of any thought except a formless desire to get to bed, and sleep.

"Well, by God!" said Con, just behind me.

Even then, I turned slowly, and stared at him with what must have been a blank and stupid look. "Where were you?" Then, my voice tautening, "How much did you hear?"

He laughed, and lounged out of the inner shed into the light. He looked quite composed, even overcomposed, and his eyes were brilliant and his expression confident. His mouth was cut a little at the corner, and a graze showed swollen, but it only served to lend him a sort of extra rakish attraction.

He came close to me, and stood there, hands deep in pockets, swaying backwards and forwards on his heels, graceful and collected. "Oh, I kept my distance! I thought that Forrest and I hadn't much to say to one another, girl dear. And I thought that maybe you'd handle him a bit better than I could. And it seems I was right, me jewel. Was it you switched the engines off?"

"Yes. As an alibi for murder it wasn't bad, on the spur of the moment, Con."

The brilliant eyes narrowed momentarily. "Who's talking about murder now?"

"I am. You switched the engines on, and the lights, so that they could be seen and heard from the house, and then you ran upstream and across the stepping stones, and met Julie in the clearing."

"And if I did?" The bright eyes were narrow and dangerous. He had stopped swaying. Suddenly I realized what I should have known even before he came so near. He was drunk. I could smell whisky on his breath. "And if I did?" he said gently.

"Adam was right. You did mean to kill her there, Con."

There was a little silence. His eyes never wavered. He said again, softly, "And if I did?"

I said steadily, "Only this, that if you thought I'd stand for anything like that, you must be a fool and an imbecile. Or don't you think at all? What sort of person d'you think I am? You said yourself not long ago that you knew I was straight, heaven help us, because otherwise you'd have been too scared of my trying to twist you in what we're doing. Well, you blundering criminal fool, did you really think I'd see you kill Julie, and not send the whole works sky-high, myself included?"

He was laughing now, completely unabashed. "All right, me darlin', murder's off the cards, is it? But you know, I'm not the fool you make me out to be. You weren't supposed to know anything about it. Oh, you might have suspected all you liked in the morning, when her poor drowned body came up on the shingle, but what could you prove? You'd have kept quiet, and held your grandpa's hand, wouldn't you?"

"Oh, my God," I said, "and to think I felt sorry for you tonight, because you were so much alone."

"Well," said Con cheerfully, "there's no harm done, is there, except a little keepsake from Forrest." He touched his cheek. "Did you manage to shut the bastard up after all?"

"I don't know."

He had begun to rock on his heels again. Somewhere behind the brilliant gaze was amusement, and wariness, and a speculation that for some reason made my skin crawl.

"'Adam,' wasn't it, now? How do you come to be calling him 'Adam,' girl dear?"

My heart gave a jerk that sickened me. I said, and was relieved to find that my voice sounded nothing but normal, and very tired, "That was one thing you and Lisa slipped up on. They must have got to Christian names. When I went today to get the strawberries, he called me 'Annabel' . . . And now I'm going in. I can't talk to you tonight. I'm tired, and you're in the wrong kind of mood. Sufficient unto the day. You're luckier than you deserve that nothing's happened; and I can't even guess what Adam Forrest'll do tomorrow, but, just at the moment, I don't care."

"That's my girl." He spoke a little thickly. Before I realized what he was doing, his hands came out and he took me by the shoulders. His eyes between the beautiful lashes were sapphire-blue and laughing, and only slightly liquid with drink. "It's beautiful you are, acushla, did you know?"

"I could hardly avoid it, with Julie in front of me all day."

His teeth showed. "Good for you. But you take the shine out of Julie, bejasus and you do. Look, now—"

I stood stiffly under his hands. "Con, you're drunk, and you're getting maudlin, and I loathe this stage Irishry anyway. If you think you can plan to murder Julie, and then bat off and drink yourself stupid, and then come and blarney me with a lot of phony Irish, you can damned well think again. And—" this as he moved, still smiling, and his hands tightened—"if you try to kiss me, that'll be another slap on the jaw you'll get, so I'm giving you fair warning."

His hands slackened, and dropped. He had flushed a little, but he still smiled. I said levelly, "Now, for heaven's sake, Con, get to bed and sleep it off, and pray to every saint in heaven that Adam Forrest chooses to hold his tongue. And take it from me, this is the last time I cover up any single thing for you. Good night."

As I reached the doorway I looked back. He was standing looking after me with an expression I could only read as amusement and affection. He looked handsome and normal and quite sober and very nice.

He smiled charmingly, "Good night, Annabel."

I said shortly, "Don't forget to put the light out," and went quickly across the yard.

CHAPTER

FOURTEEN

I wrote a letter to my love,
  And on the way I lost it;
One of you has picked it up,
  And put it in her pocket.

Traditional.

I hardly slept that night. I lay, it seemed for hours, watching the wheeling moonlight outside the open curtains, while my mind, too exhausted for sleep, scratched and fretted its way round the complications of this absurd, this crazy masquerade.

I suppose I dozed a little, for I don't remember when the moon went down and the light came. I remember realizing that the dark had slackened, and then, later, a blackbird fluted a piercing stave of song alone in the cold dawn. After he fell silent there was a deep hush, for the space of a long breath, and then, suddenly, all the birds in the world were chattering, whistling, jargoning in a mad medley of sound; the dawn chorus. I found myself smiling. It was an ill wind, indeed, that blew no good.

My moment of delight must have worked like the Ancient Mariner's spontaneous prayer, for soon afterwards I fell deeply asleep. When I looked at the window again it was full daylight, and the birds were singing normally in the lilacs. I felt wide awake, with that floating bodiless calm that sometimes comes after a night of scanty sleeping. I got up, and went over to the window.

It must be still very early. The dew was thick, grey almost as frost, on grass and leaf. The air smelled thin and cool, like polished silver. It was very still, with the promise of close and thundery heat to come. Far away, from the direction of West Lodge, I heard a cock crow thinly. Through a gap in the trees to my left I saw the distant glint of chestnut, where the Forrest colt moved, cropping the wet grass.

Sometimes, I think, our impulses come not from the past, but from the future. Before I had even clearly thought what I was doing, I had slipped into narrow grey trousers and a pale yellow shirt, had dashed cold water on my face, run a comb through my hair, and was out of my room, sliding downstairs as quietly as a shadow. The house slept on, undisturbed. I tiptoed out through the kitchen, and ten minutes later, bridle in hand, I was letting myself in through the gate of the meadow where Rowan grazed.

I kept clear of the gap in the trees, so that, even if someone else were awake at Whitescar, I couldn't be seen. I moved quietly along under the hedge, towards the horse. He had raised his handsome head as soon as I appeared, and now watched intently, ears pricked forward. I stopped under the guelder rose, where there was a gap in the hedge and a couple of railings. I sat on the top one and waited, dangling the bridle. The panicles of guelder rose, thick-coloured as Devonshire cream, spilled dew onto my shoulder, chilly through the thin shirt. I rubbed the damp patch, and shifted along the railing, so that the early sunshine struck my shoulders.

Rowan was coming. He paced forward slowly, with a sort of grave beauty, like a creature out of the pages of poetry written when the world was young and fresh, and always just waking to an April morning. His ears were pricked so far forward that the tips almost met, his eyes large and dark, and mildly curious. His nostrils were flared, and their soft edges flickered as he tested the air towards me. The long grass swished under his hoofs, scattering the dew in bright, splashing showers. The buttercup petals were falling, and his hoofs and fetlocks were flecked gold with them, plastered there by the dew.

Then he was a yard away, pausing, just a large, curious hardly broken young horse staring at me with dark eyes that showed, at the edge, that unquiet hint of white. I said, "Hi, Rowan," but I didn't move.

He stretched his neck, blew gustily, then came on. Still I didn't move. His ears twitched back, forward again, sensitive as snails' horns, as radar antennae. His nostrils were blown wide, puffing sweet breath at my legs, at my waist, at my neck. He mouthed my sleeve, then took it in his teeth and tugged it.

I put a hand on his neck, and felt the muscles run and shiver along under the warm skin. I ran the hand up to his ears, and he bent his head, blowing at my feet. My hand slipped up to the long tangled forelock, and held it. I slid slowly off the fence bar, and he didn't try to move away, but put his head down and rubbed it violently up my body, jamming me back against the railings. I laughed at him and said softly, "You beauty, you love, you lovely boy, stand still now, quiet now . . ." and then turned him, with the hand on his forelock, till his quarters were against the railings, and his forehand free. Then with my other hand, still talking, I brought the bit up to his muzzle. "Come along now, my beauty, my darling boy, come along." The bit was between his lips and against his teeth. He held them shut against it for a few seconds; I thought he was going to veer away, but he didn't. He opened his teeth, and accepted the steel warm from my hand. The bit slipped softly back into the corners of his mouth, and the bridle slid over his ears; then the rein was looped round my arm and I was fastening the cheek strap, rubbing his ears, between his eyes, sliding my hand down the springy arch of his neck.

I mounted from the top of the fence, and he came up against it and stood as if he had done it every day of his life. Then he moved away from it smoothly and softly, and only when I turned him towards the length of the field did he begin to gather himself and dance, and bunch his muscles as if to defy me to hold him. I'm not, in fact, quite sure how I did. He went at a canter, that lengthened too quickly towards a gallop, to the far corner of the long meadow, where there was a narrow wicket giving on the flat grass of the river's edge. He was biddable enough at the wicket, so that I guessed that Adam Forrest had taken him this way, and taught him his manners at the gates. But, once through the wicket, he danced again, and the sun danced and dazzled too, down through the lime leaves, and the feel of his bare back warm and shifting with muscle between my thighs was exciting, so that I went mad all at once, and laughed, and said, "All right, have it your own way," and let him go; and he went, like a bat out of hell along the flat turf of the river's edge, with that smooth lovely motion that was as easy to sit as an armchair; and I wound my right hand in his mane and stuck on like a burr to his withers with too-long-disused muscles that began to ache before long, and I said, "Hi, Rowan, it's time we got back. I don't want to get you in a lather, or there'll be questions asked. . . ."

His ears moved back to my voice, and for a second or two after I began to draw rein, he resisted, leaning on the bit, and I wondered if I could manage to check and turn him. I slackened the bit for a moment to break his stride, and, as it broke, pulled him in. He came sweetly, ears flickering back to me, and then pointing again as he turned. I sang to him, mad now as the morning, "Oh, you beauty, you beauty, you love, home now, and steady. . . ."

We had come the best part of a mile, round the great curve of the river that led to West Lodge. I had turned him just in time. The chimneys of the Lodge were showing above the nearer trees. I spared a glance for them as the horse wheeled and cantered, sober and collected now, back along the river. His neck was damp, and I smoothed it, and crooned to him, and he flowed along smoothly and beautifully, and his ears twitched to my voice, and then, halfway to his own meadow, I drew him to a walk, and we paced soberly home as if he was a hack hired for the day, and bored with it, and there had been no few minutes of mad delight there along the sward. He arched his neck demurely and fiddled with the bit, and I laughed at him and let him have it, and when we came to the wicket he stopped and moved his quarters round for me to reach, as gentle and dainty as a dancer.

I said, "All right, sweetheart, that's all for today," and slid down off him and ducked under his neck to open the wicket. He pushed through, eager now for home. I turned to shut the wicket, and Rowan wheeled with me, and then snorted and threw up his head, and dragged hard at the rein I was holding.

I said, "Steady, beautiful! What's up?" And looked up to see Adam Forrest a yard away, waiting beside the wicket, watching me.

He had been hidden from me by the thick hawthorn hedge, but of course he would have heard Rowan's hoofs, and seen us coming from some way off. He was prepared, where I was not. I actually felt the colour leave my face, and stood stock still, in the act of latching the gate, like a child in some silly game, one hand stiffly held out, the other automatically holding the startled horse.

The moment of shock snapped, and passed. The wicket clicked shut, and Adam came forward a pace and took Rowan's bridle from me. I noticed then that he had brought a bridle himself; it hung from a post in the hedge beside him, and there was a saddle perched astride a rail.

It seemed a very long time before he spoke. I don't know what I expected him to say; I know that I had time to think of his reactions as well as my own; to imagine his resentment, shame, anger, bewilderment.

What he said was merely, "Why did you do it?"

The time had gone past for evasions and pretences; in any case Adam and I had always known rather too well what the other was thinking. I said merely, "I'd have thought that was obvious. If I'd known you were still at Forrest I'd never have come. When I found I had to face you, I felt caught, scared—oh, anything you like, and when you wouldn't just write it off and let me go, I suppose I got desperate.

Then you decided I was an impostor, and I was so shaken that on the spur of the moment I let you go on thinking it. It was—easier, as long as I could persuade you to keep quiet about me."

Between us the horse threw up his head and fidgeted with the bit. Adam was staring at me as if I were some barely decipherable manuscript he was trying to read. I added, "Most of what I told you was true. I wanted to come back, and try to make it up with Grandfather. I'd thought about it for some time, but I didn't think he'd want me back. What kept me away was the worst kind of pride, I know; but he's always rather played power-politics with money—he's terribly property-conscious, like a lot of his generation—and I didn't want to be taunted with just coming back to claim my share, or to put in my claim for Mother's money." I gave a little smile. "As a matter of fact, it *was* almost the first thing he said to me. Well, there it was, partly pride, partly not being able to afford the passage . . . and, apart from all those considerations, there was you."

I paused. "But after a bit I began to see things differently. I wanted desperately to come back to England, and I wanted not to be . . . completely cut off from my home any more. I didn't write; don't ask me why. I suppose it was the same impulse that makes you turn up unexpectedly, if you have to visit a house where you're not sure of your welcome; warning them gives people too much time to think of excuses, and be wary; whereas once you're on the doorstep they've got to welcome you. Maybe you don't know about such things, being a man, but I assure you it's quite commonly done, especially if you're a person who's never sure of their welcome, like me. And as for you, I—I thought I might be able to keep out of your way. I knew that . . . things . . . would be long since over for you, but I thought you'd understand why I felt I had to come back. If I had to meet you, I'd manage to let you know I'd only come on a visit, and was going to get a job elsewhere."

Rowan jerked his head, and the bit jingled. Adam seemed unconscious of the movement. I went on, "I'd saved a bit, and when Mrs. Grey—my last employer—died, she left me a little money, three hundred dollars, along with a few trinkets for keepsakes." I smiled briefly, thinking of the gold lighter, and the car permit left so carefully for Con and Lisa to find. "She was a cripple, and I'd been with her quite a time, as a sort of housekeeper-chauffeuse. I was very fond of her. Well, with the three hundred dollars, and my savings, I managed to pay for my passage, with something left over. I came straight up to

Newcastle from Liverpool, and got myself a room, and a temporary job. I waited a day or two, trying to nerve myself to come back and see how things were. Of course, for all I knew, Grandfather was dead. . . ."

Half absently I stooped and pulled a swatch of grass, and began to wisp the horse. Adam stood without moving; I had hardly looked at him. It was queer that when a part of your life, your very self, was dead, it could still hurt you, as they say a limb does still, after it has been cut off.

"I hadn't wanted to make too many inquiries, in case Con somehow got to hear of it. I'd even taken my rooms in the name of my late employer, Mrs. Grey. I didn't know what to do, how to make my approach. I wanted to apply to the lawyers for Mother's money, you see, only I wasn't sure if I dared risk Con's finding out I was home. Well, I waited a day or two, wondering what to do—"

"Just a minute." Adam, it seemed, was listening, after all. "Why should you not 'dare' let Connor know you were home?"

I ran the wisp along Rowan's neck, and said briefly, "He tried to kill me one night, along the river, just near where we found him with Julie."

He moved at that. "He *what?*"

"He'd wanted to marry me. Grandfather wanted it, too. You knew that. Con hadn't a hope then—or so he thought—of getting the property any other way, so he used to—to harry me a bit. Well, that night he threw a bit of a scene, and I wasn't just in the mood for it; I wasn't exactly tactful, and I made it a bit too clear that he hadn't a hope, then or ever, and . . . well, he lost his temper and decided to get rid of me. He chances his arm, does Con." I lifted my eyes, briefly, from my task. "That's how I guessed, last night, that he'd have gone to find Julie. That's why I followed her."

"Why did you never tell me?"

His tone was peremptory, proprietorial, exactly as it might have been eight years ago, when he had had the right.

"There was no chance. It happened the last night I was here. I was on my way home, after I'd left you in the summerhouse. You remember how late it was. You know how I always used to go over the river by the stepping stones, and then home by the path and the bridge, so no one would know I'd been to Forrest. It was just as well I bothered, because that night I ran into Con."

"Oh, my God."

"That was the—the other reason why I ran away. Grandfather took his part, you see. He'd been angry with me for months because I wouldn't look at Con, and there'd been scenes because he'd found I was staying out late, and I'd lied once or twice about where I'd been. He—I suppose it was natural, really—he used to storm at me, and say that if I ever got into trouble, I could go, and stay away. . . ." I smiled a little. "I think it was only talk and temper; it was a bit hard on Grandfather, being saddled with an adolescent girl to look after, but of course adolescents take these things seriously. When I got home that night, after getting away from Con, I was pretty nearly hysterical. I told Grandfather about Con, and he wouldn't believe me. He knew I'd been out somewhere, and suspected I'd met somebody, and all he would say was 'where had I been?' because it was late, and he'd sent Con to find me himself. I think he just thought Con had lost his head and had been trying to kiss me, and all I was saying about murder was pure hysteria. I don't blame him, but there was a . . . pretty foul scene. There's no point in raking it all up; you can imagine the kind of things that were said. But you see why I ran away? Partly because of what had happened between you and me, and because I was scared stiff of Con . . . and now because Grandfather was taking his part, and I was afraid he and Con would start ferreting about, and discover about you. If Crystal had found out . . . the way she was just then. . . ."

Rowan put his head down, and began to graze with a jingling of metal. I paused, leaning one hand against his neck. "Well, you understand why I was afraid to come back to Whitescar, even now. If Con *had* been in charge here, alone, I'd never have dared, but once I found that Grandfather was still alive, and still playing at power-politics between me and Con and Julie, and that Julie might be exposed to exactly the same sort of danger as I had been . . ."

"And that I had gone."

"And that you had gone," I said steadily, "I knew I'd have to come back here. It would still have been a pretty sticky thing to attempt, in the teeth of Con and Lisa, and not being sure of Grandfather's reception of me, but then Con himself appeared like Lucifer out of the blue, and presented me with what looked like a nice, peaceful, Connor-proof homecoming. I rather grabbed at it. I only planned, you see, to stay here as long as Grandfather lived."

"I begin to see. How did you fall in with Connor?"

"I took a risk which I shouldn't have taken, and went to take a look at Whitescar. I didn't even get out of the bus, just went along the top road from Bellingham to Chollerford, one Sunday. I got out at Chollerford, to get the bus along the Roman Road. I—I wanted to walk along the Wall, to—to see it again."

Nothing in his face betrayed the fact that lay sharply between us; that it was on the Wall that he and I, sometimes, by chance—and oh, how carefully calculated a chance!—had met.

I said steadily, "Con saw me. He waited his chance and followed me. He recognized me, of course, or thought he did. When he came up on me I was startled, and scared stiff, and then I saw he was just doubtful enough for me to pretend he'd made a mistake. So I gave him the name I'd been using, and got away with it." I went on to tell him, then, of the interview on the Wall, and the subsequent suggestions that were made to me. "And finally, when I realized that Con was fairly well 'in' with Grandfather, and that he and Lisa had it in for Julie, and that Grandfather himself had had a stroke . . . Well, I thought to myself, this is one way of getting home with Con not lifting a finger to stop me. So I agreed. And it went off well enough, until I found that you *were* still here. . . ."

He said with sudden impatience, "That horse isn't sweating. Leave that alone. We'll turn him loose."

He began to unbuckle the cheek strap, adding, with as much emotion as if he were discussing the price of tomatoes, "Go on. When did you find I was still here?"

"Grandfather mentioned it, quite casually, the first evening. I'd managed to chisel a bit out of Con and Lisa, about the fire, and your taking Crystal to Italy, and then Vienna, and the nursing homes and everything, and her death, but you know Con, he's interested in nothing but himself, and I didn't dare press too much about you and your affairs. When I heard from Grandfather that you hadn't gone permanently, it gave me a shock. I went that night to Con and said I wanted to back down. He—threatened me. No, no, nothing like that, he just said what was true, that it had gone too far, and that a hint of the 'truth' would shock Grandfather. Of course I knew I'd told Grandfather nothing but the truth, but for all they get across one another, he thinks the sun rises and sets in Con, and it would have finished him to know what sort of a swine Con is—can be. It still would. I realized that I'd have to stay, but the thought of having to meet you was . . . terrifying. I went over to Forrest that night, the night before you came."

"To lay the ghosts?"

"I suppose so. But the next night . . . I knew you'd come, I don't know how."

You always did. . . . Nobody had said the words. He wasn't looking at me; he was sliding the bridle off, over Rowan's ears. The horse, his head free, flung it up and sideways, and swerved away from us, thrusting out into the sunlight at a trot. Then he dropped his head, and began to graze again. Adam looked down at the bridle in his hands as if he wasn't quite sure what it was, or how it had got there. Then he turned, and hung it with great care beside his own. "And when I came, you found it easier to let me think you—that Annabel was dead."

"Wasn't she?" I said.

He turned then, and for the first time we really looked at one another. "Why should you have thought so? After you'd gone, when you'd had time to think . . . there'd been so much . . . you must have known I . . ." His voice trailed away, and he looked down at his feet.

I felt something touch me, pierce almost the armour of indifference that the hurt of eight years back had shelled over me like nacre. It was not enough to have learned to live with the memory of his cruelty and indifference; I had still to care.

I said, hardly enough, "Adam, eight years ago, we quarrelled, because we were unhappy, and there was no future unless we did the sort of harm we had no right to do. I told you, I don't want to go back over it. But you remember as well as I do, what was said."

He said roughly, "Oh God, yes! Do you think I haven't lived through every minute of that quarrel since? Every word, every look, every inflection? I know why you went! Even discounting Con and your grandfather, you'd reason enough! But I still can't see why you never sent me a single word, even an angry one."

This time the silence was stretched, like a shining thread that wouldn't snap. The sun was strong now, and fell slanting over the eastward hedge to gild the tops of the grasses. Rowan rolled an eye at us, and moved further away. The tearing sound as he cropped the grass was loud in the early-morning stillness.

When I spoke, it was in a voice already heavy with knowledge; the instinct that sees pain falling like a shadow from the future. "But you had my letter."

Before he spoke, I knew the answer. The truth was in his face. "Letter? What letter?"

"I wrote from London," I said, "almost straight away."

"I got no letter." I saw him pass his tongue across his lips. "What did it . . . say?"

For eight years I had thought of what I would have liked to say. Now I only said, gently, "That if it would give you even a little happiness, I'd be your mistress, and go with you wherever you liked."

The pain went across his face as if I had hit him. I saw him shut his eyes. He put up a hand to them; it was disfigured and ugly in the clear sunlight. He dropped it, and we looked at one another.

He said, quite simply, as if exhausted, "My dear, I never even saw it."

"I realize that now. I suppose I should have realized it then, when I got no answer. I should have known you'd not have done anything quite so cruel."

"Christ," he said, without violence, "I think you should."

"I'm sorry. It never even occurred to me that the letter might have gone astray. Letters don't, as a rule. And I was so unhappy, and alone, and—and *cut off* . . . girls aren't at their most sensible at such times. Adam, don't look like that. It's over now. I waited a few days; I—I suppose I'd really only gone to London to wait for you; I'd never intended, originally, to go abroad. But then, when I telephoned—did she tell you I'd telephoned?" At his expression, I gave a little smile. "Yes, I telephoned you, too."

"Oh, my dear. And Crystal answered?"

"Yes. I pretended it was a wrong number. I didn't think she'd recognized my voice. I rang again next day, and Mrs. Rudd answered it. She didn't know who I was; she just told me the house was shut, and that you and Mrs. Forrest had gone abroad, indefinitely. It was then that I—I decided to go right away. I went to a friend of mine who was emigrating. I had some money. I went along to look after her children, and—oh, the rest doesn't matter. I didn't write to you again. I—I couldn't, could I?"

"No." He was still looking like someone who has been mortally hurt, and hasn't known it till he sees the blood draining away into the grass. "No wonder you said what you did, the other night. It seems there's even more than I thought, to be laid at my door."

"You couldn't help it, if a letter went astray! It was hardly—*Adam!*"

His eyes jerked up to mine. "What is it?"

I licked my lips, and said, hoarsely, "I wonder what did happen to that letter? We're forgetting that. I said a minute ago, letters just don't go astray, not as a rule, not for eight years. Do you suppose—" I wet my lips again—"*she* took it?"

"*Crystal?* How could—oh my God, no, surely? Don't look like that, Annabel, the damned thing's probably lying in some dusty dead-letter office somewhere on the Continent. No, my dear, she never knew. I'll swear she never knew."

"Adam, you can't be sure! If she did—"

"I tell you she didn't know! She never gave any sign of knowing! And I assure you, that if she could have found a whip like *that* to use on me, she'd have used it."

"But when she got so much worse—"

"She was no worse than neurotic for years after you went away. It was only after the fire—after I'd taken her to Florence—that you could have called her really 'mentally ill,' and I had to take her to Vienna. She never once, in all that time, mentioned any sort of suspicion of you."

"But Adam, you don't know—"

"I know quite well. Stop this, Annabel!"

"Adam, no one's ever told me—how did Crystal die?"

He said harshly, "It was nothing to do with this. You can take my word for it. For one thing, no letter turned up among her papers after her death, and you can be sure she kept everything there was."

I said, "Then she *did* kill herself?"

He seemed to stiffen himself like a man lifting a weight, only able by stark courage to hold it there. "Yes."

Another of those silences. We were standing so still that a wren flew on to a hazel close beside me, chattered a stave of shrill and angry-sounding song, then flew away. I was thinking, without drama, well, here was the end of the chapter; all the threads tied up, the explanations made. There was nothing more to say. Better say good-bye, and go home to breakfast, before tragedy dissolved in embarrassment, and the lovers who had once been ready to count the world well lost should find themselves talking about the weather.

The same thought showed momentarily in Adam's face, and with it, a sort of stubborn resolution. He took a step forward, and the maimed hands moved.

I said, "Well, I'd better be getting back before Con sees I've been on Rowan."

"Annabel—"

"Adam, don't make me keep saying it's finished."

"Don't make me keep saying it isn't! Why on earth d'you think I found myself trusting you against all reason and judgment, *liking* you— oh God, more than liking you—if I hadn't known in my blood who you really were, in spite of that bag of moonshine you handed to me so convincingly?"

"I suppose because I was like her."

"Nonsense. Julie's the image of what you were, as I knew you, and she never makes my heart miss a single beat. And tell me this, my dear dead love, why did you cry when you saw my hands?"

"Adam, no, you're not being fair!"

"You care, don't you? Still?"

"I . . . don't know. No. I can't. Not now."

He always had known what I was thinking. He said sharply, "Because of Crystal?"

"We'll never know, will we? It'd be there, between us, what we did."

He said, grimly, "I could bear that. Believe me, I made my reparations." He turned his hands over, studying them. "And this was the least painful of them. Well, my dear, what do you want to do?"

"I'll go, of course. It won't be long, you know. Grandfather's looking desperately frail. Afterwards . . . afterwards, I'll see things straight with Con, somehow, and then I'll go. If he knows I'm leaving, there'll be no danger for me. We needn't meet, Adam."

"Neither we need."

I turned away abruptly. "I'll go now."

"Take your bridle."

"What? Oh, thanks. I'm sorry I spoiled your ride, Adam."

"It doesn't matter. Rowan would much prefer it with you. I've a heavy hand."

He picked his own bridle from the post, and heaved the saddle up over one arm. Then he smiled at me. "Don't worry, my dear. I won't get under your feet. But don't go away again, without saying good-bye."

"Adam," I said rather desperately, "I can't help it. I can't *help* the way I feel. Life does just go on, and you change, and you can't go back. You have to live it the way it comes. You know that."

He said, not tragically, but as if finishing a quite ordinary conversation, "Yes, of course. But it would be very much easier to be dead. Good-bye."

He let himself through the wicket, and went away across the field without looking back.

CHAPTER

FIFTEEN

I lean'd my back unto an ak,
   I thocht it was a trustie tree;
But first it bow'd and syne it brak—
   Sae my true love did lichtlie me.

                              Ballad: *Jamie Douglas.*

Life goes on, I had told Adam. When I got back to the farm the men
were arriving for the day, and the cattle were filing into the byres. I
managed to slip into the stables and hang the bridle up again without
being seen, then went into the kitchen.

Mrs. Bates was there, waiting for the kettle to boil. She cast me a
look of surprise.

"Why, Miss Annabel! You're up early. Have you been out riding?"

"No. I just couldn't sleep."

Her bright black eyes lingered on my face. "What's to do now? You
look proper poorly."

"I'm all right. I had a bad night, that's all. I'd love a cup of tea."

"Hm." The piercing, kind little eyes surveyed me. "Piece o' nonsense,
getting up at all hours when you don't have to. You want to take care
o' yersel'."

"Nonsense, Betsy, there's nothing the matter with me."

"Never seen anything like you the day you came back." Here the
kettle boiled, and she tipped it, dexterously jetting the boiling water
into the teapot. "If you hadn't 'a' told me you was Miss Annabel, I'd
hardly 'a' knowd you, and *that's* a fact. Aye, you can smile if you like,
but that's the truth and no lie. Depend on it, I says to Bates that night,
depend on it, Miss Annabel's had a bad time of it over in America, I
says, and I'm not surprised, I says, judging by what you see on the
pictures."

"It was Canada," I said mildly.

"Well, they're all the same, aren't they?" She slapped the teapot
down on the table, which was laid ready for breakfast, whipped off the

lid, and stirred the tea vigorously. "Not but what you look a lot better than what you did, and you've begun to put a bit of weight on, aye, *and* get some of your looks back, and I'm not the only one that's noticed it. Have you noticed, says Bates to me the other day, that Miss Annabel's almost her pretty self again when she smiles. Which isn't often enough by a long chalk, I says. Well, he says, if she'd but get herself a husband and get herself settled, he says. Go on with you, I says, and her hardly home yet, give her time, I says, not but what men always thinks that's all a woman needs in 'er life to make her happy, so no offence meant, but all the same, he says to me—"

I managed a laugh that was, I hope, convincing. "Oh, Betsy dear! Let me get home first, before I start looking round!"

"Here's your tea." She pushed a steaming cup towards me. "And you did ought to take sugar in it, not a foreign black mess like that. And let me tell you that if you didn't sleep last night you'll only have yersel' to blame, with soup, and coffee, not to mention whisky and such, *as* I know by the glasses left in the kitchen bold as brass for me to find. Not that I'm one as concerns meself in things that are none of my business, but—oh, here's Mr. Con."

Con, I noticed sourly, looked attractive and wide awake even with last night's stubble on his chin, and in the clothes, carelessly hustled into, for his before-breakfast jobs. He threw me a look of surprise as he took a cup of tea from Mrs. Bates. "Good God. What are you doing up at this hour?"

"Taking a walk, she says," said Mrs. Bates, spooning sugar into his cup. "I thought she'd been riding, meself, but she says no."

His eyes flickered over my trousers and yellow shirt. "Weren't you? I should have thought Forrest's colt would have tempted you long ago."

I sipped my tea without replying. Already the scene in the meadow was growing dim, dulled, fading. . . . The hot tea was a benison, a spell against dreams. The day had started. Life goes on.

"Those things suit you," said Con. His glance held undisguised admiration, and I saw Mrs. Bates eyeing him with a sort of sour speculation. She pushed a plateful of buttered rolls towards him. "Try one o' these."

He took one, still watching me. "Are you coming out to lend a hand today?"

"That she is not," said Mrs. Bates promptly.

"I might," I said, "I'm not sure. I—I slept badly."

"You're not worrying about anything, are you?" asked Con. The blue eyes held nothing but mildly solicitous curiosity.

Mrs. Bates took his cup from him and refilled it. "She's worrying herself about her Granda, I shouldn't wonder, which is more than *you* seem to be doing, Mr. Con, *which* I may say you can think shame on yourself, for asking her to work in this heat, when you've as much help as you want up in the field, and that's the truth and no lie!"

"Well," said Con, with a glint of a smile, "I doubt if we'll get Bill Fenwick over today, so if you could relieve someone on one of the tractors some time, it would help. The weather'll break soon, you see if it doesn't. We'll have thunder before dark."

"I'll see," I said. "Will you be up there all day yourself?"

"As soon as I've had breakfast. Why?"

"I told you last night. I want to talk to you."

"So you did. Well, tonight, maybe."

"I'd rather see you before. I may come up to the field, at any rate when you stop to eat."

"Oh, sure," said Con unconcernedly, setting down his cup. "Be seeing you."

I went up to my room to change. If he hadn't been in his working clothes, I thought, he'd have smelled the horse on me. There were chestnut hairs on the grey trousers, and one or two on the shirt where Rowan had rubbed his head against me. I went along and bathed, got into a skirt and fresh blouse, and felt better.

I couldn't eat breakfast when the time came, but there was no one there to remark on the fact. Con wasn't yet in, Grandfather wasn't up, Mrs. Bates was busy elsewhere, and Lisa was invariably silent at breakfast time. Julie was taking hers in bed—this at my insistence, and more to keep her out of Con's way than for any other reason. She seemed to have completely recovered from last night's experience, and only accepted my ruling about breakfast because, she said, she had no desire to see Con again so soon, and certainly not before she had seen Donald.

Donald rang up shortly before half past eight, to ask for news of last night's truants. I told him only enough to reassure him—that Bill Fenwick's car had been involved in a mishap, and that Julie was unhurt, and wanting to see him some time that day. If, I added with a memory of the colleague from London, he was free. . . .

"Mphm," said Donald. "I'll be along in half an hour."

"Donald! Wait a minute! She's not up yet!"

"Half an hour," said Donald, and rang off.

I warned Julie, who hurled herself out of bed with a shriek and a "What shall I *wear?*" that reassured me completely as to her well-being and her feelings. I didn't see Donald arrive, but when, some half-hour later, I saw his car in the yard, I went to tell him that Julie wouldn't be long. He wasn't in the car, or indeed, anywhere to be seen; on an inspiration I slipped through the half-door of Blondie's stable, and there, sure enough, he was, stooping to prod a gentle finger into the pile of fur deep in the manger, while Tommy, sitting unconcernedly on top of the partition (which was at least half an inch wide), watched composedly, in the intervals of washing a back leg.

Donald straightened when he heard me come in. "She really is all right?" It was an unceremonious greeting, and I hoped it was symptomatic of his state of mind. He certainly betrayed no other outward signs of deep emotion.

"Perfectly. She'll be along in a minute or two."

I told him then rather more fully about the accident, but without mentioning Con, or, of course, what had happened later last night. If Julie chose to tell him, that was her affair, but I hoped she wouldn't. I wanted no more trouble until I had managed that overdue interview with Con, and after that, I hoped, all would be clear.

It was six minutes, in sober fact, before Julie came. She certainly looked none the worse for the stresses of last night. She wore her blue skirt and white blouse, and looked composed and immaculate, not in the least as if she had rushed shrieking for the bathroom only thirty-six minutes before.

She greeted Donald with a composure that amounted almost to reserve, and, when I made a move to go, held me there with a quick, imploring look that filled me with forebodings. These weren't diminished by Donald's attitude; he appeared to have retreated into silence, and, I noticed with exasperation, was even groping in his pocket for his pipe.

I said quickly, "You can't smoke in a stable, Donald. If you two are going off now—"

"Oh," said Julie, "are these Tommy's kittens? Aren't they *adorable!*"

She stooped over the bundle in the manger, exclaiming delightedly over the kittens, with every appearance of intending to remain there for some time. "And *look* at their tiny *paws!* Two black," she cried rapturously, "and three black-and-white, and *two ginger* . . . isn't it a *miracle?*"

"As a matter of fact," I said, rather sharply, "it's the ginger tom from West Lodge."

Julie had detached a ginger kitten from the tangle of fur, and was cuddling it under her chin, crooning to it. "How old are they? Oh, I'd *adore* to keep one! But they're far too tiny to take, aren't they? Six weeks, isn't it, till they can lap? Oh, isn't it a *darling*? Annabel, d'you suppose either of the ginger ones is a he?"

"They both are," said Donald.

"How do you—I mean, they're too small to *tell*, surely?"

"I should have said," amended Donald, carefully, "that the probability of both ginger kittens' being male is about ninety-nine-and-nine-tenths per cent. Possibly more. The ginger colour is a sex-linked characteristic."

The nearest we were going to get to romance today, I thought bitterly, was a discussion on genetics. And while there could, admittedly, be said to be some connection, it was getting us no further with the matter in hand. I sent Donald a quelling look, which he didn't see. He was watching Julie, who, with the kitten still cuddled close to her, was regarding him with respectful wonder.

"You mean you just *can't have* a ginger she?"

"No. I mean, yes." Donald's uncertainty was only momentary, and of the wrong kind. He stood there like a rock, pipe in hand, calm, slow-spoken, and undeniably attractive. I could have shaken him.

"Isn't that marvellous?" said Julie, awed. "Annabel, did you know that? Then I *shall* keep this one. Oh, lord, it's got claws like *pins*, and it *will* try and climb up my neck! Donald, look at it, isn't it utterly *adorable*?"

"Adorable." He still sounded infuriatingly detached and academic. "I'd be inclined to go further. I'd say beautiful, quite beautiful."

"Would you?" Julie was as surprised as I was at this sudden plunge into hyperbole. She held the kitten away from her, looking at it a shade doubtfully. "Well, it *is* the sweetest little love, of course, but do you think the pink nose is quite the *thing*? Cute, of course, with that spot on the end, but—"

"Pink?" said Donald. "I wouldn't have said it was pink."

He hadn't, I realized suddenly, even glanced at the kitten. Unnoticed at last, I began to edge away.

"But Donald, it's *glowing* pink, practically *shocking* pink, and quite hideous, actually, only so terribly sweet!"

"I was not," said Donald, "talking about the kitten."

There was a second's open-mouthed pause, then Julie, her poise in flinders, blushed a vivid scarlet and began to stammer. Donald put his pipe back into his pocket.

I said, unheeded, "We'll see you both this evening some time," and went out of the stable.

As I went, Donald was gently unhooking the kitten from the shoulder of Julie's blouse, and putting it back into the manger.

"We don't want to squash the poor little thing, do we?"

"N—no," said Julie.

Later that morning, after I had done the chores which I had taken on as my contribution to the housekeeping, I went to hunt up my gardening tools from the corner of the barn where they had always been kept. I had, of course, taken the precaution of asking Lisa where they were. The tools looked almost as if they hadn't been used since I'd last had them out more than eight years ago. It was queer to feel my hand slipping in such an assured way round the smoothed wood of the trowel, and to feel the familiar knot hole in the handle of the spade. I carried the tools along to the tractor shed and put in a little first aid on the shears, and the blades of spade and hoe, then threw the lot into a barrow, and went to see what I could do with the neglected garden.

I worked there all morning, and, since I started on the basic jobs of grass and path, it wasn't long before the place looked as if some care had been spent on it. But work, for once, didn't help. As I sheared the grass, and spaded the edges straight, and then tackled the dry, weedy beds with fork and hoe, memory, far from being dulled by the rough work, cut back at me even more painfully, as if I had sharpened that, too, along with the garden tools.

That spring and summer, eight years back . . . the March days when the soil smelled strong and damp and full of growing; May when the lilac was thick on the tree by the gate, and rain lay in each cup, scented with honey; June, with the robin scolding shrilly from the waxy blossoms of the syringa bush, as I dug and planted with my back to the house, dreaming of Adam, and our next meeting. . . .

Today, it was June again, and the soil was dry and the air heavy. The lilac was done, and the syringa bush wasn't there, dead these many years.

And Adam and I were free, but that was over.

My fork turned up a clump of bulbs, autumn crocus, flat globes covered with onion-coloured crêpe paper. I went on my knees and lifted them out carefully with my hands.

Then suddenly I remembered them, too. This clump had been in flower the last day I'd been at Whitescar. They had burned, pale lilac flames in the dusk, as I slipped out to meet Adam that last, that terrible evening. They had lain, drenched ribbons of silk, under the morning's rain when, with the first light next day, I had tiptoed down the path and away, across the bridge towards the highroad.

I found I was sitting back on my heels with the tears pouring down my face, and dripping on the dry corms held tightly in my hands.

It was still an hour short of lunch time when Betsy's voice called me from the house. I thought there was some urgency in her voice, and when I stood up and turned, I could see her, in what looked like considerable agitation, waving for me to hurry.

"Oh, Miss Annabel! Oh, Miss Annabel! Come quickly, do!"

The urgency and distress could only mean one thing. I dropped my weeding fork, and ran.

"Betsy! Is it Grandfather?"

"Aye, it is that . . . ." Her hands were twisted now into her apron, and, with her face paler than usual, and the red of the cheeks standing out like paint, and the black eyes at once alarmed and important, she looked more than ever, as she stood bobbing in the doorway, like a little wooden figure from a Noah's Ark. She was talking even more rapidly than usual, almost as if she thought she might be blamed for what had happened, and had to get her excuses in first.

". . . and he was as right as rain when I took his breakfast up, as right as a trivet he was, and *that's* the truth and no lie. 'And how many times have I tell't you,' he says, 'if you burns the toast, to give it to the birds. I'll not have this scraped stuff,' he says, 'so you can throw it out now and do some more,' *which* I did, Miss Annabel, and there he was, as right as rain . . . ."

I took her breathlessly by the shoulders, with my earthy hands. "Betsy, Betsy! What's *happened*? Is he dead?"

"Mercy, no! But it's the stroke like before, and that's how it'll end this time, Miss Annabel, my dear. . . ."

She followed me up the passage, still talking volubly. She and Lisa, I heard, had been together in the kitchen, preparing lunch, when Grandfather's bell had rung. This was an old-fashioned pulley bell, one of a row which hung on their circular springs in the kitchen. The bell had jangled violently, as if jerked in anger, or some sudden emergency. Mrs. Bates had hurried upstairs, to find the old man collapsed in the wing chair near the fireplace. He had dressed himself, all but his jacket, and must have suddenly begun to feel ill, and just managed to reach the bell pull by the hearth as he fell. Mrs. Bates and Lisa, between them, had got him to bed, and then the former had come for me.

Most of this she managed to pour out in the few moments while I ran to the kitchen and plunged my filthy hands under the tap. I had seized a towel, and was roughly drying them, when a soft step sounded in the lobby, and Lisa appeared in the doorway. She showed none of Betsy's agitation, but her impassive face was perhaps a bit sallower, and I thought I saw a kind of surreptitious excitement in her eyes.

She said abruptly, "There you are. I've got him to bed and got him covered up. He collapsed while he was dressing. I'm afraid it looks serious. Annabel, will you telephone the doctor? The number's on the pad. Mrs. Bates, that kettle's almost hot enough; fill two hot-water bottles as soon as you can. I must go back to him. When you've got Dr. Wilson, Annabel, go and fetch Con."

"Lisa, I must see him. You do the telephoning. I can—"

"You don't know what to do," she said curtly. "I do. It's happened before. Now hurry."

She turned quickly away, as if there was no more to be said. I flung the towel down, and ran to the office.

The doctor's number was written there, largely, on the pad. Luck was in, and he was at home. Yes, he would be there as quickly as possible. What was being done? Ah, Miss Dermott was with him, was she, and Mrs. Bates was there? Good, good. I was to try not to worry. He wouldn't be long. Smooth with professional reassurances, he rang off.

As I went back into the hall, Lisa appeared at the head of the stairs.

"Did you get him?"

"Yes, he's coming."

"Good. Now, will you go—?"

"I want to see him first." I was already starting up the stairs.

"There's nothing you can do." She did nothing to bar my way, but her very stolidity, as she waited for me in the middle of the way, had that effect.

I said sharply, "Is he conscious?"

"No."

It wasn't the monosyllable that halted me, three steps below her, it was the tone of it. I looked up at her. Even through my agitation I caught the surprise in her look. Heaven knows what she could read in my face and eyes. I had forgotten what lay between me and Lisa; now it whipped back at me, stinging me into intelligence, and caution.

She was saying, "There's no point in your seeing him. Go and get Con. He's in High Riggs."

"I know."

"Well, he must know straight away."

"Yes, of course," I said, and went on, past her, straight into Grandfather's room.

The curtains had been half drawn, and hung motionless, shading the sunny windows. The old man lay in bed, his only movement that of his laboured, stertorous breathing. I went across and stood beside him. If it hadn't been for the difficult breathing, I might have thought him dead already. It was as if he, the man I knew, had already gone from behind the mask that lay on the pillow. It, and we, were only waiting.

Lisa had followed me in, but I took no notice of her. I stood watching Grandfather, and trying to calm my agitated thoughts into some sort of order.

Lisa had been in the kitchen when it happened, with Betsy. It had been Betsy who had answered the bell. All that Lisa had done had been correct, and obviously genuine. And Con was far enough away, in High Riggs; had been there since early morning. . . .

I turned to meet Lisa's eyes. If I had had any doubts about the naturalness of this crisis, coming, as it had done, so pat upon the signing of the will, they were dispelled by the look on Lisa's face. It was still, as before, obscurely excited, and she made no attempt to hide the excitement from me. And it was now, also, thoroughly surprised and puzzled as she stared back at me.

I could hear Betsy chugging upstairs now, with the hot-water bottles. Lisa had moved up to my elbow. Her voice muttered in my ear, "It's a mercy, isn't it?"

"A mercy?" I glanced at her in surprise. "But he was perfectly all right—"

"Ssh, here's Mrs. B. I meant, a mercy it didn't happen yesterday, before Mr. Isaacs came. God's providence, you might say."

"You might," I said drily. Yes, I thought, it was there, clear enough to see: Lisa, single-minded, uncomplicated, initiating nothing. The stars in their courses fought for Con; Lisa need only wait. Efficient, innocent

Lisa. No doubt at all, when Doctor Wilson came, she would help him in every possible way.

I said abruptly, "I'll go and get Con."

The sun beat heavy and hot on High Riggs. A third of the field was shorn, close and green-gold and sweet-smelling. Over the rest of the wide acreage the hay stood thick and still in the heat. The clover, and the plumy tops of the grasses made shadows of lilac and madder and bronze across the gilt of the hay. There were purple vetches along the ditch, and the splashing yellow of ladies' slipper.

One tractor was at the far end of the field, with Con driving. It was moving away from me, the blades of the cutter flashing in the sun.

I began to run towards him along the edge of the cut hay. The men with rakes paused to look up at me. The cutter was turning, out from the standing hay, round, and in once more in a close circle, neatly feathering its corner and re-entering the standing hay at an exact right angle.

Con hadn't seen me. He was watching the track of the blades, but as the machine came into the straight, he glanced up ahead of him, and then lifted a hand. I stopped where I was, gasping in the heavy heat.

The tractor was coming fairly fast. Con, not apparently seeing in my visit anything out of the way, was watching the blades again. The sun glinted on the dark hair, the handsome, half-averted profile, the sinewy brown arms. He looked remote, absorbed, grave. I remember that I thought with a kind of irrelevant surprise, he looks happy.

Then I had stepped out of his path, and, as the tractor came level with me, I shouted above the noise of the motor, "Con! You'd better come to the house! It's Grandfather!"

The tractor stopped with a jerk that shook and rattled the cutter blades. The boy on the reaper hauled on the lever and they lifted, the hot light quivering on the steel. Con switched off the motor, and the silence came at us with a rush.

"What is it?"

I said, shouting, then lowering my voice as it hit the silence, "It's Grandfather. He's taken ill. You have to come."

I saw something come and go in his face, then it was still again, but no longer remote. It had gone blank, but it was as if something in him was holding its breath, in a sort of wary eagerness; there was a tautness along the upper lip, and the nostrils were slightly flared. A hunter's face.

He drew a little breath, and turned his head to the boy. "Uncouple her, Jim. I'm going down to the house. Ted!" The farm foreman came across, not hurrying, but with a curious look at me. "Ted, Mr. Winslow's ill. I'm going down now, and I may not get back today. Carry on, will you?" A few more hurried instructions, and his hand went to the starter. "Oh, and send one of the boys across to open that gate for the doctor's car. Jim, get up on the tractor here, then you can drive it back. I'll send news up with Jim, Ted, as soon as I see how he is."

As the boy obeyed, swinging up behind him, Con started the motor. He gestured with a jerk of the head to me, and I ran round and stepped up onto the back of the tractor. It went forward with a lurch, and then turned sharply away from the ridge of cut hay, and bucketed down across the uneven ground towards the gate. The men paused in their raking to watch curiously, but Con took no notice. He sent the tractor over the grid with hardly any diminution of speed. I was close beside him, standing on the bars and holding on to the high mudguard. He began to whistle between his teeth, a hissing little noise that sounded exactly what it was, a valve blowing down a head of steam. I think I hated Con then, more than I ever had before; more than when he had tried to bully me into marrying him; more than when I had wrenched away from him and run, bruised and terrified, to Grandfather; more than when he had tried to claim Adam's place as my lover; more than when he had brought me back, an interloper, to damage Julie.

He said nothing until we were getting down from the tractor in the yard.

"By the way, wasn't there something you wanted to talk to me about? What was it?"

"It'll keep," I said.

Grandfather was still unconscious. The doctor had come, stayed, and then, towards evening, had gone again to a telephone summons. This was the number . . . we were to call him back if there was any change . . . but he was afraid, Miss Winslow, Miss Dermott, he was very much afraid. . . .

He lay on his back, propped on pillows, breathing heavily, and with apparent difficulty, and sometimes the breath came in a long, heaving sigh. Now and again there seemed a pause in the breathing, and then my heart would jerk and stop as if in sympathy, to resume its erratic beating when the difficult breaths began again. . . .

I hadn't left him. I had pulled a chair up to one side of his bed. Con was on the other. He had spent the afternoon alternately in sitting still as a stone, with his eyes on the old man's face, or else in fits of restless prowling, silent, like a cat, which I had stood till I could stand it no longer, then had curtly told him to go out of the room unless he could keep still. He had shot me a quick look of surprise, which had turned to a lingering one of appraisement, then he had gone, but only to return after an hour or so, to sit on the other side of the old man's bed, waiting. And that look came again, and yet again, as the blue eyes kept coming back to my face. I didn't care. I felt so tired that emotion of any kind would have been an exercise as impossible as running to a wounded man. Heaven knows what was showing in my face. I had ceased to try and hide it from Con, and I could not, today, find it in me to care. . . .

And so the day wore on. Lisa, quiet and efficient as ever, came in and out, and helped me to do what was needed. Mrs. Bates finished her work, but offered to stay for a time, and the offer was gladly accepted. Julie hadn't come home. After the doctor's visit, Con went out and sent one of the men up in the car to West Woodburn, but on his return he reported that neither Julie nor Donald had been seen at the site since that morning. They had gone up there some time before luncheon, had walked around for a bit, then had gone off in Donald's car. Nobody had any idea where they had gone. If it was into Newcastle . . .

"Forrest Hall!" I said. "That's where they'll be! I'm sorry, Con, I'd quite forgotten." I explained quickly about the alleged Roman carving that Adam had described. "Ask him to go to Forrest Hall—he'd better go by the river path, it's quicker than taking a car up past the gates."

But the man, when he returned, had found nobody. Yes, he had found the cellars; they were accessible enough, and he thought someone had been there recently, probably today, but no one was there now. Yes, he had been right down. And there was no car parked there; he couldn't have failed to see that. Should he try West Lodge? Or Nether Shields?

"The telephone's easier," said Con.

But the telephone was no help, either. West Lodge was sorry, but Mr. Forrest was out, and had not said when he would be back. Nether Shields—with a shade of reserve—was sorry, too; no, Julie had not been there that day; yes, thank you, Bill was quite all right; they were sorry to hear about Mr. Winslow; sorry, sorry, sorry. . . .

"We'll have to leave it," I said wearily. "It's no use. They may have found something at Forrest, and all gone into Newcastle to look it up, or something; or Julie and Donald may have gone off on their own after they left Forrest Hall. But it's only an hour to supper time now, and surely they'll come then? After last night—was it really only last night?—Julie *surely* won't stay away again without letting us know?"

"Do you know, you sound really worried," said Con.

I said, "My God, what do you think—?" then looked up and met the blue eyes across the bed where Grandfather lay. They were bright and very intent. I said shortly, "Oddly enough, I am. I'm thinking of Julie. She would want to be here."

His teeth showed briefly. "I always did say you were a nice girl."

I didn't answer.

The doctor came back just before seven, stayed a while, then went again. The day drew down, the sky dark as slate, heavy with thunder, and threatening rain.

Still Julie didn't come, and still Grandfather lay there, with no change apparent in the mask-like face, except that I thought the nostrils looked pinched, and narrower, and his breathing seemed more shallow.

Con went over to the buildings shortly after the doctor had gone, and only then, leaving Mrs. Bates in Grandfather's room, did I go downstairs for a short time, while Lisa gave me soup, and something to eat.

Then I went back, to sit there, waiting, and watching the old man's face, and trying not to think.

And, well within the hour, Con was back there, too, on the other side of the bed, watching me.

Mrs. Bates went at eight, and soon afterwards, the rain began; big, single, heavy drops at first, splashing down on the stones, then all at once in sheets, real thunder-rain, flung down wholesale from celestial buckets, streaming down the windows as thickly as gelatine. Then suddenly, the room was lit by a flash, another, and the thunderstorm was with us; long flickering flashes of lightning, and drum rolls of thunder getting nearer; a summer storm, savage and heavy and soon to pass.

I went over to shut the windows, and remained there for a few moments, staring out through the shining plastic curtain of the rain. I could barely see as far as the buildings. In the frequent flashes the rain shimmered in vertical steel rods, and the ground streamed and bubbled with the water that fell too fast for the gutters to take it.

Still no Julie. They wouldn't come now. They would stay and shelter till it was past. And meanwhile Grandfather . . .

I drew the thick chintz curtains and came back to the bed. I switched on the bedside lamp and turned it away, so that no light fell on the old man's face. Con, I saw, was watching him abstractedly, with a deep frown between his brows. He said under his breath, "Listen to that, damn it to hell. It's enough to wake the dead."

I was just going to say, "Don't worry, it won't disturb him," when Con added, "It'll have the rest of High Riggs as flat as coconut matting. We'll never get the cutter into it after this."

I said drily, "No, I suppose not," and then, sharply, all else forgotten, "Con! It *has* woken him!"

Grandfather stirred, sighed, gave an odd little snore, and then opened his eyes. After a long time they seemed to focus, and he spoke without moving his head. The sounds he made were blurred, but clear enough.

"Annabel?"

"I'm here, Grandfather."

A pause. "Annabel?"

I leaned forward into the pool of light, and slid a hand under the edge of the bedclothes till it found his.

"Yes, Grandfather. I'm here. It's Annabel."

There was no movement in the fingers under mine, no perceptible expression in Grandfather's face, but I thought, somehow, that he had relaxed. I felt his fingers, thin and frail, as smooth and dry as jointed bamboo, and no more living, lying in my palm, and remembered him as he had been in my girlhood, a tall, powerful man, lean and whippy and tyrannical, and as proud as fire. And suddenly it was too much, this slow, painful ending to the day. A day that had begun with Rowan, and the brilliant morning, and a secret that was still my own; then Adam, and the knowledge of our betrayal of each other; and now this. . . .

The storm was coming nearer. Lightning played for seconds at a time, flashing like some dramatically wheeling spotlight against the shut curtains. I saw Grandfather's eyes recognize it for what it was, and said, "It's just a summer thunderstorm. I don't suppose it'll last."

"That noise. Rain?"

The thunder had paused. In the interval the rain came down with the noise of a waterfall. "Yes."

I saw his brows twitch, very faintly. "It'll flatten—High Riggs."

Something touched me that was partly wonder, and partly a sort of shame. Con was a Winslow after all, and perhaps his reaction had been truer than mine—my dumb fury of grief that was a grief for the passing of, not this old man, but my world, the world I hadn't wanted, and deserved to lose. I said, "That's just what Con was saying."

"Con?"

I nodded towards him. "He's there."

The eyes moved. "Con."

"Sir?"

"I'm—ill."

"Yes," said Con.

"Dying?"

"Yes," said Con.

I felt my lips part in a sort of gasp of protest and shock, but what I might have said was stopped by Grandfather's smile. It wasn't even the ghost of his old grin, it was nothing but the slight tightening and slackening of a muscle at the corner of his mouth; but I knew then that Con was right. Whatever had been Matthew Winslow's faults, he had never lacked dignity, and he was not the man to slide out of life on a soothing flood of women's lies. He and Con had ground where they could meet, and which was forbidden to me.

My moment of protest must have communicated itself to him through our linked hands, for his eyes moved back to me, and I thought he said, "No lies."

I didn't look at Con. "All right, Grandfather, no lies."

"Julie?"

"She'll be here soon. The storm's kept her. She's been out with Donald all day. She doesn't know you're ill."

I thought he looked a query.

"You remember Donald, darling. The Scot, Donald Seton. He's the archaeologist digging up at West Woodburn. He was here last night at—" my voice wavered, but I managed it—"your party."

I could see him concentrating, but it seemed to elude him. I had to control myself sharply, not to take a tighter hold on the frail hand in mine. I leaned nearer to him, speaking slowly, and as distinctly as I could. "You met Donald, and you liked him. He's going to marry Julie, and they'll live in London. Julie'll be very happy with him. She loves him. You needn't worry about—"

An appalling crash interrupted me. The flash, the long, growing rumble and crack of chaos, then, after it, the crash. Through all the other preoccupations in that dim room it hacked like the noise of a battleaxe.

Matthew Winslow said, "What's that?" in a voice that was startled almost back to normal.

Con was at the window, pulling back the curtains. His movements were full of a suppressed nervous excitement, which gave them more than their usual grace, like the sinewy, controlled actions of ballet. He came back to the bedside, and bent over his great-uncle. "It was a long way off. A tree, I'm pretty sure, but not here. One of the Forrest Hall trees, I'd say."

He put a hand on the bed, where Grandfather's arm lay under the blankets, and added carefully and distinctly, "You don't need to worry. I'll go out presently and find out where it was. But it's not near the buildings. And the lights are still on, you can see that. It's done no damage here."

Grandfather said, clearly, "You're a good boy, Con. It's a pity Annabel never came home. You'd have suited well together."

I said, "Grandfather—" and then stopped.

As I put my face down against the bedclothes, to hide it from him, I saw that Con had lifted his head once more and was watching me, his eyes narrow and appraising.

There was only myself and Con in the room.

CHAPTER

SIXTEEN

Nor man nor horse can go ower Tyne,
Except it were a horse of tree . . .

Ballad: *Jock o' the Side.*

It seemed a very long time before Con cleared his throat to speak.

I didn't raise my head. I could feel his scrutiny, and even through the first rush of grief, the instinct that I had been rash enough to disregard bade me hide my tears from him. I don't think I had any room, then, for conscious thought about the present danger of my position: the way my stupid, difficult safeguard against him had now become, ironically, a peril. I had known since yesterday that I would have to tell him the truth. To have discussed it today, across Grandfather's unconscious body, would have been unthinkable, like counting him already dead. And now, even if I had been ready to frame what I had to say, it was even less possible to do so.

I never knew what he was going to say. Somewhere, downstairs, a door slammed, and there were running footsteps. He checked himself, listening. I remember thinking, vaguely, that perhaps Lisa had somehow guessed what had happened. But would she have run like that? I had never seen Lisa hurry . . . somehow it seemed unlike her, even if she had cared enough . . . Julie; of course, it must be Julie. I pressed my fists hard against my temples, and tried to blot the tears off against the counterpane, steadying my thoughts as best I could. Julie was coming running, just too late, and in a moment I would have to lift my face. . . .

The steps clattered across the hall, seemed to trip at the bottom stair, then came on up, fast. Even through the thick panels of the door I could hear the hurry of sobbing breathing. She grabbed the knob with fumbling hands. It shook even as it turned.

I lifted my head sharply. There were still tears on my face, but I couldn't help that now. Here was something more. And Con had taken his eyes off me at last, and was watching the door.

It was thrust open—no sick-room entry, this—and Julie ran into the room.

She must have come in so quickly from the dark and streaming night that her eyes had barely adjusted themselves to the light. I thought for a moment that she was going to blunder straight into the bed, and came to my feet in a startled movement of protest; but she stopped just short of the bed's foot, gasping for breath.

I had been right in my swift guess: this panic-stricken haste had had nothing to do with Grandfather. She hadn't even glanced at the bed. Her look was wild, dazed almost, and she groped for a chair back, to which she clung as if that alone prevented her from falling.

Her hair, and the coat she wore, were soaked, so dark with rain that it took me a moment or two to realize, in that dim light, that the coat was streaked and filthy. The gay summer sandals were filthy, too, and there was dirt splashed over her hands and wrists, and smudged across her jawbone. The flush of haste stood out on her cheeks like paint.

She was looking wildly from me to Con while she fought for breath to speak. Her eyes, her whole head, jerked from one to the other and back again, in a kind of distraction that was painful to watch.

"Annabel . . . Con . . . Con . . ."

The appeal was whispered—the sickroom atmosphere, and whatever news Lisa had given her had overborne her own distress—but if that distress, whatever it was, had driven her to appeal to Con, then something was seriously the matter.

"Julie!" This time my movement towards her was protective. I came between her and the bed. "Darling! Whatever's the matter?"

But something in the way I moved had got through to her. For the first time, she looked past me, fully, at the bed. I saw the shock hit her, as a stone hits a man who has been knocked half silly already. She wavered, bit her lip, and said, like a child who expects to be punished for behaving badly, "I didn't know. Annabel, I didn't know."

I had an arm round her. "Yes, darling, I'm sorry. It happened just a few minutes ago. It was very sudden, and he seemed quite content. I'll tell you about it later; it's all right . . . If there's something else wrong, you can tell us now. What is it? Something else has happened? Something's wrong."

She shook in my arms. She was trying to speak, but could only manage a whispered, "Could you—please—please—you and Con—"

It was apparent that there would be no sense out of her yet. I spoke across her, deliberately raising my voice to a normal pitch, and making it sound as matter-of-fact as I could, "Con, you'd better go down and tell Lisa, then would you telephone Dr. Wilson? And you might get the brandy; Julie looks as if she needs it. Julie, don't stay in here; come along to your own room—"

"The phone's off," said Julie.

"Off?"

"Lisa says so. It went off just now, she says. She's been trying. It'll be the ivy tree. When it came down—"

"The ivy tree?" This was Con.

I said, "The old tree by the gate-house. That was what we heard come down. Never mind that. Julie—"

"It sounded nearer. Are you sure it's that one?"

"It was split. It just split in two." Julie's voice sounded thin and empty, but unsurprised, as if the questions were relevant enough. "Half came down right across the gate-house, you see. It brought the rest of the roof down, and a wall, and—"

"That's nowhere near the telephone wires," said Con. "If that was all it was, there's no real damage done."

I said, "Shut up. This is something that matters. Go on, Julie." I gave her a little shake. "*Julie!* Con, for God's sake go and get that brandy, the girl's going to faint."

"There's brandy here." He was at the bedside table. There was the splash and tinkle of liquid being poured, and he put a tumbler into my hand.

"Here, drink this." I held the rim of Grandfather's tumbler against her chattering teeth. Behind me I caught the movement as Con drew up the sheet to cover the old man's face. The moment passed, almost without significance. I said sharply, "Julie, pull yourself together. What's happened? Is it something to do with the ivy tree? Were you near the gate-house when it—oh, my God, Con, she'd have been just about passing it when we heard it come down . . . Julie, is it *Donald?*"

She nodded, and then went on nodding, like a doll. "He's down there. Underneath. Donald. The tree came down. It just split in two—"

"Is he dead?" asked Con.

Again, it seemed, his tactics worked better than mine. I felt the shock run through her, and her eyes jerked up to meet his. She said, sensibly enough, "No. I don't think so, but he's hurt, he can't get out. We have to go. . . . We were in the gate-house, you see, and the wall came down when he went down the steps, and he's hurt, there underneath. He can't get out." Abruptly she thrust the back of one grimy hand against her mouth, as if to stifle a cry. "We—we'll have to go." She looked in a kind of childish helplessness at the bed.

I said quickly, "He doesn't need us, Julie. It's all right. We'll come now. Con, where's the car?"

"I—I brought Donald's," began Julie, "only—"

Con said crisply, "You're not fit to drive. Mine's at the door. You're certain the phone's off?"

"Yes. Lisa was trying again."

"Come on, then," I said, "quickly."

It was odd—I spared a fleeting thought for it as we hurried to the door—how deeply conventions are ingrained in us. Scratch the conventional man and you find the savage; look closely at the primitive, and you see the grain of the wood from which our conventions are carved. It was incredibly hard to go out of that room in a hurry, with the mind bent on violent action. It seemed like desecration, yet only a few minutes ago this had merely been the bedroom of an arrogant, difficult, temperamental old man. By some inverted process the departure of his spirit from him had hallowed the room till, shrinelike, it had become a place where normally pitched voices and decisive actions seemed shocking.

As we reached the door, I glanced back. The sheeted shape, the single dimmed light, made of the bed a catafalque, and of the room something alien and remote. Outside was a wet night, and a fallen tree, and something urgent to do. There was no time, yet, to sit quietly, and think; either of the past, or how to meet the future. Everything has its mercies.

Lisa was in the hall, having apparently just come out of the office where the telephone was.

She stopped when she saw us. "I've been trying to get through, Julie. It's definitely gone."

Julie said: "Oh *God*," on a little sob, and stumbled, so that for a moment I thought she would pitch straight down the stairs. I gripped and held her.

"Steady up. We'll be there ourselves in a minute."

Con, behind me, said, surprisingly, "Don't worry, we'll get him out." He ran down past us, and across the hall, pausing with a hand on the baize door. "Go and get into the car. Torches and brandy, Annabel, you know where they are. I'll not be a minute. There's some pieces of timber in the barn, we may need them if there's any shoring-up to be done."

The door swung shut behind him. We ran downstairs. I paused to ask Lisa, "Are any of the men still around?"

"No. It's Bates' day off, and Jimmy left as soon as the milking was done. The others went when the rain started. There's only Con here. You'd better go too, hadn't you? I'll go upstairs."

"Lisa—" She guessed, as soon as I spoke; I saw it in her eyes. I nodded. "Yes, I'm afraid so; just a few moments ago . . . But would you go up? It seems terrible just to—to run out like this."

She said nothing. Her eyes took in my face with one of her queer, dispassionate glances, then Julie's. Then she merely nodded, and crossed the hall towards the stairs. I think, in that moment, in spite of everything, I was sincerely and deeply glad I had come home. My own isolation was one thing; Grandfather's had been another. That he had made it himself didn't matter; he had cared, and Con had given him enough . . . but without me here, now, no one at Whitescar would have mourned him.

And, ironically enough, I was at the same time glad of Lisa, calm and impassive as ever, mounting the stairs to his room.

I pushed open the green baize door, and hustled Julie through it. "Hurry. I'll bring the things. And don't worry, Julie, pet, Con'll look after him."

It didn't even strike me at the time that the tally of irony was complete.

The big Ford was there in the yard. We had hardly scrambled into it, both close together in the front seat, when Con appeared, a shadowy, purposeful figure laden with some short, solid chunks of timber that could have been thick fencing posts, together with an axe and a ditcher's spade. He heaved these into the back of the car, slid in behind the wheel, started the motor with a roar, and swung the car round in a lurching half-circle and through the yard gate all in a moment. The lights leaped out along the rising track. Rain, small now but still thick enough and wetting, sparkled and lanced in the light. I realized that the storm had withdrawn already; the lightning was only a faint flicker away to the east, and the thunder was silent.

The track was muddy, and Con drove fast. The car took a rising bend at forty, lurched hair-raisingly across a deep rut, swung into a skid that took her sideways a full yard on to turf, hit a stone with a bouncing tire, and was wrenched straight to pass between the posts of the first cattle grid, with scarcely an inch to spare on the off side.

Con said abruptly, "What happened, Julie? Try to put us right in the picture. Just where is he, how is he hurt, can we get to him?"

"It's the cellar," she said. "You know the place is a ruin; well, it had all fallen in where the old cellar stairs used to be, so they spent most of the day shifting that, and then—"

"They?" I said.

"Yes. Mr. Forrest had told Donald—"

"Mr. Forrest's there?"

I thought my voice sounded quite ordinary, even flat, but I saw Con turn to look at me, and then away again. The car roared round a curve, slid a little on the clay bankside, and then straightened up for the next grid. High Riggs now. At the edge of our lights the uncut fringe of hay along the track stood up like a horse's crest, stiff and glittering under the light rain.

"Yes," said Julie. "They'd been to the Hall cellars first—oh, well, never mind, but it turned out it was actually the cellars at the gate-house—"

"The Roman stones," I said. "Oh, dear heaven, yes, of course, they were still looking?"

"Yes, oh yes! When the ivy tree came down it brought down the chimney and most of that end wall, and the bit of the floor that those beams were holding. I—I was waiting outside, and—"

"Is he hurt?"

"I told you. He's down in the—"

"*Adam Forrest.* Is he hurt?"

"I don't know. But when the place came down they were both inside, and when I could get through the dust I tried to pull some of the stuff away from the cellar door, but Mr. Forrest—he was inside—shouted for me to hurry and get help, because Donald was hurt, and not answering him, and he didn't know how much because he hadn't found the torch yet, and couldn't get at him, and the stuff was settling. *Con, the gate's shut!*"

The car had been mounting the hill with a rush like a lift. She reached the crest, topped it, and even as Julie cried out, the lights, shooting out level now, caught the gate full on. The bars seemed to leap up out of the dark, solid as a cliff wall. Beyond, the headlamps lit a field of staring cattle.

Con jammed everything on, and the car seemed to dig in its hind wheels the way a jibbing horse digs in its hoofs, to come up all standing with her bonnet touching the bars.

Before we had stopped I was out of the car and wrenching at the stiff metal fastening. The gate went wide with a swing. As the car moved slowly forward Con, leaning out of his window, shouted, "Leave it! Get in quickly."

I obeyed him, and even before my door was shut, we had gathered speed once more.

I said, "Con. The cattle. They'll get through."

"The hell with that." I glanced at him in surprise. In the light from the dash I could see his face; it was preoccupied, and I thought it was only with the car, he was lost in the moment, in the driving, in holding the lurching, bouncing vehicle as fast as possible on an impossible road. Fast, violent action, a summons coming out of the dark like a fire alarm, that suited Con. Just as (I had had time to see it now) it suited him to save Donald; Donald would take Julie away.

"I'm sorry about that," he was saying. "I thought sure you'd have left the gate open, Julie."

"I—I came over the grid."

"But it's broken."

"I know." She gave a little gulp that might either have been a laugh or a sob. "I—I broke something off the car. There was an awful bang. Donald'll be livid with me . . . if he . . . if he—"

"Hold up," I said sharply. "We're nearly there."

"Is the top gate open?" This from Con.

"Yes."

"Okay," he said, and a moment later the Ford shot between the posts where the white gate swung wide, and skidded to a splashing halt in front of the looming, terrifying mass of debris that had been the ivy tree.

The lightning had split the great tree endways, so that it had literally fallen apart, one vast trunk coming down clear across the lane that led to the road, the other smashing straight down on to what had remained of the ruined gate-house. It was the branches, not the trunk itself, that had actually hit the building, so that the masonry was not cleanly hacked through by the one gigantic blow, but smashed and scattered by a dozen heavy limbs, and then almost buried from sight under the mass of tangled boughs and leaves, and the heavy, sour-smelling black mats of the ivy.

Con had swung the car slightly left-handed as it stopped, and he left the headlights on. They lit the scene with hard clarity; the huge clouded mass of the tree, its leaves glittering and dripping with the rain, among which the scattered masonry showed white; the raw new gash of the split trunk, where the black trail of the lightning could be clearly seen; and, sticking up through the boughs with a sickening kind of irrelevance, those fragments of the building that still stood. The surviving end wall and its chimney were intact, and half the front of the house, as far as the door with the heavy carved lintel, and the date, 1758 . . .

We thrust ourselves out of the car, and ran to the black gap of the doorway. In my haste I had only found one torch to bring, but there had been another in the car, and with this Con led the way through the doorway, where the car's headlamps served only to throw deeper shadows. Inside the wrecked walls was a black chaos of smashed masonry and tangled wet boughs and splintered beams.

Con hesitated, but Julie pushed past him, one hand up to keep the whipping boughs from her eyes as she thrust through the debris that blocked the hallway.

She called, "Donald! Donald! Are you all right?"

It was Adam who answered her, his voice sounding muffled and strained. It came from somewhere to the left of the hallway and below it. "He's all right. Have you brought help?"

"Con and Annabel. Here, Con, they're down here."

Con had shoved after her, stooping under the barrier of one biggish branch, and was kneeling by what seemed in the torchlight to be a gap in the left-hand wall of the passage. I followed him. This was, I suppose, where the door to the cellars had stood. Now there was merely a hole through the shambles of broken masonry, not quite big enough to admit a man. It gave on darkness.

Con flashed the torch into the gap, lighting the flight of cellar steps.

Twelve steps led steeply downwards, looking undisturbed, and solid enough; at the bottom was a short length of stone-flagged passage which must have led to the cellar door. Now, the doorway had disappeared. Where it had been was a pile of stones and rubble where the ceiling and one wall had collapsed, taking with them the splintered wreckage of the doorposts. But the crossbeam still held. It had fallen when the uprights collapsed, and was wedged now at an angle, within a foot or so of the floor, roofing a narrow, triangular gap of darkness which was the only way through to the cellar beyond. Above the beam pressed the weight of the broken wall, and the broken building above, all thrust down in their turn by the pressure of the fallen boughs. Stones were still falling here and there, I heard the patter of loose stuff somewhere; the other passage wall showed a frightening bulge; and there was fresh dust dancing in the torchlight.

Adam was lying right underneath the beam, face downwards. His feet were towards us, and the top half of his body was out of sight. I recognized the faded brown corduroys, his working garb, now thick with dust. For one sickening moment I thought that the great beam had fallen clean across his back, then I saw there was a gap of perhaps four inches between it and his body. He must have been somewhere on the cellar steps when the crash occurred, and he had been trying to creep under the fallen stuff to reach the place where Donald lay.

And, for the moment, the crossbeam held.

"Forrest?" Con's voice was subdued. A shout, it seemed, might bring the whole thing down, irrevocably in ruins. Even as he spoke, there was the slithering sound of something settling, and the whisper of dust chuting on to the steps below us. Somewhere, some timber creaked. I think it was only a broken bough of the ivy tree, but it lifted the hair along my arms. "Forrest?" called Con softly. "Are you all right?"

"I'm all right." Adam spoke breathlessly; it was as if he was making some violent effort, like holding up the beam with his own body; but he didn't move. "Seton's inside here; there's another pile of the—stuff —just in here, past the beam, and I can't—get any purchase—to move it. He'll be safe enough . . . it's a groined ceiling, it won't come down in there, and he's lying clear of this . . . I can just reach him if I lie flat, but I can't get—any further—and we'll not get him out till this stuff's moved. How long will the doctor be?"

"We couldn't get him. The lines are down."

"Dear God. Didn't Julie say—?"

"Look, if Seton's not badly hurt, you'll simply have to leave him, and come out, for the time being." Con had propped his torch where it could light the gap, and was already, gingerly, beginning to widen this. "You say the roof's safe over him; if you come back, we could probably shift enough stuff between us to get clear through to him. In any case, first things first, if this place isn't shored up pretty damn quick, I wouldn't give twopence for your own chances. That stuff's settling while you wait."

I heard Julie take in her breath. Adam said painfully, "My dear man, you'll have to prop it round me as best you can, and take the chance. Otherwise it's a certainty. I can't leave him. He's torn an artery."

Beside me, Julie gave a little gasp like a moan. I said, "Julie! Get a way cleared back to the car, and fetch the props. Pass them to me under that bough."

"Yes," she said, "yes," and began, with savage but barely effectual hands, to push and break a way back through the tangle to the doorway.

"I've got a tourniquet on, of a sort." Adam's voice was still muffled, so that I hoped Julie, working a yard or two away, couldn't hear it. "And it's doing the trick. I don't think he's losing much, now. But it's tricky in the dark, and I can't hold it indefinitely. You'll have to get the doctor straight away. Annabel?"

"Yes?"

"The car's there?"

"Yes."

"Will you go? If you can't find Wilson straight away—"

Julie had heard, after all. She turned among the wet branches. "The tree's down across the road, too. We can't take the car, and it's four miles."

I said, "The telephone at West Lodge, Adam? It's the same line as Whitescar, isn't it?"

"I'm afraid so."

I was on my feet. "I'll go on foot. It's all right, Julie, once I get to the road I'll get a lift."

"There's never anything along the road at this time of night," said Julie desperately, "you know there isn't! If you drove the car into the field, couldn't you get it round the tree, and—?"

"No use. We've nothing to cut the wires with, and anyway she'd bog down in a yard. We're wasting time. I'm going. I'll run all the way if I have to."

Con said: "It's more than four miles, it's nearer six. And you might get a lift or you might not. Your best chance is Nether Shields."

"But there's no bridge!" cried Julie.

"No," I said, "but I can drive right up to the footbridge at West Lodge, and then it's barely two miles up to the farm. Yes, that's it, Con." I turned quickly back. "Adam?"

"Yes?"

"Did you hear? I'm going to Nether Shields. Their telephone may be working, and I can get Dr. Wilson from there. If it's not, one of the boys will go for him. I'll send the others straight over here."

Julie said, on a sob, "Oh, God, it'll take an hour. Two miles up from West Lodge, and all uphill. You'll kill yourself, and it'll be too late!"

"Nonsense!" I said. "Run and open the gate."

"It's open. Con left it open."

"Not that one. It's quicker if I go by the top track through the Park. If I go down by Whitescar, I've to use the little track up behind the house, and there's three gates on that. Hurry, let's go!"

But she didn't move. "A horse! That's it!"

I was propping my torch where it would help Con. I turned. "What?"

"A horse! If you took the mare you could go straight across the ford and across the fields, and it's hardly any further than from West Lodge, and you'd be there much quicker!"

Con said, "That's an idea," then I saw it hit him. He paused fractionally, with his fingers curled round a lump of sandstone, and I caught his bright sidelong look up at me. He said, "The mare's not shod."

Julie cried, "That doesn't matter! What does the mare matter?"

I said impatiently, "She'd be lame in half a mile, and I'd get nowhere."

Con said, "Take Forrest's colt. He'll let you." Even then, it took me two heartbeats to realize what he was doing. Then I understood. I had been right, none of this touched him. The agonizing emergency was nothing more to him than an exciting job. In this moment of terror and imminent death, he was unscathed. By everything that had happened, he was untouched. And I had liked him for it; been grateful for it.

Well, he still had to get Adam out.

I said shortly, "It would save no time. I'd have to catch him."

Adam's voice again from beyond the beam. It sounded, now, like the voice of a man at the limits of his control. "Annabel, listen, wait, my dear . . . it's an idea. The colt's in the stable at West Lodge; I brought him in today. Take the car across there . . . if he'll face the water . . . only a few minutes to Nether Shields. He'll go, for you, I think. . . ."

The gap in the wall was open now. Con laid a stone down, and sat back on his heels. The twin torchbeams held us, Con and myself, in a round pool of limelight, one on either side of the gap. We stared at one another. He was no longer smiling.

I said to Adam, without taking my eyes off Con, "All right. I'll manage."

"The second door in the stableyard. You know where the bridles are."

"Yes. I know."

Adam said, "Take care, my dear. He doesn't like thunder."

"I'll be all right." I said it straight to that stare of Con's. "I can manage him. Don't worry about me."

"You'll take the horse?" cried Julie.

"Yes. Open the top gate for me. Hold on, Adam, darling."

As I went, I saw Con sitting there, back on his heels, staring after me.

CHAPTER

SEVENTEEN

"The water is rough and wonderful steepe,
Follow, my love, come over the strand—
And in my saddle I shall not keepe,
And I the fair flower of Northumberland."
Ballad: *The Fair Flower of Northumberland.*

It was important not to think about the scene I was leaving behind me
in the dark gate-house; to blot out Donald, his life ebbing slowly behind the wall of debris; Julie, helpless, holding panic on a thin thread;
Adam, prone in the dust under that settling mass. . . .

And Con there to help. I mustn't even remember that. I didn't know
how that quick brain would work; what he would seize for himself out
of this new situation. Con, if it suited Con, would work like a galley
slave, and do miracles; but if it didn't, God alone knew what he would
do.

But I put it out of my mind, and ran to the waiting car.

It seemed to take an hour to turn her, reversing out between the
pillars of the gateway, over mosses made slimy with rain, and liberally
strewn with fallen twigs, and fragments of rotten timber, and stray
stones scattered from the smashed lodge. I made myself take it slowly,
but even so, the wheels spun and slithered crazily among the fallen rubbish, and my hands and arms, shaking now as if with fever, seemed
powerless to control the car. I heard the ominous sound of metal scraping stone, then we were free of the driveway, and swinging to face west
again, and Julie had run across to open the gate to the upper track.

As I passed her, I called out, "Keep your eye open for the doctor's
car! He may already be on his way to see Grandfather."

I saw her nod, looking pale as a ghost in the momentary glare of
light, and her mouth shaped the one word, "*Hurry!*"

I drove my foot down as far as I dared, and tried to remember what
I could of the road.

It was eight years since I had driven along the upper track to West

Lodge. Two fields first, I remembered, then trees bordering the track, young firs, waist-high, that the forestry people had put in; for even then Adam had been trying all means to make the estate pay its way. It was a shock to run suddenly between black walls of spruce that shut out the lighter night, and towered well above the roof of the car. Time was, and they had grown a foot a year. The headlamps lit a narrow black canyon through which we ran at a fair speed, as the track was paved with pine needles which had acted as drainage, and the walls of trees had kept off the worst of the storm.

Then a gate, standing open; a long hill curling down between high banks; an avenue, planted in more leisurely days, of great beeches that soared up silver in the lights, then a twisting, up-and-down quarter-mile along the gully cut by some small stream, where all I could do was hang on grimly to the controls and hope that the track was reasonably well-drained.

It wasn't, and I soon throttled down to a safe and cowardly fifteen miles an hour, which felt slower than walking, and brought the sweat out on my body till my hands slipped on the wheel.

Then a gate, shut, hanging a little crookedly across the way.

It was almost a relief to be out of the car, and running to open it. The lever was stiff, jammed by the sagging of the hinges, but I fought it out of its socket at last, and shoved at the heavy gate. This shifted a couple of inches, and stuck. It had sagged into a muddy rut, but that was not what prevented it from opening. As I bent to heave it forcibly wider, I heard the rattle of a chain. A loop of chain, dark with rust, and with a rusty padlock tightly locked, was fastened round gate and gate post, holding them together.

A locked gate; no place to turn the car; the choice facing me of either reversing down that dreadful piece of track till I could turn for the long trail back, and round by Whitescar; or of abandoning the car and running the half-mile between here and West Lodge. Either alternative, unthinkable . . .

There are times when your body and nerves think for you. Adrenalin, they tell you nowadays. They used to say, "Needs must, when the devil drives," or even, "God helps those who help themselves."

I seized the chain and yanked at it, with the fury of desperate need, and it came off in my hands. It had only been a loop, flung loosely over the posts, to hold the gate from sagging further open. I think I stood for four precious seconds, staring at it in my hands, as if by some miracle I really had snapped its massive links like horsehair. I should have known that Adam wouldn't have let me come this way, if it had been barred.

Adam. I dropped the chain into the soaking grass by the gate post, shoved the heavy gate wide as if it had weighed an ounce, scrambled back into the car, and was through the gate and away before the grasses had stopped shaking.

A sharp rise, then, away from the trees, and here was the straight, good half-mile across a high heathy pasture where the dry gravel of the track showed white in the lights, and as clear as if it had been marked with cats' eyes.

The crest of the moor. A single birch tree, its stem flashing white and then lost again in the darkness behind. Then the sudden, sharp dip of the descent towards the river, the swift, curling drop into the sheltered saucer of land where West Lodge lay.

I had forgotten just how steep the hill was, and how sharp the turn.

As my lights met the crest of the hill, we must have been doing forty-five. I stood on the brake, but as we switch-backed over the top and dived for the river, we were still traveling like a bomb. The car went down the drop like an aircraft making for the touch-down. I saw the bend coming, drove my foot hard down on the brake, and put everything I had of strength and timing into getting her round the corner.

I felt the front wheel mounting the edge, swinging, thrown wide by the force of our turn. I had the steering wheel jammed hard over to the left. I felt the rear swing, too, mount, pause . . .

We could do it. We were round . . .

On a dry night, we might have done it, even despite my bad judgment. But the track was damp, and the grass; and the wheels, at the very verge, had met mud. . . .

The front of the car drifted, slid, swam uncontrollably wide. The wheel topped the bank, was over. The car lurched crazily as she hit the rough turf of the slope to the river. The lights struck the water ten yards away, and the mirror-flash startled my eyes.

I must have straightened the wheel instinctively as we left the track, or we would have turned over. As it was, the car plunged down the last four feet of the bank dead straight, in a dive for the river, lurched over a nine-inch drop to the shingle, hit the edge of the drop with her under-carriage, and stopped dead, with the front wheels on the gravel, and the water sliding by not a yard from the bonnet.

In the silence after the engine stalled, the river sounded as loud as thunder.

I sat there, still gripping the wheel, listening to the tick of cooling metal, and stupidly watching the wipers still wagging to and fro, to and fro, squealing across the dry glass. It had stopped raining some time back, and I hadn't noticed. . . .

I don't know how long I sat there. Not more than seconds, I think, though it seemed an age. I was unhurt, and, though I must have been shaken, I had no time to feel it. This was a pause in the movement; no more.

I clambered out of the car. The stableyard lay no more than fifty yards away, at the foot of the hill. I retained enough wit to switch the ignition off, and the headlights, and then I abandoned the car, and ran.

I had forgotten the route, and crashed Con's car in consequence, but when I got to the stable door my hand went automatically to the light switch, and, as the light snapped on, I reached for the bridle without even looking for it. Leather met my hand, and the cool jingle of metal. I lifted it from its peg, and then stood still for a moment or two, controlling my breathing, letting my eyes get used to the light, and the horse used to the sight of me.

It was no use approaching him like this. A few more seconds now, to let my heart slow down to something near its normal rate, and to control my hands . . . I hadn't realized, till I lifted down that ringing bridle, that my hands were shaking still.

I leaned back against the wall of the stable, and regarded the Forrest colt.

He was in a loose-box opposite the door. He stood across the far corner of it, facing away from me, but with his head round towards me, and ears pricked, inquiring, slightly startled.

I began to talk, and the effort to steady my voice steadied me. When I saw the ears move gently, I opened the loose-box and went in.

He didn't move, except to cock his head higher, and a little sideways, so that the great dark eyes watched me askance, showing a rim of white. I slid a gentle hand on to his neck and ran it up the crest towards his ears. He lowered his head then, and snuffled at the breast of my blouse.

I said, "Help me now, Rowan, beauty," and cupped the bit towards him. He didn't even pause to mouth it; he took it like a hungry fish taking a fly. In seven seconds after that, as smoothly as a dream, I had him bridled. In ten more, I was leading him outside into the night. I didn't take time for a saddle. I mounted from the edge of the water trough, and he stood as quietly as a donkey at the seaside.

Then I turned him towards the river. The way led to his pasture, so he went willingly and straight, with that lovely long walk of his that ate up the yards. I made myself sit quietly. Momentarily blinded by the darkness as I was, I could neither guide nor hurry him. I talked to him, of course; it seemed that this was more for my own comfort than the horse's, but it took us both as far as the faint glimmer of the river, where a path turned off towards the pastures, from the foot of the narrow wooden footbridge.

Now, I had no idea if I could get Rowan to cross the water which, swelled a bit by the recent thunder-rain, was coming down at a fair speed, and with some sound and fury over its treacherous boulders. It would be a bad enough crossing by daylight, and in the dark it was doubly hazardous. But there is no horse living, except a circus horse, that will cross the unsafe echoing of a wooden footbridge—even if I had dared put him at the triple step at either end. It was the water or nothing.

At least here we had come out from under the trees, and I could see. The bank shelved fairly steeply near the bridge. The river was a wide, broken glimmer, with shadows where the boulders thrust up, and luminous streams of bubbling foam where the freshets broke. The sound was lovely. Everything smelt fresh and vivid after the rain. As I put Rowan at the bank I could smell thyme and water mint, and the trodden turf as his hoofs cut in.

He hesitated on the edge, checked, and began to swerve away. I insisted. Good-manneredly he turned, hesitated again, then faced the drop of the bank. Then, as his fore hoofs went down the first foot of the drop, he stopped, and I saw his ears go back.

Now, when one rides without a saddle, there are certain obvious disadvantages, but there is one great advantage—one is with the horse; his muscles are joined to, melted in with, the rider's; the rider is part of the beast's power, moves with him, and can think into his body a vital split second faster than when the impulse has to be conveyed through rein and heels alone.

I felt the colt's hesitation, doubt, and momentary fear, even before the impulses had taken root in his mind, and my own impulse forward was supplied instantaneously. He snorted, then lunged forward suddenly and slithered down into the water.

I held him together as he picked his way across between the streaming boulders. I was saying love words that I thought I had forgotten. His hoofs slipped and rang on the stones, and the water swirled, shining, round his legs. It splashed against his fetlocks, then it was to his knees; he stumbled once, and in recovering sent one hoof splodging down into a pool that drenched me to the thigh. But he went steadily on, and in no time, it seemed, the small shingle was crunching under his feet, and we were across. He went up the far bank with a scramble and a heave that almost unseated me, shook his crest, then plunged forward at a rough canter to meet the track.

This ran steeply up, here, from the footbridge, and, though rutted and uneven, lay clearly enough marked in the moonlight between its verges of dark sedge. I twisted my right hand in Rowan's mane, set him at the slope, and gave him his head.

He took it fast, in that eager, plunging canter that, normally, I would have steadied and controlled. But he couldn't, tonight, go fast enough for me . . . and besides, there was this magnificent dreamlike feeling, the flying night, the surging power that was part of me, the drug of speed that felt like speed, the desperate mission soon to be accomplished. . . .

The canter lengthened, became a gallop; we were up the slope and on the level ground. There was a gate, I knew. We would have to stop and open it. Even if I hadn't been riding bare-back, I couldn't have set him to jump it in the dark. I peered ahead uncertainly, trusting the horse to see it before I did, hoping he knew just where it was. . . .

He did. I felt his stride shorten, and next moment saw—or thought I saw—the dim posts of a fence, joined with invisible wire, with the shapes of cattle beyond. Across the road, nothing. The way was clear. The gate seemed to be open . . . yes, I could see it now, set to one side of the track, as if it were lying back, wide open, against the wire fence.

Rowan flicked his ears forward, then back, and hurtled down the track at full gallop.

I had hardly time to wonder, briefly, why the cattle hadn't crowded through the gap, when we were on it, and I saw. The gate for the beasts stood to the side, and was shut, as I should have known it would be. And, clear across the way, where I had thought there was a gap, lay the cattle grid, eight feet of treacherous, clanging iron grid that, even if it didn't break his legs, would throw us both. . . .

No time to stop him now, or swerve him to face the gate. Two tremendous strides, and he was on it.

This time, he thought for me. As the grid gaped in front of his feet, looking, in the dark, like a wide pit across his path, he steadied, lifted, and was over, as smoothly as a swallow in an eddy of air.

And then all at once, ahead of us, were the massed trees, and the lights of Nether Shields.

I learned afterwards that there had been some storm damage at Nether Shields, and that after the rain was off the men—Mr. Fenwick and his two sons—had come out to take a look round. They were in the yard when I got there, and they must have heard the horse's hoofs coming up the moor at the gallop, for all three were at the gate.

The main track went by some fifty yards from Nether Shields. We cut across the corner, and I sent Rowan headlong for the gate.

It is possible that they thought the horse was bolting with me, for nobody opened the gate. Rowan came to a slithering halt with his breast almost up against the bars, and then, seeing the men, shied violently sideways and began to circle.

Someone swung the gate wide, then, and the three men stood aside. It was all I could do to get Rowan in past them, through the gate, but he went in the end, fighting every inch of the way. One of the men shut the gate behind us, and would have reached for the bridle, but I thought the horse would rear, and said, breathlessly, "Leave him. It's all right. Keep back . . ."

Someone said, "It's Forrest's," and another: "It's the Winslow girl," and then Mr. Fenwick's voice came quickly, "What is it, lass? Trouble?"

I found I could hardly speak. I was breathless from effort, but it wasn't that. My teeth were chattering as if I was chilled. I suppose it was shock catching up on me; my whole body was shaking, now, and the muscles of my thighs felt loose against the restless movements of the colt. I think that if I hadn't had a hand in his mane, I would, shamefully, have fallen off him.

I managed to say, somehow, "There's been an accident at the gate-house. Forrest Hall. A tree's down on the gate-house, and someone's hurt, and Mr. Forrest's there too. They're both trapped inside, and if they don't get help soon the whole place looks like coming down on them. The phone's off at Whitescar. Is yours working?"

Mr. Fenwick was a man of swift action and few words. He said merely, "Don't know. Sandy, go and see. Is it for the doctor?"

"Yes. Yes. Tell him a cut artery, we think, and to come quickly. And could you come yourself—all of you, straight away? There's a wall collapsing, and the men underneath, and only Con and Julie there—"

"Aye. Bill, get the Land Rover out. Ropes, torches, crowbars. Sandy, tell your mother."

Sandy went in at a run. Bill had already vanished into a shed whose doors, dragged wide, showed the gleam of the Land Rover's bonnet.

I slipped off the horse's back, and held him. "Props," I said. "Have you anything to shore the stones up?"

"What sort of length?"

"Short. Just to hold them off a man. He's lying underneath. A foot, eighteen inches, anything just to hold them clear."

"Good Christ," said the farmer.

"We had fencing posts, and Con can push them in sideways," I said, "but there weren't enough. And some for the passage, too, if you've any longer ones—"

"There's plenty stuff in the shed, all lengths." He raised his voice above the sudden roar of the Land Rover's motor. "Put your lights on, Bill!"

The lights shot out. Rowan went back in a clattering rear, almost lifting me from the ground. I saw the farmer turn, and cried, "Never mind! Get on! I can manage him!"

The Land Rover came out of the shed, and stopped just short of the yard gate, with its engine ticking over and its lights full on. Bill jumped out of the front and ran back to where his father was dragging solid lumps of sawn timber from a wood stack. I saw the gleam of a metal bar, and the shape of a heavy pick, as they were hurled into the back of the vehicle. A couple of what looked like old railway sleepers went in after them.

"The rope from the tractor shed?" asked Bill.

"Aye." The farmer threw a shovel in after the rest.

Sandy must have told his mother something as he ran to the telephone, for she appeared now in the lighted doorway of the farmhouse. "Miss Winslow? Sandy's told me of the trouble. He's on the telephone now."

"*It's working?*"

"Oh, yes."

"Dear God," I said, meaning it, and put my forehead against Rowan's hot neck.

"My dear," she said, "don't worry. It won't be long. Doctor Wilson's not at home, he's up at Haxby, but Sandy's getting through now. He'll be down at Forrest in something under twenty minutes, and the men will be there in ten. Would you like me to go with them, in case I can help?"

There came to me, the first flash of warmth in an Arctic night, a vague memory that before her marriage to Jem Fenwick of Nether Shields, she had been a nurse. He had broken a leg and spent a month in the Royal Victoria, and taken her back with him when he was discharged. A long time ago now, but if the doctor were delayed. . . .

I cried, "Oh, Mrs. Fenwick, could you go with them? *Could* you? There's Julie's young man with a cut artery, and Adam Forrest trying to hold it, and the cellar roof going to come down on them, and only Con and Julie there to try and fix it up."

She was as decisive as her husband. "Of course. I'll get some stuff and be with you. Don't you fret, child. Can you leave that horse, and come in?"

"No."

She wasted no time arguing or persuading. She must have known that I was almost grateful for the job of holding Rowan quiet amid the bustle and shouting in the yard. She turned back into the house, and I heard her calling, "Betty! Pour some of that tea into the big flask, quickly! And get the brandy. Sandy, go up and fetch blankets—what? Oh, half a dozen. Hurry, now!"

The Land Rover was loaded; Bill had pulled the gate open, and was in the driving seat. Mr. Fenwick heaved a great coil of rope into the back, and then came over to me.

"I take it you came by West Lodge?"

"Yes. The tree that's down has blocked the lane to the main road. I drove over to West Lodge, and then took the horse."

"Is the river deep?"

"In places, but it's coming down fastish, and near the bridge it's all boulders. There's no decent crossing, even for that thing."

"I doubt you're right. We can drive her down and pile the stuff across into your car. It's at the Lodge?"

"No. You can't. I—I crashed it. I'm sorry, but—"

"Good Christ," he said again. "Are you all right?"

"Yes, quite."

"Well, we'll have to go the other way. It'll not take much longer; it's a good road. Ah, here we are." This as Sandy ran past us with a load of blankets, which went on top of the tools and props. Then a girl, with what must have been the hot tea and brandy. And finally, Mrs. Fenwick, diminutive but bustlingly efficient, with a box in her hands, and about her, clad though she was in an old tweed coat, the impression of a comforting rustle of starch.

Everyone piled into the Land Rover. The farmer turned to me. "Coming? Shove the colt in the barn, he'll come to no harm. We'll make room somehow."

I hesitated, but only for a moment. "No. I'll take the horse back. Someone ought to go to Whitescar and tell Lisa. We'll have beds ready there. Don't bother about me. And—thank you."

His reply was lost in the roar of the motor. The Land Rover leaped forward, cut across the field corner, her four-wheel drive sending her through the mud churned by the cattle, as easily as if it were an arterial road. I heard Mrs. Fenwick call something shrill and reassuring, then the vehicle was nothing but a receding roar and a red light in the darkness, making for the highroad.

I only remembered then, with a curious little jolt, that I had forgotten to tell them about Grandfather.

The girl said, shyly, beside me, "Will you come in, Miss Winslow? Just for a minute? There's tea made."

"No, my dear. Thanks all the same. I must get back. Will you shut the gate behind me?"

"Surely."

It wasn't so easy to mount Rowan this time, but I managed it with the aid of the gate itself, and presently, having said good night to the girl, I turned him out of the yard to face the darkness once again.

It was now, with the job done, that nature went back on me. My muscles felt as weak as a child's, and I sat the horse so loosely that, if he had treated me to a single moment's display of temperament, I'd have slid straight down his shoulders under his hoofs.

But, the two of us alone again, he went as softly as a cat across the grass, let me open the second gate from his back, and after that he walked, with that smooth, distance-devouring stride of his, till we came to the river bank.

Sooner than have to fight or cajole him, I'd have dismounted and led him across, myself thigh-deep. But he took to the water as smoothly as a mallard slipping off her nest, and in a few minutes more, it seemed, we were striding out at a collected, easy canter for Whitescar.

He swerved only once, as we passed the crashed Ford squatting down on the river gravel, but a word reassured him, and he went smoothly on.

It was now, when I had no more effort to make, when Rowan was, so to speak, nursing me home to Whitescar, with the sound of his hoofs steady and soft on the turf of the avenue, that the spectres of imagination had time to crowd up out of the dark.

Do what's nearest . . . I had done just that, and I was right. Someone had to go to Whitescar, and warn Lisa what to prepare for. There was nothing I could have done at the gate-house. And if I could do nothing for Adam, I could at least care for his horse, who was worth, in hard cash, at least as much as the garden and West Lodge put together. . . .

But this way, I should be the last to know what had happened. And in the darkness, as Rowan (whom I would never be able to see as "hard cash" in my life) strode steadily and softly on, I was forced at last, with nerves sufficiently stripped by shock, to admit openly to myself what I had known at some other level for long enough.

It might have already happened. This night, dark and damp and sweet-smelling, might at this very moment be empty of all I cared about. All. If Adam were dead (I acknowledged it now), there was nothing else, nowhere else, nothing. They are fools indeed who are twice foolish. I had had my folly, eight years back, and again this morning in the early dewfall, and now, tonight, it might be that the chance to be a fool again was gone.

The colt stopped, lowered his head, and blew. I leaned over his neck, and pushed open the last gate. The lights of Whitescar were just below us.

A few moments later Rowan clattered into the yard, and stood still. As I slid from his back, Lisa came hurrying out. "I thought I heard a horse! Annabel! What's happened?"

I told her everything, as succinctly as I could. I must have been incoherent from sheer fatigue, but at least she knew that a bed, or beds, would be needed, and I must have made it clear that the doctor would soon be on his way. "I'll be with you in a minute," I finished wearily, "when I've put the horse in."

Only then did I notice how she looked from me to Rowan, and back again. "Yes," I said, gently, "I did manage to ride him, after all. I always did have a way with horses."

I left her standing there. As I led the lathered horse round the end of the Dutch barn, I saw her turn, and hurry back into the house.

The mare's box stood empty. I put the light on, and led Rowan in.

He went without even a nervous glance round at the strange stable. Even when Tommy lifted her head from the nest in the manger, blinking at the light, Rowan only snorted, blew, and then lowered his nose to forage for hay. I fastened the bars behind him, slipped the bridle off and hung it up, then tipped a measure of feed down in front of him. He blew again, sighed, and began to munch, rolling an eye back at me as I brought the brush and set to work on him. Tired as I was, I dared not leave him steaming, and lathered, as he was, with ripples of sweat like the wave marks on a beach.

I had my left hand flat against his neck, and was currying his back and ribs vigorously, when, suddenly, I felt the muscles under my hands go tense, and the comfortable munching stopped. Rowan put his head up, and his tail switched nervously. From the corner of my eye I saw a shadow leap from the manger to the top of the partition, and vanish without a sound. Tommy, taking cover.

I glanced over my shoulder.

In the doorway, framed by the black night, stood Con. He was alone. He came quietly into the stable, and shut the half-door behind him.

CHAPTER

EIGHTEEN

"I lo'e Brown Adam well," she says,
  "I wot sae he lo'es me;
 I wadna gie Brown Adam's love
  For nae fause knight I see."

Ballad: Brown Adam.

He stopped just inside the door, and I saw him reach back to pull the upper half shut, too.

I hardly noticed what he was doing. There was room for only one thought in my mind just then. I straightened up, saying sharply, "What's happened?"

"They got him out. The doctor got there just before I left." He was struggling with the bolt, to thrust it home, but it was rusted, and stuck. He added, over his shoulder: "I see you did get the colt over to Nether Shields. Congratulations."

"*Con!*" I couldn't believe that even Con could so casually dismiss what must even now be happening up at the gate-house. "*What's happened?* Are they all right? For heaven's *sake!*"

He abandoned the bolt, and turned. He came no nearer, but stood there, eyeing me. Beside me, Rowan stood stiffly, not eating, motionless except for that nervously switching tail. I laid an automatic hand on his neck; it was beginning to sweat again.

Con's voice was subdued, even colourless. "I told you. They got Seton out safely enough in the end. The cut in the artery wasn't too bad; he'd lost a fair amount of blood, and he got a bump on the head, but the tourniquet saved him, and the doctor says it won't be long till he's as right as rain. They'll be bringing him down soon."

So fierce was the preoccupation in my mind, that only now did Con's manner—and his begging of my question—force itself on my attention. I noticed then that he seemed totally unlike himself; quiet, oddly restrained, not tired—that I could have understood—but damped-down in some way, almost as if his mind were not on what he was saying . . . or as if he was holding back what was in the forefront of it.

It came to me, quite clearly, what he was trying not to say. My hand must have moved on Rowan's neck, for the colt shifted his quarters, and his ears flattened.

I said hoarsely, "Why did you come down like this, ahead of the rest? What are you trying to tell me?"

He looked aside, for the first time since I had known him refusing to meet my eyes—Con, who could lie his way through anything, and smile in your face while he did it. There was a horseshoe on a nail by the door; hung there for luck, perhaps, the way one sees them in stables. He fingered it idly for a moment, then lifted it down, turning it over and over in his hands, his head bent to examine it as if it were some rare treasure. He said, without looking up, "The beam came down. I'm sorry."

I must have been leaning back against the horse, because I remember how cold my own body seemed suddenly, and how gratefully the heat from the damp hide met it through my thin blouse. I began to repeat it after him, stupidly, my voice unrecognizable, "The beam . . ." Then, sharply, "*Adam?* Con, you're lying! It isn't possible! You're lying!"

He looked at me quickly, then down again at the metal in his hands. "He wouldn't come out. The beam was shifting, you saw it, but he wouldn't leave Seton, he said, he'd have to take the chance. We did what we could, but with just me and Julie there . . ." He paused, and added, "it happened just before the others got there."

While I had been riding home. It had happened then. *Then.* . . .

My hand had slid up the colt's neck, and was twisted in his mane. I think it was all that was holding me up. I said, so violently that the horse started, "So you let it happen, did you?" Con was looking at me again now. "'Before the others got there . . .' *Of course it was!* Because you let it happen! You did it, Connor Winslow, you wanted him dead!"

He said slowly, "Are you crazy? Why should I want that?"

"God knows why! Do you have to have a reason? I've stopped wondering how your mind works. I suppose it suited you to let him die, just as it suited you to get Donald out alive! You think nobody exists but yourself, you think you're God . . . every rotten murderer thinks the same! So Donald's alive, and Adam—" I stopped, as abruptly as if he had struck me across the face; then I added, quite flatly, without the faintest vestige of drama or even emotion, "You let him die, and me not there." And this time I wasn't talking to Con.

It must have been fully twenty seconds later that I noticed the silence. The quality of the silence. Then Rowan shifted his feet on the concrete, and I looked at Con again.

He was standing quite still, the horseshoe motionless in his hands. His eyes were wide open now, and very blue. He said softly, and the Irish was there, "Well, well, well . . . so it's true, is it? I thought as much, up there in your grandfather's bedroom, but I couldn't quite believe it . . . not quite; not till the clever little girl took the horse." His knuckles whitened round the horseshoe. "So that's it, is it? That's everything clear at last." He smiled. "Annabel, me darlin', what a fool you've made of me, haven't you, now?"

I didn't answer. The other thing was there in front of me still, a black questioning between myself and God. Con's voice seemed to come from a long way away, like a voice on the wireless, heard from next door through a wall. Irrelevant. A nuisance only, meaning nothing.

The horse threw up his head as Con took a step nearer. "So it was Adam Forrest, was it? Adam Forrest? Christ, who'd have thought it? What fools we all were, weren't we, and a damned adultery going on under our very noses?" All at once his face wasn't handsome at all, but convulsed, thinned, ugly. "And when you heard the wife was dead, you came back, you little bitch. You saw your chance to get me out, by God, and carry on your dirty little affair again into the bargain!"

That got through. "That's not true!" I cried.

"So, you wouldn't look at me . . . I thought there was someone, I thought there was. Your grandfather thought it was me you were meeting, but you wouldn't look at me, would you, Annabel? Oh no, it had to be Forrest of Forrest Hall, no less, not your cousin, who was only good enough to work for you . . ."

Suddenly, stupid and half-fainting (as I suppose I was) with fatigue and shock, I saw what all this time I had never even guessed: a cold rage of jealousy. Not, I am sure, because Con had ever really wanted me, but simply because I had never wanted him. It had been bad enough that I had pushed him aside without a glance, but to prefer another man . . . And the discovery of that man's identity had scored his vanity to the bone.

He took another step forward. "I suppose you thought he'd marry you?" His voice was cruel. "Was that why you came back? Was it? He's married money before, and you're well worth it now, aren't you? What was the game, Annabel? What have you been playing at? Come on, let's have it. You've been playing some game with me, and I want the truth."

He had come right up to the loose-box bar. Rowan was standing quite quietly now, head low, and tail still. But his ears moved with each inflection of our voices, and where I leaned against his shoulder I could feel the tiny tremors running up under his skin, like little flickers of flame.

"But Con . . . Con . . ." It was like groping through fog; there had been something I had to tell Con today, something about the money, that I didn't want it, and never had—that he could have it, just as he had planned, and I would take Mother's money, and go. . . . Something else, too, that I had torn up his "confession" to me, and that he was free to destroy mine, with its useless signature, "Mary Grey." . . . But above all, that he could have the money; that I was glad to let him have it for Whitescar, because Adam and I . . .

I turned my head into the horse's neck. "No, Con . . . not now. Not any more now. Just go away. *Go away.*"

For answer, he came closer. He was right up at the loose-box bar. He had one hand on it; in the other he still held the horseshoe.

"You've made a fool of me all this time, so you have." The low voice was venomous. "Do you think I'd trust you now, with what you know about me? All that crap you talked about leaving the place, making over the money—what the hell were you playing at? Stringing me along, so you could hand me over? Or contest the will?"

I said wearily, "It was true. I wanted you to have it. And you did get Whitescar."

"How do I know even that was true?" he asked savagely. "You told me, yes, but why should I believe a word you say?"

"Oh God, Con, not now. Later, if you must . . . if I ever speak to you again. Go away. Can't you see . . . ?"

"Can't *you* see?" asked Con, and something in his intonation got through to me at last. I lifted my head and looked hazily at him. "Yes," he said. "I've taken enough risks over this, and I'm taking no more. I take my chances where they come, and I'm not missing this one. Lisa'll give me all the alibi I'll need, and there'll be nothing to prove. Even clever little Annabel isn't infallible with a young, wild brute like this . . . the Fenwicks said he was all over the yard with you at Nether Shields, and they won't stop to think he's so flat out he wouldn't hurt a fly." As he spoke, he was lifting the loose-box bar. "Now do you understand?"

Instinct had understood for me, where my failing sense did not. I shrank away from Rowan's shoulder, and came back against the cold iron of the manger. Behind me I heard tiny stirring sounds in the straw, as the sleepy kittens searched for their mother. I believe that the only coherent thought in my mind was that Con mustn't be allowed to find them. . . .

He was in the box with us. I couldn't have moved if I had tried; and if I had tried, I couldn't have got away. The scene seemed to have very little to do with me. The stable was curiously dark, swimming away into an expanding, airy blackness; it was empty, except for something that moved a little, near my shoulder, and Con, coming slowly towards me with some object held in his hand, and a queer look in his eyes. I thought, but not with any sense of its meaning anything to me, he can't kill me in cold blood. Funny! he's finding it difficult. I wouldn't have thought Con would even have hesitated. . . .

His hand moved out, in slow motion, it seemed, and took me by the wrist. At that same half-conscious level I knew that he wanted to frighten me into moving, screaming, running, fighting—anything that could spark off in him the dangerous current of violence. But all I could hear was my brain, repeating the words which, since that morning, it had repeated over and over again, like a damaged record, "It would be easier to be dead. . . ."

I must have said it aloud. I saw the blue eyes widen and flicker, close to mine, then the hand tightened on my wrist. "You little fool," said Con, "he's not dead. I only said that to make you give yourself away."

The light caught the edge of the horseshoe as he lifted it. The horseshoe—this was why he had picked it up. He had intended this. This was why he came down, alone. He had lied about Adam. He was not yet a murderer. This was the truth.

Then I screamed. I wrenched violently away from him, to get my wrist free. The movement brought me hard up against the colt's side, and jerked an oath from Con as he dropped my arm, and tried to throw himself clear.

But he wasn't quite quick enough.

As I went down into the whirling blackness under the colt's belly, I heard the high scream of the horse like a grotesque mimicry of my own, saw the hoofs flash and strike as he reared straight up over me . . . and then the red gloss of blood where, a moment before, Con's blue eyes had stared murder.

They told me later that they heard the scream of the colt above the engine when they were still halfway across High Riggs.

Adam wasn't with them. He, like Con, had not waited. When the horse screamed, he was already at the yard gate, and twelve seconds later he burst into the stable to find Con, thrown clean from the box by that first tremendous slash of the forehoofs, lying in his own blood with, oddly, a loose horseshoe three yards away; and in the box Rowan standing, sweating, but quiet, with me sprawled anyhow right under his feet, and his nose down, nuzzling at my hair.

He must have let Adam into the box to pick me up.

I remember, as in a darkened dream, swimming back through the mist to see Adam's face not a foot from my own. And it was only then that I accepted Con's last statement as the truth.

"Adam. . . ."

He had carried me out of the loose-box into an adjacent stall, and he knelt there, in the straw, with my head against his shoulder. "Don't talk now. It's all right. Everything's all right. . . ."

"Adam, you're not dead."

"No, dear. Now lie quiet. Listen, there's the Land Rover coming down the hill. It's all over. You're quite safe. Donald's all right, did you know? Just lie still; the doctor's coming with them, there's nothing we can do."

"Con's dead, isn't he?"

"Yes."

"He—he was going to kill me."

"It seems he nearly succeeded," said Adam grimly. "If it hadn't been for Rowan, I'd have been too late."

"You knew?"

"I guessed."

"How?"

"God knows. The old radar still working, I suppose. When the Fenwicks turned up, they all set to work and got the cellar walls made as safe as possible, and that beam shored up, then I came out from under, and Mrs. Fenwick—she's tiny, isn't she?—managed to creep through into the cellar to fix Donald up temporarily, till the doctor came. Your cousin was still around, then. Someone had said you were making straight back for Whitescar, to warn Lisa Dermott about beds and so forth. Then the doctor arrived. He couldn't get under the beam, of course, so everyone's attention was concentrated on getting Donald out; and in the general confusion of coming and going in the dark, it was some time before I noticed that Winslow wasn't there any longer. It was only then that I realized that I'd given you away to him, and I'm afraid I didn't even stop to wonder if this might have put you in danger. I just had a strong feeling that it was high time I came down here. As it was."

I shivered, and a muscle in his arm tightened. "I thought, when I heard you scream, that I'd come just too late."

He bent his head, and kissed me. The things he said to me then, in the straw of the dusty stable, with the smells of meal, and the sweating horse, all round us, and the damp of the gate-house cellars still on his coat, and Con's body lying there in its own bright blood under the raw electric light, were the sort of thing that one only says when one's controls have been violently lifted. They are not for retelling, or even for remembering in daylight. But they belonged to that night of terror and discovery, when both of us had had to be driven to the very edge of loss, before we could accept the mercy that had saved us and allowed us to begin again. . . .

Then the Land Rover roared into the yard, and Adam lifted his head and shouted, and the world—in the persons of the doctor, the Fenwicks, and a couple of strangers who had come down with the doctor when they heard of the accident at the gate-house—bustled in on our tragic little Eden.

Adam neither moved, nor let me go. It was as if those early months of lies and subterfuge were suddenly, now, to be purged and forgotten. He knelt without moving, holding me to him, and, as they exclaimed with horror, and the doctor got down beside Con, told them precisely and in a few words what had occurred. Not the attempt at murder, never that. Simply that Con (who had come down ahead of the rest to give Lisa and me the good news) had, not realizing the danger, walked into the loose-box, tripped, and startled the colt, which had reared back and accidentally caught him with its forehoofs. And I—explained Adam —had fainted with the shock.

"And this shoe?" Mr. Fenwick had picked it up and was examining it. "He cast this?"

I had been slow to grasp the significance of Con's choice of weapon. Adam, I saw, got there straight away. If he had noticed the thing earlier, he would no doubt have removed it. He said steadily, "It doesn't look to me like one of Rowan's. It must have fallen from a nail. Was it in the box? Maybe that was what Winslow tripped over."

The farmer turned the shoe over in his hand. It was clean. He glanced at Rowan's forefeet, which were (mercifully) out of my sight. "Aye," he said, "likely enough," and put the thing up on a window sill.

It was late next afternoon when Julie and I walked up through the fields towards the old gate-house.

The air was fresh and sparkling after the storm, the light so clear that each blade of grass seemed to stand separately above its shadow, and there were wild flowers out along the roadside where yesterday there had been only dusty and yellowed turf. We let ourselves out of the gate marked WHITESCAR, and stopped there, looking at the wreckage of the lodge and the ivy tree.

Even this, the day transformed. The great cloud of oak boughs with their golden leaves as yet unfaded, the dark trails of ivy, the pink roses still rioting over what remained of the stone-work—these, in this lovely light, clothed the scene in an air of pastoral, even idyllic melancholy. Last night's near-tragedy might never have been.

But there were the marks of the tires where I had turned the car, there, a few of the timber props still lying; here, most telling of all, the clearing that the Fenwick boys had cut through the part of the tree that blocked the roadway, to let the ambulance through.

Julie and I stood looking at this in silence.

"Poor Lisa," I said at length.

"What will she do?" Her voice was subdued.

"I asked her to stay, but she's going home, she says. I suppose it's best. What's done is done, and we can only try to forget it."

"Yes." But she hesitated. I had told her, now, the story of my conspiracy with Con and Lisa, and also the truth of what had happened last night. "I still don't really understand, you know."

"Who ever does understand what drives a man to murder? You know what he thought last night, of course? He only had my word for it that Grandfather had left Whitescar to him, and when he discovered that I really was Annabel, he couldn't imagine that I'd have stood by and let Grandfather will it away from me. Then he realized that Adam had been—was still—my lover. I believe he had an immediate vision of my marrying Adam and settling here. I doubt if he took time to think anything out clearly; he just knew that I was in a position to contest the will if it *was* in his favour, and even to arraign him for trying to get money by false pretences."

"I see." She gave a little shiver. "What I can't make out is why he *didn't* just let the beam down, last night? He could have done, so easily. It would have killed them both, but I don't believe he would have cared."

"No. But he wanted Donald alive . . . and besides, you were there, watching. It wouldn't have been so easy. And Adam's death would only have solved one problem; mine solved them all. Whether I'd told the truth about the will or not, Con stood to gain by killing me. There was the money, too, remember. He wasn't sure of anything, but he wasn't risking failure at that stage, and the chance was too good to miss. I said Con was never afraid to chance his arm."

"With me, for instance, that night by the river?"

"I think so."

We were silent for a while. Then she touched my arm. "Why do you look like that?"

"I find it very hard not to blame myself."

"Blame yourself?" cried Julie. "Annabel, *darling*, what *for?*"

"I can't help feeling that what happened last night was partly my fault. If I hadn't been so tired and stupid—and if Con hadn't shaken me to pieces with that lie about Adam—I'd have managed to make him see I wasn't hatching plots to do him out of Whitescar. Or if I'd seen him earlier—or even if I hadn't tried to be so clever in the first place, and come back here to outplay him at his own game—"

"Stop this!" She gave my arm a little shake. "Be sensible, for pity's sake! All the trouble and violence there's been has come solely from Con! He's to blame from first to last for what happened last night, you know he is! He went down to the stable with the intention of murdering you, just *on the chance* that you might do him some harm! Yes, it's true, *and* you know it. Even if you'd been fit to talk to him, do you suppose he'd have listened. Not he! And as for deceiving him over the Mary Grey business, whose fault was that? If he hadn't frightened you to death eight years ago you'd never have *dreamed* of trying it! And if you hadn't thought he was a danger to Grandfather and me—which he was—you wouldn't have come at all. Oh, no, honey, let's have no nonsense about blaming yourself. Come off it!"

"All right." I smiled at her.

"Advice from Aunt Julie." She squeezed my arm lightly, then let it go. "Tit for tat. I took yours, so you take mine. Forget all about it just as soon as you can; it's the only thing to do. We've an awful lot to be thankful for, if you ask me!"

"Yes, indeed." I tilted my head back and looked up where the oak leaves glowed golden against the deep blue sky. "Do you know what I'd like to do, Julie?"

"What?"

"Rescue that blessed oak crossbeam from under this mess when they clear it up, and have something made of it, for Whitescar. Something we'll both of us use, a small table, or a headboard, or even just a shelf for Adam to keep the stud trophies on, and the cups I got for riding."

"Why not? It seems a pity to let it rot underground. It saved them both. Keep a bit for me, too." She smiled a little. "I dare say there'll be room for an ash tray or two in our London rooms. What about the tree that caused all the trouble?"

"The ivy tree?" I walked across to where it lay in its massive wreckage. "The poor old tree." I smiled, perhaps a little sadly. "Symbolic, do you think? Here lies the past—all the lies and secrecy, and what you would have called 'romance' . . . And now it'll be cleared up and carted away, and forgotten. Very neat." I put out a gentle hand to touch a leaf. "Poor old tree."

"I wish—" Julie stopped and gave a little sigh. "I was just going to say that I wished Grandfather could have known that you and Adam would be at Whitescar, but then he'd have had to know the rest, too."

We were silent, thinking of the possessive, charming old man who had delighted in domination, and who had left the strings of trouble trailing behind him, out of his grave.

Then Julie gave a sudden exclamation, and started forward past me. I said, "What is it?"

She didn't answer. She climbed onto what remained of the parapet of the old wall, and balanced there, groping into the fissure that gaped wide in the split trunk of the ivy tree. Somewhere, lost now among the crumbling, rotten wood, was the hole which the foolish lovers of so long ago had used as a letter box.

It was with a queer feeling of *déjà vue* that I watched Julie, slight and fair, and dressed in a cotton frock that I might have worn at nineteen, reach forward, scrape and pull a little at the rotten wood fragments, then draw from among them what looked like a piece of paper.

She stood there on the wall top, staring down at it. It was dirty, and stained, and a little ragged at the edges, but dry.

I said curiously, "What is it?"

"It's a—a letter."

"Julie! It can't be! Nobody else—" My voice trailed away.

She came down from the wall, and held it out to me.

I took it, glanced down unbelievingly at it, then stood staring, while the writing on it swam and danced in front of me. It was young, hurried-looking writing, and even through the blurred, barely legible ink, and the dirt and mould on the paper, I could see the urgency that had driven the pen. And I knew what the illegible letters said.

Adam Forrest, Esq.,
Forrest Hall,
Nr. Bellingham,
Northumberland.

And the blur across the top said: *"Private."*

I became conscious that Julie was speaking.

". . . and I met the postwoman at the top of the road. You remember her, old Annie? She retired that year. She gave me the Whitescar letters, and I brought them down for her. She shouldn't have done it, but that day there was just one letter for Forrest Hall, and you know how she used to, to save herself the long trail. . . . Well, I'd seen you and Adam putting notes in the ivy tree, and I suppose, being a kid, I thought it was quite the natural thing to do. . . ." Her voice wavered; I realized that I had turned and was staring at her. "So I put that one in the ivy tree. I remember now. I never thought another thing about it. I—I climbed up on the wall and shoved it in as far as it would go."

I said, "And of course, once he knew I'd gone, he'd never have looked in there again."

"Of course not. Annabel—"

"Yes?"

"Was it—do you suppose it was a particularly important letter?"

I looked down at the letter in my hand, then up at the ivy tree, where it had lain for eight years. If it had reached him, all that time ago, what would have happened? His wife ill, and heading towards complete breakdown, himself wretched, and an unhappy young girl throwing herself on his mercy and his conscience? Who was to say that it had not been better like this? The time we had lost had, most of it, not been our time. The ivy tree, that "symbol," as I had called it, of deceit, had held us apart until our time was our own, and clear. . . .

Julie was watching me anxiously. "I suppose it *might* have been important?"

"I doubt it."

"I—I'd better give it to him, and tell him, I suppose."

I smiled at her then. "I'm meeting him this evening. I'll give it to him myself."

"Oh, would you?" said Julie, thankfully. "Tell him I'm *terribly* sorry, and I hope it wasn't anything that *mattered!*"

"Even if it was," I said, "it can hardly matter now."

I might have been alone in a painted landscape.

The sky was still, and had that lovely deepening blue of early evening. The high, piled clouds over to the south seemed to hang without movement. Against their curded bases the fells curved and folded, smooth slopes of pasture, fresh from last night's rain, and golden-green in the late sunlight.

The blocks of the Roman-cut stone were warm against my back. Below me the lough dreamed and ruffled, unchanged since the day I had first sat here. Two black-faced lambs slept in the sun; the same two, it seemed, that had lain there eight years ago, when it had all begun—

Time was. Time is. . . .

I sat there, eyes shut, and remembered, in the warm green-and-blue silence. Not a lamb called; the curlews were silent; there was no breeze to stir the grasses, and the bees had gone home from the thyme. It might have been the world before life began, and I might have been the first and only woman in it, sitting there dreaming of Adam. . . .

"Annabel."

Though I had been waiting, I hadn't heard him approach. He had come quietly along the turf to the south of the Wall. He was standing close behind me. The lambs, sleepy-eyed, had not even raised their heads.

I didn't turn. I put up a hand, and when his closed over it, I drew the scarred back of it down against my cheek, and held it there.

Time is to come. . . .

WILDFIRE
AT
MIDNIGHT

All names, characters, and events in this
book are fictional, and any resemblance
which may seem to exist to real persons
is purely coincidental.

"Wildfire at midnight. In this heedless fury
He may show violence to cross himself.
I'll follow the event."

Tourneur: *The Revenger's Tragedy*

CHAPTER

ONE

৵

In the first place, I suppose, it was my parents' fault for giving me a silly name like Gianetta. It is a pretty enough name in itself, but it conjures up pictures of delectable and slightly overblown ladies in Titian's less respectable canvases, and, though I admit I have the sort of coloring that might have interested that Venetian master, I happen to be the rather inhibited product of an English country rectory. And if there is anything further removed than that from the *bagnio* Venuses of Titian's middle period, I don't know what it is.

To do my parents justice, I must confess straightaway that the *bagnio* touch was there in the family—nicely in the past, of course, but known nevertheless to be there. And my mother is just sufficiently vague, artistic, and sentimental to see nothing against calling a red-haired daughter after the Vixen Venus, the lovely redheaded Gianetta Fox, who was once the rage of London, and a Beauty in the days when beauties had a capital B, and were moreover apt to regard beauty and capital as one and the same thing. She was a nobody, the lovely Gianetta; her mother, I believe, was half Italian, and if she knew who her father was, she never admitted to him. She simply appeared, Venus rising from the scum of Victorian Whitechapel, and hit London for six in the spring of 1858. She was just seventeen. By the time she was twenty she had been painted by every painter who mattered (Landseer was the only abstainer), in every conceivable allegorical pose, and had also, it was said, been the mistress of every one of them in turn—I should be inclined here, too, to give Landseer the benefit of the doubt. And in 1861 she reaped the due reward of her peculiar virtues and married a baronet. He managed to keep her long enough to beget two children of her be-

fore she left him—for a very "modern" painter of the French school
who specialized in nudes. She left her son and daughter behind in
Sir Charles's scandalized care; the former was to be my maternal
grandfather.

So my nice, vague, artistic mother, who spends her time in our Cots-
wold rectory making dear little pots and bowls and baking them in a
kiln at the bottom of the garden, called me after my disreputable (and
famous) great-grandmother, without a thought about the possible consequences to me when I hit London in my turn, in 1945.

I was nineteen, had left school a short eight months before, and now,
fresh from a West End training course for mannequins, was ingenuously setting out on a glamorous career with a fashion house, modeling
clothes. I had a share in a bed-sitting room, a small banking account
(gift from Father), two hand-thrown pots and an ash tray (gift from
Mother), and an engagement diary (gift from my brother Lucius). I
was on top of the world.

I was still on top of the world when the Morelli Gallery acquired the
Zollner canvas called "My Lady Greensleeves," and Marco Morelli—
the Marco Morelli—decided to make a splash with it. You remember the
fuss, perhaps? Morelli's idea was, I think, to stage a sort of comeback of
art after the austerities and deprivations of the war. He could hardly
have chosen a more appropriate picture to do it with. "My Lady Greensleeves" has all the rioting bravura of Zollner's 1860 period: the gorgeous lady who languishes, life-size, in the center of the canvas is the
focus of a complicated shimmer of jewels and feathers and embroidered
silk—I doubt if any material has ever been more miraculously painted
than the coruscating damask of the big green sleeves. As an antidote to
austerity it was certainly telling. And even Zollner's peacock riot of
color could not defeat his model's triumphant vitality, or drain the fire
from that flaming hair. It was Gianetta Fox's last full-dress appearance
in canvas, and she had all the air of making the most of it.

So had Morelli, and his cousin Hugo Montefior, the dress designer,
who happened to be my employer. And there really was nothing against
the idea that Montefior should re-create the dress with the lovely green
sleeves, and that I should wear it at the showing, and that there should
be a sensation in the right circles, thereby doing the cousins a lot of
good. And, possibly, me too, though this honestly didn't occur to me
when Hugo put his idea in front of me. I was merely flattered, excited,
and terribly nervous.

So I wore the Greensleeves gown at the show, and Morelli got his sensation, and I was so scared of the fashionable crowd that when I spoke at all, it was in a tight, flat little voice that must have sounded the last word in bored, brittle sophistication. I must have looked and sounded, in fact, like a pale copy of that arrogant worldling behind me in Zollner's canvas, for that is what Nicholas Drury undoubtedly took me for, when at length he elbowed his way through the crowds and introduced himself. I had heard of him, of course, and this in no way increased my self-confidence: He had at that time—he was twenty-nine —three terrifyingly good novels to his credit, as well as a reputation for a scarifying tongue. I, for one, was so thoroughly scarified that I froze into complete stupidity, and under his sardonic look stammered some meaningless schoolgirl rubbish that, God help us both, he took for coquetry. We were married three months later.

I have no wish to dwell on the three years that followed. I was wildly, madly, dumbly in love with him, of course, a silly little star-dazzled adolescent, plunged into a life completely strange and rather terrifying. And Nicholas, it became very quickly apparent, wasn't on his own ground either. What he had meant to marry was a modern Gianetta Fox, a composed young sophisticate who could hold her own in the fast-moving society to which he was accustomed; what he'd actually got was only Gianetta Brooke, not long out of school, whose poise was a technique very recently acquired in Montefior's salons and the Mayfair mannequin factory.

Not that this initial miscasting was the cause of our little tragedy; love is a great builder of bridges, and it did seem at first as though what was between us could have spanned any gap. And Nicholas tried as hard as I. Looking back now, I can see that; if I did achieve sophistication, and a little wisdom, Nicholas struggled to rediscover tenderness. But it was too late; already, when we met, it was too late. The times were out of joint for us, the gap too wide—not the ten years' gap between our ages, but the thousand-year-long stretch of a world war that to me was only an adolescent memory hardly denting the surface of my life, but to Nicholas was a still-recurring nightmare agony leaving scars on the mind which were then only precariously skinning over. How was I, un-touched nineteen, to apprehend the sort of stresses that drove Nicho-las? And how was he to guess that, deep down under my precarious self-confidence, lurked the destroying germs of insecurity and fear?

Whatever the causes, the break came soon enough. In two years the marriage was as good as over. When Nicholas traveled, as he often did, in search of material for his books, he more and more frequently found reasons for not taking me with him, and when at length I found he was not traveling alone, I felt no surprise, but I was hurt and humiliated, and so—I have red hair, after all—blazingly outspoken.

If I had wanted to keep Nicholas, I should have done better to have held my tongue. I was no match for him on a battlefield where love had become a weakness and pride the only defense against a cynicism both brutal and unanswerable. He won very easily, and he cannot have known how cruelly. . . .

We were divorced in 1949. For the sake of my mother, who is so High Church as to be verging (according to Father), on Popish Practices, I kept Nicholas's name, and I still wore my wedding ring. I even, after a time, went back to London and to Hugo Montefior, who was angelically kind to me, worked me to death, and never once mentioned Nicholas. Nor did anyone else, except Mother, who occasionally asked after him in her letters, and even, on two occasions, wondered if we were thinking of starting a family. . . . After a year or so I even managed to find this amusing, except when I was run-down and tired, and then the gentle timelessness of Mother and Tench Abbas Rectory became more than I could bear.

So in mid-May last year, when London had been packed to suffocation for weeks with the Coronation crowds already massing for the great day, and Hugo Montefior one morning took a long look at my face, took another, and promptly told me to go away for a fortnight, I rang up Tench Abbas, and got Mother.

"A holiday?" said Mother. "The beginning of June? How lovely, darling. Are you coming down here, or will Nicholas find it too dull?"

"Mother, I—"

"Of course we haven't got television," said Mother proudly, "but we can listen to the *whole thing* on the wireless. . . ."

I spared a glance for Montefior's salon windows, which have a grandstand view of Regent Street. "That would be lovely," I said. "But, Mother dearest, would you mind if I went somewhere else for a bit first? Somewhere away from everything . . . you know, just hills and water and birds and things. I'd thought of the Lake District."

"Not far enough," said Mother promptly. "Skye."

Knowing Mother, I thought for one wild moment that she was recommending heaven as suitably remote. But then she added: "Your father was talking about it at the Dunhills' garden party the other day. It rained *all* the time, you know, and so we had to be indoors—you know how it *always* rains for the Dunhills' garden party, darling?—well, it did so *remind* Maisie Dunhill. They were there a fortnight once, and it rained *every day.*"

"Oh," I said, as light dawned. "Skye."

"And," said Mother, clinching it, "there's *no television.*"

"It sounds the very place," I said, without irony. "Did Mrs. D. give you an address?"

"There are the pips," said Mother distractedly. "We *can't* have had three minutes, and they *know* how it puts me off. What was—oh, yes, the Dunhills . . . do you know, darling, they've bought a new car, a *huge* thing, called a Jackal or a Jaeger or something, and—"

"Jaguar, Mother. But you were going to give me the address of the hotel where the Dunhills stayed."

"Oh yes, that was it. But you know Colonel Dunhill *never* drives at more than thirty-five miles an hour, and your father says—what, dear?"

I heard Father's voice speaking indistinguishably somewhere beyond her. Then she said: "Your father has it, dear, written down. I don't quite know how . . . well, here it is. The Camas Fhionnaridh Hotel—"

"*The what* hotel, Mother?"

"Camas—I'll spell it." She did. "I really don't think—I don't remember—but this *must* be the one. What did you say, dear?" This to Father again, as she turned away from the receiver, leaving me listening in some apprehension for the pips, which always reduce Mother from her normal pleasant abstraction to a state of gibbering incoherence. "Your father says it's Gaelic and pronounced Camasunary," said Mother, "and it's at the back of *beyond,* so you go there, darling, and have a lovely time with the birds and the—the water, or whatever you said you wanted."

I sat clutching the receiver, perched there above the roar of Regent Street. Before my mind's eye rose, cool and remote, a vision of rain-washed mountains.

"D'you know," I said slowly, "I think I will."

"Then that's settled," said Mother comfortably. "It sounds the very thing, darling. So *handy* having that address. It's as if it were *meant.*"

I am glad to think that Mother will never appreciate the full irony of that remark.

So it came about that, in the late afternoon of Saturday, May 30th, 1953, I found myself setting out on the last stage of my journey to Camas Fhionnaridh in the Isle of Skye. Mother, I found, had been right enough about the back of beyond. The last stage had to be undertaken by boat, there being only a rough cart road overland from Strathaird to Camas Fhionnaridh, which the solitary local bus would not tackle. This same bus had brought me as far as Elgol, on the east side of Loch Scavaig, and had more or less dumped me and my cases on the shore. And presently a boatman, rather more ceremoniously, dumped me into his boat, and set out with me, my cases, and one other passenger, across the shining sea loch towards the distant bay of Camasunary.

Nothing could have been more peaceful. The sea loch itself was one huge bay, an inlet of the Atlantic, cradled in the crescent of the mountains. The fishing village of Elgol, backed by its own heather hills, was within one tip of the crescent; from the other soared sheer from the sea a jagged wall of mountains, purple against the sunset sky. The Cuillin, the giants of the Isle of Mist.

And, locked in the great arms of the mountains, the water lay quiet as a burnished shield, reflecting in deeper blue and deeper gold the pageantry of hill and sky. One thin gleaming line, bright as a rapier, quivered between the world of reality and the water-world below. Our boat edged its way, with drowsily purring engine, along the near shore of the loch. Water lipped softly under the bows and whispered along her sides. The tide was at half ebb, its gentle washes dwindling, one after one, among the sea tangle at its edge. The seaweeds, black and rose-red and olive-green, rocked as the salt swell took them, and the smell of the sea drifted up, sharp and exciting. The shore slid past; scree and heather, overhung with summer clouds of birch, flowed by us, and our wake arrowed the silk-smooth water into ripples of copper and indigo.

And now ahead of us, in the center of the mountain crescent, I could see the dip of a bay, where a green valley cut through the hills to the sea's edge. Higher up this valley, as I knew, was a loch, where the hills crowded in and cradled the water into a deep and narrow basin. Out of this the river flowed; I could see the gleam of it, and, just discernible at that distance, a white building set among a mist of birch trees where the glittering shallows fanned out to meet the sea. The boat throbbed steadily closer. Now I could see the smoke from the hotel chimneys, a faint penciling against the darker blue of the hills. Then the glitter of water vanished as the sun slipped lower, and the enormous shadow of the Cuillin strode across the little valley. One arrogant wing of rock, thrusting itself across the sun, flung a diagonal of shadow over half the bay.

"Garsven," said the other passenger, at my elbow. I jumped. Such had been my absorption in the scene, so great the sense of solitude imposed by these awful hills, that I had forgotten I was not alone.

"I beg your pardon?"

He smiled. I saw now that he was a pleasant-looking man of perhaps thirty, with hair of an unusual dark gold color, and very blue eyes. He was tall and lightly built, but he looked strong and wiry, and his face was tanned as if he spent most of his time in the open. He was wearing an ancient ulster over what had, once, been very good tweeds. "This must be your first visit," he said.

"It is. It's a little—overpowering, wouldn't you say?"

He laughed. "Decidedly. I know the district like the back of my hand, but they still take my breath away, every time."

"They?"

"The Cuillin." He gave the word what I imagined must be its local pronunciation. His gaze had moved beyond me, and I turned to follow it. "Garsven," he said again. "That's the one at the end that sweeps straight up out of the sea at that impossible angle." His hand came over my shoulder, pointing. "And that's Sgurr nan Eag; then the big one blotting out the sun—that's the Pointed Peak, Sgurr Biorach."

"You mean Sgurr Alasdair," put in the boatman unexpectedly from behind us. He was a sturdy Skye man with a dark square face and the soft voice of the Islands. He steered the boat nonchalantly, and now and then spat to leeward. "Sgurr Alasdair," he said again.

The fair man grinned, and said something in Gaelic which brought an answering grin to the boatman's face. Then he said to me: "Murdo's right, of course. It's Alasdair on the maps—it was rechristened after some mountaineer or other; but I like the old names best. Sgurr Biorach it is, and that next to it is Sgurr Dearg, the Red Peak." His pointing finger swung towards the last towering pinnacle, black against the sunset. "Sgurr nan Gillean." He dropped his hand and gave me the sort of smile that holds the hint of an apology—the Britisher's regret for having displayed an emotion. He said lightly: "And you couldn't have had your first sight of them under better conditions. Sunset and evening star—all the works, in fact, in glorious Technicolor."

"You must be a mountaineer," I said.

"A climber? Yes, of a sort."

"He's a good man on the hill, is Mr. Grant," said Murdo.

Grant took out cigarettes, offered them to me and Murdo, then spun a spent match into the water. He said to me: "Have you come for long?"

"A week or ten days. It depends on the weather. If it stays like this, it'll be heaven."

"It won't," he said confidently. "What d'you say, Murdo?"

The boatman cast a dubious eye at the southwest, where the Atlantic merged its long and glimmering reaches into a deep blue sky. He jerked a thumb in that direction, and spoke briefly and to the point. "Rain," he said.

"Oh dear." I was dismayed. This golden prospect seemed, now that I was here, to be infinitely more desirable than the rain-washed hills of my dreams.

"Never mind," said Mr. Grant cheerfully, "it'll improve the fishing." I must have looked blank, because he added: "You do fish, of course?"

"Oh no." To my own surprise I sounded apologetic. "But I—I could learn."

His interest quickened. "You climb, then?"

"No." I felt suddenly very urban and tripperish. "Actually I came for a—a rest, and quiet. That's all."

His eye fell on my cases. "London?" He grinned. "Well, you've certainly come to the right place if you want to get out of the crowds. You'll have no neighbors except the Black Cuillin, and the nearest of them is—" He stopped abruptly.

"Nearest?" I glanced at the hotel, much closer now, islanded in its green valley, dwarfed and overborne by one great solitary mountain to the east. "That mountain? Is that one of them too? You didn't speak of it before. What's it called?"

He hesitated perceptibly. "That's Blaven."

The boatman took his cigarette from his mouth, and spat into the water. "Blah-ven," he repeated, in his soft Highland voice. "Mph—mm. . . ."

"The Blue Mountain . . ." said Grant in a voice that was almost abstracted. Then he pitched his cigarette into the water, and said abruptly: "Was London so very crowded?"

"Oh yes. It's been steadily filling up with people and excitement for months. Now it's like a great pot slowly simmering to boiling point."

Murdo turned the boat's nose neatly towards the river mouth. "London, is it?" His voice held a naïve note of wonder. "Did ye not want to stay and see the Coronation, mistress?"

"In a way, I did. But I—I've been a bit overworked, so I thought a holiday was a better idea after all."

"What made you come here?" asked Grant. His eyes were still on the Blue Mountain.

"To Skye? Oh, I don't know—everybody wants to visit Skye at some time or other, don't they? And I wanted quiet and a complete change. I shall go for long walks in the hills."

"Alone?" There was something in Murdo's expression that made me stare at him.

"Why, yes," I said in surprise.

I saw his eyes meet Grant's for a moment, then slide away to watch the approaching jetty. I laughed. "I shan't get lost," I said. "The walks won't be long enough for that—don't forget I'm a city bird. I don't suppose I'll get farther than the loch, or the lower slopes of— Blaven, was it? Nothing much can happen to me there!" I turned to Mr. Grant. "Does Murdo think I'll go astray in the mist, or run off with a water kelpie?" Then I stopped. His eyes, meeting mine, held some indefinable expression, the merest shadow, no more, but I hesitated, aware of some obscure uneasiness.

The blue eyes dropped. "I imagine Murdo means—"

But Murdo cut the engine, and the sudden silence interrupted as effectively as an explosion. "London . . ." said Murdo meditatively into the bowels of his engine. "That's a long way now! A long way, indeed, to come. . . ." The guileless wonder was back in his voice, but I got the embarrassing impression that he was talking entirely at random. And, moreover, that his air of Highland simplicity was a trifle overdone; he had, I judged, a reasonably sophisticated eye. "A very fine city, so they say. Westminster Abbey, Piccadilly Circus, the Zoo. I have seen pictures—"

"Murdo," I said suspiciously, as we bumped gently alongside a jetty, and made fast. "When did *you* last see London?"

He met my eye with a limpid gaze as he handed me out of the boat. "Eight years ago, mistress," he said in his soft voice, "on my way back frae Burma and points East. . . ."

The man called Grant had picked up my cases and had started walking up the path to the hotel. As I followed him I was conscious of Murdo staring after us for a long moment, before he turned back to his boat. That simple Skyeman act had been—what? Some kind of smoke screen? But what had there been to hide? Why had he been so anxious to change the conversation?

The path skirted the hotel to the front door, which faced the valley. As I followed my guide round the corner of the building my eye was once again, irresistibly, drawn to the great lonely bulk of the mountain in the east, stooping over the valley like a hawk.

Blaven? The Blue Mountain?

I turned my back on it and went into the hotel.

CHAPTER
TWO

ج

It was an hour later. I had washed, brushed the railway smoke out of my hair, and changed. I sat in the hotel lounge, enjoying a moment of solitude before the other guests assembled for dinner. I was sipping an excellent sherry, my feet were in front of a pleasant fire, and on three sides of the lounge the tremendous mountain scenery was mine for the gazing. I felt good.

The door of the hotel porch swung and clashed, and presently, through the glass of the lounge doors, I saw two women come into the hall and cross it towards the stairs. One I judged to be about my own age; she was shortish, dark, thickset, with her hair cropped straight and mannishly, and the climber's uniform of slacks, boots, and heavy jersey exaggerated her masculine appearance. The other was a girl of about twenty, very young-looking, with bright red cheeks and straight black hair. She did not, I thought, look particularly happy, and her shoulders strained forward under her rucksack as if she were tired. The pair of them stumped up the first flight of the stairs and round the corner.

In a minute or so they were followed by an elderly couple, both tall, thin, and a little stooping, with gentle well-bred faces and deplorable hats. They solemnly carried an empty fishing creel between them up the stairs, and on their heels another woman trudged, hands thrust deep into the pockets of an ulster. I couldn't see her face, but her hunched shoulders and lifeless step told their own story of depression or weariness.

I yawned and stretched a toe to the blaze, and drank some more sherry. Idly I turned the pages of an old society weekly which lay at my elbow. The usual flashlighted faces, cruelly caught at hunt suppers and charity balls, gaped from the glossy pages . . . beautiful horses, plain women, well-dressed men . . . the *London Telephone Directory*, I thought, would be far more interesting. I flicked the pages. There was the usual photograph of me, this time poised against an Adam mantelpiece, in one of Hugo Montefior's most inspired evening gowns . . . I remembered it well, a lovely frock. Here was the theatre page—Alec Guinness in an improbable beard, Vivien Leigh making every other woman within reach look plain, Marcia Maling giving the camera the famous three-cornered smile, staring at vacancy with those amazing eyes. . . .

The lounge door swung open and whooshed shut with a breathless little noise. Marcia Maling came in, sat down opposite me, and rang for a drink.

I blinked at her. There was no mistake. That smooth honey-gold hair, the wide lovely eyes, the patrician little nose and the by-no-means patrician mouth—this was certainly the star of that string of romantic successes that had filled one of London's biggest theatres from the first years of the war, and was still packing it today.

The drink came. Marcia Maling took it, tasted it, met my eyes across it and smiled, perfunctorily. Then the smile slid into a stare.

"Forgive me"—it was the familiar husky voice—"but haven't we met? I know you, surely?"

I smiled. "It's very brave of you to say so, Miss Maling. I imagine you usually have to dodge people who claim they've met you. But no, we've never met."

"I've seen you before, I'm sure."

I flicked the pages of the magazine with a fingernail.

"Probably. I model clothes."

Recognition dawned. "So you do! Then *that's* where! You model for Montefior, don't you?"

"More often than not—though I do a bit of free-lancing too. My name's Drury. Gianetta Drury. I know yours, of course. And of course I saw your show, *and* the one before, *and* the one before that—"

"Back to the dawn of time, my dear. I know. But how nice of you. You must have been in pigtails when we did *Wild Belles*."

I laughed. "I cut them off early. I had a living to earn."

"And how." Marcia drank gin, considering me. "But I remember where I saw you now. It wasn't in a photograph; it was at Leducq's winter show last year. I bought that divine cocktail frock—"

"The topaz velvet. I remember it. It was a heavenly dress."

She made a face over her glass. "I suppose so. But a mistake for all that. You know as well as I do that it wasn't built for a blonde."

"You weren't a blonde when you bought it," I said, fairly, before I thought. "Sorry," I added hastily, "I—"

But she laughed, a lovely joyous gurgle of sound. "Neither was I. I'd forgotten. I'd gone auburn for *Mitzi*. It didn't suit me, and *Mitzi* was a flop anyway." She stretched her exquisite legs in front of her and gave me the famous three-cornered smile. "I'm so glad you've come. I've only been here three days and I'm homesick already for town. This is the first time since I left that I've even been able to think about civilized things like clothes, and I do so adore them, don't you?"

"Of course. But as they're my job—"

"I know," she said. "But nobody here talks about *anything* but fishing or climbing, and I think they're too utterly dreary."

"Then what on earth are you doing here?" The question was involuntary, and too abrupt for politeness, but she answered without resentment.

"My dear. Resting."

"Oh, I see." I tried to sound noncommittal, but Marcia Maling lifted an eyebrow at me and laughed again.

"No," she said, "I mean it; really resting—not just out of a job. The show came off a week ago. Adrian said I positively *must vegetate*, and I had just read a divine book on Skye, so here I am."

"And doesn't Skye come up to the book?"

"In a way. The hills are quite terribly pretty and all that, and I saw some deer yesterday with the cutest baby, but the trouble is you can't really get around. Do you like walking—*rough* walking?"

"I do, rather."

"Well, I don't. And Fergus just simply refuses to take the car over some of these roads."

"Fergus? You're here with your husband, then?" I tried vainly to remember who was Marcia Maling's current man.

"My *dear!* I'm not married *at all*, just now. Isn't it heaven, for a change?" She gave a delicious little chuckle over her pink gin, and I found myself smiling back. Her charm was a tangible thing, something radiant and richly alive, investing her silliest clichés and her outdated extravagances of speech with a heart-warming quality that was as real as the blazing fire between us. "No. Fergus is my chauffeur."

"Marcia!" The name was out before I realized it; the fact that I used it was, in a way, a tribute to that charm. "You haven't brought a *car and chauffeur* here? Is that what you call vegetating?"

"Well, I hate walking," she said reasonably, "and anyway, we're not staying here all the time. I'm on a sort of tour of the Highlands and Islands. Let's have another drink. No, really, it's on me." She reached out and pressed the bell. "In a way, we came here because of Fergus. He was born here. Not that he cares much for auld lang syne and all that, but it seemed as good a place as any to come to."

I stared at her. I couldn't help it. "You're very—considerate," I said. "Your employees—"

She looked at me. This time the famous smile was definitely the one from that very naughty show *Yes, My Darling*. "Aren't I just? But Fergus—oh, a dry sherry, isn't it? And another pink gin." She gave the order and turned back to me. "D'you know, if I talked like this to anyone else in the hotel they'd freeze like—like stuffed trout."

"Who else is in the hotel?"

"Well, let's see. . . . There's Colonel and Mrs. Cowdray-Simpson. They're dim, but rather sweet. They fish all the time, day and night, and have never, to my certain knowledge, caught anything at all."

"I think I saw them come in. Elderly, with an empty creel?"

"That's them all right. Then, still talking of fish, there's Mr. and Mrs. Corrigan and Mr. Braine."

"Not Alastair Braine, by any odd chance?"

"I believe that is his name." Her glance was speculative. "A friend of yours?"

"I've met him. He's in advertising."

"Well, he's with this Corrigan couple. And," added Marcia meditatively, "if ever I could find it in me to pity a woman who's married to a man as good-looking as Hartley Corrigan, I'd pity that one."

"Why?" I asked, amused. Marcia Maling's views on marriage, delivered personally, ought to be worth listening to.

"Fish," she said, simply.

"Fish? Oh, I get it. You mean *fish?*"

"Exactly. He and Alastair Braine, they're just like the Cowdray-Simpsons. Morning, noon, and night. *Fish*. And she does nothing—*nothing*—to fight it, though she's obviously having an utterly foul time, and has been for weeks. She moons miserably about alone with her hands in her pockets."

I remembered the depressed-looking woman who had trudged upstairs in the wake of the Cowdray-Simpsons. "I think I've seen her.

She didn't look too happy, I agree. But I doubt," I said thoughtfully, "if there's a woman living who could compete with fish, once they've really got hold of a man."

Marcia Maling wriggled her lovely body deeper into her chair, and said: "No?"

"All right," I said. "You, possibly. Or Rita Hayworth. But no lesser woman."

"But she doesn't even *try!*" said Marcia indignantly. "And he—oh well, who else?"

"I saw two women—" I began.

"Oh yes, the—what's the word?—*schwärmerinen*," said Marcia, in her lovely, carrying voice. "They—"

"Marcia, *no!* You really musn't!"

But the crusading spirit seemed to be unexpectedly strong in Miss Maling. Her fine eyes flashed. "That child!" she exclaimed. "Nineteen if she's a day, and dragged everywhere by that impossible female with the mustache! My dear, she bullies her, positively!"

"If she didn't like the female," I said reasonably, "why would she come with her?"

"I told you. They're—"

"No, Marcia. It's slander, or something. Do remember this is a Scottish fishing hotel, not a theatre cocktail party."

"I suppose you're right." She sighed. "Actually, they come from the same school, or something. The little one's just started teaching there, and the other one takes P.K. or R.T. or something. I heard her actually *admitting it.*"

"Admitting what?" I asked, startled.

"Teaching this R.T. or whatever it is. What is it?"

"Muscular Christianity, I should think."

"Well, there you are," said Marcia gloomily.

"Who else is there? I met a man in the boat coming over from Elgol—"

"That would be Roderick Grant. He practically *lives* here, I believe. Tallish, nice-looking, with rather gorgeous hair?"

"That's the one. Blue eyes."

"And how," said Marcia, with feeling. "He's *definitely* interesting, that is, if it wasn't for—" She broke off and drank some gin.

Conscious of a steadily mounting curiosity to see Fergus, I said merely: "I gathered that this Roderick Grant is a fisherman too."

"What? Oh, yes, they all are," said Marcia bitterly. "But I must say, he's only spasmodic about it. Most of the time he walks, or something. He's never in the hotel."

"He's a climber," I said, amused.

"Probably. There's another climber chap called Beagle."

"Ronald Beagle?"

"I believe so. Another friend of yours?"

"No. I've never met him, but I've heard of him. He's a famous climber."

She showed a spark of interest. "Really? Yes, now you mention it, he does sit every night poring over maps and things, or glued to the radio listening to this Everest climb they're making."

"That's who it is, then. He wrote a book once on Nanga Parbat."

"Oh?" said Marcia, losing interest. "Well, he goes round with another man, a queer little type called Hubert Hay. I don't think they came together, but I gather Hay's a writer as well. He's little and round and quite, quite sorbo."

"Sorbo?"

"Yes. Unsquashable."

"I see. But what an odd word. Sorbo . . . is it Italian?"

She gave a charming little choke of laughter. "My God, but that dates me, doesn't it? I'll have to watch myself. No, darling, it's not Italian. Some way back, in the thirties, when you were in your pram, they sold unsquashable rubber balls for children. Sorbo Bouncers, they were called."

"And you used to play with them?"

"Darling," said Marcia again. "But how sweet of you. . . . Anyway, the little man's definitely sorbo in nature *and* appearance, and wears fancy waistcoats. There's another man whose name I don't know, who got here last night. I've a feeling he writes, too."

"Good heavens."

"I know. Just a galaxy of talent, haven't we? Though probably none of them are any good. Sorbo is definitely not. But this chap looks as though he might be—all dark and damn-your-eyes," said Marcia poetically, then gloomed at her gin. "Only—he fishes, too."

"It sounds a very intriguing collection of people," I said.

"Doesn't it?" she said without conviction. "Oh, and there's an aged lady who I *think* is Cowdray-Simpson's mother and who knits *all the time,* my dear, in the most ghastly colors. And three youths with bare knees who camp near the river and come in for meals and go about with hammers and sickles and things—"

"Geology students, I'll bet," I said. "And I rather doubt the sickles. There's only one thing for it, you know. You'll have to take up fishing yourself. I'm going to. I'm told it's soothing to the nerves."

She shot me a look of horror mingled with respect. "My God! How marvellous of you! But—" Then her gaze fell on my left hand, and she nodded. "I might have known. You're married. I suppose he makes you. Now, if that wretched Mrs. Corrigan—"

"I'm not married," I said.

She caught herself. "Oh, sorry, I—"

"Divorced."

"O—oh!" She relaxed and sent me a vivid smile. "You too? My dear, so'm I."

"I know."

"*Three times*, honey. Too utterly exhausting, I may tell you. Aren't they stinkers?"

"I beg your pardon?"

"Men, darling. Stinkers."

"Oh, I see."

"Don't tell me yours wasn't a stinker too?"

"He was," I said. "Definitely."

"I knew it," said Marcia happily. I thought I had never seen two pink gins go further. "What was his name?"

"Nicholas."

"The beast," she said generously. The old crusading instinct was rising again, I could see. "Have another drink, Jeanette darling, and tell me *all* about it."

"This one's on me," I said firmly, and pressed the bell. "And my name is Gianetta. Gee-ann-etta. Of Italian origin, like sorbo."

"It's pretty," said she, diverted. "How come you've an Italian name?"

"Oh, it's old history. . . ." I ordered the drinks, glad to steer the conversation in a new direction. "My great-grandmother was called Gianetta. She's the kind of ancestress one wants to keep in the family cupboard, tightly locked away, only my great-grandmamma never let herself be locked away anywhere, for a moment."

"What did she do?" asked Marcia, intrigued.

"Oh, she took the usual road to ruin. Artists' model, artists' mistress, then married a baronet, and—"

"So did I once," said Marcia cheerfully. "I left him, though. Did she?"

"Of course. She bolted with a very advanced young artist to Paris, where she made a handsome fortune—don't ask me how—then died in a nunnery at the happy old age of eighty-seven."

"Those were the days." Marcia's voice was more than a little wistful. "Not the nunnery bit, but the rest. . . . What a thoroughly worthy great-grandmother to have—especially the bit about the fortune and the title."

I laughed. "They didn't survive. Mother was the only grand-child, and Gianetta left all her money to the convent—as fire in-surance, I suppose." I put down my empty glass. "So—unlike my great-grandmamma—I wear clothes for a living."

Through the glass door I could see the Cowdray-Simpsons coming down the stairs. A maid bustled across the hall towards the dining room. Outside, behind the steep crest of Sgurr na Stri, the red of the sky was deepening to copper, its brightness throwing the jagged rock into towering relief. I saw three young men—the campers, no doubt—coming along from the river; they skirted the windows of the lounge, and a moment later I heard the porch door swing open and shut.

Somewhere, a clock struck seven.

"I'm hungry," I said. "Thank heaven it's dinnertime."

I got out of my chair, and moved to the window that faced east. Away in front of the hotel stretched the breadth of the valley floor, almost a mile of flat sheep-bitten turf, unbroken save by little peaty streams that here and there meandered seawards. The road, narrow and rutted, curved away across it, following the shore line, then lifted its grey length up through the heather and out of sight. To the right the sea murmured, pewter-dark now and unillumined in the shadow of the mountains. Far to the left, at Blaven's foot, a glimmer of water recalled the copper sky.

A late grouse shouted "Comeback!" and fell silent. A gull on the shore stretched its wings once, then settled them again upon its back. The sea seemed still. It was a prospect wild and dreary enough; no sound but a bird's call and a sheep's lament, no movement but the shake of a gull's wing and the stride of a latecomer walking unhurriedly across the grass.

Then the walker trod on the gravel of the road. The scrunch of his boot on the rough surface startled the stillness. A feeding snipe flashed up beside him, and fled up the glen in a zigzag of lightning flight. I saw the silver gleam of his underwings once, twice, against the towering menace of Blaven, then I lost him.

"Blaven . . ." I said thoughtfully. "I wonder—"

Behind me, Marcia's voice was sharp and brittle. "Not any more of that, please. D'you mind?"

I looked back at her in surprise. She was gulping the last of her third gin, and across it she met my eyes queerly. Disconcerted, and a little shaken, as one always is by rudeness, I stared back at her. I had shifted the talk rather arbitrarily, I knew, to Gianetta and her misdeeds, but then I hadn't wanted to talk about Nicholas. And she had seemed interested enough. If I had been boring her—but she had not appeared to be bored. On the contrary.

She gave an apologetic little grin. "I can't help it," she said. "But don't let's. Please."

"As you wish," I said, a little stiffly. "I'm sorry." I turned back to the window.

The mountain met me, huge and menacing. And I looked at it in sudden enlightenment. *Blaven.* It had been my mention of Blaven, not of Gianetta, that had made Marcia retreat into her gin glass like a snail into its shell. Roderick Grant, and Murdo, and now Marcia Maling . . . or was I being over-imaginative? I stared out at the gathering dusk, where the latecomer was just covering the last twenty yards to the hotel door. Then my look narrowed on him. I stiffened, and looked again. . . .

"Oh my God," I said sharply, and went back into the room like a pea from a catapult.

I stopped on the hearthrug, just in front of a goggle-eyed Marcia Maling, and drew a long, long breath.

"Oh my *dear* God," I said again.

"What's up? Is it because I—?"

"It's not you at all," I said wearily. "It's the man who's just arriving at the front door of this hotel."

"Man?" She was bewildered.

"Yes. I presume he is your nameless, dark, damn-your-eyes writer . . . except that he doesn't happen to be nameless to me. His name is Nicholas Drury."

Her mouth opened. "*No!* You mean—?"

I nodded. "Just that. My husband."

"The—the stinker?"

I smiled mirthlessly. "Quite so. As you say. This holiday," I added without any conviction whatsoever, "is going to be *fun.*"

CHAPTER

THREE

🦆

Yes, there it was, as large as life, the arrogant black signature in the visitors' book: Nicholas Drury, London. May 29th, 1953. I looked down at it for a moment, biting my lip, then my eye was caught by another entry in the same hand, high up on the preceding page: Nicholas Drury, London. April 28th, 1953. He had been here already this summer, then. I frowned down at the book, wondering what on earth he could be doing in Skye. He must, of course, be collecting material for some book; he would hardly have chosen a place like this for a holiday. This Highland fastness, all trout and misty heather and men in shabby tweeds, accorded ill with what I remembered of Nicholas. I picked up the pen, conscious that my hands were not quite steady. All the carefully acquired poise in the world was not going to make it any more possible for me to meet Nicholas Drury again with the casual camaraderie which was, no doubt, fashionable among the divorcés of his London circle.

I dipped the pen in the inkstand, hesitated, and finally wrote: Gianetta Brooke, Tench Abbas Rectory, Warwickshire. Then I tugged my wedding ring rather painfully off my finger and dropped it into my bag. I would have to tell Major Persimmon, the hotel proprietor, why Mrs. Drury had suddenly become Miss Brooke: there were, it seemed to me, altogether too many embarrassments contingent on there being a Mr. and Mrs. Drury in the same hotel. Marcia Maling had already promised to say nothing. And Nicholas was not to know that I had not become Miss Brooke again four years ago. He would probably be as annoyed and uncomfortable as I, when we met, and would surely try to pass off the awkward encounter as easily as possible.

So, at any rate, I assured myself, as I blotted and shut the book, though, remembering my handsome and incalculable husband as I did, I felt that there was very little dependence to be placed on the good behavior of Nicholas Drury.

Then I jumped like a nervous cat as a man's voice said behind me: "Janet Drury, as I live!"

I turned quickly, to see a man coming down the stairs towards me.

"Alastair! How nice to see you again! Where've you been all these years?"

Alastair Braine took both my hands and beamed down at me. He was a big, rugged-looking man, with powerful shoulders, perpetually untidy brown hair, and a disarming grin that hid an exceptionally shrewd mind. He looked anything but what he was—one of the coming men in the ruthless world of advertising.

"America mostly, with a dash of Brazil and Pakistan. You knew I was working for the Pergamon people?"

"Yes, I remember. Have you been back long?"

"About six weeks. They gave me a couple of months' leave, so I've come up here with some friends for a spot of fishing."

"It's lovely seeing you again," I said, "and I must say your tan does you credit, Alastair!"

He grinned down at me. "It's a pity I can't return the compliment, Janet, my pet. Not"—he caught himself up hastily—"that it's not lovely to see you, too, but you look a bit Londonish, if I may say so. What's happened to the schoolgirl complexion? Nick been beating you?"

I stared at him, but he appeared to notice nothing odd in my expression. He said, cheerfully: "He never told me you were joining him here, the scurvy devil."

"Oh Lord," I said. "Alastair, don't tell me you didn't know? We got a divorce."

He looked startled, even shocked. "*Divorced?* When?"

"Over four years ago now. D'you mean to tell me you hadn't heard?"

He shook his head. "Not a word. Of course, I've been abroad all the time, and I'm the world's lousiest letter witer, and Nick's the next worst, so you can see—" He broke off and whistled a little phrase between his teeth. "Ah, well. Sorry, Janet. I—well, perhaps I'm not so very surprised, after all. . . . You don't mind my saying that?"

"Don't give it a thought." My voice was light and brittle, and would do credit, I thought, to any of Nicholas's casual London lovelies. "It was just one of those things that couldn't ever have worked. It was nobody's fault; he just thought I was another kind of person altogether. You see, in my job you tend to look—well, tough and sort of well-varnished, even when you're not."

"And you're not."

"Well, I wasn't then," I said. "I've a better veneer now."

"Three years of my great friend Nicholas," said Alastair, "would sophisticate a Vestal Virgin. Bad luck, Janet. But, if I may ask, what are you doing here?"

"Having a holiday like you, and dodging the Coronation crowds. I need hardly say I had no idea Nicholas was going to be here. I was a bit run down, and wanted somewhere restful, and I heard of the hotel through some friends of the family."

"Somewhere restful." He gave a little bark of laughter. "Oh my ears and whiskers! And you have to run slap into Nick!"

"Not yet," I told him grimly. "That's a pleasure in store for us both."

"Lord, Lord," said Alastair ruefully, then began to grin again. "Don't look so scared, my child. Nick won't eat you. It's he should be nervous, not you. Look, Janet, will you let me dine at your table tonight? I'm with a couple who could probably do with having to have a little of one another's society."

"I'd love you to," I said gratefully. "But how on earth is it that Nicholas didn't tell you about us?"

"I've really seen very little of him. He's apparently in Skye collecting stuff on folklore and suchlike for a book, and he's been moving from one place to another, with this as a main base. He's out most of the time. I did ask after you, of course, and he just said: 'She's fine. She's still with Hugo, you know. They've a show due soon.' I thought nothing of it."

"When was this?"

"Oh, when I first got here and found he was staying. May the tenth, or thereabouts."

"We *were* getting a show ready then, as it happens. But how on earth did he know?"

"Search me," said Alastair cheerily, and then turned to greet the couple who were crossing the hall towards us. The woman was slight, dark, and almost nondescript save for a pair of really beautiful brown eyes, long-lidded and flecked with gold. Her dress was indifferently cut, and was a depressing shade of green. Her hair had no luster, and her mouth drooped petulantly. The man with her was a startling contrast.

He, too, was dark, but his thinness gave the impression of a great wiry strength and vitality. His eyes were blue, dark Irish blue, and he was extraordinarily handsome, though there were lines round the sensitive mouth that spoke of a temper too often given rein.

I said quickly: "The name's Brooke, Alastair, not Drury. Do remember. I thought it might be awkward—"

"I couldn't agree more. Ah"—as they came up—"Hart, Alma, this is Gianetta Brooke. Janet, Mr. and Mrs. Corrigan."

We murmured politely. I saw Mrs. Corrigan eyeing my frock; her husband's blue eyes flicked over me once, with a kind of casual interest, then they sought the lounge door, as if he were waiting for someone else.

"I'm going to desert you at dinner, Alma, if you'll forgive me." Alastair made his excuses. "Miss Brooke and I are old friends, and we've a lot to talk about."

Mrs. Corrigan looked vaguely resentful, and I wondered for a moment if she were going to invite me to join their table, until I realized that she was hesitating between two evils, the hazard of having another woman near her husband, and the loss of the society of her husband's friend. She had, in fact, the air of one for whom life has for a long time been an affair of perpetual small calculations such as this. I felt sorry for her. Through Alastair's pleasant flow of conversational nothings, I shot a glance at Hartley Corrigan, just in time to see the look on his face as the lounge door opened behind me, and Marcia Maling drifted towards us on a cloud of Chanel No. 5. My pity for Alma Corrigan became, suddenly, acute. She seemed to have no defenses. She simply stood there, dowdy, dumb, and patently resentful, while Marcia, including us all in her gay "How were the fish, my dears?" enveloped the whole group in the warm exuberance of her personality. The whole group, yes—but somehow, I thought, as I watched her, and listened to some absurd fish story she was parodying—somehow she had cut out Hartley Corrigan from the herd, and penned him as neatly as if she were champion bitch at the sheep trials, and he were a marked wether. And as for the tall Irishman, it was plain that, for all he was conscious of the rest of us, the two of them might as well have been alone.

I found I did not want to meet Alma Corrigan's eyes, and looked away. I was wishing the gong would go. The hall was full of people now; all the members of Marcia's list seemed to be assembled. There were the Cowdray-Simpsons, being attentive to an ancient white-haired lady with a hearing aid; there, in a corner, were the two oddly assorted teachers, silent and a little glum; my friend of the boat, Roderick Grant, was consulting a barometer in earnest confabulation with a stocky individual who must be Ronald Beagle; and, deep in a news-paper, sat the unmistakable Hubert Hay, dapper and rotund in the yellowest of Regency waistcoats.

Then Nicholas came quickly round the corner of the stairs, and started down the last flight into the hall.

He saw me straightaway. He paused almost imperceptibly, then descended the last few stairs and came straight across the hall.

"Alastair," I said, under my breath, furious to find that my throat felt tight and dry.

Alastair turned, saw Nicholas, and took the plunge as smoothly as an Olympic swimmer.

"Hi, Nick!" he said. "Look who's here. . . . Do you remember Janet Brooke?"

He stressed the surname ever so slightly. Nicholas's black brows lifted a fraction of an inch, and something flickered behind his eyes. Then he said: "Of course. Hello, Gianetta. How are you?"

It came back to me sharply, irrelevantly, that Nicholas was the only person who had never shortened my name. I met his eyes with an effort, and said, calmly enough: "I'm fine, thank you. And you?"

"Oh, very fit. You're here on holiday, I take it?"

"Just a short break. Hugo sent me away. . . ." It was over, the awk-ward moment, the dreaded moment, sliding past in a ripple of common-places, the easy mechanical politenesses that are so much more than empty convention; they are the greaves and cuirasses that arm the naked nerve. And now we could turn from one another in relief, as we were gathered into the group of which Marcia Maling was still the radiant point. She had been talking to Hartley Corrigan, but I could see her watching Nicholas from under her lashes, and now she said, turning to me: "Another old friend, darling?"

I had forgotten for the moment that she was an actress, and stared at her in surprise, so beautifully artless had the question been. Then I saw the amusement at the back of her eyes, and said coolly: "Yes, another old friend. My London life is catching me up even here, it seems. Nicholas, let me introduce you to Miss Marcia Maling—*the* Marcia Maling, of course. Marcia, this is Nicholas Drury."

"*The* Nicholas Drury?" Marcia cooed it in her deepest, furriest voice, as she turned the charm full on to him with something of the effect that, we are told, a cosmic ray gun has when turned on to an earthly body. But Nicholas showed no sign of immediate disintegration. He merely looked ever so slightly wary as he murmured something conventional. He had seen that amused look of Marcia's, too, I knew. He had always been as quick as a cat. Then Hartley Corrigan came in with some remark to Marcia, and, in less time than it takes to write it, the whole party was talking about fish. The men were, at any rate; Marcia was watching Hartley Corrigan, Alma Corrigan watched Marcia, and I found myself studying Nicholas.

He had changed, in four years. He would be thirty-six now, I thought, and he looked older. His kind of dark, saturnine good looks did not alter much, but he was thinner, and, though he seemed fit enough, there was tension in the way he held his shoulders, and some sort of strain about his eyes, as if the skin over his cheekbones was drawn too tightly back into the scalp. I found myself wondering what was on his mind. It couldn't just be the strain of starting a new book, though some stages, I knew, were hell. No, knowing him as I did, I knew that it must be something else, some other obscure stress that I couldn't guess at, but which was unmistakably there. Well, at any rate, I thought, this time I couldn't possibly be the cause of his mood; and neither, this time, did I have to worry about it.

I was just busily congratulating myself that I didn't have to care any more, when the gong sounded, and we all went in to dinner.

CHAPTER

FOUR

ॐ

It became more than ever obvious, after dinner, that the awkwardness of my own situation was by no means the only tension in the oddly assorted gathering at the Camasunary Hotel. I had not been overimaginative. That there were emotional undercurrents here seemed more than ever apparent, but I don't think I realized, at first, quite how strong they were. I certainly never imagined they might be dangerous.

By the time I got back into the lounge after dinner, the groups of people had broken and re-formed, and, as is the way in small country hotels, conversation had become general. I saw with a little twinge of wry amusement that Marcia Maling had deserted the Corrigans and was sitting beside Nicholas. It was, I supposed, a change for the better. She could no more help being pulled into the orbit of the nearest interesting man than she could help breathing, but I wished she would leave Hartley Corrigan alone. She had much better spend her time on Nicholas; he could look after himself.

Alastair found a chair for me in a corner, then excused himself and went off to see about weighing and dispatching the salmon he had caught that day. I saw Corrigan get up, without a word to his wife, and follow him from the room. Alma Corrigan sat without looking up, stirring and stirring her coffee.

"Will you have coffee? Black or white?"

I looked up to meet the bright gaze of the younger of the two teachers, who was standing in front of me with a cup in either hand. She had changed into a frock the color of dry sherry, with a cairngorm brooch in the lapel. It was a sophisticated color, and should not have suited her, but somehow it did; it was as if a charming child had dressed up in her elder sister's clothes. She looked younger than ever, and touchingly vulnerable.

I said: "Black, please. Thank you very much. But why should you wait on me?"

She handed me a cup. "Oh, nobody serves the coffee. They bring it all in on a huge tray, and we each get our own. You've just come, haven't you?"

"Just before dinner." I indicated the chair at my elbow. "Won't you sit down? I've been deserted for a fish."

She hesitated, and I saw her shoot a glance across the room to where her companion was apparently deep in a glossy magazine. Then she sat down, but only on the edge of the chair, remaining poised, as it were, for instant flight.

"The fish certainly have it all their own way," she admitted. "I'm Roberta Symes, by the way."

"And I'm Gianetta Brooke. I take it you don't fish?"

"No. We're walking, Marion and I—that's Marion Bradford, over there. We're together. At least, we're climbing, sort of."

"What d'you mean by sort of?" I asked, amused. The Skye hills had not struck me as being the kind you could sort of climb.

"Well, Marion's a climber, and I'm not. That's really what I mean. So we go scrambling, which is a kind of halfway solution." She looked at me ingenuously. "But I'm *dying* to learn. I'd like to be as good as Mr. Beagle, and climb on every single Cuillin in turn, including the Inaccessible Pinnacle!"

"A thoroughly unworthy ambition," said a voice above us. Roderick Grant had come across, and was standing over us, coffee cup in hand.

Roberta's eyes widened. "Unworthy? That from *you!* Why, Mr. Grant?"

He turned and, with a sweep of one arm, indicated the prospect from the lounge windows.

"Look at them," he said. "Look at them. Thirty million years ago they thrust their way up from God knows where, to be blasted by wind and ice and storm, and chiseled into the mountain shapes you walk over today. They've been there countless ages, the same rocks, standing over the same ocean, worn by the same winds. And you, who've lived out a puny little twenty or thereabouts, talk of scaling them as if they were—"

"Teeth?" said Roberta, and giggled. "I know what you mean, though. They do make one feel a bit impermanent, don't they? But then it's all the more of a challenge, don't you feel? Mere man, or worse still mere woman, conquering the—the giants of time, climbing up—"

"Everest!" Colonel Cowdray-Simpson's exclamation came so pat that I jumped, and Roberta giggled again. *The Times* rustled down an inch or two, and the Colonel peered over it at Nicholas, who was nearest the radio. "Turn on the wireless, will you, Drury? Let's hear how they're getting on."

Nicholas obeyed. The news was nearly over. We had luckily missed the conferences, the strikes, the newest atomic developments, the latest rumors from the U.S.S.R., and had come in just in time for a fuss about the seating in Westminster Abbey, a description of the arches in the Mall, and a hint of the general excitement in a London seething already towards its Coronation boiling point three days hence. And nothing yet, apparently, about Everest. . . .

Nicholas switched off.

"But I think they're going to make it," he said.

"It's too thrilling, isn't it?" said Marcia comfortably.

"It's certainly a magnificent effort," said Colonel Cowdray-Simpson. "They deserve their luck. What d'ye say, Beagle? What are the chances with the weather?"

"Fair enough." Beagle looked faintly uncomfortable at being thus appealed to in public. I remembered, with a quickening of interest, that this unassuming little man had been involved in an earlier attempt on Everest. But he seemed unwilling to pursue the subject. He groped in his jacket pocket and produced his pipe, turning the conversation abruptly. "I'd say they had a chance of better weather there than we have here, at any rate. I don't like the look of the sky. There's rain there."

"All the better for the fishing," said Mrs. Cowdray-Simpson placidly, but Roberta moaned.

"Oh *no!* And I wanted to start *really* climbing tomorrow."

"Quite determined to conquer the Cuillin, then?" said Roderick Grant.

"Quite!"

"Where d'you intend to start?"

"I don't know. I'm leaving that to Marion."

"Garsven's not hard," said someone—I think it was Alma Corrigan. "There's a way up from the Coruisk end—"

Marion Bradford interrupted: "The best first climbs are Bruach na Frithe and Sgurr na Banachdich, but they're too far away. Garsven is within reach, but of course it's just plain dull." Her flat voice and uncompromising manner fell hardly short, I considered, of being just plain rude. Alma Corrigan sat back in her chair with a little tightening of the lips. Roberta flushed slightly and leaned forward.

"Oh, but Marion, I'm sure Mrs. Corrigan's right. It doesn't look hard, and there must be a wonderful view—"

"There's a wonderful view from every single one of the Cuillins," said Marion dampingly.

"You've climbed them all?" asked Roderick gently.

"If you mean do I know what I'm talking about, the answer is yes," said Marion Bradford.

There was a little pause, in which everyone looked faintly uncomfortable, and I wondered what on earth made people behave like that without provocation. Colonel and Mrs. Cowdray-Simpson returned to *The Times* crossword, and Roderick Grant lit a cigarette, looking all at once impossibly remote and well-bred. Nicholas was looking bored, which meant, I knew, that he was irritated, and Marcia Maling winked across at me and then said something to him which made his mouth twitch. Roberta merely sat silent, fiery red and unhappy. As an exercise in Lifemanship, it had been superb.

Then Hubert Hay spoke for the first time, completely ignoring both Marion Bradford's rudeness and the hiatus in the conversation. I remembered Marcia's definition of him as sorbo, and felt amused.

"If I was you," he said cheerily to Roberta, "I'd try the Bad Step. Wait till high tide, and then you won't break your neck if you fall. You'll only drown. Much less uncomfortable, they say."

He had a curiously light, high little voice, and this, together with his odd appearance, produced a species of comic relief. Roberta laughed. "I can swim."

"In climbing boots and a rucksack?"

"Oh well, perhaps not!"

"What on earth's the Bad Step?" I asked.

Hubert Hay pointed towards the west windows. "You see that hill beyond the river's mouth, between us and the Cuillin?"

"Yes."

"That's Sgurr na Stri. It's a high tongue of land between here and

the bay at the foot of Garsven. You can take a short cut across it, if you
want a scramble. But if you follow the coast round to Loch Coruisk
and the Cuillin, you have to cross the Bad Step."

"It sounds terrible. Is it a sort of Lovers' Leap?"

"Oh no. It's only a slab of gabbro tilted at a filthy angle—about
sixty degrees—"

"Not as much," said Roderick Grant.

"No? Maybe you're right. Anyway, it hangs over the sea, and you
have to cross it by a crack in the rock, where your nails can get a good
grip."

"Your *nails?*" said Marcia, horror-stricken. "My God! D'you mean
you have to *crawl* across?"

Nicholas grinned. "No, lady. He's talking about your boots."

"It sounds just my style," announced Roberta buoyantly. "After all,
who minds drowning? Let's go round there, Marion, and come back
over Sgurr na Stri."

"I've made up my mind where we're going," said Marion, in that
flat, hard voice which carried so disastrously. "We're going up Blaven."

There was a sudden silence. I looked up sharply. I had been right,
then, in thinking that some queer reaction took place every time that
name was mentioned. This time it was unmistakable. And I was not
imagining the note of defiance in Marion Bradford's voice. She knew
that her announcement would fall on the room in just that kind of
silence.

Ronald Beagle spoke then, diffidently. "Is that quite—er, wise, Miss
Bradford? It's not exactly a beginner's scramble, is it?"

"It's easy enough up the ridge from this end," she said shortly.

"Oh, quite. But if the weather's bad—"

"A spot of rain won't hurt us. And if mist threatens we won't go.
I've got that much sense."

He said no more, and silence held the room again for a moment. I
saw Nicholas move, restlessly, and I wondered if he felt, as I did, a
discomfort in the atmosphere sharper than even Marion Bradford's
rudeness could warrant.

Apparently Marion herself sensed something of it, for she suddenly
stabbed out her cigarette viciously into an ash tray and got up.

"In any case," she said, in that tight, aggressive voice of hers, "it's
time *someone* broke the hoodoo on that blasted mountain, isn't it? Are
you coming, Roberta?"

She stalked out of the room. Roberta gave me an uncomfortable little smile, and got up to follow her. For an instant I felt like advising her to stay, then decided that, whatever the crosscurrents of emotion that were wrecking the comfort of the party, I had better not add to them. I merely smiled at her, and she went out after her friend.

There was the inevitable awkward pause, in which everyone madly wanted to discuss Marion Bradford, but, naturally, couldn't. Then Marcia, who, as I was rapidly discovering, had no inhibitions at all, said:

"Well, really! I must say—"

Colonel Cowdray-Simpson cleared his throat rather hastily, and said, across her, to Ronald Beagle: "And where do you propose to go tomorrow, Beagle?"

"Weather permitting, sir, I'm going up Sgurr nan Gillean. But I'm afraid . . ."

I got to my feet. I had had enough of this, and I felt cramped and stale after my journey. And if Murdo and Beagle were right, and it was going to rain in the morning, I might as well go out now for an hour. As I turned to put my coffee cup on the tray, I saw, to my dismay, that Nicholas had risen too, and was coming across the room in my direction. It looked very much as if he were going to speak to me, or follow me out, and I felt, just then, that a tête-à-tête with Nicholas would be the final straw. I turned quickly towards the nearest woman, who happened to be Alma Corrigan.

"I'm going out for a short walk," I said, "and I don't know my way about yet at all. I wonder if you'd care to join me?"

She looked surprised, and, I thought, a little pleased. Then the old resentful look shut down on her face again, and she shook her head.

"I'd have liked to very much." She was politely final. "But, if you'll forgive me, I'm a bit tired. We've been out all day, you know."

Since she had already told me, before dinner, that she had spent the day sitting on a boulder while the men fished the Strath na Creitheach, this was a very efficient rebuff.

"Of course," I said, feeling a fool. "Some other time, perhaps." I turned away to find Roderick Grant at my elbow.

"If I might—?" He was looking diffidently down at me. "There's a very pleasant walk up to the loch, if you'll let me be your guide. But perhaps you prefer to go alone?"

"By no means," I assured him. Nicholas had stopped when Roderick Grant spoke, and I knew that he was frowning. I smiled back at Mr. Grant. "Thanks very much. I'll be glad of your company."

Nicholas had not moved. I had to pass him on my way to the door. For a second our glances met. His eyes, hard and expressionless, held mine for a full three seconds, then he gave a twisted little smile and deliberately turned back to Marcia Maling.

I went to get my coat.

CHAPTER

FIVE

ॐ

At half past nine on a summer's evening in the Hebrides, the twilight has scarcely begun. There is, perhaps, with the slackening of the day's brilliance, a somber note overlying the clear colors of sand and grass and rock, but this is no more than the drawing of the first thin blue veil. Indeed, night itself is nothing but a faint dusting-over of the day, a wash of silver through the still-warm gold of the afternoon.

The evening was very still, and, though the rain-threatening clouds were slowly packing higher behind us in the southwest, the rest of the sky was clear and luminous. Above the ridge of Sgurr na Stri, above and beyond the jagged peaks of the Cuillin, the sun's warmth still lingered in the flushed air. Across this swimming lake of brightness one long bar of cloud lay sullenly, one thin line of purple shadow, struck from below to molten brilliance by the rays of a now invisible sun.

We turned northwards up the valley, and our steps on the short sheep turf made no sound in the stillness. The flat pasture of the estuary stretched up the glen for perhaps half a mile, then the ground rose, steep and broken, to make the lower spurs and hillocks that were Blaven's foothills. One of these, the biggest, lay straight ahead of us, a tough little heather-clad hill which blocked the center of the glen and held the southern shore of the loch. To the left of it curved the river; on the east a ridge of rock and heather joined it to the skirts of Blaven.

"Isn't there a path along the river?" I asked.

"Oh yes, but if you want to climb An't Sròn—that hill in front —for a view of the loch, we'd better keep to the Blaven side of the glen. There's a bog farther on, near the river, which isn't too pleasant."

"Dangerous, you mean, or merely wet?"

"Both. I don't know whether it would actually open and swallow you up, but the ground shakes in a beastly fashion, and you start to sink if you stand still. The deer avoid it."

"Then," I said with a shiver, "by all means let us avoid it too. It seems I ought to be very grateful to you for coming with me!"

He laughed. "It's actually pure selfishness on my part. If one loves a place very much one likes to show it off. I wasn't going to miss a fresh opportunity for taking credit to myself for this scenery. It must be one of the loveliest corners of the world."

"This particular corner, do you mean, or Skye and the Islands in general?"

"This bit of Skye." His hands were thrust deep into his pockets, but his eyes lifted briefly to the distant peaks, and to the great blue heights of Blaven dwarfing the glen where we walked. "Those."

"Is this your home, Mr. Grant?"

He shook his head. "No. I was born among mountains, but very different ones. My father was minister of a tiny parish away up in the Cairngorms, a little lost village at the back of the north wind. Auchlechtie, at the foot of Bheinn a' Bhùird. D'you know it?"

"I'm afraid not."

He grinned. "I've never yet met anyone who did. . . . Well, that's where I learned my mountain worship! I'd no mother; my father was a remote kind of man, who had very little time for me; it was miles to school, so as often as not I just ran wild in the hills."

"You must have been a very lonely little boy."

"Perhaps I was. I don't remember. I don't think I felt lonely." He grinned again. "That is, until an uncle died, and left us a lot of money, and my father made me put shoes on and go to a public school to learn manners."

"That was bad luck."

"I hated it, of course. Particularly the shoes."

"And now you spend your time climbing?"

"Pretty well. I travel a bit—but I always seem to end up here, at any rate in May and June. They're the best months in the West, although" —he flung a quick glance over his shoulder—"I think our friend Beagle was right about the weather. We'll have rain tomorrow, for certain, and once the Cuillin get a good grip on a rainstorm, they're very reluctant to let it go."

"Oh dear," I said, "and I was wanting to walk. I begin to see why people take up fishing here. It must be sheer self-defense."

"Very possibly. Watch your step, now. It's tricky going in this light."

We had reached the foot of the little hill called An't Sròn, and began to climb the rough heathery slope. A cock grouse rose with a clap from somewhere near at hand, and planed down towards the river, chakking indignantly. The light had faded perceptibly. Like an enormous storm cloud above the valley Blaven loomed, and behind his massive edge hung, now, the ghost of a white moon past the full.

Roderick Grant paused for a moment in his stride, and looked thoughtfully up at the wicked ridges shouldering the sky.

"I wonder if those two fool women will really go up there tomorrow?"

"Is it a bad climb?"

"Not if you know which way to go. Straight up the south ridge it's only a scramble. But there are nasty places even there."

"Miss Bradford said she knew her way about," I said.

A smile touched his mouth. "She did, didn't she? Well, we can't do much about it."

"I suppose not." We were more than halfway up the little hill. The going was getting steeper and rougher. "Mr. Grant," I said, a little breathlessly.

"Yes?"

I hesitated, then said flatly: "What did Miss Bradford mean about a hoodoo on Blaven? What's wrong with it?"

He stopped and glanced down at me. He looked surprised, almost blank. "Wrong with it?" He repeated the phrase half mechanically.

"Yes. Why does everyone shy off it like that? I'm sure they do. I can't be mistaken. And if it comes to that, what's wrong with the people in the hotel? Because there's *something,* and if you haven't noticed it—"

"*You* don't *know?*"

"Of course I don't know!" I said, almost irritably. "I've only just arrived. But even to me the setup seems uncomfortably like the opening of a bad problem play."

"You're not far astray at that," said Roderick Grant. "Only we're halfway through the play, and it looks as if the problem isn't going to be solved at all." He paused, and looked gravely down at me in the gathering dusk. "It's a nasty problem, too," he said. "The nastiest of all, in fact. There's been murder done."

I took a jerky little breath. "*Murder?*"

He nodded. His blue eyes, in that light, were dark under lowered brows. "Two and a half weeks ago it happened, on the thirteenth of May. It was a local girl, and she was murdered on Blaven."

"I—see." Half unbelievingly I lifted my eyes to the great mass ahead. Then I shivered and moved forward. "Let's get to the top of this hill," I said, "and then, if you don't mind, I think you'd better tell me about it."

We sat on a slab of rock, and lit cigarettes. Away below us, cradled in its purple hollow, Loch na Creitheach gleamed with a hard bright light like polished silver. Two ducks flew across it, not a foot above their own reflections.

"Who was the girl?" I asked. "And who did it?"

He answered the latter question first. "We still don't know who did it. That's what I meant when I said it was a nasty problem. The police—" He frowned down at the cigarette in his fingers, then said: "I'd better start at the beginning, hadn't I?"

"Please do."

"The girl's name was Heather Macrae. Her father's a crofter, who does some ghillying for the hotel folks in summertime. You'll probably meet him. His croft's three or four miles up the Strath na Creitheach, the river that flows into the far end of this loch. . . . Well, it seems Heather Macrae was 'keeping company' with a lad from the village, one Jamesy Farlane, and so, when she took to staying out a bit later in the long spring evenings, her folk didn't worry about it. They thought they knew who she was with."

"And it wasn't Jamesy after all?"

"Jamesy says not. He says it very loud and clear. But then, of course," said Roderick Grant, "he would."

"And if it wasn't Jamesy, who could it have been?"

"Jamesy says he and Heather had a quarrel—yes, he admits it quite openly. He says she'd begun to avoid him, and when finally he tackled her with it, she flared up and said she was going with a better chap than he was. A gentleman, Jamesy says she told him." He glanced at me. "A gentleman from the hotel."

"Oh *no!*" I said.

"I'm afraid so."

"But—that doesn't mean the man from the hotel was necessarily—"

"The murderer? I suppose not, but there's a strong probability—if, that is, he existed at all. We only have Jamesy Farlane's word for that. What we do know is that Heather Macrae went out on the evening of May the thirteenth to meet a man. She told her parents that she 'had a date.'"

"And—on Blaven, you said?"

His voice was somber. "This bit isn't nice, but I'd better tell you. At about midnight that night, some men who were out late on Loch Scavaig—I suspect they were poaching sea trout—saw what looked like a great blaze of fire halfway up Blaven. They were mystified, but of course not alarmed. It's bare rock, so they weren't afraid of its spreading. They went on with their job, whatever it was, and kept an eye on the fire. One of them had a look through some night glasses, and said it was a column of flame, like a big bonfire, but that its base was out of sight behind a rocky bluff."

He paused. "Well, they got more and more puzzled. Who on earth would light a bonfire away up there, and what on earth could he be burning there anyway? Whether they were being wise after the event, or not, I don't know, but one of them, Rhodri MacDowell, says that gradually, watching that leaping column of fire where no fire ought to be, they grew first of all uneasy, then alarmed, then downright frightened. And when the chap with the glasses reported seeing a dark figure moving in front of the flames, they decided to investigate."

He frowned down at the shining loch. "By the time they got to it, of course, the fire was out, and it was only the remains of the smoke licking up the rock face that guided them. They found a widish ledge —easy enough to get to—with the remains of charred driftwood and birch and heather blackened and scattered, deliberately it seemed, all over the rock. Lying in the middle of the blackened patch was Heather's body, flat on its back." He drew sharply on his cigarette, and his voice was flat and colorless. "She was not very much burned. She had been dead when he put her there. Ashes had been scattered over her, and her throat was cut."

"Oh dear God," I said.

"She was," said Roderick, in that flat, impersonal voice, "fully clothed, and she was lying quietly, with her hands crossed on her breast. The oddest thing was, though, that she was barefooted, and all her jewelry had been taken off."

"Jewelry?" I said, astounded. "But good heavens—"

"Oh no, not stolen," he said quickly. "She hadn't anything worth stealing, poor child, let alone worth getting herself murdered for. It was all there, in a little pile in the corner of the ledge: her shoes, a leather belt, and all the ornaments she'd been wearing—a ring, a cheap bracelet and brooch, earrings—even a couple of hair clips. Odd, don't you think?"

But I wasn't thinking about its oddness. I said savagely: "The poor kid had certainly put on all her finery for him, hadn't she?"

He shot me a look. "It's quite particularly unpleasant, isn't it?"

"It certainly is." I looked up and along the towering curve of Blaven's south ridge. "And the police: do they favor Jamesy, or the gentleman from the hotel?"

He shrugged, and ground his cigarette out on the rock. "God knows. They've been coming and going ever since that day, putting us all through it—very quietly and unobtrusively, but nevertheless thoroughly. But you see why nerves are a little bit on edge?"

"I see," I said grimly. "I must say it seems a little strange that Major Persimmon didn't warn new guests of what was going on. They might even have preferred not to come."

"Quite," said Roderick Grant. "But his line is, obviously, that Jamesy's talking nonsense to protect himself, and that it's nothing to do with the hotel. The heavy questioning is all over, and the police are in any case being very quiet about it all. You can hardly expect Bill —Major Persimmon—to ruin his season, and possibly his hotel, can you?"

"I suppose not." I squashed out my cigarette, and rose. He got up too, and stood looking down at me.

"I hope this hasn't upset you too much," he said, a little awkwardly.

"If it has," I said, "it can hardly matter, can it? It's that poor child, going up to her death on the mountain, all decked out in her best. . . ." I bit my lip, and kicked at a tuft of heather, then raised my head and looked straight at him. "Just tell me," I said, "precisely which 'gentlemen' were in this hotel on May the thirteenth?"

The blue eyes met mine levelly. "All those," he said expressionlessly, "who are here now, with the exception of Miss Maling's chauffeur."

"And which of you," I said doggedly, feeling unhappy and absurd at the same time, "has an alibi?"

"None of us that I know of." Nothing in his voice betrayed any awareness of the change of pronoun which all at once gave the story a horrible immediacy. "Two of those boys camping by the river swear they were together; the third, no. Colonel Cowdray-Simpson and Bill Persimmon are vouched for by their wives, but that counts for very little, of course. Corrigan and Braine were out fishing on Loch an Athain."

"At *midnight?*"

"Quite a lot of people do. It's never really dark at this time of the year."

"Then they were together?"

"No. They separated to different beats some time after eleven, and went back to the hotel in their own time. Mrs. Corrigan says her husband got in well before midnight."

There was an odd note in his voice, and I took him up sharply. "You don't believe her?"

"I didn't say that. I only think it was pretty good going to get back to Camasunary by midnight. Loch an Athain's another mile beyond the end of Creitheach, and the going's heavy."

"Did he let himself into the hotel?"

"It's open all night."

"How nice," I said. "And Mr. Hay?"

"In bed. A very difficult alibi to break."

"Or prove."

"As you say. Mine happens to be the same."

"I—I'm sorry," I said, feeling suddenly helpless. "This is—fantastic, isn't it? I can't *believe* . . . and anyway, I've no earthly business to be questioning you as if you were Suspect Number One. I really am sorry."

He grinned. "That's all right. And it is your business, after all, if you're going to stay here. You've got to judge whom, if anyone, you feel safe with."

I put a hand to my cheek. "Oh Lord," I said, "I suppose so. I—I hadn't thought of that."

He spoke quickly, with contrition. "And I'm a fool to have mentioned it before we got back to lights and company. . . . Come along." He took my arm and turned quickly, helping me over the boulder-strewn turf. "We'll get back to the hotel. After all, for all you know, I *might* be Suspect Number One. This way; there's a path along the top of the ridge. We'll follow it along the hill a bit before we go down."

I went with him, disconcerted to find that my heart was pumping violently. The night had grown perceptibly darker. We had our backs to the lucent west, and before us the ghost moon swam in a deepening sky, where the mass of Blaven stooped like Faustus's mountain, ready to fall on us.

And its menacing shape was repeated, oddly, in a shadow that loomed in front of us, right in our path . . . a tall pile of something, heaped on the heather as if to mark the crest of the hill. Roderick Grant guided me past it without a look, but I glanced back at it uncertainly.

"What's that? A cairn?"

He flicked a casual look over his shoulder. "That? No. It's a bonfire."

I stopped dead, and his hand fell from my arm. He turned in surprise. I noticed all at once how still the glen was, how still and lonely. The lights of the hotel seemed a very long way off.

I said: "A—a bonfire?" and my voice came out in a sort of croak.

He was staring at me. "Yes. What's up?" Then his voice changed. "Oh my God, I've done it again, haven't I? I never thought—I didn't mean to scare you. I'm a fool. . . ." He took two strides back towards me, and his hands were on my shoulders. "Miss—Janet"—I doubt if either of us really noticed his use of my name—"don't be frightened. It's only the local Coronation celebration. They've been collecting stuff for the bonfire for weeks! It's nothing more sinister than that!" He shook me gently. "And I promise you I'm not a murderer either!"

"I never thought you were," I said shakily. "It's I who'm the fool. I'm sorry."

His hands dropped to his sides, and I saw him smiling down in the dusk. "Then let's get back to the hotel, shall we?" he said.

We turned towards the lights of Camasunary.

After all, it was not so very late. The hotel was bright and warm and safe, and one or two people were still about. Through the lounge door I could see Hartley Corrigan and Alastair sitting over a last drink, and, nearby, Ronald Beagle placidly reading.

And the idea that any of the men that I had met could be guilty of a crime at once so revolting and so bizarre was fantastic enough to border on lunacy. It was on a slightly shamefaced note that I said good night to Roderick Grant, and went up to my room.

The head of the staircase opened on the central point of the main upper corridor, which was like a large E, its three branches all ending in windows facing east, over the front of the hotel. My room lay in the far southeastern corner, at the end of the lower arm of the E. The bathroom next to me was, I found, occupied, so, wrapping my white velvet housecoat round me, I set out in search of another, which I found eventually at the far end of the main corridor. I took a long time over my bath, and by the time I had finished the hotel seemed to have settled into silence for the night. I let myself quietly out of the bathroom, and padded back along the now darkened corridor.

I went softly across the head of the stairs, and was almost past before I realized that someone was standing, still and quiet, at the end of the passage opposite, silhouetted against the dim window. Almost with a start, I glanced over my shoulder.

It was two people. They had not seen me, and for a very good reason. They were in one another's arms, kissing passionately.

The woman was Marcia Maling. I recognized the fall of her pale hair even before her scent reached my nostrils. I remember vaguely thinking "Fergus?"—and then I recognized, too, the set of the man's shoulders, and the shape of his head.

Not Fergus. Nicholas.

Hurriedly I looked away, and went softly down the main corridor towards my room.

Somewhere behind me, on the other side of the passage, I heard a door shut softly.

CHAPTER

SIX

෧෨

It was precisely one forty-eight A.M. when I decided that I was not
going to be able to sleep, and sat up in bed, groping for the light
switch. The tiny illuminated face of my traveling clock stared uncompromisingly back at me from the bedside table. One forty-eight A.M.
I scowled at it, and pressed the switch. Nothing happened. Then I
remembered that the hotel made its own electricity, and that this was
turned off at midnight. There had been a candlestick, I recollected
. . . my hand groped and found it. I struck a match and lit the candle.

I scowled at the clock again, then slipped out of bed. I was jaded
and depressed, and I knew that I had already reached the stage when
my failure to sleep was so actively irritating that sleep had become
an impossibility. What was worse, I knew I was in for one of the blinding nervous headaches that had devastated me all too often in the last
three or four years. I could feel the warning now, like a tiny electric
wire thrilling behind my eyes, pain, with the elusive threat of worse
pain to come.

I sat on the edge of the bed, pressing my hands hard against my
eyes, trying to will the pain away, while still in my wincing brain
whirled and jostled the images that, conspiring to keep sleep at bay,
had switched the agonizing current along my nerves. . . . Fire at
midnight . . . fire on Blaven . . . and *a gentleman from the hotel.*
Corrigan? Roderick? Alastair? Nicholas?

I shivered, then flinched and stood up. I wasn't even going to try
to ride this one out; I was going to dope myself out of it, and quickly.
The life-saving tablets were in my handbag. I padded across the room
to get it, groping vaguely among the grotesque shadows that distorted

the corners of the room. But it wasn't on the dressing table. It wasn't on the mantelpiece. Or on the floor near the hand basin. Or by the bed. Or—it was by now a search of despair—under the bed. It wasn't anywhere in the room.

I sat down on the bed again, and made myself acknowledge the truth. I hadn't taken my handbag on that walk with Roderick Grant. I had left it in the lounge. I could see it in my mind's eye, standing there on the floor beside my chair, holding that precious pillbox, as remote from me as if it had been on a raft in the middle of the Red Sea. Because nothing, I told myself firmly, wincing from a fresh jag of pain, *nothing* was going to get me out of my room that night. If anyone was to perform the classic folly of taking a midnight stroll among the murderous gentlemen with whom the hotel was probably packed, it was not going to be me.

On this eminently sensible note I got back into bed, blew out the candle, and settled down to ride it out.

Seventeen minutes later I sat up, lit the candle again, got out of bed, and grabbed my housecoat. I had reached, in seventeen minutes of erratically increasing pain, an even more sensible decision—and how much this was a product of reason and how much of desperation I can now judge more accurately than I could then. It was quite a simple decision, and very satisfactory. I had decided that Jamesy Farlane had murdered Heather Macrae. And since Jamesy Farlane didn't live in the hotel, I could go and get my tablets in perfect safety.

Perfect safety, I told myself firmly, thrusting my feet into my slippers and knotting the girdle of my housecoat tightly round me—as long as I was *very* quick, and *very* quiet, and was prepared to scream like blazes if I saw or heard the least little thing. . . .

Without pausing to examine the logic of this corollary to my decision, I seized my candle, unlocked my door, and set off.

And at once I saw that this was not to be, after all, the classic walk through the murder-haunted house, for, although the corridor lights were of course unlit, the glimmer from the eastern windows was quite sufficient to show me my way, and to lay bare the quiet and re-assuring emptiness of the passages, flanked by their closed doors. I went softly along the main corridor, shielding my candle, until I reached the stairhead.

The staircase sank down into shadows, and I hesitated for a moment, glancing involuntarily over my shoulder towards the window where I had seen Marcia and Nicholas. No one was there, this time; the window showed an empty oblong framing the pale night. I could see, quite distinct against the nebulous near-light of the sky, the massive outline of Blaven's shoulder. The moon had gone.

Then I heard the whispering. I must have been listening to it, half unconsciously, during the few seconds I had been standing there, for when at length my conscious mind registered, with a jerk, the fact that two people were whispering behind the door to my right, I knew immediately that the sound had been going on all along.

It should have reassured me to know that someone else was still awake; it certainly shouldn't have disturbed and frightened me, but that is just what it did. There was, of course, no reason why someone else in the hotel should not be sleepless too. If Colonel Cowdray-Simpson and his wife, or the Corrigans, were wakeful, and consequently talkative, at this ungodly hour, they would certainly keep their voices down to avoid disturbing the other guests. But there was something about the quality of the whispering that was oddly disquieting. It was as if the soft, almost breathless ripple of sound in the darkness held some sort of desperation, some human urgency, whether of anger or passion or fear, which communicated itself to me through the closed panels, and made the hairs prickle along my forearms as if a draught of chilly wind had crept through a crack in the door.

I turned to go, and a board creaked as my weight shifted.

The whispering stopped. It stopped as abruptly as an engine shuts off steam. Silence dropped like a blanket, so that in a matter of seconds the memory of the sound seemed illusory, while the silence itself surged with millions of whisperings, all equally unreal. But the sense of desperation was still there, even in the silence. It was as if the stillness were a held breath, that might burst at any moment in a scream.

I moved away quickly—and tripped over a pair of shoes which had been standing in the corridor waiting to be cleaned in the morning. The carpet was thick, but the small sound, in that hush, was like thunder. I heard a muffled exclamation from behind the door, then, staccato, sibilant, the splutter of a question. A deeper voice said something in reply.

There was only one pair of shoes: a woman's. I hastily retrieved the one I had kicked over, and put it back beside its fellow. They were handmade Laforgues, exquisite, absurd things with four-inch heels. Marcia Maling's.

There was silence now behind the door. I almost ran down the stairs, plunging, heedless of the streaming candle flame, into the darker

depths of the hall. I felt angry and ashamed and sick, as if I myself
had been caught out in some questionable action. God knew, I thought
bitterly, as I crossed the hall and pushed open the glass door of the
lounge, it was none of my business, but all the same. . . . She had,
after all, only met Nicholas tonight. And where was Fergus in all this?
Surely I hadn't misread the hints she had dropped about Fergus? And
where, too, did Hartley Corrigan come in, I wondered, remembering
the look in his eyes, and, even more significantly, the look on his wife's
face.

And here I paid for my speed and my heedlessness as the swing door
rushed shut behind me and tore the flame from my candle into a long
streamer of sharp-smelling smoke. Shadows surged up towards me,
pouncing from the corners of the dim lounge, and I halted in my tracks
and put a hand back to the door, already half in retreat towards the
safety of my room. But the lounge was untenanted save by those
shadows; in the glow of the banked peat fire I could see it all now
clearly enough. I threw one haunted glance back at the hall beyond
the glass door, then I went very quietly across the lounge towards
where I knew my handbag ought to lie.

Marcia and Nicholas . . . the coupled names thrust themselves back
into my mind. The odd thing about it, I thought, was that one
couldn't dislike Marcia Maling—though I might feel differently about
it if, like Mrs. Corrigan, I had a man to lose. It was to be supposed—
I skirted a coffee table with some care—it was to be supposed that
she couldn't help it. There was a long and ugly name for her kind of
woman, but, remembering her vivid, generous beauty as she sat opposite me in this very room, I could not find it in me to dislike her.
She was impossible, she was wanton, but she was amusing, and very
lovely, and, I thought, kind. Perhaps she was even being kind to me,
in a queer way, by attracting Nicholas's attention to herself when she
guessed I wished to escape it—though this, I felt, was perhaps giving
a little too much credit to Miss Maling's disinterested crusading spirit.

I grinned wryly to myself as I stooped and groped beside the chair
for my precious handbag. My fingers met nothing. I felt anxiously
along the empty floor, sweeping my hands round in little questing
circles that grew wider and more urgent with failure . . . and then I
saw the faint glint of the bag's metal clasp, not on the floor, but on a
level with my eye as I stooped. Someone must have picked it up and put
it on the bookshelf beside the chair. I grabbed, it, yanked out with

it some magazines and a couple of books, and flew back across the
lounge with my long skirts billowing behind me.

I was actually at the glass door, and shoving it open with my shoulder, when I heard the outer door of the hotel porch open, very quietly.
I stood stock-still, clutching books and bag and dead candle to a suddenly thudding heart.

Someone came softly into the porch. I heard the scrape of a nailed
boot on the flags, and faint sounds as he moved about among the
climbing and fishing gear that always cluttered the place. I waited.
Roderick Grant had told me the hotel stayed open all night. This
was surely—*surely*—nothing more sinister than some late fisherman,
putting his things away. That was all.

But all the same, I was not going to cross the hall and climb the
stairs in full view of him, whoever he was. So I waited, trying to still
my sickening heartbeats, backing away from the glass door as I remembered my white housecoat.

Then the outer door opened and shut again, just as softly as before,
and, clear in the still night, I heard his boots crunch once, twice, on
the gravel road. I hesitated only for a moment, then I shouldered aside
the glass door and flew across the hall to the outer porch, peering
after him through the window.

The valley was mist-dimmed, and full of vague shadows, but I saw
him. He had stepped off the gravel onto the grass and was walking
quickly away, head bent, along the verge of the road towards Strathaird. A man, slim, tallish, who walked with a long, swinging stride.
I saw him pause once, and turn, looking back over his shoulder, but
his face was no more than a dim blur. Then he vanished into the
shadows.

I turned back from the window in the not-quite-darkness, gazing
round the little porch. My eyes had adjusted themselves now. I could
see the table, with its weighing machine and the white enamel trays
for fish; the wicker chairs holding rucksacks, boots, fishing nets; pale
ovals of climbing rope depending from pegs; coats and mackintoshes,
scarves and caps, fishing rods and walking sticks. . . .

Behind me the door opened without a sound, and a man came
quietly in out of the night.

I didn't scream, after all. Perhaps I couldn't. I merely dropped everything with a crash that seemed to shake the hotel, and then stood,
dumb and paralyzed, with my mouth open.

The porch door swung to with a bang behind him. He jerked out a startled oath, and then, with a click, a torch beam shot out and raked me, blindingly.

He said: "Janet!" And then laughed. "My God, but you startled me! What on earth are you doing down here at this hour?"

I blinked into the light, which went off.

"Alastair?"

"The same." He swung his haversack from his shoulder, and began to take off his Burberry. "What was that you dropped? It sounded like an atom bomb."

"Books mostly," I said. "I couldn't sleep."

"Oh." He laughed again, and pitched his coat over a chair. "You looked like a ghost standing there in that white thing. I was unmanned, but positively. I nearly screamed."

"So did I." I stooped to pick up my things. "I'd better go back to bed."

He had a foot up on one of the chairs. "If you'd stay half a minute more and hold the torch for me, Janet, I could get these blasted boot-laces undone. They're wet."

I took the torch. "Is it raining?"

"In fits and starts."

"You've been fishing, I suppose?"

"Yes. Up the Strath."

"Any luck?"

"Pretty fair. I got two or three good fish, and Hart took a beauty. One and a half pounds."

"Hart? Oh—Hartley Corrigan."

"Mm. Don't wave the light about, my girl."

"Sorry. Is Mr. Corrigan not back yet, then?"

"Lord, yes. He came back a couple of hours since, but I'd just had some good rises, so I stayed. Strictly illegal, of course, so don't tell on me, will you?"

"Illegal?"

"It's the Sabbath, my dear. Had you forgotten? I should have stopped at midnight, like Hart." He pulled his second boot off, and straightened up.

"His fish aren't in the tray," I said.

"What?" His eyes followed the torch beam to the table. "Neither are they . . . that's odd."

"Alastair."

He turned his head sharply at the note in my voice.

"Well?"

I said, baldly: "Someone came into this porch five minutes ago, messed around for a bit, and then went out again."

"What? Oh—" he laughed. "Don't sound so worried! That would be Jamesy."

"*Jamesy?*"

"Jamesy Farlane; he was out with us. He's a better walker than I am, and he was in a hurry. He lives some way over towards Strathaird."

"I see," I said. I swallowed hard.

"Did you think he was a burglar? You don't need to worry about such urban horrors here, Janet. Nobody locks their doors in the Islands. There aren't such things as thieves."

"No," I said. I put the torch down on the table, and turned to go. "Only murderers."

I heard the sharp intake of his breath.

"Who told you?"

"Roderick Grant."

"I see. Worried?"

"Naturally."

He said: "I shouldn't be. Whatever it was all about, it can't touch you."

"I wasn't worried about myself."

"Who, then?" He sounded wary.

I said, with an edge to my voice: "Heather Macrae, of course. The girl—and her people. What had she done that a filthy grotesque thing like that should catch up with her? What was it all about? There's something more than queer about it, Alastair. I can't explain just how I feel about it, but it—it's somehow particularly nasty."

He said, inadequately: "Murder's never pretty."

"But it can be plain," I said, "and this isn't just plain wicked murder. She wasn't just hit or stabbed or choked in a fit of human passion. She was deliberately done to death, and then—arranged. It was coldblooded, calculating, and—and *evil*. Yes, evil. Here, too, of all places, where you'd think that sort of perverted ugliness had no existence. It's haunting me, Alastair."

He said, a little lamely: "The police are still on it, and they won't let up, you know."

I said: "Who do you think did it?"

"Janet—"

"You must have thought about it. Who? Jamesy Farlane?"

"I—look, Janet, I wouldn't talk too much about it—"

I said: "You mean, in case it's someone in the hotel?"

He said, uncomfortably: "Well—"

"Do you think it's someone in the hotel?"

"I don't know. I—don't—know. If it frightens you, my dear, why don't you go somewhere else? Broadford, or Portree, or—"

"I'm staying here," I said. "I want to be here when they do nose out this devil, whoever he is. *Whoever* he is."

He was silent.

I said: "Good night, Alastair," and went back upstairs to my room.

I never took the tablets, after all. My dead-of-night walk among the murderers must have been the kind of shock therapy that my headache needed, for when I got back to my room I realized that the pain had completely gone.

I got into bed and surveyed the rest of my booty.

I had got, I discovered, two copies of *The Autocar*. The books were *The Bride of Lammermoor*, and the abridged edition of Frazer's *Golden Bough*.

The Bride of Lammermoor put me to sleep in something under ten minutes.

CHAPTER

SEVEN

৪৯

Next morning, sure enough, it was raining, with a small, persistent, wetting rain. The sheep grazing in the glen near the hotel looked damp and miserable, and all but the nearest landmarks were invisible. Even Sgurr na Stri, just beyond the river, was dim in its shroud of grey.

When I came down, a little late, to breakfast, the place was quiet, though this was the Sabbath quiet rather than a depression due to the weather. I could see Alastair Braine and the Corrigans sitting over newspapers in the lounge, while Mrs. Cowdray-Simpson and the old lady had already brought their knitting into play. There were, however, signs that even a wet Sunday in the Highlands could not damp some enthusiasms: Colonel Cowdray-Simpson, at the grille of the manager's office, was conducting a solemn discussion on flies with Mr. Persimmon and a big countryman in respectable black; Marion Bradford and Roberta were in the porch, staring out at the wet landscape; and near them Roderick Grant bent, absorbed, over a landing net that he was mending with a piece of string.

He looked up, saw me, and grinned. "Hullo. It's too bad it's Sunday, isn't it? Wouldn't you have loved a nice day's fishing in the rain?"

"No, thank you," I said with decision. "I suppose this is what you fishing maniacs call ideal weather?"

"Oh, excellent." He cocked an eye at the sullen prospect. "Though it mightn't prove too dismal even for laymen. This is the sort of day that can clear up in a flash. Miss Symes might get her climb after all."

"Do you think so?" Roberta turned eagerly.

"It's possible. But"—he shot a wary half glance at Marion Bradford's back, still uncompromisingly turned—"be careful if you do go, and don't get up too high. The mist can drop again just as quickly as it can rise."

He had spoken quietly, but Marion Bradford heard. She turned and sent him a smouldering look.

"More good advice?" she asked in that tense, overdefiant voice that made anything she said sound like an insult.

Roberta said quickly: "It's good of Mr. Grant to bother, Marion. He knows I know nothing about it."

Marion Bradford looked as if she would like to retort, but she merely pressed her lips together and turned back to stare out of the window. Roderick smiled at Roberta and turned his attention to his landing net. Then Ronald Beagle came out into the porch, with a rucksack on his back.

"Why," said Roberta, "Mr. Beagle's going. Are you really going up Sgurr nan Gillean in this, Mr. Beagle?"

"I think it'll clear," said Beagle. "I'm going over there anyway, and if it clears in an hour or so, as I think it will, I'll be ready." He waved vaguely to all of us, and went out into the rain.

"Well," I said to Roberta, "both the oracles have spoken, so I hope you do get your climb."

"Are you going out too?"

"My dear, I haven't even had my breakfast yet! And if I don't hurry I doubt if I'll get any!"

But as I was halfway across the hall towards the dining room I was stopped by Major Persimmon's voice calling me from the office grille. I went over. The tall, thickset countryman was still there, bending over a tray of casts, his big fingers moving them delicately.

Bill Persimmon leaned forward across the counter.

"I believe you said you wanted to hire a rod, Mrs.—er, Miss Brooke, and fish a bit?"

"Yes, I do, but I'm not quite sure when. I think I might wait a day or so, and have a look round first."

"Just as you like, of course, only—" He glanced at the other man. "If you'd really like to be shown some fishing, you might care to fix it up in advance with Dougal Macrae here. He'd be glad to go with you, I know."

The big man looked up. He had a square, brown face, deeply lined, and smallish blue eyes that looked as if, normally, they were good-tempered. Just now, they held no expression at all.

He said, in the wonderfully soft voice of the Island men: "I should be glad to show the lady how to take a fish."

"That's very good of you," I said. "Perhaps—shall we say Wednesday?"

"Wednesday iss a free day." Dougal Macrae nodded his big head. "Yess, indeed."

"Thank you very much," I said.

"Where shall I put you down for?" asked Major Persimmon.

Dougal Macrae said: "The Camasunary river, please; the upper beat. If we cannot take a fish out of there it will be a bad day indeed."

He straightened up, and picked up a well-brushed and formidable bowler hat from the office counter. "And now I must be on my way, or I shall be late at the kirk. Good day to you, mistress. Good day, Mr. Persimmon."

And he went out into the grey morning. I found myself looking after him. It had been only the most trivial of conversations, but it was my first acquaintance with the beautifully simple courtesy of the Highlander, the natural but almost royally formal bearing of the crofter who has lived all his life in the Islands. I was very much impressed with this quiet man. Dougal Macrae. Heather Macrae's father. . . .

I nodded to Major Persimmon, and went to get my belated breakfast.

I had been (rather foolishly, I suppose) dreading my next meeting with Marcia, so I was glad that she was not in the dining room. Indeed, before I had poured out my first cup of coffee, I saw a big cream-colored car come slowly past the window, and slide to a halt outside the porch door. Almost immediately Marcia, looking enchanting and very urban in royal blue, hurried out of the hotel and was ushered into the front of the car by a handsome boy in uniform, who tucked rugs round her with solicitous care. Still in expensive and effortless silence, the car moved off.

I drank coffee, wishing I had a morning paper, so that I could pretend I hadn't noticed Nicholas who, apart from Hubert Hay, was the only other occupant of the dining room.

But it was after all the latter who in a short while rose and came over to my table.

He walked with an odd, tittuping little step that made me think again of Marcia's bouncy rubber balls, or of a self-confident robin. This latter impression was heightened by the rounded expanse of scarlet pullover which enlivened his already gay green tweeds. His face was round, too, with a small pernickety mouth, and pale eyes set in a multitude of radiating wrinkles. He had neat hands, and wore a big gold ring set with a black stone.

He smiled at me, showing a flash of gold in his mouth.

"Miss—er—Brooke? My name is Hay."

"How do you do?" I murmured politely.

"I hope you don't mind me coming over to speak, Miss Brooke, but the fact is"—he hesitated, and looked at me a little shyly—"the fact is, I wanted to ask a favor."

"Of course." I wondered what on earth was coming next.

"You see," he went on, still with that bashful expression that sat comically upon his round face, "you see, I'm footloose."

"You're *what?*" I said, startled.

"Footloose."

"That's what I thought you said. But—"

"It's my nom de ploom," he said. "I'm a writer." The scarlet pullover broadened perceptibly. "Footloose."

"Oh, I see! A writer—but how very clever of you, Mr. Hay. Er, novels, is it?"

"Travel books, Miss Brooke, travel books. I bring beauty to you at the fireside—that's what we put on the covers, you know. 'To you in your armchair I bring the glories of the English countryside.' And," he added, fairly, "the Scotch. That's why I'm here."

"I see. Collecting material?"

"Takin' walks," said Hubert Hay, simply. "I go on walks, and write about them, with maps. Then I mark them A, B, or C, according as to how difficult they are, and give them one, two, or three stars according as to if they're pretty."

"How—very original," I said lamely, conscious of Nicholas sitting well within hearing. "It must take a lot of time."

"It's dead easy," said Hubert Hay frankly. "That is, if you can write like I can. I've always had the knack, somehow. And it pays all right."

"I shall look out for your books," I promised, and he beamed down at me.

"I'll send you one, I will indeed. The last one was called *Sauntering in Somerset*. You'd like it. And they're not *books* really, in a manner of speaking—they're paperbacks. I think the best I ever did was *Wandering through Wales*. I'll send you that too."

"Thank you very much."

I noticed then that he was holding an old *Tatler* and a *Country*

Life in his hand. He put the two magazines down on the table and tapped them with a forefinger.

"I saw your photo in these," he said. "It *is* you, isn't it?"

"Yes."

He leafed through *Country Life* until he found the picture. It was me, all right, a David Gallien photograph in tweeds, with a brace of lovely Irish setters stealing the picture. Hubert Hay looked at me, all at once shy again.

"I take photos for my books," he said, hesitantly.

I waited, feeling rather helpless. Out of the corner of my eye I saw Nicholas stand up, and begin leisurely to feel in his pockets for tobacco. Hubert Hay said, with a rush: "When these geology chaps take a picture of a rock, they put a hammer in to show you the scale. I thought if I took a picture of the Coolins I'd like to—to put a lady in, so that you could tell how big the hills were, and how far away."

Nicholas was grinning. I sensed rather than saw it. Hubert Hay looked at me across David Gallien's beautifully composed advertisement, and said, wistfully: "And you do photograph nice, you do really."

Nicholas said casually: "You'd better find out what she charges. I believe it comes pretty high."

Hubert Hay looked at him, and then back at me, in a kind of naïve bewilderment. "I—shouldn't I have—?"

He looked so confused, so uncharacteristically ready to be deflated, that I forgot my own embarrassment, and Hugo Montefior's probable apoplexy. I looked furiously at Nicholas. "Mr. Drury was joking," I said swiftly. "Of course you may take a picture of me if you want to, Mr. Hay. I'd love to be in your book. When shall we do it?"

He flushed with pleasure, and the scarlet pullover expanded again to its original robin-roundness. "That's very kind of you, I'm sure, very kind indeed. I'm honored, I am really. If it clears up, how about this afternoon, on Sgurr na Stri, with the Coolins behind?"

"Fine," I said firmly.

"Bill Persimmon has a spaniel." Nicholas's voice was very bland.

"Has he?" Hubert Hay took that one happily at its face value. "Maybe that's a good idea, too. I'll go and ask him if we can borrow it."

He trotted gaily off. Nicholas stood looking down at me, still with that expression of sardonic amusement that I hated.

"What's Hugo going to say when he sees you starring in *Staggering through Skye,* or whatever this masterpiece is going to be called?"

"He won't see it," I said tartly, as I rose. "The only traveling Hugo's interested in is Air France to Paris and back."

I started after Hubert Hay, but Nicholas moved, barring my way to the door.

"I want to talk to you, Gianetta."

I regarded him coldly. "I can't think that we have much to say to one another."

"I still want to talk to you."

"What about?"

"About us."

I raised my eyebrows. "There isn't any 'us,' Nicholas. Remember? We're not bracketed together any more. There's a separate you and a separate me, and nothing to join us together. Not even a name."

His mouth tightened. "I'm very well aware of that."

I said, before I realized what I was saying: "Was that you with Marcia Maling last night?"

His eyes flickered, and then went blank. He said: "Yes."

I walked past him and out of the room.

The oracles had been right. By eleven o'clock the rain had cleared, and the clouds began to lift with startling rapidity. I saw Marion Bradford and Roberta set off up the valley about half an hour later, and, not long afterwards, Nicholas went out along the track towards Strathaird.

Shortly before noon, the sun struggled out, and, in a moment, it seemed, the sky was clear and blue, and the mist was melting from the mountain tops like snow. Sedge and heather glittered with a mass of jewels, and the frail gossamers sagged between the heather tips weighted with a Titania's ransom of diamonds.

Hubert Hay and I set out with Bill Persimmon's spaniel soon after lunch. We went down through the little birch grove to the stepping-stones which spanned the Camasunary River. The birches were old and lichened, but they moved lightly in the wind, censing the bright air with raindrops, an intermittent sun-shower that we had to dodge as we took a short cut through the grove towards the river, picking our way over the wet bilberry leaves and mosses and the scattered chunks of fungus that had fallen from the trees.

We crossed the river by the steppingstones, and, after an hour or so of steep but not too difficult walking, reached the crest of Sgurr na Stri. Hubert Hay, for all his rotundity, was light on his feet, and proved, a little to my surprise, to be an entertaining companion. His knowledge and love of the countryside was not as superficial as our conversation had led me to expect; he talked knowingly of birds and deer and hill foxes, and knew, it appeared, a good deal about plants. He babbled on as he chose his "picture" and set his camera, and though he talked incessantly in clichés, I could sense that his satisfaction in what he called "the great outdoors" was deep and genuine. His resemblance to a cocky little robin became every minute more remarkable, but the quality that Marcia had called "sorbo" was, I discovered, due to an irrepressible gaiety, a delighted curiosity about everything, rather than to self-satisfaction. He was, in fact, a rather attractive little man.

We took three photographs. From the top of Sgurr na Stri you can see the whole range of the Black Cuillin, the forbidding arc that sweeps from Garsven in the south to Sgurr nan Gillean in the north, with Loch Coruisk, black as an inkwell, cupped in the roots of the mountains. I posed with the spaniel, an aristocratic but witless beast, against mountain, sky, and loch in turn, while Hubert Hay fussed with his camera and darted from one point to another with little cries of polite satisfaction.

When at length he had finished we sat down together on a rock and lit cigarettes. He seemed to have something on his mind, and smoked jerkily for a bit. Then he said:

"Miss Brooke, do you—d'you mind me saying something to you?"

"Of course not. What is it?"

"You're here alone, aren't you?"

"Yes."

His round face was worried as he looked at me earnestly. "Don't go out by yourself with anyone, Miss Brooke. You're all right with me, here, today, of course, but you weren't to know that." His rather absurd voice was somehow scarifying in its vehemence. "*But don't go with anyone else*. It's not safe."

I said nothing for a moment. I realized that I had, actually, since breakfast that morning, forgotten the sort of danger that was walking these hills.

"You don't mind me saying?" asked Hubert Hay anxiously.

"Of course not. You're perfectly right. I promise you I'll be careful." There was a certain irony about the admonition, repeating as it did Roderick Grant's warning of the night before. Could I, then, eliminate two of the suspects among the "gentlemen from the hotel," or were these warnings some subtle kind of double bluff? If I went on going for walks with the "gentlemen," no doubt I should find out soon enough. I shivered a little, and pulled the dog's ears. "It's not a very pleasant thought, is it?"

His face flushed dark red. "It's damnable! I—I beg your pardon, I'm sure. But that's the only word I can think of. Miss Brooke"—he turned to me with a queer, almost violent gesture—"that girl, Heather Macrae —she was only eighteen!"

I said nothing.

"It was her birthday." His funny high little voice held a note almost of savagery. "Her eighteenth birthday." He took a pull at his cigarette, and then spoke more calmly: "I feel it a bit, Miss Brooke. You see, I knew her."

"You knew her? Well?"

"Oh dear no. Only to speak to, as you might say. I'd stopped at the croft a couple of times, when I was out walking, and she'd made me a pot of tea. She was a pretty girl, gay and a bit cheeky, and kind of full of life. There wasn't a bit of badness in her. Nothing to ask for— what she got."

"*You* didn't get any hint as to who she was going with?" It was a silly question, of course, as the police would have gone over the ground with meticulous thoroughness, but he answered without impatience: "No, none at all."

But his voice had altered subtly, so that I glanced at him. "You got *something?*"

"A very little hint," he said carefully. "I told her that I was writing a book, of course, and she was interested. People usually are. . . . She said that quite a lot of folks came around the crofts, one way and another, asking questions about local customs and superstitions and the like. I asked her if she had any special superstitions—just joking-like —and she said no, of course not, she was a modern girl. Then I said wasn't there any magic still going on in the Islands like there used to be, and"—he turned pale round eyes on me—"she shut up like an oyster, and pretty near hustled me out of the kitchen."

"*Magic?*" I said. "But that's absurd!"

He nodded. "I know. But, you know, I can't help having a feeling about this murder. It must have been all *planned*, you see. The stuff he'd used for the bonfire must have been taken up there, bit by bit, quite deliberately. There was heather and peat and branches of birchwood, and a big chunk of oak hardly charred, and a lot of that dry fungus—agaric—that you get on birch trees."

I made an exclamation, but he hadn't heard me. "Then, when he is ready, he gets the girl up there. . . . Just think a minute, if you'll excuse me bringing it up again . . . the fire, and the shoes and things in a neat pile, all tidy, and the girl laid out with her throat cut and her hands crossed, and ashes on her face. . . . Why, it's like a—a *sacrifice!*"

The last word came out with a jerk. I was on my feet staring down at him, with my spine prickling.

"But that's *crazy!*"

The pale, troubled eyes glanced up. "That's just it, isn't it? Whoever did it must be just plain crazy. And he looks and acts just as sane as you or me . . . except sometimes." He got to his feet and regarded me solemnly. "So I wouldn't go for walks with anybody, if I was you."

"I won't," I said fervently. "In fact, I'm beginning to think that I might go back to London, after all."

"It wouldn't be a bad idea, at that," said he, picking up his camera, and turning to follow me down the hill.

CHAPTER

EIGHT

ৡ৶

I was still wondering if it wouldn't, after all, be wisest to leave the hotel, when something happened that made me decide, at any rate for the time being, that I must stay.

It was in the lounge, after dinner, that the first stirring of a new uneasiness began to make itself plain. Alastair Braine, carrying coffee cups, paused in the middle of the room and said, on a slight note of surprise: "Hullo, aren't the climbers back yet?"

"They weren't at dinner," said Alma Corrigan.

Colonel Cowdray-Simpson said: "Good God, neither were they. I hope there's nothing amiss."

"That fool woman!" said Mrs. Cowdray-Simpson, roundly. "She shouldn't have gone up on a day like this."

Alastair said reassuringly: "I shouldn't worry. They've probably only gone a little farther than they meant to, and after all, it's still light."

Nicholas looked up from a letter he was writing. "The weather was clearing nicely when they went, and there's been no mist on Blaven this afternoon. They'll be all right."

"If only," said Marcia Maling, "if only that *awful* woman hasn't gone and done something silly, just to impress! That *poor* child Roberta—"

Roderick Grant said quietly: "Miss Bradford is actually a very accomplished climber. She wouldn't take any risks with a beginner. And Drury is quite right about the weather. After all, Ronald Beagle went up Sgurr nan Gillean, and he certainly wouldn't have gone if it hadn't been all right."

"He's not back either," said Hubert Hay.

There was a little silence. I sensed discomfort and uneasiness growing.

"Neither is he," said Alma Corrigan, rather stupidly. "Well, I suppose—"

"Where's your husband?" asked Mrs. Cowdray-Simpson.

The question sounded abrupt, but there was nothing in it to make Alma Corrigan flush scarlet, as she did. "He—he went out walking."

She was so obviously embarrassed that everybody else began to feel embarrassed too, without knowing the reason. Alastair said quickly: "We all went out after lunch to walk up to the ridge for the view over Loch Slapin. I brought Mrs. Corrigan back, but Hart went farther."

"Oh, you went that way? Did you see the women, then, on Blaven?" asked Colonel Cowdray-Simpson.

"Not a sign. We saw someone—I believe it was Drury—in the distance, but not another living soul."

"I wasn't on Blaven," said Nicholas, "so I didn't see them either."

Roderick Grant put down his coffee cup and got to his feet. "It's only eight thirty, and I don't personally think we need to worry yet, but they certainly should have got back by this. I think I'll have a word with Bill. They may have told him if they were going to be late."

He went quickly into the hall, where I could see him leaning over the office counter, in earnest conversation with Major Persimmon.

"Sensible chap," said Colonel Cowdray-Simpson. "No point in starting a fuss."

But Marcia was not to be stopped so easily. "This is *too* ghastly, isn't it? What d'you suppose *could* have happened to them?"

"Plenty of things can happen in the Cuillin," said Alma Corrigan, rather tartly, "and altogether too many things *have* been happening lately."

"*That* affair?" said Alastair. "That can hardly have any connection—"

"I'm not talking about the murder," said Alma brutally. I heard Marcia give a little gasp. "I'm talking about climbing accidents." She looked round the circle of faces, her fine eyes serious and a little frightened. "Do you realize how many people have been killed by the Cuillin, this year alone?"

Her use of the preposition gave the sentence an oddly macabre twist, and I saw Marcia glance over her shoulder to where the great hills towered against the massed clouds of evening. "Is it—a lot?" She sounded a little awe-stricken.

"Four," said Alma Corrigan, and added, almost absently, "so far. . . ."

I felt the little cold caress of fear along the back of my neck, and was grateful for the Colonel's brisk interposition. "Well," he said, practically, "if people will go wandering out in these mountains with only the haziest ideas about how to climb them, they must expect accidents. In almost every case these mishaps are brought about by ignorance or carelessness, and I'm sure we can acquit Beagle and Miss Bradford on both those grounds. We're making an unnecessary fuss, and I think we'd better stop talking about it and frightening ourselves."

He turned to Alastair with some remark about tomorrow's sport, and in a few minutes tension seemed to be relieved, and people were chatting generally.

I turned to Marcia Maling. "Where did you go today?"

"To Portree, my dear"—her face lit up with the familiar warm *gamine* charm—"along the most *ghastly* roads, with poor dear Fergus snarling like a tomcat all the way because he'd just washed the car!"

"I thought there was an excellent road from Broadford?"

"Oh, there is. But it goes *snaking* about with the most *ghastly* hairpin bends and cliffs and things—"

"But, Marcia, the views—"

The views were dismissed with a wave of her cigarette. "It was divine, of course," she said quickly, "only it was raining. And then Portree on a Sunday is the utter *end*. But I got some marvellous tweed there on Friday. I'll show it to you tonight. It's a sort of misty purple, and quite gorgeous."

But here Roderick came back into the lounge, and there was a lull in the conversation as eyes turned towards him.

"Bill Persimmon says there's no earthly reason to worry," he said reassuringly, but, as he crossed the room towards me, I thought I saw uneasiness in the glance he cast at the sky outside.

Someone switched on the radio, and the lugubrious weather report insinuated itself into the conversation. Colonel Cowdray-Simpson moved nearer to listen.

"Waiting for news of Everest," said Roderick to me with a grin. "That, with the notable absence of fish in the rivers, seems to be the Colonel's main preoccupation."

"He's rather sweet." I said. "I'd hate him to be disappointed, but, you know, I have the oddest feeling about Everest. . . . I believe I'd be almost sorry to see it climbed."

"Sorry?" He looked at me curiously. "Why on earth?"

I laughed. "Not really, I suppose. But I'd always imagined it as the last inviolate spot that arrogant man hadn't smeared himself over, sort of remote and white and unattainable. Immaculate, that's the word I want. I somehow think it would be a pity to see man's footmarks in the snow."

"I didn't know you were a poet, Gianetta," said Nicholas's voice above me, lazily mocking. He had come over to the window just behind my chair.

I felt myself flushing, and Roderick looked a little annoyed.

"Why should you? I didn't know you knew Miss Brooke."

His voice was curt. Nicholas eyed him for a moment.

"Why should you?" he echoed, unpleasantly, and turned away to the window. "And here, if I'm not mistaken, is our friend Beagle at last."

"Alone?" asked Mrs. Cowdray-Simpson.

"Yes . . . that's odd."

"What's odd?" asked Alastair, joining him.

"He's coming down the glen from Loch na Creitheach. I thought he went up Sgurr nan Gillean," said Nicholas thoughtfully. "Wouldn't it have been easier for him to come down the west side of the glen and over the steppingstones?"

"There's nothing in it," said Alastair. "That's a shorter way, certainly, but the going's terrible, while there's a path down the Blaven side of Creitheach."

Roderick said: "He may have seen the two women, if he's come along the glen. It's still light enough to see someone on the south ridge."

But Beagle, when he came in, denied that he had seen anyone. And the worried look that came over his face when he heard that the two girls were still out, brought back with a rush the apprehensions that we had been trying to dismiss. He went to change and eat a late meal, and we all sat, talking in fits and starts, and trying not to look out of the window too often, for another half hour of steadily mounting anxiety.

By half past nine it was pretty dark. Rain clouds had massed in great indigo banks right across the sky, shutting out any speck of residual light that might linger in the west. Wisps of wet mist scudded underneath the higher cloud, and the fingers of the gusty wind clawed at the windows, flinging rain in spasmodic handfuls against the glass. By now everybody, I think, was convinced that something had happened to the two women, and it was almost a relief when, at nine thirty exactly, Bill Persimmon came into the lounge and said, without preamble: "I think we'd better go out and look for them. Mr. Corrigan has just come in with Dougal, and they say there's still no sign of them coming down the glen."

The men were on their feet.

"You're sure they went up Blaven?"

Persimmon said: "Certain. They—"

"They might have changed their minds," said Nicholas.

Bill Persimmon looked at him, queerly, I thought. He said, slowly: "They went to Blaven, all right. They were seen on it."

"Seen?" said Roderick. "When? Whereabouts?"

"At the Sputan Dhu," said Persimmon dryly.

Ronald Beagle started forward. "At the—but *my God*, man, that's no place for a beginner! The Black Spout! That's a devilish tricky climb. Are you sure, Persimmon?"

We all stared at Bill Persimmon, while our imagined fears gradually assumed a horrible reality.

"Who saw them?" asked Nicholas quickly.

Bill looked at him again. "Dougal Macrae. He saw them making for the gully at about four o'clock. All three of them."

My throat was suddenly dry. I heard myself say in a strange voice: "All *three* of them?"

He nodded and his eyes went round the group of faces where a new sort of fear was beginning to dawn. He said: "Dougal says there were three. And . . . everybody else is back. Odd, isn't it?"

"Perhaps they had a guide," said Nicholas.

"They set out without one," said Roderick.

Bill Persimmon backed to the swing door, thrusting it open with his shoulder. "We'll discuss it after we've found them and brought them in," he said. "The ladies would be well advised to stay indoors. Will the men be ready in five minutes? Come along to the kitchen then, and my wife'll have sandwiches and coffee ready."

I got up. "Can't we help there?"

"That would be very good of you, ma'am. I expect she'd be glad of a hand."

Then he pushed through the door with the other men after him.

When, at length, they had all gone out into the gusty dark, I went slowly back to the lounge. I was thinking, not very coherently, about Dougal Macrae's story. Three climbers? *Three?*

There could be no possible connection, of course—but I found myself wondering what Jamesy Farlane looked like.

Alma Corrigan had gone to bed, and Mrs. Cowdray-Simpson was upstairs with her mother-in-law. Marcia and I were alone again in the lounge. The curtains had been drawn to shut out the storm, but the rain was hurtling against the windows in fistfuls, and the wind sounded vicious. Behind its spasmodic bursts of violence droned the steady sound of the sea.

Marcia shivered, and stretched her legs to the fire. Her eyes looked big and scared.

"Isn't this too utterly ghastly?" she said, and through the outworn extravagance of the phrase I could hear the strain plucking at her throat.

"I'm afraid it does look as if something had happened," I said. "Look, I brought us both a drink, Marcia."

"Oh, you angel." She took the glass and drank a generous mouthful. "My God, I needed that!" She leaned forward in her chair. The big eyes seemed bigger than ever. "Janet, do you believe there *is* a hoodoo on that mountain?"

I gave a laugh that was probably not very convincing. "No, of course not. They just went climbing in too hard a place and got stuck. It's always happening. They'll turn up all right."

"But—the other climber?"

"Whoever it was," I said robustly, "it certainly wasn't a ghost."

She gave a little sigh. "Well, the quicker they're found the sooner to sleep. I hope to heaven nothing's happened to that Roberta child. She's rather sweet—pathetic, in a way. I wonder—"

"It was the other one I found pathetic," I said, and then realized with a shock that I had spoken in the past tense.

But Marcia had not noticed. "That ghastly Bradford woman? But, my dear, she's *impossible!* Not that I'd want anything to happen to her, but really—!"

"She must be a very unhappy woman," I said, "to be like that. She must know she's making everybody dislike her, and yet some devil inside her drives her perpetually to antagonize everyone she meets."

"Frustrated," said Marcia cruelly, "*and* how. She's in love with Roderick Grant."

I set down my glass with a click, and spoke almost angrily. "Marcia! That's absurd!"

She giggled. She looked like a very pretty cat. "It is not. Haven't you seen the way she looks at him?"

I said sharply: "Don't talk nonsense. She was abominably rude to him, both last night and this morning. I heard her."

"Uh-huh," said Marcia, on a rising note of mockery. "All the same, you watch the way she looks at him. It's just about as noticeable as the way he *doesn't* look at her—just looks down his nose in that charming well-bred way he has, and then jumps at the chance of taking *you* for a walk! If I were you, darling, I'd keep out of her range."

"Oh, nonsense," I said again, feeling horribly uncomfortable. I got up. "I think I'll go to bed."

Marcia uncurled herself, and drained her glass. "I'll come too. I'm certainly not going to sit down here alone. I imagine we'll hear them coming back, and'll find out what's happened then."

She linked her arm in mine as we went up the stairs, and grinned at me. "Annoyed with me?"

"Of course not. Why should I be?"

"Honey, on account of I say things I oughtn't. And that reminds me—I'm afraid I gave you away tonight. I didn't mean to."

"Gave me away? What d'you mean?"

"I let out to Roderick Grant that you and Nicky had been divorced. I forget how it came up—it was during the shemozzle tonight, when you were in the kitchen. I'm sorry, truly I am."

"It's all right." Nicky, I thought. Nicky. I'll bet she spells it Nikki. . . .

"I hope it doesn't matter," said Marcia.

I laughed. "Why should it? I don't suppose he'll tell anyone else."

"Oh, well. . . ." We had reached the stairhead. "*That's* all right, then. Come and see my tweed before you go to bed."

I followed her along the passage to her room. The window at the end showed, tonight, only a square of roaring grey against which our reflections glimmered, distorted and pale. Marcia pushed her door open and went in, groping for the light switch.

"Just a sec., I'll see—" The light went on.

I heard her gasp. She was standing as if frozen, her back to me, her hands up to her throat.

Then she screamed, a high, tearing scream.

For a paralyzed, horrified moment I couldn't move. My body turned to ice and I stood there, without breath.

Then she screamed again, and whirled round to face me, one hand flung out in a gesture of terror, the other clutching her throat.

I moved then. I jumped forward and seized the hand. I said: "Marcia, for God's sake, what is it?"

Her breath came roughly, in gasps. "*The murderer. Oh my God, the murderer. . . .*"

"Marcia, there's no one here."

She was shaking violently. She grabbed my arm and held it tightly. She pointed to the bed, her lips shaking so much that she couldn't speak coherently.

I stared down at the bed, while the slow goose flesh pricked up my spine.

Lying on the coverlet was a doll, the kind of frivolous doll in a flounced skirt that the Marcias of this world love to have sprawling about on divans and sofas among the satin cushions. I had seen dozens of them—flaxen-headed, blue-eyed, pink and white and silken.

But this one was different.

It was lying flat on its back on the bed, with its legs straight out and its hands crossed on its breast. The contents of an ash tray had been scattered over it, and a great red gash gleamed across its neck, where its throat was cut from ear to ear.

CHAPTER

NINE

෭෨

They found no trace, that night, of either Marion Bradford or Roberta. The night had been black and wild, and after several fruitless and exhausting hours of climbing and shouting in the blustering darkness, the searchers had straggled home in the early hours of daylight, to snatch food and a little sleep before setting out, haggard-eyed and weary, for a further search. Bill Persimmon had telephoned for the local rescue team, and, at about nine the next morning, a force some twenty strong set out once again for what must now certainly be reckoned the scene of an accident.

This time, I went with them. Even if I couldn't rock-climb, I would at least provide another pair of eyes, and I could help to cover some of the vast areas of scree and rough heather bordering the Black Spout.

The morning—I remembered with vague surprise that it was the eve of Coronation Day—had broken grey and forbidding. The wind still lurched among the cairns and heather braes with inconsequent violence, and the frequent showers of rain were arrow-sharp and heavy. We were all muffled to the eyes, and trudged our way up the sodden glen with heads bent to meet the vicious stabbing of the rain.

It was a little better as we came under the shelter of the hill where Roderick and I had talked two nights ago, but, as we struggled on to the crest of it, the wind met us again in force. The raindrops drove like nails before it, and I turned my back to it for a moment's respite. The storm gust leaped past me, wrenching at my coat, and fled down the valley towards the sea.

The hotel looked far away and small and lonely, with, behind it, the sea loch whitening under the racing feet of the wind. I saw a car move slowly away from the porch, and creep along the storm-lashed track to Strathaird. It was a big car, cream, with a black convertible top.

"Marcia Maling's car," said a voice at my elbow. It was Alma Corrigan, looking businesslike in Burberry and scarlet scarf and enormous nailed boots. She looked also, I noticed, decidedly attractive, now that the wind had whipped red into her cheeks and a sparkle into her fine eyes. She added, with a touch of contempt, as we turned to make our way along the top of the spur: "I suppose it would be too much to expect her to come along as well, but she needn't have taken the chauffeur away with her. Every man we can get—"

"She's leaving," I said.

She checked in her stride. "Leaving? You mean going home?"

"Yes. She's going back to London. She told me so last night."

"But I thought she planned to stay a week at least! I suppose this affair, on top of the other business—"

"I suppose so," I said, noncommittally. I was certainly not going to tell anyone the reason for Marcia's sudden decision. Mrs. Persimmon knew, and Mrs. Cowdray-Simpson, but if Marcia's hysterics had not disturbed Alma Corrigan the night before, so much the better. And I was more than ever certain that I, myself, was going home tomorrow. But since I had not, like Marcia, been, so to speak, warned away, I felt I could hardly go without finding out what had happened to Marion and Roberta.

"Well!" said Mrs. Corrigan, on an odd note which was three parts relief and one of something else I could not identify. "I can't pretend I'm broken hearted to see her go. She's only been here five days, and"—she broke off and sent me a sidelong glance up from under her long lashes—"you'd understand how I feel, if you were a married woman, Miss Brooke."

"No doubt." I added gently: "She couldn't help it, you know. . . . She's been spoiled, I suppose, and she *is* such a lovely creature."

"You're more charitable than I am," said Alma Corrigan, a little grimly. "But then, you haven't so much to lose."

I didn't pretend to misunderstand her. "She had to have men's admiration," I said, "all the time, no matter who got hurt in the process. I—forgive me, but I'd put it behind you, if I were you. Can't you begin to pretend it never happened?"

She laughed a little, hardly. "It's easy to see you don't know much about dealing with men."

I didn't speak for a moment. I wondered irritably why married women so often adopted that tone, almost of superior satisfaction in the things they had to suffer. Then I told myself that she was probably right. I had after all failed utterly to deal with the man I had married, so who was I to give her advice? I thought wryly that nobody ever wanted advice anyway; all that most people sought was a ratification of their own views.

We were passing the Coronation bonfire, and I changed the subject. "I suppose they'll hardly light that bonfire now. I mean, celebrations won't exactly be in keeping, if anything's happened to these two girls."

She said morosely: "The sticks'll be wet, anyway," and added, with the determined gloom of a mouse returning to its accustomed tread-mill: "But how can Hart just expect to go on the way he has? He's been following her round like a lap dog, making a fool of me, ever since she came. Oh, you haven't seen much of it. She switched to that Drury man last night, but *really*—I mean, *everybody* must have noticed. It's all very well saying she can't help it, but what about Hart? Why should Hart be allowed to get away with that sort of thing? I've a damned good mind to—"

I said abruptly: "Do you want to keep your husband or don't you?"

"I—of course I want to keep him! What a silly question!"

"Then leave him alone," I said. "Don't you know yet that there's no room for pride in marriage? You have to choose between the two. If you can't keep quiet, then you must make up your mind to lose him. If you want *him*, then swallow your pride and shut up. It'll heal over; everything does, given time enough and a bit of peace."

She opened her mouth, probably to ask me what I knew about it anyway.

"We're getting left behind," I said, almost roughly. "Let's hurry."

I broke away from her and forged ahead up the rapidly steepening path.

We had climbed to a good height already, and I was thankful to notice, as we began to thread our way up the deer tracks on the westerly flanks of Blaven itself, that the force of the wind was lessening. The gusts were less frequent and less violent, and, by the time we had reached the base of the first scree slopes, the rain had stopped, shut off as suddenly as if by the turning of a tap.

The party was strung out now in single file, forging at a steeply climbing angle along the mountainside. Most of the men carried packs;

several had coils of rope. The going got harder; the deer paths narrowed and steepened. These were foot-wide depressions—no more—in the knee-deep heather, and they were treacherous with the rain. Occasionally we found ourselves having to skirt great outcrops of rock, clinging precariously to roots and tufts of heather, with our feet slithering, slipping on the narrow ledge of mud which was all that remained of the path.

Above us towered the enormous cliffs of the south ridge, gleaming-black with rain, rearing steeply out of the precipitous scree like a roach-backed monster from the waves. The scree itself was terrifying enough. It fell away from the foot of the upper cliffs, hundreds of feet of fallen stone, slippery and overgrown and treacherous with hidden holes and loose rocks, which looked as if a false step might bring half the mountainside down in one murderous avalanche.

The place where Dougal Macrae had seen the climbers was about halfway along Blaven's western face. There the crest of the mountain stands up above the scree in an enormous hogback of serrated peaks, two thousand feet and more of grim and naked rock, shouldering up the scudding sky. I stopped and looked up. Streams of wind-torn mist raced and broke round the buttresses of the dreadful rock; against its sheer precipices the driven clouds wrecked themselves in swirls of smoke; and, black and terrible, above the movement of the storm, behind the racing riot of grey cloud, loomed and vanished and loomed again the great devil's pinnacles that broke the sky and split the winds into streaming rack. Blaven flew its storms like a banner.

And from some high black corrie among the peaks spilled the tiny trickle of water that was to form the gully of the Sputan Dhu. I could just see it, away up on some remote and fearful face of rock—a thin white line, no more, traced across the grey, a slender, steady line that seemed not to move at all save when the force of the wind took it and made it waver a little, like gossamer in the breeze. And the slowly falling gossamer line of white water had cut, century by century, deep into the living rock, slashing a dark fissure for itself down the side of the mountain. Through this it slid, and rushed, and slid again, now hidden, now leaping clear, but all the time growing and loudening and gathering force until it reached the lowest pitch of the mountain and sank clamorously out of sight in the cleft that split the upper edge of the precipice above the scree.

And then at last it sprang free of the mountain. From the base of the cleft, some hundred feet up the face, it leaped as from a gutter-spout, a narrow jet of roaring water that jumped clear of the rock to plunge the last hundred feet in one sheer white leap of foam. And then it vanished into the loud depths of the gully it had bitten through the scree.

Up the edge of this gully the rescue party slowly picked its way. At intervals, someone shouted, but the only answer was the bark of a startled raven, which wheeled out from the cliff above, calling hoarsely among the mocking echoes.

I clawed my way over the wet rocks, my shoes slipping on slimy tufts of grass and thrift, my breath coming in uneven gasps, my face damp and burning with exertion in spite of the intermittent buffets of the chill wet wind. The men forged steadily ahead, their seemingly care-less slouch covering the ground at a remarkable speed. I clambered and gasped in their wake, lifting my eyes occasionally to the menace of those black cliffs ahead that rode, implacably grim and remote, above the flying tails of the storm. Down to our left, at the bottom of the gully, the water brawled and bellowed and swirled in its devil's pot-holes. Here was a veritable demon's cleft; a black fissure, seventy feet deep, bisecting the scree slope. Its walls were sheer, black and dripping, its floor a mass of boulders and wrestling water.

Suddenly, and for the first time clearly, I realized that somewhere here, in this wilderness of cruel rock and weltering water, two young women were probably lying dead. Or, at best, alive and maimed and unable, above the intermittent roar of wind and water, to make them-selves heard.

I found myself repeating, breathlessly, stupidly, in a whisper: "Ro-berta . . . Roberta. . . ."

The man directly in front of me was Alastair. He turned and gave me a quick, reassuring smile, and reached out a big hand to steady me up the slope.

"Don't go too near the edge, Janet . . . that's better. We'll soon get them now, if Dougal was right. These rescue chaps know every inch of the place, you know."

"But . . . Alastair"—exertion had made me only half articulate—"they can't be alive still. They must have—must be—"

"If they managed to creep into shelter, they could quite easily be alive, providing they weren't seriously hurt by a fall. It wasn't cold last night."

"Do you believe there were three of them?"

"Dougal Macrae isn't exactly given to flights of fancy," said Alastair.
"Are any of the local men missing?"

"I'm told not."

"Then, if there *were* three people, the third climber must be someone
from the hotel. And nobody's missing from there either."

"Exactly so," said Alastair, in a blank noncommittal sort of voice.

"And if nobody from the hotel reported the accident, then it
means—"

"Exactly so," said Alastair again. He paused and took my arm. Then
with his free hand he pointed upwards, and a little to the right of
where we were standing.

"That's where the bonfire was, that night," he said. Then he dropped
my arm and addressed himself to the climb again.

I followed, numbly. Murder? Again? Who on earth would want to
murder Marion and Roberta? It was absurd. But then what reason
could there have been for the murder of Heather Macrae—and such a
murder? But again (I told myself) between the two incidents there
could be no possible similarity. The disappearance of two climbers was,
if not normal, at any rate not tainted with the fantastic, almost ritual
air of the other death. Or was it? When we found the bodies. . . .

I pushed the wet hair back from my face with an unsteady hand,
and looked up.

The men ahead had stopped climbing, and were gathered on the edge
of the gully at the point where the waterfall leaped its final hundred
feet or so from the upper cliff. Someone was pointing downwards.
Ropes were being uncoiled.

I hauled myself up the last step of rock and paused. Then I walked
slowly forward to join them.

I was afraid, horribly afraid. I felt that no power on earth would
make me look down over that edge of rock to see Roberta staring up
at me with sightless eyes, with her throat cut like that of Marcia's silken
doll, and the bright blood splashed into pink by the rain, crawling
between the clumps of blossoming thrift.

But it appeared that no sign of either Roberta or Marion had yet
been seen, though anxious eyes scanned the depths of the black gully.
Dougal Macrae pointed out to the rest of the men the place where
he had seen the climbers—he had not, it is true, seen them actually
on the cliff, but they were making for it at an angle which suggested

that they intended either to climb on the face of the Spout itself or to cross above the fall by the upper rocks.

Roderick Grant turned his head and saw me, and came over, tugging a battered pack of cigarettes from some inner pocket. He handed me one, and we lit up—no easy process this, as the force of the gusty wind had not appreciably diminished.

"What are they going to do?" I asked anxiously.

"If Dougal's right, and they were starting to climb across the Spout, then the first move is to do the same climb. There may be some traces in the rocks above the gully, or the climbers may be able to see down below the fall."

"Did you get this far last night?"

"Yes, but of course it was no use in the dark. All we could do was shout."

I looked down into the cleft, where the white water leaped and wrangled. The sides of the gully gleamed and dripped, the hanging tufts of fern and heather tossing in the currents of wind that roared up the cleft like air in a wind tunnel. With each gust the water of the fall was blown back, and flattened in its own spray against the rock. The echo was uncanny.

I shivered, and then looked up again at the grim pitch above us. "Is it a very bad place to climb?"

He was grave. "It's pretty bad for anyone, and for a beginner it's—well, it's sheer lunacy."

"Can the men get down into the gully if they—if they have to?" I asked fearfully.

"Oh, yes. Beagle says he'll go, and Rhodri MacDowell is going with him. He's a local chap and a pretty good climber."

I peered down again into the echoing depths. "Doesn't the gully flatten out farther down the mountain? I mean, couldn't they start down there, and work their way up the bottom of it?"

"This is quicker. It would take hours to work up from below. The stream goes down in leaps, you see—anything from seven to twenty feet at a time. It's much simpler to go straight down here."

Operations were beginning at the foot of the cliff. Three of the men, of whom Beagle was one, were roping themselves together, preparatory to making the climb across the Spout. The rest of the group had split up, and small parties of men seemed to be casting back along the hillside, among the smaller clefts and fissures in the scree.

"What do we do?" I asked Roderick.

"I should wait here. If they do find them, injured, you might be able to help." He smiled at me reassuringly. "The odds aren't quite as bad as they look, Janet. It won't be long before we have them safely back at the hotel."

Then he was gone, and I was left with Alma Corrigan and the little group of men who remained to watch the climb across the gully.

CHAPTER

TEN

ॐ

I don't pretend to know anything about the art of rock-climbing. The three men who were climbing out across the face of the Sputan Dhu were all, it appeared, experts at the job; and indeed, they moved so easily and smoothly on the rock that it was hard to believe the traverse was as dangerous as Roderick had made out.

I had gone farther up the scree to a point near the start of the climb, and sat, watching and nervously smoking, while the three climbers moved steadily, turn and turn about, across the wet cliff. The route they followed took them at a steep angle up the rock face, at one point straddling the narrow cleft above the spout of water. Even to my ignorant eyes it was obvious that the wet rock and gusty wind must add considerably to the risks of the climb, but the climbers appeared unaffected by the conditions. Ronald Beagle was first on the rope, leading with a smooth precision that was beautiful to watch. The other two, Rhodri MacDowell and a lad called Iain, were members of the local rescue team. All three—it seemed to me—took the climb very slowly, with long pauses between each man's move, when, I imagine, they were looking for traces of the other climbers. They gave no sign, however, of having found any, but moved on, unhurriedly, up and across the dreadful gap.

Dougal Macrae said, just behind me: "That's a bonny climber."

Ronald Beagle was halfway up what looked like a perpendicular slab of gleaming rock—a hideously exposed pitch, as the slab was set clear above the gully. He climbed rhythmically and easily, making for the next stance, which was an intilted ledge some fifteen feet above him.

"I think he's wonderful," I said warmly. "I don't know anything about climbing, but it looks uncommonly tricky to me."

"It's a fery nasty place," said Dougal. "And that bit that Mr. Beagle is on now—that is the worst."

"It looks like it."

"He must be right out over the gully. Ah, he's up. He's belaying now."

Beagle had swung himself easily onto the ledge, and was busy looping himself in some way to a jut of rock beside him. Then he turned and called down something to the men below. I couldn't hear what it was, but he must have been telling them to wait, for neither of them moved from their stances. Beagle turned to face outwards and, crouching in the support of the belayed rope, he bent to peer down into the gully.

I cried out involuntarily: "But they can't be down there, Mr. Macrae! It's impossible!"

He looked somberly down over his pipe. "If they fell from yon piece of rock that's where they'll be."

"That's what I mean." I fumbled with chilled fingers for another cigarette. "They'd never have crossed that piece of rock. That girl, Roberta Symes—she'd never have tackled a climb like that. She'd never climbed before!"

His brows drew down. "D'ye say so?"

"That's what she told us. And Miss Bradford was apparently a good climber. She'd never have let Roberta try this route—surely she wouldn't!"

"No. You'd think not." He raised troubled eyes again to the dangerous pitch. "No. But it was for this place they were making when I saw them. It did look indeed as if they were planning to cross the Sputan Dhu—ah, they've moved again."

Rhodri MacDowell, the middle man, was now on Beagle's ledge, while Beagle himself was out of sight round an overhang which beetled over the far side of the gully. Iain, who was last on the rope, was moving up.

I dragged on my cigarette with a nervous movement, and shifted on the wet stone. "I—I wonder if they've seen anything—down there?" The words, tremulous and reluctant, were snatched into nothing by the wet wind.

"We'll hope ye're right, and that they'd never let the lassie try the place. It may be—"

"They?" I turned on him quickly. "It was you who said there were three climbers, wasn't it? I suppose you couldn't have made a mistake, could you? You're really sure about it?"

"Oh, aye." The soft voice was decisive. "There were three, sure enough."

"And the third one—was it a man or a woman?"

"I don't know. At that distance I could not tell very much about them, and nowadays all the ladies wear trousers on the hill, it seems. There was not anything I could be picking out, except that the middle one had a red jacket on."

"That would be Miss Symes," I said, and remembered with a pang how the scarlet windbreaker had suited Roberta's bright Dutch-doll face and black hair.

"It would make it easy enough to find her now, you'd think," said Dougal.

"I—I suppose so." The second climber had disappeared now. The rope gleamed in a pale penciled line across the overhang to where Iain was working his way up to the ledge. He gained it presently, and belayed. I heard him call something and soon Ronald Beagle reappeared some way beyond him, making for what looked like the end of the climb, a widish ledge above the scree at the far side of the gully, from which the descent was only an easy scramble.

In a very few minutes more all three climbers had foregathered on the ledge, and seemed to be holding some sort of a conference. The people on our side of the gully, Alma Corrigan, Dougal Macrae, myself, and the handful of men who had not gone to search the scree slopes, watched in stony silence, frozen into a dismal set piece of foreboding. I sat there with my forgotten cigarette burning one-sidedly between wet fingers, stupidly straining eyes and ears to interpret the distant sounds and gestures of the men's conversation.

Dougal said suddenly: "I think they must have seen something in the gully."

"No," I said, and then again, foolishly, as if I could somehow push the truth further away from me, "no."

"Rhodri MacDowell is pointing. I thought he had seen something when he was on the cliff."

I blinked against the wet wind, and saw that one of the men was, indeed, gesturing back towards the gully. The three of them had disengaged themselves from the rope, and now began to make a rapid way down the scree towards the far side of the gully. There was about them a purposeful air that gave Dougal's guess the dismal ring of truth.

Then Alma Corrigan turned abruptly from the little group nearby, and strode across to us.

"They're down there," she announced baldly.

I just stared at her, unable to speak, but I got stiffly to my feet. Behind her the hotel proprietor, Bill Persimmon, said quickly: "We don't know for certain, but it does seem as if they've seen something."

"Ye'll be going down the gully then," said Dougal Macrae.

"I suppose so." Bill Persimmon turned back to watch the climbers' approach.

Behind us we heard the rasp and slither of boots on wet heather. Nicholas came down the slope, with Roderick not far in the rear. Nicholas's eyes, narrowed against the rain, were intent on Beagle as he approached the opposite side of the gully.

"It's time someone else took a turn," he said abruptly. "If they've been seen in the gully, I'll go down. What about you, Bill?"

"I think," began Major Persimmon, "that perhaps we ought—"

"Did they see anything down there?" Roderick's voice cut anxiously across his. "We came back because it looked as if—we thought—" He saw my face, and stopped; then he came over quickly to stand beside me, giving me a little smile of reassurance.

But I shook my head at it. "I'm afraid they did," I said under my breath. "Dougal says one of the men saw something."

"Yes. Rhodri. We saw him pointing. I'm very much afraid—" He stopped again, and bit his underlip. "Why don't you go back to the hotel, Janet?"

"Good Lord," I said, almost savagely, "don't worry about *me*. *I'm* all right."

And now the three climbers were at the edge of the gully. Beagle's voice came gustily across the fitful noises of wind and water.

". . . Below the pool . . . couldn't really see . . . might be . . . a leg . . . going down now. . . ."

I sat down again, rather suddenly, on my stone. I think I was surprised that, now it had happened, I felt no horror, only numbness. The small things—the sluggish misery of wet shoes, the chilly drizzle, my handkerchief sodden in my coat pocket—each petty detail of discomfort seemed in turn to nag at my attention, and fix it, dazedly, upon myself. I suppose it is one kind of automatic defense; it may be a variety of shock; at any rate I just sat there, dumbly working my fingers into my damp gloves, while all round me preparations were made for the final horror of discovery.

Beagle and Rhodri MacDowell went down after all. To me, watching them with that same detached, almost childish interest, it seemed an amazing operation. They were so incredibly quick. Beagle was still shouting his information across the gully when Rhodri and the lad Iain had thrown the rope over a little pylon of rock that jutted up beside them. The ends of the doubled rope snaked down into the depths, touched bottom, and hung there. Rhodri said something to Iain, heaved the rope somehow between his legs and over his shoulder, and then simply walked backwards over the cliff. He backed down it rapidly, leaning out, as it were, against the rope that acted as a sliding cradle. It looked simple—and crazy. I must have made some kind of exclamation, because, beside me, Roderick gave a little laugh.

"It's called abseiling. . . ." He himself was busy with a rope. "Quite a normal method of descent, and much the quickest. . . . No, Bill, I'll go. We'll shout up fast enough if we want reinforcements."

Rhodri had vanished. The boy Iain stayed by the spike of rock that anchored the rope, and Beagle was already on his way down. Nicholas turned back from the edge.

"I'm coming down," he said briefly.

Roderick, bending to anchor his own rope, shot him a swift upward look and hesitated. "You? I didn't know you climbed."

"No?" said Nicholas, not very pleasantly. Roderick's eyes flickered, but he merely said, mildly enough: "I'd better go first, perhaps."

And as quickly as Rhodri—and rather more smoothly—he was gone. Nicholas watched him down, with his back squarely turned to me where I sat huddled on my wet stone. Then, at a shout from below, he, too, laid hold of the ropes, and carefully lowered himself over the edge.

The little group of waiting men had moved forward to the brink of the gully, and once more there was about them, peering down into the echoing depths, that air of foreboding that gradually freezes through dread to certainty. I got up and moved to join them.

And almost at once a shout came from below—a wordless sound whose message was nevertheless hideously clear. I started forward, and felt Dougal Macrae's big hand close on my arm.

"Steady now!"

"He's found them!" I cried.

"Aye, I think so."

Major Persimmon was kneeling at the gully's edge; there were further exchanges of shouting, which the wind swept into nothingness. Then the group of men broke from its immobility into rapid and practiced activity, two more of the local rescue team preparing to descend, while the main party made off at some speed down the scree.

"Where are they going?"

"For the stretchers," said Dougal.

I suppose hope dies hard. My passionate hope, and my ignorance, between them, made me blind to his tone, and to the expressions of the other men. I pulled myself eagerly out of his grip, starting forward to the edge of the gully.

"Stretchers? They're alive? Can they possibly be still alive?"

Then I saw what was at the bottom of the gully. Beagle and Nicholas were carrying it between them, slowly making their awkward way across the slabs that funneled the rush of water. And there was no possible misapprehension about the burden that they were hauling from the fringes of the cascade. . . . I had forgotten that a dead body would be stiff, locked like some grotesque wood carving in the last pathetic posture of death. Navy trousers, blue jacket smeared and soaked almost to black, filthy yellow mittens on horror-splayed fingers . . . Marion Bradford. But it was no longer Marion Bradford; it was a hideous wooden doll that the men held between them, a doll whose head dangled loosely from a lolling neck. . . .

I went very quietly back to my stone, and sat down, staring at my feet.

Even when the stretchers came, I did not move. There was nothing I could do, but I somehow shrank from going back to the hotel now, alone—and Alma Corrigan showed no disposition to leave the place. So I stayed where I was, smoking too hard and looking away from the gully, along the grey flank of the mountain, while from behind me came the sounds of the rescue that was a rescue no longer. The creak and scrape of rope; a soft rush of Gaelic; grunts of effort; a call from Roderick, strained and distant; Beagle's voice, lifted in a sharp shout; Major Persimmon's, nearby, saying "*What? My God!*" then another splutter of Gaelic close beside me—this time so excited that I stirred uneasily and then looked round.

It was Dougal who had exclaimed. He and Major Persimmon were on their knees side by side, peering down into the gully. I heard Persimmon say again: "*My God!*" and then the two men got slowly to their feet, eyeing one another.

"He's right, Dougal."

Dougal said nothing. His face was like granite.

"What is it? What are they yelling about down there?" Alma Corrigan's voice rose sharply.

Bill Persimmon said: "She fell from the slab all right. The rope is still on her body. And it's been cut."

Her face was sallow under the bright scarf. "What—what d'you mean?"

He lifted a shoulder, and said wearily: "Just what I say. Someone cut the rope, and she fell."

Alma Corrigan said, in a dry little whisper: "*Murder. . . .*"

I said: "And Roberta Symes?"

His gaze flicked me absently as he turned back to the cliff's edge. "They haven't found her yet."

And they did not find her, though they searched that dreadful gully from end to end, and though for the rest of the day they toiled once more up and down the endless scree.

CHAPTER

ELEVEN

ɜ❦

The search went on all day. Towards late afternoon the wind dropped, only wakening from time to time in fitful gusts. The rain stopped, but great slate-colored clouds hung low, blotting out the Cuillin and crowding sullenly over the crest of Blaven. Marsco, away to the north, was invisible, and a long way below us, Loch na Creitheach lay dull and pewter-grey.

They finally got Marion Bradford's body down to the mouth of the gully at about four o'clock. From high up on the scree, I watched the somber little procession bumping its difficult way over the wet heather, with the sad clouds sagging overhead. It reached the lower spur of An't Sròn and wound drearily along its crest, past the pathetic irony of the celebration bonfire, and out of sight over the end of the hill.

Dispiritedly I turned back to the grey scree, fishing for another cigarette. The Coronation bonfire . . . and tomorrow, in London, the bells would be ringing and the bands playing, while here—there would be no celebration here, tomorrow. The lonely bubbling call of the curlew, the infinitely sad pipe of the golden plover, the distant drone of the sea, these were the sounds that would hold Camasunary glen tomorrow, as they did now. And if Roberta were still missing. . . .

I heard the scrape of boot on rock above me, and looked up to see Roderick Grant edging his way down one of the innumerable ledges that ran up to the cliff above the Sputan Dhu. His head was bare, and the fair hair was dark with the rain. He looked indescribably weary and depressed, and one of his hands was bleeding. I remembered what Marcia had told me, and wondered suddenly if he had known of Marion

Bradford's *penchant* for him, and was feeling now some odd sort of self-reproach.

His expression lightened a little when he saw me, then the mask of strain dropped over it again. His eyes looked slate-blue in the uncertain light.

"You should have gone back to the hotel," he said abruptly. "You look done in."

"I suppose so," I said wearily. My hands were wet and cold, and I was fumbling ineptly with matches. He took me gently by the shoulders and pushed me down to a seat on a boulder. I sat thankfully, while he flicked his lighter into flame and lit my cigarette, then he pulled open his haversack and produced a package.

"What have you had to eat?"

"Oh, sandwiches. I forget."

"Because it was far too long ago," said he. "Here—I got a double chukker. Help me eat these. Did you have some coffee?"

"Yes."

He held out a flat silver flask. "Have a drop of this; it'll do the trick."

It did. It was neat Scotch, and it kicked me back to consciousness in five seconds flat. I sat up on my rock and took another sandwich.

He was eyeing me. "That's better. But all the same, I think you'd better go back to the hotel."

I shook my head. "I can't. Not yet. I'd never be able to settle down and wait, not now. We've got to find Roberta. Another night on the hill—"

His voice was gentle. "I doubt if another night will make much difference to Roberta, Janet."

"She *must* be alive," I said stubbornly. "If she'd fallen into the gully with Marion Bradford, she'd have been found. Dougal Macrae said she could have been stopped higher up, by a ledge or something. There must be places near the top of the gully—"

"I've raked the whole of the upper gully twice over," he said wearily. "Drury and I and Corrigan have been there all day. There's no sign of her."

"She must be somewhere." My voice sounded dogged and stupid. "She must have been hurt, or she'd have answered you; and if she was hurt, she can't have gone far. Unless—"

I felt my muscles tightening nervously as, perhaps for the first time, the possible significance of that severed rope end fully presented itself. I turned scared eyes to him.

"Roderick"—I used his name without thinking—"you were down in the gully. You saw Marion's climbing rope. That cut rope can only mean one thing, can't it?"

He dragged hard on his cigarette, and expelled a cloud of smoke like a great sigh. "Yes. Murder—again. . . ."

I said slowly: "And Dougal swears there *was* a third climber, but whether it was a man or woman he can't say."

He made a slight impatient gesture. "If he's to be believed."

"Oh, I think he is. If anyone in this world's dependable, I'd say it was Dougal Macrae. If there wasn't a third climber, then we've got to believe that it was Roberta who cut the rope, and that's fantastic."

"But is it?"

My eyes widened. "You can't believe that *Roberta*—"

"She was a beginner. If Marion fell, and was pulling her loose from her hold, she might panic, and—"

"I don't believe it! And what's more, neither do you!"

He gave a wry little smile. "No."

"So there *was* a third climber," I said, "and he cut the rope, so he's a murderer. He was there when Marion fell. And Roberta—whether she fell or not—can't be found. It doesn't add up to anything very pretty, does it?"

"You think *the murderer* removed Roberta?"

"What else can we think? We can't find her. If she was dead, he could safely have left her. If she was only injured, he'd have to silence her. He may have killed her and hidden her, hoping that the delay in finding the bodies would help him in some way or other." I fetched a sigh. "I don't know. I'm just in a dreary sort of whirl, praying she's all right and—oh God, yes, knowing all the time she can't be."

I got to my feet.

"Let's get on with this," I said.

The dark drew down, and all along the mountain slopes, indefatigably, the searchers toiled. Beagle and Rhodri MacDowell, who had been down with the stretcher, returned bringing food, soup, coffee, and torches from the hotel. We ate and drank, standing round in the gathering darkness. There was not much said; the men's faces were drawn and strained, their movements heavy. What little conversation there was related simply to accounts of areas searched and suggestions for further reconnaissance.

I found myself beside Ronald Beagle, who, despite the exacting role he had played in the rescue, was showing very little sign of strain. He was draining his mug of hot coffee as Alastair came up, seeming to loom over the smaller man in the darkness.

"That gully below the Sputan Dhu," he said abruptly. "What's the bottom like?"

Beagle glanced up at him. There was mild surprise in his voice. "Pretty rough. All devil's potholes and fallen boulders. The stream drops down a series of cascades to the foot of the scree. Why? I assure you we couldn't have missed her."

"Any caves or fissures in the sides of the gully?"

"Plenty." Ronald Beagle bent to put his coffee mug in the hotel's basket. "But there were four of us, and I assure you—"

"Can you assure me," said Alastair evenly, "that at least two of you searched each of these fissures?"

There was silence for a moment; I saw the rapid glow and fade, glow and fade, of Alastair's cigarette. Then another cigarette glowed beside it. Roderick's voice spoke from behind it.

"Why? What are you suggesting?"

"I'm suggesting that one of us here is a murderer," said Alastair brutally.

Hartley Corrigan's voice broke in. "That's a filthy thing to say! It's tantamount to accusing Beagle or Grant or Drury—"

"He's quite right, you know," said Beagle mildly. "It could quite easily be one of us. But why should it be in the murderer's interest to conceal the second body, once the first was found? It would certainly be to his interest to be the first to find her if she were still alive, so that he could silence her." He looked up at Alastair again. "But he didn't. I imagine every crevice in that gully was searched, solo and chorus, by every one of us."

"And that's a fact." Rhodri MacDowell spoke unexpectedly out of the darkness.

"Okay, okay," said Alastair. He looked at Beagle. "You know how it is. . . ."

"I know. It's quite all right."

The group was moving now, breaking and re-forming its knots of shadow-shapes, as men gathered once more into their parties for the search. I found Nicholas beside me.

He said shortly, his voice rough with fatigue: "This is absurd, Gianetta. Get back to the hotel at once."

I was too tired to resent his tone. "I can't give up yet," I said dully. "I couldn't stand sitting about waiting, listening with the Cowdray-Simpsons for the Everest news, and just wondering and wondering what was happening on the hill."

"There's no sense in your staying here," said Ronald Beagle. "You want to get back and rest, and find some way of taking your mind off this business. And talking of Everest—" He gave a jerk to his haversack and raised his voice. I saw his teeth gleam in an unexpected grin. "I forgot to tell you," he said to the dim groups scattered round him, "that the news came through on the A.F.N. a short while ago. They've done it. By God they have. They've climbed Everest."

There was a buzz of excitement, and for a moment the grim nature of the quest on which we were engaged was forgotten, as a host of eager questions was flung at him. He answered with his usual calm, but soon moved off, alone, and immediately afterwards the group broke up, and the parties vanished in various directions in the darkness to resume their search. I heard their voices as they moved away, animatedly discussing Beagle's announcement. He had, it seemed to me, deliberately kept back his news and then used it to galvanize the weary searchers into fresh activity. My respect for him increased.

Beside me, Nicholas spoke again, angrily: "Now look here, Gianetta—"

Roderick broke across it: "Leave her alone."

"What the hell do you mean?"

Torches were flashing nearby, and in their fitful flickering I could see Roderick's face. It was quite white, and blazing with a kind of nervous fury. His eyes were on Nicholas, and in that light they looked black and dangerous.

"What I said. What Janet does is nothing to do with you, and I rather fancy she prefers you to leave her alone."

It was a nasty, snarling little scene, and it had all blown up so quickly that I stood, gaping, between the pair of them, for a good fifteen seconds before I realized what was happening. This was Marcia's doing, blast her.

"Stop it, you two," I said sharply. "What I do is my own affair and nobody else's." I took hold of Roderick's arm, and gave it a little shake. "But he's right, Roderick. I'm no use here, and I'm going back now. So both of you leave me alone." I pulled my woolen gloves out of a pocket and began to drag them on over cold hands. "We're all tired and edgy, so for heaven's sake don't let's have a scene. I'm going to pack these thermos flasks and things, and take them straight down to the hotel, and then I'm going to bed."

I knelt down and began to pack mugs into the basket. I hadn't even glanced at Nicholas. He didn't say a word, but I saw him pitch his cigarette savagely down the hillside, then he turned in silence and plunged off into the darkness after Ronald Beagle. Above me, Roderick said hesitatingly:

"Have you got a torch?"

"Yes," I said. "Don't worry about me, I know my way. Go and help the others." I looked up then at him uncertainly. "And—Roderick."

"Yes?" His voice was still tight and grim.

"Find her, won't you?"

"I'll try." Then he, too, was gone. I packed all the debris I could find by the light of my torch, and then I sat down for a few minutes and lit another cigarette. I had just finished smoking one, but my nerves were still jumping, and the last little scene, with all its curious overtones, had upset me more than I wanted to admit.

It was quite dark now. Behind me the hill flashed with scattered torchlight, and I could hear, distorted by the gusts of wind, the occasional shouts of the searchers. In the intervals of the wind I heard the scrape of boots on rock, and, twice, away to my left, a sharp bark that I took to be the cry of a hill fox.

I got up at last, ground out my cigarette with my heel, lifted the basket, and began to pick my way down the mountainside. I gave the gully a very wide berth, and scrambled slowly and carefully, with the aid of my torch, down through the tumbled boulders of the scree. Half-way down, I knew, I would come upon the deer track that led, roughly but safely, to the lower spur of An't Sròn. Away below, a flock of oyster catchers flew up the glen from the shore, wrangling noisily among themselves. I could hear their cheery vulgar chirking echoing along the water of the loch, then falling silent. The wind blew strongly on my face, with its clear tang of sea and grass and peat. I let myself carefully down onto a muddy ledge and found that I was on the deer track.

Going was easier now, but I still went slowly and cautiously, hampered by basket and torch, which left me no hand free in case I slipped. It must have been well over an hour after I started my journey back, before I found myself, with relief, walking on the heather of the ridge that joined Blaven with An't Sròn.

I had been so afraid of stumbling, or of losing the deer track, that I had come down the hillside with my eyes glued to the little circle of ground that my torch lit at my feet. But as I reached the level heather of the ridge, I became conscious of a new element in the tangy wind that blew against my face. Even when I identified this as the smell of smoke, I still walked forward unalarmed, unrealizing.

Until I lifted my eyes and saw it, a pale climbing column of smoke, no more than a hundred yards ahead.

The bonfire. Someone had lit the bonfire. The smoke from the damp wood towered and billowed, ghostly against the black night, but there was a flickering glare at the heart of the smoke, and I heard the crackle as a flame leapt.

I suppose I stood there, looking at it, for a full half minute, while my slow brain registered the fact that somebody, who had not heard about the accident, had lit the celebration bonfire. Then another branch crackled, the smoke billowed up redly, and across in front of the glow moved the black figure of a man.

It was as if a shutter in my brain had clicked, and, in place of this, an older picture had flashed in front of me. A column of flame, with a man's shadow dancing grotesquely in front of it. A blackened pyre, with the body of a murdered girl lying across it like a careful sacrifice. . . .

Roberta!

It was for this that the murderer had kept Roberta.

I dropped the basket with a crash, and ran like a mad thing towards the smoking pyre. I don't know what I hoped to do. I was acting purely by instinct. I hurled myself forward, shouting as I ran, and I had the heavy torch gripped in my hand like a hammer.

There was an answering shout from the hill behind—close behind—but I hardly heeded it. I ran on, desperately, silent now but for my sobbing, tearing breath. The fire was taking hold. The smoke belched sideways in the wind, and whirled over me in a choking cloud.

I was there. The smoke swirled round me, billowing up into the black sky. The flames snaked up with the crack of little whips, and the criss-cross of burning boughs stood out in front of them like bars.

I came to a slithering, choking halt at the very foot of the pyre, and tried to shield my eyes as I gazed upwards.

I saw the smoke fanning out under something that was laid across the top of the pile. I saw the glass of a wrist watch gleam red in the flame. I saw a boot dangling, the nails in the sole shining like points of fire.

I flung myself at the burning pile and clawed upwards at the arm and leg.

Then a shadow loomed behind me out of the smoke. A man's strong hands seized me and dragged me back. I whirled and struck out with the torch. He swore, and then he had me in a crippling grip. I struggled wildly, and I think I screamed. His grip crushed me. Then he tripped, and I was flung down into the wet heather, with my attacker's heavy body bearing me down.

Dimly, I heard shouting, the thud of feet, a voice saying hoarsely: *"Gianetta!"* Then someone dragged my assailant off me. I heard Alastair's voice say, in stupefaction: *"Jamesy Farlane!* What goes on, in the name of God?" as he took the young man in a vicious grip. It was Dougal Macrae who hauled me onto my feet. I was shivering and, I think, crying. He said: "Are ye all right, mistress?"

I clung to him, and whispered through shaking lips: "On the fire—Roberta—*hurry.*"

He put an arm round me. His big body was trembling too, and as I realized why, my pity for him gave me the strength to pull myself together. I said, more calmly: "Is she dead?"

Another voice spoke. I looked up hazily. There was a man standing a little way from the bonfire. It was Hartley Corrigan, and he was looking down at the thing that lay at his feet.

His voice was without expression. He said: "It's not Roberta Symes. It's Beagle. And someone has cut his throat."

CHAPTER

TWELVE

೭ಾ

I slept late next morning, after a night of nightmares, and woke to a bright world. Mist still haunted the mountain tops, lying like snow-drifts in crevice and corrie, but the wind had dropped, and the sun was out. Blaven looked blue, and the sea sparkled.

But it was with no corresponding lift of the spirits that, at length, I went downstairs, to be met by the news that Roberta had not yet been found, and that the police had arrived. I could not eat anything, but drank coffee and stared out of the window of the empty dining room, until Bill Persimmon, looking tired and grave, came and told me that the police would like a word with me.

As luck would have it, the officer in charge of the Macrae murder had come over from Elgol that morning, to pursue some further inquiries relating to the earlier case. So, hotter upon the heels of the new de-velopment than any murderer could have expected, came the quiet-eyed Inspector Mackenzie from Inverness, and with him an enormous redheaded young sergeant called Hector Munro. A doctor, hastily sum-moned in the small hours by telephone, had already examined the bodies of Marion and Beagle, and a constable had been dispatched to the site of the new bonfire, to guard whatever clues might be there for the Inspector to pick up, when he should have finished his preliminary questions at the hotel.

This information was relayed to me hastily by Bill Persimmon, as he led me to a little sitting room beside the residents' lounge, where the Inspector had his temporary headquarters.

Absurdly enough, I was nervous, and was in no way reassured when the Inspector turned out to be a kind-looking middle-aged man with greying hair and deeply set grey eyes, their corners crinkled as if he laughed a good deal. He got up when I entered, and we shook hands formally. I sat down in the chair he indicated, so that we faced each other across a small table. At his elbow the enormous redheaded sergeant, solemnly waiting with a notebook, dwarfed the table, his own spindly chair, and, indeed, the whole room.

"Well now, Miss Brooke. . . ." The Inspector glanced down at a pile of papers in front of him, as if he were vague about my identity, and had to reassure himself. "I understand that you only arrived here on Saturday afternoon?"

"Yes, Inspector."

"And, before you came here, had you heard anything about the murder of Heather Macrae?"

I was surprised, and showed it. "Why—no."

"Not even read about it in the papers?"

"Not that I recollect."

"Ah. . . ." He was still looking down at the table, talking casually. "And who told you about it?"

I said carefully, wondering what he was getting at: "I gathered, from hints that various people let drop, that something awful had happened, so I asked Mr. Grant about it, and he told me."

"That would be Mr. Roderick Grant?" He flicked over a couple of papers, and the sergeant made a note.

"Yes. And then Mr. Hay talked of it again next morning." I added politely, to the sergeant: "Mr. Hubert Hay. Footloose."

"Quite so." The Inspector's eyes crinkled momentarily at the corners. "Well, we'll let that go for the moment. I understand that it was you who found Mr. Beagle's body on the bonfire last night?"

"Yes. At least, I was first on the scene. I don't know who pulled him off the bonfire."

The Inspector looked straight at me for the first time, and I saw that his eyes were quite impersonal, remote, even, and very cold. The effect, in his homely pleasant face, was disconcerting and a little frightening. He said: "When was it that you first noticed that the fire had been lit?"

"Not until I was quite close to it. Do you know the hill, Inspector Mackenzie?"

"I've been on it a good bit in the past three weeks."

"Of course. How stupid of me."

He smiled suddenly. "And Hecky and I have a map. Now, Miss

Brooke, just tell me in your own words what happened on your way down from the hill."

So I told him. He listened quietly, his grey eyes placidly inquiring. At his elbow the redheaded sergeant—equally placid—made notes in a competent shorthand.

". . . And then I saw a shadow, like a man, near the bonfire."

"Only one?"

"Yes."

"I take it that you didn't recognize him?"

"No."

"Was he carrying or hauling a body then?"

"Oh no. He was just moving about on the fringe of the smoke—it was billowing here and there, you know, in the wind. I remembered the—the other murder, and I thought it was Roberta being murdered this time—"

"Roberta?"

"Roberta Symes, the girl who's missing. Inspector, oughtn't we all to be out looking—?"

He said quietly: "There are men out now on the hill. Go on."

"That's all there is. I just ran towards the bonfire. I don't know what I imagined I could do. I saw there was something—a body—on top of it, and then just as I tried to get to the body before the fire did, the murderer attacked me."

"In actual fact," said the Inspector calmly, "it was Jamesy Farlane who attacked you."

I stared at him. "I know that. Surely—?"

He interrupted me. "Now. Let's get this picture right. You realize no doubt that Mr. Beagle cannot have been killed very long before you found him. You met or passed nobody at all on your way down to An't Sròn?"

"No one."

"Did you hear anything? Any footsteps, or—?"

"Nothing. I could hear the men shouting occasionally away above on the scree, but nothing else. When I saw the bonfire and screamed, someone shouted quite close behind me, but I hadn't heard him till then. The wind was strongish, you see, and—"

"Quite so." Once more he appeared to contemplate the table in front of him. "You last saw Mr. Beagle alive when the group broke up for the final search last night?"

"I— Are you allowed to ask leading questions, Inspector?"

He grinned. "I've already heard the answer to this one a dozen times. I'm saving time. Did you?"

"Yes."

"Did you see which way he went?"

"Downhill."

"Alone?"

"Yes."

"Sure?"

I regarded him levelly. "Quite."

"I see. Now let's get back to the bonfire, shall we? You ran towards it, and screamed. Did you recognize the shout that answered you—from close behind you, I think you said?"

"No, I didn't. But I assumed it was Alastair—Mr. Braine—because it was he who pulled Jamesy Farlane off me. He must have got there pretty quickly. Dougal Macrae was there too."

"Mr. Alastair Braine, then, was first on the scene—and very prompt." His voice was contemplative and pleasant. I felt my muscles tightening. "Who else was there?"

"Mr. Corrigan. He was standing by the bonfire. He—he must have pulled the body off." I swallowed, and added quickly: "He and Alastair probably came down together."

"No," said the Inspector gently to the table top. "Both gentlemen tell me they arrived independently." His grey eyes lifted to mine, suddenly hard and bright. "Who else was there?"

"Why nobody."

"Jamesy Farlane and Dougal Macrae, Mr. Braine and Mr. Corrigan, all there within seconds of your scream. Who else?"

I looked at him. "That was all. I saw nobody else."

The grey eyes regarded me, then dropped. "Just so," said the Inspector vaguely, but I had the most uncomfortable impression of some conclusion reached in the last five minutes which was anything but vague. He shuffled a few papers in a desultory way, and said, without looking at me: "You booked your room a week ago?"

"I—yes."

"After the murder of Heather Macrae."

"I suppose so. I didn't know—"

"Quite. Sergeant Munro has your statement to that effect. . . . You booked your room, Miss Brooke, in the name of Drury, Mrs. Nicholas Drury."

It was absurd that he should be treating me as if I were a hostile witness, absurd that I should sit there with jumping nerves and tight-clasped hands just because his manner was no longer friendly.

I said, sounding both guilty and defiant: "That is my name."

"Then why did you change it to Brooke as soon as you got here? And why have you and your husband been at some pains to ignore one another's presence?"

"He's—not my husband." I found myself hurrying to explain. "We were divorced four years ago. I didn't know he was here. When I saw him the first evening I was horribly embarrassed, and I changed to my maiden name to avoid questions."

"I—see." Then, suddenly, he smiled. "I'm sorry if I've distressed you, Miss Brooke. And you've been very helpful—very helpful indeed."

But this, oddly enough, was far from reassuring me. I said sharply: "But why does all this matter? Surely it's all settled? You've got the murderer, and—"

His brows shot up. "Got the murderer?"

"Jamesy Farlane!" I cried. "Jamesy Farlane! Who else could it be? He was at the bonfire, and he attacked me there. What more do you want?"

"A bit more," said Inspector Mackenzie, with a little smile. "Farlane's story is that he was going back from the hotel after bringing the stretcher in. He was at the foot of An't Sròn when he saw the bonfire go up. He went up the hill as fast as he could, and was nearly at the top when he heard you scream, and then you came running and, he says, flung yourself at the bonfire. He thought you were going to be burned, and he jumped in and hauled you off. You hit at him, and in the ensuing struggle you both fell down the heather slope. . . . Is that right, Hecky?"

"That's right, sir." Hector Munro nodded his red head.

"You see?" said Inspector Mackenzie to me.

"It might even be true," I said.

He grinned. "So it might. Especially as Dougal Macrae was with him at the time."

There was a sharp little silence. Then he rose and began to gather up his papers. I stood up.

"If I may," he said, "I'll see you again later, but just at present I'd better get up onto An't Sròn." He held the door for me with punctilious courtesy. "You'll be about all day, I take it?"

"I'll be up on the hill myself," I said, and was unable to keep the asperity out of my voice. "There's still somebody missing, you know."

"I hadn't forgotten," he said gravely, and shut the door behind me.

CHAPTER

THIRTEEN

Two nights and a day—it was a very long time to be out on the mountainside. I think that, by now, we had all given up all prospect of finding Roberta alive. I had, to begin with, built a lot of hope upon the fact that there had been no trace of her within range of Marion Bradford's dead body. A direct fall in the same place must have killed her. The fact that she was nowhere near appeared to indicate some not-too-serious injury which had allowed her to crawl away into shelter. But, of course, if she were still conscious, she must have heard the search parties. And two nights and a day, even in summer weather, was a very long time. . . .

I had by now abandoned my grisly theory that the murderer—the third climber—had taken Roberta away, alive or dead, for reasons of his own. If the murderer of the bonfires and the murderer of the cut climbing rope were one and the same—which was so probable as to be a certainty—then, surely, he would hardly have killed poor Beagle for his second bonfire if he had had Roberta's body handy.

That he had any real motive for killing Ronald Beagle I could not believe. It seemed more than ever certain that we were dealing with a maniac. There was a causeless crazy flavor about the killings that was nauseating. Hubert Hay's word "sacrifice" occurred to me again, with shuddering force.

But where these two apparently ritual killings fitted with the deaths of Marion and Roberta I had no idea. At least, I thought, trudging once again up the deer track behind Hubert Hay, there was something we could *do*. The finding of Roberta, or Roberta's body, might help the police a little in their hunt for what was patently a madman.

The sun was still brilliant in the blue heaven. Yesterday, under the heavy grey sky, it had been easy to see the mountainside as the background to tragedy, but today, with the sunlight tracing its gold-foil arabesques on the young bracken, and drawing the hot coconut smell from the gorse, Blaven was no longer the sinister mountain that it had been yesterday. It was alive with the summer. The mountain linnets were playing over scrubs of bright furze, chirping and trilling, and everywhere in the corners of the grey rock glowed the vivid rose-purple of the early bell heather.

The search parties seemed at last to have abandoned the Black Spout, and were scattered about the mountain, still searching the screes and slopes of deep heather. One of the parties, Hubert Hay told me, had climbed higher up the cliffs above the Sputan Dhu, and was out of sight in the upper reaches of the mountain. I realized, as I scanned once again the acre upon acre of steep rocky scree, split by its gullies and fissures, how people could lie for a week, a month, out in the mountains, and their bodies not be found. And there were still, Hubert Hay told me, climbers lost years ago, of whom no trace had yet come to light.

As we reached the point where, yesterday, I had met Roderick climbing down from the Black Spout, we heard a shout, and saw, away to our right, a small party of men, one of whom—it looked like Hartley Corrigan—waved his arm and called something.

"Do you suppose they've found her?" I asked breathlessly.

"It doesn't look like it," returned Hubert Hay. "They may have decided on some new plan of search. I'll go along and have a word with them."

He began to make his way towards the other party, and I, left alone, stood for a while gazing up at the rocks above me. I was, I noticed, almost directly below the spot where Heather Macrae had been found. For a moment I dallied with the macabre fancy that there, upon that blackened ledge, we would find Roberta lying. Then I shook the thought away like the rags of last night's bad dream, and turned my eyes instead to the more accessible route which led towards the climb over the Black Spout.

I knew that the area had been searched already; searched, moreover, by a team of men who knew far more about the hill than I. But there is something in all of us which refuses to be satisfied with another report, however reliable, that someone else has looked for something and failed to find it. We cannot rest until we have looked for ourselves. And it was surely possible, I told myself, that some corner or hole or crevice of this awful country might have been overlooked.

I began doggedly to scramble up towards the tumble of rocks and heather at the side of the Sputan Dhu.

It was terrible going. The rock was dry today, and there was no wind, but each boulder represented a major scramble, and between the rocks were treacherous holes, thinly hidden by sedge and heather. I was soon sweating freely, and my head was swimming from too much peering under slabs and down the chutes of small scree that tunneled below the larger rocks. I struggled on, without realizing how high I had climbed, until exhaustion made me pause and straighten up to look back down the way I had come.

And almost at once something caught my eye—a tiny point of light among the heather, a sparkle as of an infinitesimal amber star. I saw the gleam of metal, and stooped to look more closely.

It was a brooch of a kind very common in souvenir shops in Scotland, a circle of silvery metal set with a cairngorm. I stooped for it, suddenly excited. Roberta—surely Roberta had been wearing this on that first evening at the hotel? I wiped the dirt off it, then lit a cigarette and sat down with the brooch in my hand, considering it. It meant no more, of course, than that Roberta had been this way—and that I already knew from Dougal Macrae's testimony. But for me that winking amber star had somehow the excitement of discovery about it that set me scanning the empty slopes about me with renewed hope.

I was out of sight of the party, and could no longer hear their voices. The only sounds that held the summer air were the rush of the waterfall and the sudden rich burst of song from an ouzel I had disturbed from his perch. I frowned up at the steep pitch of rock above the gully, trying to picture what might have happened there two days ago.

Looking back now, I can realize that this was perhaps one of the queerest moments in the whole affair. If I had not been so abysmally ignorant—and so stupid—over the business of that climb across the Sputan Dhu, if I had worked on the evidence plainly available (as the others were even now working), I, too, would have abandoned the gully and searched elsewhere, and the story would have had a very different ending. But I sat there in the sun, smoking and piecing together my own bits of evidence, and deciding that, come what may, I had to finish seeing for myself if Roberta was on this side of the Sputan Dhu. So I stubbed out my cigarette and got up to resume my search.

I have no idea how long I took. I clambered and slithered and peered, pushing aside mats of heather and wood rush, and crawling into the most unlikely places. At first I called occasionally, my breathless *"Roberta!"* ringing queerly back from the cliffs above. Soon I was too exhausted to call but climbed and searched in a grim, hard-breathing silence, brought, minute by minute, to acknowledge that Roderick had been right when he said that he had searched every inch of the place. Roberta was not there.

At length, when I was all but giving up, my foot slipped when I was investigating a ledge. This was wide enough, and I suppose I was in no actual danger, but the brink of the ledge overhung the gully itself, and I was so badly frightened that I had to sit down, my back pressed against the wall of the rock, to collect my wits and my courage.

The sun poured down, slashing the rock with purple shadows. The towering cliffs shut out all sound but the rush of the lonely water. I might have been hundreds of miles from anywhere. The stillness was thick, frightening, uncanny. I sat still, listening to my own heartbeats.

It was then that I heard the moan.

From somewhere to my left it came, to the left and behind me.

I was on my feet in a flash, fatigue and fright alike forgotten.

"Roberta!" My voice was shrill and breathless. I waited.

It came again, a tiny animal whimpering. It seemed to come from somewhere along the ledge, somewhere back from it, inside the very rock. . . . I turned my back resolutely to the gully and my face to the cliff, and went as quickly as I dared towards the sound.

I came to a jutting rock, a corner, and peered round it, with my heart thudding in my throat. Beyond the buttress the ledge ran along the gully side, rising gradually and dwindling to a mere crack in the cliff. I could see the whole of it from where I stood. There was nothing there. Nothing.

I called again: *"Roberta!"*

I waited. There was no sound. The sun beat upon the empty rock. *"Roberta!"*

There it was again, the tiny moaning.

I squeezed cautiously past the corner, and along the ledge. This was wide enough at first even for me, who am not used to mountains, but when I found it growing narrower, and taking a nasty outward slant at the same time, I stopped, bewildered and, once more, afraid. There was certainly nothing on the ledge. And, just as certainly, this ledge had already been searched. I had seen the imprint of boots which led as far as the corner. I was imagining things.

In that moment I heard the little whimper of pain again, but this time back to my left.

I looked back the way I had come, almost giddy now with bewilderment and excitement, my heart thudding, and my legs and wrists none too steady.

Then I saw the answer to the riddle. I had pressed past the jutting buttress of rock at the corner, without seeing that behind it, and running sharply back into the face of the cliff, was a narrow fissure. Most of the opening was masked by a hanging mat of weeds and heather, but there was a little space below this, through which someone might have crawled. . . .

I tore at the heather mat with desperate hands. It was tough, but chunks of it came away, and I flung it down the gully. Pebbles and peat spattered down onto the ledge. I yanked at a great trail of green and threw it down, so that the sunlight streamed past me into what was, in effect, a small dry cave.

She was there, all right. She was lying in a little curled huddle, her back against the wall of the cave. One leg stuck out at an ugly angle, and her hands were torn and covered with dirt and dried blood.

But she was alive. I flew across the cave to kneel beside her. Her eyes were shut, and the bright face that I remembered was a frightening grey-white, with a film of sweat over it like cellophane. The flesh was pulled back from the bones, so that her nose jutted out as sharp as a snipe's beak.

I thrust a shaking hand inside the brave red jacket and tried to find her heart. . . .

A man's shadow fell across the floor of the cave.

CHAPTER

FOURTEEN

ट॰

Roderick's voice said: "My God, you've found her!"

I turned with a great sob of relief. "Oh, Roderick—oh, thank heaven someone's come! She's alive, and—"

"*Alive?*" His voice was incredulous. He took a stride across the cave, towering over us both. "*Alive?*"

"Yes. Yes, she is! I heard her moaning—that's how I found her."

He was down on his knees beside me now, his hands moving over Roberta. His face was grim.

"Yes, she's alive, but only just, Janet. I'm very much afraid—" He broke off, while his hands gently explored her head. She whimpered and moved a little. I said: "I'll stay with her, Roderick. You go and get the others. You'll go faster than me!"

He hardly seemed to hear me; he was still intent on Roberta. He looked remote, absorbed. When he spoke, it was with suddenly impersonal authority. "Janet, I left my haversack at the end of the ledge. You'll find my brandy flask in the pocket. Get it, will you?"

I went quickly. The sunshine met me in a dazzle of light and warmth as I stepped through the cave door. Behind me Roberta whimpered again, and said something in the blurred little voice of delirium. I caught the word "*Marion. . . .*"

It halted me in mid-stride, as the implications—the terrifying implications—of our discovery of Roberta came fully to me for the first time. I swung round. Roderick turned his head, and my frightened eyes met his. And beneath their still impersonal coolness I saw the same thought that was driving my heart in sickening jerks against my ribs.

"Roderick. . . ." I almost whispered it. "Roderick, she—she knows who did it."

There was a grim twist to his mouth. "I realize that," he said. "And by God she's going to stay alive till she tells us. Get that brandy, please."

"We ought to wrap her up first. Have my coat. . . . We've got to get her warm somehow until we can call the others." I began to take off my coat. He followed suit rapidly, and I knelt down to wrap the now quiescent Roberta as warmly as I could in the two garments.

He added, still with that grim note to his voice: "And I'm not going for help either, to leave you here with this amount of potential dynamite; nor are you going to wander this hill alone any more, my dear. You fetch that brandy while I have a look at her leg, and then you'd better get along above the end of the ledge and just yell bloody murder till somebody comes. And if you don't like the look of whoever comes just yell bloody murder for me." He smiled suddenly. "And I'll be there. Now hurry."

"All right," I said. But as I tucked Roberta's cold hands gently inside my coat and made to rise, she began to stir once more, restlessly. The grey lips parted again in a whimper, and I saw that her eyelids were flickering.

"She's coming to," I whispered. My heart began to thump violently. Roderick's hand gripped my shoulder.

Then Roberta's eyes opened wide; they were dark and filled with pain, but sensible. For a moment she stared at me, as if bewildered, then her gaze moved beyond me.

Someone else was coming along the ledge.

Roberta's hands moved feebly under mine, like frightened animals. Her eyes dilated in an unmistakable look of pure terror. Then she fainted again.

I looked around. Framed in the narrow doorway of the cave was Hartley Corrigan, with Nicholas just behind him. And I could hear Alastair's voice as he followed the others along the ledge.

Alma Corrigan was waiting at the end of the ledge, and was now summoned with a shout. With the coming of the others my responsibility had lightened, and I had time to feel the slackening of nervous tension that comes with reaction. All at once exhaustion seemed to sweep over me like a drowning wave, and it was with feelings of unmixed thankfulness that I found myself elbowed aside by Mrs. Corrigan as she proceeded, with Roderick, to take charge of Roberta. I heard her giving rapid orders for first aid, while Roderick curtly deputed Nicholas to go and summon the other searchers and commandeer a stretcher.

The cave was now uncommonly crowded, but, remembering that look of terror in Roberta's eyes, I stayed where I was. I did go out onto the ledge, but there I remained, leaning against the rock in the sunlight, watching the others inside. If any of those people was the murderer who had sent Roberta to her death, it hardly seemed likely that he could finish his work here and now before she could speak and identify him—but I was taking no risks. I leaned there against the warm rock, and watched the others in the cave ministering to Roberta.

Presently I heard a shout from Nicholas, away up near the main cliff. This was answered by a more distant call. And after that, it did not seem so very long before the stretcher party arrived, and I could at last abandon my post and leave the ledge to them.

Dougal Macrae was with them, and the boy Iain, and Hubert Hay, who was certainly not the third climber, since he had been with me on Sgurr na Stri when Marion fell to her death. Roberta would be safe enough now—that is, if the murderer's work had not been already done too well, and she were to die of exposure.

But at least she had been found. The long strain was over. I sat among the heather, waiting for the stretcher to be brought off the ledge, and lifted my face to the sun, shutting my eyes and feeling, for the first time for two days, a sense of relaxation. The warm, sweet heather-smelling afternoon insisted, with every lark note, every linnet call, on the normality of the day and place. Even when, with mutterings, and cautious scrapings of boot on stone, the stretcher was maneuvered along the ledge and balanced onto the scree, even then I still felt strangely lighthearted, as though the worst were over.

I had forgotten that Roberta had only to open her mouth and speak, and that a man—a man I knew—would hang by the neck until he was dead and then be buried in quicklime in a prison yard.

Inspector Mackenzie, with the enormous Hecky and Neill, the young local constable, was on An't Sròn when the stretcher was brought down. Hecky stayed where he was, and continued what was apparently a minute examination of the ground round the bonfire, but Inspector Mackenzie, after one glance at Roberta, summoned young Neill from his job, and with him accompanied the stretcher back to the hotel.

As soon as he was told that I had found Roberta, he dropped back from the main party with me, and began to question me. I told him, as exactly as I could, what had passed. He listened quietly, and as soon as I had finished, he took me through it all again, putting a question here and there, until I must have repeated every action and every word from the moment I heard the first moan, to the arrival of the stretcher party. As I told my story, trudging wearily beside him down the valley, I found that the precarious tranquillity that had lit my little hour upon the hillside had already vanished, a snow-on-the-desert passing that left me picking my old lonely way through the grey wastes of uncertainty and desolation. And that little cold wind of terror fumbled and plucked again, ice-fingered, at my sleeve, so that I stumbled once or twice in my narrative. But I recounted, honestly and flatly enough, all that I remembered, and left him to draw what conclusions he would.

Then he surprised me. He looked sideways at me and said abruptly: "I'm putting young Neill on to guard yon lassie, and we'll send for a nurse straightaway. But we'll not get one before tomorrow at soonest, as the doctor told me this morning that the district nurse is tied up just now with a tricky case. So someone's got to look after Miss Symes till a nurse comes. Do you know anything about nursing?"

"A little, I suppose, but—"

"That's fine. Will you do it? Stay with her tonight and watch her for me?"

"Why, of course," I said. "But surely someone else—I mean isn't there anyone more competent, more practiced, perhaps, than I am? Mrs. Corrigan seems to know her stuff, and I imagine Mrs. Persimmon—"

"No doubt," he said drily. "But has it not struck you, ma'am, that you're the only woman in the hotel who wasn't here at the time of the first murder?"

"I—I suppose I am. But, Inspector, you can't suspect a *woman*, surely? I mean—"

"Maybe not," he said, "but Mrs. Corrigan and Mrs. Persimmon have husbands. And I want *no one* in that room who might be in any way— er—involved." He shot me a queer look. "No one, on any excuse whatever. You follow me?"

"If you mean Nicholas," I said tartly, "I'm hardly 'involved' with him, and I assure you he's not likely to be admitted."

His mouth relaxed a little. "Now, now, lassie," he said, almost indulgently, "I wasn't meaning any such thing. Then I take it you'll do it?"

"Of course." I looked at him curiously. "Do you mean to tell me that I'm the only person here you don't suspect?"

"Let's say," he said cautiously, "that I don't suspect you of wanting to kill Roberta Symes."

And with that, we reached the hotel. Since Marion Bradford's body was in the room which she had shared with Roberta, and this had been locked by the police, I suggested that Roberta should be given the other bed in my room. The offer was approved by the Inspector, and accepted gratefully by the Persimmons, who were already harassed beyond belief. I left her being tucked up by Mrs. Persimmon and Mrs. Cowdray-Simpson, with Neill and the Inspector in attendance, and went along to have a bath.

When eventually I got back to my room I found that a bright fire had been kindled on the hearth, and that a kettle was already singing on the bars. All the apparatus for making hot drinks was there, and a half bottle of brandy gleamed on the bedside table.

The Inspector had gone, but Mrs. Persimmon was still busy over something by the hearth, and Neill rose from the chair by the fire and grinned shyly at me. He was a tall, overgrown lad of perhaps twenty, with graceful coltish movements, and the black hair and blue eyes of the true Celt. He said: "The doctor will be here soon, Mistress Brooke. Inspector Mackenzie told me to tell you. He says will you stay here with me till then?"

"Of course. Do we do anything for her meanwhile?"

Mrs. Persimmon rose to her feet. "We've packed her in hot-water bottles," she said. "She's as warm as we can get her, so all we can do now is wait for the doctor." She bent in a harassed way over Roberta's bed, twitching the blankets unnecessarily into place. She was a small woman, with a round face that normally was good-humored, and wispy, untidy brown hair. Her eyes were of the true glass-grey that you so seldom see, clear and lovely, but just now they were puckered and clouded with worry. "If she comes round enough to swallow, you could give her a little sweet tea—and I'll go down now and make some really good clear broth. But that's all we can do for the moment."

"Except," said Neill softly, "to watch her."

We both looked at him. I said uncertainly: "It all sounds very—very frightening, Neill. Does he really expect the murderer to try and get her in here?"

He spread out calloused, beautifully shaped hands. "If she talks, we can hang him," he said simply.

I went over to the bed and looked at her. She was lying very quietly now, and though I fancied that her skin had lost some of its icy glaze, it still had a tight-stretched pallor that was frightening. Her face was pinched and small; her body, too, was still and small in its packed blankets. Not dangerous; not "potential dynamite"; not worth the ghastly risk of silencing her. . . . It seemed impossible that those dry lips should ever speak again.

But even as I turned from the bedside she stirred and moaned and her eyelids fluttered. The dark head shifted restlessly on the pillow.

"Here," said Mrs. Persimmon from the hearth. "Here's the tea."

With anxious concentration we fed a few drops of the weak sweet stuff between her lips, and saw with delight the faint ripple of the throat muscles as she swallowed. I began, spoonful by spoonful, to pour the life-giving glucose into her, watching anxiously for any sign of change in that effigy of a face.

"I'll go and see about the broth," said Mrs. Persimmon at length, and went out.

The telephone rang. I jumped violently, spilling tea on the bed-clothes. Neil lifted the receiver, listened and then said to me: "The Inspector's on his way up, ma'am. The doctor's here."

"Thank heaven for that!" I said fervently.

"Yes indeed."

A minute later we admitted Inspector Mackenzie and the doctor, and thankfully watched the competent way in which the latter examined Roberta. At length he pulled the bedclothes back over her, and looked across the bed at the Inspector.

"I can't find anything wrong except the leg," he said brusquely. "Bruises and lacerations, yes; they'll heal, given time. But we'll have to deal with the leg now. I'll need Mary Persimmon to help me, and someone else."

He glanced at me from under inquiring brows, but the Inspector intervened. "No, Miss Brooke's done enough for today, and besides, she has to be night nurse. Tell Mrs. Persimmon to bring one of the maids up with her, and I'll stay here myself. There's a telephone, doctor, if you want to give your orders."

"What? Oh, ah, yes." The doctor lifted the receiver, and began to dictate a list of his requirements.

Inspector Mackenzie turned to me. "I've asked the cook to give you something to eat as soon as possible," he said. "It'll be ready in the kitchen in ten minutes or so. You go on down, lassie. I'll call you when we want you back."

I gave another look at the small figure in the bed, and then made my way downstairs to the lounge.

CHAPTER

FIFTEEN

ॐ

Roderick was in the hall. He must have been waiting for me, because, as soon as I appeared, he strode towards the foot of the stairs, looking anxious.

"Is she all right? What does the doctor say?"

"He didn't say very much," I replied. "He's found no actual damage beyond the broken leg, but I imagine it's the two nights in the cave that will kill her if anything does."

"What does he think of her chances?"

"He didn't say. I suppose she has as good a chance as anyone could have after what she's been through. She's young and very strong, and she did find herself a dry corner out of the wind and rain."

"She's still unconscious, of course?"

"Oh yes."

"She'll pull through it," he said confidently. "Once they get the leg set—I suppose they're doing that now?"

"Yes. Mrs. Persimmon's helping. They sent me down, I'm glad to say."

"And I'm glad they did. You look washed out, Janet."

I smiled. "Thank you for nothing."

"Sorry, but it's true." He was still looking worried. "You won't have to go back and sit with her, will you?"

"I think the Inspector wants me to stay in the room tonight."

"But that's absurd!" he said angrily. "You've done more than enough for one day! Why can't Mrs. Corrigan stay with her?"

"She's done quite as much as I have."

"Well, Mrs. Cowdray-Simpson, then?"

I said, carefully: "Inspector Mackenzie has allowed me to understand that he doesn't include me in his list of suspects."

"He doesn't—?" He broke off, and his blue eyes narrowed. "Surely he doesn't suspect *any* of the women?"

"I rather think he suspects everybody," I said, uncomfortably. "At any rate, I'm not married to a suspect either, you see."

He opened his mouth as if to speak, and then shut it again in a hard line. His eyes slid away from mine and he studied the pattern of the carpet.

I swallowed, and said hastily: "I'll be all right, Roderick. All I have to do is give her a drink every now and again, and I can get some sleep between times. In fact it's terribly snug in there, with a fire, and a kettle to make tea, and all the works!"

"Does the Inspector—?" He paused, and shot a quick glance round the hall, then lowered his voice. "Does the Inspector think there's still any danger to Roberta from—him?"

The last syllable fell queerly, whispered in the empty hall. I found myself lowering my voice in reply.

"I think so. But he's taking precautions. Roberta'll be safe enough, and, by the same token, so will I." I smiled at him again. "So don't worry!"

"Very well, then, I won't. As a matter of fact"—his voice was suddenly grave, and a little abstracted—"as a matter of fact, I think you're probably the only person in the hotel who isn't—"

"Suspected of murder?"

"No. Who isn't in danger from the murderer."

He looked at me then, with a strange hesitant look that seemed to be mingled of both pity and dread, and something else that I found it hard to read. I felt my heart jump and twist painfully inside my ribs, and I could not meet his look. I turned sharply away towards the lounge door, saying in a tight, flat little voice: "I'll go and ring for a drink."

There seemed to be a crowd of people in the lounge, all gathered into small groups near the blazing fire. The air was a hiss of whispered conversations, which ceased abruptly as I came in. Heads swiveled, eyes stared, and then a fusillade of questions met me.

"How is she?" came simultaneously from Mrs. Cowdray-Simpson, her husband, Hubert Hay, and Alastair. Alma Corrigan's quick "*Has she said anything yet?*" cut across it like a knife.

I crossed to the fire and held my hands to the blaze. "The doctor's with her now, setting her leg. Apart from that, the damage appears to be superficial, and the doctor said nothing to me about her chances of recovery from the exposure." I looked at Alma Corrigan, who was twisting an empty whisky glass round and round in her fingers. She looked, I thought, frightened. I said: "I don't think she's said anything yet."

As I turned to ring for a drink, I saw that Hartley Corrigan had moved up near his wife, and had sat down on the arm of her chair. It made a nice change, anyway, I thought, and wondered, a trifle sardonically, where Marcia was at this moment. One thing was certain, she was well out of whatever was going on here, though just now I would have welcomed the company of one other person in the same equivocal position as myself. There was nothing overt in the manner of anyone in the room to suggest that they knew or resented the fact that I alone was free from police suspicion, but still I felt isolated among them, uncomfortably a sheep in the middle of the goats. And there had been something oddly protective about that gesture of Hartley Corrigan's.

Mrs. Cowdray-Simpson looked up again from the inevitable knitting. "I presume—I hope—the police will take adequate precautions to protect that girl from this beast that's loose among us?"

The phrase sounded curiously shocking, and the speaker seemed to realize this, for the pale eyes behind her spectacles moved round the group, and she said, almost defensively: "There's a murderer in the room. You can't get away from that fact."

"Not necessarily," said Alastair, rather drily. "We're not all here. Grant, Drury, Persimmon, not to mention Jamesy Farlane . . . they lengthen the odds a little, Mrs. Cowdray-Simpson." He gave a hard little laugh that held no trace of amusement.

"What odds do I lengthen a little?" This was from Roderick, pushing through the swing doors with a glass in either hand.

"We're just beginning to take seriously the fact that someone in this hotel is a murderer," said Alastair.

Roderick gave me a glass, and his eyes met mine in a quick look. He said, a little coldly: "Is anything to be gained by discussing it here? I imagine the police have it pretty well in hand. They can usually be trusted to do their own job."

"If they only look after that girl Roberta, and pull her round," said Mrs. Cowdray-Simpson, "she'll do the job for them."

"There'll be a constable watching her all night," I said.

"Young Neill Graham? Is that quite—adequate?"

I hesitated, and then said: "I'm staying with her too." I added, lamely: "She's in my room."

"Oh. . . ." Once again I felt the imperceptible withdrawal of the group, leaving me, as it were, marooned alone on the hearthrug, isolated by my innocence.

"Won't you be frightened?" This from Alma Corrigan. Was there, or was I imagining it, a trace of malice in her tone?

"I don't think so." I took a drink, and gave the group a quick look over the rim of my glass. "Where's Mr. Drury?"

"I think he went out to the garage." It was Hubert Hay who answered. "He's lost a book, and he thinks he left it in his car."

"Why?" asked Alma Corrigan, and this time I certainly heard the venom in her voice. "Has the Inspector asked for a report on our movements?"

I felt myself go scarlet, but I held onto my temper, and said, very evenly: "I am not, as you imply, Mrs. Corrigan, appointed by the police to spy on you all. I happen to be in the lucky position of not being a suspect, simply because I wasn't here when the first murder was committed, and since the odds are that we only have one murderer and not two, I can't be guilty. So the Inspector can leave me with Roberta until the nurse comes."

"It's monstrous to suggest—" began Roderick, hotly, to Alma Corrigan, but I cut across him.

"It's all right, Roderick. And the suggestion isn't so very monstrous after all. I'm certainly co-operating with the police—I hope we all are. And if that includes giving the Inspector an account of anyone's movements at any time, I'll do my utmost to describe them for him."

"Well!" said Alma Corrigan. "I must say—" Her husband dropped a hand on her arm, and she broke off. I said to her, coldly: "I should hardly need to point out that this isn't a case of the police *versus* a bunch of suspects. It's a case of the murderer *versus* every single other person here."

"Good for you!" said Hubert Hay unexpectedly.

Colonel Cowdray-Simpson cleared his throat. His face looked all at once remote and austere, with a curious withdrawn intelligence that his gentleness had hidden before. It was a look both forbidding and compassionate, the look of a judge rather than of a soldier. I found myself wondering if he were a magistrate. "It is more than that, my dear young lady," he said to me. "Each case of murder is a case of the murderer *versus* every civilized human being. Once a man has put his hand to murder he is automatically outcast. I would go further than that. I would assert that once the very idea of extreme physical violence has occurred to a man as an acceptable solution to any problem, then he is in danger of forfeiting his claim to consideration as a civilized being."

"That's a strong statement, sir," said Roderick.

"I happen to feel strongly about it," retorted the Colonel.

"Do you apply the same principle to nations as to individuals? You, a military man?"

"I do."

"To acts of war?"

"To acts of aggression. It seems to me a denial of the intellectual progress of centuries, for a nation to consider violence as a tool of policy."

"All the same," said Alma Corrigan mulishly, "it's absurd that we should all be treated as suspects. The police *must* have some idea who did it."

"If they haven't now," said Hubert Hay, "they certainly will have as soon as Roberta Symes opens her mouth."

There was a nasty little silence.

I set down my glass with a *click* on the glass-topped table. "Well," I said, "for the sake of everybody here who isn't a murderer, I promise you that Roberta will be kept safe until she *does* open her mouth."

Then I walked out of the room.

It didn't take much, I thought, to skin the veneer of politeness and sophistication off people who were in some kind of danger. There had been some strong undercurrents there in the lounge tonight, and I had a feeling that, if one had been able to trace them out, one would be a fair way to solving the mystery. On the face of it, I thought (as I crossed the hall and started down the dark passage towards the kitchens and back premises), I would be inclined to absolve the Colonel. He had delivered himself so convincingly of his principles; but then (I added a despairing rider), that, surely, might be just what a murderer would do? And, heaven knew, our murderer was clever. He was an actor who could hide the instincts of a werewolf under an impeccably civilized exterior. Nobody in the lounge tonight, hearing his own condemnation, the statement of his utter isolation from the rest of us, had so much as batted an eyelid. But then, of course, the murderer might not have been in the lounge. . . . There were other possibilities, as Alastair had pointed out.

I turned a corner of the passage and ran straight into Nicholas. Literally ran into him, I mean. He caught me by the arms and steadied me, peering down in the dimness of the passage.

"Why," he said softly, "it's our little copper's nark. The Inspector's not down this way, darling."

I did lose my temper then. I blazed at him, pulling against the pressure of his hands. "Let me go, damn you! *Let me go!* Don't you dare to speak to me like that! You've no right—"

"So you keep telling me. Where are you going?"

"That's none of your damned business!"

"It's anybody's business in this murderous locality to stop you from wandering about in the dark alone."

"I'm going to the kitchen to get some food," I said waspishly, "and I'm in a hurry."

He did not move. "Where's the boy friend?"

"What d'you mean?"

"Your *preux chevalier* with the golden hair. Why isn't he playing bodyguard?"

"You always did have a filthy tongue, Nicholas," I said bitterly.

"I did, didn't I?" He grinned sardonically. "You could say it's a valuable stock in trade as a writer, though perhaps as a husband—"

"Exactly. Now let me go."

"Just a moment. I'm quite serious, as it happens, Gianetta. It seems to me you're altogether too fond of wandering about the place alone— or with somebody you don't know. If you had a grain of sense you'd know this chap meant business. Aren't you scared?"

"I wasn't," I said tartly, "until three minutes ago."

I don't know what made me say it. The instant the words were out I regretted them, but it was too late. He dropped his hands from my arms and stood looking down at me in the semidarkness. I thought he must hear the thudding of my heart.

"O—ho . . ." he said at length, and then, very softly: "Sits the wind in that quarter?"

I was silent. I wanted to run from him, towards the lights and warmth of the kitchen, but I was held there, nailed to the passage wall by the hammer blows of my own heart.

Nicholas said: "So you're afraid I'll kill you, Gianetta *mia*? . . . Do you really think I'd do that, Gianetta? Cut that pretty throat, Gianetta . . . and all for what? Auld lang syne?"

"Do you need a reason?" My voice was a whisper that sounded strange to me. This could not be happening; this fantastic conversation could not be taking place. . . . "Do you need a reason?" I whispered.

He did not reply. He stood looking at me in silence, his face, in that uncertain light, quite inscrutable. At length he said, in quite a different tone: "What's your proof?"

I almost jumped. "I haven't any."

"If you had, would you hand me over—for auld lang syne?"

Fantasy . . . thickening round us like the spinning of a spider's web. He might have been asking if I wanted more housekeeping money. I put a hand to my head. "I—don't know, Nicholas."

"You—don't—know." His tone brought the blood to my face.

"Nicholas," I said desperately, "try to understand—"

"You were my wife."

"I know, but—"

"You always used to say that you didn't believe in divorce."

"I know," I said again, a little drearily. It was auld lang syne all right. Every quarrel we had ever had, had ended with my being forced on the defensive. I heard the familiar note of excuse creeping into my voice again now, feebly, infuriatingly: "But it wasn't my fault we got divorced."

"Even so, according to what you used to say, you should think of yourself as still bound to me . . . or do you—*now?*"

"Now? I don't follow."

"No? I was harking back to the blond boy friend."

"Damn you, Nicholas!"

He gave a hard little laugh. "You've got a nasty problem, haven't you, Gianetta? Moral loyalty *versus* civic duty . . . or does the situation simplify itself now into the old love *versus* the new? It would save you a lot of trouble if you could hand me over this minute, wouldn't it?"

The outrage that swept over me was as real, as physical, as shock. I went cold. My voice dropped to a flat icy calm. "If you had been in the lounge just now, you'd have heard Colonel Cowdray-Simpson expressing what happen to be my views. He said that by an act of violence, like murder, a man cuts himself off from his fellows, and forfeits his—his human rights. If I were still your wife"—I put my hands against the wall behind me, feeling for its solid bracing comfort—"if I were still—legally—your wife, I shouldn't help to incriminate you, even if I could, because, as your wife, I should be identified with you in all you did . . .

but I would leave you. I couldn't stay with you, knowing you were—"

"Cain?"

"I—yes."

There was an odd note in his voice. "And as it is?"

"As it is—" I stopped, and to my horror my voice caught on a little sob. "As it is," I said raggedly, "I don't know, God damn you. Now let me by."

He moved without a word, and I ran past him, and down the passage to the kitchen.

CHAPTER

SIXTEEN

ॐ

In the kitchen there was light, and warmth, and the good smell of food. The cook was busy over the stove, and one of the girls who waited at table was bustling about with stacks of plates.

I hesitated inside the doorway, conscious suddenly of my shaking hands and the tears in my eyes, but Cook looked up, gave me a flushed, fat smile, and pointed to a place set at one end of the big scrubbed table.

"If it's nae odds, mistress," she said in a brisk Lowland voice, "ye can hae yer denner in here. Ye'll get it hetter and quicker. Yon Inspector telt me ye'd want it the noo."

"It's very good of you. I hope it's not too much of a nuisance."

"Nae trouble at all," said Cook comfortably, not moving from the range. "Effie, gie the lady some soup."

Effie was thin and dark, with enormous eyes that devoured me with curiosity. She brought me a plate of steaming soup, putting it down in front of me warily, almost as if I might bite. Then she backed off a step or two, gripping the front of her apron.

"Noo, Effie!" This sharply, from Cook. "Gang awa' intae the dining room wi' the breed!"

Effie went, casting a longing, lingering look behind. As the kitchen door swung to behind her, Cook put down her ladle, and said, in a hoarse, impressive whisper: "Sic a cairry-on, mistress, wi' a' them murrders! It's fair awesome. It garrs yer bluid rin cauld!"

I agreed mechanically. The hot soup was wonderfully comforting, and the bright warmth of the kitchen rapidly helped to dispel the effect of that fantastic little interview in the passage. Cook leaned her plump red fists on the opposite end of the table and regarded me with a sort of professional pleasure.

"Noo, they're grand broth, aren't they?"

"They're—it's excellent, Cook."

"They're pittin' a bit reid intae yer cheeks. Ye looked fair weshed oot and shilpit-like when ye cam' in, I'll say. They were sayin' it was you found her?"

"Yes, I was lucky."

"It was her that was lucky, the puir lassie, to be livin' the day." She nodded heavily. "Mony's the yin that hasnae been sae lucky—and I canna mind a waur simmer."

"Well," I said, "it isn't every year you get—murder."

"No. Guid be thankit. But I wasna' meanin' that." She whipped away my empty soup plate and substituted a lamb chop flanked with peas and roast potatoes. "It was the accidents on the hill I was meanin'."

"Oh?" I remembered something somebody else had said. "Has this year really been worse than usual?"

"Aye, that it has, miss. Thae twa lassies"—she jerked her head vaguely towards the ceiling—"they're the third casualties we've had this season, no' countin' murrders."

"Who were the others?"

"Well, there was a pair frae London—the daft craturs went into the Cuillins wi' neither map nor compass. They were no' fun' till a week after, lyin' at the fit o' a pressypiece."

"How dreadful! Had the mist come down on them?"

"The day they went up it was as clear as consommay," said Cook. "Naebody kens what happened."

"It's a big price to pay for a bit of carelessness," I said.

"Aye, it's that. But them hills are no' to be taen lightly . . . aye, and that puir man lyin' upstairs, he's mony a time said the verra same, and a grand climber he was an' a'. Aipple tairt."

"I beg your pardon? Oh, I see. Thank you, Cook. This is very good."

"It's no' sae bad," said Cook complacently, watching me sample her rich, flyaway pastry. "Then there was twa o' them students, frae the College at Oxford-and-Cambridge. They baith tummled doon frae a muckle rock—gey near the same bit."

"Dead?"

"Aye, deid as a stane. The rope snappit."

I put my spoon and fork down carefully, side by side, on my empty plate, and stared at them for a moment. But I wasn't seeing them. I was seeing, in a queer fugitive vision, two pairs of climbers climbing in the Cuillin . . . but in each case, another climber moved with them; the third climber, in whose presence ropes snapped, and bodies hurtled to their death. . . .

"A cup o' coffee noo?" suggested Cook.

"I'd love one," I said, "but I think I'd better take it upstairs to drink. The doctor must have finished up there, and Mrs. Persimmon'll want to come down."

"Hoo was the lassie when ye left her?" She set a large blue cup on the table, and began to pour coffee.

"Not too good. But I've a feeling she's going to be all right."

"Thank guidness. I've gien ye the big cup. Ye'd better tak' it quick, while it's warm. Sugar?"

"Please. Thank you very much, Cook. That was excellent. I feel a whole lot better."

"Aye, an' ye look it," said Cook. "Mind ye keep the door lockit the nicht, ma lassie."

"I certainly will," I said fervently, and got up as she turned back to her stove.

There was no one in the passage. I went quickly along it, round the corner with my heart beating a little jerkily, then out into the open hall. Nicholas was there, leaning over the reception desk talking in an undertone to Bill Persimmon. He saw me, but beyond a slight twitch of his black brows he gave no sign. I ignored him, and almost ran up the stairs, balancing my cup of coffee carefully.

I met Mrs. Persimmon and a maid on the landing.

"Oh, there you are, Miss Brooke!" Mrs. Persimmon still sounded harassed, which was hardly surprising. "Did you get some dinner?"

"Yes, thank you, I've done very well."

"Oh, good, good. Well, the police are expecting you now, I think."

"How's Miss Symes?"

"I hardly know. Still unconscious, and the doctor won't say very much. Oh dear, oh dear. . . ." And she plunged downstairs, followed by the maid laden with crumpled linen. I heard her still lamenting faintly as I went along to my room and knocked on the door.

The Inspector opened it.

"Ah, Miss Brooke. Come away in."

He shut the door carefully behind me. The doctor had gone. Roberta, in her blankets, looked very white and still, so white that I exclaimed anxiously: "Inspector Mackenzie, is she all right?"

He nodded. "The doctor thinks so. He says she'll pull through."

"That's wonderful!"

His eye was on Roberta's quiet, shuttered face. "Aye," he said, his voice expressionless. Then he turned to me. "And you? Did you get some food?"

"Yes. Cook fed me in the kitchen."

"Good. How do you feel now?"

I smiled. "Ready for anything—But I hope you're going to tell me what to do, before I'm left alone with the patient."

"The doctor left instructions, and I wrote them down for you." He indicated a paper on the bedside table. "But it's mostly a case of keeping the hot bottles filled and the room warm. You can give her a little broth, or tea with a dash of brandy in, whenever she'll take it. The doctor had a confinement due, so he had to go, but if you get at all worried, you can get hold of me, and I'll ring up the Broadford hospital for advice."

"D'you mean I'm to send Neill for you?"

"No. Use the telephone. I'm using Miss Maling's room. I'll probably be up most of the night, but when I do go upstairs, I'll switch it through to there. Don't hesitate to ring up if you're in the least nervous or worried. We'll be about all night."

"I won't."

"Good. Well, now"—he turned to Neill, who had appeared in the doorway—"Neill, you know what to do. Make yourself comfortable. Sergeant Munro'll relieve you at two o'clock, and I'll be along myself now and again to see everything's all right. I doubt if any of us'll get much sleep tonight." He crossed to the window and stood looking out. "There's a mist coming up. A pity. It's never a help on this kind of job. I think. . . ." He reached a hand up and latched the window shut. "That disposes of *that*. D'you mind being a trifle stuffy?"

"Under the circumstances, not at all."

"That's all right, then. Well, I'll leave you. I'm afraid you've a long night ahead of you, but I think it's a safe night. And—oh, yes, Major Persimmon is to keep the dynamo running all night, so the lights will be on. All right, Neill?"

"Yes, sir."

He turned to me. "Are you a light sleeper, lassie?"

"I think so."

"There's no need for you to stay awake all night, you know. She'll sleep, and if she wants you, Neill will wake you. Get some rest yourself between whiles. Right?"

"Right."

"Well, good night, lassie."

"Inspector Mackenzie—"

He was already at the door. He turned with his hand on the knob. "Yes?"

"There are some things—I have a few things you ought to know."

"Important?"

"I—I'm not sure."

"Anything that'll enable me to arrest our murderer here and now?"

"Oh no. No."

His eyes considered me, queerly. "You've located him, haven't you?"

"*No!*" The single syllable came violently, surprising me as much as the Inspector.

He looked at me for a moment. "Then I dare say it'll keep till morning, ma'am," he said.

He went out. I went quickly across the room and turned the key. The whirr and click of the wards was reassuring, and the *chock* as the bolt slid home punctuated our security with sharp finality.

CHAPTER

SEVENTEEN

෪

The long evening dragged through and the night came. I nodded over the fire with *The Bride of Lammermoor*, fighting off the feeling of desperate tiredness that threatened to overwhelm me. Neill sat in the shadows beside Roberta's bed, his long body still and relaxed in the wicker chair, his back to me and the rest of the room. Roberta stirred once or twice, but her breathing seemed every moment more natural and her color improved, so that it was with a reasonably quiet mind that I eventually put down my book and decided to try to get some sleep.

I crossed the room softly towards my bed. "Good night, Neill."

"Good night, miss," he answered, without turning his head, and, absurdly enough, I felt a wave of relief pass over me at the quiet reply. It was as if one of the still shadows of the room had offered reassurance; and it brought home to me the unwelcome realization that, in spite of all precautions, in spite of Neill's very presence, I was really very nervous indeed. I chided myself sharply as I wound up my little bedside clock and slid my feet out of my slippers. The room was locked, door and window, and Neill, solid dependable Neill, was here with me; and there, at arm's length, on the other end of the telephone, was Inspector Mackenzie.

I turned back the eiderdown and crept underneath it, wrapping the full skirt of my housecoat round me. My whole body ached with weariness, but I had no fear that I should sleep too soundly to hear Roberta moving. There were other fears that would keep me too near the edge of consciousness for that. . . .

I was quite right. I dozed and waked, and dozed again—little uneasy snatches of sleep that might have been of a minute's or of an hour's duration. Twice, Roberta stirred and whimpered and had me up on my elbow in a flash; but each time she subsided once more into sleep. Once, some time soon after midnight, she seemed to rouse more fully, so I got up and heated broth, and Neill and I managed to make her swallow half a dozen spoonfuls before she turned her head away with a tiny petulant movement, and subsided again into sleep. Another time I remember boiling more water for bottles, and I recollect, dimly, the quiet change-over of watchers, as Hector Munro relieved Neill at two o'clock; and I remember twice, as in a recurrent dream, the Inspector's voice outside the locked door, asking how we did. Some time during the dead hours Hecky made a cup of tea—strong, this time—and I drank it curled up warmly under my eiderdown before I got up yet again to fill hot-water bottles.

I did my job efficiently enough, I know, but I must have moved through that firelit fantasy in a state suspended between wakefulness and dream, so that, looking back now, I can hardly tell where the reality ended and the nightmare began. Indeed, my memory now is of a night of continuous nightmare, where the ordinariness of the tasks which engaged me could not hold at bay the shadows haunting, uneasily, the corners of the firelit room. The ticking of my little clock, the workaday hum of the singing kettle—these homely sounds became, to me lying dozing through the small, crawling hours, distorted into the very stuff of nightmare—manifestations as eerie and terror-filled as the shadows that gibbered across the fire-flickering ceiling above my head. Shadows and fire . . . shadows across the glare . . . shadows coalescing even as I watched into the image of a murderer gesticulating before the flames, dancing crazily round a pyre that grew and swelled and dilated into a gigantic smoking shape, a red-hot Paracutin of a bonfire, a veritable hell's mountain. . . . And now it was Blaven itself that loomed over me, lit with flames. And a solitary, faceless climber straddled that devil's gully, pulling after him a length of cut rope. Somewhere, a knife gleamed, and I heard the soft stutter of two voices in counterpoint, wavering through the sound of falling water. . . . *You used to be my wife.* . . . *You've located him, haven't you?* . . . *You've got a nasty problem, haven't you?* . . . *You've located him, haven't you?* . . . *haven't you?* . . .

My own "No!" woke me finally, with such a jerk that I wondered if I had spoken aloud, and strained my ears for the vibration of my own voice among the shadows. Or was it Hecky who had spoken? Or Roberta? I pushed myself up onto my elbow and looked across at her. She was moving, making fretful little noises of pain, but it was not this that made my heart jump and my body stiffen in its little nest under the eiderdown. Hecky wasn't there.

Even as I reacted to this in a manner that betrayed the lamentable state of my nerves, I turned my head and saw him, like the specter of my dream, in front of the fire. But this fire threw no terrifying shadow back into the room, and for the worst of reasons. It was almost out.

A glance at my clock told me that it was quarter past four. I had not been asleep long, and Hecky had presumably not been to sleep at all, but in spite of us the peat fire, inexpertly stacked, had dwindled and died into an inert-looking mass of black sods.

Now a peat fire is a tricky thing for an amateur to manage. Once it is going well, it is wonderfully hot, a red glowing mass like the heart of a blast furnace. Mrs. Persimmon had banked this one expertly, and Neill, too, had known what to do with it, but Hecky was a townsman and a Lowlander, while I was the most helpless of amateurs. Between us we must have handled it very clumsily, for it had burned itself almost out, and as Hecky stirred it the peat crumbled, and fell away into fragments that rapidly began to blacken.

I swung myself off the bed, thrust my feet into my slippers, and went softly across to the fireplace.

"Won't it go at all, Sergeant?"

"It will not."

"Isn't there any more peat?"

"Och, yes, there's plenty. It's the putting it on that's tricky. Have you the way of it at all, miss?"

"Far from it, but we've got to try." There was a small pile of fresh peats on the hearth. I knelt down beside Hecky and together we stacked them over the embers and tried to blow them to a flame. But to no avail; the red ash waned and darkened, and the peats steamed sullenly, black and unresponsive. The room felt cold.

"It's no good," I said. "It's going out."

We looked at one another in some dismay, then I stood up, biting my lip. I had to put fresh bottles in Roberta's bed. I had to be ready to make her another drink. I had to get the room warm against the chill hours of daybreak.

"I'm sorry," said Hecky. "I—"

"It's my fault as much as yours. In fact, neither of us is to blame if we can't manage the dashed thing. What we should have done is to ask

Mrs. Persimmon for some wood to help us keep it going. I'm afraid it didn't occur to me."

He stood up, dusting his hands lightly together. "Will I get Inspector Mackenzie to bring some wood, then?"

"There should be some somewhere," I said. "The lounge fire was made up with logs, I remember. Perhaps—"

"I ken fine where it is." He was at the telephone now. "We've been all over this place at one time and another, you'll mind. It's oot the back." . . . He put the receiver back and looked at me. "No answer. He'll be taking a look around, likely enough."

"Then—had we better wait?"

He glanced at the black fireplace. "That'll be oot in five minutes. I'd best go myself."

I said doubtfully: "Should you, d'you think?"

"You've got to get this fire going, have ye no'?"

"Yes. Yes, I have."

"Well, then, I reckon I'd better go. And if you don't open the door till I get back, there'll be no harm done."

"I—I suppose not. How am I going to be sure it's you when you come back?"

"I'll knock—this way." He moved nearer. His hand went out to the mantelpiece beside me. A finger fluttered. I heard a tiny tapping, the sort that might be made by a grasshopper's feet landing a little raggedly on a leaf: *tap—taptap—taptaptap—tap*. . . . Nobody else but I, with my ear some nine inches away, could possibly have heard it.

"Right," I said. "Don't be long, for goodness' sake. And—oh, Sergeant—"

"Yes, miss?"

"If there's a kettle hot on the stove, you might bring it up. It'll save time."

"O.K., miss."

"You—you'll be all right?"

He grinned down at me. "Don't worry about me, now. I'd give a year's pay to meet that chap, whoever he is, down by the woodshed! I'll no' be more than five minutes, miss, and if I see Inspector Mackenzie prowling around, I'll send him along."

He let himself out, and I locked and bolted the door again behind him. I heard him go softly down the passage. Silence.

My heart was beating uncomfortably hard, and once again I had to take myself sharply to task. I turned resolutely from the door, and went over to have a look at Roberta. She seemed to have relaxed a little, and her breathing was less shallow, but her eyelids twitched from time to time, as if the light troubled her. I took my green silk scarf out of a drawer and dropped it over her bedside light, then went back to nurse my little core of red fire till Hecky should come back.

He was surprisingly quick. I had ripped some pages from the *Autocar* and with these and some small crumblings of peat, was getting a nice little lick of flame, when I heard the soft tap at the door.

I was halfway across the room before I realized that the sound had not been the grasshopper tapping that Hecky and I had arranged.

It came again, a tiny sound: *Tap-tap-tap.*

I was standing three feet from the door, with my hands, in rigid fists, pressed down against the front of my thighs. My heart began to jerk in slow, sickening thuds. I stood, turned to marble, with my eyes on the door, while the seconds ticked madly by on the little bedside clock.

Ever so gently, the door handle turned. Ever so softly, the door rattled as somebody pressed against it.

If I screamed, I thought, people would wake up, and they would catch him there . . . the murderer, trying to get at Roberta.

But if I screamed, it might penetrate that still slumber of Roberta's, and I had no idea of the possible effect of such a shock. It was not a risk that I felt I had any right to take.

Then I was at the door.

"Hullo?" I was surprised that my voice sounded so normal. "Is that you, Sergeant?"

Of course it wasn't; but if he said it was. . . .

"No." The vigorous whisper was certainly not Hecky's. "It's Inspector Mackenzie. I came to take a look at her. Open up, will you, lassie?"

Even as I accepted the statement with a quick uprush of relief, I surprised myself again. I heard my voice saying calmly: "Just a minute, Inspector. I'll get a dressing gown on."

In three strides I was at the telephone, and had lifted the receiver. My little clock chittered the seconds crazily away beside me . . . two, four, seven seconds, seven dragging light-years before I heard the *click* of the other receiver being lifted, and Inspector Mackenzie's voice, soft but alert, saying sharply: "Mackenzie here. What is it?"

I cupped a hand round the mouthpiece and whispered into it: "Come quickly! *Quickly! He's at the door!*"

The line went dead. My knees gave way under me, and I sat down slowly on my bed, with the receiver still clutched in my hand. My head turned, stiff as a doll's head, to watch the door.

There was no sound, no rattle, no movement of the handle. The door stood blind, bland in its smooth white paint, telling nothing.

There was a swift stealthy rush of feet up the corridor. A voice. "Inspector? Is anything the matter?"

"Where the devil have you been, Hector Munro?"

"To get wood. I'm sorry, sir. Is something wrong?"

Doors opened. I heard Hartley Corrigan's voice, raw-edged with nerves. "What the devil's going on here?" Then his wife's scared whisper: "Has something—happened?"

"Nothing, madam. Please go back to bed." The Inspector's voice sank to a reassuring mumble, and, since I could now hear three or four voices murmuring in the corridor, I opened my door.

The Corrigans were just withdrawing into their room, which was opposite my own. The only other people who seemed to have been disturbed were Colonel Cowdray-Simpson and Hubert Hay, whose rooms were just round the corner from our passage, in the main corridor. As I opened the door, Hecky, standing rather shamefacedly before the Inspector with a bundle of wood under one arm and a still-steaming kettle in the other, turned and saw me, and came hurrying down the passage in some relief.

Inspector Mackenzie whipped round after him. His voice was still low, but clear and urgent.

"Hecky! Don't touch that door! Miss Brooke, stand away from the door, please."

"Look here, Inspector"—this was Colonel Cowdray-Simpson, still surprisingly authoritative in a deplorable old dressing gown, and without his teeth—"what's wrong?"

"Please accept my assurance that there's nothing wrong, sir. You can reassure Mrs. Cowdray-Simpson. And you, Mr. Hay. I promise you that if I want help I'll ask for it, but just at the moment—"

"O.K. I'm off." And Hubert Hay, resplendent in Paisley silk, disappeared reluctantly.

The Inspector came swiftly down to where I was still standing. "Now, what's all this?"

It was so much the conventional policeman's opening that I felt an absurd desire to laugh. I said, shakily: "He—he was at the door. The murderer. He said—he said—"

He took my arm and drew me gently into the room towards my bed. "You sit down there. Don't try to talk." He shot a rapid glance at Roberta, and was apparently satisfied. "Hecky, get that fire going. . . . No, on second thoughts, let me do it. You go to my room and get my bag and give that door a going-over." He looked at me. "You said he was at the door. I suppose he touched it?"

"Yes. He pushed it, and turned the knob."

He gave a small grunt of satisfaction. "The knob, Hecky. No, man, leave it standing open, then no ghosts can wipe it clean before you come back. Aah!"

This was an exclamation of satisfaction as the dry sticks caught alight, and the flames roared up the chimney in a crackling blaze.

"I suppose there wasn't a sign of anybody when you came?" I said.

"No." He was expertly stacking peat.

"He must have heard me telephoning you. I'm sorry."

"On the contrary, you did very well."

"Well, I'm sorry I made Hecky go downstairs, then. It was my fault for letting the fire down, but I had to get it going again."

He pushed the kettle down among the now blazing peats, and stood up. "It might have been a lucky stroke," he said, "if we *had* seen the murderer. Now, supposing you tell me what happened."

I told him about it, while Hecky busied himself over the surface of the door, and Roberta lay quietly in her blankets in the little green glow of the bedside lamp.

He listened in silence, his eyes on my face. "Hum," he said at length. "He must either have heard Hecky go, or have see him go out across the yard. It doesn't get us much forrarder, except for one thing."

"What's that?"

"It proves that Miss Symes can convict him. He was our third climber, all right. He cut that rope."

I said flatly: "Inspector, do you know who this murderer is?"

"Have you finished, Hecky?"

"Aye, sir. Juist aboot it."

"Inspector, please—"

"Any luck, Hecky?"

Hecky straightened up. His face was rueful. "No, sir. It's been wiped."

"*What?*" The Inspector was across the room in three strides, and was examining the door. His mouth was thin and hard. "Damn!" he said explosively, then added: "All right, Hecky. Shut the door and get back to your chair." He came back into the room looking angry. "Bang goes my proof," he said bitterly.

"Proof?" I said. "Then you *do* know who it is?"

"Know? Hardly that, perhaps. Call it a pretty sure guess. . . . But a guess is no good to a policeman, and we've no proof at all—not a shred; and if yon lassie on the bed doesn't open her mouth soon, I'm afraid of what may happen. Look at tonight, for instance. Look at the kind of chance he takes—and might very well get away with, God help us, because nobody in their right senses would expect him to take a risk like that."

"He'll tempt his luck once too often," I said.

"*Luck!*" His voice seemed to explode on the word. "He murders Heather Macrae with a twenty-foot blaze of fire on the open side of Blaven. He kills Miss Bradford in full sight of Camasunary glen in the middle of the afternoon. He cuts Beagle's throat within yards— *yards*—of witnesses. And now this!" He looked at me, and added, quietly: "I've been on this corridor all night. I only went downstairs to the office twenty minutes ago. And then—only then—your fire goes out, and he sees Hecky Munro going off and leaving you alone."

"I—I'm sorry," I said feebly.

He smiled at that. "Don't say that, lassie. I told you it wasn't your fault. You've been quite a useful recruit to the Force, indeed you have. . . . That kettle's boiling. Shall I do those for you?"

"I can manage, thanks." I began to fill Roberta's bottles.

He was standing by her bed, staring down at her face as if he would draw her secret from behind the pale barrier of her brow. His own forehead was creased, his hair tousled, his chin grey with unshaven stubble. His fists were thrust deep into his pockets, and his shoulders were rounded. He looked like any worried middle-aged man wakened out of sleep by the baby's wailing. Then he turned his head, and the quiet intelligent eyes gave the picture the lie. "Do you mind finishing your watch now?"

"No."

"Don't send Hecky away any more."

"I certainly won't!"

"I shan't be on the end of the telephone. I have—a few things to do. But don't worry. And who knows, it may all be over sooner than you think. We'll get him. Oh yes, we'll get him. . . ." And his eyes were no longer kind, but cold and frightening.

CHAPTER

EIGHTEEN

When, once again, I had locked and bolted the door behind him, I busied myself over Roberta. It was a full twenty minutes before I had finished my tasks, and, when I had done, all desire for sleep had gone.

I drew a curtain aside and looked out of the window. It was still misty. I could see the faint grey of the first morning light filtering hazily through the veil like light through a pearl. It looked dank and chilly, and I was glad to be able to turn back to the firelit room.

Hecky had made more tea, and I took a cup back to bed with me, wishing yet again that I had something reasonable to read. At this hour of the morning, my heart failed me at the thought of *The Bride of Lammermoor*, and I had torn up most of the *Autocars* to light the fire. There remained *The Golden Bough*—an odd thing, surely, to find in a remote hotel in Scotland? It was a pleasant title, I thought, but I had a vague feeling that it was as heavy going, in its own way, as *The Bride of Lammermoor*. Something to do with primitive religions . . . hardly a bedside book, and hardly, I thought, picking it up incuriously, the sort of book with which to while away even the wettest day in Skye. Except, of course, Sunday, when there was no fishing.

But someone had been reading it. There was a bookmark, an old envelope, thrust between the pages, and, of its own accord, the heavy book fell open at the place thus marked. It opened in the ready and accustomed manner of a book much handled at that particular page.

I looked at it, mildly curious.

The Beltane Fires, I read. *In the Central Highlands of Scotland bonfires, known as the Beltane fires, were formerly kindled with great ceremony on the first of May, and traces of human sacrifices at them were particularly clear and unequivocal. . . .*

I sat up, staring unbelievingly at the page, my brain whirling. It was as if the words had exploded into the silence of the room, and I glanced across at Hecky Munro's broad back, hardly able to believe that he could be unconscious of their impact. My eye skipped down the cold, precise print. From it, as if they had been scrawled in luminous paint, words and phrases leapt out at me. . . . *Their sacrifices were therefore offered in the open air, frequently upon the tops of hills . . . a pile of wood or other fuel . . . in the islands of Skye, Mull and Tiree . . . they applied a species of agaric which grows on old birch trees and is very combustible. . . .*

There flashed between me and the printed page a vivid memory: the birch grove, silver gilt and summer lace, with broken pieces of fungus still littering the wet ground between the smooth-skinned trees. And the brown fans of agaric pushing, palms up, from some of the sleek boles. *Very combustible. . . .*

I read on, the cool detached prose bringing to my racing mind picture after picture: *in the Hebrides, in Wales, in Ireland*—in the queer Celtic corners of the land those fires were lit, and rites were performed that echoed grotesquely, though innocently, the grim and bloody rites of an older day. May day fires, Midsummer fires, Hallowe'en fires—for countless years these had purified the ground, protected the cattle from plague, burned the witches. . . .

Burned the witches. Another memory swam up, sickeningly: a young girl lying in the embers with her throat cut; Hubert Hay's voice talking of magic and folklore and writers who questioned Heather Macrae about old superstitions.

I found that my hands were wet with perspiration, and the print was seesawing in front of my eyes. It was absurd. *Absurd.* No modern young woman of eighteen, even if she did live in a lonely corner of the earth, was going to be sacrificed as a witch. *That* part of it was nonsense, anyway. But why had she been killed, then, and in that unmistakably ritual manner? Hardly in order to protect the crops. Even Jamesy Farlane, born and bred in the mountains, could no longer believe—

I jerked myself out of my thoughts, and read on. I read how, when the sacrificial fire was built, it was lighted, not from "tame" fire, but from new fire, "needfire," the living wildfire struck afresh from dry oak, and fed with wild agaric. I read how those who struck the living fire "would turn their pockets inside out, and see that every piece of money and all metals were off their persons." I read how, in some localities, the one who made the wildfire must be young and chaste. . . .

The print swam away from me finally then in a wild and drowning dance of words. I put my hands to my face and thought, in a slow painful enlightenment, of Heather Macrae, who was young and chaste, and who divested herself of her pathetic little gewgaws to make the needfire for her murderer. She must have thought the whole affair crazy, I mused bitterly, but she thought it was fun, it was "different," it was the sort of romantic craziness that a clever bookish gentleman from London might indulge in.

My thoughts skidded away from that same clever gentleman from London, as I tried, vainly, to fit the other killings into the same framework of primitive ritual. Where, in the plans of this primeval throwback of a murderer, did Beagle's murder fit? Or Marion Bradford's cut rope? Or the students from Oxford and Cambridge? Or Marcia Maling's doll?

It became more than ever certain, on the evidence of this book, that the only kind of logic that could knit together crimes so various must be the cracked logic of madness. And that the book was evidence there was no doubt. There were too many parallels between its calm statements and the crazy ritual murder on Blaven hill. Nor could it be mere coincidence that the book itself was here, in this hotel. There was the probability that it was the murderer's own: a man whose studies had made him sufficiently familiar with such rites and customs—a man of unstable mind—might, when that mind finally overturned, wallow in just such a blotched travesty of ritual as Heather's murder now showed itself to be. Or it was possible—

I was, I found, still clutching in my damp fist the crumpled envelope that had marked the page. My hand shook a little as I smoothed it out.

I sat looking at it for a very long time.

The envelope was in my father's handwriting. It had no stamp, but it bore, in his clear, beautiful hand, a name and address:

> *Nicholas Drury, Esq.,*
> *at the Camas Fhionnaridh Hotel,*
> *Isle of Skye,*
> *Inverness-shire.*

CHAPTER

NINETEEN

ॡ

The morning brought misty sunshine and the nurse. She was a young-ish, square-built woman, who looked kind and immensely capable. With relief I abandoned Roberta to her and went down to breakfast.

As I went into the dining room, heads turned, and Mrs. Cowdray-Simpson asked quickly: "The girl—how is she?"

I smiled. "All right so far, thank you. The nurse is with her now, and says she's getting on well."

"I'm so glad! I was so afraid that all that disturbance in the night—"

"It was nothing," I said. "I let the fire out, and the Inspector heard Sergeant Munro prowling down the stairs to get wood for me."

Nobody else spoke to me while I ate my breakfast, for which I was grateful. I found myself being careful not to catch anybody's eye. I had just poured my second cup of coffee when Effie, round-eyed, appeared at my elbow.

"If you please, miss, the Inspector says—when you're ready, he says, but not to be interrupting yourself—"

Her voice was high-pitched and possessed remarkable carrying power. It was into a dead and listening silence that I replied: "I'll go and see the Inspector at once. Thank you, Effie."

I picked up *The Golden Bough*, which I had wrapped in yet another piece of *The Autocar*, took my cup of coffee in the other hand, and walked out of the dining room, still in that uncomfortable silence. My face was flaming. Last night's quarantine seemed still to be isolating me, Nicholas's mocking phrase to be whispering me out of the room. In each look that followed me I could sense the same resentment. In one pair of eyes there might also be fear. My cheeks were still flying scarlet banners when I got to the Inspector's temporary office.

He greeted me cheerfully, with a shrewd glance at my face which provoked me into saying, tartly: "I could do without the distinction of not being a suspect, Inspector Mackenzie!"

He was unperturbed. "Is that so? Don't they like it?"

"Of course they don't! I feel—cut off . . . and the funny thing is that it's *I* who feel guilty. I wish it was all over!"

"I'm with you there." He stretched out a hand. "Is that for me?"

I handed him *The Golden Bough*. In some curious way I felt that, by doing so, I had committed myself to something, had started down a path from which there was no turning back. I sat down. "I've marked the place," I said.

I bent my head over my coffee cup, stirring it unnecessarily, concentrating on the brown swirl of the liquid against the blue sides of the cup. I heard the Inspector make an odd little sound, then he said sharply: "Where did you find this?"

I told him.

"And when did you see this marked section?"

"Last night." I told him about that, too. But not about the crumpled envelope. It was in my pocket. I could not go quite so far down the path. Not yet.

"It was you who marked these passages?"

"Yes."

"Do you know whose book this is?"

The envelope burned in my pocket. "No."

There was a pause. I looked up to find his eyes watching me. He said: "You had other things to tell me, I believe. You told me so, before you found this book. Now, Miss Brooke"—he was being very formal this morning—"what is it that you think I ought to know?"

"The first thing," I said, "concerns the cut climbing rope that killed Marion Bradford."

"Yes?"

I began to tell him about my trip downstairs in the darkness on my first night in the hotel, and how both Jamesy Farlane and Alastair Braine had been in the hotel porch.

"And Mr. Corrigan had been fishing with them," I said slowly. "Alastair said he'd already come back—but yesterday his wife said he didn't get in that night till three o'clock. It was about half past two when I spoke to Alastair."

The Inspector was writing rapidly. He looked up when I fell silent. "What you're trying to tell me is that each one of these three men had the opportunity to damage the girls' climbing rope the night before the climb."

"Yes," I said, miserably.

"Then where does Dougal Macrae's third climber come in?"

"He might be innocent," I said, "and just be frightened! When he saw them fall—"

"Aye, aye, lassie," said the Inspector drily, and, again, gave me that long considering look. "And had you anything else to tell me?"

I hesitated. The envelope? Not yet, I told myself, not yet. . . . And the other thing? The half-lie I had told about what happened by the second bonfire? It wasn't proof, I assured myself desperately, and proof was all he wanted. Surely I didn't have to tell him? Not yet. . . . He was watching me steadily across the table. I began rather hurriedly to tell him about the episode of Marcia's doll. Finally I sat back, and looked unhappily across the table at him. "But perhaps you knew?"

He nodded. "Mrs. Persimmon told me about that. But you can forget it. It's not a mystery any longer, and it never was a piece of this mystery in any case. I think I may tell you that it was part of a little private feud between Mrs. Corrigan and Miss Maling."

"Oh? You mean *Alma Corrigan* did it?"

"Yes. She told me this morning. She did it to frighten Miss Maling away from the hotel for—er, reasons of her own."

"I—see." I was remembering Alma Corrigan's face as she watched Marcia's car driving away across the glen. "Well, it appears to have worked."

His mouth relaxed a little. "Quite so." Then he looked down at his notes. "Well, I'm much obliged to you for telling me these things. I think you were right to do so. Is there anything else?"

"No," I said, but I was not well enough guarded yet, and his eyes lifted quickly to my face. They had sharpened with interest.

He said flatly: "You're lying to me, aren't you? There is something else."

"No." But I said it too loudly.

He looked at me very gravely for a few long seconds. Then he laid the pencil carefully down on his papers, and put his hands, palm downwards, flat on the desk. "Lassie"—his tone was no longer official; it was very kind—"I think you told me a lie last night, didn't you?"

"I? A lie? What—"

"When you said you hadn't guessed who the murderer was."

I bit my lip and sat rigid, my eyes on the floor.

He said: "Do you really think a woman of Marion Bradford's experience wouldn't have noticed if the rope was damaged when she put it on? Do you really think that rope was cut in the hotel porch that night?"

"I—it might have been."

"It might. But you don't think it was."

"N—no."

He paused. "I'll tell you how we think this murder was done," he said at length. "You realized, of course, that Roberta Symes never climbed across the Sputan Dhu at all?"

He added, as I stared at him: "There was no rope on her body, was there?"

I said slowly. "No. No, there wasn't. Of course . . . if she'd been middle man on the rope the murderer *couldn't* have cut it between her and Marion. D'you know, I never worked that out? How stupid of me!"

"It's just as well you didn't, or you'd have left the Sputan Dhu to look for her elsewhere."

"What did happen, then?"

"We think he offered to do the climb with Marion Bradford, Roberta watching. When he got Miss Bradford to the one pitch that's out of sight of the other side—there's an overhang—"

"I know. I noticed it. He could have cut the rope then without being seen."

He nodded. "He pulled her off and cut the rope. Roberta would see an 'accident,' see her fall. Then she would hear him shout that he was coming back. He could get back quite easily alone by going higher above the gully. She would wait for him in who knows what agony of mind, there by the gully's edge. And in her turn, when he came there, he would throw her down. She must have fallen out of sight, or, if he'd suspected she wasn't dead, he'd have gone down to finish her."

I said nothing. I couldn't speak, couldn't think. I believe I shut my eyes. I know I was trembling.

"Lassie," he said, very gently, "if a man's a murderer, and a murderer like this one, crazy and—yes, vicious and crazy, he's not fit to defend, you know."

I said chokily: "Loyalty—"

"Doesn't enter into it. He's an outlaw. Your loyalty is to the rest of us, the sane ordinary people who want him locked up so that they can be safe."

"Well, why don't you arrest him, if you're so sure?"

"I told you. I can't possibly move without proof. I'm waiting for some information to come from London. Or—there's Roberta."

"Why did you leave me with her, if you're so sure I'd shield the murderer?" I cried.

"Because I'm a good enough judge of people to know that, when it comes to the point, you'll be on the right side, whatever your—loyalties."

"My instincts, you mean," I said bitterly. "If you'd been in the lounge last night, you'd have heard me talking very fine and large about my principles, but now—" I got up. "Has no one ever told you that people mean more to women than principles? I'm a woman, Inspector Mackenzie."

He had risen, and his eyes met mine levelly. "So was Heather Macrae."

I blazed at him at that. "I don't know why you're treating me to a sermon on loyalty, Inspector Mackenzie! Even if I *did* guess who your murderer was it's only a guess! How am I supposed to be able to help you catch him? I've told you everything—"

"No." His voice was soft, but it brought me up short. "I still don't believe you." He surveyed me grimly. "And if this fact—whatever it is—that you are keeping back, is one that will give me the proof I want, then I must warn you—"

"Proof? I haven't any proof! I swear I haven't! And if I had—oh God, I must have time to think," I said shakily, and almost ran out of the room.

There may have been people in the hall; I never saw them. I went blindly across it, making without coherent thought for the glass porch, and the fresh air and freedom of the glen. But when I pushed my way through the swing doors into the porch I came face to face with Dougal Macrae coming in. He greeted me gravely.

"Good morning, mistress. It's a grand morning for it, forby a bit of mist coming up frae the bay. Are you wanting to go right away?"

"Go?" I looked at him blankly.

"It was today I was taking you fishing, Mistress Brooke. Had you forgotten?"

"Fishing? Oh—" I began to laugh, rather weakly, and then apologized. "I'm sorry; but it seems odd to be thinking of fishing after—after all this."

"To be sure it does. But ye canna juist be sitting round to wait for what's going to happen, mistress. Ye'll be better out in the clear air fishing the Abhainn Camas Fhionnaridh and taking your mind off things. Fine I know it."

"Yes, I suppose you do. . . . All right, Mr. Macrae, I'll come. Give me five minutes."

Three-quarters of an hour later, as I stood on the heather where the Camasunary River flows out of Loch na Creitheach, I knew that Dougal had been right.

The mist that, earlier that morning, had blanketed the glen, had now lifted and rolled back, to lie in long vapor veils on the lower slopes of Blaven and Sgurr na Stri. Just beside us, An't Sròn was all but invisible in its shroud, and from its feet the loch stretched northwards, pale-glimmering, to merge with the mist above it in a shifting opalescent haze. Marsco had vanished; the Cuillin had withdrawn behind the same invisible cloak, but directly above our heads the sky was blue and clear, and the sun shone warmly down. The river, sliding out of the loch in a great slithering fan of silver, narrowed where we stood into a deeper channel, wrangling and glittering among boulders that broke it into foam or shouldered it up in glossy curves for all the world like the backs of leaping salmon. Close under the banks, in the little backwaters, piles of froth bobbed and swayed on water brown as beer. The smell of drying heather and peaty water, strong and fresh, was laced with the pungent odor of bog myrtle.

Dougal was a good instructor. He soon showed me how to assemble my hired rod, how to fix the reel and tie the fly, and then, with infinite patience, he began to teach me how to cast. Neither of us spoke a word about anything but the matter in hand, and very few, even, about that. It was not long before I found, to my own surprise, that the difficult art I was attempting had, indeed, a powerful fascination, before which the past faded, the future receded, and the whole of experience narrowed down to this stretch of glancing, glimmering water, and the fly I was trying to cast across it. The timeless scene and the eternal voice of the water created between them a powerful hypnosis under whose influence the hotel with its inmates and its problems seemed far away and relatively unimportant.

And even if my own problem did not recede with the others, it did—so passionately did I refuse to face it—relax a little of its claw-hold on my mind.

Dougal had put up his own rod, but did not at first use it. He sat on the bank, smoking and watching me, occasionally getting up to demonstrate a cast. Of course I never caught anything; I did not get even the suspicion of a bite. But so powerfully had the peace and timelessness of the place worked upon me that when at length Dougal began to unwrap sandwiches for lunch I was able to think and speak with tolerable composure.

We ate at first in silence, while the water ran bubbling brown past our feet, and a dipper flew zit-zitting up and down the center of the river. A fish leaped in a flashing silver arc.

"That's just where I was fishing," I said humbly. "I must have been casting over him all the time, and never caught him."

"You might yet. I've known stranger things happen," said Dougal. It could hardly be called an encouraging answer, but I supposed that, from a Highlander, it might even be accounted praise. He looked up at the sky. "It's a bit overbright for the fish, in fact. If the mist came down a little, and took some of the glare off, it might be better."

"It seems a pity to wish the sun away."

"You'll not notice, once you're fishing again."

We finished our lunch in silence, then Dougal got out his ancient pipe, while I fished in my pocket for cigarettes. As my fingers closed over the remains of yesterday's rather battered packet of Players, they encountered something else, something metallic and unfamiliar.

I gave an exclamation as I remembered what it was. Dougal turned an inquiring eye in my direction, through a small fog of pipe smoke.

"I ought to have given this to the Inspector, I suppose," I said, withdrawing my hand from my pocket with the cairngorm brooch. "I'd forgotten all about it. It's Roberta's, and—"

"*Where did ye get that?*" The big Scotsman's voice was harsh. His pipe fell unheeded into the heather, and his hand shot out and grabbed the brooch from my palm. He turned it over and over in a hand that shook.

"Why—up on the hill, yesterday," I said, uncertainly. "On the scree near the Sputan Dhu. I—I thought Miss Symes must have dropped it there."

"It was Heather's." Dougal's voice was unsteady too.

"*Heather's?*" Confusedly I tried to remember where I had picked it up. . . . Yes, it had been lying on the scree below the ledge where she had been found. Could it have dropped or been kicked off that little pile of metal in the corner? . . . I turned to look back at Blaven, only to find that the mist was, indeed, rolling down the slopes behind us like a tide of smoking lava. Blaven was already invisible, and a great wall of mist bore steadily across the glen behind us, obliterating the afternoon.

"I gave it to her for her birthday," said Dougal, his voice unnaturally loud and harsh. "She was wearing it when she went out that night. . . ." He stared at it for a moment longer, then thrust it back at me." You'd best take it, mistress. Give it to the Inspector and tell him where you found it. God knows it won't help him, but—" He broke off, and turned with bent head to hunt for his pipe. By the time he had got it alight again his face was once more impassive, and his hands steady. He glanced round at the silently advancing mist.

"This'll be better for the fish," he said, and relapsed into silence.

The sun had gone, and with it, the peace of the place had vanished too. The finding of that pathetic brooch had brought back, only too vividly, the horrors which had beset this lovely glen. My own miserable doubts and fears began again to press in on me as the grey mist was pressing. The other side of the river was invisible now. We seemed, Dougal and I, to be in the center of a world of rolling grey cloud, islanded between the loud river and the lake, whose still and somber glimmer dwindled, by degrees, into a grey haze of nothing.

I shivered. "Don't you think we ought to go back, Mr. Macrae? I think I ought to give the brooch to the Inspector straightaway."

He got up. "It's as you wish, mistress. Shall I take down the rods, then?"

I hesitated. Perhaps it was only the eeriness of the mist-wrapped glen, but, suddenly, violently, I wanted to be gone. I could escape this thing no longer; I must face my problem now, and take whatever uneasy peace was left to me.

"We must go back," I said at length. "There are—other reasons— why I should see the Inspector. I mustn't put it off any more. And I—I don't like the mist."

"We can't lose our way along the riverbank even in this. Don't worry your head about the mist. Just bide still a minute while I get my rod, then we'll get away back."

He turned downriver, and before he had gone ten yards, was swallowed in the mist. I stubbed out my cigarette on the now chilly stone, and watched the grey swirl where he had disappeared. The obliterating cloud pressed closer, on heather, on rock, on the chuckling water.

The dipper warned me first. It burst from under the fog, fleeing upstream with a rattle of alarm notes that made my nerves jump and tingle.

Then through the blank wall of the mist there tore a cry. A curse. A thudding, gasping noise, and the sickening sound of a blow. And a sharp yell from Dougal.

"Lassie! Run!"

Then the horrible sound of harsh breath choking, rasping in a crushed throat; another thud; and silence.

CHAPTER

TWENTY

ε‰

Of course I screamed. The sound was like a bright knife of panic, slashing at the mist. But the grey swirls deadened it; then they were all round me, clawing and fingering at me, as I stumbled forward towards where Dougal's voice had been.

I am not brave. I was horribly frightened, with a chill and nauseating terror. But I don't think anybody normal would unhesitatingly run *away* if they heard a friend being attacked nearby.

So I leaped forward, only to falter and trip before I had gone five yards, so blinding now was the mist that shrouded the moor. Even the edge of the river was invisible, and a hasty step could result in a broken ankle, or, at best, a plunge into the rock-ridden swirl of waters. I put out my hands, foolishly, gropingly, as if they could pull aside the pale blanket of the mist. I plunged another four yards into it, then I stepped on nothing, and went hurtling down a bank to land on my knees in deep heather.

It was only then that I noticed how complete was the silence. The sounds of the struggle had ceased. Even the river, cut off from me by the bank, ran muted under the mist. I crouched there, shaken and terrified, clutching the wet heather stems, and straining with wide, blind eyes into the blankness around me. I found I was turning my head from side to side with a blind weaving motion, like a newborn beast scenting the air. The mist pressed close, the bewildering, sense-blotting nothingness of the mist, so that I no longer knew which way the river ran, or where I had heard the men fighting, or—where the murderer might, now, be supposed to be.

Then I heard him breathing.

There was a soft step; another. Water drops spattered off the heather; the stiff sedge rustled, and was still. Silence.

He had been ahead of me, to the right. Of that I was certain, but how near . . . ?

The breathing surely came from behind me now. My head jerked round on neck muscles as tight and dry as rope. I could feel my eyes straining wider, my mouth slackening in panic. My hands tightened on the heather stems till I thought he must hear the bones cracking.

And now the breathing had stopped. Somewhere, the river poured its unheeding waters along under the peat banks. Behind me? Before? To the right? I found I could no longer trust my senses, and on the heels of that betrayal panic came.

All at once the mist was full of noises. The rustle of heather was the murderer's breathing, the thud of my own frightened heart his footstep; the surging of blood in my temples blended with the rush of the invisible river, eddying, wavering, distorted by the dizzying mist into the very stuff of terror. . . .

There was salt on my tongue; blood. My lip throbbed painfully where I had bitten it, but the pain had checked the panic. I flattened myself in the long heather, closed my eyes, and listened.

He was there; there had been no illusion about that. He was fairly close, moving towards me, but a little way to one side, between me and the river. I could hear the water now, quite clearly, some few yards away on the right. I went lower in the heather, flat in my form like a hunted animal, glad now of the bewildering mist which was the friend of the hunted more than of the hunter. I had only to keep still; perhaps, when he had passed me, I could break cover and run, and . . .

He was level with me now, between me and the river. His breathing was shallow, rapid, excited. He stopped.

Then, farther away, down along the riverbank, I heard something else. Footsteps, heavy, uncertain footsteps that thudded on heather and then scraped on rock. Dougal Macrae's voice called, thickly: "Lassie . . . lassie, are ye there?"

A great sob of thankfulness tore at my throat, but I choked it back, wondering wildly what to do. If I answered. . . . The murderer was within six yards of me, I knew. I heard his harsh indrawn breath; sensed the tensing of his muscles as he realized that he had failed to eliminate Dougal. If I called to Dougal, was there anything to save my throat from that bright butcher's knife not twenty feet away? A

knife which could dispatch me in a matter of seconds, and then turn
its dripping point to wait for Dougal to answer my call. . . .

But I must call. . . . Not for help, but for warning. I must cry out,
and tell Dougal that he is here, the killer is here, just beside me. *Somehow I must cry out,* and then run, run into the lovely blinding mist,
away from the knife and the excited hands of the butcher coming behind me.

And Dougal was coming. He plunged towards us, as bold and heavy
as an angry bull. I was on my knees, and my mouth was gaping to
shout a warning, when suddenly the murderer turned, and was running
upriver like a stag. I could hear him bounding, sure as a deer, through
the long heather. And Dougal heard him too. He let out a yell that
was a curse, and flung himself after the escaping man. I saw him looming through the fog. I caught the gleam of a blade in his lifted fist,
and I saw in his face such a white blaze of anger as to make him unrecognizable. He looked like some avenging giant out of an old myth.

I gasped out something as he plunged past me, but he paid no heed.
He brushed by me as if I were not there, and blundered on into the
mist after the killer. Even as I cried, in panic: *"Dougal!"* he vanished
upriver into the fog. He must have glimpsed or heard his quarry, because my cry was drowned in a harsh eerie yell that startled the sullen
heather with its pagan echoes, and sent a flock of oyster catchers
screaming up into the mist like witches.

"*A mhurtair! A mhich an diabhil! Aie!* You bloody murthering
bastard! *Aie!*"

One of the birds rocketed over my head with the screech of a damned
soul, the mist streaming from its wings in swaths like grey grass under
the scythe.

It vanished, and the mist swept down in its wake, and the sound
of the men's running was blotted out once more by the muffled silence.

I turned and ran blindly in the opposite direction.

I do not know how long that stumbling terrified flight through
the heather lasted. I had succumbed finally to pure panic—mindless,
senseless, sobbing panic. I was no longer frightened of the killer. Reason
had stayed with me just long enough to show me that he was no longer
concerned with me. Attacking an unsuspecting man out of the mist
was one thing; facing an armed Highlander, fighting-mad on his own
ground, was quite another. No, the murderer had to lose Dougal very

effectively in the fog before he dared turn back to me—and then he
had to find me.

But panic has nothing to do with reason. Reason, now, had slipped
her cogs, and my brain was spinning sickeningly, uselessly, out of control. I ran and jumped and slithered, and the salt tears slid down my
face with the wet mist drops, and flicked into my open mouth onto my
tongue. The white mist met me like a blank wall; my hands were out
like a blind man's; the skin of my face and my palms was wincing as I
thrust myself wildly against the intangible barrier. And as I ran I chattered crazily to myself: *"No—oh no—oh no. . . ."*

What brought me up, all standing, with the panic knocked out of
me as at the slash of a whip, was the fact that the ground over which
I blundered was shaking beneath my feet.

Half-dazedly I peered at the tufted mosses over which I had been
running. Tentatively I took another step. The ground shivered, and I
backed quickly, only to feel the surface of the moor rocking like the
bottom boards of a punt.

I stood very still.

There was a small dreadful sound beneath my feet, as if the ground
had sucked in a bubbling breath.

CHAPTER

TWENTY-ONE

ट॰

My lapse from reason had cost me dearly enough. I was well out in the bog of which Roderick had once spoken, and how far out, I had, I found, no idea. Nor could I tell at all accurately from what direction I had been running when I made this last frightening discovery.

Fear flickered its bats' wings at me afresh, but I shook my head sharply, as if by doing so I could drive it away. I stood exactly where I was, trying to ignore the ominous trembling of the earth, and listened for the sound of the river.

But it was of no use. The more I strained my ears, the more confused were the sounds that eddied and swung round me in the mist. I heard, faintly, the muted murmur of flowing water, but it seemed to come from every quarter at once, reflected off the banks of fog, and, over it, all the time, whispered and clucked the invisible life of the bog—small lippings, suckings, a million tiny bubbles popping, uneasy breaths. . . .

My feet were sinking. With an almost physical effort, I gathered the last rags of my self-control round me, then stepped quietly towards a tussock of heather a couple of yards away. The feel of its tough, resistant stems under my feet did much to steady my nerves, but my body was shaking uncontrollably now, and my teeth were chattering. I stood islanded on my little tump of heather, peering vainly along the ground in every direction and being met, in every direction, by the same few feet of boggy green, swimming and shifting under the treacherous mist.

But I knew that I must move, must leave my little tuft of safety and go in some direction—any direction. I told myself that the bog was unlikely to be really dangerous, but here, again, reason was no real help.

I think it was the fact of being blinded that brought panic pressing so persistently close. If I could have seen even four yards in front of me, seen where my feet were going five steps ahead, it would not have been so bad. But I should be moving blindly over this hideous, shivering bog, ignorant of the real gravity of the danger, and moving, possibly, farther out into a worse place. . . .

I clenched my hands into icy knots, turned in what I imagined to be the direction of the river, and walked slowly forward.

The sheer effort of self-control needed to make me move slowly was so enormous that, mercifully, I could not think about anything else. I wanted to run—dear God, how I wanted to run! But I made myself go slowly, testing each step. Once I trod unwarily on a patch of lighter green, and went up to the knee into black mud. And by the time I had skirted the light patch, stepping warily from one moss hag to the next, I had completely lost all sense of direction again, so that, when a ghostly skeleton shape floated out of the mist beside me, my whole body jerked like a marionette's with fear. It was only the pale ghost of a young birch, a bone-bare branch that lay rotting on the bog—touchwood, crumbling to decay; but in that misty morass it looked solid, and where it lay the tufted reeds were tall and dark and promised safety.

And I drew a breath of hope. The shape that showed so insubstantial through the fog was one I had seen before. Surely Roderick and I had passed quite near a fallen birch on that first evening's walk? It had lain on our left, not many yards away, between us and the river. I had only to remember which way it had lain in relation to our path, and I could make without delay for the safe ground.

I trod towards it warily, trying to see it again in my mind's eye as I had noticed it the first night. It was quite possibly not the same tree, but in the mind-annihilating swirl of mist even this frail compass was as sure as the pillar of fire in the wilderness. I stood by it, anchored by its deceptive solidity, and tried to remember, steadying myself quite deliberately with hope.

It had been lying, roughly, north and south. Of that I felt sure. And surely I must still be to the river side of it? In which case the safe ground was beyond it, about thirty yards beyond. If I could once reach that, I would, sooner or later, find a sheep track that would lead me down the glen, to within sound of the sea. Or I might find some trickle of running water that would lead me safely to the river and the hotel.

A black shape shot out of the mist at my back, and skimmed, whirring, into invisibility. A grouse. I swore at it under my breath, and quieted my hammering pulses once again. Then I stepped carefully over the birch tree and took what I thought were my bearings, straining my eyes once more against the mist.

It was only then that I became fully conscious of something that had been tugging at the skirts of my senses for a little time. The ground was shaking. I was standing perfectly still, but the ground was shaking.

So complete had been my absorption in my new fear that I had actually forgotten that, somewhere out in the blind world, there was a murderer looking for me with a knife. . . . And here he was, moving steadily across the quaking bog.

I dropped to my face behind the skeleton of the birch. The rushes were thick and tall. Beneath me the ground shivered and breathed. I lay frozen, this time not even frightened, simply frozen, icy, numb. I doubt if even the knife, ripping down through the mist, would have had the power to move me.

"*Gianetta.* . . ." It was a tiny whisper, no more than a harsh breath. It could have been the breathing of the bog, the exhaling of the marsh gas in its million tiny bubbles.

"*Gianetta.* . . ." It was nearer now. "*Gianetta.* . . ." The mist was rustling with my name. It floated in little dry whispers like falling leaves, swirling lightly down to rest on the shivering ground.

He was moving slowly; under my body I could feel the measured vibrations of his tread. His hands would be out in front of him, groping for me; his whispering probed the silence, reaching out to trap me.

I recognized it, of course. Oh yes, I knew him now, beyond all doubt. I knew now that my unhappy guessing had been right enough; knew now why the Inspector had pitied me; and why Alastair, two nights ago, had given me that look of unexpressed compassion.

"*Gianetta.* . . ." There it was again, that name—the name that no one else ever called me . . . the name I had heard shouted through the darkness beside Ronald Beagle's funeral pyre. . . . His voice floated down through the mist, a little fainter now, as if he had turned his head away. "*Gianetta,* where are you? In God's name, *where are you?*"

Roderick had guessed, too, of course. I wondered, pressing my body closer to the wet ground, why he had been so sure that I, alone of all the people at Camasunary, would be unharmed.

"Are you there, Gianetta? *Don't be afraid.* . . ."

I don't think I was afraid, now that I knew for certain it was Nicholas. It wasn't that I believed, with Roderick, that, because of the past, Nicholas would never hurt me. It was just that, as that terrible whispering brought my suspicions to life and made them into truth, I didn't care any more. Not about anything.

"Gianetta . . . Gianetta . . . Gianetta. . . ." The syllables pattered down through the mist in a fantastic muttered counterpoint. I put my cold cheek down on the soggy grasses, and cried silently, while the fog wavered and whispered with my name, and its ghostly grey fingers pressed me into the marsh.

And then he was gone. The groping voice had faded, echoed and faded again. The quaking of the bog had ceased. A bird had slipped silently and unalarmed across the grass. He was gone.

I got up stiffly, and, myself moving like a weary ghost, trudged uncaring, heedless, mindless, across the bog, away from the last mocking echo of his voice.

And almost at once I was on firm ground, among stones and long heather. I quickened my pace instinctively. The ground was rising steadily away from the bog, and presently I found the mist was wavering and dwindling round me. I plunged up the slope at an increasing rate as my range of vision extended. The fog thinned, shrank, and ebbed away behind me.

As suddenly as a swimmer diving up through the foam of a wave to meet the air, I burst out of the last swirl of mist into the vivid sunshine.

CHAPTER

TWENTY-TWO

The relief was so colossal, the change so unbelievable, that I could only stand, blinking, in the clear light of the afternoon sun. My eyes, blinded with mist, and still dazzled with crying, took several seconds to get used to the flood of light. Then I saw where I was. I had clambered a little way up the lower slope of Blaven, at a point where a great dyke of rock bisected the scree, a wall laid uphill like an enormous buttress against the upper cliffs.

The foot of this buttress was lipped by the fog, which held the lower ground still invisible under its pale tide. The glen itself, the loch, the long Atlantic bay, all lay hidden, drowned under the mist which stretched like a still white lake from Blaven to Sgurr na Stri, from Garsven to Marsco. And out of it, on every hand, the mountains rose, blue and purple and golden-green in the sunlight, swimming above the vaporous sea like fabulous islands. Below, blind terror might grope still in the choking grey; here above, where I stood, was a new and golden world. I might have been alone in the dawn of time, watching the first mountains rear themselves out of the clouds of chaos. . . .

But I was not alone.

Hardly had my eyes adjusted themselves to the brilliant spaciousness of my new world above the clouds, when I became aware of someone about fifty yards away. He had not seen me, but was standing near the foot of the great rock buttress, gazing past it, away from me, towards the open horizon of the southwest. It was Roderick Grant. I could see the dark-gold gleam of his hair in the sunlight.

I called: "Roderick!" and was amazed at the harsh croak that my stiff throat produced.

He did not move. My knees were shaking, and it was with difficult, uncertain steps that I made my way towards him over the rough ground. I said his name again: "Roderick!" He heard then. He swung round. He said: "Yes?" and then: "*Janet!*" His voice sounded raw with shock, but at that I could hardly feel surprised. God knows what I looked like, death-white and shaking, wet and filthy, with the ghosts of terror and despair still looking out of my eyes.

He took two swift strides to meet me, and caught hold of my hands, or I would have fallen. He thrust me down onto a flat rock with my back against the warm stone of the buttress. I shut my eyes, and the sunlight beat against the lids in swirls of red and gold and violet. I could feel its heat washing over me in great reviving waves, and I relaxed in it, drawing my breath more smoothly. Then at length I opened my eyes and looked up at Roderick.

He was standing in front of me, watching me, and in those blue eyes I saw, again, that dreadful look of compassion. I knew what it meant, now, and I could not meet it. I looked away from him, and busied myself pulling off my sodden shoes and unfastening my coat, which slid off my shoulders to lie in a wet huddle on the rock. My blouse was hardly damp, and the grateful heat poured through it onto my shoulders.

He spoke then: "You don't—know?"

I nodded.

He said slowly, an odd note in his voice: "I told you that you would not be hurt. I shouldn't have said it. It was—"

"It hardly matters," I said, wearily. "Though why you thought, after what Nicholas put me through when we got divorced, that he'd have any scruples about me now, I don't know." My left hand was flat on the hot rock. The line where my wedding ring had been showed clear and white on the third finger. I said, still with the weight of dreariness pressing on me: "It was wrong of me to try to protect him, suspecting what he was. I see that now. One shouldn't really put people before principles. Not when the people are—outlaws."

My voice dwindled and stopped. He had turned away from me, and his eyes were on the distant peaks of the Cuillin, where they swam above the vaporous lake.

"Why did you do it?"

I blinked stupidly. "Why did I do what?"

"Protect—him." There was a curious light tone to his voice that might have been relief.

I hesitated, then said flatly: "Because I'm his wife."

He turned his head sharply. "Divorced."

"Oh yes. But—but that made no difference to some things. I mean, one has loyalties—"

He said harshly: "Loyalties? Why call it loyalty when you mean love?"

I said nothing.

"Don't you?"

"I suppose so."

He was silent. Then he said abruptly: "What happened down there? How did you find out?"

"He was looking for me in the mist. He called me. I knew his voice."

"He *called* you! But surely—"

"I was with Dougal Macrae, fishing, when the mist came down. Dougal had gone to get his rod. I heard a struggle, and Dougal must have been knocked out, then he—Nicholas—started looking for me. Only, Dougal recovered and went after him. They both chased off into the mist, and I ran away, but I got lost. And then—and then—"

"Yes?"

"I heard him coming across the bog, calling for me. Not calling, really, only whispering. I suppose he'd given Dougal the slip, and had doubled back to look for me. And he daren't call loudly in case Dougal heard him."

"He must know that you've guessed who—what—he is."

I shivered a little. "Yes."

He was peering down now at the thick pall that covered the valley. "So Drury is down there. In that?"

"Yes."

"How far away?"

"I don't know. I suppose it was only a few minutes ago that—"

He swung round on me, so suddenly that I was startled.

"Come on," he said, abruptly, almost roughly. "We've got to get out of this. Get your shoes."

He had hold of my wrist, and pulled me to my feet.

"Down into that?" I said, doubtfully. "Shouldn't we wait till it clears a little? He's got—"

"Down? Of course not. We're going up."

"What on earth d'you mean?"

He laughed, almost gaily. "*I will lift up mine eyes unto the hills. . . .*"

He seized my coat where it lay on the rock, and shook out its damp folds. Something tinkled sharply onto a boulder, and rolled aside with a glint. "Don't ask questions, Janet. Do as I say. What's that?"

"Oh!" I cried, stooping after it. "It's Heather's brooch!"

"Heather's brooch?" His tone was casual, so casual that I looked at him in some surprise.

"Yes. I found it yesterday under that dreadful ledge. I thought it was Roberta's, but Dougal said—"

Once again my voice dwindled and died in my throat. I stood up, the brooch in my hand, and looked up into his eyes.

I said: "The first night I was here, you told me about Heather's murder. You told me about the little pile of jewelry that was found on the ledge. A bracelet, you said, and a brooch, and—oh, other things. But the brooch *wasn't* on the ledge when she was found. And since she had only been given it that day, for her birthday, you couldn't have known about it, *unless you saw her wearing it yourself. Unless you, yourself, put it onto that little pile on the ledge beside the bonfire.*"

High up, somewhere, a lark was singing. Round us, serene above the mist, the mountains swam. Roderick Grant smiled down at me, his blue eyes very bright.

"Yes," he said gently. "Of course. But what a pity you remembered, isn't it?"

CHAPTER

TWENTY-THREE

ટુ♥

So we faced each other, the murderer and I, marooned together on our island Ararat above the flood of cloud; alone together, above the silent world, on the mountain where already he had sent three people to their deaths.

He was smiling still, and I saw in his face again the look of compassion that, now, I understood. He liked me, and he was going to kill me. He was sorry, but he was going to kill me.

But, just for a moment, even this knowledge was crowded out by the one glorious surge of elation that swept through me. The whole of that silent, cloud-top world was drenched with the light of the sun and the song of the lark—and the knowledge that I had been criminally, stupidly, cruelly wrong about Nicholas. I think that for two full minutes I stared into Roderick Grant's mad blue eyes and thought, not: "I am here alone with a maniac killer," but: "It was not Nicholas, *it was not Nicholas. . . .*"

Roderick said, regretfully: "I'm so sorry, Janet. I really am, you know. I knew when I heard you talking to Dougal by the river, that sooner or later you'd remember. I didn't really mean to, but of course I'll have to kill you now."

I found to my surprise that my voice was quite calm. I said: "It won't help you if you do, Roderick. The Inspector knows."

He frowned. "I don't believe you."

"He told me so. He said he was just waiting for information from London to confirm what he knew. And of course there's Roberta."

His face darkened. "Yes. Roberta."

The vivid eyes hooded themselves as he brooded over his failure with Roberta. I wondered if he had killed Dougal, or if Dougal, with Nicholas, were still hunting through the mist below us . . . the lovely safe mist, not many yards below us.

"Don't try and run away," said Roderick. "I'd only have to bring you back again. And don't scream, Janet, because then I'd have to throttle you, and"—he smiled gently at me—"I always cut their throats, if I can. It's the best way."

I backed against the cliff of the buttress. It was warm and solid, and there were tiny tufts of saxifrage in the clefts under my fingers. Real. Normal. I forced my stiff lips to smile back at Roderick. At all costs, I must try to keep him talking. Keep him in this mad, gentle mood. I must speak smoothly and calmly. If I should panic again, my fear might be the spark that would touch off the crazy train of his murderer's mind.

So I smiled. "Why do you do it at all, Roderick? Why did you kill Heather Macrae?"

He looked at me in surprise. "They wanted it."

"They?"

"The mountains." He made an oddly beautiful gesture. "All these years, these ages, they've waited, dreaming like this, above the clouds, watching over the green life of the valleys. Once, long ago, men paid them worship, lit fires for them, gave them the yearly sacrifice of life, but now"—his voice had an absent, brooding tone—"now they have to take for themselves what they can. A life a year, that's what they need . . . blood and fire, and the May day sacrifices that men paid them when the world was young and simple, and men knew the gods that lived on the mountains."

He looked at me. It was uncanny and horrible, to look at someone's familiar face, to listen to someone's familiar voice, and to see a complete stranger looking out of his eyes.

"She helped me carry the wood and the peat. Together we collected the nine woods and the wild agaric and the oak to make the wildfire. She made the fire for me, and then I cut her throat and—"

I had to stop him. I said abruptly: "But why did you kill Marion Bradford?"

His face darkened with anger. "Those two women! You heard the little one—Roberta—that night. You heard her talking sacrilege, you heard how she chattered of conquering—*conquering*—these." Again the flowing gesture that embraced the dreaming peaks. "And the other one —Miss Bradford—she was the same." He laughed suddenly, and sounded all at once perfectly normal and charming. "It was quite easy. The elder one, that dreadful, stupid woman, she was a little in love with me, I think. She was pleased and flattered when I met them on the mountain and offered to show her the climb across the Sputan Dhu."

"I suppose you thought they were both dead when you left them."

"They should have been," he said. "Wasn't it bad luck?"

"Very," I said drily. My eyes went past him, scanning the fringes of the mist. No one. Nothing.

He was frowning at a sprig of heather that he had pulled. "That ledge where you found Roberta," he said. "I'd been along the damned thing three times already, but I never went farther than the corner when I saw the ledge was empty. I wanted to find her first, of course."

"Of course." The lark had stopped singing. There was no sound in the blue-and-gold day but the grotesque exchange of our pleasant, polite voices, talking about murder.

"But *you* found her." The cock of his eyebrow was almost whimsical. "And you nearly—oh so nearly—gave me the chance I wanted, Janet."

I forgot about being calm and quiet. I cried out: "When you sent me to get the flask! You were going to kill her then!"

He nodded. "I was going to kill her then. A little pressure on the throat, and—" This time the gesture was horrible. "But you came back, Janet."

I licked my lips. "When she opened her eyes," I said hoarsely, "it was *you* she saw. *You*, standing behind me."

"Of course." He laughed. "You thought it was Drury, didn't you? Just as you thought it was Drury who killed Ronald Beagle—"

"Why did you do that?"

He hesitated, and into the blue eyes came a look of naïve surprise. "D'you know, I don't quite know, Janet. I'd hated him for a long time, of course, because I knew that to his mind *they* were just so many peaks to be climbed, so many names to be recorded. And then he came among us that night, on the mountain, talking so glibly of Everest—Everest conquered, those untouchable snows defiled and trampled, where I had thought no man could ever put his sacrilegious feet. . . . *You* said that, Janet. You remember? You spoke like that about it once, and, because of that, I thought that I could never hurt you. . . . But Beagle—I followed him down the hill. I caught him from behind and killed him." His eyes met mine ingenuously. "I think," he said, "I must have been a little mad."

I said nothing. I was watching the edge of the mist, where it frothed along the empty mountainside.

"And now," said Roderick, feeling in his coat pocket, "where's my knife?" He patted his coat carefully, as a man does when he is wondering where he has put his pipe. The sun gleamed on his dark-gold hair. "It doesn't seem to be—oh yes, I remember now. I was sharpening it. I put it down somewhere. . . ." He smiled at me, then he turned and scanned the heather anxiously. "Can you see it, Janet, my dear?"

Little bubbles of hysteria rose in my throat. My fingers dug and scraped at the rock behind me. I stiffened myself with a jerk and flung out an arm, pointing at the ground beyond him.

"There, Roderick! There it is!"

He swung round, peering.

I couldn't get past him, down into the mist. I had to go up.

I went up the end of that buttress like a cat, like a lizard, finding holds where no holds were, gripping the rough rock with stockinged feet and fingers which seemed endowed with miraculous, prehensile strength.

I heard him shout "*Janet!*" and the sound acted like the crack of a whip on a bolting horse. I went up ten feet of rock in one incredible, swarming scramble, to haul myself, spreadeagled, onto the flat crest of the buttress.

The enormous wing of rock soared in front of me up to the high crags. Its top was, perhaps, eight feet wide, and strode upwards at a dizzy angle, in giant steps and serrations, like an enormous ruined staircase. I had landed, somehow, on the lowest tread, and I flung myself frantically at the face of the next step, just as the ring of boots on rock told me that he had started after me.

How I got up what seemed to be twenty feet of perpendicular rock, I do not know. But my mad impetus still drove me, holding me against the cliff, clamping my hands instinctively into crannies, bracing my feet against juts of safe rock, propelling me upwards as thoughtlessly and as safely as if I were a fly walking up a wall.

With a heave and a jerk I dragged myself onto the wider ledge that marked the second step. And, inexorably, the next perpendicular barred my way, this time gashed from summit to foot by a vertical crack, or chimney. I flew at this, only to be brought up short as I saw that the rock on which I stood was a stack, a chunk split off the main buttress, and between me and the next upright there yawned a gap which dropped sheer away to the level of the scree.

The gap was perhaps four feet wide, no more. And at the other side, on one wall of the chimney, was a smallish, triangular ledge, above which a deep crevice held a slash of shadow.

There was my handhold, there the ledge for my feet, if I could only get across that dreadful gap. . . . But I was nearly foundered, and I knew it. My breath was coming in painful gasps; I had knocked one of my feet; my hands were bleeding.

I hesitated there, on the brink of the split in the rock. Then I heard the rattle of pebbles behind me—close behind. I turned, a terrified thing at bay, my eyes desperately searching for another way off the top of the stack. To left, to right, a sheer drop of thirty feet to the scree. Before me, the chasm. A hand swung up over the edge of the platform where I stood. A dark-gold head rose after it. Mad blue eyes, rinsed of all humanity, stared into mine.

I turned and leaped the gap without a second's thought. I landed on the little ledge. My knee bumped rock, but I hardly felt it as my hands, clawing wildly, found a safe anchorage in the crevice above. Then my knee was in the crevice. With a heave and a wriggle I pulled my body up to it, and was in the chimney, which was narrow enough to let me wedge myself against one side of it while I sought for holds in the other. I swarmed up it like a chimney boy whose master had lit a fire beneath him.

Then my hand slid into a deep grip; I braced myself and with one last heave, one final convulsion, dragged myself out of the chimney and onto a deep ledge sheltered by an overhang.

And this time I was cornered. I knew it. Even if I could have climbed the overhang that bulged above me, the impulse had given out; nature had swung back on me. I was finished. And the place where I now found myself was no more than a ledge of rock, some four feet by ten, piled with small boulders and blazing with bell heather.

I crouched among the scented flowers and peered down.

Roderick was standing twenty feet below me at the edge of the gap, his convulsed face lifted to mine. His breathing was ragged and horrible. I saw the sweat gleaming on his flushed cheekbones, and on the knuckles of the hand in which he held the knife. . . .

I screamed then. The sound splintered against the rocks into a million jarring, tearing echoes that ripped the silence of the afternoon into tatters. The raven swept out from high above me with a frightened bark.

Something flashed past my cheek with the whistle of a whiplash. The wind of it seared my face. Roderick's knife struck the cliff behind me, and shattered into a hundred little tinkling notes that were whirled into the bellow of the echo as I screamed again.

The empty rock flung my terror back at me, hollow, reverberating. The raven swung up, yelling, into the empty blue air. Away to the west, in the greater emptiness, the Cuillin dreamed on indifferently. I crouched in my eyrie high above the sea of cloud, an insignificant insect clinging to a crack in a wall.

Roderick swore harshly below me, and his now empty hands lifted, the fingers crooked like claws.

"I'm coming up," he said on a savage, breathless note, and I saw his knees flex for the leap across the gap.

My fingers scrabbled at the heather, caught up a big jagged rock, and held it poised on the brink of the ledge.

"Keep off!" My voice was a croak. "Stay where you are, or I'll smash your head in!"

He glanced up again, and I saw him recoil half a pace. Then he laughed, and with the laugh the whole situation split up, and re-formed into a yet crazier pattern, for the laughter was genuine and full of amusement. From the face he lifted to me, all the savagery had been wiped clean; it held the familiar gaiety and charm, and—yes, affection.

He said rucfully: "I broke my knife, Janet. Let me come up."

I held onto the rags of my own sanity. "No! Stay where you are or I'll throw this down on you!"

He shook the hair out of his eyes. "You wouldn't do a thing like that, Janet darling," he said, and leaped the gap like a deer.

Then he was standing on the little triangular ledge below me, one hand locked in the crevice. I saw his muscles tense as he prepared to heave himself up the chimney after me.

His head was back; his blue eyes held mine.

"You couldn't do a thing like that, could you?" he said.

And, God help me, I couldn't. My fingers clutched the jagged boulder. I lifted it, ready to heave it down . . . but something held me—the imagined impact of rock on flesh, the smashing of bone and eyes and hair into a splintered nothing . . . I couldn't do it. I turned sick and dizzy, and the rock slipped from my hands back onto the ledge among the flowers.

"No," I said, and I put out both my hands as if to ward off the sight of the violence I could not do. "No—I can't. . . ."

He laughed again, and I saw the knuckles of his left hand whiten for the upward pull. Then something smashed into the rock not six inches from his head. The report of the gun slammed against the echoing mountain with a roar like an express bursting from a tunnel.

"Don't worry, Gianetta, I can," said Nicholas grimly, and fired again.

CHAPTER

TWENTY-FOUR

૨≫

Only then did I become aware that, a little way to the north, the edge of the mist was broken and swirling at last, as men thrust out of it and began to race along the hillside: the Inspector, Hecky, Neill, and Jamesy Farlane, all making at the double for the foot of the stack.

Nicholas, well ahead of them, had already reached the base of the buttress. The slam of his second shot tore the echoes apart, and now the rock by Roderick's hand splintered into fragments. I heard the whine of a ricocheting bullet, and I saw Roderick flinch and, momentarily, freeze against the rock.

The other men, running at a dangerous pace along the scree, had almost come up with Nicholas. I heard the Inspector shout something.

Roderick half turned on his little ledge, braced himself for an instant, then flung himself, from a stand, back across the gap between the ledge and the stack. The nails of his boots ripped screaming along the rocky platform, then they gripped. In the same moment I heard the scrape and clink of boots as the pursuers, spreading out, started to climb the north face of the buttress.

Roderick paused for an instant, balanced, as it were, in mid-flight on the top of the stack. The sun glinted on his gold hair as he glanced quickly this way, that way. . . . Then he leaped for the south side of the stack, swung himself over, and disappeared from view.

Someone yelled. Hecky was half up a lower step of the buttress, and had seen him. I saw him cling and point, shouting, before he addressed himself even more desperately to the cliff.

But Roderick had a good start, and he climbed like a chamois. In less time than it takes to tell, I saw him dart out onto the scree south of the buttress, and turn downhill. He was making for the mist, with that swift leaping stride of his, and I heard the Inspector curse as he, too, started to run downhill.

But Nicholas had moved faster. He must have heard Roderick jump down onto the scree, for only a few seconds after he began his dash for the shelter of the mist, Nicholas had turned and started down the north side of the buttress.

From my dizzy eyrie, I could see them both. To that incredible day, the race provided as fantastic a climax as could well be imagined. There was the great dike, swooping down the side of the mountain, to lose itself in the sea of fog; and there, on either side of it, ran hunter and hunted, law and outlaw, slithering, leaping, glissading down the breakneck scree in a last mad duel of speed.

Once, Roderick slipped, and fell to one knee, saving himself with his hands. Nicholas gained four long strides before he was up again and hurtling downhill, unhurt, to gain the shelter of the mist. Not far to go now . . . thirty yards, twenty . . . the buttress had dwindled between them to a ridge, a low wall . . . then Roderick saw Nicholas, and swerved, heading for safety at an angle away from him.

I saw Nicholas thrust out a foot, and brake to a slithering ski turn in a flurry of loose shale. Something gleamed in his hand.

The Inspector's yell came from somewhere out of sight below me. "*Don't use that gun!*"

The gun flashed down into the heather as Nicholas put a hand to the low dike and vaulted it. Roderick gave one quick glance over his shoulder, and in three great bounds reached the margin of the mist. It swirled and broke around his bolting form, then swallowed him into invisibility.

Twenty seconds later the same patch swayed and broke as Nicholas thrust into it, and vanished.

Then, all around me, the cliffs and the clear blue air swung and swayed, dissolving like the mist itself. The scent of the heather enveloped me, sickening-sweet as the fumes of ether, and the sunlight whirled into a million spinning flecks of light, a vortex into which, helpless, I was being sucked. An eddy, a whirlpool . . . and I was in it. I was as light as a cork, as light as a feather, as insubstantial as blown dust. . . .

Then out of the spinning chaos came Inspector Mackenzie's voice, calm, matter-of-fact, and quite near at hand.

He said: "Wake up, lassie, it's time we got you down from there."

I found that my hands were pressed to my eyes. I took them away, and the boiling light slowly cleared. The world swung back into place, and I looked down.

Inspector Mackenzie was on the top of the stack, standing where Roderick had stood, and Jamesy Farlane was with him. "How in the world did you get up there, anyway?"

"I don't remember," I said truthfully. I sat there on my cushion of heather and looked down at the two men, feeling suddenly absurd. "I—I can't get down, Inspector."

He was brisk. "Well, lassie, you'll have to be fetched. Stay where you are." The pair of them became busy with ropes, and then Jamesy approached my cliff. He got across the gap with ludicrous ease, and paused there, examining the chimney.

The Inspector, I saw, was looking back over his shoulder.

"Nicholas—" I said hoarsely, but he cut me short.

"Hoots awa' wi' ye"—it was the one conventionally Scottish expression that I ever heard him use—"don't worry about that. Hecky and Neill both went after him, as you'd have seen if you hadn't been so busy fainting. Your man's safe enough, my dear."

And, even as he finished speaking, I saw Nicholas come slowly up out of the mist. He moved stiffly, like a very tired man, but he seemed to be unhurt. He raised his head and looked up towards us, then quickened his pace, lifting a hand in some sort of gesture which I could not interpret, but which seemed to satisfy the Inspector, for he grunted, and gave a little nod as he turned back to watch Jamesy's progress.

I cannot pretend that I was anything but an appalling nuisance to poor Jamesy, when at last he appeared beside me on the ledge with a rope, and attempted to show me how to descend from my eyrie. In fact, I can't now remember how this descent was eventually accomplished. I remember his tying the rope round me, and passing it round his own body, and round a spike of rock; I also remember a calming flood of instructions being poured over my head as I started my climb, but whether I obeyed them or not I have no idea. I suspect not; in fact, I think that for the main part of the descent he had to lower me, helplessly swinging, on the end of the rope. And since I could not possibly have jumped the gap to the stack, Jamesy lowered me straight down the other thirty feet or so into the bottom of the cleft itself. I remember the sudden chill that struck me as I passed from the sunlit chimney into the shadow of the narrow gully.

Then my feet touched the scree, and, at the same moment, someone took hold of me, and held me hard.

I said: "Oh, Nicholas—" and everything slid away from me again into a spinning, sun-shot oblivion.

CHAPTER

TWENTY-FIVE

৯৯

When Nicholas dived into the pool of mist after Roderick, he was not much more than twenty yards behind him, and, though the mist was still thick enough to be blinding, he could hear the noise of his flight quite distinctly. It is probable that Roderick still believed Nicholas to have a gun, while he himself, having lost his knife, was unarmed; he may, too, have heard Neill and Hecky thudding down the hillside in Nicholas's wake; or he may, simply, have given way at last to panic and, once running, have been unable to stop—at any rate, he made no attempt to attack his pursuer, but fled ahead of him through the fog, until at length they reached the level turf of the glen.

Here going was easier, but soon Nicholas realized he was rapidly overhauling his quarry. Roderick, it will be remembered, had already had to exert himself considerably that afternoon, and now he flagged quickly; the panic impulse gave out and robbed him of momentum. Nicholas was closing in, fifteen yards, ten, seven . . . as the gap closed, panic supervened again, and Roderick turned and sprang at his pursuer out of the fog.

It was a sharp, nasty little struggle, no holds barred. It was also not quite equal, for whereas Nicholas had only, so to speak, a mandate to stop the murderer getting away, the murderer wanted quite simply to kill his pursuer if possible. How it would have ended is hard to guess, but Neill and Hecky, guided by the sounds of the struggle, arrived in a very short time, and Roderick, fighting literally like a madman, was overpowered. And when Dougal Macrae, still breathing fire and slaughter, suddenly materialized out of the fog as well, the thing

was over. Roderick, unresisting now, was taken by the three men back
to the hotel, where he would be held until transport arrived. Nicholas,
breathing hard, and dabbing at a cut on his cheek, watched the mist
close round them, then he turned and made his way back up the hillside into the sun.

So much I had learned, sitting beside Nicholas on the heather at
the foot of the buttress, with my back against its warm flank. I had
been fortified with whisky and a cigarette, and was content, for the
moment, to rest there in the sun before attempting the tramp back
to the hotel.

The Inspector, it appeared, was to set off immediately with his prisoner for Inverness. He paused before us as he turned to go.

"Are you sure you're all right, lassie?"

"Quite, thank you," I said, and smiled at him through the smoke
of my cigarette.

He glanced from me to Nicholas, and back again. "It seems I was
wrong," he said drily.

"What d'you mean?"

"In thinking you were withholding evidence that mattered."

I felt myself flushing. "What did you imagine I knew that I hadn't
told you?"

"I thought you'd recognized the man you saw in front of the bonfire."

"Oh. No, I hadn't. I hadn't, really."

"I believe you. . . ." But his glance was speculative and I felt the
flush deepen. "Even so, I could almost have sworn you were lying just
then about something."

"I was," I said, "but not about that. It was something I heard, not
something I saw."

His gaze flicked to Nicholas once more, and he smiled. "Ah," he
said. "Just so. Well, I'll be away. I'm glad to be leaving you in such
good hands. Take care of her, sir. She's had a rough time."

"I will," said Nicholas.

"One thing"—Inspector Mackenzie regarded him with some severity
—"you have, of course, got a license for your gun?"

"Gun?" said Nicholas, blankly. "What gun?"

The Inspector nodded. "I thought as much," he said drily. "Well,
see you get one."

And, with another nod, he turned and was presently swallowed up
in the mist.

And we were alone on the mountainside, islanded in the pool of mist, where, on every hand in the golden distance, the mountaintops drifted, drowsing in their own halcyon dreams. Sweet and pungent, the honey smells of rockrose and heather thickened round us in the heat, and, once more, the lark launched himself into the upper sky, on a wake of bubble-silver song.

I drew a little sigh, and settled my shoulders gratefully against the warm rock.

"It's all over," I said. "I can hardly believe it, but it's all over."

"My God, but you had me worried!" said Nicholas. "I knew Grant had gone out, but the Inspector had put Neill on to watch him, and then when the mist dropped like that, all in a moment, and Neill came back and said he'd lost his man. . . ." He glanced briefly down at me. "I knew where you and Dougal were fishing, so I made upriver as fast as I could. The police turned straight out after Grant. Then I heard a yell from Dougal, and you screamed, and I ran like blazes. I found your fishing rods, but you'd gone, so I started hunting you. I went across the bog—"

"I know. I heard you. I was hiding quite near."

"Silly little devil."

"Well, I was scared. I thought you were the murderer and you didn't help by whispering my name in that blood-curdling way."

He laughed ruefully. "I'm sorry. But I knew Grant might be nearer you than I was, and if you'd called out from too far away he might have reached you first. No, I wanted to get you safe under my wing, and then—"

"So you *knew* it was Roderick."

He glanced down sideways at me. "Then, yes. I'd been wondering about him for quite some time, and so had Inspector Mackenzie, but there was no proof."

"What was the information he was waiting for from London? Or—no, you'd better start at the beginning, Nicholas. Tell me—"

"That *is* the beginning. The information that came today is really the beginning of the story. It concerns Roderick Grant's family. Did you know his father was a minister?"

"He told me a little bit about it. I felt rather sorry for him, a lonely little boy all by himself at the back of the north wind—that was what he called his home."

"It's not a bad description either. I've been through Auchlechtie. It's a tiny hamlet of a dozen cottages in a valley near Bheinn a' Bhùird.

The manse, where the Grants lived, was four miles even from the village, up beside the ruins of the old church and its primitive grave-yard. The new church had been built down in the village itself, but the minister's house had no one for neighbor except that little square of turf, walled off from the heather, and filled with crumbling head-stones and mounds covered with ivy and brambles and old, split yews deformed by the wind."

"And he told me he lived alone with his father."

"So he did. His mother died when he was born and his grand-mother, his father's mother, brought him up till he was nine. Then she died—in an asylum."

"Oh Nicholas, how dreadful. So his father—his father's family—"

"Exactly. His father had always been the stern, unbending, austere kind of godly Presbyterian that used to be common in fiction and, possibly, even in fact. In him the—the taint showed itself at first only in an increasing remoteness and austerity, a passionate absorption in his studies of the past which, gradually, took complete possession of him, and became more real than the real life round him—if you can apply the term 'real life' to that tiny hamlet, four miles down the empty glen. The history of the long-dead bones in that long-dead grave-yard became, year by year, the only thing that meant anything to him. And the little boy only mattered as being someone to whom he could pour out his half-learned, half-crank theories about the ancient cus-toms and legends of the Highlands."

"Roderick told me that he learned to worship the mountains," I said. "I never guessed he meant it literally."

"But he did, quite literally. He must have spent a large part of his childhood listening to his father's stories and theories, imbibing his mad, garbled versions of the old folk customs of the North, the sort of half-connected, inaccurate rubbish you said he was telling you to-day. He must have built, bit by bit in his crazed mind, a new sort of mythology for himself, of which the so-called 'ritual' murder of Heather Macrae was a concrete example; a jumble of facts from books and from his father's researches, half-remembered, distorted bits of folklore that shook together like glass in a kaleidoscope and made a picture of violence that seemed, to a madman's brain, to be quite logi-cal."

"I know. I found some of the bits in *The Golden Bough*."

"Oh yes, my *Golden Bough!* The Inspector told me you had it. I was looking all over the place for it last night. I thought I'd left it in my car."

"I'd taken it to read, quite by accident." I told him about it. He glanced down at me with an enigmatic expression.

"So you handed it to the Inspector. If you'd known it was mine—"

"But I did. There was an envelope in it addressed to you in Daddy's writing. I have it in my pocket."

"Have you indeed?" I could feel his eyes on me still, but I would not meet them. "Why didn't you give that to the Inspector, if you knew the book was mine?"

"I—I don't know."

The lark was descending now, in lovely little curves of sound. "How did Daddy know you were here, anyway?"

"What?" He sounded oddly disconcerted. "Oh, I wrote to him and asked him to lend me his copy of the book. There was no one in my flat, so I couldn't send for my own copy. You see, Grant had made one or two remarks that had made me wonder about him—queer little misstatements and inaccuracies that sounded like half-remembered quotations from Frazer and the older books that were Frazer's sources. And when I saw how some of Frazer's details checked with poor Heather Macrae's May-day sacrifice—"

"May Day?"

"May the thirteenth *is* May Day, according to the old calendar. Ancient lore again, you see. Oh, everything fitted, even though it did so in a queer mad way; so, of course, I showed the book to Inspector Mackenzie."

"You did what?" I exclaimed. "When was this?"

"Last week."

"Then he *knew* the book was yours!"

"Of course."

"Then why—" A memory flashed back at me, of the Inspector's kind, compassionate gaze. "Did he never suspect *you*, Nicholas?"

"He may have done, to begin with, and, of course, even after I turned up the evidence of *The Golden Bough* he may have kept me under suspicion, along with Hubert Hay, since we two, as well as Grant, have made some sort of study of local folklore. But Hay had an alibi—with you—for Marion's murder, while I, if you discount the intolerable possibilities of bluff and double bluff, had indicated my innocence by giving evidence to the police. Which left Grant."

"Then why," I said again, "was the Inspector so—so kind, and so *sorry* for me, this morning? He talked about loyalties, and—"

"And you thought he was warning you that I was guilty? Why should you assume that your loyalty should be directed towards me, Gianetta?"

Abruptly, between one wingbeat and the next, the lark's song ceased. He shut his wings and dropped like a flake of shadow into the heather. I said, stupidly: "D'you mean he thought it was *Roderick* I saw by the bonfire?"

"Of course. He thought you were falling for Roderick Grant. That was my fault, I'm afraid. I'd told him so—on very little evidence except that Grant, in his own way, was quite patently interested in you."

I was stupefied. "You told the Inspector that I was in love with Roderick Grant?"

"I did, more or less. Sorry, Gianetta. Sheer dog-in-the-manger stuff. Jealousy exaggerates, you know."

I let that one pass. After a moment he went on: "The Inspector could only take my word for it, and when you seemed to be protecting Grant he thought you suspected him yourself, but hesitated to give him away."

"But that's absurd! Of course I was never in love with him! I liked him, yes. I thought he was very charming—but *in love!*" I spoke hotly, indignantly. "It's fantastic nonsense!"

"Why?" The question was bland as cream.

"*Why?* Because—" I stopped short, and bit my lip. I felt the color flooding my cheeks, and shot a quick glance at him. His eyes, narrowed against the smoke from his cigarette, were fixed dreamily, almost inattentively, on the long glimmering verge of the mist where it lay along the far sea's edge. But there was a smile touching the corner of his mouth. I said hurriedly: "But when did the Inspector finally fix on Roderick? Surely the others at the hotel were suspect too?"

"Of course. Any of the other men—Braine, Corrigan, Persimmon, Beagle, could have had an unconfessed interest in folklore, but Marion's murder, remember, narrowed the field down sharply, since it demanded that the murderer also be an efficient climber. And soon afterwards the only climber of the group—poor Beagle—was murdered too."

"Which leaves us with Roderick again."

"As you say. When the Inspector came over yesterday morning he found Roderick, so to speak, leading the field and hardly anyone else running, but still without a thing that could be pinned on him. Then you found Roberta, and he might have got his proof, but he didn't dare wait much longer for her to open her mouth. He put another hurried call through to London for any information about Grant that they could rake up. He was going to risk pulling him in on suspicion if he got anything from them that could justify him. But nothing came through till this morning."

"The fact that his grandmother had died insane? Was that enough?"

"It wasn't all," said Nicholas soberly. "His father died in a mental home two years ago."

"Oh God," I said.

"Quite enough," said Nicholas grimly, "to warrant his being detained—got somehow out of circulation till Roberta could talk. But it was too late. That damned fog came down like a curtain, and Grant gave Neill the slip, and went out looking for you." His arm, somehow, was round my shoulders. "Bloody little fool," he said angrily, his mouth against my hair.

"I'd have been all right with Dougal if the mist hadn't come down," I said defensively. "Nicholas, tell me something."

"Yes?"

"Dougal—he had a knife. I saw it. Did he—down there when you caught Roderick—he didn't—hurt him?"

His arm tightened, as if in protection. "No," he said soberly. "He came up spitting fire and brimstone and revenge, poor devil, but he shut up as soon as he saw Grant."

"Why?"

"Grant collapsed. When I caught him first, he fought like a wildcat, but when Dougal got there as well, and he saw it was hopeless, he just seemed to deflate. To break. He went suddenly quite helpless and gentle, and—I can't describe it, quite. It was rather beastly. He seemed to change character all in an instant."

"He did it with me."

"Did he? Then you'll know just how unspeakable it was. I'd just hit him on the jaw, and then there he was smiling at me like a nice child, and wiping the blood away."

"Don't think about it, Nicholas. He wouldn't remember you'd just hit him."

"I suppose not. He just smiled at all of us. That was when Dougal put his knife away and took him by the arm and said, 'Come on, laddie. Ye'd best be getting back oot of the fog. . . .' He went quite happily with the three of them." He dragged at his cigarette. "After they'd gone a little way off, into the fog, I heard him singing."

"Singing?" I stared at him.

"Well, crooning a tune, half to himself." His eyes met mine. " 'I *to the hills will lift mine eyes, From whence doth come mine aid. . . .*' " He looked away. "Poor devil. Poor crazy devil. . . ."

I said swiftly: "They'll never hang him, Nicholas."

"No."

He ground out his cigarette on a stone, and pitched it away as if with it he could extinguish and discard the memory of that nasty little scene. Then he turned his head again, and his voice changed abruptly.

"You saw me with Marcia Maling, didn't you?"

"Yes."

"I heard you go past us when she—when we were kissing outside her room."

"You heard me? But I hardly made a sound."

He smiled crookedly. "My dear girl, my instincts work overtime where you're concerned. Even in the dark, and when I'm kissing another woman."

"Perhaps even more when you're kissing another woman," I said drily, and got a wry look from him.

"I suppose I deserve that one. But this time, I promise you, I was more kissed against than kissing."

"All night?" I said.

His brows shot up. "What the devil d'you mean?"

I told him how I had heard a man's voice in her room later that night. "So of course I assumed it was you. And when I asked you next morning—"

"I—see. I thought you were just referring to the kiss you'd seen. No, Gianetta, I did not spend the night with her. I merely got—how shall I put it?—momentarily waylaid, through no intention of my own."

"I'm sure you struggled madly."

He grinned, and said nothing.

"I suppose the man in her room was Hartley Corrigan? Oh yes, I *see!* That was why he came home early from fishing that night, and yet Alma Corrigan said he didn't get to bed till three!"

"I think so. And when she realized what had happened she took her lipstick and murdered Marcia's doll with it."

"Poor Alma."

"Yes. Well, it's over for her, too. I rather think they've both had a fright, and they realize that they do matter to each other after all. . . ." He paused for a moment, looking down at me under lowered brows. "And now," he said, in a totally different voice, "shall we talk about us?"

I did not reply. My heart was beating lightly and rapidly somewhere up in my throat, and I could not trust my voice. I could feel his eyes on me again, and when he spoke, he did so slowly and deliberately, as if with some difficulty.

He said: "I'm not going to begin with apologies and self-abasement, though God knows you have plenty to forgive me for, and God knows, too, why you have apparently forgiven me. I'll say all that to you later on. No, don't speak. Let me finish. . . . What I want to say to you now is quite simple, and it's all that matters in the world to me. I want you back, Gianetta. I do most damnably want you back. I suppose I knew I'd been a fool—a criminal, brutal fool—about two days after you'd gone, and then my pride stepped in and stopped me coming after you."

I remembered how I had told Alma Corrigan that there was no room for pride in marriage. His next words were almost an echo—almost. He said: "But pride and love won't go together, Gianetta. I discovered that. And I do love you, my darling. I don't think I ever stopped." He took me gently by the shoulders, and turned me so that I had to face him. "Will you have me back, Gianetta? Please?"

"I never did have any pride where you were concerned, Nicholas," I said, and kissed him.

Later—a long time later—he said, rather shakily: "Are you sure? Are you sure, my darling?"

"Quite sure." The words were decided enough, but my voice was uncertain as his. I added, foolishly: "Darling Nicholas."

"Gianetta *mia*. . . ."

Later—a rather longer time later—he held me away from him, and laughed.

"At least, this time, there's no doubting the solid worth of my affections!"

"Why not?"

He looked down at me with the old, mocking look. "If you could see yourself, my Lady Greensleeves, you wouldn't ask me that! And if Hugo were here—"

"Which God forbid—"

"Amen. . . . No, don't try and tidy yourself up. It couldn't be done, and in any case I like you dirty, wet, and semiragged. I want to concentrate on your beautiful soul."

"So I noticed."

He grinned, and his arm tightened round my shoulders.

"It wasn't just coincidence that I met you here, you know."

"Wasn't it? But how—?"

"Your father," he said succinctly.

"D'you mean to tell me—?"

He nodded, still grinning. "I got into touch with your people again some time ago. As you know, the divorce upset them very much, and they were only too anxious to help me put things straight." He smiled down at me. "Poor Gianetta, you didn't stand much chance. Your father told me flatly that you'd never be happy without me, and your mother—well, I don't think she ever has quite grasped the fact that we were divorced, has she?"

"No. For Mother, divorce just doesn't exist."

"That's what I understood. Well, I was here at the beginning of May, and I happened to write to your father from this address, to ask him about *The Golden Bough*. A little later I rang him up—I was at Armadale then—and he told me you were due for a holiday, and that he'd contrived—"

"Contrived!" I said dazedly. I began to laugh. "The—the old Macchiavelli! And Mother said it must have been 'meant'!"

"It was meant all right," said Nicholas grimly. "I thought that all I needed was a chance really to talk to you. . . ." He smiled ruefully. "And then you ran away from me and I thought that perhaps your father was wrong and it really was all finished. I'd been so sure . . . I deserved a setdown, by God I did. And I got it. You came—and I couldn't get near you. . . ."

He gave a bitter little laugh. "So of course I behaved just about as badly as I could. I said some pretty filthy things to you, didn't I? I've no excuse, except that I thought I'd go crazy, being so near you, and having no—no claim. Somehow the biggest shock to my egoism was when I found you'd even discarded my name, and my ring."

"I only dropped them when I saw your name in the register. Look." I held out my left hand. The white circle on the third finger stood out sharp and clear against the tan. Nicholas looked at it for a moment, while a muscle twitched at the corner of his mouth, then he turned again and pulled me into his arms. His voice was rough against my hair. "So you're going to let me walk straight back into your life? After what I did? After—"

"You said we'd not talk about that."

"No, I like things made easy, don't I? It would serve me right if you turned on me now, and told me to get back where I belonged, and stop making a mess of your life."

"No," I said.

The lark had left his nest again, and was bubbling up through the clear air. I touched Nicholas's hand softly. "Just don't—don't ever leave me again, Nicholas. I don't think I could bear it."

His arms tightened. He said, almost with ferocity: "No, Gianetta, never again."

The lark rocked, feather-light, snowflake-light, on the crystal bubbles of his song. The great hills drowsed, drifting head under wing in the luminous haze.

I stirred in his arms and drew a little breath of pure happiness.

"What d'you bet," I said, "that when we arrive at Tench Abbas, Mother'll meet us just as if nothing had ever happened, and serenely show us both into the spare room?"

"Then we'd better be married again before we get there," said Nicholas, "or I won't answer for the consequences."

And so we were.